THE
SAVAGE

KRIS NEDY

For more information:
https://krisnedy.com/

ISBN 978-1-0688212-0-2

To all the people in the world
Who seek the holy truth out there.
To those who once believed in wonders
And had big dreams, but never dared.

To atheists and to believers;
To the wise, the good, and the obscene;
To everyone who wants to know
What's going on behind the scenes;

To those who want to figure out
What "Know thyself" was meant to mean;
What is the purpose of existence
And the failure of the human being:

To all of them, I give this story,
A tale of wisdom, truth, and pain.
I hope they'll find their source of worry
And they won't spend their lives in vain.

"Know thyself!"
Delphic maxim

*"And then you will know the truth and
the truth will make you free."*
John 8:32

CONTENTS

PROLOGUE

The two-masted junk rocked up and down, tossed by the waves like a child's toy. It floated helplessly in the pitch-black night, lashed by the stormy winds and whipped by the stinging rain. The nine surviving sailors were all on deck, trying in vain to regain control of the ship.

"Fai Che, keep her steady as she goes! Ease her to windward! Bear east!" shouted Cho Li over the roaring gale. Fai Che, a young man with no experience in steering, pulled hard on the helm in response.

"Chang, Chao! What are you doing? Move your asses, you fools! Furl the jib!"

Both rushed toward the bow just as Cho Li bellowed, "Watch out!"

An enormous mass of water surged onto the deck, sweeping away everything in its path. Cho Li was flung backward and hit his head on the foremast as Chang and Chao landed on top of him, smashing into his stomach and legs. A second later, they sprang up and lunged forward again. Cho Li rose slowly, doubled over in pain. He staggered and grabbed a rope dangling from the mast.

"Dragon's egg," he spat through clenched teeth. "I've had enough of this journey!"

Desperate and dizzy, he rubbed his head and went down to the mess deck, where he collapsed on the long table. It was pitch dark inside. The ship heaved and plunged, creaking and shuddering as if she would burst apart at any moment. Cho Li's head was spinning. He moaned, grabbed his temples with both hands, anchored his elbows firmly against the table, and closed his eyes.

It had been about three moons since they had lost the rest of the flotilla, and their situation was worsening with each passing day. His thoughts drifted back to the past...

Dragon's Wing consisted of eighty sailors and about two hundred boys and girls. The ship was part of the Xu Fu fleet that had set sail two years before for the legendary Seven Islands in search of the Elixir of Life. The expedition comprised about sixty ships, manned by thousands of sailors and carrying teenage virgins, both boys and girls. Their mission was to find the so-called *Immortal Mountain*, full of everlasting creatures, and gather herbs that only grew there. Afterward, they were to take the plants to the emperor's magicians, who would mix them and cast the incantations to create the elixir of immortality or the so-called Elixir of Life.

The start of the journey had been fantastic, with several weeks of blue skies, calm sea, and a festive mood. The hold was full of food and livestock—mainly fowl, goats, and pigs, so they had nothing to worry about. There was even a cage with live snakes, which the priest used when he performed his religious rituals. Occasionally, they stopped at some remote island to resupply with fresh water and fruits, or simply to stretch their legs a bit.

But even then, far before the peaceful voyage had come to an abrupt end, and all hell broke loose, Cho Li knew that something was wrong.

First, nobody knew for sure the location of the Seven Islands, so the sailors had only a vague idea where they were going, relying on myths, rumors, and legends about the place.

Second, all those youngsters got on Cho Li's nerves with their noisy capriciousness. He agreed, of course, with the concept that the plants for the elixir had to be gathered only by virgins, as they were supposed to be the purest of human beings. The problem was, he strongly doubted that most of the passengers were as pure as they claimed to be.

"Maidens, my eye," he muttered, and spat at the floor. He knew at least three girls who were not virgins at all; he had personally seen to that himself in the hold's darkness, and, considering the rumors and hints overheard here and there, he suspected that half of the sailors had done the same. There were so many skirts onboard and so eager at that. Now, he couldn't help but ask himself if this fornication had not been the reason for all their misfortunes. After all, it had all started when he was doing his third victim, that pussy with big, pouty lips and raven black hair. He remembered the girl below him, lying on her back on sacks of rice, her dress above her legs, her white thighs gleaming in the gloom. She moaned, his hand on her mouth to muffle the sounds, and he passionately kissed her sweaty, childish face while his little prick wiggled inside her, thrusting in and out faster and faster, when a mighty quake rolled them both over.

Shouts and footsteps pounded on the deck above, and the big gong started sounding. Cho Li hastily pulled on his pants and ran up, tightening his belt as he went. On deck, everyone was on the port side, staring at the water below. Cho Li squeezed his way through, reached the bulwarks, looked down, and the blood froze in his veins. The sea was foaming, churning, and gurgling. Amid the whirlpool stirred a gigantic, octopus-shaped creature. It was whitish and slimy, with hundreds of tentacles around a sucking mouth and an ugly head in the midst of a shapeless, jellylike body. A thick fog crawled up from the sea, wrapping the ship in its bony white hands. Suddenly, the monster hit the junk so hard that several people fell down, screaming. The *Dragon's Wing* slid through the water with incredible speed, hauled away by the disgusting thing.

Cho Li cocked his head and listened. The rocking had diminished, and the ship's creaking wasn't so noisy.

"The wind abates," he muttered and sank into his thoughts again.

The weather was misty and stormy back then, and the monster had towed them further and further away into uncharted waters. They did everything to gain control over the bloody junk, but all was in vain. Finally, after many days, the ship halted abruptly, and everybody rushed to see what was happening. As they craned their necks over the bulwarks, *Dragon's Wing* suddenly rocked and rose almost vertically on her bow. With terrifying screams, a third of the crew and nearly all the passengers disappeared into the churning water, straight into the monster's maw. The whirlpool turned red, and limbs floated everywhere. Cho Li shuddered. It had been a terrible sight. The ship fell back to her usual position, but the dread continued. The tentacles of the awful creature swiftly darted in and out with a swishing sound, grabbing the sailors and dragging them into the sea. This time, however, the men fought back, brandishing their swords and slashing at the thick, slimy tentacles until the monster let go. Eventually, it vanished the same way it had come, without a trace, sinking into the depths of the ocean.

Now they were free, but the aftermath of the attack was disastrous. All the passengers were gone, and of eighty crew members, only twenty-five had survived, all of them seamen before the mast except Cho Li who, as a boatswain, had to take charge of the ship.

With the captain and all officers dead and with no information about the course, they floated for weeks, surrounded only by the blue immensity of the sea. On top of that, the sky was cloudy all the time, so they could not use the stars to navigate. Cho Li, however, had an intuition to keep heading east, and he listened to it. Besides, there was nothing better to do.

Cho Li was a short, sullen man in his forties, and the crew did not like him much. Several youngsters had started snapping at him, openly challenging his authority, but while a mutiny was brewing, an unknown disease mowed down half of the remaining crew. Nobody could have understood what had hit them so hard, and by the time they discovered that the monster's slimy secretions had contaminated one of the water barrels, only fourteen men remained alive.

"As if some ominous curse follows us everywhere," Cho Li muttered. The death claimed his mates' lives by all sorts of unfortunate events. Dong and Daquan fell overboard in stormy weather. Zhang hanged himself on the yardarm during his watch, and Ji and Gen, both excellent sailors, threw themselves into the sea on the same day (though not simultaneously). They both swore to have heard enchanting songs and seen beautiful mermaids swimming alongside the ship and waving at them. Cho Li suspected that the water shortage had severely addled their brains.

"I should've known better," he sighed in the darkness. "If I'd tied them to the mast, I could have saved them from imaginary mermaids."

He slammed his fist against the wooden table. So many mistakes and no chance to rectify them. If he could have turned back time…

"Bugger that," he grunted. "There's no going back. One thing I know for sure—if we don't find land within five days, we're all dead men. At least the rain gives us a little fresh water, but for how long? And after all the ordeals and misery, when we eventually had a glimmer of hope, this bloody storm started up! Such shitty luck!" He hit the table again, his face distorted with rage.

Two days before, they had spotted land at last. Oh, what a joy it was, and such a relief when the lookout had cried, "Land ho!"

It was a small group of islands resembling a gigantic turtle from afar. In the late afternoon sun, each isle outlined distinct parts of the animal—the smaller ones formed the head and the neck, the shell was a big chunk of land with a high hill in the center, and three little atolls shaped the tail.

The crew was elated, and the hope returned to their eyes as they finally envisioned the end of their troubles.

"Straight ahead to the shell, mateys!" Cho Li cried out joyfully. "Hands aloft to hoist the topsails! Keep her steady, Fai!"

It was not meant to be. Cho Li had sensed it from the start, this nasty feeling of impending doom. A sudden, strong headwind drove them far away from their desired destination. The gale raged and within an hour, the poor seamen were forced to change course, losing sight of the land they so coveted.

"Hey Cho Li, where are you?" He turned his head, listening. Chang shouted from above, "Did the wind blow you overboard, old man? Where are you, by thunder?"

Cho Li sighed, hauled himself up, and headed for the main deck.

* * *

In the morning, the storm died away and the dawn bathed the sea in light. Dead tired, the sailors lay scattered on the deck, snoring soundly. Cho Li remained behind the helm, the only man awake aside from Kang, the lookout. His gaze lingered on the horizon. The wind fondled his face, and the shimmering water reflected a golden glare from the rising sun. The view aroused in him a sad longing for bygone days.

He should have been tired after being up all night fighting the storm, but strangely enough, his head was clear, and he was in excellent shape. Not exactly young and strong as he once was, but almost...

"Land ho!" cried Kang from above, and Cho Li jumped, startled. He shaded his eyes and looked ahead at the dark little spot, visible despite the distance.

"At last," he grunted and dashed toward the bronze gong. The giant disk shone like red gold in the morning sun, and the silver snakes decorating the center looked like they were alive. Cho Li grabbed the heavy club dangling beneath the gong and started hitting it, mad with joy.

A while later, all the seamen leaned against the bulwarks and watched the looming island with excitement. It appeared enchantingly beautiful from afar—a crescent of green land with three steep hills rising in the middle stood out amid the azure sea. The bay, enclosed by the two ends of the sickle, was large enough to shelter a fleet. As the ship approached, they could discern a broad sandy beach and scattered palm trees, friendly waving their green fronds. It seemed to be a calm, uninhabited place, with no sign of human activity.

"Take down the sails and drop anchor!" cried Cho Li, his voice muffled by the whipping of the canvas. "Do you see the reef? We can't get any closer."

The waves broke into white foam about a hundred yards from the shore, clearly outlining the stretch of the shoals.

"You must be blind not to notice it," grunted Feng, a tall, gaunt sailor who hated Cho Li's guts more than anyone else did.

"Up to the crow's nest, Feng, and fast! Let's see if your eyes are as sharp as your tongue. Tell us what you can perceive aloft!" commanded Cho Li. Feng shot him a nasty look and slouched toward the mainmast, emphasizing his lack of enthusiasm with every step.

"Come, mateys, cheer the slug up!" Cho Li shouted. Feng started slowly climbing the mast among the chuckles and whistling of the others. Halfway up, he stopped and made an obscene gesture at them, which lightened their mood even more. Once he got to the top, he observed the land for a while, then cried, "There's a flock of birds circling above the center of the jungle. And a wide green patch at the foot of the hills, probably a clearing. Not sure, though. I see something that looks like thin smoke rising over there, but it could be a play of the light... Maybe one of you scoundrels with better eyes should climb up here and look?"

"All right, get down. We've heard enough!" Cho Li shouted back. He waited until Feng had descended, then commanded, "We need to see how the land lies. Chang, Chao, and Feng are coming with me ashore, and the other of you wait here. If we don't come back by the time the big sandglass is turned over thrice[1], it means that something's gone wrong, right? If you don't spot a fire or any sign of us by nightfall, you double your vigilance, and if there is still no trace of us tomorrow, don't go ashore to look for us, but hoist the sails and leave. Now, get the sampan ready."

They lowered the boat and the four sailors got in. As it glided over the water, nobody uttered a word. Cho Li inhaled the salty smell of the ocean while he listened to the gentle oars splash, the swishing of the wind, and the piercing cries of the seagulls. He felt happy as a child, surrounded by the colors of the day, as lively as they had been in his youth. And just like in his teenage years, the roar of the surf brought him the excitement of starting an incredible new adventure. They passed the reef in silence, admiring the pinkish coral formations jutting out here and there above the sea. Once ashore, they jumped out of the boat, splashing the water around them. They dragged the sampan inland, making sure that the tide could not reach it. Then, still panting from the effort, they wiped their faces and looked around.

The beach was about 20 yards wide, studded with palms and some crooked, unfamiliar trees with small leaves. Beyond the sandy strip was the dense, tangled wall of foliage where the tropical jungle began. Cho Li and his company crossed the beach and stopped beneath the first of the tall trees.

"All right, first we need to find fresh water and fruit," Cho Li said. "We can manage without more meat for now—we still have three hogs and two goats alive on the ship. So, let's focus on searching for a river or some other freshwater source. And stick together, right! Nobody wanders off! Let's go!"

He drew his jian[2] and walked into the jungle, followed by his comrades.

---

1 About six hours.

2 A short, bronze, double-edged straight sword.

Creepers, shrubs, intertwined vines, and fallen trunks were tangled in such an incredible mess that it was almost impossible to advance. Drenched with sweat, they hewed their way, cutting left and right. The branches whipped and scratched their faces, and the scorching heat melted their brains. The damp air, the birds' screeches, the shrieks of unknown animals, and the buzzing of insects, which thrust themselves in their mouths and nostrils, only added to their frustrated desperation. Now and then, Cho Li turned sharply, scanning nervously through the trees around.

"Pretty jumpy, Cap'n?" Chang called mockingly.

"Honestly, I don't like this place," Cho Li replied. "I sense some ominous presence, as though somebody's watching. Do you feel it?"

"I rather feel like taking a shit," said Chang, and all but Cho Li burst into laughter.

"Hey, look, there's a path over there!" Chao cried out.

The thick foliage thinned out on their left, outlining a narrow trail. They followed it, penetrating deeper into the jungle, and gradually the track grew wider until it led them to a vast clearing.

"Turtle's egg," Cho Li whispered and stopped dead.

In the middle of the clearing rose a gigantic ancient tree. Its trunk was dark green and so large that a score of men holding hands could scarcely have encircled it. Just below the branches, its upper part was studded with spears, axes, knives, daggers, and maces of different sizes and shapes.

The massive boughs, every one of them as big as a tree in its own right, spread horizontally in all directions. In addition to the dense, broad green leaves, the branches were festooned with impaled skulls and putrid parts of human bodies, which dangled here and there, swinging slowly in the faint breeze. Hundreds of black birds, resembling crows but considerably bigger, flocked above the crown, letting out sharp cries and occasionally swooping at the corpses.

Before the grisly tree, a flat, rectangular stone had been set atop a rocky outcropping. It was carved all over with notches, grooves, and strange symbols. Sun-bleached bones and skulls were heaped around it.

The seamen stood thunderstruck, unable to believe their eyes. Confused and completely lacking any sense of time, they stared for a prolonged period, until a gust of wind brought to them a terrible stench of carrion. Cho Li stepped away and bent double to throw up. When the last convulsion passed and he lifted his eyes again, he jumped backward, and a thin trickle ran along his left leg. Scores of swarthy men came noiselessly out of the forest, each clutching a spear in his hand.

Cho Li pivoted quickly. They were everywhere, blending in with the shadows of the trees and staring ominously at the sailors. They were all naked, except for loincloths, with mighty physiques. Each man stood a head taller than the sailors, slender and brawny, with shaved skulls and bodies covered with tattoos depicting the same gigantic tree, crania, or battle scenes. Small human bones dangled from their noses and ears, their faces emanating the cruelty and strength of feral animals.

"*Sheer savages,*" whispered Cho Li.

He met the stare of a broad-shouldered man with a missing ear, and froze with horror, for he read his own death in the man's dreadful black eyes, connected with the deepest darkness.

At this moment, his stomach churned and he shit himself. With a wet arse and a banging heart, red in the face with shame, he slowly raised his hands in the air and dropped his sword from a height, then slumped to his knees and said in a trembling voice, "We come to you in peace, to look for water and food. If you'd be so kind to allow us to replenish our supplies a little, we will generously acknowledge our gratitude. We'll give you anything you want. Just let us go, please."

He touched the earth with his forehead in a sign of profound humility, followed by Chang, Chao, and Feng, who mimicked him to the slightest details.

The locals understood nothing of what Cho Li said. His body language, however, was eloquent enough. A tall, fierce-looking man stepped forward and shouted in the tribe's native tongue: *"Tie them up! They alone found their path to sacrifice. The Great Kepolo led them to the Sacred Tree, which means only one thing: he is claiming their lives. As to the others in the big boat, they will be our slaves. I want them alive, well-fed, and pampered all the time. They should lack nothing because these strangers will teach us how to build such big boats, and we will become the most powerful people in the Turtle Archipelago!"*

The seamen, who were not able to discern even a single word, focused intently on the dark man's intonation. There was nothing peaceful in it. As he spoke, the savage progressively raised his voice and finished in a high-pitched crescendo, lifting his spear. The others responded with similar cries and hoisted their spears as one. Then, several men lunged at the poor sailors, tied them up, and dragged them toward the enormous tree. As they stretched Cho Li on the flat stone and fastened his limbs, the last thought that passed through his mind was:

There it goes, bloody Elixir of Life.

I

MANIHA KOMO

CHAPTER I

AKAMUI

—1677 AD, MANIHA KOMO ("HALF-MOON ISLAND")

"You performed a great feat at the last battle, young Akamui," said Hamaki. "If not for you, they would have overturned us! But you fought like five men! Not to mention that you saved my life, and that is something I'll never forget."

The inside of Hamaki's bamboo hut was dim and dusty. The only light seeped through cracks in the straw curtain that covered the entrance. Besides two shelves with wooden and clay bowls along the wall, and a bucket with fresh water in the corner, there was nothing in the room. The two men sat face-to-face, cross-legged on shark pelts stretched over the earthen floor. Hamaki leaned on the central column that supported the thatch roof. At Hamaki's words, Akamui's face flushed with pleasure.

"Anyone would do the same in my place," said Akamui.

"No, no, don't underestimate yourself," Hamaki objected. "Every brave deed deserves a reward and you shall have yours. I've decided to recommend you as a candidate for the Council in the next elections."

Akamui's eyes widened and his mouth dropped open. He tried to say something, but Hamaki stopped him with an imperial gesture.

"I know you think you're too young, that you don't have enough experience. Well, all that is nonsense. Take Ahaki, for instance. He is a little older than you, but he has been on the Council for years. The elders can choose any man, no matter the age, in virtue of his special merit among the tribe. Ah, stick with me, lad, and you'll never lose; I've been on the Council for a long time and, believe me, my word carries weight there."

"I don't have the words to express my gratitude, wise Hamaki." Akamui rose and bowed. "It is such a great honor for me." He kneeled and kissed Hamaki's foot.

"Sit down, sit down, don't be ridiculous." Hamaki patted him on the cheek. "You are a respectful boy. It's the least I can do for you. Lima!" he shouted.

A graceful young woman, naked save for a loincloth, parted one of the straw curtains that separated the room from the rest of the hut. Hamaki had one of the biggest dwellings in the village, large enough to house his three wives and five children. By the tribe's standards, he was one of the richest men in Maniha Komo, obviously a result of his long tenure on the Council.

"Do you know Lima, my third wife?" asked Hamaki and tapped her behind.

"Of course I do," muttered Akamui, smiling uneasily. "She is good friends with Kalia, my wife."

"Oh, really? I didn't know that."

"You certainly did; you even met her once here, remember?" said Lima.

"Yeah, maybe," Hamaki scratched his head. "At my age and with all the responsibilities of the Council, I may forget things." He tapped her again. "Bring us some *tuka,* sweetheart. We have a lot to celebrate!"

Lima nodded and glided lithely out of the room, flashing a smile at Akamui.

"I have the best palm wine on Maniha Komo, you'll see," said Hamaki.

Somebody called from outside the entrance. "May I have a word with you, wise Hamaki?"

"That must be Arataki," muttered Hamaki, standing. "Stay here; I'll be back in a moment."

He hurriedly stepped out. Akamui gazed at the gently swinging straw-mat and strained his ears in a vain attempt to catch some of the muffled conversation. Something rustled behind him, and Lima returned from one of the other rooms, bringing two wooden cups full of transparent liquid. She scanned the room, approached Akamui, and pressed her bare leg to his shoulder.

"Where is he?" she whispered.

"Just went outside to speak with the chieftain."

She bent over to lay the cups on the floor, her naked breast swinging close to Akamui's face. She lingered for a while in this position, then swiftly kissed him on the lips and stood upright, her eyes shining.

"Are you crazy?!" he hissed.

"I missed you so much, my heart! I kneeled before Rakapi and prayed day and night to our god for you. 'Please Almighty Kepolo,' I said, 'bring my beloved Akamui safe and sound back home because he is the sun and air to me.'"

"This is insanity, Lima. We must stop it once and for all! What if he finds out? Didn't you hear that he wants to make me a member of the Council?"

"Well, I also heard that you saved his life. He certainly wouldn't mind sharing his third wife with you as a sign of his gratitude," Lima giggled, her perfect white teeth flashing in the dusk.

"Yeah, he'll certainly kill both of us," Akamui grunted.

"Oh, I see. My hero is afraid of some old limp-dick," Lima giggled again. "Listen, tomorrow morning he said he would be in the Hive; the Council is gathering. I will be waiting for you at our place when the sun reaches its highest point…"

Hamaki rushed in. He was a big, stout man, but the age had slackened his muscles and his short hair had already turned gray.

"Sorry about that, my young friend," he said, resuming his seat. "Tribe's duties all the time. Ah, the wine is here, wonderful!"

"Yes. I just asked our guest how Kalia was doing," Lima chirruped. "She is expecting a baby, you know… It's a special time for women."

"Good for you!" Hamaki tapped Akamui on the shoulder. "I wish for you to have a healthy boy who will become a great warrior, just like you!" He turned to Lima. "You can leave us now, my sweet butterfly. We have something important to discuss."

* * *

It was almost dark when Akamui got home. When he saw him, Kalia's face brightened. She threw herself into his arms and kissed him fondly.

"I'm so happy you're back, my love," she whispered. "I've been waiting the whole day for your return. Where have you been? You must be hungry. Come, sit! I've cooked you something delicious!"

Akamui grunted and slumped on the straw mat that covered the floor of his hut. He was dead tired. After returning from the raid yesterday, he'd had to go out early the following morning, so they hadn't seen each other much. In the flickering, soft firelight of the torch that cast playful shadows around the room, he watched her absentmindedly while she bustled around. The tiny place was hot and stuffy, with a large hammock in the middle that took up almost the entire space.

So small, compared with Hamaki's hut, Akamui thought. *You could die from suffocation in here. Well, that will change, once they accept me in the Council.*

Kalia brought the meal on a wooden tray, kneeled, and laid it before her husband. She was beautiful and young, still slender despite her protruding abdomen. As Akamui eyed her sullenly, she smiled at him, flicked a lock from her face, and shook her long black hair, which reached to the small of her back. Her full, sensitive lips and shining black eyes could inflame every man on the island. Everyone but

Akamui. Her deep love toward him, her willingness to be a devoted and submissive spouse, and her readiness to satisfy his slightest whims filled him with disgust. In fact, he had never loved her. She had been very young when he took her as a wife, and he did it only to please his father, who was in debt to Tanuli, one of the Council's members.

One day, one that Akamui would never forget, his father called him. When Akamui entered the hut, he found Tanuli sitting there. He was a tall man in his late forties, with short white hair and a long necklace made of the phalanges of his foes.

"I have six girls, and I have to find a match for each one of them," he began, after the usual exchange of pleasantries. "It's an enormous burden for every father to find even a single good guy to protect his daughter, let alone for six. But you are a good boy, Akamui, and I understand why your father is so proud of you. I have been observing you for a long time, and I think you will be a perfect fit for my youngest daughter, Kalia."

Tanuli looked up at his father. The latter looked pleased. He smiled and said, "I am sure that my son will take good care of your Kalia. She will be happy with him."

Akamui hadn't been sure that he wanted the deal—at least not until he met his father's stern stare, which eloquently spoke in favor of the proposition. He had bowed his head and said that he gladly accepted and would be honored to marry Tanuli's daughter. What else could he have done, anyway? However, when he saw Kalia for the first time, his first thought was, *What I'm supposed to do with this child? Should I fuck her or feed her first?*

Kalia was a virgin and was soon crazy about him. In the beginning, he enjoyed her vehement love, her wild sexual passion, and her almost slavish attitude. She had never raised her voice to him and had never contradicted him. Year after year, she was growing up and her body blossomed into curvy, womanly shapes. His friends' mockery gradually died away, and one day Akamui realized that all of them envied him for his beautiful wife. He was glad back then to have married her and had considered himself a lucky man.

Then Lima emerged and turned his world upside-down. She was Kalia's best friend, two years older than she was, and her attitude hinted toward a rich experience with men. Lima was playful and flirted jokingly with him now and then, but he had never taken her seriously. Not until the day she set up a meeting with Kalia by Butterfly Waterfall and went straight to Akamui's hut instead, playing innocent and looking for her friend. Akamui had a hard time catching her drift; taking hints was not his strong suit. Finally, Lima lost patience, grabbed his cock, and put it in her mouth. What happened then between them was so intense, so superb and incredible, that it forever changed Akamui's perception of sex.

From that day on, he stopped being interested in Kalia. Sex with her was so boring, so conventional. Lima knew how to make him feel like a real man. Fulfilled. Gratified. Satiated. As he was too poor to afford more than one wife, he seriously leaned toward the decision of dumping Kalia and replacing her with Lima.

Destiny, however, had decided otherwise. About eight full moons ago, the news that Lima would become Hamaki's third wife broke simultaneously with the announcement of Kalia's pregnancy. When Akamui learned he would be a father, his heart softened toward his spouse. Kalia was so radiant, so beautiful the day she announced the news to him. He had taken her scarlet, tear-stained face between his hands, had looked straight into her shining eyes, from which emanated all the happiness in the world, and had kissed her on the lips.

"I'm so lucky to have you, my love," he had whispered. "You will bear me a son, a great warrior, the pride of the entire Tipihao tribe…"

"Are you listening to me at all, or you're drifting off?" Kalia touched Akamui's hand, and he looked up, startled out of his reverie. "Eat! What are you waiting for?"

The meal still lay untasted before him. Akamui attacked it vigorously, noisily sipping the hot fish-broth and devouring the large swordfish steak.

"So, as I was saying," said Kalia, "you told me this morning that you'd be back before noon. I was waiting all day for you. Where have you been, my heart?"

"I met Hamaki, and he invited me to his hut. It was just for a quick chat, but then he took out his famous *tuka* and the time flew."

"Oh, it's nice of him to welcome you to his home," said Kalia. "Did you see Lima over there?"

"I did. She sent you her regards," said Akamui, and added quickly, "Can you believe that Tanuli wants to propose me for membership on the Council at the next election?"

"Really?" Kalia looked impressed. "This is wonderful news, my love! How come he's suddenly so kind to you?"

"He owes me something," snorted Akamui and lapsed into silence. Kalia peered at him lovingly. To her, he was the most handsome man on the island. To the rest of her acquaintances, her husband was a pretty dreadful creature.

Akamui was in his early twenties, brawny and tall (almost a head taller than the average Tipihao man), with impressive bulging muscles and taut sinews. A tattoo of a man dangling upside down from a tree, his body being pecked by a large bird with spread wings, covered the left part of his torso, beginning from the shoulder and creeping to his chest and abdomen. As was true of most of Maniha Komo's warriors, he had shaved his head down to the skin and it shone in the torchlight like a gigantic oily egg. A low forehead, full lips, and a flat nose, with a small white bone-ring through the left nostril, and similar rings hanging on both of his ears, gave him a fierce look. However, the most terrifying thing about him was his cold, murderous stare. His black eyes flashed with insane flame when he got furious, and nobody dared to confront him when he was in this state of mind.

Akamui finished his meal, wiped his mouth with the back of his hand, burped, and stretched in the corner. Kalia cleared the wooden bowl and plate and snuggled up to him.

"Did you miss me, my love?" she whispered, eagerly pressing her naked body to his.

"Of course I did," Akamui answered sleepily.

"Both of us? Do you want to feel him kicking?" She took his hand and gently lay his palm on her stomach. Akamui was not in the mood. He snorted and pushed her lightly.

"He is asleep like I am," he grunted.

After a brief silence, Kalia asked in a hurt voice, "So, how was the raid? The moon waxed and waned and became full again since you left. I heard you performed impressive feats there. It seems that everybody knows about them, but me! Tell me about Hamaki. What does he owe you?"

"Let's leave that for tomorrow, shall we?" Akamui muttered. "I want to sleep now, but I'll be all yours in the morning, fresh for a chat."

He pushed her again, hauled himself up, extinguished the torch, and climbed into the hammock. A while later, she heard him snoring. She stared at the darkness for a long time, tears rolling down her cheeks.

The next morning Akamui got up late. He had not slept well. He'd dreamed of having sex with Lima and woke up in the middle of the night with a hard-on. Kalia lay beside him, her bottom turned to him, but he did not touch her. The image of Lima, just coming out from the lake under Butterfly Waterfall, wet, gorgeous, and naked, with shiny hair and a luring smile, was burning his heart. He realized he must end all this. It was too dangerous to continue seeing her, especially now that he was in Hamaki's good grace.

My chances would be ruined in a twinkling if he found out, he brooded. Still, he could not restrain his lust. It took him a long time to fall asleep again, and when he woke up in the morning, the desire to see Lima was unbearable.

"Just this one last time, and then I'll end it," he muttered, not convinced at all. The hut was quiet and empty. Kalia was nowhere to be seen.

Perfect, Akamui thought and jumped from the hammock. He put on a small waistband of foliage that hardly covered his sex, slung a leather strap with a stone knife stuck into a wooden sheath over his shoulder, and fastened his bamboo sandals with their fiber laces. He glanced at the corner where three boiled seagull's eggs, a slice of dry meat, and a bunch of bananas waited for him enticingly, hesitated for a while, shook his head, and then ran outside. The sun was high in the sky, and he was sure that Lima was already awaiting him.

Akamui's hut was at the end of the village and he rushed straight into the jungle. The moment he reached the first trees, Kalia emerged on her way toward the hut, coming from the heart of the village, bringing a basket full of fruit. She saw her husband disappearing hurriedly into the forest, and her jaw dropped.

But where he's going? She wondered as she rushed into the hut to leave her load and stopped short, stupefied: for the first time since they were together, Akamui had not touched his breakfast.

She quickly assessed the situation.

Yesterday he said we would talk in the morning. He overslept, so obviously there was not anything pressing… What's the rush, then? He seemed scared, worried about something…

Grim anxiety hit her in the stomach, and piercing pain stabbed her heart. She got out and dashed toward the jungle, following Akamui's path.

Her father had taught her to read the trail, and Kalia followed the almost-invisible path of bent and crushed blades of grass that wound through the lush greenery, where branches made a compact, low tunnel. The thick canopy blocked the sun, letting through occasional flashes of bouncing light. It was dusky and grim, and the hot, damp air made her breathing difficult.

Kalia faltered, often tripping against snags and roots, her sharp eyes scanning for crumpled grass or snapped twigs. She stopped now and then, panting, drenched in sweat, pressing her belly with both hands. The heavy load in her womb exhausted her. The baby fidgeted and kicked, agitated, and her heart thumped wildly. Every single step became a burden, and she slowed down.

"Please, Great Kepolo, watch over him, don't let him be hurt," her lips moved silently as disastrous scenarios passed one after another through her head. She took a sharp turn but lost the trail and stopped, straining her ears. Leaves rustling; birds screeching; wings fluttering; insects buzzing; toads croaking. The song of the jungle, as the old-timers called it, the sounds she had grown up with. Yet she detected something in the distance, a faint constant humming.

"Butterfly Waterfall," she exclaimed and ran again.

This path must lead straight there. How dumb I am not to have guessed it earlier! I always take the other way, that's why… But why would he go there?

The tangle of foliage lashed her face and body, but she hardly felt it. The humming was getting louder and louder, gradually turning into a roar, and the path grew larger. All of a sudden, the jungle ended, and she found herself in a small clearing, lit up by the shining sun and studded with tropical flowers.

A narrow mass of water fell with a deafening noise from a high, almost vertical cliff into a round lake. Kalia took a step forward and waded into the soft, succulent grass, whereupon an iridescent cloud of butterflies rose around her. There were everywhere, lovely and colorful as flying flowers, fluttering all over the glade and alighting now and then on the bright tropical blossoms, tinted in red, orange, yellow, and cream-white. She stopped short, enchanted by the breathtaking picture. This spot was her favorite, the place where she had played as a kid and had spent the happiest moments of her life. The sweet scent, wafting in the air, and the roar of the waterfall, made her dizzy and carried her back to her childhood.

And then, a loud moan coming from her left brought her back to reality. She turned sharply. Lima, her best friend, leaned against a solitary palm tree near the lake, her legs wrapped around Akamui's waist and her arms folded around his neck. She was groaning and shouting as if mad, while Akamui thrust into her, moving back and forth faster and faster. Kalia's jaw dropped open. She watched them, stunned: two wild animals clinging tightly to each other, burning with passion. Fiery rage burst in her chest and hit her brain, incinerating her insides. In that moment, she hated Lima so powerfully that the desire to kill her was the only driving force that made sense.

"Fucking betrayer!" Kalia bellowed. Blind with rage, she bent down, grabbed a thick, knotty piece of wood, and ran toward them. Akamui was just easing Lima to the ground when both of them turned, startled by the inhuman scream coming from Kalia's lungs. She fell upon them, lashing the club at Lima's head. Akamui flung himself to shield her, and the club landed heavily on his shoulder. He hollered in pain but did not flinch. Kalia lifted her gnarled weapon again with an effort, preparing for a new blow, and staggered, losing her balance under its weight. Quick as a flash, Akamui took a step forward and backhanded her across the face, knocking her onto her back. Kalia hit her head on the edge of a protruding stone and then remained still.

Akamui and Lima watched with terror as a red pool slowly spread from beneath her head. Lima gave out a shrill scream. Akamui kneeled down, lifted Kalia's head, and started caressing her, muttering gentle words. Her eyes were wide open, staring at the sky, her face distorted in a grimace of pain and hatred.

Lima flung herself hysterically at Akamui, drumming his back with her small fists. Patiently, he lay Kalia on the ground, turned around, and tried to catch Lima's hands. She wrung herself free and jumped forward, attempting to claw his face. He pushed her roughly. She fell, wailing loudly, sobbing and tearing at her hair.

Shock and confusion seized Akamui, and for a moment, he just stayed there, rooted to the ground, staring at Kalia's dead body. He was aware of the consequence of killing a woman, especially a pregnant one…

Sharp pain in his left forearm brought him out of his stupor. Lima had flung herself at him again and had just bitten him. Her squalls were driving him crazy. He grabbed her, lifted her to her feet, and stared at her wandering eyes.

"Listen to me," he said, shaking her. She was still absent, her look vacant. Akamui slapped her tear-stained face.

"Are you listening now, you stupid fish?" he cried, irritated. "She's dead, all right! There's nothing to do about it. Go to your house and play innocent. Did anybody see you coming?" He slapped her again. "Answer me! Did anyone—"

"I don't know," sobbed Lima, "leave me alone, please…"

"Listen to me carefully now. You go straight home and stay there as if nothing happened. If anybody asks you where you've been, tell him you just went to gather herbs, all right?" He smacked her one more time and shouted, "Look at me! Do you understand? If Hamaki suspects that we have been meeting in secret, we're as good as dead. Got it? Stop crying now!"

Lima's look gradually cleared up.

"What will you do?" she sobbed.

"Don't worry about me. Do what I say and leave everything else to me. Go now, run!"

She jumped and ran, brushing away her tears. When she disappeared into the forest, Akamui looked at Kalia—the woman who loved him so much and who had been ready to sacrifice her life for him. He felt nothing for her. No more than for any other person who he had killed or raped during his life. It was different for the baby, though. He had longed for a son, and now everything was falling apart…

I'll bring her to my mother. Maybe she can still save the baby, he thought.

He lifted Kalia and flung her across his shoulder, feeling her still-warm blood dripping onto his neck.

"What a mess!" he muttered and set out for the village, desperately shaking his head.

* * *

Several hours later, Akamui stood before the Council in the huge bee-hive-like bamboo hut, known by the locals as "The Hive." The elders were sitting in a tight semi-circle in the middle of the room around a large round stone hearth. Akamui stood on the opposite side, his head bowed. The smoke from the hearth was biting his eyes and tears trickled down his cheeks. The elders smoked their pipes and nodded in agreement with Hamaki's speech.

"We all know that killing a woman is a terrible crime, punishable by death," Hamaki was saying. "The women are precious, and we have to take care of them. They bring us strength and comfort and are the most important source of inspiration in our life. For ages, all the wars break out over women, as foreign women bring fresh blood to the tribe and give us strong, healthy babies, which is crucial for our survival and prosperity.

"So, wise elders, the crime carried out by the young Akamui is out-rageous. We all know that the punishment for such a misdeed is death. However, as the highly respectable Council can see, the death of poor Kalia was a pure accident. She had struck her husband with a club in her rage, the evidence of which is visible on Akamui's left shoulder, and he had hit her back in self-defense. Sometimes our otherwise gen-tle spouses get irritated during their childbearing, don't they?

"Here I want to emphasize the honesty and the courage of this young fellow, who immediately brought Kalia to his mother and did everything possible to at least save the baby. He did not hesitate after-ward to come to us and to tell us the truth, thus taking responsibility for the demise of his beautiful wife. I'd like to draw your attention to the fact that the young Akamui struck only one blow at Kalia. It was fatal, it's true, but come on, who hasn't ever thrashed his wife or daughter now and then? It's necessary sometimes, you know, just to keep them on the right track.

"With that said, I ask the Council to consider carefully the fate of this brave, smart, and fearless warrior, who is an irrefutable asset to Tipihao's army. I don't think it's time now to deprive our troops of his might and cunning and to ruin his bright future because of this unfortunate accident.

"Thus, I respectfully request that the respectable Council not to be too hard on this young man. I suggest sending him in exile for two years to the remote outpost atolls as a lookout for the enemy's boats. Thank you for listening to me, wise elders. My talk is over."

An agitated murmur met the suggestion. Hamaki bowed to the Council and sat down. Akamui did not budge. Kerully, the oldest of the elders, rose slowly, leaning on a long bamboo stick and shaking all over. He was bald, slightly stooped with age, and so skinny that could barely stand on his feet.

"I don't want to contradict the wise Hamaki, but I must point out that the sentence he proposes is too clement, given the severity of the crime. I'd like to offer my condolences to my old friend Tanuli." Kerully bowed to the man who was staring at the ground, crushed with sorrow, before continuing. "The blood of his precious child is calling for justice. Let's not forget that only three full moons ago we sentenced to death Tamali, a precious warrior, for a similar misdeed—he had beaten his wife so severely that she passed away from her wounds. So, I'm telling you now: this beating must stop once and for all. It's true that in the case of Akamui it was more of an accident than murder, and I agree that a bright future lies ahead for him. But justice is justice. Two years is too short a punishment for such a crime. I vote for at least five to seven years in exile on the Coral Beck. Life is hard over there, at our most remote atoll on the northern boundary. Akamui will serve his time, building the great stone watchtower along with the slaves and the other law-breakers. His youth will fade in hardship and repentance and he will return wiser, stronger, and atoned for his misdeeds. Thank you, wise elders. My talk is over."

Kerully slumped back in his seat, apparently exhausted. Each of the elders took their turn to speak, before taking a vote. As the debate grew more and more heated, they eventually agreed to leave it to the sacred smoke to decide the length of the sentence. After careful observation of its direction, Akamui was sentenced to five years in exile at the Coral Beck atoll.

CHAPTER II

LELANI

ince time immemorial, the Tipihao tribe inhabited Maniha Komu, which in their native language meant "Half-Moon Island." It was one of the biggest islands in Kepula Penu[3], which was comprised of scores of isles, grouped around a formation resembling, as the name suggested, a gigantic loggerhead turtle.

The word "tipiho" in the tribe's dialect meant a "savage," "wild," "intractable," and "bellicose" warrior—a perfect description of Tipihao men. Nobody could compare with their ferocity and force. For hundreds of years, they kept the other tribes in subjugation, thanks to their perfect military organization, iron discipline, and the possession of knowledge that nobody else had—the secret of building big sailing boats, far more rapid than the primitive canoes used by the other peoples.

The Tipihaos often sailed to the nearby islands, where they sowed devastation, death, and dread. All tribes paid them tribute, making gifts of everything from trade goods—such as animal pelts, weapons, woven clothes and mats, bamboo, wine, fruits, dry meat, and raw materials—to young women, children, and slaves.

---

3 The Turtle Archipelago.

The Tipihao tribe integrated the foreign women and children and inured them to their customs. The slaves, mostly captive warriors, were forced to build boats and huts or hew trees in the jungle. When, after prolonged inhumane treatment, the slaves were on the brink of physical and mental exhaustion, they were sacrificed to the tribe's god Kepolo before Rakapi, which literally meant "sacred tree."

Life on the island was simple and had changed little since the time of the first ancestors. The men hunted, fished, made war, and governed. The women took care of the children and did all the hard work related to the household. Their social status was not much better than that of the slaves, as they had no right to vote or to take part in any issue related to the tribe's rules.

The hierarchy was democratically organized. All the men would gather once every two years and would elect the twelve members of the Council of Elders, based on wisdom and merit. The Council made all the important decisions related to the tribe's governance, justice, and politics. They would also approve the nominees for the next election and select the chieftain, who was usually one of the Council members. The chieftain fulfilled the roles of military leader and shaman.

By the time of Akamui's return, the Tipihao tribe consisted of about five thousand people who lived in bamboo huts in the island's heart. The largest dwellings, occupied by the chieftain and the elders, were at the foot of the central ridge, so-called *Carapace Hill*. The rest of the village's huts, considerably smaller, were crowded on the slopes of the two neighboring heights—*Whelk Hill* to the west and *Egg Hill*, situated eastward of *Carapace Hill*.

It was almost ten moons since Akamui returned from exile. His punishment had taken its toll on him. The days on the atoll were long and tedious, and the labor hard and exhausting. His life was a burden, as he was doomed to endure living in complete wilderness, without woman or friend, surrounded only by morons and slaves—sheer losers punished for their stupidity and cowardice. He rapidly showed them his superiority, and after several fierce thrashings, nobody ever dared to bother him.

The nights were even worse. In the silence of the darkness, broke only by the loud snoring of his roommates, Akamui stayed up, staring into the void and fretting until dawn about the unfortunate events that led to his punishment.

But he was tough and never gave up. The spite was making him stronger, and after the hard daily work, he spent hours training his body and transforming it into an incredible mass of muscles. Broad shoulders, enormous dorsals, and bulging biceps made every man think twice before arguing with him. He kept himself in perfect shape, preparing for the big day of his return.

Unfortunately, things did not work out the way he expected. To his surprise, once back on the island, he discovered that his old friends now preferred to keep their distance. The worst of them was Hamaki, who didn't even greet him for his homecoming. The youngsters, especially those unfamiliar with Akamui's former feats, followed the common demeanor of the older warriors and paid him no respect.

It must be that fucking dotard Tanuli who's incited the others against me, Akamui seethed.

Soon, he realized that nobody liked him. In consequence, he became sullen and short-fused, dangerous, and unpredictable until he found himself alone, isolated, and depressed, just as he had been in exile.

* * *

After a few days of not seeing Akamui around the village, his mother Lalago woke up one morning with a pang of anxiety in her stomach, feeling that something was wrong with her son. With a racing heart, she hurried up the hillside to his hut, terrified of what she might discover.

Lalago was a good-tempered, smiling, chubby woman. People adored and highly respected her because of her kindness and her famous healing skills. Her knowledge of herbs, infusions, and salves was so legendary that her fame had reached beyond the boundary of Half-Moon Island and had spread all around the Turtle Archipelago.

The moment Lalago stepped into Akamui's hut, she wrinkled her nose and gasped in shock. Her beloved son lay motionless, flat on his stomach, with his fists clenched and his face buried in the seating rug. All around him was a mess of leftover food, scattered empty flasks, cups, and broken pottery vessels. Flies swarmed the interior of the hut, and the stench was overwhelming.

Lalago bent down, grabbed Akamui by the shoulders, and rolled him on his back. After quickly scanning the room, she snatched a half-full bucket of water from the corner and splashed it over Akamui's face. He jumped with a cry, brandishing his knife and staggering, still dizzy from the wine.

"What are you doing?!" he shouted, once he recognized his mother.

"No, what are *you* doing?" Lalago yelled back. "When are you going to stop making a fool of yourself and start acting like a real man? Where did my brave, smart son disappear to? Or did they suck out your brain with a bamboo straw on Coral Beck to turn you into a good-for-nothing wretch?"

"I'm desperate, mother," muttered Akamui. He slumped on the ground and thrust his knife up to the hilt into the earth floor. "The men make fun of me behind my back. They never took me on a raid with them, and this was my only hope to prove my name again and find a foreign gal for the locals are fleeing from me like frightened birds..."

"Stop whining like a woman!" Lalago cried out angrily. "Are you a man, or aren't you? I know what you should do, and you will listen to your mother as you always did, and then you will thank me, as usual."

"What do you mean?" grunted Akamui.

"Go to Kepolo tonight and beg him forgiveness. You must propitiate him and offer him a sacrifice. Then, you must ask him what you should do to gain the respect of your tribe again!"

"A sacrifice? What sacrifice, mother? Kepolo likes our foes dismembered before Rakapi. Where would I find a foreign warrior right now?"

"Well, if you don't have a foe to offer him, then you should promise him one. The important thing is to do it sincerely, with all your heart—thus, Kepolo will know that you mean it and he will help you. That's the way it works. Now, don't be crestfallen! Go to the brook and wash yourself; you stink like a boar in rut. Meanwhile, I will clean up all this mess and prepare you something to eat."

* * *

Akamui squeezed his way through the dense greenery. The gray blanket of twilight was falling over the forest, but his eyes were strong in the dark and the waxing moon was already rising in the east. He occasionally stopped and listened to the familiar noises of the jungle. It was the quietest period in the tropical forest—the deafening concert of piercing cries ebbed away as the diurnal animals went to sleep, and the nocturnal ones had not still come out.

Akamui hurried. Prayers before Rakapi took place a little after the sunset when the big red fireball sank in the ocean and darkness covered the place. The twilight was a special, magical time for Tipihaos. He looked up at the stars. Alina, the brightest one, was pale, meaning that he still had time. A glance ahead reassured him that he was approaching his final destination as the trees thinned out, giving way to shrubs and high grass. And sure enough, a moment later, he brushed aside the last of the ferns to emerge into a vast clearing, called by the natives the *Sacred Zone* or *Kepolo's Belt*.

Rakapi, the gigantic Sacred Tree and the dwelling of the tribe's god Kepolo, was a black silhouette against the dark sky. Its boughs spread in all directions, almost reaching the extremities of the clearing, where multiple cages were built into the crowns of the surrounding trees.

The Council's building, known as *the Hive,* stood out as a huge domed beehive on the far left side of the Sacred Tree.

Every time Akamui faced the Tree, a wave of awe and dread filled his heart.

He prostrated himself and glued his front to the ground. He paused in this position for a moment, then got up and advanced toward the enormous trunk. The hundreds of skulls impaled on its branches gleamed softly in the moonshine. Dangling bones rattled gently in the faint night breeze, which also brought a disgusting stench of carrion. Akamui shuddered and wrinkled his nose. Even though he had grown up with this smell, the first moment was never easy.

A big black bird flew out from inside the treetop with a piercing croak, flapping its wings. Akamui jumped nervously and hit his shin on the stone altar.

"Bloody *burkans,*" he cursed and stepped forward, rubbing his leg.

He kneeled and pressed his forehead against the trunk, feeling the cool, rough bark. A scent of moisture and something astringent filled his nostrils. Akamui knew what it was—a fluorescent mushroom that grew only on the bark of the Sacred Tree. The shamans used it for smoking or chewing and put it in the palm wine during the sacrifices. Akamui reached out and broke a small luminous piece from the large mushroom just above his head, then put it in his mouth and chewed it slowly. It tasted sour at first, and then the strong, bitter savor stung his tongue. He stayed still for a while with his eyes closed. His head was spinning and his thoughts drifted away. After a long moment of silence, he whispered: "Please, Great Kepolo, the strongest of all gods, listen to my prayer. I beg you on my knees, oh, Almighty: help me win back the respect of my tribe; make me an elder or a chieftain; please give me a woman who will bring me a son, Almighty; only you know how much I covet a boy! If you do that for me, I swear to sacrifice to you three young boys from the Taraho tribe… Please, give me a sign, greatest of the greatest gods, and show me the way to my destiny…"

Akamui stayed in a daze for a long time, staring at the green-brownish bark. His lips continued moving, but no sound was coming out. The world reeled before his eyes and made him heave.

He focused all his attention on the rustling of the leaves. Now, the clarity of his hearing was incredible—he could discern every single sound to such a degree that he had the impression that he could hear the ants walking on the branches. The rattle of the bones above him was banging in his head, stronger than the big gong. The clanging overwhelmed him and carried him away. Now he felt light as a feather, free of his body, like a loose leaf from the tree, tossed by the wind and floating aimlessly in the air. At one moment, he was scudding down, almost touching the ground; the next he flew up and drifted high above the crown; then, he descended earthward and lost himself in the green, rustling leaves… Two firebugs were chasing each other just in front of him. He fixed his mind on the blinking yellow lights, which grew bigger and bigger until a bright light exploded in his brain and he found himself in front of Lalago's hut. His mother was weeping. She handed him a crying baby, wrapped in bloody clothes, and in his head rang her sobbing voice,

"It's a boy… I'm so sorry, son!"

Akamui was about to ask her why she was sorry for such good news when the scene changed abruptly, and he saw himself hunting into the jungle with an eight- or nine-year-old curly-haired boy, clutching a spear in his hand. They were after a wild boar and Akamui was teaching him how to read the trail.

The setting shifted again, and a third vision appeared. Now the boy was tied to the big stony altar, his legs and arms spread horizontally. Heavy rain poured down. A flash of lightning lit up the hundreds of warriors with burning torches who swung their bodies under the rhythm of the drums. The Sacred Tree hung ominously over his son while Akamui raised his knife to sacrifice him to Kepolo.

"No!" Akamui cried out and shook his head, crossing the distance from the future to present in a blink of an eye. He lay under the tree again, numb with shock. A deep, guttural voice, coming from the rustling leaves, whispered in his ears.

"Soon you'll have a son, brave Akamui. This boy belongs to me. I want you to sacrifice him to me the moment he succeeds in his warrior's proof. Once he kills his first foe, he must taste human flesh and drink his enemy's blood before I accept him."

"Please, spare me, Almighty Kepolo," whispered Akamui, shaking from head to toe. "I know you are great in your plans. Let my son be!"

"I'll give you five sons, brave Akamui," the leaves rustled in his ears. "I claim the first one. He will be your gift for me. Prove your respect, and tomorrow, before the day runs out, I'll make you a member of the Council. Furthermore, the day you sacrifice your son to me, you'll become the new chieftain. Promise me your firstborn, young Akamui. Be my faithful warrior!"

"Do I have a choice, Almighty?" Akamui whispered.

"Of course, you do," the leaves hissed. "That is the beauty of being human—you can choose your path. Your side. Free will, as it is… But do you have guts to stand against me, little Akamui? Stick with me and I'll lift you to eminence. Refuse to serve me and I will crush you. You will be a miserable coward, despised and repudiated by everyone. Do we have an agreement, young Akamui? Make your vow now."

Akamui was trembling like a leaf. Atavistic fear crept inside him, giving him goosebumps. The top of his head was prickling and, if he hadn't shaved his hair to the skin, it would have been standing straight. He had never felt so afraid.

Unable to move, with a heart torn with grief, he uttered, "Let your will be done, Almighty Kepolo, ruler of our destiny and master of our tribe. I will sacrifice my firstborn son to you right after his warrior's proof."

A strong blast of wind swished in the crown of the great tree, and in a flash, another vision swam before Akamui's eyes. A girl crept out of the sea and crawled on the sandy shore.

"I see your sincerity," whispered *Rakapi's* leaves. "Go to the South shore and find Lelani."

And then deep blackness wrapped Akamui in a gentle hug.

When he came to his senses, the moon was shining brightly, high in the sky. He blinked and rubbed his temples as if waking up from a heavy dream. He rose, bowed to *Rakapi,* and the vision of a lying on the sand girl flashed in his mind. *Go find Lelani,* rustled the leaves and he rushed toward the beach. Dizzy and confused, not aware of the twigs and branches lashing at his naked body, he ran in the darkness, moving deftly through the jungle, as though led by an invisible force. When finally the cool night breeze whipped his face and he heard the roar of the surf echoing in the distance, he realized that he had reached the shore, although he could not remember for the life of him which path he had chosen. The moonlight cast a mild glow over the beach, bathing the ocean in shimmering gold and making the sands white and lucent. A big round crab scuttled majestically, followed by several smaller whitish ones on their way toward the water. Akamui sank his feet into the cool sand and looked around. About fifty yards away, he saw the outline of a dark bulk near the water. He took out his knife as he approached it cautiously.

It was a girl in her teens, lying prone, half wrapped in long, tangled hair, her face buried in the sand. Akamui sheathed his knife and squatted beside her. He took her by the shoulders, rolled her over, and gazed at her swollen, covered with sand face, all in bruises and scratches. It was hard to tell who she was. Akamui slapped her across the face, but she gave no sign of life. He looked around.

How did she get here? he thought. *I see no boat or raft... Weird... I'll take her home.*

He swung the girl with ease on his shoulder and set off stealthily toward his hut. Luckily, he met no one on his way.

Living on the outskirts has its advantages, he thought, as he lay the girl on the floor. He took a small open pot filled with shark oil from the shelf and hit two flints together several times to give out a spark. The wick caught fire and mild light suffused the room. He brought the lamp close to the limp body, bent down, and moved aside her tangled black hair, staring at the pinched, exhausted face. He pressed his palm to her cool forehead. She was young, almost a child.

Yes, this is Lelani, indeed... Akamui thought.

He knew her. She was the eldest daughter of an old friend of his, Lairo, who had been killed some time ago. Akamui helped Lairo's wife now and then since he returned from exile, usually supplying her with food when she and her three children were starving. Lelani had disappeared about six moons ago, and nobody had a clue what had happened to her. The Council of Elders conducted a meticulous investigation. They had thoroughly interrogated all her relatives and friends, and combed the entire island for several days without results.

Akamui detached the wooden flask dangling at his waist and sprinkled Lelani's face with water. As he wet her cracked lips, she slowly opened her eyes.

"Glad to see you again, Lelani," Akamui said, "it's been a long time. Where have you been, girl?"

Lelani did not answer. She turned her head and closed her eyes, drifting back into unconsciousness. Akamui pushed her several times and slapped her lightly across the face, but she did not come around.

"I need my mother," he decided and rushed out.

Lalago lived down the hill. When Akamui got in her place, he was met by loud snoring. He grasped her shoulder and shook her.

"Wake up, mother! Get your basket of herbs and ointments and come with me. Somebody needs your help."

"What's going on?" asked Lalago sleepily. "What are you doing here? How did the praying go? Did Kepolo give you a sign?"

"He did. Hurry up!" snarled Akamui. He helped her gather her remedies, grabbed the small covered basket, and hurried out. She trotted behind him, still half-asleep.

When Lalago saw Lelani where Akamui had left her, she let out a cry and muttered, "Poor thing."

She kneeled and turned Lelani flat on her stomach, then pulled a small wooden box from the basket. She scooped up a small amount of ointment with the tips of her fingers and rubbed it vigorously onto Lelani's back. Within seconds, the girl opened her eyes. Lalago rolled her over and, supporting her head, poured some liquid into her mouth. Lelani's eyes brightened, and she gradually came to her senses.

"Water…" she whispered, and Akamui passed her his flask. She rose a little, leaned on Lalago, and drank eagerly, staring at Akamui, who had bent down, impatiently waiting for her to finish. As she lowered the flask, a wan smile slid onto her lips.

"Thank you, master Akamui," she whispered.

"Where have you been, Lelani? We've been looking for you for a long time. Tell me what happened to you!" asked Akamui anxiously.

"I came from Rocky Island," croaked Lelani in a husky voice. "I've been living there since I left Maniha Komu."

"What the fuck did you do there?"

"I married a man of the Taraho tribe."

"You what?" shouted Akamui. "You eloped with a man from Rocky Island? Are you out of your mind? Don't you know this deed is punishable by death?"

"I do," uttered Lelani, "and that's why I'm here. I brought you some important information, Master Akamui. It's so crucial for the survival of our tribe that I hope bringing it back to the Elders will mean they treat me with clemency."

"Speak up, girl!" said Akamui, his eyes throwing thunderbolts. "How come you ran away with a Taraho jerk in the first place? Where did you find him?"

"He was a slave here; they kept him in the cages at *Kepolo's belt*. His name was Triko…" Lelani spoke slowly, with a great effort.

Akamui nodded. "I remember the fool."

"The moment I laid my eyes on him, I knew he was the man of my life," Lelani continued. "I was ready to die for him… I helped him escape… It was a hardship to get there, and all that for nothing…"

"What are you babbling on about, kid?" Akamui shouted.

Lelani squinted and whispered, "Our people are in deadly danger, master Akamui. The chieftains of the Four Islands have allied against Tipihaos. Now there are fifteen or more tribes, all around the Kepula Penu. They have raised an enormous army, ten times ours, maybe even more…"

"Toadshit!" Akamui yelled. "Where is this army?"

"They rallied on Rocky Island and by the full moon, after they perform their ceremony dedicated to the Moon Goddess, they will set off for Maniha Komo. They vowed to the Moon Goddess to slay us all this time, even the women and the children. Not a single Tipihao alive—this is their oath."

Akamui leaned at the hut entrance and sat silent for a long time, his gaze boring into the darkness.

"Full moon is in three sunsets," he muttered to himself, glancing at the sky, where the waxing moon glowed. He turned to Lelani. "Tell me, slut, why did you return? Why did you not stay with your man on Rocky Island?"

"He is dead, that's why," said Lelani grimly.

"Go on! What happened?" barked Akamui.

"There was a quarrel about me, between him and a man from Starfish Island," Lelani brushed her eyes. "The son of a snake leered at me all the time and even groped me more than once. I held my mouth shut. I wanted no trouble… It was not a big deal anyway, but Triko saw him touching me, and…" her voice trailed off. Lalago sat beside her and hugged her, gently grooming her dirty hair.

"They fought, and Triko plunged his knife in the bugger's ribs," Lelani continued after a while, sniffing and brushing her eyes. "The jerk fell and didn't budge. Then my beloved wiped his knife on his stinking body and bent to tear his necklace, as the winners do. Then, suddenly, the dead man came to life and thrust his knife into Triko's throat… They both died in a pool of blood, one piled over the other. And all that because of me," Lelani burst into tears and buried her face in Lalago's breast.

"It's all right, sweetie," murmured Lalago, rocking her gently and caressing her. "It's not your fault. The men have no brains, only instincts, these morons; you will understand all that with time. But don't fret too much about Triko—you didn't belong to him, that's why Kepolo gave him a sudden death. You are young; you'll make it through. Here you'll find a strong, handsome man, close to your kin."

Akamui was losing patience. "Cut the crap, will you?" he yelled at his mother. "And you, stop crying and keep talking," he snarled at the girl. "When did your man get killed?"

"It was right after the half-moon, about six or seven sunsets ago," said Lelani, sniffling. "I panicked, didn't know what to do. They would have torn me apart if they found out that two warriors were dead because of me. I ran to the shore and took the same canoe we used when we fled from here. Afterward, I don't remember much—I followed Alina, I drank rainwater and ate nothing for many sunsets. Then my boat hit the reef, and I thought I was dying."

Lelani stopped speaking abruptly and drifted off. Akamui glanced at his mother, who nodded and said, "Go! I'll take care of her."

Akamui ran to the center of the village, straight to the Snakes' Gong. The large, reddish disk with carved wriggling silvery snakes gleamed in the moonlight, hanging from a solitary tree. Nobody knew for sure how this strange object had arrived in the village. The story went that it belonged to some pale-skin sailors, who came in ancient times to Maniha Komu in a big sailing boat. According to the legend, these men taught Tipihaos how to build and steer such boats, cultivate flax, and weave linen sails. They also brought many strange plants and animals, species like boars and snakes, which could be seen nowhere else around the Archipelago but on Maniha Komu. Moreover, the same seamen trained them to make pottery and taught them numbers and the lunar calendar. Based on that, a Tipihao year began with the rainy season, the time of the most intensive rains, and lasted between eleven and twelve full moons.

Akamui dashed straight to the gong. He took the heavy club, which was kept leaning against the tree, and hit the copper disk three times in quick succession—the signal for an emergency meeting of the Council of Elders. After a brief interval, he repeated it two times more, threw the club down, and blended into the forest. Somebody shouted at him from a distance, but Akamui was not interested in discussing his act. Summoning the Council was the prerogative of its members, except in cases of imminent danger. He knew they would go to Kepolo's belt to check out what was going on, so he rushed to the clearing and hid amongst the shadow of the trees, waiting and keeping a sharp eye on the entrance of the Hive.

The chieftain, Arataki, came first. He opened the heavy wooden door, made of interlaced rods, and left it wide open. From his hiding place, Akamui watched him kneel in the center to strike flints over tinder to light the sacred fire. Akamui remembered the hearth from the time he had been brought before the elders after killing Kalia. It was built in a circle from evenly-sized stones, and the nasty smoke had stung his eyes many times.

The elders used the fire to foretell the will of Kepolo, hence its name: "the foreshadowing fire." The chieftain always used dry twigs and branches fallen from the Sacred Tree to kindle it. The fire must burn the whole meeting and its purpose was purely practical: during the debates, the elders examined the smoke, thus guessing Kepolo's will. If it rose straight upward and passed through the small outlet at the top of the roof, it meant that the god agreed with their decisions. Any disturbance in the smoke such as winding, wriggling, or whirling indicated that Kepolo was not pleased and that they must change their decision until the god was satisfied and the smoke began rising straight up again. Akamui remembered how a disturbance in the fumes during his trial had prompted the elders to harshen his sentence.

While the chieftain kindled the fire, the other elders arrived one by one and took their positions around the hearth. Akamui counted nine. He knew there was one vacant place in the Council since *karuli*, the most dangerous snake on the island, bit the old Afari.

As the last two elders appeared and hurried into the Hive, Akamui slipped in after them.

Arataki was standing up and gesticulating nervously, saying in an irritated voice, "… and if none of us summoned this meeting, then who—"

"I have," said Akamui, stepping forward. "I'm the one who hit the gong."

He scanned the men who were sitting cross-legged on shark-skin rugs in a semicircle around the hearth. They all gazed at him in dismay.

"And who are you to do that?" cried out Arataki, "Don't you know that nobody is supposed to touch the Snakes' gong unless it's a matter of life and death?"

"And it is, indeed! I have some crucial information to share with you tonight, and after you hear it, you will all agree that I have acted the right way," said Akamui. His face was passive, but his eyes burned like two black coals in the dark room.

"Speak out then. Come here, before the hearth!" said Arataki.

Akamui stepped up. "Before I reveal to the honorable elders the facts I was given, I want to refer to the law of our ancestors and to claim the vacant place in the Council until the next election," he said firmly.

Silence lingered. Kerully rose with difficulty, supporting himself with his stick, and said in a hoarse voice, "An appointed place on the Council belongs to a man with special merit to his tribe. Tell us what you know; if your tale is worth something and the smoke approves you, we will vote in your favor. However, if you speak nonsense, your punishment will be fifty lashes for summoning us without a justifiable reason. Do the wise elders concur with my proposition?"

The men nodded in silence.

"And you, young Akamui? Do you agree to my terms?"

"I have always appreciated your wisdom and fairness, sagacious Ker-ully," said Akamui, bowing. "Let it be as you wish, then. I have been informed that the Four Islands have made a military alliance with the other tribes of Kepula Penu and have gathered considerable forces on Rocky Island. They will wait for the full moon to rise, and after they make their offerings to the Moon Goddess, they will leave for our land, firmly determined to kill us off. I already have an action plan, and if the Council would kindly accept me as a member, I would be glad to share it with you."

"How do you know all this?" barked Tanuli, who still detested Akamui as strongly as in the day he lost his daughter.

Akamui expected the question. "The almighty Kepolo gave me his signs and led me to the source of my knowledge. Early tonight I went to *Rakapi* to prey, and I had a vision of a girl lying on the south shore. Kepolo told me she had a secret to convey. I ran to the beach and there she was. It turned out to be Lelani."

Agitated whispering met these words.

"Lelani?" exclaimed Arataki. "Wasn't she the girl who disappeared some time ago? Where had she been hiding?"

"She told me she had eloped with one captive from Rocky Island."

"Who exactly?" asked Hamaki, who was in charge of the slaves.

"Triko," Akamui said.

"Triko? I remember him. He cut trees in the forest with the other slave trash before disappearing mysteriously into thin air," Hamaki barked.

"Yes, that one," confirmed Akamui. "The girl admitted that she had helped him flee. Fell in love with him and all that crap. He's dead now, and she came back with the warning to try to redeem herself. I promised her that nobody would hurt her for her previous mistakes."

"And who you are to absolve her?" Tanuli shouted. "You have neither the right nor the power to make such a promise! You should have brought her here, instead, so that we could cross-examine her. We should punish her for her betrayal; our law is unequivocal on that matter."

"And are we sure she's telling the truth? Imagine if it's a trap?" asked Ahaki.

"Listen, the girl is very weak. She's useless right now," said Akamui.

"How so?" barked Tanuli.

"She lies unconscious, and my mother takes care of her," Akamui explained. "As for the doubts expressed by the young Ahaki, I am strongly convinced that she is telling the truth because I believe that the Great Kepolo sent her to us as a messenger.

Kerully leaned on his stick, his old body shaking uncontrollably, and croaked, "Some things make sense in this story. First, those fools, the Tarahos and Toragos, do worship the moon. They think everything undertaken at full moon will be crowned with success. Second, Kedia foresaw that the destruction of our tribe would come from Rocky Island. Fortunately, Kepolo is the strongest of all gods. He keeps watch over us and makes us invincible. So, if the girl tells the truth, we need to be prepared. We have to take immediate precautions and lay an ambush for our enemies. Once they set their foot on Maniha Komo, we will strike and kill them off. That is my proposition, wise elders. My talk is over."

"With all due respect for the wise Kerully, I dare to say that his plan is far from good," objected Akamui. "We must not allow our enemies to come and trap us like wild boars in their dens. Lelani told me they outnumber us ten to one. If they attack us on Maniha Komu, they could set the island on fire and chase us like animals. I say we must surprise these stinking frogs the way our ancestors once did. We must go to Rocky Island and hit them when they expect it the least—on the eve of their departure. As I mentioned already, I have a plan on how to do that and if the honorable Council deigns to listen to it…"

"But this is an incredible impudence," said Keko, a fierce-looking giant whose left ear was missing. He leaped to his feet, licked his thick lips, and brushed his wide, flat nose, from which a bone ring was dangling. "First, Akamui is not a member of the Council, so he has no right to participate in the debates. Second, instead of telling us what to do, let's make him bring this girl here. We must question her, as the Wise Tanuli suggested! What if she's lying? What if this is a trap intended to draw us away from familiar territory and help our enemies take the island? The full moon is almost set. We don't have time to go to Rocky Island and leave our women and children unprotected. My opinion is that the best precaution would be to stay here and to organize our defense. My talk is over."

Keko slumped down, snorting angrily.

"With all due respect to the Honorable Council, I think Akamui's plan is excellent," rose Ahaki.

Akamui looked at him, astonished. Ahaki was in his late twenties, the youngest member of the Council, which was unusual, considering that the appropriate age for this position was at least ten years older. He was of medium height, with short hair, and the only one in the room with no tattoos or dangling bones on his body. His only decoration was a necklace of wild boar tusks, about a dozen, attached on a leather strap. Between the tusks were strung beads of shark teeth. Akamui had heard that Ahaki killed all the beasts only with his knife, a remarkable feat in any case.

"It's a fair play," he liked to say. "They have their teeth, and I have my knife. Let the best one win." Thus, he received the nickname Kailalele, which meant "The fair hunter." Ahaki was highly esteemed for his ingenuity, bravery, and intellect, but the exact merit that had ensured him a place in the Council was a mystery for Akamui.

"There are still three days to the full moon," continued Ahaki, "If we set off tonight with our fastest sailing boats, we will reach Rocky Island the night before their departure. Nobody would expect us, and they will all die, once and for all."

"What about the outposts? How are we to go unnoticed past the lookouts?" shouted Hamaki.

"As I said, I have a plan…" started Akamui, but his voice was drowned by the din that exploded. Now everybody was speaking simultaneously, gesticulating, crying, rolling their eyes, spitting on the floor, and nobody listened to anybody else. The hubbub was getting out of hand when Arataki bellowed, "Enough!"

Silence reigned over the room.

"There is only one way to find out if the girl lies and which plan is better," snapped Arataki. "We need to perform the ritual and to ask Kepolo through the foreshadowing fire!"

They all nodded in agreement. The chieftain walked to the remote corner of the room. Arataki was in his late thirties, tall and slender, taunt like a bow-string and quick as a snake. Unlike the other Tipi-haos, his hair was shoulder-length, something regarded as being very unpractical for the fighting tactic. The women, however, went crazy for him—he was the only man with five official wives on the island, not to mention the countless mistresses.

Arataki reached the far end of the room, where on a grayish-white sharkskin stood an about a height of a man replica of the Sacred Tree. Around the trunk were scattered many objects, amid them a long pipe, several small leather purses, necklaces made of small bones, a few shapeless wooden objects, and a leather hat with a crane affixed to its top. A spear with an impaled skull leaned against the trunk. Just beside it lay an impressive headdress, consisting of a semicircle of long colorful feathers.

Arataki put the headdress on, took the long pipe, stuffed it with some herbs from one of the leather purses, snatched the long spear, and returned, walking solemnly. The feathers, which belonged to the divine parrots named *manuka lani*, were remarkable, colored from deep red through bright yellow to deep blue, each one of them two handspans long or longer.

Transformed into a swaying parrot's tail, Arataki approached the hearth with ceremonial steps, raising the spear up and down. He circled the hearth three times on the left and three times on the right, then stopped, thrust the spear into the ground, squatted, and lit the pipe with a coal from the glowing ambers. He took a deep draw and puffed out a great amount of reeking smoke, then passed it to the oldest of the elders, Kerully, who inhaled before handing it to Tanuli, the next oldest, and so on.

During this ritual, Akamui stood upright and watched them. Nobody gave him the pipe. It circled three times, and finally Ahaki passed it back to the chieftain, who laid it on the ground. Arataki took the spear and circled the hearth three times left and right again. Having done that, he stopped in front of the elders, turned toward the miniature *Rakapi*, kneeled, raised the spear, and cried out:

"Oh, God Kepolo, the greatest of the greatest gods, the one who gives us strength and power to rule over our foes. Show us the way, Almighty, and lay your wisdom upon us. We ask you now with all the humbleness in the world: should we accept Akamui, a skillful warrior and a brave man, as a member of the Council?"

The flame flickered slightly, but the smoke moved up straight.

"Almighty Kepolo looks favorably on Akamui's demand," cried out Arataki. "Does it mean that Lelani's story is true and we are in deadly danger?"

The smoke did not change.

"Give us your will, All-Powerful Kepolo, leader of our destiny and protector of our people. Tell us how we ought to confront our foes. Should we take the advice of the old and wise Kerully and wait for them at home?"

The flames suddenly swung, as if a drought passed through the hut. The smoke whirled around and crawled toward Kerully. All the men let out a gasp.

Arataki cried excitedly, "Give us a sign, oh, Almighty, the greatest God of all times! Should we go to Rocky Island and surprise our enemies there?"

The smoke rose straight through the outlet.

"Thank you, god Kepolo, our protector and wise advisor! We understood your signs and we'll obey your will," cried Arataki, raising the spear higher, its feathers swinging widely as he bowed. All the men did the same thing. Then Arataki stood up and walked at a solemn pace to return the spear, the headdress, and the pipe to their places in the corner. Once there, he kneeled and bowed again to the Sacred Tree.

When he returned to the hearth, he hugged Akamui and said, "Welcome to the Council of Elders, warrior Akamui. We are glad to accept such a smart and noble man between us."

All the elders but Tanuli got up one by one and congratulated Akamui, who was glowing with pride, his eyes shining in the darkness. He took the vacant place between Ahaki and Hamaki and, with a thumping heart, tried to focus his attention on the chieftain.

"Ahaki will prepare the boats," said Arataki. "We will sail before dawn, and thus we will be able to get to Rocky Island in time to surprise them at the moment they perform their ceremony. Keko will organize the men—I want everyone who has passed his warrior's proof to be a part of the expedition. Hamaki and Tanati, you will go to Kedia's cave for confirmation.

"Considering that warrior Akamui is now in Kepolo's good grace, and as we are all aware of his former feats and his miracles of courage, I appoint him as my first commander. We will be glad to hear your plan, brave Akamui, and create a detailed attack strategy."

CHAPTER III

LAIA

The colossal cliff of Petrel's Atoll towered above the shimmering water. From three distinct vantage points, the lookouts of the Taraho tribe watched with raising concern the approaching boat, her bow decorated with a full yellow moon—the totem of their allies, the Torago people. Impeded by the falling twilight, they could not make out the painted faces of the men in the boat, but they could see the white warpaint in the darkness.

Kimo, the commander of the Taraho lookouts, didn't like it. According to plan, it had been at least ten sunsets since the Toragos arrived at Rocky Island, so a boat drifting alone at night was more than suspicious. Kimo whistled sharply, and eight men gathered at the cliff overhanging the sea within a minute.

"I smell a rat, boys," Kimo said. "Keep your eyes peeled and be extremely careful. These three are probably from Torago tribe like they claim to be, but the timing is weird."

"All the Toragos are already on Rocky Island. There's something wrong here," grunted one of the guards.

"Aho and Liko, you go down the cliff and keep your bows ready to cover the others," ordered Kimo. "Amari, take four men and hide in the bushes around the shore. You'll lay in ambush, and once they beach the canoe, you'll swoop down on them, tie them up, and bring them here. We'll take them to Rocky Island to see what their story is. Akeru, you stay with me!"

The men gave stern nods and disappeared in different directions while the commander and Akeru worked their way up until they reached a patch of small flat ground, the highest point on the atoll and an excellent observation spot. A huge stack of wood sheltered with big stones was set up there, ready to be lit. This was the signal fire, which the lookouts had to ignite if it appeared that Rocky Island might be in danger.

Akeru and Kimo crawled toward the edge of the cliff and looked at the shore. The full moon was rising from the east, bathing the sea in soft golden light, and they had a clear view of the boat coming toward the island.

"The cloudless night is a good omen," said Kimo, observing the sky. "We have to set off immediately after we capture our visitors if we want to attend the ritual. I'll leave only Amari with two men for the night watch."

"Do you think we'll get there on time?" asked Akeru.

"I hope we will. The ceremony will start when the moon levels with the Albatross's Peak, so we have plenty of time. Right after the sacrifice, if the omens are favorable, we will set off for Half-Moon Island."

While they talked, the boat reached the shore, and the three men inside jumped in the water. As soon as they dragged her up on the beach, the guards leaped out of hiding and charged with their spears raised.

"Lie down! Put your hands behind your heads!" barked Amari.

The strangers from the boat obeyed at once. "It's all right, we're your allies, from the Torago tribe," shouted one of them in the common archipelago language. "We left late, and the current carried us away, so we lost the course. Take us to the chieftain Moholi, he'll confirm."

"My intention, precisely," smirked Amari. "Tie them up!"

"Seriously, men! What a hearty welcome! Where are your manners?" the captive complained while the lookouts were tying their hands behind their backs.

Something's wrong here. Amari's mind was racing as he pressed his knee between the man's shoulders and deftly fastened the rope. *I've never seen such submissive jerks, mocking and arrogant instead of scary or angry. All their heads shaved… But wait, all Toragos have a shoulder-length—*

A wild yank at his hair broke his stream of thought, and a sharp pain burst in his throat. The blood gushed out and choked his horrified scream.

* * *

Akeru and Kimo lay flat on their stomachs on the bare cliff and watched as their men tied up the intruders. The evening breeze lashed their faces and roared in their ears, so they avoided speaking. With brisk movements, Akeru touched the commander's hand and pointed at the beach.

"There's something weird about these Toragos, but I can't figure out what is it," he said, putting his mouth close to Kimo's ear.

"Yeah, they're somehow different," Kimo replied. "Yes, I know what! It's the hair. The men of the Torago tribe never shave their heads, they braid their—"

"Toadshit!" exclaimed Akeru.

As the guards were binding the captives' hands, a dozen black shadows crawled from the water. Noiseless and quick, they pounced at the lookouts and slit their throats, then cut the ropes around their friends' wrists before all of them disappeared together into the jungle. It happened so fast that both men watching the scene barely had time to grasp what was going on.

"Tipihao cannibals," whispered Akeru, horrified. "Moon Goddess, we're doomed."

"Run to the bonfire! Move!" shouted Kimo.

They dashed madly toward the pile of logs, kneeled, and fervently started striking the flints with shaking hands. Once the tinder caught fire and the dry grass crackled, they bent and blew until the first flame began licking the thick lumber.

Meanwhile, the Tipihaos, who could smell the smoke from a mile away, were already there. Akeru and Kimo didn't even hear them coming. They were still blowing on their knees when several spears hit them in their backs and sent them into the pile of wood. The logs scattered as their blood extinguished the fire.

A sturdy man, tattooed from head to toe, straddled the dead men and urinated over the corpses, giving his contribution to the putting out of the smoldering wood. Satisfied, the man lingered there as his friends dispersed down the cliff in search of other survivors, watching the shore, when suddenly the last two enemy lookouts, Aho and Liko, appeared from the forest. They sprinted toward their own beached canoes, waving their bows.

The man brought his fingers to his mouth, whistled sharply two times, and ran toward the shore. The escapees pushed one of the canoes into the water and started rowing desperately when several Tipihaos appeared at the beach and threw themselves into the sea. They swam with rhythmic strokes, shortening the distance swiftly. Soon they reached the boat and turned it upside down. The water churned and boiled, and then everything went still.

A little later, after thoroughly combing the atoll for survivors, the Tipihaos set off for Rocky Island, where they would deal with the guards in the same fashion as at the Petrel's Atoll outpost. The tactic was simple, but it always worked perfectly. At first sight of land the men dived, leaving only two or three on board. The divers approached the shore invisibly, thanks to thin bamboo pipes which they used to breathe whilst hiding under the water until the perfect moment to strike.

The tattooed man who pissed on fire took one of the lookouts' canoes and rowed in the opposite direction for a long time before reaching Seagull Islet, a bare rock crowded with sea birds. It was the most remote piece of land westward of the Turtle Archipelago, which was not claimed by any tribe. Now instead of seagulls, it teemed with Tipihao's sailing barks. The man neared the first one and cried to the men inside, "The way is clear!"

* * *

The hammock swung gently in the hut's darkness. Laia clung tightly to Keoni's naked body and listened to his calm, even breathing, hot tears running down her face. For a long time, she stared into the dark, trying to control her anxiety. It was their last time together on Rocky Island before her beloved Keoni, the man of her life, would set off toward his destiny. The sacrificial ceremony would commence at any moment, and she was surprised that she had not heard the assembly drums yet.

The last evening before the raid was free of duty, allowing the warriors to make their proper leave-taking with their dear ones. Laia knew that many of them had left their wives and girlfriends on their native islands, but Keoni was a lucky one. As the eldest daughter of the Torago's chieftain, she had begged for permission to come and stay with her hero until the last moment of his departure. Now the time had come, and a grim feeling of impending calamity was slowly turning into a growing lump in her throat. For hours the same thoughts circled in her head:

*What if they kill him over there? If I never see him again? What will happen to all of us if the evil cannibals wi*n...?

She started coughing, choked with grief.

Something is wrong. I can feel it in my bones, she thought.

Damned Tipihaos, with all their wars and cruelty! She had witnessed so many deaths during her life. But for the first time now, the odds were good, and the alliance could finish off this ferocious tribe once and for all.

She had heard her father saying that such an enormous army had never been formed before. And if they won this war, all this atrocity would be over at last, and peace and harmony would prevail among people. If only her beloved Keoni could stay with her instead of going there… But he was the bravest hunter and warrior she ever knew, and his place was in the battle, not in her lap.

She stared at his open, handsome face and ran her hand through his shoulder-length hair. He did not seem to care much about the upcoming battle. As she watched him, his lids twitched, and a slight smile glided onto his lips. A wave of love suffused her heart, and she started kissing him fervently, waking him up. He folded her in his arms, and she climbed on top of him, grabbed his pulsating member, and directed it inside her. The hammock began to swing wildly. She moaned, clinging to Keoni so tightly that the moment he finished, he pushed her aside, gasping for breath.

"What's wrong with you?" he said, panting heavily. "Do you want to kill me just before the battle?"

"I won't let you go!" said Laia, continuing kissing him. "You'll stay with me, and we'll escape to Hot Spring Island, and I'll bear you many children, and we'll live a long and happy life together, forever and ever."

"Hot Spring Island," Keoni chuckled. "How did you come up with that one? Nobody leaves there."

"That's my point! It will be only the two of us in the entire world and our beautiful kids." Laia's eyes shone in the darkness.

"Yeah, and our kids will go as a tribute to the bloody cannibals," said Keoni. "We cannot continue living like this, my heart. We have to get rid of this pest once and for all. And then freedom, harmony, and peace will reign all over the Turtle Archipelago and our children will grow up happy and safe."

"You know that it's not going to happen," said Laia quietly. "Do you think it's so easy to get rid of them? They have dominated us since time immemorial despite the countless attempts to gain our freedom, and everybody knows why."

"I don't," said Keoni. There was a hint of mockery in his voice. Laia bristled.

"Of course you do! It's all because of their god Kepolo, the same one that makes them kill and eat humans, the one that gives them supernatural force. My grandmother had said once that the only way to beat them would be to accept their god."

"That's old woman's talk, pure nonsense," said Keoni angrily. "How do you see us adopt their disgusting rituals? Becoming servants of evil? Giving up on the Moon Goddess who brings us love and harmony? No, my love. It's time to stop talking and start acting, and we have to do it now because tomorrow will be too late. The omens are good, and even their prophecy says that the destruction of the Tipihao tribe will begin from Rocky Island."

His blazing eyes and glowing face made him so handsome! She knew that he firmly believed in every word that he spoke. A wave of hot, burning love welled up in her again, a passion that she had never felt before.

"Stay with me, my love," she whispered, tears streaming down her cheeks. "I can't bear to lose you... I love you so much..."

The curtain of the hut entrance flew open, and Akamui rushed in, followed by three other men. Keoni pushed Laia aside and reached for his pike, but it was too late—Akamui plunged his spear into Keoni's chest with such a force that the tip emerged through his back. The hammock overturned, and Laia fell to the ground with a terrible scream. She jumped to her feet and flung herself toward Keoni. One of the men met her with a fierce backhand strike. She flew back, banging her head on the hut's central support column, and fell unconscious. Akamui looked her over and nodded with approval.

"Nice chick," he said. He removed his necklace and put it on Laia's neck, then turned to the warrior who hit her.

"Tie her up and bring her to my boat," he ordered. "Let nobody touch her, understood? This one will be mine."

* * *

Akamui's plan had worked well. The Tipihaos had neutralized all outposts, debarked on Rocky Island, and sneaked into each hut, killing the men, and tying and gagging the women and children. As most of the warriors had gathered unarmed (as the custom required) for the ceremony, they did not even know what had hit them. The cannibals attacked them in the rear and slaughtered them to the last man, "as a sacrifice to the Moon Goddess," as they put it later, laughing. Flushed with excitement after their victory, the savages ravaged the island the whole night, raping the women and burning everything that could catch fire.

The first sunbeams revealed a terrible picture of still smoldering, collapsing huts, and dead bodies scattered all around. Wails of bound women and cries of children were filling the air. The women constituted the main part of the captives, along with a few surrendered warriors and three of the surviving tribes' chieftains. All of them had been dragged to the shore and loaded into the canoes.

Laia was gradually coming to her senses. The ground heaved up and down, making her head spin and her stomach churn. A soft splashing of oars and agitated talk in a strange dialect were the first sounds she heard as she came round.

She opened her eyes, and the bright sunlight exploded into her brain, forcing her to shut them again. She attempted to bring her hand to her face, but she couldn't. She writhed her body and realized that her arms and legs were bound.

Laia let out a low moan of pain. Slit-eyed and trembling, she couldn't see much more than the two pairs of bare men's legs just in front of her, and she realized that she was in the bottom of a canoe. The events of the last night came back to her in slow motion: laying in Keoni's arms; four men rushing in; Keoni with a spear sticking out from his chest...

Laia let out a shrill shriek. Roaring laughter shook the canoe.

"Ah, look who just woke up," said a mocking voice. A toned, brawny forearm brought a wooden flask to her lips. "Drink! Akamui wants you alive."

Soon the boat slowed down. Laia sensed a cool blade gliding between her hands and ankles and cutting the ropes that tied her. She got up, shivering, stretching her numb limbs. They were drawing near to a substantially bigger boat with a pole stuck in the middle and a large square piece of cloth attached to it.

Laia had heard many times about the famous cannibals' sailing boats, driven by the force of the wind, but she had never seen one. A rope dangled from the hull, and one of the men motioned for her to grab it. Somebody hauled her over the edge and she jumped on board. It was swarming with men who were shouting, cursing, spitting, and scurrying back and forth. Some of them climbed the only short mast, fiddling with the ropes as they hoisted the sail. As she watched them, Laia sensed shivers crawling down her spine and her hair started slowly lifting from the back of her head.

"Mother Moon, what abominable creatures," she whispered, staring hypnotized at these bald men whose strong tattooed bodies were still covered with the blood of their victims. The wild, primitive force of feral beasts emanated from their ugly faces, and their eyes streamed pitiless cruelty, death, and horror.

The world started swinging before her, and she focused on the face of a man, frozen in a dreadful grimace of anguish. There was something wrong in these bulging eyes and the half-opened mouth, full of pointed teeth. Blood trickled down from its corner toward his... neck? Laia squinted at the sun, gazing at his broad back and unable to understand how a man with his back turned could also be facing her.

Just as she realized she had been looking at a tattoo of a face on the back of his head, he turned around. His real face was covered with dried blood. A thin human bone passed straight across his nose. His lustful eyes bored into her as he licked his lips and grinned, revealing the same pointed, filed-down teeth. The second their eyes met, Laia visualized the endless rape, beatings, and misery that awaited her from now on.

She screamed at the top of her lungs and darted toward the port side with the firm intent to throw herself into the water. She had almost reached the edge of the boat when a fat man knocked her down. She wriggled desperately facedown while he pressed his knee to her back and started tying her up. Akamui approached and licked his lips again.

"Eh, careful with the fish," he said. "I want her in good shape, right?"

The fat one chuckled. "We know the chick is yours, Akamui, only you are so handsome that she got a little jumpy."

He lifted her and turned her around, forcing her into a sitting position. Akamui bent down and pressed her face between his hands.

"Yeah, I don't think she appreciated my new tattoo. I'll certainly have to teach her some manners, with an emphasis on discipline," he said, looking her straight in the eyes. His stare was insane. Laia did not understand a word, but she had never seen such hatred in someone's gaze. She diverted her eyes.

Akamui tossed her aside disparagingly and said, "Put her with the others."

The fat man grabbed her and carried her aft, where he threw her on a pile of tied and gagged women, crammed together like a stack of fish.

Laia closed her eyes and thought,

What I'd give to have died with my beloved Keoni.

* * *

The shore swarmed with people who had come out to meet the triumphant winners. They shouted and cheered, raising their spears, while the sailing boats dropped anchor in the bay and the canoes sped toward the shore, passing over the reef. Once they reached the beach, the warriors jumped into the water and hauled the canoes onto the sand under the shouts of the throng.

The captives, still tied up, were tossed on the ground, women apart from men.

With tight jaws and clenched fists, Tipihao wives stared narrow-eyed at their foreign rivals, who would soon share their huts and the hammocks of their husbands.

In their spite, some of them kicked the poor newcomers, spat at them, or hit them with rocks and rotten fruit.

"Here we go again," muttered Arataki, while dragging aside two young women under the murderous looks of his wives. They had clustered together, all five of them, and their stares bode nothing good for the days to come.

Whenever the men brought foreign women to the island, it created turmoil. Brawls, fights, and violent beatings inevitably broke out, often ending in the death of the intruders. The jealousy among locals was so wild that there was no force in existence that could prevent the natural storm unleashed by the disturbed hierarchy. The irony was that the men, so strong and mighty on the battlefield, were helpless when it came to keeping a tight rein on their sweethearts—despite all the restrictions and bans, the first several full moons were always a nightmare for men and women alike. It all eventually calmed down when the foreigners began getting pregnant—it was unheard of for anyone to mistreat an expectant mother.

Arataki turned to the crowd and lifted his hand, his long black hair flying majestically in the breeze. When the silence reigned, he shouted over the surf, "Thank you for the hearty welcome, sons and daughters of Kepolo. In this crucial battle, when all other tribes united against us and plotted our destruction, we prove once again that there is no-one stronger, braver, and smarter than us, the Tipihaos!"

The crowd roared in agreement, raising their spears and waving clenched fists.

"Led by our God, the Almighty Kepolo, the One who gives us wisdom, strength, and power to rule over the others, the One who has always protected and supported us, we taught a good lesson to our enemies, and smashed all of those miserable toads with birds' hearts."

More cheers and applause.

"This victory will be perpetuated in songs and legends for years to come, and everybody will remember the day when the Almighty Kepolo crushed once again the fake Moonlight Goddess and all of her worshipers."

He rose his spear and wild cries swept over the shore.

"Tonight will be a celebration time," continued Arataki, when the cheers died. "Our foes will be sacrificed before *Rakapi*, as a sign of our deepest gratitude to the Glorious Kepolo. We'll drink their blood and eat their hearts, and their strength will become our strength, and their spirits will strengthen our spirits!"

Amid the roar of the crowd, Arataki turned to the nearby man and ordered, "Take all the captives to the cages now!"

Laia lay on the sandy shore in utter confusion. She listened to the brisk, seagull-like shouts of the chieftain. Right after his last words, a man standing next to her brusquely drew his knife and bent over her. She shut her eyes, terrified. The stone blade touched the skin between her wrists, and the rope loosened. The man grabbed her under the arms and lifted her onto her feet. She opened her eyes, feeling sick.

The Tipihaos were setting the enslaved women in rows and were attaching wooden hoops around their necks. The one who had set Laia free pushed her into the middle of a row of eight women and fit her with a similar ring, leaving it just loose enough to breathe. Another warrior passed a long rope through all hoops and girded it around each captive's waist. Linked that way, nobody could escape, as every step aside would drag the entire row in the escapee's direction.

A crack of the whip announced the start of the journey. In the beginning, all of them stumbled and staggered until they grew accustomed to keeping synchronizing every movement with each other. Laia shambled, confused and dizzy, listening to the heavy breathing of the girl behind her. She was moving as if in a nightmare, hoping desperately to wake up at any moment, only it continued on and on—a strange separated reality of scorching heat and a swarm of insects buzzing into her ears and thrusting themselves into her mouth, nostrils, and eyes.

The path was narrow, and the twigs left scratches all over her face and body. Thick creepers tangled around her feet and made her stumble every step or so, which often provoked the lash of a whip over her naked body. The bites of the leather strap formed small bloody grooves around her back and shoulders, and the thirsty insects clung to her wounds, sucking them mercilessly.

Gradually, Laia fell into a state of profound indifference toward everything that happened around her, and her mind drifted back to the lush meadows of her native island, strolling hand in hand with Keoni.

"I'm coming to you, my love," she whispered. "Nobody can keep me away from you. I'll kill myself at the first chance I get, and we will be together forever…"

The narrow path ended and the row of captives found themselves in a vast clearing bathed in sunshine. Laia jerked out of her daze and squinted, unable to believe her eyes. The nightmare was getting brighter and more surrealistic, with many wretched details incomprehensible to normal human thinking. Just in front of her, hundreds of black birds were circling the most gigantic tree she had ever seen, bristling with embedded weapons and adorned with bones.

The awful smell made Laia step aside and vomit. She heard an angry shout, and a swish of the whip burned her shoulder. She was forced back into step with the other captives, and they marched toward a score of bamboo cages perched over the branches of the trees surrounding the clearing.

On their way, the captives passed an unlit pyre. Around it the grass had long been burned away, and their shuffling feet caused white bones to roll over the dirt, gleaming in the sunshine.

The guards stopped below the cages, took the hoops off the women's necks, and disentangled the ropes. The leader of the convoy beckoned to several old men and young boys who had been waiting nearby.

"Who is in charge of the wardens?" he asked.

"It's me, master Hakahili," said a skinny old man with a bow.

"Nice to see you, Tanagora," replied Hakahili, bowing back. "Look now, these eight go together. They are for the elders, and these two here belong to Arataki. Another six chosen are coming too, for the rest of the elders, so you put them in a separate cage."

"And those over there, master Hakahili? There is not enough space for all of them," asked Tanagora, nodding at the crowd of women who had just spilled into the clearing.

"I don't care for them much. They are destined for the warriors after a toss-up, so do whatever you want with them," Hakahili chuckled meaningfully.

The old man stretched his lips in a sad toothless grin and turned to the boys. "Didn't you hear, sluggards? Take care of the ladies!"

"Hey, careful with this one," warned Hakahili, pushing Laia aside. He touched the necklace around her neck. "Do you recognize this?"

Tanagora shook his head.

"She belongs to Akamui," Hakahili explained.

"Excellent choice, indeed," chuckled Tanagora, his eyes gleaming. "I hope she'll live longer than his last wife. It was high time for him to find a woman, though. He's become pretty creepy lately…"

"Absolutely," sneered Hakahili. "See you tonight, old man."

After another toothless grin, accompanied by a friendly wave, Tanagora clutched Laia's elbow and snapped at a boy, "What are you staring at, as if you've never seen a woman? Send her with the others over there!"

The boy pushed Laia toward a cage to their right, where a long rope ladder dangled from several feet above the ground.

"Climb!" he shouted in the archipelago language. Laia grabbed the ladder and tried to pull herself up, struggling with the ropes, but she was too feeble. She felt the boy's hand between her legs, squeezing her hard, heard his disgusting chuckle, and felt his stinking breath blowing in her neck. He lifted her with a mighty push, and she found the first rung under her trembling feet. The ladder swung on the wind as she struggled to climb.

A second boy emerged from a square opening in the cage's floor and reached down to give her a hand. Laia found herself in a large dark room made of interlaced bamboo sticks. After the all women climbed, the guard counted them and slipped out, closing the hole and bolting it from below.

The sun was high, casting scorching heat upon the clearing. Most of the warriors retreated for a well-deserved rest. Only five guards remained, hiding in the shadow below the cages.

The women in the cage were silent. They sat on the floor with their backs leaned against the wall and stared blankly ahead of them. Some were very young, almost children. Suddenly, a slender beauty with gorgeous long wavy hair broke in tears.

"They said they'll draw lo—lots for us," she sobbed. "Wha—what will our life be from now on? With these animals? Ca-nni-bals? Damn them!"

"Stop whining," snarled a chubby girl with a split, bloody upper lip and a black, half-closed eye. "Nobody will draw lots for you. We've already been allotted to the elders, so relax."

"I think she's destined for the chieftain," said a skinny girl with a parrot's feather in her hair, nodding at the sobbing one. "Did you see how all his wives looked at us? I wish you good luck with them—

they'll eat you alive, with all your snot and tears. As for me, I hope to be given to the oldest one, won't fuck me too often."

"If you ask me, the men are the least of our problems," said a small woman with a cute face. "Think about it. How long does a man stay home? They are always outside, hunting or fighting, or whatever. Their wives, though, are the real trouble for us. If I have to deal with only one, I'm sure I'll get along with her, but if more allied against me, it would be really tough…"

"*The men are the least of our problems…*" mimicked a tall, heavily built, hard-faced woman. "What nonsense! I know these men well and I would not be surprised if we end up roasted tonight. Being someone's wife is far preferable to being eaten alive."

The world whirled around Laia. The heat, the exhaustion and all the terrible events from the last days took its toll on her. The women's voices rang loudly in her ears and she fainted.

When she came round, it was twilight. The tall woman was pushing at her shoulder again and again.

"Water," whispered Laia in a hoarse voice. Her mouth was dry, her lips cracked and stiff.

"There is no water here, honey," said the hard-faced woman. "I just wondered if you're still alive. You need to wake up, 'cause they'll start the sacrifice ceremony soon, and right after that we'll be brought to their stupid tree for acceptance."

"How do you know?" asked the girl with the parrot's feather.

"I've already been through this," said the tall woman. "They abducted me and made me marry one of them. How I hated the brute! I counted every bloody sunset and made plan after plan until I managed to escape. And all that for naught—only to come back again."

"How did you escape?" asked the girl with the wavy hair.

"I promised my man that I'd give him the best sex of his life if he takes me on a trip to Jellyfish Atoll. And there, while he was inside me, I drew his knife and stabbed him in the throat. It was so sublime…

I've never come like that before, and I doubt I will ever again… Then I took his canoe and reached my native island, and he fed the sharks, the bloody wretch."

Long silence lingered in the air.

"Wow," said the girl with the split lip, with a hint of respect in her voice. "I can say that living with cannibals made you quite blood-thirsty… A bit like them."

"Do you think they'll recognize you?" asked the girl with the feather.

"Nah, they are really stupid, you'll see," said the tall woman blithely. "Just consider their procedure of acceptance: they think if their wacky god is to claim you, the bark of the tree will glow, and they must scarify you. It's never happened, though. Otherwise, if the bark remains unchanged, you belong to the man who has chosen you. Pure non-sense!"

Laia drew her limp body near the interlaced poles and peered through the gaps. The area down below teemed with people, hustling to and fro in preparation for the forthcoming ritual. Older men, kids, and women dragged wood and piled it up, building a huge pyre not far away from the cages. The faint rhythm of drums sounded far away.

A bunch of men had gathered beneath the gigantic tree. They swayed in front of a flat rectangular stone and let out strange sounds, something between grunting, wailing, and singing. The chieftain, who was easily recognizable by his long hair, wore a weird cylindrical hat with a skull fastened on the top. He was going around the stone, mumbling and sprinkling red liquid from a coconut shell. And just behind the stone, the horrible tree seemed even more ominous in the twilight.

Laia shuddered, feeling a growing terror creep in her. She had heard hundreds of legends about this famous tree, the god of the canni-bals, but this… Its gigantic size, the nightmarish black birds, swoop-ing down and pecking at the swinging bodies, the terrible stench of carrion, floating around and causing her constant nausea—all these wretched details had widely surpassed her worst fears.

The beat grew louder and soon a couple of men with drums appeared from the jungle, followed by hundreds of people who flooded the clearing. Then the drums stopped, and the chieftain addressed the crowd in his weird barking language. He spoke for a long time, often drowned out by the wild cries of the throng.

The drums started again. The chieftain rose a burning torch, then walked solemnly to the pyre and lit it. The flames licked thirstily at the pile of wood, rapidly growing bigger.

Meanwhile, a captive was brought and stretched over the altar. Arataki lifted his torch and passed the fire to one of the surrounding men, who, in his turn, handed it to the next. Within seconds, the place was bathed with bright light. The drums increased their rhythm.

The chieftain turned to the altar and placed his torch in a special aperture in the stone. He raised both his hands interlocked in a fist, clutching a long knife. The blade was outlined in the light of the flames. The crowd started rocking back and forth and humming a long-drawn-out melody.

Laia screamed and shut her eyes. She twisted and vomited on the feet of the woman beside her, who jumped up as if stung.

"Fucking fish," she shouted.

"I'm sorry," Laia murmured. She leaned on the wall and started crying, then passed out again.When she came to, it was pitch dark. The beat of the drums rammed tediously into her head. The other women were missing from the cage. Laia looked outside. The bonfire burned out, and the glowing embers cast purple gleams on the lawn. Around it, men and women were dancing in wild ecstasy. In the air drifted the foul smell of burnt flesh. Through the darkness above the clearing floated moans, screams, and giggles.

The cage squeaked and rocked. The cover moved up and aside, and the ugly head of the tall man from the boat popped up through the hole. He squeezed up to the waist and moved his torch inside. As he saw Laia, who retreated into the corner like a wounded animal, he grunted something and motioned for her to approach.

"I wanted to attend to bring you personally to my God," Akamui barked in perfect archipelago language. "You are the last; all the women passed already. Come with me. Kepolo must accept you."

He disappeared through the opening below. Laia crawled toward the orifice, turned backward, and searched with her legs for the ladder's steps. Having found the uppermost rung, she slowly descended. Akamui watched her graceful body while the ladder swung on the night breeze. When she leaped on the ground, he grabbed her by the hand and yanked her toward the Tree.

"Go kneel before the trunk and embrace it," he instructed and pushed her rudely.

Laia advanced, all of her attention focused on suppressing the urge to throw up, and did exactly what she was said to. The moment she laid her forehead on the cool green bark, a deafening boom came from the heavens, and everybody looked up to see a blazing shooting star, falling with unbelievable speed and leaving a red trace across the black sky. It exploded just above the clearing with a blinding light and, in a twinkle, the whole place became bright as day. A rain of dazzling sparks and scattered lights sprinkled over all the Sacred Zone, and everybody let out cries of surprise and acclamation.

Gradually, the sky turned black again, and nobody but Laia noticed that the tree's bark was glowing with a soft purple color, claiming her life. She took a quick step back and glanced at Akamui, who was still gaping at the sky. She bowed her head in acceptance.

It's finally over, she thought in a flash. A second later, a wave of incredible energy overwhelmed her body and shook her like a thunderbolt. A mighty impulse to live ran in her veins and, in a split second, she realized that she had some mission in this world and that she must live to accomplish it.

Without even understanding what she was doing, she ran toward Akamui, threw herself on his neck, and kissed him. He looked bewildered in the first moment, then kissed her too.

"Let's go to my hut," he said, gripping her firmly by the hand, and dragged her toward the jungle. Laia glimpsed at the Tree—the bark was dark again.

Akamui walked confidently in the darkness, impatiently pulling her out every time she tripped.

"Watch your step, numbskull," he yelled at her every trip.

Laia was in shock. "*Slut! Whore!*" a voice screamed in her head. "*What did you do? Where is your honor? Your dignity? These cannibals killed your beloved and you are ready to spread your legs for them? Such a tramp like you doesn't deserve to live. Kill yourself! Right now!*"

She wrenched herself free of Akamui and darted into the darkness, but collided with a tree, bounced off, and stumbled on a root, falling back into Akamui's hands. He grabbed her by the neck and she started screaming.

"Wanna play games, do you?" he hissed in her year. His mouth stank terribly. "Don't worry, sweetheart, soon we'll play games. I bet you'll like them very, very much."

He slapped her on the back of her head to stun her, then lifted her across his shoulders and carried her home as though she were a hunting trophy.

Once in the hut, he dropped her on the floor and poured a bucket of water over her face. Laia jumped and withdrew to the corner, bristling. Akamui calmly lit the lamp and leaned on the supporting pole, scrutinizing her. She was gorgeous, upper class, far more beautiful than Kalia, and still resembling her somehow. Slender and tall, with long curly hair, full sensuous lips, small nose, and big black shiny eyes, Laia possessed some particular inner beauty, some humility that made her face glow from inside. At this moment, though, her look emanated only wild, rudimentary fear.

"Come here!" Akamui hissed menacingly in the archipelago language. "From now on you will be my wife and you must satisfy all my needs, understood?"

"I'd rather die," snarled Laia.

"Oh, you'll die for sure, if you don't obey… Like my first wife… Come here! I need a woman right now."

Laia did not move. Quick as a flash, Akamui lunged at her, grasped her throat, and lifted her in the air. She kneed him in the groin, and he doubled over with a yell, hurling her to the ground. They rolled over, she madly scrambling to escape, and he trying to keep her back, pulling at her hair. Amid shouts and curses, Akamui was the first to regain his feet. He clutched Laia in his mighty arms, threw her flat on her back, pressed his knee to her chest, and began slapping her rhythmically with heavy cutting blows. Laia screamed, blood gushing from her nose and mouth. At this moment, Lalago entered the hut and yelled at her son something that Laia did not understand. Akamui stopped at once.

"Leave her alone!" shouted Lalago angrily. "What do you want, to kill her like you did Kalia?"

"She has to obey," said Akamui through clenched teeth.

"She's coming with me!" snapped Lalago. "She will sleep in my hut tonight! Don't you see how weak is she, still in shock? She needs to be healed; she is not ready for the stupid phantasms buzzing in your head. I'll talk with her, woman to woman, and she will understand. Get out of the way, now!"

Lalago stepped forward and pushed her son aside. She extended her hand to Laia and lifted her to her feet. The youthful woman was trembling and staggering.

Under Akamui's stunned look, Lalago pulled Laia's arm over her shoulders and the two of them left the hut.

Akamui watched them crossly as they walked down the path, hesitating what to do. His groin ached, but he had immense respect for his mother, so eventually, he let them go. When they passed out of sight, he muttered, "Women," and went back into the dark room.

* * *

It seemed to Laia that it took forever to get to Lalago's hut, and the moment they went in, she collapsed on the floor. Lalago dragged her to the corner and prepared a bed for her from straw mats. After quenching her thirst, Laia swallowed hot fish broth, so delicious that she couldn't compare it with anything she had ever eaten before. When she finished her meal, Lalago made her stretch on the floor, cleaned all her wounds and bruises, and rubbed her body with some soothing ointment.

"It will appease your pain and calm you down. Tomorrow you'll feel a lot better, you'll see," she said to Laia, smiling at her. She continued in a confidential voice: "Listen, he's not so bad, my son. The problem with him is that he is a bit short-tempered, but once you get to know him, you'll be surprised how easy it is to get along with him."

"I don't want him," moaned Laia. "I'd rather die."

"I hear you, girl, but everything will be all right, you'll see. I'll teach you some tricks and, in a brief time, you'll be able to wrap him around your little finger. Don't forget that it was me who has raised him, and I know him better than anyone. Don't worry now. Get some rest, and tomorrow will be another day."

The soothing words didn't reach Laia. The ointment was taking effect, and she started drifting away. The events of the last days passed in quick succession through her mind, and she wriggled and tossed in her sleep. Little by little, the dream steadied, and she walked hand-in-hand with Keoni in a large green meadow studded with colorful tropical flowers.

"Listen, Laia," Keoni whispered in her ear. "You must accept Akamui for your husband. I know how difficult it is for you, but you have to do it. We have a child, my love, a boy who was conceived on our last night together, right before they killed me. It's crucial to give birth to this boy, my heart. It's a matter of life and death…"

Laia moaned loudly in her sleep, rocking her head left and right. From her hammock, Lalago watched her suspiciously.

"Do you remember when I said that the time has come for us to crush this cursed tribe?" whispered Keoni. "This boy is the key. He is precious… He will change their thinking, and from bloodthirsty cannibals they will be made into peaceful people, as in the time before Kepolo, when they worshiped the Moon Goddess. Yes, my love, our son will be a great man. But I can see that his life is in great danger. If you kill yourself or let Akamui kill you, everything would be lost. That's why you have a great responsibility, and you must be braver than any warrior on the battlefield. Akamui has to think he is the father of the child; otherwise, he'll kill both of you. Do whatever it takes to gain his confidence, Laia! Do it, if you love me…"

The meadow disappeared and Laia gradually woke up. In the hut's darkness, the only sound was Lalago's steady breathing. Laia propped herself up on an elbow and gasped, her eyes wide open—Keoni, gleaming in the dark, stood in front of her. His hair was matted and his near-naked body smeared with blood. In the middle of his chest gaped a large bloody hole.

"Don't make a sound," said his voice, which she heard inside her head. "Don't touch me, either! Just think in your mind, ask whatever you want and be quick, because we don't have much time. Do you remember the dream?"

Laia nodded.

"Every single word?"

She nodded again and said with her thoughts, "Are you real?"

"Of course, I am. The dead are as real as the living. You can't imagine what a beautiful world awaits you after your death, my love. It's amazing! I met my parents and my brother… Not everyone has the same fate, though. Some people are doomed to suffer… Listen Laia, the only reason you can see me now is because I have to convey to you the message about our child. I see you are not convinced at all... You must accept Akamui as your husband and you need to sleep with him right away. I know it's hard, my beautiful flower, but no suspicion about the child's parentage must be raised. He has to believe that the boy is his blood, understand?"

"I can't stand this man," whispered Laia, and she shuddered, tears rolling down her cheek. "Just the thought of him makes me sick..."

"You have to accept your destiny!" Keoni said firmly. "You must give birth to this child, whatever it takes. There is nothing more important than that. This is the bitter cup from which you must drink to the last dregs. Do whatever it takes and remember that I love you with all my heart. Don't even think about suicide, as it's one of the most terrible things you could possibly do. I'll help you in your endeavor. Look here, I'm giving you my shark-teeth bracelet. Every time you need my help, just press it to your heart, and I'll come to you and give you strength. I know that you can do it, my love... Can I count on you?"

Laia nodded and Keoni disappeared. She drifted away. When she woke up again, the sun was already high in the sky.

She looked around. The hut was empty. The dream was still vivid in her memory, only in daylight, it seemed more unreal than ever.

She sat up, contemplating how to run away when something clattered in her lap. She looked down, startled, and froze. On the earthen floor gleamed a white bracelet. She stared at it for a long time, then she reached down to pick it up, observing the sharp shark's teeth strung on a leather strap.

She knew the story behind it: One day, while Keoni was out to sea fishing, the beast attacked his canoe and overturned it. The assault was so sudden that most of his weapons sank to the ocean's bottom and he faced the shark with only his knife, which he always wore attached at his waist. The battle was epic. Keoni's left shoulder was torn to the bone, and the traces of the beast's teeth were visible on his upper back and thighs thereafter. Other men from his tribe were nearby and came to his aid. When they approached, the shark was already dead. Keoni took its head and later made the bracelet.

Now, as Laia looked at it, her eyes filled with tears and an overwhelming love suffused her heart.

"But how is it possible?" she muttered, fiddling with it thoughtfully. She was sure that when Keoni got killed, the bracelet was fastened as usual around his wrist because she remembered it scratched her back while they made love…

"… *Every time you need my help, just press it to your heart*," resounded his voice inside her head.

She clutched the bracelet and clasped it firmly to her chest. In the blink of an eye, she saw a curly little boy with mild features and big shiny black eyes, who smiled at her. The resemblance to her was so striking that she gasped. An immense wave of love swelled in her, and at that moment, she was ready to do anything for this child. She got up and strode decisively toward the entrance. Her eyes were full of tears but shone with unbending intent. She stepped out and met Lalago, who was sitting before the hut, basking in the morning sun.

"Are you all right, girl?" she asked, surprised when she saw Laia.

"I am," nodded Laia and smiled. "Thank you for having me overnight; your hospitality helped me to think everything over. Now I must accept my destiny. I'm ready to be your son's wife, and I'm going to tell him my decision right away. From now on, you will become a mother for me, and I will be your daughter."

Lalago gaped at her, unable to believe her ears. Laia smiled and motioned to the path that ascended the hill.

"As far as I recall, I have to follow this track, right? Goodbye for now."

She bent over, took the old woman's wrinkled hand, and kissed it, then turned around and hurried away, leaving the stunned Lalago gawping after her for a long time.

"Well, well," she said at last. "What a change! It must be the special soothing ointment I rubbed her with."

CHAPTER IV

KAMOLEA

Laia panted as she climbed the steep narrow path. The long pole across her shoulders, with two bulky buckets filled with water attached at either end, had already left bruises on her back and neck. She felt heavy and clumsy and sweated profusely in the late morning heat.

It had been almost nine full moons since she had resigned herself to becoming Akamui's wife. Until now, she could never explain what had seized her when she quit Lalago's hut and set off to meet her future husband. That day was stamped so deeply on her memory! Every detail of what happened next, so clear and vivid, ceaselessly stung her heart in cruel torture, and every single night she woke up, crying bitterly.

Laia had found Akamui sitting in front of his hut and stripping a long stick of its bark for a new spear. When he saw her approaching, he lifted an eyebrow and smirked. She strode decisively toward him and told him that she accepted to be his wife. He rose, took her by the hand, and led her into the hut. Once inside, he grabbed her rudely and shoved her on the floor. She hit her head against the earthen floor and his heavy, two hundred pounds body of iron muscles crashed on top of her. Dizzy and helpless, sickened by his reeking breath, she left him to do what he wanted. Akamui was like an animal in heat. He had sex with her for hours, with only brief breaks. During all that time Laia had completely detached from herself. By the end, after one of Akamui's violent pushes, she found herself peering from above at their naked bodies, lying entwined on the floor.

This is me, and yet it's not, she thought. She watched how Akamui, who had satiated his passion at last, got up and left the hut without a second glance at her.

I won't return in this disgusting, stinking shell, filled with his slimy liquids, she decided. She felt light and happy without her body, like a bright ball of light, boiling with energy.

Soon she discovered that she could move through the air. It was enough just to fix her attention on something and she started floating toward it. She made a tour around the hut, lingering a bit at the central pole and the ceiling, and then focused on the wall.

Somehow, she knew that the wall would not stop her on her way to freedom and she decided to go through it. At this instant, the room filled with light. As in haze, Laia noticed a weird old man, clad in red, with white, shoulder-length hair and a bearded face. He smiled at her and shook his head, then lifted his hand and pointed to her. With incredible speed, she flew toward the lying woman below. She sensed the wind blow through her nostrils and woke up with a gasp in her mutilated body.

As she opened her eyes, a wave of despair and hatred toward herself overwhelmed her. Feeling filthy and humiliated, grief seized her in a firm grip, and she remained lying on the floor, unable to move, crying and pressing Keoni's bracelet to her heart.

When Akamui returned hungry and sullen at sunset, he found her huddled in the corner. He kicked her in the ribs and bellowed, "Where is my supper!?"

The first two months were a nightmare—sulky and disgruntled, Akamui never showed affection and was always displeased with her. Her feelings were reciprocal. She had never realized that he was

Keoni's killer, but all the same, she loathed him so vehemently that even looking at him caused her pain. In her eyes, Akamui was an embodiment of evil. The brute had not even a single positive quality. He projected hatred, arrogance, spite, cruelty, and death. In the beginning, he almost killed her several times. Occasional snap or slow execution of his whims led to violent trashing. Beaten to a pulp, she often ran away to Lalago to seek protection, for she had discovered that Akamui would never dare to oppose his mother.

That was the worst period in Laia's existence, when her life was hanging by a thread, either because she was always on the brink of suicide or in the constant danger of Akamui's wrath.

However, in the most critical moments, some strange waves of energy overwhelmed her, stopping her thoughts and giving her strength. During such a hard time, she fervently kissed Keoni's bracelet, pressed it to her heart, cried for hours, and then she felt purified and resigned, gaining the strength to continue her dreadful reality.

As time went by, Akamui gradually relented. It was not clear what had softened his heart toward her, but the beatings had been replaced by occasional slaps and the shouts by growls. One day she yelled at him not to touch a pot, still stewing on the fire, and braced herself for the inevitable blow. To her surprise, however, he retreated, grunting discontentedly.

But the actual change occurred when she told him she was expecting a baby. From that day on, he never raised his hand against her. On the contrary, he became attentive, caring and made his mother come more often to help Laia with the household chores. In her presence, Laia regained her courage and often gave Akamui back-talk or even snapped at him, which he endured, even though she noticed his glare sometimes.

"I don't recognize your son. He's become so patient, so self-controlled," she confided to Lalago once.

"You know why?" whispered Lalago back, casting a furtive glance about. "He told me recently that every time he wants to hit you, Kalia, his previous wife, emerges soaked in blood before his eyes, as though her spirit restrains him from doing it."

And once Akamui, softened after several cups of tuka, told her, "There is nothing more important than my child and you. All my life I've been dreaming to have a strong, handsome son, blood of my blood, and flesh of my flesh. I'll make him a great warrior, and the entire Archipelago will sing songs about his feats."

"And if it's a girl?" she teased him with a playful smile.

"No, it will be a boy, believe me," said Akamui convincingly.

For the first time since the death of Keoni, Laia lived something similar to a normal life. The moon waxed and waned, and she felt her child growing in her. As it wriggled and kicked inside her womb, the desire for suicide faded away, replaced by her admiration of the wonder of life and the joy of having a baby. Her mother's instincts were so profound that every single thought and desire was dedicated to the child inside her.

Now, carrying the heavy buckets and panting on her way to the hut, she whispered to herself:

"If it's a boy, I'll call him Keoni, after his father. And if it turns out to be a girl, I'll give her the name… I don't know, maybe Aloa… I need to speak to Lalago first, to hear her opinion on the matter… And then, we need to check with her crazy son… Although the brute told me once that he had not come up with a name and will leave it up to me, he'll just give his approval…"

The baby gave her a sharp kick, cutting off her thoughts, and she doubled in pain. She dropped to her knees, the buckets hitting the ground and rolling over. The water spilled and was thirstily absorbed by the dry, cracked earth. Yellow lights danced in front of Laia's eyes. Something warm gushed down her thighs and she started screaming, paralyzed with terror: "Help! My baby! Help me, please!"

Several men and women rushed from the nearby huts and bent over her.

"It's all right, her water broke," said one of the elderly women after examining her. "Let's take her to Lalago."

* * *

Akamui had been waiting for the birth for hours in front of Lalalgo's hut. He heard the cry of the baby coming from inside a long time ago, but when he tried to enter, all three women inside shouted in one voice: "Get out!"

"What the fuck are they doing?" muttered Akamui, pacing nervously around the entrance. The sun was dragging lazily over the blue sky, and the stagnation drove him crazy. It was almost sunset when Lalago finally emerged, clutching a large purple bundle in her hands. She handed the baby to him and said in a tired voice, "It's a boy..." Then she brushed a tear from beneath her eye and sobbed, "I'm so sorry, Son!"

In a flash, a sense of déjà vu suffused Akamui's mind. He stared at his mother, but mentally he was under the Sacred Tree, praying, and seeing Lalago giving him a baby, as the ominous voice of the rustling leaves told him he would have a son who he must sacrifice to Kepolo.

In fact, Akamui had completely forgotten about his vision, as often happened to the Tipihaos when they came out of a trance.

"Akamui, do you hear me, Son?" Lalago was crying, her body rocking with sobs.

"What was that? What did you say?" he asked, shaking off the weird memory, his look wandering like a person who had just woke up from a terrible nightmare.

"She's gone," repeated Lalago, her eyes fixed upon the ground. "She passed away."

"She's dead?" uttered Akamui, his face whitened. "What have you done?"

"We tried everything," said Lalago, wiping her eyes. "I don't know what happened… The blood gushed out and we could not stop it. She lost too much blood… I'm so sorry, Son."

"Let me see her," hissed Akamui. Absentmindedly he pushed the baby back into Lalago's hands and got into the half-dark hut. He stepped over a bucket full of water and leaned over a pile of dirty clothes smeared with bloody stains. Laia lay in the center of the room, mostly covered with rugs. At the gleams of the torches, Akamui looked at her pale, exhausted face. Her left hand clutched Keoni's bracelet. Akamui took a lock of wavy hair away from her face and touched her forehead, still bedewed with small drops of sweat. He remained still for a moment, then lifted her up and strode away.

At the entrance, he told his mother, "Take care of my son. I'll lay her down below Rakapi and pray to the Great Kepolo to let her dwell in the Tree's mighty crown along with our ancestors. I hope our god will accept her, even though she was a foreigner."

∗ ∗ ∗

After Akamui left, Lalago went up the hill to see Oliana, a young woman whose son Anuro Lalago helped deliver about a full moon ago. It was already dark when she reached there, and there were no signs of life in the hut. Lalago pulled the curtain aside and peeped inside.

"Oliana," she hissed. Someone fidgeted. A baby started crying. The boy in Lalago's hands took up as if in sympathy. Oliana emerged from the hut, rocking her baby with one hand and rubbing her puffy eyes with the other.

"What's up," she asked, yawning.

"Laia's dead," whispered Lalago. "Could you feed her baby and keep him for the night? I'll take him tomorrow."

"I don't know," muttered Oliana. "Mine is already a nightmare. I've barely slept a wink since this one was born, and you want to give me another baby? Pity about the girl, though. She seemed really nice."

"I understand that it's hard, but it's only for tonight," Lalago insisted. "The baby shouldn't stay where his mother died. I'll purify the place at sunrise, and he can remain with me afterward. Do you have enough milk?"

"More than enough," Oliana nodded. "Afterwards, you can bring him here to breastfeed if you like, as long as you keep him at night. What's his name?"

"We haven't named him yet," Lalago muttered.

"All right, give him to me."

"Thanks, Oliana. See you in the morning," said Lalago with a wan smile, handing her the baby.

As she reached her hut, she was already on the brink of exhaustion. It took her a lot of time to clean up all the mess. When she finished, she collapsed on the ground, not even able to reach her hammock, and immediately sank into a deep sleep.

That night she had a strange dream. She had kneeled before the Sacred Tree and rhythmically swung her body back and forth, touching the ground with her forehead in fervent prayer. She begged Kepolo to give her grandson health and strength and to make him a brave and mighty warrior. Suddenly she was wrapped by complete darkness and started groping in her blindness. Then a single ray of sunshine lit her up, tearing open the blackness. A strong, echoing voice came from above, speaking so loudly that Lalago pressed her palms to her ears, but that didn't help, as she felt the voice vibrate inside her.

"Today a boy was born," it thundered. "He will have neither mother nor father. You will take care of him as your own precious son until the time is right. Then I will take over. He will be my son, and I will teach him knowledge and wisdom. He will become a great chieftain and will lead his tribe to a new life. His name shall be Kamolea!"

The light moved away from Lalago and lit up the Sacred Tree. A blinding thunderbolt ripped through the black sky and hit Rakapi, splitting its trunk in two and setting the crown on fire. Then a terrible earthquake struck, and the ground swung.

Lalago woke up, moaning and rolling on the floor. Feverish and frightened, she sat up for a long time, staring ahead in the darkness. In her ears kept ringing the words *"His name shall be Kamolea!"* She shuddered. In their language, the name Kamolea meant "a new beginning."

* * *

The next morning, Lalago met Oliana, who looked even more exhausted than before. The baby, to the contrary, was in a good mood, well-fed and crowing. When Oliana gave Lalago a wooden flask filled with breast milk, the latter thanked her one more time and wended her way to Akamui. She found him sitting before his hut, looking thoughtfully at a black beetle crawling near his foot.

"Here he is, your son," she said, smiling, handing the small bundle to Akamui.

"What do you want me to do with this baby?" Akamui snorted. "He needs his mother now, not me. Look after him until he grows up, then the fun will begin. You'll see what an outstanding warrior I'll make of him. They'll call him the brave… the brave what? What was the name Laia proposed? I liked it …"

"That's exactly what I'd like to talk with you about," began Lalago cautiously. "Laia's name was good, but it's not relevant now."

"Why not?" grunted Akamui.

"Last night, I had a dream about it," Lalago replied. "Your son must be really special, as God Kepolo himself came into my dream and spoke to me about him. He ordered me to give him the name Kamolea."

"Kamolea? Bats' droppings, how did you make up this one?" barked Akamui. "Have you ever heard of someone with such a name?"

"I know, it's a weird one, but it's not my fault," snapped Lalago. "It was Kepolo's will, pure and simple!" And she told him her dream.

"Hmm, very strange," said Akamui. "I like the part about how he'll become a great chieftain, but why would Rakapi split open and set on fire? It doesn't make sense. In fact, Kepolo also gave me a sign about this boy; only there was nothing about making him a chieftain or anything. It's pretty confusing, isn't it?"

"What sign was it?" asked Lalago suspiciously.

"I'd rather not to tell, Mother," muttered Akamui. "Not now, anyway. I have to think it all over because, honestly, I understand nothing."

Lalago remained silent for a while.

"The whims of gods are often dimmed and unclear for mortals like us," she said at last, "but we need to follow the will of Almighty Kepolo and give your son the name he has bid. He also ordered me to take care of him like a mother, so we must respect that, too. No matter how many wives you have from now on, I want you to promise me that only I will be responsible for his upbringing. If not, we would draw Kepolo's wrath upon us."

"Have it your way, then!" said Akamui reluctantly. "Kamolea! What a stupid name! I do count on you to look after him, though. As my wives die like flies, I don't think I'll get another one soon, anyway."

Lalago nodded.

"Leave everything to me, Son, and don't worry about a thing," she said and waddled toward her hut with Kamolea in her hands.

* * *

Kamolea's early childhood was the happiest period of his life. Raised by Lalago and surrounded by friends, he had no care in the world. The resemblance to his mother was obvious: he had the same high, prominent forehead, curly hair, small nose, full lips, and big, black shiny eyes. His mild features considerably distinguished him from the other kids of the Tipihao tribe. Oh, how strongly he loathed his small locks! As he was the only "curly" person on the island, to be different in such a small community posed serious problems, and he was a constant object of ridicule because of his hair.

Akamui loved his son madly, and although he was a busy man with many responsibilities in the Council, he always found time for Kamolea. Scarcely had the latter reached the age of five before Akamui began to take him to the forest and teach him the language of the jungle. Under his training, Kamolea learned to hunt, set snares, read tracks, shoot with a bow, throw knife and spear, know where snakes nest, beware of spiders and other dangerous insects, and how to find birds' eggs and water in the roots of the trees.

Another part of his practice took place in the sea. There he acquired abilities like swimming, diving, fishing with spear and knife, breathing whilst under the water with a straw in his mouth, keeping away from sharks, sailing a raft, and so on.

"A Tipihao warrior is never afraid of death," Akamui repeated during his lessons. "There is no greater honor for us than to die in a battle. Then Almighty Kepolo will graciously accept our spirit and he will incarnate us in a newborn body. Thus, we will become stronger and braver thanks to our previous experience. And one day, after many incarnations, when we will finally reach absolute perfection as warriors, we will dwell eternally in the mighty crown of Rakapi, where our ancestors live forever and enjoy our sacrifice along with us. So, remember our motto, Son: *Kill or die! No mercy for our enemies! No pity for their wives and children! Nobody is stronger than us! Win or die!*"

As Kamolea grew up, Akamui became increasingly amazed by his son's intelligence. He was a quick learner, and after every successfully completed lesson, Akamui couldn't resist bragging to his friends about how clever Kamolea was and how he would become a chieftain one day.

Sometimes, however, late at night, Akamui's thoughts whirled in his mind, not giving him rest and raising serious concern about his son. At seven, Kamolea began to manifest strange behaviors. Something was not quite right with him. Akamui could not explain it, yet, he could feel it in his bones.

It began with this cursed boar's hunt. Kamolea was mad with joy at the prospect of hunting his first boar. He had begged his father so many times to do it that finally Akamui, who was aware of the danger and had intended to postpone the hunt until Kamolea got a little older, reluctantly gave in. They hunted in the jungle around Carapace Hill. During the trek, Akamui explained to Kamolea the beast's habits and different tricks for finding its lair.

"Maniha Komu is the only place in the entire Archipelago where such animals live," Akamui pointed out, smiling inwardly at Kamolea's eager expression.

"Why so, Father?" Kamolea asked.

"Well, as the saying goes, some people with pale skin brought them in ancient times, along with the cursed snake."

They spent two days in the jungle, in rain, scorching heat, suffocating dampness, and eaten alive by the mosquitos, finding and losing the boars' usual trail, when finally they came upon a fresh wild boar's track. They sneaked as they followed the lead, visible through the crumpled grass and bushes. It was already late afternoon on the second day, and they hoped to catch a boar before nightfall.

Suddenly, Akamui touched Kamolea's elbow and gestured forward. Under a palm tree, with her brown, bristly back turned to them, a massive female swine was thrusting her snout into the dirt, grunting quietly as she dug for roots. Kamolea's young eyes widened—the animal looked enormous to him.

Akamui advanced noiselessly, hiding behind the trees, with Kamolea following into his steps. Now they were no farther than five yards, but the subtle breeze blew against them and the boar still had not scented out the danger. Akamui nodded toward the boar and Kamolea raised his spear. He drew his arm backward and arched his back, exactly the way his father had taught him, his sinews taut, his muscles bulging, ready to deliver the mortal blow. Akamui was waiting, content with his performance. A couple of seconds passed. Kamolea had frozen in the perfect position to fling the spear, but did nothing. The swine raised her head and started sniffing the air. Kamolea slacked his posture and lowered his weapon. Akamui gaped, flabbergasted.

"I can't kill her," whispered Kamolea. "Please, Father! She has seven babies in her stomach."

"What?" shouted Akamui. The wild boar dashed into the jungle and he ran after her. Kamolea did not move. Soon Akamui returned, dragging the dead swine with him. Kamolea stood rooted to the ground, staring at his feet.

"What's wrong with you?" Akamui yelled. "What is this nonsense? You failed your first boar's hunt. What a shame! A son of mine should never behave like this! What were you afraid of?"

"I'm not afraid, Father," said Kamolea quietly. "I'm just… sad."

"Sad? Girls get sad, not men. Listen to me now! You're a boy who will become an outstanding man, a brave and strong warrior, a hunter. If you pity your prey, you and your family will end up starving to death. If you have mercy on your foes, their spears will overthrow you and you'll feed the *burkans*, lying in disgrace in a pool of blood. Remember, mercy is equal to weakness, and weakness equals death. Understood?"

Kamolea swallowed and looked at his feet. His eyes were full of tears.

"It was not fair to kill her, Father," he whispered. "She was about to give life to seven babies."

Akamui's eyes narrowed. He made two rapid steps and delivered a hard backhand blow to Kamolea's face. Kamolea fell with a heavy thud, his lip split in two, blood dripping from his nose.

"This was to know your place," said Akamui through clenched teeth. "Never contradict me, you milksop! Are we clear?"

Kamolea nodded fearfully and wiped his bleeding nose.

"Good," said Akamui. "Now I'll rip up her belly and you'll see that the things you imagine have nothing to do with reality."

He drew his knife, kneeled, and plunged it in the boar's belly. When he ripped it open, blood spouted, soaking into the soil and forming a pool. Akamui pulled the entrails out onto the ground, and amid them fell seven mouse-like piglets.

* * *

Right after the boar hunt, there was a series of unfortunate events, which brought Kamolea to the brink of despair. His father, angry and confused by Kamolea's correct guess about the baby boars, decided to direct his son's attention to serious things and to knock any stupid ideas out of his head.

"I intend to make of you a real man, not a sissy boy," Akamui told him. "I think it's about time to start getting familiar with our customs. When the next sacrifice takes place, I'll bring you to Kepolo's belt and show you what destiny awaits all traitors and cowards."

The opportunity presented itself a score of sunsets later, when a young slave was caught in an attempt to escape and sentenced to death.

Kamolea would never forget the ominous sentiment he experienced that moonless night. Thick clouds hung in the dark, overhanging sky, and not a leaf stirred in the still air. The *Sacred Zone* echoed with the drum of timpani as the crowd swung their bodies back and forth, humming in sync. Akamui pushed Kamolea to the front row to watch the ceremony at close quarters.

The gigantic Sacred Tree had an overwhelming effect on the little boy, as he felt so small in front of it. A rudimentary fear crawled in Kamolea and he started swaying with the others. After some time, four Tipihaos dragged out the poor victim, a handsome young man. They hurled him onto the altar and tied his limbs to the four corners of the rectangular stone. The humming grew louder, the torches swayed faster and faster, and the crowd fell into a trance, rocking their bodies as one.

The chieftain approached, carrying a torch in one hand and a long sacrificial knife in the other. Akamui pulled Kamolea aside and clutched his shoulder.

"This is your initiation into real life, Son," he hissed in his ear. "The scene is hard to watch, but you must not look aside. Be brave and don't flinch! Be my worthy heir, my pride, and my glory!"

Kamolea nodded, determined. He would not even dream of disgracing his father. He would do everything he was required to, like a real man… He looked at the chieftain, who wore a funny tall hat with a skull perched on top of it. The chieftain placed his torch into a slot on the altar near the victim's head, slowly raised the knife that he clutched with both hands, and began singing a weird song, resembling the crowing of a *burkan*.

Kamolea's heart started banging against his chest. Everything reeled before his eyes and he got the feeling that he was being sucked into a gigantic whirling funnel of wind. He floated now far beyond the clouds, watching the black sky studded with millions of stars. An incredibly bright star attracted his attention and he sped toward it.

"Kamolea, remember Alina and her three children." A booming voice vibrated in his entire being, and he noticed three stars in a row, near to the brightest star in the sky. And then all those countless stars around him whirled him in a staggering dance and formed a silhouette of a beautiful woman, which starry eyes pierced through Kamolea's heart.

A sharp sting on his cheek brought him back to his senses. He opened his eyes and found himself lying on the ground. Akamui was bending over him and had just slapped him again.

"Wake up, you coward," cried Akamui, beside himself with rage. "That's exactly what you get when an old woman raises a child—a sissy boy and a worthless wretch. I forbid you to live with your grandmother anymore. You move into my hut tonight. From now on, your education will be my priority."

Kamolea was ill with shame. He could see the terrible disappointment in his father's eyes.

"I'm so sorry, Father," he whispered. "I didn't mean to let you down. I just… I don't know what happened."

He glanced at the altar. It was covered with blood, but the man was gone.

Akamui shook his head. "Go straight to my hut. Tell Kalima that you shall live with us, to feed you and to find you a place to sleep."

"I don't want to live with her, Father. She hates me…"

"I don't care what you want," Akamui barked. "Do what I say. Hey, Ahaki, are you going to the village?"

"I am," Ahaki said with a nod.

"Could you take my son with you through the forest, please? Afterward, he knows the path. I need to stay here a little longer. Thank you, wise Ahaki."

"Always my pleasure, Master Akamui," nodded Ahaki. He grabbed Kamolea by his arms and lifted him to sit on his shoulders.

"Just watch your head," he told him and strode away.

In the forest, it was quiet and dark. Ahaki walked in silence, sunk in his thoughts. Kamolea had wrapped his hands around Ahaki's neck and laid his chin on the top of his head. He could not stop thinking about his failure. After a while, his body rocked with sobs.

"What is it, Kamolea?" asked Ahaki. He bent and put him down.

"I failed my father so badly tonight," Kamolea said, weeping. "He wanted me to watch the sacrifice, but I fainted like the world's greatest coward…"

"Oh, come on, don't be too hard on yourself," said Ahaki with a smile. "It happens to the best of us, especially the first time at a sacrifice."

"Did you pass out as well?" asked Kamolea, astounded.

"I did," nodded Ahaki. "And I was even older than you are now. Not only did I faint, but I had a strange vision."

"What's a vision?"

"It's something like a vivid dream, only you're awake when it happens... Anyway, my father was not pleased, to put it mildly, just like yours today." Ahaki chuckled, took Kamolea's hand and they continued walking.

"I also had a vision," said Kamolea proudly after a moment of contemplation. "Was yours something about the stars?"

"Nah, mine was weird. I had swum up from the bottom of the sea and paced toward the shore, water dripping off me. And on my shoulders, I carried a mighty warrior with a face covered in scars, who was gripping a big ax in his hand."

"Wow," Kamolea said. "That's so cool. My vision was stupid, just some stars..."

Ahaki cut him off. "I think it's time to part company, my little friend. Here's your father's home."

"Thank you, Master Ahaki." Kamolea bowed and ran toward his new home.

* * *

Several days later, Kamolea was running toward the north shore. Tears mixed with blood streamed down his face. When he reached the shore, he threw himself in the sea and, taking advantage of the high tide, swam to his favorite spot: a cave, situated in the middle of a jagged cliff.

The cliff was about two hundred yards away from the hilly shore, and the strong current and the submerged boulders made it difficult to reach, but Kamolea knew the way like the back of his hand. The spray rose a misty veil around the slippery rock, and he groped for a crack or prong to hold on. The whirlpool spun him in a boiling swirl, but he managed to hook his fingers into a crevice and resist the draught. Then, using the surge, he caught the protruded rock, hoisted himself up, and rolled over on the cave's stone floor, panting. He lay on his back for a long while, listening to the roaring wind and the breakers that crashed relentlessly against the rock.

Recently, he had been spending more and more time in the cave, away from his father and friends. It was small and cozy, always dry and pleasantly warm, located high enough, so the tide heaved just a little below the entrance.

Kamolea adored the place. He felt calm and secure in it, as though an invisible presence watched over him and gave him strength and reassurance. The damp scent of the sea and its constant booming would make his thoughts stop and carry him away, and he would spend hours staring at the unceasing whirl of the white foam until he himself turned into a droplet of the splashing water, floating in the ocean's infinity.

Now Kamolea felt anxious and hurt. He hauled himself up and sat cross-legged, his body trembling and his head almost touching the ceiling of the tiny oval space. He ran his fingers over his clawed face, sniffed, and fixed his gaze on the horizon, where the water merged with the sky. Today he had blundered again, and he was not eager to face his father when the latter got home at dusk.

The day began as usual. When he woke up, Kalima, his stepmother, was nursing his second half-brother Lelando. Kamolea got up and walked past her on his way to the shelf to get something to eat when from the corner of his eye, he caught some shadow, similar to a big black fish, which was twisting its body in the air. Kamolea gaped and stared at it. With every twirl, the shadow was getting bigger and bigger, reaching up to the ceiling, and suddenly it lunged toward Kamolea. Frightened, he violently jumped back and collided with Kalima, who dropped the baby. A terrible din broke out... She screamed like mad at him and clawed at his face, neck, and shoulder. He ran away, aghast and humiliated, leaving behind him a fine trail of bloody droplets, and he did not stop until he reached the cave.

Kamolea brushed a rolling tear and almost jumped as he heard Akamui's voice bellow inside his head: *"Men don't cry!"*

"Why am I so weird?" he whispered in the darkness. "My father won't love me anymore. I bring only shame on him."

He stretched out in the corner and listened to the surf, which lulled him, and his eyelids grew heavy. Suddenly, the cave started to glow inside, as though the morning light was chasing the gloom. Kamolea sensed someone's presence. He was aware of everything around him, yet he knew he was dreaming because he could not open his eyes.

To his left, near the entrance, appeared a man. A strange, pale-skinned man, his entire face covered with white hairs. Kamolea found that curious, as all the men on the island were beardless. His hair, long and white, reached to his shoulders. He was wrapped in a red robe richly decorated with golden crosses, which trailed on the cave's floor. In his left hand, which he kept close to his chest, he clutched a strange, black object with a white cross and several signs carved on it. His presence was somehow reassuring and, instead of being afraid, Kamolea felt elated, as though some source of happiness touched his heart. The old man smiled at him, his eyes streaming light and goodness.

"Go see Lalago tonight and ask her about Kedia and the legend of your tribe," resounded his deep voice in Kamolea's head. The words were spoken in the perfect Tipihao language. "Tell her that the prophecy has been set in motion!"

Kamolea jerked and sat up. Nobody was in the cave, and it was dark, meaning he had slept for a long time. In a panic, he jumped in the water and crawled toward the shore with mighty strokes.

* * *

When Kamolea reached Lalago's hut it was already night, and he presumed that she was fast asleep. It had been a while since he last visited her and, as he didn't want to scare her, he sneaked to the entrance and peeped inside. To his surprise, Lalago was up. She was kneeling over a mat covered in dried herbs, and she crumbled them between her palms into a wooden bowl. The faint flame of the lamp flickered next to her. When she saw Kamolea, she let out a cry of surprise.

"What are you doing here?" she scolded. "You know what your father said…"

"I don't want to return there, Grandma," said Kamolea. "Can I stay here tonight? Look at what Kalima did to me…"

"She did that!?" exclaimed Lalago, as she drew the lamp near to his clawed face. "That snake! Tell me what happened?"

"I bumped into her and she dropped the baby. Can I stay, Grandma?" Kamolea pleaded again.

"All right, all right," said Lalago. "Your father will be angry, but stay if you'd like. Your hammock is always waiting for you, even though it's getting a little short for you already. Are you hungry?"

"I am," Kamolea admitted.

"Good. Give me just a moment to finish with these herbs and I'll bring you your favorite fish broth."

After Kamolea finished his meal, he stretched on the hammock and said, "It's good to be with you, Grandma. Could you tell me the legend of our tribe one more time, please? How did we become so strong and subdue all other tribes? How did it come to be that our god Kepolo chose us and made us invincible?"

"Well, I've told you that story a few times already," Lalago said reluctantly.

"True, but I was little then and don't remember. Tell me again, please."

"It's late and I'm tired now," Lalago said. "Let's leave it for another time."

"It must be tonight, Granny," insisted Kamolea.

"Why?"

"Because the hairy man said so," cried Kamolea

"The hairy man? Who is this?" asked Lalago suspiciously.

Kamolea didn't respond.

"Speak out, boy!" Lalago yelled.

"The legend first," Kamolea said stubbornly.

"All right, then," sighed Lalago. "In ancient times, many, many years ago, so many that nobody could ever count to such a big number, Maniha Komo was a beautiful place where everybody lived in harmony and peace. The legend says that our ancestors came by huge rafts from a large earth that lies far away, in the direction of the rising sun. They were peaceful and meek and worshipped the Sun God and his wife, the Moon Goddess. At that time, nobody killed his neighbor, and the war was an unknown word."

"How so? What was wrong with them?" Kamolea cried out.

"It's not wrong to live in peace, boy. Yes, it was a calm time for a long time, and Maniha Komo was a glorious place, the most important center of the Turtle Archipelago." Lalago smiled dreamily. "Our ancestors worshipped the Moon Goddess, and women ruled our tribe."

"Whaaat?!" Kamolea looked scandalized. "How come men accepted that? Who would obey a woman in the first place?"

"And why not?" Lalago retorted. "Aren't women better than men? They give birth, and they realize how precious life is. They carry their children for nine full moons, and when the baby is born, they feel it like a part of them, bone of their bones and flesh of their flesh. And here is the thing—they take care of their sons until they grow up, only to see them slaughtered in battle afterward. Isn't that insane?

"But at the time it wasn't like that. Everything was thriving and Maniha Komo was at the height of its glory. And the happiest days were during the time of the highest Moon Priestess Alina, who it was said was so tightly connected to the Moon Goddess that she received everything she asked for. The other tribes even considered Maniha Komo a holy piece of land, a blessed gift from the Moon Goddess to her people. Unfortunately, it was so long ago that nobody can even remember our first real tribe's name. What people did remember, though, was the immense love and respect they had toward Alina, who was not only a priestess but also a chieftain. She ruled for a long time, but even at her ripe age she looked beautiful and young. The people started to say that she was eternal, a goddess herself. Her three daughters were also incredibly gorgeous and goddess-like. Everything within her touch was in harmony and filled with beauty."

Kamolea listened intently. The name of Alina sounded familiar, and he racked his brain, trying to remember where he had heard it.

"Everything was perfect until the day when cruel, violent men invaded the Turtle Archipelago." The voice of Lalago became brisk. "They were killers and rapists who brought war and devastation with them. Nobody knew who they were or where they had come from. They started taking the islands of Kepula Penu and enslaving the people. Caught by surprise and softened by the long peaceful period, nobody was ready to resist them. When they landed on Maniha Komo, Alina met them with peace and tried to propitiate them. How did they respond to her kindness? Well, they raped and killed her in the cruelest fashion, along with her daughters. However, Alina and her offspring were so pure and beautiful that their spirits ascended straight to the sky and turned into bright stars, which always shine over Maniha Komo."

Lalago sniffed and brushed a tear from the corner of her eye. Kamolea was the embodiment of concentration. His eyes shone in the darkness and his mouth was slightly open.

"Alina the star! I remember now!" he exclaimed. "I asked my father about it some time ago, because I flew to it when… Never mind. My father pointed it out for me, the brightest star of all, and said that if someday I get lost, I need only to follow it and it will bring me back home."

"My son showed you Alina? Really? He said the name?" asked Lalago in disbelief.

"Yes, Granny, and he also told me that stupid old women consider her to be our ancestor and protector, just like you said. Do you think he meant you?" Kamolea giggled.

"Well, the men don't like this legend because it contradicts Kepolo's teaching—he wants war and she loved peace. However, you need to know this part of our history in order to understand that once we were different. As I told you, though, don't mention it to your father."

"And how came the Almighty Kepolo to replace the Moon Goddess and become our god?" Kamolea asked.

"Well, you know already this part of the story. After Alina was killed and the entire tribe massacred, only a few children and elderly people escaped into the heart of the jungle. They hid in the crown of the enormous tree. From the top, they watched with sinking hearts how the assailants dragged their mothers and sisters across the sandy shore, threw them into their boats, and rowed away. Some of the invaders, however, stayed longer, searching for survivors.

"Afraid to leave their hiding place, the escapees spent several days in the tree, drinking rainwater from its hollows, eating mushrooms and insects from its bark and leaves, and the small red fruit growing on its branches. It's not clear whether the mushrooms or the fruit or maybe the combination of both is what had a strange effect on them. One night, they shared a vision: A gigantic man of darkness, engulfed in flames, rose in the middle of the forest, and all the trees around their hiding place burned up.

"The man spoke in a pure Tipihao language. 'Don't be afraid, future children of darkness! Today I choose you as my people and you'll accept me as your god. I'll save you from your invaders and will make you strong, mighty warriors. You'll be a horror to anybody who dares to challenge you. From now on, your tribe's name will be Tipihao, and everyone will bow down to you. Here, around this tree, I'm tracing my belt, and may this clearing be your *Sacred Zone*. Honor the tree that saved your lives, give me your foes as sacrifice to me beneath its branches, respect my commandments, and glorify my name: Kepolo. That is all you need to do to have my goodwill and protection.'

"With these words, the man disappeared. The blazing trees burned the whole night and, in the morning, the newborn tribe saw a perfect circle of ashes around their hiding tree. It was as though the fire purified and strengthened our people, petrified their hearts, and tempered their bodies. They became brave and bold, and even though they were only children and old men and women, they feared nothing. They climbed down the tree and went through the island, but they found no-one, because all of the assailants were gone.

"Thus began the transformation of our peaceful ancestors into pitiless warriors. They began to worship Kepolo, the Dark One, as the meaning of his name implies. They deified the tree that saved their lives as he commanded, calling it *Rakapi*, or the Sacred Tree. Thus, Rakapi became the temple of their new god Kepolo, who was also known as '*The Master of the Tree*.'

Lalago stopped for a moment and looked at Kamolea. He had propped himself up on an elbow in his slightly swinging hammock and watched her without blinking, absorbing every word.

She smiled at him and went on:

"Meanwhile, the invaders retreated to the other islands, where they killed off some of the local tribes, leaving alive only the youthful women, who brought to the world their offspring, cruel and belligerent as their fathers were. War broke out across Kepula Penu, and violence became a way of living. Our ancestors had no choice but to become impeccable warriors. Led by an invisible force, they trained themselves in all the arts of war: bow shooting, spear and slingshot throwing, the setting of snares and traps, fist fighting, and blending into the forest. The young warriors, still merely children, developed their rapidity, endurance, and boldness, and, most importantly, their philosophy of superiority without a shred of mercy. A soft attitude toward foes had been regarded as great weakness and a sign of cowardliness. All their exercises took place around Rakapi, where they prayed to Kepolo to give them strength and wisdom, patiently biding their time.

"And the day of their revenge eventually came after the moon waned and waxed many, many times. The boys had become strong and fearless men by then. One day, several of the same cruel men came to Maniha Komu to look for food and supplies. They had taken no precautions, as they were sure nobody was living there. The Tipihaos took them by surprise and killed them off, all of them.

"The next morning, our ancestors decided to strike their enemies first before they suspected that anything was wrong. They reached their island in two sunsets and crawled onto the shore at nightfall. Nobody expected the horror that would follow.

"In the middle of the night, the Tipihaos silently entered each hut and slew every man; afterward, they set the entire village on fire. They took away most of the women and, in doing so, they recognized in some of them their abducted sisters and mothers. The chieftain of the massacred tribe and a few surrendered men were taken as a special gift to Kepolo.

"On their way back home, the weather was perfect and the sea was calm. Several sunsets later, they saw many black points on the horizon and realized that a horde of them were coming for revenge. Led by Almighty Kepolo, Tipihaos built an altar under Rakapi and killed the captured chieftain with a fervent prayer for victory in the forthcoming battle. Then something incredible happened: a violent storm arose and overturned most of the boats, which made our ancestors insane with joy. Most of the invaders drowned, and those who reached the shore were immediately captured or slain.

"That very day, at sunset, the Tipihaos performed their famous ritual for the first time. They stretched their foes over the altar and executed them, and then they drank their blood and ate their flesh. They decorated the branches of the Sacred Tree with the captives' heads and danced their famous dance of death until the sun chased away the gloom of the night sky.

"And from that day on, my boy, nothing was the same. Why? Because the god Kepolo looked favorably at this custom. The signs and omens were clear that the warriors had to continue doing this ritual. In return, Kepolo made the Tipihaos the greatest, the bravest, and the strongest tribe in the Turtle Archipelago. From then on, with his help, the Tipihaos rule over the other tribes, which fear us and tremble with dread at the mention of our name."

Lalago glanced at Kamolea. He had tilted his head, staring dreamily at the ceiling.

"So," Lalago said, "what about this hairy man?"

"Yes, he was very weird. He had pale skin, and white hair was growing from his head and face," Kamolea chuckled. "And he had wrapped himself with a red cloth, and in his hand he held something black, like a piece of wood or something… Have you seen someone like him ever before, Grandma?"

"Never." Lalago rose in the hammock, looking suspiciously at him. "Where did you meet him?"

"In my secret hiding place. At first, I thought it was a dream, and he wasn't real, but then he spoke to me as though he was."

"And what did he say?" asked Lalago, smiling. She obviously did not take any of this seriously.

"He mentioned the name of some woman… Kelia… or Kebia…," Kamolea scratched his head, trying to remember.

"Kedia," said Lalago, the blood draining from her face and her smile fading.

"That's it exactly!" exclaimed Kamolea happily. "And he said also that something was put in motion or whatever... Who is she, Grandma?"

"How do you know about Kedia?" whispered Lalago, her voice trembling.

"I know nothing, Grandma. The pale man told me to ask you about her."

"Look, I think we should stop with the legends for now," said Lalago firmly. "Go to sleep and go straight to your father in the morning. He must be worried about you. And remember: if you want to stay alive, forget about Kedia and never—I repeat, never—mention her name again. And get this pale man out of your head! He does not exist. You imagine things, and this is not good. Not good at all, boy, understand? Do you know what they do with such people? I assume you don't want to finish hanged on Rakapi, do you? Not a word about that till the end of your life!"

Kamolea looked at his grandmother with astonishment. He had never seen her in such mood—angry and shuddering.

She's scared to death, he thought, but nodded in agreement to her last words and soon sank into a deep sleep.

CHAPTER V

LAGGI

The next several years of Kamolea's life passed under Akamui's strict surveillance, who watched closely that his son's behavior conformed to the common rules and customs of the tribe. Now Kamolea attended all sacred ceremonies and took part in activities related to his warrior's proof, which quickly approached.

The warrior's proof took place when boys reached the age of thirteen. It was the most important event in a Tipihao man's life, aiming to change every boy into a man and a valiant warrior. It consisted of capturing another tribe's soldier and bringing him to the Sacred Tree as a trophy. To accomplish that, the boys were taken to one of the numerous islands in the Turtle Archipelago and were left there only with their weapons and a flask of water. The task was difficult: they had to survive in the heart of the enemy territory, find a man, and return to their native island, transporting the captive in a stolen canoe or raft. Sometimes they came back victorious, but often they never returned.

The preparation for this remarkable test took up most of Kamolea's time: day after day, he learned fighting skills and developed his bloodthirsty instincts. Under the pressure of the training, he became stronger and more supple. His shoulders broadened, his legs toughened up, and although he was not very tall, he projected the vital strength of a wild animal. The development of his body inevitably led to another major change, which was a source of constant trouble throughout every man's life. It started suddenly and without warning. One night, he woke up with a hard-on, his groin aching, and naked women and erotic scenes swarming inside his head. Several days after he had his first wet dream, and he understood that the blissful time of his childhood was irrevocably gone.

His best friend, Anuro, experienced similar processes, and his obsession with the opposite sex had reached an alarming height.

One day, he met Kamolea by the Great Hollow Tree, which had been their secret spot for years. Situated on Whelk Hill, the *Great Hollow Tree* was actually a formation of several Banyan trees that had tangled their thin root-like trunks around each other into an impossible mess, thus forming a unique gigantic bole. It rose, huge and solitary, surrounded by a small glade, as its long branches spread all the way up to the forest, casting a shadow so thick that no other plants could grow under it. At the middle of this phenomenal tree formation, two separated trunks weaved their boughs together, creating a large hollow that started from ground level and reached high above their heads. It was so vast that it could easily shelter a dozen men comfortably stretched out.

Anuro, Oliana's son, was slightly taller than Kamolea and a full moon older. The boys were "milk brothers" as they had both drank Oliana's milk, which made their connection special, much stronger than an ordinary friendship. Anuro was turbulent, mischievous, light-headed, and had an incredible sense of humor. He was noisy and talked all the time, his head always crowded with new projects, which he was never able to accomplish, as he had trouble concentrating on anything for long. His character was the exact opposite of the calm, reserved Kamolea, but the two friends complemented one another perfectly.

This morning Anuro was agitated more than usual.

"You know what?" he began as soon as he saw Kamolea. "I've just overheard my sister speaking to her girlfriends. They're going swimming in Frog Lake."

"So what?" asked Kamolea.

"Are you slow, or what? They'll swim in the lake! Naked!"

"But they are almost naked all the time," Kamolea said.

"Yeah, exactly, *almost*. And now they will be completely naked." Anuro's eyes shone with excitement. "I've always wanted to see my sister's pussy, but at home, I've never had a chance. Many times I tried to peep out, but one day my old man caught me and beat the shit out of me. Now I know better, especially when he's around. So, what are we waiting for? Let's go!"

"I don't know, man," Kamolea said. "I have to meet my father in the afternoon..."

"We'll be back by then. Come on, Kami, don't leave me alone!" Anuro took him by the hand and dragged him toward the tiny path that winded uphill.

They rushed westward, where Frog Lake lay amidst the jungle.

"I like my sister very much," explained Anuro, while they fought their way through the tangled greenery. "I think I'm in love with her. I agree it's kinda wrong, but she's actually my half-sister, so it doesn't count... I dream of marrying her one day."

"My grandma says it's wrong to do that," Kamolea said. "The babies are not healthy that way."

"I hear you, mate," agreed Anuro, "but what can I do? She's so gorgeous! I don't know how to tell her, though. I heard the older boys saying that if you like some girl, you just take her in the jungle and you tell her you wanna be with her, and that's it, you're together."

"What if she doesn't want you?" Kamolea asked. Anuro was obviously an expert in this field.

"Well, if she pulls away, you just slap her several times, until she likes you," explained Anuro. "It's not complicated, see. But when it's your sister, it doesn't work that way. My father will kill me if I touch her. He's saving her for somebody rich and with influence, I heard him say once. On top of that, Kala is older than me, and she'll laugh her head off if I confess my love to her…"

"Shh," Kamolea said, because the trees had thinned out and the path abruptly ended.

The boys threw themselves behind a fallen trunk and cautiously crawled forward. Frog Lake lay about seven yards below. It was a round pond, fed by a small waterfall, formed by the river coming downhill, that jumped gaily over several superimposed boulders at the far side of the lake.

The clear water, reflecting the unblemished blue sky, the spray, which diffracted the light into thousands of brilliant drops, and the deep green of the surrounding trees, gave a sense of magical enchantment to the scene.

The breeze brought to them the sound of the waterfall, ringing laughter, casual shouts, and splashes. Three girls chased each other through the water, giggling, yelling, and splashing around. They crept in turn up the boulders to the waterfall, then let the swift current pour them over into the lake as they shrieked with joy. The boys lay prone and watched them, hidden behind the thick trunk.

"Who are the other girls?" Kamolea asked.

"Kalani and Illima. They're sisters, actually. Kalani is about my sister's age, and Illima is about ours…"

Kamolea stiffed a yawn. "It's boring to watch them like this, till they've had their fun. Wanna get down and join them?" he asked casually.

"Don't you dare! You'll ruin everything. They'll get out soon, you'll see," hissed Anuro.

It was not so soon, but eventually they swam to the shore and crawled out of the water.

"Isn't she gorgeous?" whispered Anuro, his eyes boring into Kala's naked body.

"Divine," uttered Kamolea, but he didn't mean Anuro's sister. He stared, enchanted, at the youngest girl, Illima, and the magical feelings of bliss, euphoria, and awe overwhelmed his entire being.

The nude girl was nothing special, in fact. She was slim and slender, her body still unshaped, breastless, child-like. Her hair was long, black, and straight, her face small and slightly elongated. Bathed in sunshine, she was glowing, smiling, and radiant. Kamolea couldn't discern her features, but at that moment, a magical, indescribable feeling touched his heart, and he perceived her as the most splendid creature in the world. Unable to tear his eyes off, he had lost track of time.

Meanwhile, the girls put their straw skirts on and the leis they had woven and set off for the village amid giggles and joyful cries. As they disappeared into the jungle, Kamolea shook off his stupor and turned around. Anuro was on his knees, fiddling with his member, his eyes shining with satisfaction.

"I couldn't resist," he said with a wide grin.

"You jerked off?" Kamolea cried. "You are so disgusting, you stupid—"

"Sorry about that, man," Anuro cut him off, wiping his palm against the grass. "But did you see her? Divine, as you said."

"You are a hopeless case, my friend," said Kamolea, shaking his head. "Let's go; my father will be waiting for me."

From that day on, Kamolea could not get Illima out of his mind. When he slept, he dreamt about her. When he was awake, he saw her everywhere. He looked up at the sky and she was in the clouds. He practiced with his father, and her face was printed in the trees and bushes all around. Illima turned into an obsession and he racked his brain to figure out which feat to do to impress her. He had such a hard time focusing on his training that Akamui started to get seriously upset.

"What's the matter with you?" he yelled at Kamolea. "Why are you so distracted? Your life is at stake here, understood? Let's start this exercise again and this time pay attention or I'll smash your face in."

But nothing helped. Kamolea was losing not only his strength, but also his mind. When he told Anuro about his pangs of love, his friend rolled on the ground, rocking with laughter until tears started running down his eyes.

"You're such a jerk," he said to Kamolea, after he finally calmed down. "Illima! Why did you fall in love with her? She's not even pretty, that eel. Flat as a board…"

"Oh, shut up, dickhead. I don't give a shit about your opinion. The question is what should I do now? I have trouble sleeping at night and if it continues like this…"

"*What should I do… I have trouble sleeping…* Too many wet dreams…" Anuro mimicked in a high-pitched voice, rolling his big black eyes. "You're dumb as a rock, man. Just tell her, then screw her as many times as you like, and then, I guarantee you, you'll sleep like a baby."

"Well, I don't want it to be like that," Kamolea muttered. "I want it to be a special moment… To make a romantic declaration of love, you know…"

Anuro snorted. "Honestly, I don't know," he said. "But listen, I was in the same position as you with my sister. I had the same trouble sleeping, eating, even focusing on something other than her. I couldn't stand it anymore, so one day I went to Kala and confessed my love to her. She laughed at me and told me to fuck off. I cornered her and grabbed her by the pussy. She clawed at my face, and I slapped her two-three times. She slid down, holding up her hands, shielding her face, whimpering. Then I kneeled and started groping her, and kissing her on the mouth… She bit me first, but then yielded… Eventually, we had sex, and it was the greatest day of my life."

"Wow! When did it happen?" Kamolea was impressed.

"Around the last full moon—about ten sunsets ago."

"And why didn't you tell me anything?"

"Well, it's kind of secret… She's so afraid that Father will find out… Don't tell anyone about it, or we're as good as dead."

"Don't worry. But I find it disgusting to fuck your sister..."

"Why? Isn't she pretty?"

"She is, indeed, but that's not the point..."

"What then?"

"I don't know, man," sighed Kamolea. "I just feel that it's terribly wrong. So, your advice is that I should tell Illima that I'm into her, right?"

"I see no way around it," shrugged Anuro with mischievous glitter in his eyes, watching Kamolea as if he were some weird creature. "Even a five-year-old kid would tell you the same thing."

* * *

Kamolea slept badly. Hundreds of times, he played in his mind the encounter with Illima: he meets her by chance while she is plucking flowers, and he hands her one himself, then he says to her beautiful, ardent words of love. She gazes at him, enchanted, and listens spellbound with shiny eyes. A sunbeam lightens her face and she looks like a heavenly alien creature. He bends over and kisses her, sweet, honey kiss...

Kamolea woke up with a hard-on, drenched in sweat. It was hot, late in the morning. He got up and staggered, his head spinning, and his thoughts swirling chaotically:

I'll go for a quick dip in the sea, and hopefully I'll find her on the beach; if not, I'll go to her hut and suggest we go for a walk... I can't continue like this anymore; it's driving me crazy. What a bloody disease love is. Today will be the day that I confess my love to her and come what may.

It was a gorgeous sunny day, which reflected his mood perfectly. Elated and dreamy, feeling light like a feather, Kamolea set off for the beach. The moment he buried his feet into the scorching sand and his look wandered off into the blue immensity of the sea, his heart fluttered with happiness. A second later, the blood receded from his face and he already regretted his decision. At the far end of the beach, gathered under the shadow of a crooked tree, a bunch of boys stared in his direction.

"Bloody Laggi's gang," muttered Kamolea. Unruly and dirty, about the same age as him, they were the most famous troublemakers on the island. A broken rule, raped girl, or boy beaten to a pulp—in all cases, usually a member of Laggi's gang was involved.

When Kamolea noticed them, his first instinct was to retreat into the jungle, but it was too late—they had already spotted him and to run away was never an option. He was sure that if he chickened out they would find and torture him anyway, as they had done once with one of his acquaintances. The poor boy ended up killing himself and everybody knew it was because of them. What troubled Kamolea most was that they always got away with their mischief thanks to Laggi, who was the youngest son of the chieftain Momo, who had replaced Arataki about a year ago after Arataki had been killed by one of his mistresses out of jealousy.

Kamolea sighed, waved in a friendly way in the gang's direction, and continued toward the sea with the firm decision to swim away and return to shore as far down as possible. Two of the boys detached from the group and ran toward him. Kamolea recognized Loto, sturdy, fierce-looking thug with a scar from a knife cut on his left cheek. His friend, a tall, broad-shouldered tough with a low forehead and dull stare, was unfamiliar to Kamolea. The rest of the gang slouched lazily behind them.

"Whoa, look who's here. The curly boy. How are you, Curly?" Loto drawled, still panting from the run.

"Hi, there! Just passing by for a quick dip and going back to the village," said Kamolea amiably, suspiciously eyeing the long knife that dangled from Loto's waistband.

"Well, for now, I'm afraid you have to skip the dip," Loto said casually. "It's still not that hot, all right?"

"And who will stop me?" Kamolea asked. A dangerous glitter flashed in his eyes.

"Maybe I will," said Loto and pushed him with one hand in the chest. Kamolea took a step back. He looked around and quickly assessed the situation. Loto's companion was grinning stupidly, but his fingers fiddled with his knife's hilt. The other five were closing in. Kamolea sighed and looked Loto in the eyes.

"Touch me one more time and you're a dead man," he said through clenched teeth.

"Well, we'll see how that goes," said Loto mockingly. He made another step toward Kamolea and reached to push him again. Quick as lightning, Kamolea grabbed his hand, kicked his ankles, and sent him down onto his back. He jumped over Loto's outstretched body, pressed his knee down on his chest, and grabbed him by the throat. Then Kamolea's hair was yanked back and a sharp stony blade was pressed to his throat.

A gale of laughter exploded as he heard somebody yelling, "Leave him alone, Kamani! I said quit it! Put the knife away."

The blade withdrew from under Kamolea's chin and the grip on his hair was released. He got up, surrounded by the gang. Loto jumped to his feet and lunged toward Kamolea, but the others pulled them apart.

"We saw enough of your bravery, Loto," drawled a tall, handsome boy, grinning. "It's lucky you have Kamani watching your back, isn't it? If not, you'd be dead by now… Strangulated…"

He grabbed his own throat, stuck his tongue out, and rolled his eyes in a comical grimace. The boys doubled with laughter, and even Kamani smiled. Loto's eyes narrowed.

"Watch your mouth, Laggi," he hissed. Then he snarled at Kamolea, "We aren't done with you."

"Whenever you want," Kamolea responded.

"Be careful, Loto," said one boy. "Don't forget who his father is."

"I don't care!" shouted Loto.

"Since we're more evenly matched now," said Laggi, cutting Loto off, "we could settle our argument from a little while ago. Will you play tug of war with us, Kamolea?"

"Well, I'm kind of in a hurry," began Kamolea, but Laggi approached him and put his arm around his shoulders.

"Don't spoil our fun, okay? I'm sure you're happy to play with us. We need to be evenly matched, so you'll be on my team against Loto, Kamani, Hemi, and Taneo. Did somebody bring the rope? No, as usual. I have to think about everything. Go fetch the rope, Taneo!"

Taneo, short and stocky, darted back to the crooked tree where they'd been hanging out earlier. While they waited, Kamolea watched Laggi and secretly admired him. *It's hard to tell him no, and I highly doubt he has sleeping problems because of a girl!* he thought.

Bold, overbearing, and a natural leader, Laggi was the oldest of the gang. He was tall, strong and muscular, with a handsome, open face and black, shoulder-length, shining hair. He bore a striking resemblance to the former chieftain Arataki, who had spread his seed all over Maniha Komo. Rumor had it that Chieftain Momo, who was short and plump, was not actually Laggi's biological father and that Laggi's mother had narrowly missed being killed at the time by her husband for her playful attitude.

He has incredible hair, Kamolea thought, looking with envy at Laggi. In fact, all the boys still had long hair, which meant that none of them had passed their warrior's proof yet.

I want to see their ugly faces the day they have to shave their heads and prepare for a battle, he brooded. His own thick curls had always been his biggest complex.

Meanwhile, Taneo was back with the long, knotty rope and the game began. Soon Kamolea was shouting and laughing along with the others, his bare feet buried in the hot sand, sweat dripping over his face, his palms burning and sore from the rough rope, and his sinews strained to the breaking point. He felt happy and carefree, and for the first time since he saw Illima, he completely forgot about her.

The competition was tight, and the strength of the two teams was equal. When Hemi, on Loto's team, finally let the rope go and they all rolled over the sand amid breaking laughter and shouts, it was already about noon. The sun was at its highest point and the scorching heat chased them off the beach and under the shadow of the trees.

Laggi raised his hand and shouted in a bossy voice, "Listen to me, guys!"

All of them pressed tightly around him.

He paused dramatically for a while, then cried, "Let's see if the divine parrots have hatched."

Loud cheers and whistles met his words.

"Laggi is the best!" shouted one.

"Laggi is the greatest!" shrieked another.

"Three times hurray for Laggi!" And a thunderous "hurray!" rent the air.

The parrots in question, called *manuka lani* in the tribe's dialect, were the most beautiful birds on the island. The size of a seagull, with enormous, powerful beaks, they burst with incredible colors, a combination of bright red, yellow, green, and blue. The Tipihaos deified them and considered them a symbol of bravery and selflessness. The tribe's law protected the parrots, and those who dared to kill a bird were subject to severe punishment, but even that couldn't prevent the parrots from being killed occasionally.

The roots of the *manuka lanis'* troubles lay in the legend of one of the first Tipihao chieftains, whose war name was Manuli, which meant "The Blue Parrot." Manuli was skinny and short, qualities that usually would secure no one a chieftain's position. In compensation, he was sly and clever, with a rich imagination.

At that time, the chieftain was not chosen by elections, but in a direct fight to the death, and Manuli was aware that his chances were zero in a straight clash with one of his mighty opponents. However, he wanted to become a chieftain so badly that he was ready to pay even with his life for it. He brooded over some other solution for a long time and, just before the day of the contest, he proposed that the fight be replaced with something completely different: a competition where the winner would be the one who, within one day from sunrise to sunset, was first to bring back a chick from the parrots' nest.

Luckily for Manuli, the others did not see the trap. They laughed heartily at his proposition, calling him a coward and a jerk, but because secretly nobody wanted to fight to the death, they agreed to the challenge.

The result was more than surprising: two of the men lost their lives, falling from the crown of the tree, and the third one lost his eye, pierced by the sharp beak of a parrot. Nobody but Manuli took into consideration the ferocity of the birds during their nesting season, so he was the only one who had taken the necessary precautions. He had protected his head with a special wooden cage and so had managed to steal a *manuka lani* chick from its nest.

After he became the chieftain of the Tipihao tribe, he abolished the fights to the death and introduced elections as the only legitimate way of choosing a new chieftain. He had defied the parrots, unified the chieftain and shaman positions, and accomplished many incredible feats—and thus his cunning became legendary. The only problem was that defying *manuka lani* brought big trouble for these birds through the years, as young boys considered stealing a chick from the nest a matter of honor and proof of bravery, despite the risk of severe punishment.

Laggi's suggestion made the boys wild with excitement. Kamolea was carried away; he had never felt so exhilarated. He ran along with the others with a thumping heart, burning ears, and shining eyes.

Squeezing their way through the forest, snapping branches and cutting bushes, the boys rushed as fast as they could and soon stopped by a tall, branchy tree in the middle of the jungle. Panting for air and scratched from head to toe, they gathered around the trunk.

Laggi raised his hand for silence and said, "Listen up, bastards! I will climb the tree to see if the chicks have already hatched. You wait for me here!"

"And you wouldn't dare to touch them, right?" said Loto menacingly. "All of us need an equal start!"

"Of course I won't touch them! What do you take me for?!" cried Laggi. "If the chicks are there, I'll get down and all of us will start from here..." He took his knife out and scored a deep line on the ground. "All right? Now, wait for my return!"

Laggi jumped up into the tree and soon disappeared inside its crown. He wriggled his way through the dense leaves, nimbly pulling his body up and swinging from branch to branch. The twigs scraped his face, and soon his hands were black and sticky from the resinous bark. Toward the top, the branches thinned out, and it was hard to hold on. Clinging to a fork and buffeted by the wind, he looked around and spotted the nest. It was situated at the bough of the nearby tree, a little lower than his actual position, but reachable also from his tree.

Three hatchlings—little fluffy balls of yellowish down—huddled and pressed against each other. Next to them, their mother glided her huge, brownish beak over her body, smoothing her colorful feathers. Soon the male, considerably bigger than her, landed in the nest and folded his large wings. He was carrying some food, and the babies craned their necks and opened their little beaks, letting out sharp squeals.

Satisfied, Laggi began the downward climb.

Meanwhile, something strange happened to Kamolea, who gazed up along with the others at the thick greenery of the tree's crown. Like a fog dispersed by the sunny beams, his enthusiasm and high spirit gradually evaporated in the air, replaced by sheer dread that slowly crept into his bones and blocked his senses. A sharp pain stabbed his heart and a feeling of impending calamity drove him numb with terror. Seized by a chilling, animal fear, he hardly mastered his urge to run away. Kamolea had never experienced such dread before. Fatality lingered in the air and he felt a desperate urge to do something to stop the horror that was coming.

"Run away! Beat it! As fast as you can!" his entire being was screaming. He glanced at the others, who were burning with excitement, shifting impatiently from leg to leg, ready to attack the tree.

What's wrong with me? Kamolea thought. *Only cowards run away like that. There's nothing to fear, damn it…*

A rustle in the low branches interrupted his thoughts. Laggi slid swiftly on the ground, pointed towards the top of the tree, and touched his lips with one forefinger, signifying that they should keep quiet.

"Three chicks," he whispered, goggling his eyes. "The nest is between these two trees, very high, but it's accessible from both of them. So, are you ready? We'll all start on my signal, on three, right? So, one, two—"

"Wait!" Kamolea shouted. A flock of birds flew up from the nearby branches, frightened by his voice. The boys stopped short and looked at him, as though seeing him for the first time.

"Don't do that!" Kamolea cried. His voice echoed in the strange silence that reigned around him. "Something terrible will happen, believe me! Somebody is going to die! Let's get out of here! Right now!"

Seven pairs of eyes stared at him, perplexed at first, then gradually changing to mocking and scornful expressions.

Loto took a step toward him.

"What did you say?" he asked, watching him like a snake fixing its gaze onto its victim.

"Somebody will die!" repeated Kamolea.

"Yeah, maybe you—from fear," said Loto. Everybody laughed.

"Don't do that, Laggi!" Kamolea said stubbornly, looking straight at their leader.

"Well then, chicken out, pussy!" snapped Kamani. "We don't need cowards like you!"

"Yeah, curly boy, you're just a good-for-nothing wretch," shouted Taneo. "We'll be sure to let everyone in the village know how brave you were, just as soon as we get back."

The others giggled, casting contemptuous glances at Kamolea, and resumed their places at the starting line. Only Laggi remained silent and didn't budge.

"Who's going to die?" he asked quietly at last.

"I don't know," muttered Kamolea, red in the face. "Don't let them do it, Laggi. It's a bad omen to touch these birds…"

"Eh, Laggi, are you coming or are you going to listen to this nonsense all day long? Or maybe I should give the starting signal?" Loto drawled.

The burst of laughter was enough for Laggi to make up his mind. He turned to the others and shouted, "All right, guys, one, two, three, go!"

The boys rushed to ascend, shouting and pushing each other. Laggi chose the tree he'd just climbed, with Taneo and Hemi rushing at his heels. Loto and the others were crawling up the next trunk. Soon Loto and Kaleo gained the lead, quickly ascending via their distinct routes up the immense tree. When they approached the nest, Laggi was already there.

Frightened, the parrots had flown from the nest and now circled around the tree, letting out shrill squawks. Laggi hung from a branch slightly above the nest, stretched out his arm, and grabbed one of the chicks. At that moment, the female attacked with a piercing cry. She flew at Laggi with all her weight and stuck her enormous beak into his face. Laggi screamed with pain, dropped the chick into the nest, and raised his hand to defend himself. The female flew back and made a turn, ready to attack again. At the same time, Laggi heard a mighty flapping of wings coming from his left. A wave of hot air ruffled his hair, and he pivoted to face the male parrot swooping at him. Instinctively, Laggi twisted his body in panic, lost his balance, staggered, and then the female hit him again, burying her beak in his temple. Laggi dropped from the tree with a terrible scream. Kamolea, who was the only one left under the tree, jumped back, horrified, when Laggi landed on his back next to him with a loud thud, hitting his head on the thick roots.

Shaking with shock, Kamolea bent down and lifted the body. Laggi's head hung at an unnatural angle and almost touched his back. His face, distorted in a terrible grimace and covered with blood, was unrecognizable.

Kamolea started shaking.

"Laggi's dead," he shouted. There was a silence, then Loto's voice came somewhere from above.

"What did you say, coward?"

"Laggi fell; he's dead," cried Kamolea in a trembling voice. "Get down now, guys!"

"No way!" Loto bellowed. "Let's take revenge for Laggi!"

Loto climbed further and reached the closest position to the nest. The female was in the nest, protecting her chicks. Balancing unsteadily and squeezing the branch between his thighs to hold on, Loto drew his knife out and brandished it, shooing her away. She flew, squawking angrily, and he grabbed one of the babies with his other hand. The male swooped down on him, and Loto plunged his knife into its breast. The female attacked and hit Loto's head with its beak. Loto reeled, dropped the chick, and grabbed a branch to keep his balance.

The male parrot thudded on the ground several yards from Laggi's body, followed by the little chick. Kamolea rushed to them, only to find that they were dead.

Up the tree, Loto saw how Kaleo and Kamani, who had both reached the nest in the meantime, grabbed one baby chick each and climbed down, followed by the envious eyes of the other boys. In the distance echoed the piercing cry of the mother, filled with grief.

When everybody was back on the ground, they all gathered around Laggi. Loto bent, took the dead parrot, and threw it over Laggi's dead body.

"You are avenged, Lag," he said. After a brief silence, he turned to the others. "From now on, I'm the leader. Any objections?"

"You ain't got no chick. I've got one, so I deserve to lead the pack," said Kamani, watching him spitefully.

"Let's settle it now, then," hissed Loto and drew his knife. Kamani did the same with a wicked grin.

"Drop it, Loto!" cried Taneo. "We don't have time for that! One dead is enough, don't you think? Look up at these thick black clouds; the wind is picking up, and the storm is coming."

"What will we do with Laggi?" asked Hemi anxiously.

"We'll take him to the village," answered Loto, glancing at Kamani as sheathing his knife. "Let's go!"

* * *

When the chieftain Momo saw his son's dead body, he couldn't believe his eyes, nor could he believe his ears. He made the boys repeat the story three times, getting angrier and angrier. However, on the third time, somebody recalled Kamolea's warning that something terrible would happen and somebody would die. When Momo heard that, he went berserk.

"Where is he?!" bellowed the chieftain, his bulging eyes roving in all directions. "Where is the curly wretch? Bring him to me right away! And lock Loto in a cage! He must answer for killing the manuka lani!"

While two men dragged Loto to Kepolo's belt, everybody spilled around to look for Kamolea. Meanwhile, a mighty blast of wind raised dry leaves and dirt from the ground and a blinding flash of lightning cut through the sky. The earth quaked, and within minutes, a wild storm arose.

* * *

Kamolea ran away shortly after he saw the body of the dead parrot hit the ground. A sense of doom and hopelessness deepened in him, as he immediately knew that he would be blamed for Laggi's death.

I should have kept my big mouth shut, he thought, as he scrambled through the trees, choosing the most remote paths to avoid the village. Once he reached the shore, he ran as fast as he could, following the curve of the sand. The sky blackened, the wind grew stronger, and the rain started to come down furiously. The sea ran high, and immense waves broke with a roaring noise, reaching almost the middle of the beach.

Kamolea plunged into the sea without hesitation. With mighty strokes, he crawled towards the cliff nestling his cave, cleaving the waves that tossed him up and down. He sank sharply again and again in swirls of foamy abyss until the crest of the next billowing wave raised him up. It took him almost three times longer than usual to reach his small cave.

Exhausted, he could barely cling to the slippery rock, washed away by the raging breakers every time he tried to climb. Finally, a monstrous surge hoisted him to the edge of his rocky shelter. In a blink of an eye, he managed to grab at the fringe and, hauling himself up, rolled over into the warm, cozy space of the cave.

Lying on his back and panting heavily, he listened to the roar of the wind and the thunder of the sea. It was dark and soothing inside, but his heart was still racing. Before his eyes passed in quick succession the events of the day—the play at the beach, the rush in the jungle, the unforgettable feeling of extreme happiness, later replaced by the one of impending doom, the thud of Laggi's dead body, the shrill squawks of the sacred parrots… And Illima, who he had planned to meet today. He was supposed to tell her about his feelings, instead of all this insanity… His heart sank as he thought about Illima. What about her now? She would hear from the others what a miserable coward he was, and she would never like him or take him seriously.

"Who wants to have a craven fool for a boyfriend?" he muttered in the darkness. Shame and despair overwhelmed him, followed by the urge to throw himself in the sea and end his miserable life. As soon as this thought passed through his mind, a sharp cackle split his brain, making him jump.

You'd better do it now and die with dignity, you fucking loser! a shrill voice screamed out inside his head. *How will you return to the village with such heavy guilt? It was the chieftain's son, not just anybody! Act like a real man and do what it takes to redeem yourself. Go ahead, do it*!

Kamolea felt goosebumps crawling down his neck and back. As in a daze, he sat up, shivering. Sometimes he did hear voices, especially when he was tired, but they were all familiar ones, belonging to his father, granny, or friends. This voice now, high-pitched and unpleasant, was completely unknown and scared the wits out of him.

Still trembling, Kamolea began to rise, firmly resolved to end his life, when suddenly the small cave filled up with light, and near to the entrance emerged a woman clad in a long white dress. Her silhouette emanated a soft glow that illuminated the cave. Kamolea, who had never seen a dressed woman, immediately noticed that she bore a striking resemblance to him: long curly hair, prominent forehead, and big black shiny eyes.

"Mother?" he whispered.

The woman reached towards him.

"How handsome and brave you grew up to be, Kamolea." Her voice, soft and gentle as a rippling brook, rang in his ears. "And how stupid, as well. Have you really decided to kill yourself? Never dare to listen to the deceitful voice screaming in your head. Be afraid of nothing, my son. Your destiny will be hard, but noble, and your name will be a legend for generations to come. Today is an extraordinary day for you—you foretold the truth, and you tried to save a human life regardless of the consequences or others' opinions. Today was your spiritual birthday, your prophetic victory, and you have proved that you are ready to fulfill your destiny."

Kamolea shut and rubbed his eyes. When he reopened them, the woman was still there, smiling at him.

"I understand that it's hard to believe that you are speaking with your dead mother." She stepped forward and sat beside him. "I came to you from very far away because I see how desperate you have become. And that, believe me, is just the beginning. Heed my words, my son! Hard days lie ahead, and to survive you need to be stronger than flint and braver than a *manuka lani*.

"Remember two important things from me. First, you are not a Tip-ihao. You are a descendant of the Torago tribe. Your grandfather was a great chieftain, and your father was an exceptional hunter and warrior. His name was Keoni, and he was a man of honor and kindness, not a butcher and bloodthirsty killer like the one who you call your father now. I brought you a gift from your father: his favorite bracelet, the symbol of his audacity. Put it on your left wrist and thus, he will always be with you; this bracelet will guide you and protect you the same way that it saved me at the time.

"Second, no matter how hard things seem or how desperate you feel, the thought of killing yourself must never cross your mind. Don't listen to the deceptive voice in your head because it does not belong to you. It tries to impede God's plans for you. This God has assigned you an important mission, which you have to bring to an end. Let Him guide you, trust in Him, be brave and fair, and never give up, as you don't know what the future holds for you."

With these words, Laia disappeared, and the cave became somber and bleak. Outside was dark, even though it was still late afternoon. The storm continued to rage. Kamolea crawled to the place where his mother had stood. At that moment, a lightning bolt split the sky and Kamolea caught a glimpse of some gleaming object. He took it and turned it in his hands. It was a white bracelet made of shark teeth. He fiddled with it for a while, then slipped it on his left wrist. Calm and bliss suffused his body. At that moment, he forgot all about his troubles and drifted into a deep slumber.

* * *

In the morning, the wind had died out, and the sun shone in the unblemished sky. When Kamolea reached the village, he noticed with a sinking heart that everybody whose path he crossed eyed him suspiciously.

He entered Akamui's hut, dreading the encounter. As he stepped in, two men materialized from nowhere and seized him. In a blink of an eye, he lay prone on the floor with his hands bound behind his back. The men dragged him outside and brought him to the Sacred Zone. On his way toward the cage, he passed Loto, who lay beside the altar, beaten to a pulp but still alive, his body a messy jelly of blood and broken bones.

A mighty push took him out of his stupor.

"Up there!" bellowed one of his guards.

Kamolea grabbed the rope ladder and climbed nimbly to the cage that perched on the fork of ancient koa. Once locked in the cage, for the first time he realized how serious his situation was. In their religious beliefs, the Tipihaos considered talking to someone about their own death to be a grim omen, which could bring ill fortune to the person concerned.

If they blame me for Laggi's death, I'm done, he thought.

The elders came one by one and entered the Hive.

An eternity seemed to pass before the guards brought Kamolea before the Council. The elders sat in a semicircle around the hearth and smoked their pipes. The chieftain Momo was the only one standing. He motioned for Kamolea to approach.

Paralyzed with fear, Kamolea stepped forward and then froze with his head bowed while the elders examined him for a long time like a rare species of an insect.

"Tell us what happened yesterday, Kamolea! Start from the beginning and don't lie, because we know everything!" barked Momo.

With a broken voice, Kamolea told them everything, repeatedly answering the same questions: "How did you realize that something terrible would happen? That someone would die? Did you know who would die? Why did you not stop them?"

"I don't know how I knew it; I just felt it," repeated Kamolea for the tenth time. "And I did try to stop them, but nobody listened. They called me pussy and coward. What could I have done?"

"I think you are the one to blame for Laggi's death!" Momo said finally, his voice grim and menacing. "Your stupid premonition brought the misfortune upon my son. I vote for the death penalty."

Akamui jumped to his feet. "This is ridiculous!" he cried. "Nothing proves that my son should be blamed for the death of yours! Kamolea never mentioned Laggi's name, so he could not bring ill to him. He even warned them to go away! It's not his fault they didn't listen!"

Hardly had he spoken these words when an argument broke out. Everybody was talking, and nobody was listening. After a heated debate, the elders eventually decided that Kamolea had nothing to be accused of and let him go.

CHAPTER VI

ILLIMA

Right after his release, Kamolea went to see Lalago. He stepped into the room and asked her without any pleasantries, "What was my mother like? Describe her to the slightest detail, please."

"Why do you bring this up?" Lalago was genuinely surprised. She was sitting on the ground, grinding some herbs in a wooden mortar. "First, tell me what happened to you. What was all that fuss about the chieftain's boy? I heard he's dead. Is it true?"

"Laggi died because of his stupidity," said Kamolea with a shrug. "The problem was that I foresaw it. I told him not to mess with the divine parrots, but he didn't listen. Later I'll tell you everything, exactly the way it happened." He waved impatiently. "Now, what about my mother?"

Lalago fell silent for a moment.

"Give me a hand up, will you?" she said at last.

"Tell me, Granny! Was she pretty? Do you remember her?" insisted Kamolea as he hauled her up.

"Of course I do," sighed the old woman. "I can see her in my mind as clearly as if it was yesterday."

"Did she have long wavy hair and black eyes? A little bit taller than I am? With a tiny beauty spot on the left cheek?"

"That's exactly her. How do you know such details?"

"I dreamed about her," Kamolea muttered.

"You resemble her a lot, you know... Wait, what is this on your wrist? Where did you find it?" Lalago exclaimed, grabbing his left wrist and staring at the bracelet.

Kamolea muttered something.

"What are you mumbling?" cried Lalago. "This bracelet belonged to your mother! I searched for it everywhere after Laia passed away, but it had disappeared into thin air. How do you have it now?"

"I found it in my father's hut, stuck between the reeds," lied Kamolea, blushing.

"Ah, I've always suspected that he must have taken it." She shook her head disapprovingly. "I asked him several times, though, and he always denied it."

"Tell me something about my mother," Kamolea begged.

"Well, she was a fine woman," Lalago said, "beautiful and gentle, but a fragile flower, refined, not fit to survive in the rough setting of Maniha Komu. She told me once she was the daughter of a Torago chieftain and she behaved as such."

"She was spoiled, you mean?"

"Well, not exactly. Different, I would say. She looked down on us and never accepted our customs. She was not much into your father, either. I loved her a lot, though, despite her haughtiness, and I was heartbroken when she passed away."

"What about my father," Kamolea asked. "Did he love her?"

"Oh, he adored her, no doubt about it." There was a firm conviction in Lalago's voice. "At the beginning, they had their ups and downs, as every normal couple does, but eventually, things smoothed out."

"I know how my father smooths things out," muttered Kamolea. "Did he beat her a lot?"

"Well, there was some thrashing, especially the first moon or so," Lalago sighed. "Poor thing, she always came to me, seeking protection from my mad son. He used to get unhinged back then; I don't understand what seized him, really. It all stopped when he found out she was pregnant with you. Didn't raise his bloody hand to her anymore. It tore my heart out when she cried, always clutching this bracelet and pressing it to her chest."

Kamolea tried to imagine the life of the beautiful woman he had seen in the cave with a tough man like Akamui. Unfortunately, Lalago wasn't able to give him any information about Laia's life before Half-Moon Island, and when it came to the question of Akamui's parenthood, he simply didn't dare to ask.

The days dragged, one after another, and Laia's words gradually faded in his memory, replaced by other problems.

He had overheard people saying that he was bringing bad luck to the island and provoked misfortune. Everybody, from children to old men, had started avoiding him. Illima was another source of constant pain and fretting. He thought about her all the time, but he knew it was a hopeless case. *I'm so ashamed of myself that I'll never dare to approach her again. What shitty luck I had to meet Laggi's gang that cursed day... I should have gone directly to her instead. I'd better stop brooding over her; it wasn't meant to be...*

Each night he fell asleep having made the same decision, and each morning he woke up longing to see her.

Last but not least, Akamui was still mad at him about Laggi's death. Despite Laia's words, which he had almost forgotten, Kamolea still considered Akamui his father and the most significant person in his life. He respected and admired him more than anyone else, and Akamui's opinion was of crucial importance, so Kamolea constantly racked his brain to find a way to appease the man he called his father. One sleepless night he came up with a solution: he would go alone into the jungle and kill a wild boar as a gift to him. To hunt out a boar was challenging even for a skilled man, let alone an inexperienced boy. Still, if Kamolea succeeded, he was sure that he would be forgiven.

"When I bring the beast to him and throw it at his feet, he will love and respect me again," he whispered to himself.

At dawn, he was up. He took his hunter's gear—a leather bag, a flask of water, a rope, his large, double-edged hunting knife, and his personally made spear with a pointed flint spearhead—and set off for the hills.

It was a beautiful, sunny morning. Kamolea established a quick pace, mentally calculating the distance to the peak of the Carapace Hill where the wild boars were more likely to be found.

Soon after he had taken the narrow path that wound through the dense forest, a snap of a twig to his left made him freeze, listening. There was a strange noise coming from the trees. He advanced cautiously, alert, his body taut as a string, his spear raised for a blow. Several yards ahead, he noticed a girl squatting under an aged tree. She hummed and plucked flowers, arranging them in a reed basket. Kamolea let out a gasp of surprise and lowered his spear. The girl jumped to her feet and turned around to face him. As he recognized her, his heart started pounding and the blood rushed to his head.

He hadn't seen Illima since Laggi's death. She seemed to be taller now, her shape fuller, more pronounced. Her thick, long, black hair glistened under the sun's glare. A flower lei around her neck covered the upper part of her body, hiding her naked breasts. A scant straw skirt and sandals completed her clothing.

Such an enchanting beauty, Kamolea thought as his legs grew soft. He swallowed nervously, not knowing what to do. She smiled and beckoned to him, then bent and lifted the basket full of flowers.

"Hi, Kamiolea," she said with a sweet smile and brushed away an unruly lock of hair. She looked neither surprised nor afraid.

"Hi, Illima," said Kamolea, his face burning. "What are you doing in the jungle alone?"

"Oh, I'm going to Butterfly Waterfall," she chirruped blithely. "Would you like to walk me there? To be my protector? It's dangerous for a girl to be alone in the jungle, you know?" She sent him a charming smile, revealing two rows of perfect white teeth.

"That's my point exactly," stammered Kamolea. "You must be courageous, rambling like that!" She just smiled and shrugged.

"What will you do at the waterfall, anyway? Do you have somebody to meet there?" Kamolea went on.

"Maybe…" she smiled. "If you come with me, you'll see…"

"Absolutely! I'll never let you go alone. What if you come across Loto's gang? Let's go!" Kamolea took charge of the situation and wiped his bedewed front.

They set off for the fall, walking in awkward silence, and the more time passed, the more embarrassed Kamolea got. He tried to think of a conversation he could start, but no words came to his lips. He had imagined this scene so many times and now couldn't come up with a single sentence that made sense. Angry and frustrated with himself, he glanced at Illima. She was humming, occasionally bending to pluck a flower and putting it in the basket. She didn't seem to mind his silence. Now and then, she cast a playful look at him and flashed him a smile, unequivocally inviting him to say something.

Kamolea was getting desperate. *"You're as dumb as a rock, man,"* Anuro's mocking voice said in his mind, and he couldn't have agreed more. Finally, as he recalled one of his dreams, he snapped off a yellow *plumeria*[4] and handed it to her.

"Thank you, Kamolea," she chirped and stuck it in her hair. "You aren't very talkative, are you? Where were you off to, so heavily armed?"

"I'm going hunting a boar," Kamolea said proudly.

"Oh, I see. Isn't that dangerous?"

"It is," he said with a nod.

"And why would you do that?"

---

4 A tropical flour with bright colors.

"It will be a gift for my father. Lately, he's been mad at me, so I want to please him."

"I heard he's not the only one angry at you," Illima said casually, casting him a sideways glance. "Is that the reason I don't see you anymore in the village?"

"Well, I feel like I'm not very welcome there, after… you know."

She nodded. "Where do you hang out, then?"

"I don't have much time for fooling around. My warrior's proof is the next full moon, so I train a lot with my father."

"And besides that? Do you have some secret hiding place?"

"I do," said Kamolea. "Why do you ask?"

"Well, maybe I would like to come and visit it sometime," said Illima carefully. "If you don't mind, of course."

"I… would be thrilled if you did," said Kamolea, flushing.

The rumble of Butterfly Waterfall was audible now.

"I spoke with Anuro recently," Illima said casually. "His sister is a good friend of my sister, and we see them often now, since… they are together…"

"I thought it was a secret," Kamolea muttered.

"It is," Illima confirmed, her face serious, "but friends share secrets sometimes. Anuro shared with me a secret about you, as well."

Kamolea bristled. He knew all about Anuro's big mouth. Before he could ask anything else, they emerged into the small glade, which was covered with splendid, sweet-scented flowers. A swarm of colorful butterflies fluttered everywhere. In front of them, the narrow mass of water was falling from the high cliff with a deafening sound into the pond, as it had for thousands of years. Fine mist rose from the churning whirlpool and diffracted the sunbeams into a gorgeous rainbow that curved above the crystalline water.

"Look how beautiful it is, Kamolea," said Illima quietly and took him by the hand. By her touch, a jolt of excitement ran through his body. She led him several steps toward the water, stopped, and turned to him. Kamolea stood speechless. She watched him tenderly now, her big black eyes mesmerizing, filled with moisture and longing.

"This place has always filled me with happiness," she said, her face inches from his, as she tried to speak near to his ear. "It is the most romantic, beautiful, and breathtaking scenery, a perfect setting for us to start our love story. A new beginning—that's your name's meaning, isn't it, Kamolea?" She squeezed his hand and smiled at him, her gaze intense, drinking him in with her eyes. She lifted herself on tiptoes, kissed him on the mouth, and slowly withdrew. Kamolea stayed dumbstruck, his mouth half-opened, his cheeks burning.

"I love you, Kamolea," he heard her say, and before he fully understood what was going on, their lips melted into each other. At that moment, the heavens opened and a ray of incredible happiness lit up Kamolea's heart. The roar of the waterfall, the sweet scent in the air, the butterflies, the rainbow, and the honey taste of Illima's lips spun him in a magic whirl and exploded in his chest like a volcano of glowing lava.

The next thing he remembered was that they lay on the soft meadow, wrapped in a cover of flowers and losing themselves in each other's eyes. The buzzing of the insects and the fragrance of the blossoms made them dizzy with happiness. With many breaks between long, passionate kisses, Illima told him how once Anuro, trying to impress his half-sister, spilled the beans about Kamolea's secret love. Kala, naturally, reported it to Kalani who immediately blabbed it out to Illima. The latter couldn't believe her luck, as she had liked Kamolea since the moment she met him for the first time in Anuro's hut a long time ago. Kamolea didn't remember their first meeting.

"Oh, I'm not surprised, we were still kids, but you impressed me a lot back then," Illima said and fondled his face.

He told her in turn how he had sneaked up on her at the Frog Lake and fallen in love with her.

"I wanted to tell you so many times, but I never dare to do it, especially after Laggi's death," he said. "But tell me, Illima, how did you know where to meet me today?"

"I've been stalking you for days," she admitted. "Every morning I sneaked around your hut and waited to see what you were doing and where you were going. I suspected you had some kind of hidden place on the north shore, but you were always so quick I never could catch up with you… Besides, I wanted to bring you to Butterfly Waterfall, and your place was in the opposite direction. But last night, I had a dream, and a voice explained to me what I should do to meet you…"

"Tell me about that!" cried Kamolea excitedly.

"It was so weird! You had been gone for a long, long time and I had been waiting for you day after day, longing, watching the horizon, and begging the sea to return you to me safe and sound. I was sure you'd be back one day, but it took an eternity, and my patience was wearing thin. Then I heard a voice coming from above that told me I must wait for you, whatever it takes, and that I'm not to give myself to any other man but you.

"Next, I found myself in a terrible place. I think it was a cave, dark and hot, with steam coming from the earth. There was some awful creature with me, something between animal and human, hardly reaching my chest in height. It screamed like mad. Along with this thing, I prayed for your return to some weird god that was not Kepolo. And then, one day, you came back, strong and handsome, even though your face was disfigured and covered with terrible scars. Despite that, I loved you so much! Finally, the same voice told me to meet you in the morning in the jungle.

"'Tell him about your feelings, because you're running out of time,' it resounded in my head, and I saw the exact place under that tree where you found me today, can you imagine?"

"Yes, I agree that's weird," Kamolea said. "Listen, it's getting hot. Let's take a dip in the lake."

"Superb idea!"

They ran and jumped into the water with joyful cries. The rainbow shone above their heads like a celestial gate. They slipped under the roaring jet, and hugged and kissed as the water drummed over their heads, but when Kamolea began to grope her more aggressively, she wriggled like an eel and got out.

They spent the entire day together, talking and kissing until the sun sank, and the first stars started winking in the ink-blue sky.

The night brought unknown magic to their passion. During the day, Illima firmly refused his advances beyond kisses, but now he started kissing her fervently and his hands were all over her. His groin ached and he couldn't wait anymore. Only, his lack of experience was obvious. He tried to climb on top of her, reaching between her legs, but she suddenly stopped kissing him, pushed him slightly, grabbed his hand, and firmly put it aside.

"Let's not do it on our first meeting," she said. "I want our memory of it to be romantic and perfect."

"Let's do it tomorrow then?" Kamolea proposed.

"No, I'm still not feeling ready," said Illima, smiling shyly. "I'd prefer it if we did it after your warrior's proof—this way, you will be already a real man, not a boy, and it means that you could take care of me. And you have to ask my father for permission; there's no way around that."

"Do you think he'll agree? I mean, with all the stupid rumors about me floating around the village…"

"Don't worry about that." Illima waved her hand dismissively. "The only thing that matters to him is that Akamui is your father. He is so desperate to work his way up, my poor dad."

They sank into silence for a while, staring at the stars.

"Do you see the brightest star just above us?" asked Illima at last. "That is my favorite one. Sometimes I pray to her instead of Kepolo, and I think it works better."

"Yes, Lalago told me that its name is Alina. Do you know the legend?" asked Kamolea.

"I do. But I'm surprised that you know it, too. Men don't like it, and women keep it to themselves."

"Yes, my granny warned me about that. But my father said this is only old women's talk, pure nonsense."

"I don't care," said Illima. "But I promise you now before Alina the Brightest and her three daughters that I'll be your faithful spouse forever, no matter what others say or think about you. And if my dream happens to be true and I need to wait for you to return, I vow that I'll be waiting for you until my death, praying to Alina day and night to bring you back home safe and sound."

"And I will be your hero, always faithful to you, and you'll be my beloved wife until my death!" Kamolea exclaimed, and they sealed their vows with a passionate kiss.

They lay still for some time, then Kamolea said, "I'm getting hungry, my love. It's been a long day. Let's go to the village."

"Shh. Don't speak about grub, silly! You'll spoil everything." Illima kissed him and pressed her forefinger to his lips. "Don't protest, my love. We'll spend the night here, lying under the stars, praying to Alina to give us a long and happy life together and many children."

CHAPTER VII

THE OLD MAN

The raft drifted aimlessly, swinging gently on the sea's rippling surface. Kamolea sat cross-legged, leaning against the mast, and thoughtfully watched the distant sickle of hilly green land, wrapped in the shimmering haze.

If only I could somehow get away from this terrible place, he thought.

That morning he'd left before sunrise under the pretext of going fishing, but truthfully he couldn't have cared less about fishing. All he'd wanted was to be alone. He'd hurried to the shore and dragged his raft into the water. The dawn found him in the open sea, wrapped by silence, broken now and then only by the shrill cries of the soaring birds.

Kamolea hauled down the sail, left the raft drifting, and remained still for a long time, immersed in thoughts, his gaze wandering into the distance and the breeze fondling his face.

Tomorrow was his warrior's proof—the biggest day of his life, the turning point when he would become a man. Afterward, nothing would be the same. A crucial change was coming, and he was convinced that it boded no good.

Yesterday he undertook the final exam of his long and exhausting training. It was a tough one—he had to surprise Akamui during the daylight and bring him down in a close-up fight, simulating his killing with a wooden knife.

At sunrise, Kamolea was already lying in ambush around Akamui's dwelling. He stalked him all morning without a result—Akamui was alert and jumpy and didn't move far from his hut. About noon, Kamolea was beginning to lose hope when he heard the big bronze gong echo to announce an assembly of the Council.

"Perfect," he muttered as the plan formed in a flash in his head.

He ran through the jungle and climbed to an enormous spreading tree, the branches of which overhung the path that Akamui always took on his way to the Heave. There he lay flat on a large bough, blending in with the dense greenery and biding his time. Soon Akamui appeared, walking stealthily. He stopped every several steps, listening closely. As Kamolea spotted him through the thick screen of leaves, he pulled out his knife and clenched it between his teeth. The moment Akamui passed below Kamolea's position, the latter lunged at his back, grabbed him by the throat, and they both rolled over on the ground. Quick as a snake, Akamui tried to shake him off, but Kamolea clung to his neck with a powerful chokehold and stabbed his father lightly in the ribs.

At that precise moment, his heart sank. He sensed that something in the conception of his training was very wrong, and he realized that he couldn't kill anyone, even if his life depended on it.

Akamui was pleased. He hadn't noticed Kamolea's inner struggle, and his eyes gleamed with pride and satisfaction. He tapped his son on the cheek and called him a brave boy.

Terrified and deeply ashamed of himself, Kamolea didn't get a wink of sleep all night, fretting about what a hopeless coward he was. Now, in the lull of the bobbing raft, his thought drifted to Illima.

They met in secret every evening, and the more he got to know her, the more deeply he fell in love. Whatever he did, he always asked himself whether she would approve it, and if she would be proud of him. *She certainly would not like a sissy boy, afraid to kill.*

He tried to imagine what his life would be like after killing an innocent person and, even worse, tasting his body to inherit his strength. At the mental image of this act, his stomach churned and black bile welled up in his throat. He flung himself at the edge of the raft and heaved, wheezing with a choking cough.

He lay prone for a long time, his eyes closed. The raft bobbed more strongly as the breeze increased in force. Suddenly a storm-bird swooped over his head with a piercing cry. Kamolea jerked up and looked around. The sun had passed its highest point long ago and was now creeping toward the horizon, its light reflecting off the water in a thousand dazzling gleams. The current had carried the raft away and the island was a small dot on the horizon.

How long have I been here? Kamolea thought, horrified. *It'll be dark before I get home. I was supposed to meet Father this afternoon; he'll go berserk!* He quickly hoisted the sail and set off for Maniha Komo.

* * *

The next day, Kamolea woke up with a headache and a heavy heart. It was still dark and unusually quiet in the hut. The moment he opened his eyes, a shrill voice screamed in his head:

"The day has come, wretch! Get up and face your destiny!"

In a flash, he visualized himself in a bloody scene, clutching the throat of an unknown man and stabbing him in the chest repeatedly. The blood dripped from his knife. He bared his teeth and brought his face, smeared with blood, to the neck of his victim…

Kamolea shook off his terrible vision.

"I never wanted that, but a man's gotta do what a man's gotta do," he muttered and sat up in his hammock. He looked around and realized that he was in Lalago's place.

Kamolea squinted, trying to remember why he was there, and the scene from the previous evening slowly emerged. He had returned late from the shore and was surprised to see Lalago waiting for him at the entrance of the village. She rushed toward him, took him by the hand, hushed him, and dragged him to her hut.

"You should stay here overnight until your father calms down," she told him. "I don't want him to kill you just before your big day tomorrow. He was looking for you all day and you can't imagine how angry he was."

Kamolea sighed.

I hope today he'll be in a better mood, he thought, looking at Lalago's empty hammock. His grandma often got up at sunrise to gather herbs. "At dawn, they have the strongest healing effect," she often said, sometimes mentioning something about magic.

Kamolea perked up his ears, alert. He couldn't shake the feeling that there was someone in the room. In the gloom of the corner near the cold hearth, the shadows of the pottery shelves were taking strange fluent, incessantly changing shapes. The moment they seemed to resolve into a stable form, they would change again into elongated animals or branchy trees, and then back to shelves again... Gradually, they steadied, outlining a glowing human silhouette. Kamolea blinked several times as the hut filled with mild light, and gasped, as a strangely familiar old man with pale skin, clad in red, materialized in front of him. The dense fog of Kamolea's memory slowly cleared and he remembered where he had seen him.

"Kedia," he whispered.

Before his eyes swam the gloomy cave, the smell of the sea, the hopelessness after Kalima had clawed his face... and the weird old man, who had appeared then just as he emerged now. He clutched the same black object near his chest and moved his right hand left and right, and up and down. Now that he was up-close, Kamolea could take a better look at his red garment and his bearded, gleaming face, and even catch the man's odor, which was pleasant and very calming.

The old man's look was stern in contradiction to his soft voice, which rang in Kamolea's ears:

"The time has come, Kamolea. From now on, I will be your master and your protector. I will steer the boat of your destiny through the stormy sea of life until you understand the purpose of your existence. Wisdom and humility are hard to learn, but once you step on the path of knowledge, there is no way back."

"What?" Kamolea wanted to shout, but his lips remained glued.

"The true God, the Ultimate Judge of Good and Evil, will no more tolerate the abominations happening on this island," continued the old man. "He has decided to destroy this place and to annihilate the entire tribe. For thousands of years, He has waited in vain for them to repent, to stop their atrocities, and to become better people. Now, the blood of thousands of innocent men slain by Tipihaos are calling for revenge. Thousands of raped and murdered women wait to be repaid. The days of this island are numbered, my young apprentice.

"However, God is forgiving and forbearing even to monsters like the Tipihaos. There are still good people in this place who do not deserve to die with the other sinners. God saw in you an opportunity to incline this bloodthirsty tribe toward Good, thus saving it from destruction. You must make them change their habits, show them the right path, and teach them wisdom. Remember, if you fail, their blood will be on you, for an earthquake will sweep away the island, leaving none alive."

Kamolea stared at the old man. Not a single thought was forming in his head and he only opened and closed his mouth like a fish out of water.

"Today will be your warrior's proof, but it won't happen the way you imagine," the old man continued. His brown eyes shone in the darkness, boring into Kamolea. "You must stand against Akamui and Chief Momo and refuse to leave the island. You shall tell everyone that the True God forbids killing, and the worshipping of trees, and that Kepolo is not a god!"

Impossible! screamed a shrill voice inside Kamolea's head.

Kamolea heard steps and muffled voices approaching the hut. The old man smiled for the first time.

"Take your first test with spirit and audacity, young Kamolea! Do it like a real man and remember that nothing is impossible when God supports you!"

With these words, the old man disappeared, just when Akamui rushed in, followed by Itaki and Lelando, his two younger sons. Kamolea jumped quickly out of the hammock and greeted them.

"Here he is, hiding behind his granny's skirt," said Akamui derisively. "Where were you yesterday? We had to pay our respect to Kepolo, waiting under Rakapi for his revelation about your warrior's proof."

"I apologize, Father," said Kamolea, keeping his gaze on the floor. "I wanted to be alone and prepare mentally for the big trial…"

"I understand," nodded Akamui. "I hope Kepolo will not be angry with you and will help you in your endeavor." He cast a glare at his sons, who are snorting and hiccoughing, trying to suppress their giggles. "Are you ready now?"

"I am," answered Kamolea, his heart pounding.

Akamui took a step forward and handed him a knife in a brand new leather sheath with fringes on the edges. Kamolea's eyes widened. He slowly pulled the knife out of the sheath—the long blade was of polished flint, very sharp, and slightly curved toward the point. The wooden handle was exquisitely carved in the shape of a parrot's head.

"Thank you, Father," Kamolea said, moved.

Akamui patted him on the cheek.

"You are a good boy," he said. "Let this knife bring you luck and cut many heads as a new decoration for Rakapi. Remember, Son: no one is braver, sharper, and quicker than you are. I am convinced that you will succeed with excellence in your proof and will never bring shame on me."

Akamui's verbal outpouring was so unusual that Kamolea was genuinely pleased.

"Thank you, Father," he said again, his heart overwhelmed with gratitude. "I'll never disgrace you, I promise! You'll be the proudest father in Kepula Penu; otherwise, I'd rather die!"

"Let's go," Akamui said, smiling. "The others are expecting us."

Kamolea slung the leather strap with his new knife over his shoulder, hung a wooden flask full of water on the opposite side, picked up his spear, and they set off for the beach.

The day was breaking, but it was gloomy outside. The heavy sky and the rising wind portended a storm. The shore was already crowded with people, mainly relatives and friends of the future warriors, along with some idlers who had come to see the event. They stood in small groups and talked agitatedly, sometimes raising their voices to shouts and cheers.

"Kamolea!" called someone to his left. He turned and saw Anuro, Kala, Kalani, and Illima clustered together and waving at him.

"I'll go see Anuro, Father," Kamolea told Akamui.

"You'd better hurry up; the others are already waiting," grunted Akamui and motioned toward six boys who had gathered around the canoes just a few yards away from the water.

"I will," nodded Kamolea before dashing toward his friends.

"Here he comes, the horror of Kepula Penu," cried Anuro, googling his eyes as he always did when the girls were around. Kala and Kalani giggled. Illima looked at Kamolea lovingly and smiled.

"Hello everyone," Kamolea said. "It's very kind of you to come."

"Hey, they came to see me, not you," Anuro shouted.

"It's not true. I came for you," said Illima, smiling shyly. She took his hand and pulled him a bit farther away from the others.

"I brought you a present for luck," she said and handed him a bracelet of pinkish seashells. Her face was radiant and her black eyes shone like brilliant stars.

Today she's extremely beautiful, Kamolea thought.

Out loud, he said, "Thank you, my love. I'll put it on my left wrist, closer to my heart."

"Let me do it." Illima glided the pinkish bracelet over his hand, fixing it next to the white gleaming one. "Thus, you'll have two protectors: your mother's gift and mine."

"Come on, Kamolea, we gotta go," Anuro cried out.

"Good luck, my heart," said Illima. She squeezed his hand and kissed him quickly on the cheek.

Anuro approached and tapped him on the shoulder. "Let's go," he said.

"I love you, Illima," Kamolea said, fondling her face. "Wait for my return and I'll make you the happiest girl in the world."

"I promise," she said, smiling, and he couldn't tear his eyes away from her.

"Come on! Great feats await us!" said Anuro impatiently and tugged him by the arm. The moment Kamolea turned his back on Illima, he felt as if a fireball had hit him in the stomach, and his heart sank with a terrible feeling of foreboding calamity.

Once a coward, always a coward, he thought, desperately trying to get a grip on himself.

They set off toward the group of boys, who had meanwhile increased in number. The future warriors would depart in different directions, accompanied by several men, and everybody would be left on a different island in the Archipelago. The boys were overexcited, keen to start the journey, and to prove themselves. As Anuro and Kamolea neared, the latter caught sight of Lalago in the crowd, who was speaking with two other women.

They joined the others just when a plump boy named Fetu was saying,

"... And if they see you, it won't be easy..."

"Oh, come on, it will be child's play to capture someone who isn't expecting you," bragged Tamati, a stout boy almost a head taller than

Kamolea and twice as strong. "The real challenge comes after that. How will you bring him to Maniha Komo? How will you steal a canoe without being seen by the lookouts?"

"Yeah and how will you find the way back, especially if the sky is starless?" Fetu put in.

"Stop whining like a maiden, Fatty! I feel like taking a shit when I listen to you," cried Loto. Kamolea looked at him curiously. He hadn't seen him since the day Loto had been left lifeless beside the altar, smashed to a bloody pulp.

He's a tough one, Kamolea thought with admiration. Loto was older than he was, but obviously, his recovery after the beating had not allowed him to accomplish earlier his warrior's proof.

"What are we waiting for?" Tamati shouted. "Who's still missing?"

"Lacki, he's coming, over there," said Fetu, waving toward a short and skinny boy who looked a lot younger than the others did. He approached and muttered a torpid greeting. The lack of enthusiasm in his eyes was obvious.

"Is everybody here?" cried Chief Momo from a distance.

"Yes, Chieftain," Loto shouted back.

"Listen up!" Momo raised his right hand and waited until the yelling and laughing subsided. Anuro's facial muscles were jumping nervously; he could hardly suppress his smile. The chieftain was stumpy, fat, and smelly, with a big paunch, bulging eyes, and no neck. He fitted neither with the tribe's concept of male beauty nor of a warrior in good shape. However, his fierceness and cruelty, combined with his rhetorical skills and an unambiguous sign of Kepolo, had tipped the balance in his favor during the last election.

The crowd calmed down, and the only sounds were the roar of the wind, the waves' splashing, and the birds' piercing cries.

"People of the Tipihao tribe!" boomed Momo's voice. "Today is the most important day for these young boys, who are on the verge of becoming brave and strong men. After they bring back our foes and decorate Rakapi with their heads, and after they drink their blood and inherit their strength, the children you see here will become fearless warriors, and their names will ring over Kepula Penu to the horror of anyone who dares to challenge the great Tipihaos! Let's wish them good luck, and may Almighty Kepolo help them return home safe and sound, covered with glory!"

The roar of cheers was muffled by the blasting wind, which got up more with every word of the chieftain. The waves rose their foamy heads higher and higher, crashing furiously against the shore. Everybody watched the sea with growing concern.

"It seems that a storm is brewing, but that won't stop our brave young fighters," Momo concluded his speech and turned to the boys, who trembled with anticipation. "Let's get started! Go to the boats!"

The men chosen to escort the youngsters dragged eight canoes and waded into the water, struggling in the waves to keep the canoes straight. The boys darted off with war cries, splashing into the water, and then jumped in the boats. All but Kamolea.

He stood rooted to the ground, unable to move. His stomach churned. A fireball was burning in his chest, blocking his senses, as his heart was racing faster and faster. He stared at the rough sea and couldn't believe his eyes.

The old man from this morning was walking on water. Now he was a giant, towering above the waves, ten times taller than a normal human being. Kamolea discerned every detail of his bearded face and pale, delicate skin. His white hair flew back majestically and his red cloak was flapping in the wind. He wore red leather boots, which Kamolea hadn't noticed until then. In his left hand, he held, as usual, the black rectangular object. A large gleaming cross flashed in his other hand. The old man looked frightful and menacing. He stopped about 30 feet from the shore and raised the cross. The wind ceased and the sea calmed. From the cross, a bolt of lightning flew out toward Kamolea and blinded him, forcing him to shut his eyes. As he opened them again, he had the feeling that the heavens opened and time froze. In that instant, Kamolea felt eternity.

He sensed the presence of an incredible force that controlled the entire universe, and he understood in a fraction of a second that this power was pure energy, conscious and self-aware, alive and breathing, giving life to countless creatures and capable of creating or destroying worlds. He realized that God, whatever He was, was a personification of this majestic force and an enormous wave of awe and humility suffused him. He felt insignificant, helpless like a fly and smaller than a speck of dust.

"Who are you to defy the Power who created you?" boomed a voice. "God raises mountains, makes the Earth tremble and the stars fall. Who are you to disobey Him? Do as you were told! Refuse to kill!"

Kamolea fell on his knees, shaking all over. Then the old man vanished, the sky closed, and the world started spinning again.

The enlightenment lasted only a few seconds, but to Kamolea it was equal to an entire life. His heart was brimming over with joy. What his father or anyone else thought didn't matter to him anymore. All that mattered was to obey the great force, and he was ready to die for it.

The boys were already in the boats, and all eyes turned at Kamolea. He was still kneeling with a dreamy expression on his face.

"Look, he dropped on his knees and the wind abated," somebody called out.

"What's going on, Son? What are you waiting for?" shouted Akamui.

Kamolea rose slowly, as if in a trance, his eyes still wandering off to sea.

"I'm not going anywhere!" he cried and threw aside his spear. "It's wrong to kill people and I refuse to do it."

"What's this shit?" yelled Momo. "Do not speak like that; you'll vex our god."

"Such a god does not exist," shouted Kamolea. "I'm going on a great journey, and when I return, I will fell *Rakapi*. Then you will realize that you, fools, have always worshipped an ordinary tree and deified an imaginary god."

"You will die for those words right now, you little shit," cried Momo. He raised his spear to throw it. Kamolea shut his eyes, bracing himself for the sharp pain.

It's over, he thought.

He heard the crowd let out a collective gasp. Nothing happened. There was no way that the chieftain would miss from such a close distance. Kamolea opened his eyes. Momo lay prone, his fists buried in the sand, his spear next to him. Several men and women, including Akamui and Lalago, leaped toward the motionless body and rolled him over, feverishly trying to bring him around. Lalago bent over and put her ear to his chest.

"He's dead," she said. "His heart does not beat."

"You are the one to blame!" shouted Akamui at Kamolea, drawing his knife. "My son or not, I'll slit your bloody throat and hang your head on *Rakapi*, as an example for everyone who dares to defame our god!"

He pounced upon Kamolea. As he took his first step, a great crash of thunder rent the air, and a bolt of lightning struck the ground before his feet. He leaped back, dodging the loose sparks spilling over him. The lightning hissed on the ground like a glowing snake and disappeared in the sand.

Akamui stood rooted for a while, taken aback, hesitating. Finally, he turned to the crowd and shouted:

"Nobody should ignore the fire falling from the sky. You all saw what happened. This boy calmed the sea and killed our chieftain. It's obvious that the elements defend him. The death of Chief Momo is a bad omen and the departure should be postponed until we understand what is going on. I convoke the Council of Elders right away."

He pointed at Kamolea and said to the men nearby, "Take him away. Lock him in a cage until the Council decides his fate."

CHAPTER VIII

KEDIA

For the second time, Kamolea watched through the tangled sticks of the cage as the elders rushed one after another into the Hive. Soon the white smoke started rising through the outlet on the top of the thatched roof.

They have to choose a new chieftain, Kamolea thought. *I hope it's Father, although it's clear that even he couldn't let me off the hook. I can't believe I said all that nonsense. That damn old man, he bewitched me… I even don't remember what I said exactly, but I didn't mean it, that's for sure. And now, everybody will think of me as a craven traitor, and I'll end up torn apart like a fish on the altar in honor of Almighty Kepolo, despised by everyone.*

The tears welled up in his eyes.

In the Hive, all the elders were on their feet, shouting and speaking simultaneously. Hamaki, as the eldest one, attempted to outshout the din to assume control of the situation.

"Listen up, everybody! Pay attention. Let's sit down and hear each other out." He waited as the last conversations died away, and continued. "We have to choose the next chieftain and to decide Kamolea's fate. After the death of Momo and the thunderbolt that stopped Akamui, I'm not sure there will be many volunteers to kill him. I suppose that you made the connection between today's events and the troubles of Kedia's time. Unfortunately, Kerully, the only witness of that turbulent period, is no longer among us, may his spirit dwell forever at Rakapi's crown. Now we are on our own in this hard situation and we need all our cunning to resolve it. First, let's vote for a new chieftain! Silence, over there! Do I have your attention, please?! Ahaki, bring *nahiwa koho,* please."

Ahaki went to the sacred corner and brought twelve wood slabs with a drawn totem of each elder and a bunch of wood chips with a carved image of the totems.

"Thank you, wise Ahaki," said Hamaki. "I won't compete, though; I'm getting too old for this. Does anyone else wish to abstain?"

"I'm out too. I won't deal with all the weird things that are going around," grunted Tanuli.

"Will all others stay on course?"

Everybody nodded. After distributing the chips, letting out those of the abstained members, Hamaki said, "All right, let's vote. Don't forget that you may not propose yourself."

After each of the elders threw a chip into a large bowl, Hamaki counted them twice and cried out, "Toad's shit, I can't believe it. We have a tie of four! It's never been seen before. Three voices for Keko, three for Ahaki, three for Kelani, and three for Akamui!"

The news provoked an agitated murmur.

"I don't know who the morons are that voted for Akamui," growled Tanuli. "As the father of the young Kamolea, he must not be allowed to compete for chieftain because it creates a conflict of interest. At the time he did not pay the full price for killing my daughter; he helped his son get away with Laggi's death; and if you elect him now, he will do the same thing again."

"Wrong!" Akamui jumped to his feet and raised his hand. "Listen to me, everybody! Chieftain or not, tonight I will sacrifice my son Kamolea to Almighty Kepolo. He insulted our God and disgraced me in front of the entire tribe. Such a traitor and coward does not deserve to live among us. He put stigma not only on me, but also on the name of Tipihao. I swear to the Great Kepolo that tonight will be his last day!"

"The tie is a tie and we have to break it," said Hamaki firmly. "There is no way to veto Akamui's participation, it's his right and his privilege as a member of the Council. Does anyone wish to change their vote to break the tie?"

Nobody moved, all of them staring stubbornly ahead.

"In this case, we have no choice but to use the foreshadowing fire and to ask Kepolo to decide, as our ancestors did in times of emergency."

The four contestants stood abreast before the hearth, at three strides' distance from one another, as follows: Keko, Kelani, Akamui, and Ahaki. The others sat cross-legged around the fire. Hamaki took the long pipe and the spear with the skull from the corner, then circled the hearth as the ritual required and passed the pipe to everyone but the nominees, who waited patiently.

Once that was done, Hamaki cried, "Oh, Almighty Kepolo, Greatest of the Greatest Gods, show us who should be the next Tipihao chieftain. Let the foreshadowing fire lay its smoke on the men you'll reject and leave untouched the one you chose." He threw a handful of grains and powdered bark from the Sacred Tree into the fire.

The flames flared and flickered, producing thick black smoke. It started crawling left, reaching for Keko and Kelani. It wrapped them in a dense veil, so intense that they started coughing. While everybody expected that the smoke would touch Akamui next, an invisible draft bent the flames to the right. A fleecy puff crept toward Ahaki, touched him lightly, and dissolved in the air to astounded exclamations from all present. Whilst the elders waited to see what would happen next, the flames swung again, and the smoke went straight into the face of Tanuli, who shut his eyes and began coughing.

"Thank you for your unequivocal signs, Great Kepolo," Hamaki cried out. "Your choice is clear to us, as you showed us who should be eliminated and who has displeased you by speaking against your favorite. We humbly accept your desire, Almighty! We greet Akamui, the Tipihao's new chieftain, with joyful hearts."

The elders got up and started congratulating Akamui for his new position, but he raised his hand and cried, "Thank you for your support, wise elders, but the sunset approaches, and we don't have time for celebration. Let's summon the tribe, because I want to sacrifice the little traitor to the Great Kepolo as soon as possible."

* * *

Kamolea lay prone on the cage's floor and watched the Hive's entrance. Some time after the smoke stopped winding through the thatched outlet, his father emerged surrounded by other elders. The chieftain's necklace of bones dangled around Akamui's neck and he clutched the spear with the skull. He motioned to the stone altar, and Kamolea's heart sank.

Here we go, he thought. *At least they elected him, despite everything I've done.*

The elders disappeared into the jungle on their way to the village. The guards switched shifts below and soon only two of them remained in the clearing. A gloom fell over the place, and fat drops of rain started drumming against the roof of the cage. Kamolea heard men's voices. He put his ear on the crack of the floor and focused on the muffled sounds below.

"Here, it's a perfect shelter from the rain," said a thin teenage voice. "So, you said they chose Akamui?"

"Yes, yes, Akamui is the new chieftain," responded an excited voice with a bass timbre. "But you know what? There's a rumor that his son's behavior is similar to Kedia's, and if that's true, things are getting really interesting!"

"Who is Kedia?"

"You don't know who Kedia is? Man, are you living under a rock?"

"I've never heard that name, mate."

"Seriously? No wonder, though, you're still young, and the elders try to keep the entire story a secret. Even so, everybody knows about Kedia. In her youth, she started foretelling incredible things. Her moment of glory came when, just before one crucial battle, she had foreseen that the chieftain would perish and the Tipihaos would lose, unless they obeyed a simple warrior named Zilony."

"The legendary Zilony? So, she guessed right, I assume?" the youngster cried excitedly.

"She did," confirmed the other. "Everything happened exactly the way she predicted. The chieftain was killed, Zilony took over, the Tipihaos won the battle, and Kedia became a national hero. She was the first woman to become an official priestess of Kepolo and nothing was undertaken without her approval. She not only had the gift of being able to foresee the future; she was also a great healer; she could connect with the spirits of the dead and could find lost objects and children. I'm telling you, mate, people went crazy about her; they adored her. Everybody came to her for advice and the entire tribe worshipped her, even more than Kepolo."

"What an incredible story!" exclaimed the boyish voice.

"Hold on, the incredible bit's coming right up!" the bass replied. "In a blaze of her glory, something weird occurred—Kedia began saying things that contradicted Kepolo's teaching."

"Really? How so?"

"I don't know, man. One day, she simply lost her mind and started screaming that Kepolo was a fake god and Rakapi was a simple tree that we shouldn't worship. She said that God is a spirit and we must accept him; otherwise, we'll all perish in agony."

"But this is unbelievable," exclaimed the young guard. "Kamolea said almost the same things about Rakapi!"

"See the connection? Wait till you hear the rest! The elders didn't know what to do. They were afraid of killing her because the people would tear them to pieces. Besides, her foretelling gift came in handy when they had to make crucial decisions. So, they got together and decided to lock her up in a cave somewhere high in the hills, in a secret place known only by the chosen. They've kept her there ever since, but I heard the Council regularly turn to her for important decisions. Rumor has it that just before our last grand victory, when we surprised the alliance on Rocky Island, they went and asked her if they would win, even though Kepolo's signs were unambiguous on that matter. She also confirmed the victory but with a warning that everybody secretly repeats now:

"You'll win the battle but after then,
For all the men of our island,
Starts the beginning of the end
And the final act of this tribe violent."

"Weird," said the young one. "Who speaks like that? It's not a normal way to convey a story…"

"There's nothing normal when it comes to Kedia," said the bass voice gravely. "They said she spoke in verse from the moment they locked her in the cave. I knew one of her guards and he swore to me that her voice changed to a man's when she began to prophesy. It's very strange, I'm telling you…"

"Hey, you two, why are you hiding under the tree, losers?" yelled a rough voice from a distance. "Hakui, up to the cage and get the prisoner ready for the ceremony. And you, dotard, keep your eyes peeled; the boy is very dangerous!"

Kamolea smelled smoke and resin in the air and looked outside. Under the veil of a slight drizzle, hundreds of men were coming from the jungle and spilling into the clearing. Everybody carried an unlit torch in hand. Next to the stone altar, a blazing fire raised bright, lively tongues higher and higher.

The cage shook and swayed. The rectangular trapdoor moved aside and a man's head popped up. He was in his twenties, his face entirely tattooed. Kamolea had seen him speak with his father several times, who had said once that the young Hakui was a bright one and would go far.

"Cut the crap and behave yourself, all right?" he warned Kamolea. "Your father is the new chieftain, so don't disgrace him more than you already did. We're going down now; watch your step."

He gave Kamolea a shove, who then squeezed through the opening and deftly swung on the rope ladder, swiftly climbing down. An old warrior waited for him below, and a minute later, Hakui came down too. The two guards took Kamolea by his arms and dragged him toward the throng. The rain lashed Kamolea's face, the wind roared in his ears, and his heart was banging in his chest. He heard Akamui's voice from a distance. All of a sudden, the entire place became as bright as daylight as everyone raised a burning torch.

"Make way!" bellowed Hakui. The crowd split and the guards passed through, hauling Kamolea. A flash tore the sky, illuminating the rectangular flint plate covered with grooves. The overhung branches of the Sacred Tree waved ominously, studded with skulls and bones. Akamui stood before the altar, holding the long ritual knife in his right hand and the spear with the impaled skull in the other.

"… We are calling for justice and vengeance for Chief Momo," he shouted furiously. "His death occurred because of my son, who deserves the most severe punishment. Many years ago, I had a vision that he would be sacrificed for the greater glory of Almighty Kepolo. This day has now come. I will show you tonight that even though Kamolea is my blood, he will be treated as an ordinary traitor. He insulted our god and his skull will decorate Rakapi as a warning to anyone who dares to do it again. There he is, coming! Bring the traitor and bind him over here!"

As the two guards dragged Kamolea toward the flint slate, a flash ripped the sky and a thunderbolt hit the altar. Blinding sparks flew as the slate split in two and fell off its stone base with a crash.

A flying piece of rock hit Hakui in the skull. He slumped down with a cry and remained unconscious, releasing Kamolea's arm. The old guard jumped away, terrified, as a big fireball formed in the air and hit him in the chest. He collapsed lifeless next to Hakui. The crowd fell silent, flabbergasted. Nobody dared to touch Kamolea, who stepped up free and faced Akamui.

"Kill me," he shouted. "You are right, I disgrace you and my people, and I deserve to die. Let Kepolo's will be done! Go ahead! Thrust the spear into my heart and it'll be over!"

All eyes turned to Akamui, who stood as still as a graven image. A flash rent the sky and lit his stony face, his lips tightly pressed together, rain streaming down his cheeks. He slowly raised the spear, but then lowered it and shouted:

"The boy is cursed, so we must not kill him on the island. If we do that, his enchanted spirit may bring a colossal disaster to our land. We need to ask Almighty Kepolo for further clarification on how to proceed. Tonight, I postpone the sacrifice. Tomorrow, I'll summon the Council again and announce our ultimate decision to you. Go to your places now! My talk is over!"

The crowd broke up with a low grumble, and it took a long time for the clearing to become deserted, save for the elders and Kamolea's guards.

They all stood in the pouring rain around the broken altar, soaked to the skin.

"Why aren't we going to the Hive?" asked Hamaki, irritated.

"We don't need to," Akamui responded. "I know what Kepolo's will is. We have to take him to Kedia."

"What?" exclaimed Keko. "How did you decide that? We need to vote!"

"I saw it," said Akamui darkly. "As soon as I kill him, there will be an earthquake and our island will disappear under the water. The vision was terrible. Everybody screamed with horror as gigantic waves swept over every living creature on the island. Then I heard a voice, telling me that I must bring Kamolea to Kedia and obey her prophesy, otherwise total destruction awaits us. Enough talking now! This time we'll skip the vote. I want only Ahaki with me, as a witness, and two guards to keep Kamolea secure. Tomorrow I'll tell you what Kedia wills. We'll leave for the Steamy Cave right now."

The elders looked stunned. Paying no more attention to them, Akamui pointed at two men standing nearby.

"You two, take the prisoner and come with me! From now on, you answer with your lives if he escapes. Are you ready, Ahaki? Do you know the place well? It won't be easy to find the way in this pouring rain."

"Don't worry, Master Akamui, we'll get by. Let's go!"

Akamui turned to leave, but Hamaki said, "One more thing, Chieftain Akamui."

Akamui turned around. "What is it?"

Hamaki pulled him out of Ahaki's earshot. The elders stood in a circle, almost touching their foreheads.

"There must be no witnesses to your meeting with Kedia," Hauni whispered. "The last time there was a leak and we cannot afford other rumors about her to creep around the village. I heard that some people reject our god because of her. I have even overheard the words 'resistance' and 'prophecy' several times. We have to be extremely cautious, for this boy could provoke a riot. So, nobody besides you and Ahaki should know about this visit, understand?"

"I question even Ahaki's pertinence here," said Aleki cautiously. "He's also acting weirdly sometimes…"

"Ahaki is all right," said Akamui firmly. "As long as I am a chieftain, nobody will touch him. However, sometimes he is oversensitive, so for now it's better not to show awareness of the situation. As for the guards, I have to admit you have a point here. Fewer witnesses, the better. Let's get it over with!"

"May Kepolo keep you safe, Chieftain Akamui," said Hamaki, bowing.

* * *

The rain poured over the small group of men who advanced slowly, hewing the dense, soaked greenery. The flame of the torches flickered, blew by the strong wind in the otherwise pitch-black night. The *Steamy Cave* was at the top of *Carapace Hill*. There was no path or trail to this hidden place; they climbed with great effort, regularly tripping over shrubs, snags, and stones, as branches and thorny twigs whipped their naked bodies and scratched their faces.

Ahaki was in the lead, followed by Kamolea's guards, and the latter between them. His hands were tied in front of him and the rope was twisted around his waist and the wrist of each one of his keepers. Akamui brought up the rear.

After an eternity, Ahaki halted and raised his hand. A bolt of lightning lit up an area of stony ground, the other side of which rose to a high, almost vertical cliff, covered with bushes and small trees. The flashing lightning lit up dense globular clusters of mist. As the men cautiously approached, they discerned the small entrance of the cave, hidden by shrubs and creepers.

"Who's there?" shouted somebody from inside.

"I'm the new chieftain, Akamui. We came to see Kedia on an urgent matter," Akamui shouted back.

"Say the password," came out the voice.

"Password? What password," muttered Akamui and looked at Ahaki.

"Oh, it's 'hot spring'," said Ahaki quickly.

"Hot spring," cried Akamui.

Two sturdy, tough-looking men, armed to the teeth, emerged from the dark cave's mouth. Kedia's wardens were usually punished warriors who, after serving their time, swore an oath never to reveal what they had witnessed under the threat of decapitation.

"Greetings to you, Chieftain Akamui," said one of them with a bow. "We knew nothing about the change. What happened to Chief Momo?"

"Momo is dead. We want to speak to Kedia," Akamui said brusquely. "What is this mist, all around? It stinks as though something farted after three days of constipation…"

"It comes from the brook," said the other guard. "There's a spring with hot water that flows just under the cavern, and the steam rises from there. I agree the smell is terrible, though. No wonder that the crazy witch is getting worse with every passing day."

He had hardly finished these words when a horrid wail, something between a scream and howl, came from the cave. Akamui's blood froze in his veins. For the first time in his life, he looked terrified.

"Come in, don't stay out in the rain," said the first guard with a faint smile, motioning toward the entrance. The others followed him in silence. Akamui caught himself trembling.

Come on, it's only an old woman, he thought and turned to Kamolea's guards

"Both of you stay here at the entrance, keep watch, and don't let anyone in. From now on Kamolea will be my responsibility." He took the rope from them.

"With your permission, Chieftain, I'll stay with them too. You don't need me over there," said the man who had explained about the steam. "Talluti is as strong as two men, he'll get you there."

"Fair enough," Akamui grunted. "Let's see this crazy hag. Lead us, warden!"

With raised torches, Ahaki and Akamui followed Talluti. Kamolea slouched between the chieftain and the elder, trying to wake up from the surrealistic nightmare that was going on. Wrapped by the dense vapor, he waddled in puddles of warm water, feeling like a blind man, as despite the flickering flames of the torches he saw almost nothing but steam. The moisture penetrated his body, and the smell of sulfur pierced his brain. The constant dripping of water was driving him crazy. He was focusing on the hypnotic drip-drip-drip sound, mixed with the splashing noise of their steps, when he hit his head against a stalactite descending from the low ceiling.

"Nice place to live." Akamui's voice echoed hollowly in the darkness.

A sharp scream resounded in the compact space: "*Cooommiiiiiing.*"

Kamolea started shaking from head to toe.

This can't be real, he thought. *It would have been a hundred times better if they'd killed me tonight.*

They stopped in front of a bamboo wall, which blocked the way. Talluti pulled a heavy latch and took out two rods from the middle. They squeezed one after another through the narrow opening and advanced with raised torches toward the middle of a vast room. The flames cast dancing shadows on the cave's walls. The steam was less intense there, allowing a clearer view. From the ceiling, sharp stalactites hung ominously like crooked fingers. In the center ascended a big egg-shaped stone with a flat upper surface, formed by stalagmites; to its right, a small spring bubbled. Clay cups and small animal and fish bones were scattered around.

Something stirred just behind the stone, and they all jumped back as the most terrifying creature they had ever seen dashed out with a piercing scream.

The short, animal-like figure of an old woman dashed towards them, then leaped immediately out of the reach of the guard, who had swung his spear at her. She was naked, covered only by her long white hair that trailed on the ground, and so skinny that her bones jutted out and threatened to pierce her skin from the inside. Her ugly, wizened face was as old as the hills but at the same time very expressive.

It's all in her eyes, Kamolea thought, staring at her big brown eyes, which shone with incredible intelligence. Her face was lit by an inner light and looked alive and spiritual.

Kedia crawled back, took a sip from the spring, and fixed her eyes on Kamolea. She crept toward him, humming under her breath and often touching the moist stone floor with her forehead to express her submission. As she got closer, she stretched a bony hand and crooked fingers, with long, curved nails, wrapped around Kamolea's ankle. Writhing like a worm, she lifted his foot, put her head underneath, and pressed it on her neck. All the men watched, stunned. She froze in this position for a moment, emitting strange gurgling sounds, which got louder until, finally, they turned into hoarse, hardly-recognizable words:

"He came, he came, the boy with scars here came,
The one who'll change forever the thinking of all men,
The one who'll cut the Tree; he glorious will be,
As God supports him strongly, and he will make us free."

She removed his foot from her neck and began to retreat, keeping her eyes on Kamolea.

"So many lengthy years I waited for this day,
The day when he'll appear with a mighty ax in hand,
The day of New Beginning, as stated by his name,
The day I'll pass away and suffocate my flame."

Akamui snorted.

"What the fuck was that?" he yelled. "I understand nothing of your babble, woman. Can't you speak like a normal person? We came to ask you what we should do with my son Kamolea because, apparently, we aren't able to kill him. He betrayed our God and disgraced me, and he deserves to die, but the elements protect him and thunderbolts kill the people who try to punish him."

The ugly creature leaped on the top of the egg-shaped rock and kneeled. Her body shook uncontrollably and she began to scream. The echo bounced off the walls and resounded in the cave ten times more loudly. Akamui and Ahaki looked at each other, terrified.

"Don't be afraid, Chieftain, she's just laughing," said Talluti with a tinge of mockery in his voice.

Kedia halted and tilted her head to one side. Her face was distorted into a ghastly grimace and her eyes rolled until only the sclera were visible. She stayed still for a moment and then from her mouth came a bass male voice:

"Oh, stupid mortal people, impossible it will be
That such a boy can master the elements and the sea,
However, I agree, indeed he has the key.
This island pretty small is for his great destiny.

So, put him in a boat supplied with food and water,
Enough for him for three days in order to survive,
Then kick him off the island instead of being slaughtered,
And may the elements and God take care of his life.

But never dare to kill him, as never you'll be able
To bend him or extinguish the divine spark in him.
And shall a single hair of his head touch the ground,
Tremendous calamity awaits you for your sin,

And natural disaster will meet this land with fury,
And everyone will perish in awful pain and blood.
You'd better let the boy, who the Lord supports truly,
Go and pull you out of your disgusting mud."

She ended the last sentence with an awful scream, fell flat on her back, and remained motionless. The quiet rippling of the brook was the only sound breaking the portentous silence that lingered in the air.

Akamui looked helplessly at the others.

"Is she dead?"

"Nah, she's just recovering from her trance. It's gonna be a while until she comes around," Talluti replied.

"Did you catch any of that nonsense?" The voice of Akamui trembled with rage.

"I did, and her words confirmed your vision, Chieftain Akamui," Ahaki replied. "We need to put your son in a boat with food and water for three days and leave him at the mercy of the elements. In no case should we kill him, as that would provoke a colossal disaster."

"Did you hear the same thing?" Akamui asked the guard.

"That's what she said, precisely," he answered, hardly able to keep a straight face.

"Let's go then," muttered Akamui, casting a murderous look at the guard. One by one, they squeezed their way out of the room. Kedia was still lying unconscious, wrapped in vapor.

As they advanced, Akamui whispered in Ahaki's ear,

"Take Kamolea and our men and wait for me at the end of the path. I have some business to finish with Kedia's wardens."

Ahaki nodded and took Kamolea's rope. As they reached the entrance, he beckoned to Kamolea's guards, bowed to the others, and hurried outside.

"So, it's time for us to go now," Akamui said to Kedia's keepers. "Thank you for your help and hospitality, I highly appreciate it. When you finish your sentence, come and see me and you will be richly rewarded."

"It was a pleasure for us to help you, Chieftain Akamui," said Talluti with a broad grin. "It was an amazing night. She's terrible, this witch, ain't she?"

"A horrible old hag," agreed Akamui. "I never imagined such a disgusting creature. Goodbye, then."

The two guards bowed slightly. Quick as a snake, Akamui drew his long knife and with one fierce stroke almost cut off the head of the still grinning Talluti. The other one jumped aside and drew his own knife, but he was too slow—with a mighty fling, Akamui thrust his spear into the guard's chest. The latter dropped his knife, staggering. Blood spurted out of his mouth and he collapsed onto the ground. Akamui yanked out the spear, cast a quick look around, and dragged the corpses into a low niche inside the cave.

"I hope no-one finds them right away," he muttered as he hurried to join Ahaki and the others, who waited for him by the treeline.

"Let's go," he grunted. "The day is breaking and I don't want to meet the new shift. Ahaki will take care of Kamolea, and you two bring up the rear."

They ran through the forest. Suddenly Akamui turned, gave a sign to Ahaki to continue, and disappeared into the dense thicket on the left. The guards appeared several yards after Kamolea and, as they passed the place where Akamui vanished, there was a swishing sound and a sharp cry rent the air. One man fell, writhing in agony, a spear sticking from his throat. His friend leaped to help him and another scream resounded, as Akamui's knife flew out and thrust up to the hilt into his chest. Ahaki and Kamolea returned in a wild run and found Akamui squatting beside the corpses, wiping his knife with a tuft of grass.

Ahaki said nothing. He suspected that something was wrong from the moment the elders called Akamui for a private talk just before their departure. When the chieftain returned from Steamy Cave without the two wardens, Ahaki was already sure.

"Let's hide them and move on," grunted Akamui, and dragged one body in the shrubs. Ahaki tugged the rope, but Kamolea didn't budge.

For the first time, his admiration for his father was replaced by boiling resentment toward all these meaningless killings.

"Do you hear me?" bellowed Akamui from afar. "Move your asses, bring the other!"

"Why did you kill these men?" shouted Kamolea, beside himself with rage. "They had done nothing bad, had they? You don't even know their names…"

Akamui jumped out from the bushes and swooped at Kamolea. "You, fucking son of a snake, it's your fault they are dead. How you dare to speak at all, you filthy worm?"

He gave him a hard backhand blow. Kamolea rolled over, his upper lip split in two.

"Not a word from your mouth, you fucking coward, or I'll wring your neck despite all the bloody signs and warnings," he hissed and spat on him, then rushed to haul away the other corpse.

The return journey passed in complete silence as they ran as fast as they could until they reached Kepolo's belt.

As all bad things come in threes, once again, Kamolea was locked up in a cage, and the Council was summoned. Akamui and Ahaki explained Kedia's message. At the beginning nobody agreed with her words, and even Akamui was hesitant, but Ahaki fought fiercely and, after a long debate, convinced the elders that they had no choice but to respect her decision.

"However, we need to be sure that this boy will never come back to our land," Hamaki pointed out.

"Well, I think sending him alone in the boundless sea in an oarless boat, with a scarce supply of food and water, is pretty equal to death," said Ahaki. "I suggest leaving him at the north side where the currents are stronger and he will have no chance of returning safely. Even better, let's paint the boat with the Tipihao signs of war, and even if he reaches another island, the other tribes will know that he is one of us and will kill him immediately."

"Excellent idea," said Hauni approvingly.

"One thing I know for sure," said Keko, standing. "Once we cast the traitor off, he will be our enemy forever; he will no longer belong to our tribe, and if he dares to set foot on our land again, he will be doomed."

"Let's vote, then," Hamaki sighed. "I don't want to be the one to announce our decision, though. I can imagine the comments: The son of the chieftain gets away with treason and the former chieftain's death…"

"Don't worry, leave that to me," said Akamui. "I will convince them it's Kepolo's will, and let's see if anyone dares to challenge me."

"We shouldn't go to extremes," Aleki put in. "We're all behind you in this decision. The most important thing is that nobody mentions Kedia's name. Let's vote now."

* * *

The north shore was crowded with people who had come to see Kamolea's fate. Everybody was surprised that the gathering was not, as usual, at the Sacred Zone, and the rumors that the Council had decided to drown Kamolea in the sea as a sacrifice to the Sea God Akuakai circulated everywhere.

The rain had stopped, but grey rags of clouds dragged along the sky. It was windy and hot. With a bent head, his hands tied in front of him, Kamolea stood near the water beside a canoe, painted on the bow with the totem of the Tipihao tribe: a tree with a dangling skull.

Kamolea looked haggard and miserable. Shame and despair burned his insides and tore his heart apart. The lump in his throat grew bigger and bigger, almost suffocating him. He ducked whenever a stone or chunk of wood was thrown at him from the crowd. Spiteful and derisive stares bored into him, and the desultory shouts of "traitor," "coward," "shame," "worthless," "kill him," and "sacrifice him" stabbed his heart as if with a knife.

He glimpsed Lalago but he was fervently searching for Illima. She had surely witnessed yesterday's mess, and he was not sure what she would think about all this. Did she still love him, or consider him a coward and a traitor like everybody else? If she was not here now, then the latter was more probable…

A stone hit his shoulder and broke his thoughts. He leaped aside to avoid another one and a seagull's egg landed on his neck. Dizzy and humiliated, he wished he could clean his neck of the slimy, dripping yolk. At that moment, the crowd parted, and the guards stepped aside to make a place for Akamui, who walked toward him, followed by the elders.

Everybody fell silent, watching the chieftain.

"Proud Tipihaos," he shouted. "Do you see this boy? Until yesterday, he was my beloved son, my pride, and my hope. Today he is the worst traitor and coward ever to have been born on Maniha Komu. The shame he brought is not only mine; he is a disgrace to our tribe and our god."

Wild boos and catcalls accompanied his speech.

"You all know what happened yesterday," continued Akamui. "It was a terrible day for all of us. After realizing that it is impossible to kill Kamolea, we prayed all night to Almighty Kepolo in hope that he would lead us to the right decision. And he, as always, showed us the way and gave us his signs, so that we finally learned the truth. Kamolea is bewitched. An evil spirit, planted in him by our enemies through magic, possesses him.

"According to the revelation we received from the Great Kepolo, we must not kill the boy on the islands, as his enchanted spirit will provoke a terrible natural disaster. Our God told us to cast Kamolea off. We will put him in the unmanageable boat without oars, with minimal supplies, and leave him in the sea at the mercy of the elements and the sharks. His chances of survival are practically nil. But even if he somehow survives, he must never return to our native land, as death will always await him here. My talk is over!"

Without waiting for a reaction, he turned to the guards and ordered, "Take him to the boat!"

"It's not enough," shouted someone from the crowd. "He deserves to die!"

"Don't protect your son!" yelled another.

"Yeah, death for him," echoed scattered shouts.

"He will die anyway," cried Akamui. "There are things you don't understand, folks; don't forget that I am also a shaman of the Almighty Kepolo and if someone challenges my decision, he is going directly against our god."

The grumbling was getting louder and louder, but nobody dared to defy Akamui, who stood firmly set, his legs slightly apart, his dark, sturdy silhouette outlined against the cloudy sky. His posture projected wild, rudimentary strength that nobody wanted to test.

One of the guards pushed Kamolea toward the water with the blunt end of his spear, while another one pulled the canoe into the sea.

"Get in the boat," Akamui shouted.

Kamolea cast a glance at the throng and met Illima's gaze. She was in the first row and stared at him intently, her eyes streaming pity and love. When she caught his eyes, she smiled at him, brought her fingers to her lips, and blew him a kiss. Kamolea's heart fluttered.

"She still loves me!" he wanted to cry out to all these gruesome, croaking people with faces distorted by hatred. At that moment he didn't care what they were thinking or yelling. The only thing that mattered was the look on Illima's lovely face and the gesture of love she had sent to him. It was like a salve on his wounded, torn-apart soul. In response to her kiss, he raised his left hand and pressed his lips to her bracelet.

"Get in the fucking boat," bellowed the guard, who then struck him in the face.

Kamolea waded in the water and climbed into the bobbing canoe, which was already attached to a considerably bigger boat with six men inside, ready at the oars. Heartbroken and miserable, blood dripping from his nose, his gaze swept to the cliff with his little cave and back to the crowd where Anuro, Illima, and Lalago waved him goodbye. The sorrow suffocated him as he realized that he'd never see them again.

The warriors pulled at the oars, the little canoe rocked, and Maniha Komo gradually receded.

Thousands of memories started buzzing in Kamolea's head. In quick succession, before his eyes, rolled scenes from his childhood: a walk with his grandmother, a hunt with his father, training in the jungle, the games played with his peers, his first kiss with Illima at Butterfly Waterfall. Tears started rolling down his face and he sobbed uncontrollably.

The boat cleaved the waves faster and faster. Maniha Komu had disappeared from view a long time ago. The Tipihaos, hauling the canoe, cast contemptuous glances at the crying boy who had never had the chance to become a man. They rowed tirelessly toward the horizon until the last birds vanished, and everything was water and heaven as far as the eye could see.

Then the canoe slowed down as one of the rowers cut it adrift. The big boat faded away in Maniha Komo's direction, leaving Kamolea alone in the middle of the infinite blue immensity.

IN THE OPEN SEA

CHAPTER IX

WHITE SHARK

Yellow spots danced in front of Kamolea's eyes. The sun, high at its zenith, seemed to have stopped its path across the unblemished sky, mercilessly casting fire over the sea.

"*What a loser,*" he heard Akamui's angry voice say. "*Worthless jerk. I waited for you all night long…*"

"*Kamolea, where have you been?*" It was Lalago's voice. "*Your father is mad with fury. You'd better stay here overnight…*"

"*You are so nice, not like the other fools,*" Illima whispered. "*I'll always be waiting for you…*"

Kamolea moaned in his half-conscious, half-mad state.

It had been many sunsets already since he drifted in the sea. In the beginning everything was fine—the weather was gorgeous and when the scorching heat got unbearable he dipped in the water.

He ate very little, but he was thirsty all the time. The fresh water depleted on the third day and the lack of it addled Kamolea's brain. Consequently, one mistake followed another.

One morning, a fat flying fish landed in the canoe with a hollow thud. Kamolea, happy that food was falling from the sky, grabbed it eagerly and immediately dropped it with a sharp cry, clasping his hands. The long fin had stabbed his palm, and blood started gushing, soaking the boat's bottom. Kamolea immediately dipped his hand into the sea, and the soothing, analgesic relief of the salt calmed him down.

He left his hand trailing for a while. Suddenly, the water stirred, and the boat swung. He yanked his hurt palm away just in time: two shark fins glided toward the canoe, and it rocked violently a moment later.

The sharks circled, joined in a trice by three others, and more followed. Finally, Kamolea stopped counting them, desperately watching the encircling siege from his little floating fortress.

I should have known better, he thought, irritated. *Father says those beasts can sniff blood as far away as Coral Beck.*

He spent the night on tenterhooks, jerking at every jolt of the boat. The next day, despite his hope that they would leave him alone, the sharks were still there, and he couldn't bathe in the ocean. The glaring sun hurt his eyes as its heat sucked up the moisture through his skin. Thirst rending his insides, his mood darkened and his mind became foggy.

Gradually, he got delirious. Voices of his closest people, fragmentary and unclear, were ringing in his head. In contrast, a screaming, shrill voice was always clear and consistent. It heaped reproaches and insults onto him and ceaselessly incited him to commit suicide.

"Are you out of your fucking mind, you stupid jerk?" it echoed angrily in his head. *"Why did you listen to that crazy old man? Where is he now to answer for what he's done to you, eh? Of course, he's not here because he simply doesn't exist! Why didn't you obey your tribe, your father, your god? What will you do now, surrounded by sharks, alone in the sea? I'll tell you what—jump in the water and feed the fish. End your miserable existence! What's the use of living, anyway? Kamolea the coward—a new beginning for losers and fools."*

"What I am waiting for, indeed?" Kamolea agreed. "Cowards like me don't deserve to live. Who cares if I live, anyway? The faster I get this done, the better!"

"*He hears voi-i-i-ces,*" the shrill voice was screaming, drawling the words. "*He se-e-e-e-es old do-o-tards who nobody else do-o-e-es. He's a complete lo-o-o-o-ny.*"

Kamolea lay on the boat's bottom, semi-conscious, torn with grief, and unable to move. The swish of the wind, the lulling rumble of the sea, and the occasional gentle splash of the fish were the only sounds around him. He felt death approaching, its steps echoing in his ears with every heave of the boat.

Why did he have the impression that the sea swelled? He propped himself up on an elbow and exclaimed, "Finally saved!"

A beautiful island, full of trees heavy with fruit and a gorgeous waterfall falling from a soaring cliff, danced before his eyes. Colorful birds flew around a deep blue lake. The shore was swarming with people who waved at him and smiled. Illima and Lalago were there.

"Water," he moaned. The island approached. Wasn't that Chief Momo? Looking rather menacing? Awaiting him with his spear ready, keeping the precious water away from him? And his father, his face distorted in a mask of disdain, his brows knitted angrily? Wild, rudimentary fear welled up inside Kamolea. Fear of death. Dread of being buried under the ground, unable to see a single sunbeam again… He started panting for breath, stretching his arm toward Lalago.

"What happens to us when we die?" he wanted to ask his granny, but suddenly the island disappeared, and a shrill giggle split his brain. He sat upright… and then he saw *it*.

It stood in the canoe's bottom, in front of Kamolea, within arm's reach. It was definitely the ugliest creature in the world—three hand-spans tall, with a large frog-like mouth and bulging, unmoving, brown eyes that stared at Kamolea. Its skinny body, with short, almost stunted arms and crooked legs, sharply contrasted with its big bald head, glued directly to its shoulders. Two tiny protuberances, forming miniature horns, stuck out from its pate. Its color kept changing from pale gray through brown to black and then back to gray again, and its features fluctuated all the time.

It was so grotesque that Kamolea couldn't tear his eyes away from it.

"What are you gawking at, sucker?" the ugly thing shrieked. "Don't you like what you see?

"Who are you?" Kamolea wanted to ask, but his chapped, bleeding lips refused to budge.

"Nobody! I don't exist, loser," snapped the creature. "You aren't supposed to see me. I'm an invention of your sick brain, a figment of your imagination, right? Same as the old fool who messed up your life. Why did you even listen to him?"

I'm so sorry, thought Kamolea, his heart torn apart. *I really don't know what on earth seized me to do such stupid things. If I could turn back time, I'd certainly never do it again.*

"That's the way to go!" cried the weird thing and jumped toward Kamolea. In a split second, Kamolea felt a puff of air and a slight tingling sensation in his chest, realizing that *it* entered his body. Then, an ear-spitting giggle pierced his brain, and a range of negative feelings welled up inside him. A fireball of anger, desperation, jealousy, and spite grew bigger and bigger inside his chest until a mighty explosion tore him into hundreds of pieces and he fell unconscious.

The small, nutshell-like canoe, left at the mercy of the elements, drifted in the infinite sea, tossed by the waves and drawn by the currents toward its dim destiny.

* * *

White Shark cleaved the waves at full speed as her bow plunged forward, making a foamy whirl that raised a fine cloud of spray around a figurine of a full-sized grinning shark. The three-masted frigate outlined majestically against the blue sky, swelling out her sails with the fair wind. It had been two days since they tried to outrun the Spanish galleon that spotted them near El Callao. Although *White Shark* was far lighter and faster, it was a tight run, so they had been forced to tack downwind, changing the course south-west and throwing everything unnecessary from the hold to lighten the load. They had lost the galleon from sight some time ago, and everybody was on a high—at least until the frigate slowed considerably. Bobo El Tuerto[5] directed his single eye toward the dangling canvas.

"Slack as a drained cock," he muttered, as he scrutinized the small, white, fluffy cloud hanging in the blue sky. "Don't like it at all."

"What the bloody hell!?" barked Captain Gonzalez, popping out of the great cabin. One glance upward was enough for him to assess the situation.

"All hands on deck!" he bellowed. "Bos'n, blow the pipe!"

Diego de Sylva's sharp whistle brought a commotion of running feet onto the main deck.

"All hands aloft!" shouted the boatswain. "Man the braces! Strike sail!"

In a matter of seconds, all the sailors were upon the masts, dousing the sheets. Meanwhile, the blue sky turned gradually to an ominous grey as black clouds flocked from the east.

"Coxswain, ready to lie ahull!" the captain cried.

Bobo El Tuerto fixed the helm, getting ready for lying to. A blinding glare tore through the sky, and heavy drops started pounding the deck.

"Heave to!" shouted Gonzalez. The gale drowned out his words as the heavens opened, letting go torrents of lashing rain. The waves crashed over the deck, sweeping everything before them. The ship heaved and rocked, then plunged bow first, almost keeling over, and Diente De Oro[6] fell off the spar, screaming. A mighty blast caught the still unlowered topsail, ripped it to pieces, and crashed like a toothpick the upper

---

5 The One-Eyed.

6 Goldtooth.

part of the mizzenmast, which landed in slow motion upon the cursing sailors below, tangled rigging and all. The hurricane swelled the sea, and the Pacific roared like a wounded beast.

* * *

Three days later, Captain Gonzalez and the quartermaster, Lars van Halle, were bent over a large map spread out across a huge square desk in the great cabin. The storm had finally calmed, but it had done such severe damage that they urgently needed to mend the ship.

"How the hell did we go so far?" Gonzalez growled, stabbing his finger at the map. "We veered westward because of the bloody galleon, but it was only two days sailing from El Callao. How come we found ourselves in the middle of nowhere?"

"If my calculations are right, we are at least two weeks from Lima," replied Van Halle who, amongst other tasks, was in charge of the navigation. "Apparently, the currents are strong in this part of the ocean and carried us away while we lay ahull."

"Blood and thunder! We didn't need this shit!" grunted Gonzalez.

"Nah, especially with all the fatigue and frustration going around," muttered Van Halle.

"What do you mean?" asked Gonzalez, alert.

"The crew ain't happy, Cap'n. Two months in the open sea, with no booty in sight, and now lost in these uncharted waters... I smell trouble..."

"What kind of trouble? Speak out, quartermaster!"

"I suspect a mutiny is brewing..."

"Let 'em try, lubberheads," Gonzalez snarled. "Is it my fault that the ship is so undermanned, by thunder? We were ninety-eight in the beginning, and after the ambush, when we lost half of the crew, it was already hard to handle her. Now we are thirty-six, and in heavy weather, she's almost unmanageable."

"Thirty-five," corrected Van Halle, "I told you we lost Diente De Oro in the storm."

"Sink me, I completely forgot! How come? Was he drunk, the rascal?"

"He fell aloft when the topmast broke," said Van Halle matter-of-factly.

"Diente de Oro, the old bucko." Captain Gonzalez shook his head in desperation. "Thirty-five, blood and thunder! They'll work their asses for four and shut their traps at that, or I'll blow out the head of the first lubber who dares to challenge my authority, even if it means in the end, I have to steer this beauty alone."

"I hear you, Cap'n. You know you can always count on me," said Lars van Halle quickly.

"The hell I know! So, first we need to find a shore and mend her," continued the captain. "With our mizzen topmast broken, and the hull leaking from three different places, we won't get far."

"Boat ho! Larboard side, abeam!" resounded the cry of the lookout, followed by the piercing whistle of the boatswain pipe.

"What is it now!?" grunted Gonzalez, and the both of them rushed to the quarterdeck. The sailors piled up, leaning on the port rails at the waist. It was a gorgeous, sunny morning, and the boundless blue sea, calm and shimmering, cast back a golden glare.

"It's a boat, Cap'n; just over there," said the boatswain.

Captain Gonzalez snapped open his spyglass and peered at the small canoe floating adrift. A swarthy, skinny boy lay prone on the bottom, seemingly lifeless.

"A lad, unconscious, in a drifting canoe," concluded Gonzalez. "Bos'n, ready about!"

"Hard-a-lee! Man the topgallant gear! Clew down!" called out Diego De Sylva.

The ship started turning her bow clumsily toward the canoe.

"Lower a boat and haul him out!" ordered the captain.

"Hopefully there's land lying nearby, and if he's alive, he'll lead us there," said Van Halle, while the sailors carried out the commands. Soon, both boat and boy were hoisted aboard. The men spread the limp body on the deck and crowded round it, watching him with great interest.

"Is it a negro?" asked Ron O'Reilly, scratching his head through the worn-out, discolored kerchief that lay atop his red hair.

"Nah, he's not one of us," said Bobo El Tuerto, a bald, black giant of a man with a leather patch over his left eye and a large ring in his left ear. "He rather looks like a mongrel, a mulatto, or a mestizo…"[7]

"Or even worse, a zambo,[8] sprouted out of the womb of some Indian bitch!" cried out Alfonso El Cucharón,[9] the ship's cook, who was always in a good mood.

Everybody chuckled.

"What's that on his wrist?" O'Reilly squatted beside him and took his limp hand. "Two bracelets, one of shark's teeth, the other a pretty womanish one."

"Shark's teeth? It's an omen, that!" exclaimed Benito El Creyente.[10]

"Aye, everything connected to the sharks brings us luck," confirmed the old Calisto.

"It's weird, his face," said Hugo La Daga,[11] raising his brawny, mer-maid-tattooed arm and running his hand through his long hair. "His features are like a white person, his hair is curly like a quadroon, and his skin is not too dark. It's tough to tell. I would say some mulatto, but no way a mestizo or zambo…"

"Pour a bucket over his face, and we'll find out fast enough," ordered the captain.

---

7 Born of Indians and white people.

8 Born of Indians and African ancestry.

9 Alfonso The Ladle.

10 Benito The Believer.

11 Hugo The Dagger.

The first pail had no effect, but the boy jerked and opened his eyes after the second hit his face. He propped up on one elbow, stretched his hand, and moaned something in an unfamiliar language.

"Give him water," commanded Gonzalez.

Benito kneeled and brought his canteen to the boy's lips. He grabbed it and started gulping like mad, his eyes bulging from the effort. He emptied it within seconds and motioned for more.

"Hey, not so fast, you're gonna get stomach cramps," Benito said.

"Shiver me timbers, seems this one has spent a lot of time at open sea," exclaimed Juan Carlos.

The boy tried to rise, but his legs failed him and he remained prostrate.

"Where is your homeland, lad? Is it nearby? Show us where are you coming from?" pressed Captain Gonzalez.

The curly fellow offered no answer and just stared at him. The sailors watched with bated breath, waiting for the outburst, as they knew their captain and his famed lack of patience.

"Hey, Gabacho[12], bring your brush and make this one speak, or blimey, I'll throw him back in the sea!" growled Gonzalez.

"Aye-Aye, Cap'n!" replied a tall man with a palpable Spanish accent and disappeared down the hatch. He had been born François, but now only his mother remembered it, as nobody had addressed him by his real name in years. He returned with a piece of canvas, a paintbrush, and a small round box filled with red paint. He spread the sheet and drew a picture of an island with a palm tree in the middle. This time, the youngster seemed to understand. His eyes gleamed for a moment, but then he shook his head in despair.

"Where is it?" shouted Gonzalez. "Heave him here!"

Bobo El Tuerto lifted the skinny boy like a feather and pressed him to the larboard edge.

---

12 Frenchy.

"Where is your land? Is it over there?" Gonzalez waved towards the southeast, the direction they first had noticed the boat.

The boy's gaze lingered on the horizon, then he slowly turned his head, tracking something visible only to his eyes. He disentangled himself from Bobo's hands and strode aft, staggering and reeling, then mounted the quarterdeck and grabbed the mizzen starboard shrouds to steady himself. Staring into the distance, he raised his hand and pointed northwest.

"Impossible!" cried Van Halle. "No way to come from thence! Look at the current, the wind; it's ridiculous!"

Quiescent but confident, with one hand tangled around the shrouds and the other decisively indicating northwest, the boy's posture was an embodiment of determination and assurance, and Captain Gonzalez, who trusted nobody, somehow believed him.

"Are you sure, lad? Your land's over yonder?" he asked him quietly.

The boy's chest started heaving fast. He turned his head slowly towards the captain, and his eyes blazed with a yellow, inhuman glare. He nodded, and from his mouth came a thick, hoarse bass voice, speaking Spanish,

"*Dos dias en tierra.*" [13]

The voice had nothing in common with the youngster's previous timbre. Gonzalez's jaw dropped open and goosebumps crawled down his spine.

"Who are you?" he whispered.

Instead of a response, the boy released his grip and collapsed unconscious.

"Benito, O'Reilly, over here!" Gonzalez shouted. "Take this fellow to the focs'l, find him a place to sleep, feed him, quench his thirst, and see he lacks nothing. Coxswain, at the helm! Bos'n, ready to go about! We tack northwest!"

---

13 Two days ashore.

"Big mistake, Captain," Lars van Halle objected. "According to my calculations…"

"I'll take a chance," interrupted Gonzalez, patting him on the back. "Wanna' wager two escudos [14] that the boy is telling the truth?"

Van Halle grunted discontentedly and turned his back. Captain Gonzalez smirked and muttered to himself, "And if he is, I swear I'll make him a fine seaman and my favorite attendant."

* * *

Kamolea woke with a start. His first impression was that he was in his hut on Maniha Komo, swinging in his hammock, but it quickly dissipated as the unfamiliar smell of tar hit his nostrils. His eyes flew open, and his jaw dropped—a mess of taut ropes, dense as a spider's web, tangled above his head. He hauled himself up and looked around. Large pieces of canvas were flapping in the wind; men were climbing poles so high that their tops reached the sky; shouts and pounding feet echoed around. Kamolea stepped carefully onto the wooden deck. The floor heaved up and down, and he staggered as he took several steps towards the midship. Beyond the bulwarks, the sea stretched to the horizon, boundless and everlasting.

"What an immense boat," he mumbled, dumbstruck. Everything looked so enormous, so sophisticated…

"Almighty Kepolo, what *is* this thing?" he whispered, staring flabbergasted at the capstan. The round black wheel on the reel-like base had six metal poles sticking out of it, and was so impressive that, for some reason, he decided that this structure was the place for sacrifice and torture. Memories of past events started running through his mind.

How did I get to this place? he frowned, rubbing his forehead. He had been cast off, all right—he clearly recollected that. Then he was alone

---

14 Gold coins.

in the canoe, encircled by sharks, his hand bleeding… And that was the last thing he remembered. As he was racking his brains, somebody tapped him on the shoulder, and he jumped, frightened.

"Ahoy, matey!" cried out a short, plump, jolly man in his forties, clad in drab, baggy trousers and a threadbare, once-white shirt. Kamolea immediately liked his round face as it stretched into a broad smile across his rosy cheeks, which were covered by large bushy whiskers. "Hey, old drunkards, look who's swelling sails here! The scourge of the Seven Seas has awakened."

"What are you babbling on about, Cucharón?" shouted back a burly fellow in a bleached open shirt and a faded bandana wrapped over short-sticking pigtails.

"Tell the bos'n to blow muster. Our tiger's aroused, and everybody deserves to see him!"

"The lad is up. The chap awakened," echoed a few voices around the ship. Within minutes, all the sailors had gathered on deck and surrounded Kamolea, staring at him as though he was some strange animal. Kamolea gawked back, unable to conceal his stupefaction, but calculating at the same time his chances against each one of them.

The tall black one with the bulging muscles and the eye patch looks pretty scary. The one with pigtails has an ear missing and could be dangerous. The man tattooed with the fish-tailed woman doesn't seem too strong; neither does the one with the wooden leg…

They all were tough-looking men with weather-beaten faces furrowed with wrinkles and scars. Their beards were bushy, and their hair was plaited in queues under tricorn or brimmed hats, or bound with bandanas and faded kerchiefs.

More pale men, Kamolea shuddered, recalling the bearded man from his vision. Their clothes, however, differed considerably from the old man's gorgeous, richly embroidered red cloak. This lot wore plain ragged linen shirts and canvas doublets, knee-long breeches or baggy trousers, strapped sandals, and leather boots. Some were barefooted, just like Kamolea was. Their fierce, proud, derisive eyes, which conveyed the message that no other law existed but the one they had chosen to obey, reminded him of his tribesmen.

He did not understand the conversation that flowed, but it was obviously something funny, for they were all laughing their heads off, shaking and clutching their bellies, even bent double and gasping for breath. Ron O'Reilly pointed at Kamolea's skinny biceps and cried,

"Look at these bulging muscles! So strong and healthy, as he is, he'll do the job! But what about his ribs? They're about to split his skin open."

"Pretty handsome, curly lad, I'd say!" panted Alfonso.

"Wanna become a privateer?" cried Hugo the Dagger, taking over the roars of the others. "It's a lot of fun, you'll see! Rum, lasses, and booty all day long! But first, get your sea legs, matey!"

The long period of starvation had sapped Kamolea's strength, and his muscles had disappeared, so his boyish body had become ridiculously skinny. Now he looked so grotesque that the pirates were dying with delight. He jumped and spun, following the direction of the shouting, a stupid smile plastered across his face, his white teeth flashing against his dark skin, his eyes darting from one man to another, and his curly head swinging comically atop his long neck.

Suddenly, a gunshot rang out, and Captain Gonzalez's voice thundered:

"Avast!" All the men shut up and parted. "Aye, caramba! Who's in charge here, you scallywags?"

"Cap'n Gonzalez forever!" roared back the crew.

"Bring the monkey before your Cap'n then!"

Santiago and Andreas grabbed Kamolea and tossed him at Gonzalez's feet. Captain Gonzalez was a huge man. Long black locks spilled over his mighty shoulders and framed his pale, handsome face, which was decorated with an aquiline nose, thin lips, and a short-boxed beard. His aristocratic features, which betrayed a man of noble birth, now emanated the cruelty of a bird of prey. He wore a thigh-long black coat, with two pistols and a dagger sticking out from his belt, in addition to a dangling saber on his waist. Although his black eyes gleamed mischievously, the crew was tense, clearly displaying that their captain was not a man to be trifled with.

"Kneel down!" he bellowed at Kamolea, who did not react. Tom Brady kicked his shin from behind and he fell to his knees.

"*Never kneel before your foes,*" Akamui's angry voice rang in his ears, and he attempted to rise. Captain Gonzalez yanked his cutlass free and raised it high. Kamolea dropped in response, bowed his head in submission, and closed his eyes, bracing himself for the mighty impact. He heard the blade swish, but it hardly touched him. He looked up at the towering man, who had laid his weapon upon his right shoulder.

"Men, do you see this boy?" Gonzalez cried. "Two days ago, he set a new course and predicted that we would reach land today. Luckily, I listened to him, and sure enough, now we are approaching land—you all saw the hovering petrels and seagulls. So," he continued in a solemn voice, "today I nominate you, little savage, as ship's boy and my first attendant. And as we don't know your name, and because nobody bloody cares what it is, and as you have no more brain than my favorite, sadly departed monkey, I'm giving you his name–Junu. Therefore, in the monkey's honor and the glory of our great *Rey Car-los El Hechizado*,[15] I dub you a knight. From this day on, you will be known as *Caballero Junu El Gran*,[16] the scourge of the Seven Seas and the dumbest sailor in the universe!"

The cutlass tapped Kamolea's right shoulder, before swinging narrowly over his head and touching his left. The crew burst out laughing and cheering.

---

15 King Charles the Bewitched (the nickname of King Charles II of Spain).

16 Sir Junu the Great.

"Let's make El Caballero swear allegiance!" cried Ron O'Reilly.

They grabbed the boy under the armpits and dragged him toward the captain where, across a large keg, lay a huge, bleached shark's skull, complete with a gaping jaw and two well-preserved rows of sharp teeth. Just underneath it was a crossed pistol and dagger. Dizzy and confused, Kamolea was forced onto his knees before the keg, facing the maw of the grinning beast. Somebody put his right hand on the top of the skull and bent his head down, pressing his face to kiss the weapons amid more shouts and laughter.

"Let's brand him now!" proposed Tom Brady. "Tuerto, bring the brazier!"

"My pleasure," grinned Bobo.

"Land ho! Dead ahead!" shouted the lookout from the main top.

The men dropped Kamolea, and everybody ran to the bow. Sure enough, the hazy outline of a shore lay far ahead.

"I knew it!" cried Captain Gonzalez, delighted. "Everybody, take your places! Coxswain, steady as she goes!"

He brought the spyglass to his eye, and with a thin smile, he observed the approaching land as he muttered to himself,

"My favorite cabin boy ever."

CHAPTER X

DIEGO DE SYLVA

It was a small island, densely covered with palm trees. After Captain Gonzalez ordered the men to lower the gigs, the sailors disembarked ashore and spilled across the beach to see how the land lay. Soon they discovered that the large, sandy expanse was abundant with turtles and crabs. The palm trees scattered around were heavy with coconuts, and a small brook flowed through the jungle nearby.

"Nothing more to wish," said Captain Gonzalez, pleased, turning to the crew carpenter. "What do you think, Tom? Is the inlet good enough to careen her?"

"It's perfect, indeed," nodded Tom Brady. "Pure sand on the bottom, no cliffs and crags in sight, and the high tide will haul her ashore, nice and sweet. We'll tie her to the palms over there, tip her on the port side and scrape the barnacles. Once that's done, we're gonna mend the hull."

"Let's do it then!" barked Gonzalez. "Quartermaster, we settle here. Take some hands to the ship and start discharging her. Once she's lightened, see that Andreas, Mathias, and Ron O'Reilly set the cables, so we can use the high tide to haul her onshore. Lively now; move!"

"Aye aye, Cap'n," replied Lars van Halle.

A few hours later, two boats attached to the ship's bow towed *White Shark* towards the shore, as the rest of the sailors waded through the water and pulled at the cables, crying as one: "heave-ho!" From the beach, Kamolea watched with admiration at the bulging muscles and outlined sinews taut to breaking point, as with every strain the men drew the ship nearer to the beach.

Engrossed in the action, he heard somebody shouting to his left, but paid no attention until a tap on his back made him jump. He turned and found himself face to face with Alfonso the Ladle.

"How many times do I have to call you, little monkey?" he said crossly. He jabbed Kamolea with his forefinger and articulated, "*Tu eres Junu. Tu nombre es Junu. JUNU. Comprende?*"[17]

Kamolea grinned and repeated, "*Comprende.*" Alfonso rolled his eyes. He took Kamolea's hand and put it against his breast.

"*Alfonso,*" he said, then directed Kamolea's hand back to his chest and said,

"*Junu.*"

Finally, Kamolea understood. He pointed back to Alfonso and repeated,

"Alfonso."

"Si![18] And you—Junu! Repeat: Ju-nu! That's right. See, you're not so stupid after all. Come with me, now!" Alfonso beckoned him, and Kamolea followed. After a brief reflection, he said in Tipihao's language, "My name is Kamolea." The Laddle ignored him, as he was gesturing towards the jungle, trying to explain to the youngster to go and gather woods for the fire.

When Kamolea came back, loaded with sticks, the high tide had already been retreating. The sailors had keeled the *White Shark* over and were about to fasten the topmasts to the nearby palm trees, using a system of pulleys.

Kamolea dropped the sticks at Alfonso's feet.

---

17 You are Junu. Your name is Junu. JUNU. Understand?

18 Yes!

"Go fetch more, but thicker, like this one," ordered the cook, as he showed him a short log and handled him a hatchet. On his return, he found the Laddle filling a large hole he had just dug with stones and pebbles. Kamolea helped him build support of sticks above the hearth, where Alfonso hung a kettle full of water and built a fire, arranging the logs in a pyramid shape. As the sticks crackled and the flames twisted gaily, licking the bottom of the kettle, The Ladle started chopping turtle legs, babbling ceaselessly as he did.

"Soon, you'll taste the most delicious turtle soup in the world," he said, and Kamolea grinned in agreement, not understanding a word but responding to his cheerful intonation.

The twilight was descending rapidly upon the beach. The place was ringing with the merry shouts and laughter of the seamen, who were busy setting up tents, gathering turtles, and still securing the ship. In the evening, they all gathered around the fire, and that first night spent with the crew remained embedded in Kamolea's memory as one of the best experiences of his life. Under the blinking stars and the roar of the surf, the pirates drank an incredible quantity of rum and sang shanty after shanty. The increase in empty bottles led to a competition to see who could jump over the highest flames, all accompanied by wild dancing. After midnight, the level of celebration, laughing, and shouting got so frenzied that Kamolea assumed that his new chums were the happiest people in the world. The festive mood mentally transported him back to Maniha Komo, where his tribe had performed similar celebrations around the pyre after the sacrificial ceremony.

At least these here don't eat people, otherwise, I would have ended up boiling in the kettle, he thought. The turtle broth, which was delicious indeed, strengthened his force, warmed his heart, and made him feel happy for the first time since he had left his island. And several swigs of rum offered fine assistance to the mood until, peering into the fire, content and satiated, he dozed off.

In the morning, the seagulls' piercing screams and the booming surf woke him up before dawn. His head was pounding in unison with the waves' crashes, and his dry mouth craved water. He got up, still dizzy, and looked around for something that might quench his thirst. The buccaneers were scattered all around the dying fire, snoring loudly amid rolling empty bottles, flasks, and pannikins.

"Must go to the brook; they've drained dry everything that's here," Kamolea muttered, chuckling at the memories of the night before.

It was terrific, all that dancing and singing… I'm so grateful that these jolly folks found me! He was still grinning when, in a flash, an idea dawned on him.

"Eggs for breakfast! That's exactly what I'm gonna do to express my gratitude to the men who saved my life," he whispered. He bent down and grabbed Hugo's large tricorn hat from next to its wheezing owner, then rushed toward the woods. After he quenched his thirst from the brook, he used the skills he had gained on his native island to detect the locations of the bird's nests. That early morning, he climbed a great many trees, but his efforts were rewarded by a hat full of eggs.

Happy with the accomplishment, Kamolea returned to the camp, where he found Alfonso scratching his head about what to prepare for breakfast. As Kamolea showed him his harvest, the Ladle's face glowed with pleasure.

"Smart lad." He tapped his shoulder. "Stick with me, help me with my daily stint, and I swear nobody will trouble you."

As the buccaneers ate scrambled eggs with salt beef a little later, they all praised Kamolea's wits, and he knew he had won their hearts. However, his first days on the island were particularly hard, as he understood nothing and permanently messed up in every possible situation. Most of the pirates tolerated his clumsiness, laughing and joking around, but some were less patient, and his errors were met with occasional slaps and raised voices. The physical abuse did not surprise him much as initially, he had considered himself to be a slave and, remembering the cruel attitude and constant thrashing of Tipihao's captives, he had expected to be killed at any moment. He felt, however, that something was wrong, as the sailors' behavior towards him did not befit their masters' status.

They are so cool, these guys! It's fun to be their slave! he thought. *They certainly work harder than me and treat me mostly as a friend and equal. I wonder if they are stupid or weak. They are pretty sloppy if I think about it—I could kill them all while they sleep. But why would I do that? I like them so much!*

The more time passed, the more the crew softened towards him, and the less he had the impression that he was being kept against his will, so he eventually found himself wondering what his real status in the crew was. Gradually, his responsibilities increased, and besides his chores as Captain Gonzalez's servant, he had to help Alfonso supply and prepare meals, as well as take the sailors their water, tobacco, and rum.

Several men, however, had taken a dislike to Kamolea from the very beginning, and for no apparent reason at that. O'Reilly, a red-haired rascal with a round, freckled face and small, piggy eyes streaming cruelty and arrogance, was the worst of them. He was of medium height but stocky and brawny, with impressively broad shoulders and heavy fists, the weight of which almost every crewmate had felt. Always disgruntled and ready for a brawl, he loved nobody, and consequently, nobody loved him back. When he addressed Kamolea, he did not bother even to open his mouth, preferring instead to "speak" to him with gestures. Of course, if Kamolea failed to understand his message, he would receive a swift punch, always to the left shoulder. It happened three times in the first few days, and his left arm started dangling as though it had been separated from his body. When Captain Gonzalez noticed the blue bruise on his shoulder, he summoned the crew, and after a quick investigation, discovered the culprit. He pushed O'Reilly into the center and said,

"You, scoundrel, just touch my cabin boy again, and you'll meet the rope end. Do you hear, all of you? Fifteen cats will scourge the back of the one who dares to raise his hand against this lad. Am I clear?"

"Aye-aye, Cap'n," responded the crew.

"Did you get that, Ron O'Reilly?"

"Aye-aye, Cap'n," muttered O'Reilly through gritted teeth, hate streaming from his eyes.

"Good. I won't flog you now, but I warn you that your punishment will be doubled the next time you hit Junu, or my name isn't Enrique Gonzalez Castaneda Delgado El Feroz. Back to work now, all of you!"

Mending the ship was a hard, demanding job. After the sailors cut down scores of trees, trimmed off the branches, and made logs to support the vessel, they plugged the cracks and holes, scraped off the barnacles, and tarred the hull.

Once that was done, they searched for a suitable tree to replace the broken mizzen topmast, and under Tom Brady's guidance, repaired all the broken spars and rigging.

Finally, after almost a month of hard work, the ship was mended, loaded, and ready to set sail. It was a relaxing last day on shore, dedicated to the final preparations before the morning high tide. In the afternoon, El Gabacho was honing his Spanish rapier when he caught Kamolea's curious stare.

"Do you like it?" Francois asked, grinning at him. Kamolea nodded, smiling back shyly.

"Wanna try it?" He handed him the sword. Kamolea took it, his eyes gleaming with excitement. It was a long, exquisite weapon with a sophisticated handle, consisting of twisted knuckle-bow and a shiny hemispherical cup-hilt—a real piece of work, compared with most of the short, uncouth cutlasses of the others.

"Let me see you brandish it." Diego de Sylva's harsh voice startled him. Kamolea looked up and met his mocking gaze. There was something deeply disturbing in those narrow, mean eyes. Kamolea could not understand what it was about, but it was not the first time he had caught De Sylva's stare boring into him like a dagger. His leer puzzled and disquieted him a great deal because the boatswain watched him the same way the Tipihao men ogled the young women on Maniha Komo. Only Kamolea definitely wasn't a woman. Perhaps he resembled one? Something was terribly wrong, but he could not put his finger on it. On his native island, he knew only one way of having sex, and it had never crossed his mind that a sexual attraction between men could exist. He could not even imagine such a thing—only the thought of it made him heave. Yet this look… He smiled awkwardly and averted his eyes, suppressing a shudder.

Diego De Sylva was disgusting. He had recently recovered from yellow jack, and his jaundiced skin matched his rotten, tan teeth. He was tall and gaunt, in his thirties, with long, matted hair that receded from his forehead into a tangled plait that stretched down to his waistline. His jaw was set to permanent work, chewing tobacco ceaselessly, while his jutting Adam's apple jumped back and forth. The awful smell coming from him was a cause for constant squabbling with some of his shipmates who, although not very clean themselves, felt offended by De Sylva's lack of hygiene.

"Could you give me your sword, Diego?" François asked. "Junu likes my rapier, and the timing is perfect for initiating him in fencing."

"That's a brilliant idea," grinned the boatswain. He drew his cutlass and handed it to the Frenchman.

"Now, Junu, would you like to try 'my sweetheart?'" François smiled at Kamolea's eager expression as he passed him the épée, hilt first. "When I say 'en garde,' you hold it like that. Put your right leg forward, slightly bent, your left leg brought back, your left hand raised above your head like this…"

After about an hour of teaching posture, footwork, greeting, advance, lunge, and parry, which drew the entire crew to watch and laugh, Kamolea, proud of his new achievement, handed the rapier back to his owner and rushed towards the jungle to obey the call of nature.

He found a low place near the brook and squatted. The bushes rustled at his right, and he pricked up his ears, but he wasn't really worried about what could be lurking around—living with the pirates had blunted his instincts. Yet, he had the nasty feeling that he was observed. He finished his deed, wiped himself with several palm leaves, and took the path on his way back when Diego de Sylva emerged in front of him. Skinny and pale, he looked like a ghost. He licked his lips, scratched his groin, and stepped closer to the surprised boy, his brown eyes boring into him with an insane gleam. With a brusque move, he grabbed the lapel of Kamolea's shirt and jerked him closer, their faces almost touching.

"Nice ass, hearty," he hissed. The stench of his breath was unbearable. "You shake it so sweetly when you fence, but I enjoy it far better while I watch you wipe it. Your fucking asshole… I wouldn't mind getting in there someday, you know… Must be wonderful in there."

Still clutching his shirt with one hand, he grasped Kamolea's bottom with the other one and licked his cheek, starting from his chin up to his temple. Kamolea hollered with disgust, wriggled, and tried to break away. Although he hadn't understood the buccaneer's slur, Diego de Sylva's gestures were unambiguous.

"Fuck off, freak!" he yelled in his native language. A flock of frightened birds flew out with sharp squawks, and Diego de Sylva lost his focus for a second. Kamolea twisted his body and punched him in the stomach with all his might. De Sylva doubled in pain, releasing his grip, and Kamolea yanked himself free, darting like crazy toward the camp.

Trembling from head to toe, his cheeks burning with shame, it took him a long time to calm down. He spent the rest of the evening attached to Alfonso and surrounded by the other sailors, as far away as possible from Diego de Sylva. Still, he caught his stare and abominable leer on several occasions, which horrified him even more.

When the night fell, Kamolea did not dare to sleep on the beach. Instead, he took one of the Laddle's kitchen knives and sneaked into the woods, where he climbed into the hollow of a large tree he had discovered on his raids for birds' eggs. There, listening to the rustling of leaves and the crazy concert of the jungle's nocturnal animals, he jerked endlessly, frightened by every sudden sound. De Sylva's ugly face, with his nasty yellow teeth, danced ceaselessly before his eyes, and the awful stench coming from the boatswain's mouth still lingered in his nostrils.

After some time, the darkness calmed him down, and Kamolea was about to drift off when the high-pitched voice that had tortured him in the canoe screamed inside his head, splitting his brain and making him jump.

"Such a beauty! Are you ready to get laid, gorgeous sissy boy? What a shame on the great Tipihao tribe! Kamolea, the new beginning, proud of his torn ass!" Kamolea pressed his palms against his ears. The nasty cackle drove him crazy. *"Never would a Tipihao warrior leave such an insult unpunished. The jerk deserves to die. Kill him and prove that you're not a worthless wretch! Do it right away, coward!"*

But the burning feelings of hate and shame were so strong that Kamolea lay, paralyzed, staring into the darkness with a pounding heart. That whole night, he was unable to get a wink of sleep, and when dawn broke, he was grateful that the horror was finally over.

When he got back to the camp, everybody was already up and waiting for the high tide to begin. The sky was dyed in crimson, promising an excellent sunny day. A steady sea breeze was rippling across the water, and the pirates, fed up with standing ashore and eager for new adventures, were overexcited. As the water flooded the beach, they knocked out the logs that supported the *White Shark*, and the voice of Lars van Halle rang in the air.

"Cut her loose!"

The ropes that had kept the ship keeled over slackened, and she rose majestically above the water. As everyone got onboard, Captain Gonzalez cried,

"Keep her clause-hauled, Bobo! Beat to windward! All hands, stand by to go about!"

"Man the braces! Set the fore and topgallants!" ordered Lars van Halle. "Ready for port tack! Coxswain, lee ho!"

The frigate turned slowly, her bow upwind, as the sails puffed and whipped until, finally, they swelled, catching the fair wind.

"Full sail for El Callao!" called out Gonzalez, and all hands replied as one,

"Aye-aye, Cap'n!"

As White Shark glided majestically in the open sea towards the endless horizon, Kamolea leaned against the bulwarks and watched the small island gradually fading away. The bright sun had chased away his awful memory from the previous day, and his heart fluttered with excitement at the thought of the incredible adventures that lay ahead.

* * *

A moon later, in the late afternoon, Kamolea watched the setting sun while sitting on the main topgallant yardarm. Entangled in the lanyards, he stared into the infinity, feeling happy and free as a seabird. The ship's bow hove and plunged, and the wind roared in his ears, lashing furiously at his face. He glanced to the dwarf-like seamen below and thought,

What a lucky guy I am! I'm ready to spend my entire life on this ship!

The journey was not a bed of roses, though, and now, sitting just above the main-top, the memories of the previous days onboard started swirling in his head. He remembered how swiftly his initial admiration of the ship had vanished, replaced by utter exhaustion and despair, as he realized that being a sailor was a hard and overwhelming job.

Once in the open sea, the new reality hit him hard from day one. He ran ceaselessly fore and aft, climbing the masts, bracing, trimming, and setting all tangled rigging and sails, washing and scrubbing the deck, cleaning Captain Gonzalez's berth, and helping Alfonso in the galley. And when the next exhausting day was over, and he, dog-tired, tried to get some sleep, the shouts of the sailors were still ringing in his ears.

"Cabin boy, aloft to brace the gallants!"

"Junu, go scrub the quarterdeck!"

"Monkey, off down the caboose to help with the meal!"

"Savage, bring water from the scuttlebutt!"

"Knave, up the bowsprit!"

And so on, and so on. Kamolea had no time to think—he was learning everything in motion amid a lot of yelling and occasional slaps and punches. Although he had tremendous difficulties with the Spanish language, he was a quick learner, and after some time at sea, he knew almost everything expected of him. The pirates liked his positive attitude, humility, and willingness to help, and most of them considered him to be the ship's charm. In turn, Kamolea did not consider himself to be their slave any longer—he had the same rights as the others and even better, for he was exempted from lookout duty.

The evenings were his favorite time, as, during dogwatches, all sailors gathered for supper, and the daily chores yielded to sheer fun. Sometimes, after supper, some of the buccaneers taught him pirate skills. Thus, Hugo the Dagger trained him in subtleties of the knife fight, Alfonso was his shooting teacher, and El Gabacho, his fencing master. Their lessons took place at the forecastle, where the crew gathered to watch him, and when he accomplished a sophisticated move or accurate shot, a volley of cheers and applauses tore through the air.

"I'll make of you the best dagger fighter, or, by thunder, I'll change my name of Hugo la Chica,"[19] cried Hugo.

Sitting on the yardarm and gazing into ocean's boundless vastness, Kamolea smiled inwardly.

He's so cool, this Hugo. And Calisto also, with his bushy beard and enormous whiskers… But Benito is definitely my favorite.

As he thought about Benito, he recalled their conversation from yesterday. It was one of those special days on the ship, which the seamen

---

19 Hugo the Wench.

called "Domingo[20]", when everybody except the lookouts was idle.

Kamolea spotted Creyente Benito, who was leaning cross-legged on the foremast and staring at some strange object. He was so engrossed that he did not hear Kamolea approaching and jumped, startled when the latter asked him,

"What are you doing?"

"What?" he said, perplexed.

Kamolea could not suppress a grin. He watched him and thought, *He's so funny, this Benito!*

In his late thirties, of medium height but perfectly built, Benito looked somehow delicate and fragile. This impression was reinforced by his round face, with carefully maintained mustache and round wire spectacles which, combined with his short chestnut hair, gave him the refined look of a bookkeeper rather than a pirate. These intelligent, delicate features and his unimposing physique made him look out of place, in sharp contrast with the other pirates' rugged appearances.

His shipmates called him *"El Creyente"* because he never missed the opportunity to emphasize his firm belief in God and preach to the others about the deep meaning of the gospels. Considering himself smarter and more educated, Benito had adopted a slightly haughty attitude toward his ignorant, uncouth, and boorish comrades. In their turn, they repaid him with cruel jokes and taunts, which he endured with no more than the occasional roll of the eyes and the stoic face of a martyr.

"You do what?" Kamolea asked him again.

"I'm reading, silly." Benito smiled at him. "You don't know what it is, do you?"

Kamolea shook his head.

"Of course you don't. Nobody ever reads here. Look now, we call this a book, see?"

---

20 Sunday.

He closed the book and raised it. It was black, with a white cross engraved on the cover.

But this is the thing the powerful old magician who can calm the sea holds in his hand sometimes, Kamolea thought and added out loud, "What it do, Benito?"

"Do you see these black dots on the page inside?" smirked Benito, glad of this sudden enthusiasm. "They are called letters. Every sound of our speech is recorded as a letter. The letters make words, the words make sentences, and all this is written on paper. If you could read, you would understand what a pleasure it is to discover new worlds through books."

"But what for? It's easier speak. Why write?"

"Aye, it's true, but how would you pass on your knowledge and experience to others? How would they learn what has happened to you when you are no longer in this world? There is much wisdom inside books, lad, and that makes them priceless!"

"And most priceless they are, when you're sitting in the head,[21] looking for something to wipe your arse!" called out Ron O'Reilly as he passed by with Santiago and Andreas, who both burst out laughing.

"Hey, Junu, don't listen to nutty Benito," drawled Andreas. "The more books you read, the crazier you become. A real man does not read books; he drinks rum, robs ships, and has fun with lasses. Bugger them books; they give you nothing, only fill your head with bubbles, and in no time, you'll start resembling this lubberhead."

They walked away, shaking with laughter. Benito shook his head disapprovingly.

"Do you see how stupid they are? I'm telling you, matey, books are the most important invention of man. There is magic in them—they carry us away to unknown worlds and teach us how to live. And this one here is the Holy Bible, the greatest and wisest of all books. For

---

21 Ship's toilet.

sixteen hundred years, everyone, be they prince, king, or beggar, has been familiar with it."

"Why so interesting?" Kamolea asked.

"Because it's about God, good and evil, and wisdom beyond our comprehension." While he was speaking, Benito's voice trembled, but his eyes shone. He removed his glasses and mopped his dewy face. "It explains the creation of the world, how death fell upon mankind, the Lord's commands that He conveyed to people, and so on."

Kamolea considered this information for a moment.

"Sound good. Is Kepolo there?" he asked.

"Kepo what?" Benito asked, confused.

"For sure he there," decided Kamolea. "I like read someday. You teach me?"

"It will be my pleasure, my little savage," smiled Benito. "Whenever you want…"

Caught by a surge, the ship lurched and plunged headlong, bathing the White Shark figurehead in fine spray and bringing Kamolea back to the present. He reeled and grabbed the lanyard, his bottom sliding from his seat.

"Junu! Where are you, lad? Come here and I'll spin you a yarn," called One-eyed's voice from the quarterdeck.

"He's here, just above," cried François, who was a lookout on the main-top. Kamolea shook off his thoughts, swiftly climbed down, and rushed towards Bobo El Tuerto. Lately, he had found an exciting interlocutor in the coxswain's person, and he adored keeping him company and watching him operate the big double steering wheel. Sometimes, when he was in a good mood, Bobo allowed him to try it. It was a heavy beast that creaked and squeaked, and Kamolea had to strain with all his might to keep it straight, admiring One-eyed's strength as he did.

It's not by chance that his biceps are twice as big as anyone else's; even Ron O'Reilly thinks twice before snarling at him.

"Hola Bobo," Kamolea greeted him. One-eyed flashed him a smile, his white teeth gleaming in the falling twilight. A glint of a silver chain resting on his mighty breast underneath his open shirt, attracted Kamolea's attention. As the coxswain seemed happy tonight, smoking his pipe and humming some merry shanty, Kamolea plucked up his courage and asked him something he had intended to for a long time.

"What's that thing dangling on your neck?"

Bobo chuckled,

"This, my boy, is my rainy day's insurance."

"Why, no rain in sight?" asked Kamolea, confused.

"Sink me, matey, you're dumb as a spar," Bobo grinned. "You don't know what the key is, do you?"

He removed the heavy chain and pointed to a small silver key attached to it. He handed it to Kamolea, who scrutinized it and fiddled with it, then scratched his head and shrugged, disappointed.

"No comprendo," he said, giving the chain back to his owner.

"Do you see this object here?" Bobo pointed to the key, casting a furtive glance around him, then bent over Kamolea and whispered, "Can you keep a secret, lad? I'll tell you something, but you have to promise me you're gonna be silent as the grave. Are you?"

Kamolea nodded.

"This thing here opens a chest with buried treasure—*my* treasure, matey. I'm the richest man on this bloody ship, and once we get to Panama, I'll say goodbye to all them muttonheads and leave *White Shark* for good. I'm done with all that shit, lad! And then, believe it or not, I'll spend the rest of my life like a prince, living in a palace, sleeping in a feather bed, eating fancy food, and my servants will pander to my every whim."

"How so?" exclaimed Kamolea, not really catching the meaning but getting excited by Bobo's anxious whispering, nonetheless.

The coxswain smirked.

"I've always wanted to share my darned story with somebody without being afraid that he'd stab me in the back and go find the buried treasure for himself. That's why I'm lying to all them losers that the silver key is a gift from a gorgeous señorita, who gave it to me as a reminder that I unlocked her heart. But you, savage, are the perfect outlet to pour my soul into—dumb, ignorant, and unlettered, catching little to naught of our talk. Couldn't wish for better, could I?"

"Thank you, Tuerto, I very grateful you think high of me," said Kamolea, moved. From the pirate's story, he had only fully understood the last phrase.

"No problem," Bobo chortled, "but you keep your hatch-trap tightly shut, right? Nobody would believe you, anyway." He paused before continuing. "So, at the time, I sailed with Captain Morgan—the greatest captain of all time, matey. We had our ups and downs under his command, but the raid on Panama was something unbelievable. Listen, when we took Panama, the convoy with the plunder was so long that it stretched as far as you can see. But it wasn't milk and honey, and you may lay to that. We went through the jungle for days, starving, our bones rotting under the damp and the pouring rain, and gnats eating us alive… We only slept for a few hours now and then, and the first night was the most terrible. Tough men and all, we almost shat our pants that night, as the woods echoed with a horrifying roar. We looked at each other, terrified, trembling like virgin maidens, wondering what kind of dreadful beast would jump out on us. But the next day, we laughed our heads off, as it turned out to be nothing but a stupid monkey!"

Bobo choked, shaking with laughter, and brushed a tear from his only eye. He attached the helm with a rope and sat beside Kamolea, still rocking and chortling.

"They call them Howlers, the laziest monkeys in the world. So weary they are, that they prefer to howl instead of stirring their asses and protecting their territory like any other beast. It was funny, though, to see us frightened to death of such a harmless creature!"

Although he had never seen a monkey, Kamolea chuckled with delight.

"And then, matey, we finally reached Panama City, we did. Oh, they were waiting for us, sure enough, thousands of men, infantry, and cavalry, and hundreds of bulls, and all. They bloody outnumbered us at least five to one, and we crushed them like a huddle of señoritas. I lost my deadlight in this damned battle, but it was worth it, for after we seized Panama, my pockets were heavy with gold and silver. It was a pure stroke of luck, though. My shipmate Carlos and I, we strayed away from the herd of ravaging rogues in search of some liquor to splice the mainbrace, and we came upon this gorgeous three-story house. We went down straight into the cellar, and there, instead of booze, we found… guess what? A couple of rich merchants and their families hid inside a secret chamber in the cool basement. So frightened they were as they saw us coming," Tuerto grinned in the darkness, his voice betraying a level of amusement. "Now, they had tucked away a lot of dough with them, so to spare their lives, we *obtained* that splendid casket full of gold, gems, and silver. That was a pretty convincing ransom, matey, so we let them go, with their wives and children, and all. Then we stuffed our pockets with pesos and hid all the rest, for if the others had found out, they would've deprived us of every last piece of eight and then keelhauled us 'til our entrails spilled out to feed the fish. To keep the swag to yourself is punishable by death in any case, you must know that. Anyway, we did well to hide our little treasure, for when Captain Morgan vanished with the booty, all our fools of shipmates were left only with their fingers stuck in their asses." He laughed, then added, "Damned Captain Morgan, he was some piece of work…"

"Curly monkey, report for duty," resounded Captain Gonzalez's voice, sounding slightly tipsy. Kamolea jumped up immediately, waved Bobo goodbye, and ran towards the great cabin.

* * *

The night was cloudy and moonless, and that perfectly suited Diego de Sylva. He lay still behind the coiled rigging near the capstan, waiting patiently as the port watch passed stemwards, then resumed crawling aft. Going to the captain's quarters was already an immense risk, and he realized the craziness of the whole situation, yet he could not resist.

The bloody savage, he thought, grinding his teeth. *From the first day I saw him as if a bolt of lightning had hit me. Couldn't think of anything else but his ass, couldn't sleep anymore… And he's cunning, the bastard, always surrounded by his fucking friends, always moving, and the damned captain keeps his watch over him like a hatcher over her chicken… But enough is enough. Tonight I'll bloody get him, the bilge rat. I'll gag him, tie him in the forehold and fuck him as much as I wish. And when I'm satiated and fed up with him, I'll slit his throat and send him to find Davy Jones' Locker. Then I'll find my peace again.*

The hustle and bustle of the passing days made Kamolea almost forget about Diego de Sylva's assault to the point where he didn't realize his life was hanging by a frail thread. The only reason he was still alive was Captain Gonzalez's order to move him just beside the entrance to the great cabin. There, in the remote corner below the quarterdeck, Kamolea had stretched out his hammock and set his sea chest, making himself available day and night for his captain's whims. It turned out that Captain Gonzalez had disturbed sleep and often awoke in the heart of the night with a sharp cry, imme-diately searching for his cabin boy to comfort him and keep him company until he drifted off to sleep again. Sometimes Gonzalez would ask him for a bottle of rum or send him to the galley to bring him food or some sugar to "sweeten his sour taste," as he liked to say. After finishing a good deal of rum, the captain would talk for hours, telling Kamolea incredible stories about his sea adventures, buried treasures, and the people he had killed. Kamolea observed his handsome, cruel face and nodded occasionally, but he understood nothing of his drunken slur. Gonzalez usually fell asleep again at the break of dawn, by which time Kamolea was already expected on deck, and the next long day would begin.

Diego de Sylva reached the quarterdeck's stair and skulked behind it, cursing Gonzalez in his mind. In the end, the captain had had Ron O'Reilly flogged because the latter had hit Kamolea again, and since then, nobody had dared to touch his protégé. After the whipping, De Sylva had overheard O'Reilly say that the days of the savage were numbered, and he would personally see to it.

Not so quickly, mate, the boatswain thought. *I have personal business to square with the sucker.*

He strained his eyes but could not see Kamolea. Instead, he listened to his steady breathing for a while, and the mere proximity of the young boy aroused him. A hot wave stirred up inside him, and his cock stiffened and started pulsating.

Here we go, he thought, swallowing nervously. *Now or never!*

He drew his knife, clutching in his other hand a rope and a dirty piece of cloth, all prepared for gaging his victim. Carefully, he took two steps and stretched his arm out, groping about in the darkness. Then, he stopped short. There was noise coming from the captain's quarters. Diego de Sylva quickly stepped back and ducked under the stairs. The door to the great cabin flew open, and Gonzalez shouted,

"Junu, bring me rum and get ready for a long night! I've had enough of these nightmares!"

Then, he slammed the door and retreated inside the room. As Kamolea staggered towards the cabin, rubbing his puffy eyes with one hand and holding in the other a bottle of rum that he always kept at the ready behind his sea chest, Diego de Sylva withdrew, hissing,

I'll bloody kill him, the filthy son of a gun!

* * *

The days dragged endlessly, tedious and identical. It was already a month and a half since the pirates had hauled anchor, and although they had seen sails several times, the ships were too far away, and they quickly had lost them. The headwind had considerably slowed them on their way back to El Callao, but now they had finally neared the Galapagos Islands, and the traffic had become busier. Everybody was unusually agitated, nervous, and irritated. The lack of action, booty, and women was driving the men crazy, and constant yelling, accompanied now and then by brawls and fistfights, was becoming more of a regularity. The flogging of the instigators did not yield any satisfying results, though, so Captain Gonzalez declared he would blow out the brains of the next man who dared to start a fight.

"At least there will be some action," commented Ron O'Reilly, one of the craziest men onboard.

And, sure enough, that hectic day came at last, like a torrent after a long drought. Kamolea was scrubbing the deck early in the morning when Benito, who was on kitchen duty, appeared from the caboose with a bucket in his hand. He beckoned Kamolea and started explaining slowly, gesticulating,

"Junu, take this bucket, go down to the hold, and fill it with salt beef from the second barrel of your left." He pointed to the bucket, opened the hatch, and waved down into the darkness. "Savvy?"

Kamolea flashed a smile.

"Salt beef for Creyente. Junu know barrel." He was proud that he recognized all the words of the assignment.

"It's for El Cocharoné, not for me. Hurry up, as he's not very patient." Benito moved his body, imitating running.

"Aye, Cap'n!" cried Kamolea and grabbed the bucket.

Benito rolled his eyes.

"Hopeless savage," he said, smiling.

Kamolea rushed downstairs. In the damp, gloomy hold, the air was hot and stale. It was crammed with barrels, sacks, caskets, chests, old canvas, and rigging. Below, he heard the gentle splash of the water that had accumulated in the bilge. Three days before, he had descended to drain it with Benito and Hugo, and he shuddered with repulsion at the memory of the dead rats and the stench of carrion and stagnant seawater.

It was so repugnant down there... I hope I never have such a lousy experience again. Which one did he say was the beef? Irritated at his short memory, he wandered between the barrels and stopped before a butt, a foot taller than him. As he struggled to open the lid, something rustled behind him. He turned his head toward the noise, and somebody grabbed him by the neck. A sturdy hand pressed him in a tight chokehold, almost suffocating him, and he felt a cold steel blade against his throat.

"Shh," a husky voice whispered in his ear, and he immediately recognized Diego de Sylva. From his mouth wafted the same stench he could never forget. "One cry, and I'll stick you like a pig. Easy now, my lovely, we have something to square. Don't jerk or move too briskly, will you?"

He removed the blade from Kamolea's throat and cut the cord of his baggy trousers, which slackened and slowly slid down. His naked skin sensed the hard member of the gaunt buccaneer pressing on his behind through the rough dock fabric. He desperately tried to wriggle free, but De Sylva shoved him prone over the pile of sacks and pressed his knee into the small of his back. Despite his skinny physique, he was surprisingly strong, all muscles and sinews. Kamolea's spine cracked under the force. He sensed the blade under his chin, first pressing lightly, then more and more firmly.

"Now you'll be a sweet lad, won't ya?" whispered De Sylva, his voice husky and strained. "It won't hurt much, you'll see. In the beginning, maybe..." Kamolea sensed his pants moving downward, "... but then you'll even like it..." He slowly released his knee from Kamolea's back, clutching his hair now, the blade still on his throat.

Akamui's face swam before Kamolea's eyes, full of contempt and disgust, his cruel eyes casting thunderbolts. He could hear his angry voice:

"Worthless wretch! You're a disgrace—to allow someone to fuck you like a woman! Get out of my sight!"

Kamolea felt the boatswain's naked member touching his thigh on its way toward his buttocks.

"Nooo!" he roared and shoved himself backward, smashing the back of his head into De Sylva's face while grabbing his armed hand. They rolled over, and the dagger sunk into Kamolea's left shoulder.

"Ah!" he bellowed, mad with pain and fury, and delivered a mighty blow to Diego's nose. The crunching sound from the sailor's facial bones wrung a terrible bawl from his lungs. He grabbed his face, releasing his grip on Kamolea, who jumped up, kicked him in the groin, and attempted to run, but De Sylva's hand yanked at his ankle, and he fell with a scream, landing face down. He twisted as De Sylva lunged at him and plunged his dagger into the wooden floor, a few inches from Kamolea's head. In a heartbeat, the boatswain raised it for another blow, but another figure jerked at his plait and sent him on his back. "Leave the boy alone, you fucking scum!" Benito's angry voice resounded in the gloom. "You're as good as dead when the captain learns what you did."

De Sylva rose, pulled his trousers up, and charged like a raging bull. Benito met him with a mighty kick in the groin, sending him down onto his knees, groaning. Then, he drew his pistol and cocked it at the boatswain's head.

"One more step, and that's it," he warned De Sylva. "Get up and scuttle off before I blow off your ugly head." De Sylva spat on the floor, wiped his bloody face, and climbed up the hold's stairs, hissing something under his breath.

"Are you all right?" Benito turned to the trembling Kamolea, who was in the process of pulling his trousers back up.

He nodded. In the faint light coming from above, tears gleamed in his eyes.

"Gracias," he uttered, frustrated that he could not express his gratitude properly. His look, however, was eloquent enough. Benito smiled at him and patted him on the cheek.

"Don't worry, lad. Everything will be settled." He picked the lantern he had brought with him, raised it, and exclaimed, "Gosh, but you're bleeding!"

He handed him the light, tore a piece of canvas, and fastened it firmly around Kamolea's shoulder.

"It's gonna hurt a bit," he said. "Come, let's go see the captain now." Kamolea rocked his head violently in refusal.

"Hey, Benito, what happened with the beef? Are you grazing it or what?" the voice of the Ladle came from above.

"Blimey, completely forgot," muttered Benito. "Coming!" he shouted and spun around, looking for the bucket. As he turned his back, Kamolea slipped behind him, climbed the stairs, wriggled through the hatch, and popped up on deck. Ashamed, perplexed, and angry, he wanted to hide somewhere and be left alone, so he flung himself at the ratlines of the mainmast, climbed quickly up over the head of the main-top, and reached the royal yard where he sat, clutching the thick pole of the mast.

His face, lashed by the gale, burned like a hot iron. The bandage over his shoulder was soaked with blood, but he didn't feel any pain. All he felt was a seething rage and wild hatred that made his ears ring. His stomach churn, and his heart boom wildly, as the fury hissed like a poisonous snake inside his chest.

This time, I've had enough, he thought. *Tonight, I'll kill the son of a snake, and nothing will stop me.*

He shuddered and wrapped the yardarm's brace tightly around his wrist.

"I'll fucking kill him!" he repeated aloud through clenched teeth. He forced himself into thinking clearly as he tried to plan the assault.

Today he's on the middle watch. I'll lure him to the rails, then cut his throat and push him overboard. Hugo El Dagga taught me how to catch him unprepared. The moon is waning, so it'll be pitch dark, and nobody will notice. And then I'm taking on that swain O'Reilly. The same fate for the red-haired jerk—throat cut and thrown overboard. From now on, nobody will mess with me. I won't cast shame on my father and Tipihao's name anymore. No, they will be proud of me—tonight, my warrior's proof will happen at last...

The moment he mentioned his warrior's proof, the old man emerged before his eyes. He was gigantic, hovering over the water, and Kamolea watched him, confused, unable to understand if this was his memory or reality. The majestic man towered in front of Kamolea, looking menacing and angry.

"We've already been through all this," his voice boomed inside Kamolea's head. "Did you forget that I explicitly forbade you to kill?"

"I don't care!" shouted Kamolea. "And you don't exist! Scram, you bloody apparition! The two jerks will die tonight, whether you like it or not. It's my decision, and you can't stop me. For me, it's a question of self-respect. Ain't no one messing with me anymore."

The old man stretched his hand toward Kamolea, and the latter sensed how all his spite, anger, and frustration were fading away. He experienced a strange detachment from himself as though he were watching himself from a distance. At this moment, it was all the same to him if Diego de Sylva lived or died, even after what he had done to him. But there was something more, something that he could not explain for the life of him, but it was there—an instantaneous flashing of light inside him, which made him suddenly realize why it was so wrong to kill. For a fraction of a second, he understood that everyone had a strictly defined destiny and that any interference in it would bring a cruel punishment on the killer.

"No one will die tonight, at least not by your hand," the old man's voice vibrated inside Kamolea. "The way you just felt about Diego de Sylva is how sages perceived their foes, and you will achieve this perfection under my training. Respect my commandments, and I will always be here for you. Promise me you won't kill anybody, and I will give you a small present to compensate you for your bravery."

"This is cowardice, not bravery," Kamolea muttered, but then his curiosity took over.

"What present?" he asked.

"I see how much trouble you are having learning the new language, so I'll open a part of your brain, usually inaccessible by humans, which will allow you to read thoughts and understand everyone directly, on an energy level, as animals do," the old man replied. "This will be a temporary measure that will make you sensitive to outside influences, to which ordinary people are unsusceptible, but it will speed up your learning skills, and in a matter of weeks, you'll be able to speak properly."

Kamolea felt his head spinning. He closed his eyes, and heard Benito shouting from below, "Junu, where are you?" He looked down and met Benito's stare.

"Come, get down!" he beckoned him. At this moment, the lookout shouted below,

"Sail ho! Port bow!"

Startled, Kamolea looked around. The old man had disappeared.

CHAPTER XI

BENITO EL CREYENTE

A mighty clamor commenced on deck. With excited cries, the sailors ran to the war chests to gather their weapons and climbed the masts to hoist sails. They stared at the horizon with gleaming eyes, licking their lips like a pack of skinny wolves that had just caught a whiff of an elk at the tail end of winter.

The ship was still too far away, a small dot in the distance, but there was no doubt: *White Shark* was closing in rapidly. Soon, they could make out the topgallants, then the topsails, and finally the hull, which was looming larger with each passing minute.

"Three-masted merchant caravel, a small one!" barked Lars van Halle, watching through his telescope from the quarterdeck. Next to him, Captain Gonzalez was guiding Bobo El Tuerto, who was at the helm as usual.

"Piece of cake," nodded Gonzalez. "Look, she's going about."

The ship slowly turned her stern towards them, clearly displaying its lack of keenness for a meeting.

"They don't have time to outsail us, the fools," said Bobo. "We're running full speed before the wind, and we have twice the sheets."

"Her name is *Santa Maria de Gracia*," said Lars van Halle. "May Santa Maria have mercy on them; they're certainly gonna need it."

Captain Gonzalez chuckled.

"Junu, come here," he beckoned him. "Strike his Catholic Majesty colors and hoist the grinning shark!"

He winked at Lars van Halle and said, "He brings us luck, this little savage."

Kamolea rushed to the mainmast, lowered the red and white crossed flag, and hauled up a black piece of cloth depicting a white shark with its jaws clamped shut across the midriff of a man writhing in pain. Just below the shark were two crossed cutlasses. As he hoisted the flag, he saw how the crew of *Santa Maria* was gripped by sheer panic. Everybody started scurrying about and climbing fervently aloft, bracing the sails. The caravel tacked her course, turning her broadside and preparing for a battle.

"They've realized they have no chance to outsail us," Lars van Halle said and passed his spyglass to Gonzalez. "Look, Captain, they have a squad of soldiers on board. About thirty muskets or so, already moving into position."

"Don't worry about them 'lubbers. We shall sweep them out in no time." Captain Gonzalez shut the telescope with a snap and bellowed, "All hands, beat to quarters! Gun crews and boarding parties, at the ready!"

With a mad flame burning in their eyes, some pirates were already crouched, hidden behind the bulwarks, clutching their bare cutlasses and daggers, the shiny steel glaring ominously in the bright sun. Others nervously checked their pistols and blunderbusses' firing pins or charged their crossbows with grappling hooks instead of arrows. On the gun deck below, the gunners were fervently hauling off the tarpaulins and ramming the guns' muzzles with powder and round shots. The artillery of the White Shark comprised thirty-six twelve-pound cannons, eighteen at each broadside, but considering that the ship was desperately undermanned, only seven of them could be used effectively in the battle. Two swivel guns on the open deck complemented the arsenal.

As Kamolea descended the mainmast, he rushed to his place under the quarterdeck and opened his sea chest, the heritage of a sailor named Diente De Oro, who had died several days before Kamolea had been found. After a short rummage inside, during which he dug out various small gifts, including three blue beads, a yellow cord for fastening the pantaloons, a small mirror, a pipe, an extra pair of shirt and pants, and a spyglass that old Calisto had given him as a present, he reached the bottom and pulled out the gift of Hugo El Daga with a happy cry. It was a quite exquisite dagger with a nacreous hilt and a shiny blade, about eight inches long. The sheath was missing, though, so Kamolea couldn't carry it while he did his chores.

If I had had it today, Diego de Sylva would have been lying with a slit throat by now, he thought bitterly and dashed back, his eyes sweeping the deck in search of a suitable position.

"Hey, Junu, over here," Benito called to him from the left, and he plunged behind the bulwarks next to him. "I was looking for you. I told the captain what happened today, and he wants to hear the whole story from your mouth. Where have you been?"

"I prefer be alone," muttered Kamolea.

"I understand that." Benito nodded and squeezed his hand. "Lighten up, matey. Don't fret too much. Everything will be all right, you'll see. Are you ready for your first battle?"

"Aye! Look what I got! Hugo give to me." His eyes shone proudly.

At that moment, the caravels' cannons went off. Two cannonballs hit the hull just above the waterline, the rest splashing into the water, unable to reach their target.

The pirates returned a gale of laughter.

"They've poked the bear!" cried out Alfonso. "I'm telling you, mateys, these guys are asking for trouble!"

"Hey, Powder Monkey, down to the hold to fetch ammunition for the gun crews!" rasped Captain Gonzalez and Kamolea flew out, propelled by his angry voice.

He swiftly opened the aft hatch and plunged into the gloom. The magazine was way down below the waterline. He took as many cartridge buckets as he could carry and rushed back to the gun deck, where the guns were already loaded and ready for the first shot. Kamolea placed the small containers stuffed with powder next to each gun.

"That's enough for now," grunted Alejandro, nicknamed El Cojo[22] because of the wooden leg that ran up past his right shin. He wiped his brow and asked Kamolea, "Stay here to help me with the charge, will you? It's hard for me with this peg leg."

Meanwhile, the *White Shark* gained swiftly on *Santa Maria*, plunging headlong before the wind, her bow aiming at the middle of the caravel's hull.

"Coxswain, hard to larboard!" hollered Captain Gonzalez. Bobo leaned with all his weight on the helm, and Lars van Halle helped him, working on the other side of the double wheel. The ship rocked and keeled over, so everybody gripped a rope to steady himself as the frigate sharply tilted sideways and slowly came about, exposing her broadside to the caravel. The two ships were now parallel to each other, rapidly closing the gap between them and creating a foamy whirl in the water underneath.

"Take your aim!" shouted Captain Gonzalez. The gunners opened the gun ports and rolled the cannons. Kamolea pushed the heavy gun along with Alejandro, who looked outside through the small opening and adjusted the muzzle a few degrees higher.

"Fire!" Gonzalez bellowed from above. Miguel the Blunderbuss rushed with a linstock and brought the slow match to the touch hole. The cannon roared, followed by several others in quick succession.

---

22 The Lame.

The ship shook violently, and dense smoke filled the room. Kamolea jumped back as the gun recoiled, his ears ringing and his head spinning. The smell of powder elated him.

My first battle! Now I shall prove myself a warrior! He wanted to cry out, overexcited, his heart banging wildly against his chest, but the moment he opened his mouth, a loud boom tore through the air, and a burst of shots smashed against the *White Shark's* hull. Splinters exploded just over the gunners' heads and rained down upon them, causing Kamolea to shriek with pain as a chip of wood thrust into his thigh. He pulled it out, still howling, the blood gushing from his leg. Through the lingering smoke that filled the room, he discerned several sailors convulsing, shouting, and moaning, crushed under cannons and lumber.

"Sponge, hearty!" cried Alejandro between two coughs. In the utter confusion that followed the volley, Kamolea grabbed a wallowing long stick with a wet lambskin on its end and frantically started rubbing it inside the muzzle.

"Enough!" shouted Alejandro. He took a powder cartridge from the bucket, crammed it inside the barrel, then added a wad of old rags.

"Ram now!" he yelled. Kamolea grasped a massive wooden staff and thrust it into the muzzle. El Cojo put in the twelve-pound round shot, and he rammed again.

"Fire!" hollered Captain Gonzalez from the quarterdeck, and the guns spewed blazing hail one after another. The response did not delay, and the rain of splinters burst forth once again. The frigate rocked and rolled like a wounded beast.

"Junu, load the gun!" cried Alejandro. Kamolea sponged and rammed again. His ears rang so loudly that he hardly heard Captain Gonzalez's order,

"Crossbow shooters, grappling hooks, now!"

On the deck above, Benito, Matias, François, and Santiago jumped to their feet and aimed their crossbows, loaded with hooks, at the caravel shrouds. The grapnels flew out with a swishing sound, uncoiling their attached ropes with a wild speed, and tangling themselves in the foe's rigging.

"Two, six, heave!" Ron O'Reilly cried out.

"Heave, ho!" echoed the others, pulling hard at the ropes and inching their vessel toward the enemy ship. As she neared, more grappling irons shot out, landing on the railing and the bulwarks. A volley of bullets met the pirates. Santiago staggered, dropped the line, grabbed himself by the chest, and collapsed on the deck along with Calisto and Hidalgo, who writhed and moaned with pain. Bullets whizzed and swooshed everywhere, ricocheting off the masts and the hull and bursting into tiny splinters.

Through the gun port, Kamolea saw the caravel looming swiftly.

"Ready to board!" roared Gonzalez.

"Stow that ramming, matey! After me, fast!" cried out Alejandro. He drew his cutlass and limped clumsily towards the ladder leading above, followed by the few surviving gunners. Kamolea hurled the ramrod away, clutched his dagger white-knuckled, and stumped along after the others to the main deck. Through the dissipating mist, he saw that *Santa Maria de Gracia* was blown pretty badly—the mainmast, broken in two, had crashed across the deck, crushing several groaning sailors. Men, smeared with blood, scurried back and forth in sheer panic. The helm had been swept away along with the helmsman, and the Spanish ship had tipped over, unmanageable. *White Shark*, on the contrary, was in rather good shape—aside from the riddled bulwarks and the several men lying dead around the waist, the damage to the pirate's ship was insignificant, and the rigging remained intact. As he noticed the fallen sailors, Kamolea let out a wail and, limping, reached midships, where the old Calisto lay prone with clenched fists. The boy rolled him over on his back, and his gray beard bristled up, all stained with blood. Tears welled up in Kamolea's eyes, but he brushed them away quickly as he heard Akamui's angry voice shouting, "Men don't cry!"

He was still kneeling beside his friend when the hulls clashed with a screeching sound, and the buccaneers leaped at the caravel's rigging, throwing over planks and gangways with cries,

"Boarders, away!"

"At'em all hands!"

"Kill'em off!"

"Attaack!"

The sight of the pirates climbing and jumping on deck with cutlasses, knives, and dirks clenched between their teeth, paralyzed the remaining soldiers, who discharged their muskets chaotically, causing no significant damage. In a panic, they drew their sabers to meet the wave of the raging bandits.

Kamolea hobbled along with the others, blood still dripping from his thigh, but he felt no pain. Hollering and brandishing his dagger, he stepped on the gangway, grabbed the main shrouds, and jumped with a triumphant cry on Santa Maria's deck. Ahead of him, Bobo El Tuerto hurled himself into the melee, wielding a heavy mace and sweeping three men with a mighty swing as he cleaved through the crowd towards the quarterdeck. Captain Gonzalez was cutting left and right, leaving a trail of bodies along his way, and in no time, the deck became slimy with blood and large chunks of severed limbs.

At Kamolea's left, O'Reilly was engaged in a furious duel with a young soldier, who yielded his sword so vigorously that sparks flew off every clash of metal. Another marine popped up in front of Kamolea and lashed out at him, his rapier flashing ominously in the sun. Kamolea jumped left and collided with O'Reilly's partner. As they both rolled over, O'Reilly turned to face Kamolea's attacker, yelling, "Savage, finish him off!"

Quick as a flash, Kamolea twisted and got onto his knees, grabbing the soldier's hand. To his surprise, the man offered no resistance, and Kamolea noticed he was bleeding from the stomach. Like a wolf sniffing blood, his most primitive instincts unlocked themselves from within, and he raised his dagger with a beast-like roar, but then he met the horrified look of the marine and froze for a second. Before his eyes emerged a vision of the same man wearing civilian clothes and taking a tiny pink bundle of a baby from the hands of a beautiful young woman with shoulder-length raven hair. Kamolea's dagger was already halfway to the soldier's throat when the voice of the old man screamed in his head,

"Spare him!"

As if its course had been deviated by an invisible force, the dagger hit the deck with a hollow thud a few inches aside from the marine's head,. In the heat of the moment, Kamolea yanked it back and raised it again, following his bloodthirsty impulse, but someone grabbed his wrist, twisted it, and hurled him onto his back. The dagger flew out and clattered several yards from him. From his sprawling position and blinded by the glare of the bright sun, Kamolea glimpsed Diego de Sylva's face, distorted in an awful grimace of hatred and spite. He clutched Kamolea's throat and lifted his knife to deliver the mortal blow when a shot resounded. De Sylva remained motionless for a second, then his grip loosened, his body went limp, and he collapsed on top of Kamolea, who pushed him aside and rolled him over. A red rose had bloomed on the boatswain's forehead, his face still frozen in the same hateful grimace. Kamolea turned around, looking for the man who had saved his life, but saw only a group of soldiers who had clustered together. With hands raised, they cried in unison,

"Nos rendimos! Misericordia! No nos mates!"[23]

* * *

Santa Maria de Gracia was a mess of crashed masts, a shattered upper hull, and dead and injured bodies.

---

23 We surrender! Mercy! Don't kill us!

"Take all the captives over there!" shouted Lars van Halle, waving towards the waist deck, and turned his attention to the several bleeding sailors who crawled and groaned under the broken rigging.

"Shoot and throw overboard all those who can't walk," he rasped as Gonzalez strode towards the two dozen surviving men who awaited their fate with bowed heads.

"Where is your captain, swabs?" he asked, watching them derisively.

"There he is, señor," stammered a sailor in his twenties, his face white as a sheet, and pointed to a body in a blue coat, rolling in a pool of blood.

"Address me as Captain, lad. Somebody else from the command?" Gonzalez asked.

"They're all dead, Cap'n," said the youth.

"Where are you coming from, and where are you bound for?"

"From El Callao to Panama, Cap'n."

"What about your freight?"

"We've got tobacco, sugar, cacao, and rum."

"That's not so interesting," Gonzalez growled. "Gold, silver, and pearls; that's what I'm after."

The young man hesitated for a moment.

"Speak out!" hollered Gonzalez. He drew his cutlass with a brusque movement and pressed the blade to the man's throat.

"Nada señor. Know nothing about that," he said, trembling, and stared down, defeated.

Capitan Gonzalez watched him like a cat stalking a mouse.

"Listen up, everybody!" he roared. "Take the captives to the *White Shark* and sweep this ship from stem to stern. I want every nook and cranny thoroughly searched and everything of value reported to me personally. You have four glasses to do it, after which we scuttle her. And you," he turned to the youngster and increased the pressure of the blade on his throat, "if you're lying to me, you'll be the first to walk the plank!"

"Cap'n, look who we found hiding in the hold," cried out Matias, pushing forward five young women and one middle-aged man. Two of the women were clad in gorgeous, richly embroidered gowns and obviously belonged to the upper class, in contrast to the other three, who wore simple bodices and skirts. The man's light-brown leather jerking was pretty chafed, his breeches worn out, and there was a hole in the lower part of his left stocking.

A simple servant, concluded Captain Gonzalez, disappointed, and he flashed a glare at the pirates who had flocked around them, their eyes gleaming wolfishly.

"Off with you, scoundrels! I said four glasses, and your time's running out! Find me these hidden pieces of eight, and fast!" he shouted, and everybody scurried in different directions. "Saludos señor, señoritas," he returned to the newcomers, suddenly turning into a model of courtesy. He bowed, taking off his hat and making a semicircle before him with his hand. "Who do I have the honor of addressing, señor?"

"Felipe de Belmonte, majordomo of Don Diego de la Cruz, and in charge of trade operations," replied the man. He was in his fifties, chunky and with a well-shaped belly. Little drops bedewed his bald head and trickled down his front.

"Just the man I was looking for! And could you present to us these splendid señoritas, por favor?" asked Gonzalez.

"Señorita Isabella Diaz de la Cruz," said Belmonte pompously, pointing to a slender beautiful woman in her twenties with black, shoulder-length wavy hair that spilled over her pale blue dress, "her cousin, Senorita Sara Pérez Fernandez," a plump, cheerful girl in her late teens made a curtsy with a charming smile, "and their servants, Catalina, Andrea and Julieta."

The women, all of them swarthy, with tightened black hair and pleasant countenances, bowed one after the other, looking terrified.

"So, as far as I have understood, you are bound for Panama?" Gonzalez went on. "Tell me now, Señor Felipe, what the aim of your journey is, and what do you have as a load?"

"This ship belongs to my father, and you, a rabble of rogues, had no right to destroy it, nor to touch our goods! Be sure he'll see that all you rascals dance the hempen jig!" cried Señorita Isabella, her face distorted with rage, leaving the majordomo with a half-open mouth.

"What a fiery temperament!" exclaimed Gonzalez, mockingly lifting his right brow. "You truly scared me out of my wits, señorita. May I ask who your powerful father is?" Isabella pursed her lips, realizing the huge mistake of her outburst.

"What is his name?" pressed Gonzalez, turning to Felipe de Belmonte, who swallowed nervously. Matias pushed him rudely.

"Speak out!" he yelled.

"Don Diego de la Cruz," he replied reluctantly.

"Very well. And why should I be afraid of Don Diego? Hey, Bobo, come here!"

The black giant approached, carrying a small metal chest.

"Look what we found in the great cabin, Cap'n," he said, grinning, and opened the lid. A pile of golden doubloons gleamed in the sunshine.

"Splendid! That's exactly what I'm talking about! Give it to me, Bobo, I'll take personal care," growled Gonzalez.

"There are rumors that a load of pearls and a sea chest full of pieces of eight are hidden somewhere," said Bobo.

"Rumors?" asked Gonzalez.

"One of the crew is ready to join us, and he's spilled the beans..."

"Bueno![24] What else do we have?"

"Nothing much. In the hold, we found tobacco, sugar, cacao, woolen fabric, crates with bottles of rum, a score kegs of wine..."

"Oh, wine? We have smugglers then? Breaking His Majesty's order of a wine trade ban?" Gonzalez cut him off.

---

24 Good.

"No, no smugglers, Capitan," protested Señor Felipe. "The wine is a gift from Don Diego's brother, Don Pedro Fernandez, as gratitude for hosting his daughter, Señorita Sara."

"Don Diego? That name rings the bells somehow…" said Bobo.

"You were with Captain Morgan when he sacked Panama, weren't you?" Gonzalez asked him.

"I was," confirmed Bobo.

"Did you hear the name of Don Diego de la Cruz over there?"

"Blimey, Cap'n! Don Diego, the sugar king? One of the richest and most powerful men in Panama. His sugar plantation was a few hours from the city, but even Cap'n Morgan didn't dare try his luck with him."

"Oh, really?" Captain Gonzalez's face glowed. "Look here, the lovely señoritas before you are his daughter and niece."

The only eye of Bobo el Tuerto blinked with disbelief.

"Shiver me timbers! If this is true, Cap'n, it smells at least of a hundred thousand pieces of eight in ransom," he said, and they both burst out laughing.

"Hugo, come here!" cried Gonzalez, his body still rocking. "You and Bobo, lock the two noble señoritas in the free berth next to Lars van Halle's and see that nobody touches them. The other three…" he cast a quick look around and called out, "All hands, come here!"

The pirates gathered within seconds.

"Do you like these lovely birds?" asked Gonzalez.

"We certainly do," responded Tom Brady.

"We adore them, Cap'n! We'll take good care of them," cried Jose-Louis, leering and scattered chortles, chuckles, and sneers supporting his eagerness.

Captain Gonzalez looked at their worn-out faces, which were smeared with blood and powder, and pity touched his heart.

"You did well today," he said. "Cunning like foxes, and brave like tigers, that's my crew! I reckon you deserve some fun now. I give you these splendid creatures as a prize for your bravery and dedication. Enjoy yourselves, you old salts!"

Wild cheers met his words, and Hugo cried,

"Three times hurray for the greatest captain ever!"

After the ovation subsided, Bobo El Tuerto and Hugo El Dagga led the women to the White Shark, as the others spilled out again in search of the hidden pieces of eight.

"You, O'Reilly, fasten Don Felipe to the foremast and beat out the shit of him until he tells us when the silver is. I hate dishonest scoundrels like him!" Gonzalez ordered and strode toward his cabin carrying the gold-filled chest.

* * *

Later that evening, *Santa Maria de la Gracia* burst into flames and illuminated the dark sky, casting bright sparkles across the falling twilight. The pirates, most of them already drunk with the rum they had uncovered in the caravel's hold, were in a great mood after finding the sea chest full of silver and the bag of pearls, which Don Felipe had handed over willingly after clapping eyes on the cat-o'-nine-tails.

As *White Shark* slowly glided away, Kamolea watched the burning ship with rapt adoration. The wounds on his shoulder and thigh, now washed out and freshly dressed, hurt pretty badly, and his ears still rang from the gunshots, but his heart brimmed with joy and relief at the thought of Diego de Sylva, lying stone dead on Santa Maria, shriveling and dwindling in the scorching flames. The blaze took him back to his native islands, where sacrificial pyres were pretty common.

May Kepolo accept his bloody ashes as a gift from me, he thought. A woman's scream made him tear his eyes away from the fire and direct his attention to the lower deck, where he could hear drunken grunts, shouts, and wails. Kamolea walked to the stairs leading to the gun deck, descended two steps, and stopped, surprised by the crowd below. The gun deck was crammed with men lining up to have their way with the handmaids. Amid the cannons and the tables, where the crew would usually eat, three improvised compartments had been fashioned, which his shipmates called fuck berths—small spaces separated with blankets and fabrics, seized as a prize from *Santa Maria*'s hold. A thick layer of the same material was spread out on the floor, making almost-comfortable beds. Kamolea noticed that the line for the middle berth was twice as long as the other two and immediately suspected why.

"Big tits?" he asked Juan Carlos, who was the last man waiting in the long queue and made a rounding gesture before his chest.

"Si, si.[25] The taller one, the gorgeous," replied Juan Carlos with a grin.

"I wait for her too," decided Kamolea, grinning back. "You last?"

"Hey, Junu, what are you doing there?" Benito yelled from above. He quickly descended the ladder and seized him by the elbow. Kamolea looked up, startled. Benito's face was still smeared with blood, his glasses askew, and he was swinging a bottle of rum in his hand.

"Why, I wanna fuck," explained Kamolea. "Big tits over there…"

"Scupper that! You're coming with me, and right now! I need a mate for a drink. Come on, we're gonna splice the mainbrace!" He yanked at his arm, and Kamolea almost fell.

"Leave me alone!" he said pleadingly. "I wanna fuck."

"No, you don't! Off with you, little fool! You know better than that!" Benito grabbed his upper arm and dragged him up, then aft. Although he looked frail and delicate, Kamolea was surprised by the strength of his grip. "I ain't gonna let you rape no one for a life of mine, or my name ain't Benito El Creyente."

"Why not? It's fun…"

"Shut up! One day, your memory will chase you and torture you for all the awful things you've done. Then you'll be grateful that I didn't let you do this."

---

25 Yes, yes.

"But…."

"Gag it, I said! Just hours ago, Diego de Sylva would have torn your ass." Benito chuckled. "Maybe I should have let him do it; then you would understand what kind of fun this is."

Kamolea fell silent, chewing on this—it had never crossed his mind to look at it from the victim's perspective. A few seconds later, they reached the mizzenmast. The rigging was coiled around the pole, and some wool sacks were piled up to protect from stray enemy bullets. Benito slumped heavily and leaned his back against the mast, grabbing Kamolea's hand and forcing him to sit beside him. The latter, still frustrated by the missed opportunity, looked at Benito and said crossly,

"Now what?"

"We drop anchor here, matey," Benito said, slurring and spitting saliva through his teeth. "I'm three sheets to the wind, but who cares," he hiccupped, then he leaned in and whispered in Kamolea's year, his breath stinking of rum.

"Listen, Junu, no man before the mast is supposed to come so close to the captain's quarters, but your hammock is hung just over there, so if somebody's asking, I've only come to look for you, right?" He gulped from the bottle and handed it to Kamolea. "Take a quaff, my curly savage. Raise a toast to your first ship scuttled and sent to Davy Jones' locker."

Kamolea swigged and felt the fiery liquid flowing pleasantly down to his stomach. A moment later, his head started spinning.

"There," muttered Benito, "how do you feel, lad? Don't fuck those whores; have no regret about it. All my troubles came because of them, bloody harlots. God forbid, what a sinner I was…"

They sat in the darkness for a while, in complete silence. The din of the party coming from below was muffled by the howling wind and the splash of the sea. The ship creaked and groaned like a living thing, and the mizzen course whipped at the wind just above their heads.

Suddenly, a woman's scream, filled with horror, pierced the night. Kamolea chuckled.

"It must be Bobo El Tuerto's turn to fuck," he said, grinning. "He terrible enough to frighten poor thing…"

"I get sick of all that," said Benito. "These beautiful, frail creatures, so defenseless… Poor girls! It's disgusting, a sheer abomination. If I were a captain, I would've never allowed that."

He took another mighty gulp and passed the bottle to Kamolea.

"Last night, I had a horrible dream. I faced a court to answer why I've killed so many people and ain't respected the Scriptures. 'Thou shalt not kill,' you know—the fifth commandment. Their spirits chased me in my nightmare. They pointed at me and blamed me for their lost lives, for their dreams cut short, for their orphans and widows. I sensed all their anguish and suffering, and I saw what their life would have been if I hadn't killed them; how many children they would have had, what joys and sorrows they would have experienced… That's why today I tried to kill nobody. Well, almost…"

Something weird was going on inside Kamolea's head. After the second swig, a window opened before his eyes, and he watched the battle from that day from afar, stunned. He saw himself on top of the young soldier from before, but it was as if he was watching through someone else's eyes. The moment Diego de Sylva attacked him, he saw this other person drawing his pistol and shooting the boatswain in the head.

"…Shot him like a fucking dog and ain't no remorse for him, the bilge rat," Benito was saying near his ear.

"Oh, it was *you* who kill the cur!" Kamolea exclaimed. "You save me twice today, then!"

"I knew he'd try again and claim afterward you had died in the battle. A flogging awaited him if you reported to the captain. I know how they think, them scum, Satan's children. So, I kept an eye on him…"

"Gracias," Kamolea said, frustrated again by his limited language.

He wanted to say so much to his savior but instead, he could only grip his hand firmly.

"Don't mention it." Benito squeezed his hand back and swung the bottle to his mouth again.

They lapsed into silence. A loud giggle and a chime of glasses came from the great cabin.

"My life is running out, matey," said Benito after a while. "I feel the cord tightens around my neck. I'm just wondering how, from a noble, educated man, born in a palace, I became a useless swab and got to the very bottom of the society."

He sniffed, took his glasses off brusquely, and wiped his eyes.

"You know, I'm a descendent of an old noble family. I was a first-born son, rich heir, rolling in dough, a bright future ahead, and all that shit. And my life? A string of balls, hunting, stage plays, sprees, and debauchery. Was I happy? The hell I wasn't. I felt like a bird in a golden cage. Too many compromises in the upper class, matey. Too many calculations, intrigues, and all that hypocrisy. Now, I ask you frankly, man to man—did we come into this bloody world only to eat, shit, and spoil ourselves? There must be something else, I say. Whatever..."

He quaffed, but this time he didn't offer it to his interlocutor, who, lulled by Benito's voice, was gradually drifting off.

"And then they fucking killed my Ana Maria... Suffocated her with a pillow, with my child in her womb. I never forgave my bloody parents. How could they do this to me? And why? Because of this ugly cow, Duchess Angelina Amador de Castilla, I was betrothed to. What the fuck did I care that she was a distant cousin of the king? Ana Maria was my mother's servant, true enough, but she was worth more than all the queens in the world. But it's my fault, all that. I knew they wouldn't allow me to marry her, but she was so dazzling that I couldn't resist..."

He took another swig, pulled his legs against his chest, and wrapped his arms around them, bringing his knees to his chin.

"As soon as I buried her, I left them," he continued after a while. "I was so disgusted by the secular life that I decided to become a monk. But first, I wanted to go to the Holy Sepulcher in Jerusalem and purify myself, so I set out for Valencia. On my way, I met some Spanish nobles, and among them this outstanding man, Pastor Mendoza." Benito hiccupped again, staring into his past, oblivious of his company. "Turned out he was traveling to Athos, in Greece. They call it the Holy Mountain there, you know… He told me he had received the Lord's revelation in his dream and followed His orders—to meet a monk in Athos, who will reveal to him a secret weapon that will help the people in their fight with the Evil One."

By the mention of the name of the evil, Kamolea jerked and perked his ears up.

"Who this?" he asked.

"The Evil One? We also call him the Devil and Satan. He is a creature that makes people do bad things," Benito finished his sentence with a mighty burp.

"What bad?" Kamolea asked.

"Killing, stealing, raping, beating, all that is bad," Benito said.

"Why, that men do?" asked Kamolea proudly. After a moment of silence, he continued,

"Why say it bad? At home, we do only that. And eating our foes, too. Is eating men bad?"

"Oh, shut up, disgusting savage! Have you done something so dreadful already?"

Kamolea shook his head.

"My father do," he said. "I not man yet."

"So, you're telling me you aren't able to recognize good from evil? Such an animal you are, you primitive cannibal!"

Kamolea grinned broadly.

"You kill, and steal, and beat, no? Benito is real man. When I kill, I real man too!"

That statement threw Benito into deep reflection. After a long silence, he said,

"You hit the mark here, my little barbarian, and I have to admit you've put me in a tight spot, for we are no better than you. We are even worse 'cause we are all aware that we do wrong, and yet we still don't have the strength to change our bloody lives."

He sank into his thoughts. It was already the deep of night, and the starry sky cast silent magic over the deck. The hubbub had calmed, and everybody was snoring, save the lookouts. The canvas flapped at the wind and the ship's bow cleaved the waves, relentlessly plunging and heaving into the white whirl. The swell was getting stronger, lulling Kamolea into slumber again. Benito finished the bottle and threw it away.

"You are so stupid, amigo. Dumber than a jib-boom… Yet I feel good sharing my damned story with you," he slurred and hiccupped, shaking his head. "Look now, this Pastor Mendoza was one of a kind. He taught me the meaning of Christianity and the wisdom of the Bible and everything. I'll never forget his farewell words: 'Find the Lord, and He will cure your wounded soul.' Nobody ever has told me better words."

As Kamolea did not respond, he continued.

"Then the bloody Turks attacked the ship, and I killed for the first time. Ah, it was a massacre, lad, and blimey, only five of us survived. They shackled us and put us at the oars. Two years as a galley slave, matey… Two bloody years of redemption. Rowing from dawn to sunset with a pack of naked, stinking sweaty wretches and the bites of the warder's whip turning into bloody grooves over our bodies. An unbearable stench, my hearty, the stink of the bilge is a fragrance compared to it. Sometimes I wake up at night, and this smell still clings to me like barnacles on the hull.

"Two fucking years!" he repeated. "And then finally came the escape. There was a Moor, a sturdy one, who somehow unshackled himself and choked the guard with his chain, then took the keys and freed us all. We jumped on the Turks and wrung their necks and tore their throats like wild animals. In short, we took control of the ship, and we set sails to Malta, one of the few places that were not under the Ottoman's yataghan.

"And we reached there, blood and thunder, but what a journey it was! On our way, we crossed a Venetian ship, bound for the Silk Road. We sacked her, short and swift, and the booty we found there changed my life forever. A load of pearls, gold, and plate was my share, and I felt free and rich like a king. And when we landed on Malta after so much time in shackles… blimey, matey, I blew all the money on broads and booze and gambling. I'll be damned, but I had fun for four, every night with a different whore, man. Fucked them so hard they had no force to get up in the morning…"

A loud snore made Benito jerk.

"What?" he snarled and pushed Kamolea, who rolled over the deck. "You filthy son of a gun. I saved twice your life today, and you dare to sleep when I tell you my story? Pay attention, sucker; there's a moral to be retained."

"What's that moral?" muttered Kamolea, rubbing his eyes. "Your story boring, and I get nothing. Speak slow, at least."

"Yeah, here is the moral," said Benito crossly. "When I was on a roll, and fair gale swelled my sheets from one tavern to another, I had this dream of Pastor Mendoza, telling me to leave Malta immediately and to sail to Kattavia,[26] where he'll be waiting for me. '*Don't forget the purpose of your journey,*' he said in my dream. '*Don't give up on your desire to become a monk and to serve God, because right now you're ruining your life and serving the Evil one. Come while you still can, you're running out of time…*'

Benito fell silent, peering through the darkness.

"And then?" Kamolea urged him on.

---

26 A small village on Rhodes Island.

"Then… the damned dice rolled, and my fate turned into a shitty mess. What wouldn't I give to turn back time and follow Pastor Mendoza's words. Often, after the next terrible nightmare, I wake up crying his name. He was the only one who could have helped me save my soul…

"But what have I done, instead? On the same morning when I had this dream, I woke up with another slut in my bed. I rummaged in my purse to pay her, and I couldn't believe my eyes—of all my fortune, only a few pieces of eight and one double *doubloon*[27] were left. I'll never forget this cursed coin, lad. I stared at it for so long that it enchanted me. And that fatal night, instead of using the gold to pay a ferryman to take me to Rhodes, I was back to the tavern to gamble again. It's just incredible how one wrong decision can change your life forever."

Suddenly, another vision revealed itself to Kamolea, who looked on in dismay at the scene before him. Benito El Creyente, a slender youth, sat at a table in a room with stone walls, facing a tall, long-haired man, clad in a black cloak, adorned with a white cross on his chest. They drank from wooden mugs, and between them, in the center of the table, lay a pile of golden coins. The young Benito laughed heartily and shook a small wooden cup vigorously, then he brusquely turned it upside down and lifted it slowly. They both stared at the six dice, then Benito lifted his eyes, which were filled with despair, his gaze betraying the pain of a wounded animal.

"It's over," said his companion. "You threw it all in, and you lost. You could have won the pile of gold, but instead, you've just lost your freedom."

"Never!" yelled Benito and jumped, flipping the table on its side. The mugs flew off, and the gold spilled on the floor. Benito tried to escape, but several men, including the one wearing the mantel with the cross, swooped over him and knocked him unconscious on the slab stone floor.

---

27 Gold coin, equal to 8 escudos or 16 pieces of eight.

"The fucking Hospitaller[28] sold me to those scumbags!" Kamolea heard the present-day Benito muttering under his breath next to him, as the scene changed. They were on a ship now, and the knight shoved him toward a richly clad man. Two sailors grabbed him and dragged him to the hold, where they shackled him along with many black men and women, crammed like sardines in the tiny space below. Then, Benito's memories switched to a sea battle against a schooner with a black flag, where rovers similar to White shark's crew boarded his ship in the same fashion they had done that morning. The pirates slaughtered most of the sailors and freed the slaves, who gladly accepted the chance to join them.

"I liked this life very much, lad; I really did," Benito was mumbling. "This feeling of freedom, to feel the elements, far from bloody society—even now it brings me such incredible joy and happiness that you are yet to discover… Free like a birdie and finally able to forget my beloved Ana Maria…"

Before Kamolea's eyes, more battle scenes played out, with Benito cutting throats, stabbing, and shooting many men. A sailor with a bleeding face was lying on the deck, begging him for mercy, stretching his arm out to him.

"*He will be judged for that*," boomed a deep voice as Benito lifted his cutlass and, with a powerful strike, cut the man's head clean off.

"It was in self-defense," the real Benito moaned, and sobs rocked his body. He wrapped his head in his hands and leaned on Kamolea, who jerked, having completely forgotten that the buccaneer was in fact sitting next to him.

They ceased talking and only stared blankly ahead. The magic was gone, and Kamolea couldn't see what was going in Benito's head anymore, but it wasn't pleasant for sure, as the latter continued moaning now and then.

---

28 Knight who belongs to the Order of Knights of the Hospital of Saint John of Jerusalem.

Suddenly, the captain's door banged open, and Gonzalez's voice rang out in the darkness,

"Junu," he roared, "where are you, bloody monkey? Come here right now, you savage!"

Kamolea jumped like he had been stung and darted off towards the cabin.

"Go fetch me rum, and quick, cause it's warming up here," he growled, staggering, clutching the door with one hand and waving the other. "La señorita would like to grease her throat. Run, curly monkey, run!" And he started laughing like a mad man.

Kamolea dashed to the hold and returned with a bottle of rum. The door was closed, and he knocked timidly. Gonzalez swung it open, bare-chested, clad only in underwear. He snatched the bottles and spluttered,

"Off with you, sucker!"

He staggered back, and Kamolea glimpsed a woman lying naked on the bed. The next second, Gonzalez slammed the door in his face, and Kamolea heard him bellowing,

"Now we'll have fun, lassie!"

CHAPTER XII

THE LAST BATTLE

Kamolea woke with a start at the sound of the boatswain's pipe. The sun rose above the horizon, telling him that he had overslept. Some of the pirates were getting up slowly, stretching their stiff limbs; others still lay dead-drunk all over the deck, empty bottles and pannikins rolling around them.

Kamolea stood up with difficulty. Every single bit of his body ached, but his shoulder and leg were worse. As he hobbled fore towards the scuttlebutt, thirsty and rubbing his pounding head, the memories of the previous evening floated gradually to the surface of his mind, and a wave of sheer gratitude towards Benito suffused him.

He saved my life twice in one day, he thought, as his eyes swept the deck for his new friend. The high-pitched whistle of the pipe shrieked again, followed by Van Halle's voice.

"All hands on the waist deck!"

The men gathered in the vast low space between the forecastle and the quarterdeck. Although still sleepy, they were in an excellent mood, in unison with the perfect, sunny morning.

Captain Gonzalez emerged on the quarterdeck, clad in black, staggering, and puffy.

"Listen up, everybody!" he cried. "Yesterday was a day of celebration. Did you have fun?"

A hail of cheers met the question.

"I gave you three beautiful young women to entertain yourselves with, but I made a huge mistake, as I did not take into account what a pack of bloodthirsty wolves you are. The night watch reported to me that Señorita Andrea, the short one with the wavy hair, was found lifeless, strangled to death. Blood and thunder, but what the hell have you done, you dumbasses? Is that your idea of fun? Does it befit us to behave like savages toward these frail creatures? Who was the mental dwarf who killed the woman?"

Nobody moved.

"Ay, caramba!" Once in motion, Gonzalez's wrath seemed to charge itself more and more with every single word. "Who was with her last night? Speak out, or I'll bloody keelhaul you one by one until you remember! So? Nobody? Who's the first to be hooked up? O'Reilly's the perfect start, I reckon?"

The menace of the keelhauling was taking effect as the sailors stirred, moving left and right and leaving in the center a group of four men—Jose Luis, Tom Brady, Miguel the Blunderbuss, and Alejandro the Lame, the latter leaning heavily on his crutch.

"Blimey, Captain, always unjust toward me!" O'Reilly cried. "I didn't touch the short one for the life of me! Have nothing to do with her death, by storm and thunder! Ask the peg leg man, he lingered with her a lot."

"Wow, wow, hold your bloody water!" cried Alejandro. "I was just after Jose Luis, and when I finished, she was still in pretty good shape."

"Who was last?" asked Captain Gonzalez.

"I was," said Miguel the Blunderbuss quietly, a sturdy man in his thirties with raven-black, greasy hair. His black eyes were permanently shaped into mean slits, and his enormous nose protruded under his bushy black beard like the barrel of his namesake. Nevertheless, it wasn't quite clear whether his nose was the reason for the nickname, or his stupidity.

"Did you kill the poor thing?" asked Gonzalez.

"I can't tell, Captain," mumbled Miguel, his stare riveted on the deck's planks. "I was drunk and don't remember much; had a kinda blackout, you know… But she was alive before, and then she wasn't …"

A wave of murmuring passed through the gathered men.

"You, stupid bilge rat!" cried Gonzalez. "You deprived us of a valuable ransom and committed an outrageous crime! I said to have fun with them, not to *kill* them!"

He bent, grabbed a coiled rope, and threw it into Miguel's hands.

"Attached this rope around your waist. I'll bloody drag you under the keel five times, and if you survive, you'll be deprived of half of your prize."

"Beg for mercy, Cap'n," Miguel's voice trembled. "I didn't mean to kill her. It was an accident."

Captain Gonzalez drew his pistol.

"Obey the order, sailor! O'Reilly, Hugo, take out his arms and bring him to the mast."

Miguel drew his cutlass, but instead of handing it to Hugo the Dagger, he lunged toward him. Gonzalez's pistol roared in an instant, blowing his head off.

"Throw him overboard!" he ordered and continued unperturbed as he put his still smoking weapon back into his belt. "From now on, anyone who touches a woman will have the swab's fate! The last night I promised Señorita Isabella that the fair sex would live in the empty cabin at mate's quarter, and nobody would bother them anymore. Am I clear enough?"

The men nodded, not looking happy.

"Now, the second point: walking the plank. Bring the captives here!"

O'Reilly, Hugo the Dagger, and Matias went to the fore-hold and brought a score of surviving sailors back. The wretched prisoners shuffled, crestfallen and despaired, but otherwise with minor injuries, as the more aggravated cases had been already shot and thrown overboard. They formed a single row on the waist, lining up abreast, their legs slightly apart, and their heads bowed.

"Come on now," Captain Gonzalez growled, "we'll do the press-gang, and Bobo will brand all who choose to join us. Shark on your breast and the odor of burned flesh in your nose—that's what I call a fresh start for a better life." Scattered chortles and whistles confirmed the captain's words.

"Right after that, we'll divide the booty," continued Gonzalez. "The quartermaster will appoint three witnesses, and everybody will get his fair share under my surveillance. All square, my tigers?"

"Aye-aye, Cap'n!" roared the crew.

"All right, then!" declared Gonzalez and turned to the captives. "The future gentlemen of fortune, who choose the life of liberty and fun, two steps forward."

Nobody moved.

"Maybe I didn't express myself properly," said Gonzalez, drawing his cutlass. "Do you see that plank over there?" He pointed with his saber to a large, three-yard-long plank attached to the bulwarks and overhanging the sea. "The men who refuse to become part of our small privateer's community will take a walk with their eyes fastened 'til they find the chest of Davy Jones. You can pray to God or your Bewitched King[29] to save you, but I guarantee you that neither one will lift his little finger for you. So, now I repeat–all future sharks, two steps forward."

Ten men took two steps; another one joined them after a short inner fight.

"Excellent!" Gonzalez said. "Go there and stay by. Now, those who are ready to die, one step forward."

---

29 The nickname of King Charles II of Spain.

A huge, burly man with impressively broad shoulders, covered by long blond hair, took a step. Four others followed, and the remaining three did not react.

The giant's bright blue eyes cast thunderbolts. Kamolea had never seen such a handsome, sculptured man. He spat at Gonzalez's feet and said boldly, with a thick Spanish accent.

"My great grandfathers were the horror of the sea back in time! They never kneeled before some miserable Dagos. You, wretches, prove your bravery and take me on in a fair fight! Man to man, and fist to fist. I stand against your depraved way of life, to the glory of my King William the Third, and in defense of God's commandments! The right is on my side, and I am invincible!"

The crew sank in awkward silence. Captain Gonzalez let out an amused chuckle.

"Brave but delusional chap," he said. "Say, my man, what kind of gringo mongrel are you?"

"Better mongrel than a Dago cur like you!" the blonde spat again.

"He is the personal bodyguard of Lord Pettigrew," said one of the recruits, waving at the last three men, who stood rooted like logs.

"Who are these jesters?" Gonzalez asked.

"They are English, Cap'n. They understand nothing of our talk," responded the first one.

"Englishmen like O'Reilly? That's why they look so stupid? What funny clothes!" The captain waited until the gale of laughter subsided, then yelled, "O'Reilly, come here and translate in your bloody language what it is all about."

"First, I'm Irish, not English," specified O'Reilly, while shuffling towards the three men, "but as far as the English stupidity, I'll give you that one." He glanced at Tom Brady and leered, giving him a wink.

The three men looked entirely out of context. The eldest, a man in his sixties, wore a white periwig that reached to his shoulders. He was a nobleman, no doubt about that; clad in tawny petticoat breeches and a sophisticated, richly embroidered red coat with golden thread and garish yellow buttons. The other two were considerably younger, and their simple, worn clothes betrayed their servants' status.

O'Reilly struck up a chat with the youngest.

"This is Lord Pettigrew with his two attendants," he reported to Gonzalez. "They are bound for Portobello, where a ship for London awaits them. The Lord promised us five hundred golden guineas as a ransom for them three."

"Where's the money?" growled Gonzalez.

"He has a man of confidence on the ship in Portobello who keeps it for him."

Gonzalez contemplated for a minute.

"Only we ain't going to Portobello; it's on the other ocean. Did you search His Lordship properly? He must've had some pieces of eight with him."

"I ransacked them thoroughly, Cap'n; turned their pockets upside-down, didn't find a dime," said Jose Luis, a handsome young man with a motley bandana tightened over his head.

"Well, that's a pity," shrugged Gonzalez. He approached them slowly, his eyes gleaming mischievously. "Ask them for the last time, O'Reilly: where are their belongings?"

"They are all gone with the destroyed ship, Cap'n," translated O'Reilly, as Lord Pettigrew nodded vigorously in confirmation.

"Convincing and very convenient," said Gonzalez, "but his lordship's wig is slightly askew."

He took a step forward, grabbed Lord Pettigrew's wig, and jerked it from his head. Lord Pettigrew's bald head shone in the bright sun, revealing a leather purse glued on the top of his crown.

"I think we don't need to go as far as Portobello," the captain cried, and with one strike of the blunt edge of his cutlass, he knocked the purse off the man's head. It landed at Tom Brady's feet, who swooped on it like a bird of prey and fervently detached it.

"Gold guineas!" he shouted and lifted a coin in the air. The pirates all cheered back.

"Give it to the quartermaster to put it with the plunder!" ordered Gonzalez. "We'll send Lord Pettigrew and his servants into the hold to keep Señor Belmonte company. Considering his lordship's higher rank, I reckon he can do better than this with the ransom. As for the others, let's have fun now. All you rookies, show us what you're capable of! Make these fools walk the plank. Bare hands only, no weapons allowed. Eleven to five! Give us good entertainment, go!"

After brief hesitation and quick gesticulation, six of the future pirates swooped over the blond giant as the others attacked the others in single combat. The blond met the first of his attackers with a mighty uppercut, and he flew backward, felling two others in the process. A kick to the groin made the next one double up with pain. Quick as a flash, Lord Pettigrew's bodyguard grabbed him and hurled him against the rest of the assailants, then fiercely started kicking and punching everybody who was already on the ground.

"Such incredible force," muttered Gonzalez, delighted. "This bear of a man is strong for seven, el Diablo… Pity that he has chosen the wrong side. With one like him in my crew, I would've been invincible."

Meanwhile, all honest men had won their sparring and arranged themselves around the blond Englishman, ready to continue the fight, as their partners rolled over the deck, moaning and clutching their bloody faces.

The pirates watched in silence, impressed by the men's bravery and force. Captain Gonzalez, though, was not pleased.

"Enough! Kill them all!" he cried.

Like a pack of wolves, the Shark's crew closed on the sailors with drawn daggers and swords. The cruel butchery lasted only a minute, leaving a bunch of mutilated corpses and a stream of blood.

"In the end, nobody walked the plank, but I wouldn't say the day was dull!" said Gonzalez. "All right, drop them overboard and swab the deck. Bobo, go get the brazier!"

While the pirates were cleaning the deck, One-Eyed and Jose Luis went to the bow, returning with a heavy iron brazier attached to a metal tripod. Bobo filled it with wooden coals, lit it, and took out a metal bar shaped like a plate at the top, with an embossed shark's head. When the flames got stronger, he positioned the stick in his enormous paw, making it look like a toothpick, and plunged it into the live coals, where he left it until the plate turned white-hot.

Then, the ceremony began. The future pirates passed before a big barrel with the familiar shark's skull with a grinning jaw and the crossed pistol and dagger below. They took it in turns to kiss the bleached forehead first, then the weapons, declaring aloud that they would be faithful to their captain and crew. After they finished, they lined up before the brazier and bared their chests, awaiting the brand. As he watched them, Kamolea remembered his own initiation and realized that he had skipped the branding part himself. Afraid that somebody would remember this detail, he scooted off right after the awful scream of the first sailor as his breast hissed under the red iron. The breeze carried the foul smell of burnt flesh to Kamolea's nose, bringing flashbacks of his native island to his mind. He slipped swiftly into the great cabin, shut the door, and dropped to his knees, clutching his wounded leg and moaning in pain. The memories of his childhood flew at him like angry wasps. A huge pyre loomed before his eyes, and he found himself in the Sacred Zone, shaking with fear and staring at the flames in rapt adoration. Then, in a split second, the pyre turned into *White Shark*, burning in the darkness, the blazing fiery tongs reaching the sky. The feeling of impending doom, the same as the day of Laggi's death, swooped over him, and the familiar old man's voice echoed in his mind:

"Kamolea, go save the women!"

The vision vanished, leaving only a disquieting feeling, and he looked around. Although the windows took up almost the entire wall, it was still crepuscular inside the cabin as they sailed northeast with the sun already high in the sky. It stank of rum and sweat and something else, sharp and unfamiliar. Two empty bottles rolled over the floor, and a torn piece of white bodice hung on the chair.

In normal times, Captain Gonzalez's berth was a separate room within the great cabin, but now the bulkheads were knocked away as they were every time a battle took place, so his bed—the only real one on the ship, covered with sheets at that—lay messy and weird in the far right corner.

Kamolea picked up the scattered clothes and the bottles, then stopped and listened intently. Muffled female voices and sobs were coming from the cabin on his left. He advanced to hear better when a sharp knock on the door made him jump.

As he approached cautiously, there was another rap, and the door cracked open a bit.

"Junu?" Benito's voice hissed. "Are you there, lad?"

"What's up, Creyente?" Kamolea asked, letting a sigh of relief. "You scared me, man!"

Benito slipped inside. He was very pale and shivering, his front dewed by drops of sweat. A small tarpaulin satchel of a faded green color dangled over his shoulder.

"I followed you when you left the gathering," he explained. "Listen, last night, after I finished my story, I had another dream. We were both kneeling before my sea chest, and I took the Bible out and gave it to you with the words: 'Keep it as the apple of your eye!' And then there was a gunshot volley, and the *White Shark* exploded. We all died but you, for the Bible protected you, and you just flew up to the sky, far away from all this madness." He blinked heavily and croaked, "We're all doomed, lad, and I'm sure my end is coming. But here's the thing—when I die, my shipmates will break my sea chest in an old sailor's custom and share my stuff and all. I know the Holy Book won't be in good hands then... So take it, now! I'm following my dream by giving it to you."

While he was speaking, Benito took off the satchel and hung it across Kamolea's shoulder.

"What for?" Kamolea protested. "I want it not. I know no read. Gimme this pistol of yours, not this thing."

"You'll keep the Scripture for me until we get ashore, and then I'll take it back. No, no, don't protest! You owe me that, lad! Remember that you are alive only because of me, so you'll take care of it, right? And I swear to God, if He spares my miserable life one more time, I will immediately quit this enterprise and become a monk. Do we have a deal, Junu?"

"Aye, aye," said Kamolea and sighed. "If you insist so much, I keep it for you, I promise."

"Good… What was that?" cried Benito. A low rumble came from afar, followed by a loud crash, and the ship rocked violently.

The voice of the lookout hit their ears.

"Sail ho! Starboard beam!"

"Here we go!" cried Benito and rushed toward the door.

Kamolea followed him, dragging his leg. The sailors pressed against the starboard rail to see the ship that had just fired the shot. She was over 2000 yards away, and her dimensions were impressive, even from that distance. The cannonball that had landed near the forecastle had done no significant damage, but considering how far it had traveled, it was incredible that it had even reached the ship. The long range meant only one thing—a perfectly equipped warship.

"Look at her, Cap'n," said Van Halle, watching through his spyglass. "A monstrous man-of-war—three-decker, four masts, about 1000 tons, and at least a hundred 42 pounders. Fortunately, she's up the wind, so we still have a chance to outsail her if we tack…"

"Sail ho! Port bow, two points!" cried the lookout again.

"Bloody hell!" shouted Gonzalez, turning 180 degrees and bringing his telescope to his eye. "That's *Santa Lucia*, the galleon that chased us at El Callao. Look, she's closing on us swiftly. How did you, fools, allow them to trap us like fucking rats? Where were the lookouts? These ships were visible for at least two glasses!"

"Juan Carlos was supposed to be on watch…" muttered Lars van Halle.

"Was he? He was down here, watching the morning show! And why is the grinning shark still waving above? Why did nobody strike it down and hoist his Catholic Majesty's colors? It should have been done yesterday!"

"I'm sorry, Cap'n," whispered Lars van Halle, turning crimson. "This girl softened my brain last night…"

"Oh, you're sorry now!" bawled out Gonzalez, seething with rage. "Wait till all this is over, then you'll be sorry for sure! All hands, full sail! Coxswain, hard-a-port! Keep her close-hauled! Ready to go about!"

"We don't have time to beat to windward, Cap'n. *Santa Lucia* is bearing down on us at full tilt; she'll plunge at us bow first," warned Bobo, trying to keep port as the raised sails caught the fair wind and the White Shark floated north-west, straight towards the man-of-war.

"We have to face her and flee from this monster ahead!" cried Gonzalez. "All hands, stand by for club hauling! Get ready to drop the kedge!"

Meanwhile, the man-of-war had shortened the distance by about five hundred yards and was slowly coming about, aligning its broadside with the White shark. All of a sudden, its gunports sprang opened, and the tell-tale black muzzles popped out.

"Brace yourself!" yelled Juan Carlos, as the guns spewed out fire and smoke. A hail of splinters and iron swept the White Shark's deck, followed by the cries of injured and dying men. The mainmast cracked and fell out in slow motion, dragging the sails and rigging down with it.

"They've fired chain-shots, bloody curs!" shouted Alfonso, but another volley, this time from the galleon on the port side, drained his cry. Alfonso flew off his feet, hit by a round shot, and landed on a sticking spar, which sprang out from his chest.

"Gunnery crew, at the ready! Stand by to fall in range!" bellowed Captain Gonzalez.

"We cannot survive this crossfire, Cap'n. Let's raise the white!" cried Lars van Halle.

"Over my dead body, coward!" shouted Gonzalez back. "All hands, lively, get down to the gun deck!"

Kamolea ran toward the hatch where the pirates were disappearing one after another, when a loud moan made him stop dead in his tracks. He turned around and saw Bobo El Tuerto, jammed under the heavy helm, writhing in pain and struggling to free himself. Kamolea limped back aft and grabbed the gigantic wheel. An inhuman force filled his body, his veins strained, and his muscles bulged as he struggled to lift it. The sharp pain in his shoulder stabbed him like a knife, but with a scream, he overturned the helm and fell beside the smashed coxswain, red spots dancing before his eyes.

Bobo's face was covered with blood. He struggled to move, howling in pain, but his legs were numb and dangling off him as if they did not belong to his body. Kamolea rose to his knees and put his hand behind the coxswain's neck, cradling his head as he tried to hoist him.

"Belay this, matey," whispered Bobo. He grabbed Kamolea's shirt and dragged him near to his face. His fat lips started moving in indistinct, delirious babble. Kamolea strained his ears to catch something, but all that he got were a few fragmentary words. "Iglesia de la Merced…," he whispered, "Panama… buried it… the big tree southeast of the church… de la Merced…"

Kamolea squeezed his hand to give him courage. Suddenly, everything went black, and before him, the same window as the one from the previous night opened, just as it had when he had been speaking with Benito. But this time, he was inside Bobo's head. It was night, and the moon was approaching fullness, casting a mild glow over an enormous tree. A massive fire was blazing in the distance, reducing a tall house to ashes. Nearby, another dwelling lay in ruins, already burnt to the ground but still smoking. Watching through Bobo's single eye, Kamolea saw a bearded man, panting with the effort as he dug a hole under the tree. Close to him lay a casket gleaming in the soft moonlight. When the hole was deep and big enough, the man, whose name (according to Bobo's thoughts) was Carlos, pointed to the casket and Bobo laid it inside. Kamolea was fascinated—he was an embodiment of Bobo, with his thoughts and feelings, but a part of him knew his own identity.

Yesterday it wasn't exactly like this, he thought. Meanwhile, they both started burying the casket. At that moment, the One-Eyed looked towards a tall building with a cross perched on a gable roof, situated not far away.

"May Nuestra Señora de la Merced forgive me," he whispered, then lifted the spade and hit his shipmate around the back of the head.

A new explosion of round shots brought Kamolea back to reality, and he started, as though waking up from a nightmare. A second later, the *White Shark's* guns roared in response.

"Kamolea, save the women!" echoed the old man's voice again. Kamolea glanced at Bobo and saw the flame of life dying away in his eye.

He dragged himself to the sterncastle and tried to open the cabin next to Van Halle's berth. It was locked. He lunged himself against the heavy oak door, but he bounced straight off.

"Didn't budge," Kamolea muttered and kicked it, but all he gained was a searing pain in his foot and he fell, seething with rage at his impotence. He put his dagger inside the lock, attempting to break it, but still the door didn't move even an inch. The frightened women's wails coming from inside were getting stronger. Kamolea looked around desperately and shuffled back to the main deck, searching for something to help him break the door. Near the mizzenmast, he spotted a metal rod that the sailors used to taut the cables. He grabbed it, returned to the berth, thrust it between the door and the bulkhead, and pushed against it with all his force. The door flew open, and he burst inside. The señoritas had all huddled in the furthest corner like a flock of terrified sheep, and Kamolea's heart filled with pity at the look of their haggard faces, covered with bruises and their dirty, torn dresses. Señorita Catalina, the one Kamolea had had his eye on, was a terrible picture, her left eye half-closed and purplish-blue, her nose broken and smeared with curdled blood. The others didn't look much better, except Señorita Isabella who, aside from her torn dress that lay around the shoulders, did not bear traces of any physical injuries.

"Come with me, run!" Kamolea cried, beckoning them. They rushed after him as the guns exploded again and rain of splinter burst into the room, leaving a big gap in the hull precisely in the place they had been standing a moment before. Amid the terrifying screams of the women, the mizzenmast broke in half, and sails and tangled rigging crashed down, nearly missing them. Only three guns fired back in tepid response, and Kamolea's heart sank. He grabbed Señorita Isabella's hand and, forgetting his pain, dragged her through the mast's debris towards the midship. In turn, she clutched Señorita Sara's hand, and the two servants followed at a short distance. As they reached the waist, Kamolea kneeled and tore the huge foresail with his dagger, at the same time cutting the lanyards attached to the broken pole, thus liberating the access to the hatch. He lifted the heavy trapdoor and cried,

"Get inside, señoritas, and hide in the hold!"

They descended, passed between decks, and reached another ladder.

"In the hold? Never! It's pitch dark and full of rats..." protested Señorita Isabella, but Kamolea pushed her forward and shouted,

"Get down or die!"

Something in his intonation made the women obey with no further protests. After they descended, he rushed to the gun deck, where he found a dozen bodies, either dead or badly injured, pressed under overturned guns and piles of debris amid the lingering smoke and powder smell. Through a large hole in the hull, Kamolea saw an immense beast of a ship looming. The shooting had stopped, and he glanced around, trying to understand what was wrong. The remaining guns had been left unmanned, and sponges, rammers, and round shots were rolling around the deck.

Is everybody dead? he asked himself and rushed upstairs. On the main deck, seven survivors had gathered and Benito, mounted onto the scuttled butt, waved his white shirt attached to a broken pole and desperately yelled,

"Avast! Do not fire! We surrender!"

The other six—Ron O'Reilly, Andreas, Juan Carlos, Lars van Halle, El Gabacho, and Tom Brady—looked crestfallen and miserable. Captain Gonzalez lay prone to one side, firmly clutching his cutlass, his head lying next to his body amid a pool of blood, having been severed by a chain shot. Hugo the Dagger lay a bit further away, riddled with bullets. A sharp pain pierced Kamolea's heart as he comprehended that he would never see his friends again. But he had no time for grief—the ship rocked and screeched as *Santa Lucia* rubbed her hull against the *White Shark*. A minute later, the soldiers threw over their gangways and started boarding. The man-of-war closed in from the starboard, and its name, *Providencia,* now clearly visible, boded nothing good for the days to come. Kamolea raised his hands, following the example of his shipmates, fell to his knees, and prepared to face his destiny.

CHAPTER XIII

THE TRIAL

The dark, hot hold stank of stagnant seawater, must, urine, and sweat. The water splashed endlessly in the bilge below, the rats squealed, and stomping feet pounded above the captives' heads. They lay motionless, listening to the ship's creaking, their hands tied behind their backs and their legs bound with a long iron chain that finished with an 18-pound round shot. The rats, initially timid, got cocky over time and drove the sailors crazy. Nobody dared fall asleep, and the chain often shook violently, accompanied by a wild cry, as a rodent started gnawing at somebody's ear, nose, or toe. A sentry descended with a lantern now and then and gave them water or a piece of rusk, usually followed by a spiteful kick.

Kamolea lay in a daze, shaking from head to toe. He burnt with fever, his lips were cracked, and his face was red hot. The shame and humiliation he felt when he had relieved himself directly into his pants was a hard blow for his young self-esteem, but of course, he had no way of knowing that the urine had in fact prevented the deep cut on his thigh from sustaining further infection, thus saving him from certain death. Unfortunately, the same wasn't true for his shoulder. His shirt, soaked in blood, was tightly glued to his sore skin and amalgamated with his inflamed wound, which leaked white pus in the center and turned blue at the periphery. It worsened with every single day, as did his fits, which shook him so violently that his teeth chattered while his feverish mind wandered, depicting weird, distorted scenes. He was in the Maniha Komo jungle now, and Illima's ringing laugh echoed in his ears. She beckoned him, playfully tossing her head back, her long hair waving in the breeze. He followed her, filled with joy at seeing her again, but she disappeared between the trees. He ran, scrambling through the woods, his heart pounding with fear that he would lose her. Suddenly the earth shook, the trees swung in a wild whirl, and he found himself in a vast clearing, studded with flowers. In the distance, he noticed a silhouette of a vaguely familiar woman approaching. As she got closer, his eyes widened in surprise.

"Granny?" he whispered.

"Kamolea, what are you doing here?" Lalago gasped and grabbed him by the hand. She was in her thirties, slim and beautiful, nothing like he remembered her.

"Why are you so different?" he asked her.

"You aren't supposed to be here!" she retorted without answering his question. "Your time has not yet come. Here is between worlds, the place of the dead. Go away, get back to the world of the living!"

She pushed him in the chest, then again, harder. Kamolea woke up after a third kick in the ribs. A soldier had bent over him, detaching the chain from his leg.

"Stand up!" he barked. "Come with me!"

He grabbed him unceremoniously and lifted him to his feet. Kamolea staggered as the soldier pushed him toward the hatch.

"What a stench! I hope you all die from suffocation before we reach Panama, you bloody curs," Kamolea heard him muttering under his breath.

They walked out onto the open deck, and the bright daylight exploded in his eyes. The breeze caressed his face, and he lingered for a second, eagerly inhaling the fresh sea air. A bump in the back directed him aft, as the guard shouted,

"Keep walking!"

Kamolea advanced, shivering. Although feverish, he was impressed by the dimensions of the immense ship with her multiple high decks crammed with sailors in dark-blue navy coats.

She's far larger than White Shark, his mind told him. *Pity our beautiful frigate, though. Burned and scuttled on her turn and delivered as a gift to the sea god.* They had been forced to watch the White Shark's destruction before being transferred to the man-of-war and shoved in the hold.

The guard led Kamolea to the aftercastle and pushed him into a spacious cabin, where Señorita Isabella, her cousin, and three navy officers were having breakfast around a round table. In the middle sat a man, distinguished from the others by his splendid crimson coat with golden buttons. He bore such a striking resemblance to Captain Gonzalez—the same aquiline nose, trimmed beard and mustache, and a sharp, stern look—that Kamolea's addled brain mistook him for his former captain, and he grinned happily at him.

They didn't smile back; only stared silently at him. Señorita Sara wrinkled her nose and pressed her handkerchief to her mouth.

"That's him, Captain," she said. "If it were not for him, we all would've been dead by now."

"That's the chap with the Bible, Captain," chimed in one of the officers.

"Oh, it was him?" Gonzalez's double boomed in a deep voice and lifted his eyebrows in astonishment. "But he looks like a sheer savage to me. I doubt he can even speak properly, let alone read. What's your name, lad?"

Kamolea's grin had vanished, and he only stared back at them, his ears ringing, unable to open his mouth.

"He doesn't look well," noticed Señorita Isabella. She got up and grabbed his arm. At her slightest touch, Kamolea collapsed to the floor.

"Bring the ship surgeon, fast!" the captain cried, and the guard who had brought him ran to carry out the order.

* * *

Kamolea was slowly coming to his senses. As he opened his eyes, he ascertained he was again in the dark hold, chained between the French and Juan Carlos. He felt much better now—the fever had gone, and his head was clear again. A fresh bandage was tightened around his cleaned wounds, and although he was exhausted, he was hungry for the first time in many days.

He sat up, listening to the even breathing of the surrounding men. A mighty fart came from behind him, adding its contribution to the awful stench. O'Reilly was snoring loudly at the front end of the chain, letting out grunting sounds at equal intervals.

Kamolea hesitated for a moment, then plucked up his courage and whispered, "Benito?"

Nobody responded.

"Benito! Are you alive?" he said aloud.

Somebody stirred. "Junu? Thank God! Are you all right, matey? We'd given up on you; nobody believed you would survive," came Benito's voice behind him.

"Survive!" snorted Andreas somewhere ahead. "What's the point of surviving only to be hanged like a dog?"

"Always keep a tiny spark of gleaming hope in your hearts," said Benito in a singsong manner.

"The hell I will do," grunted Tom Brady. "I bet my worn boots that they bring us to Panama, and believe me, there will be no quarter for us."

"Aye, if even a tenth of all the stories that El Tuerto told us about the raid of Captain Morgan are true, they won't meet us with hugs and flowers, for sure," bemoaned Juan Carlos.

"Nah, they'd rather invite us to dance the hempen jig. Just the thought of it makes my neck stiff," muttered François.

"Hey, do you hear that?" said Lars van Halle. Everybody strained their ears. The monotone of the splashing water had diminished, and the creaking of the hull had almost stopped. There was only one explanation—the ship was coming to a halt. And sure enough, a while later, the chain of the anchor rattled, followed by a big splash. The hatch above banged open, and several soldiers came down, barking orders and kicking them to rise.

The pirates climbed the ladder to the open deck, their aching limbs exuding stiffness. Their legs were still chained together, and their hands bound with ropes. It was about noon, and a thick layer of white cloud covered the sky. The canvas whipped on the steady breeze as the sailors hauled them down. On deck was a flurry of scurrying, climbing, yelling men. The pipe whistled sharply, and the drums started beating at an even pace.

"Fall in!" shouted a tall officer, and the soldiers formed in two rows.

The pirates remain near the bulwarks on the port side, surrounded by several guards. They filled their lungs with the fresh sea air and watched the breathtaking scenery with an inner darkness, knowing that nothing bode well for them in the days to come.

Providence had just dropped anchor in the picturesque Panama bay, where several more ships were moored, including *Santa Lucia*. In the distance, hazy, low spreading mountains outlined against the sky, reminding Kamolea of his native island. In the bosom of a considerably closer, steep green hill, scores of beautiful buildings with red, pointed roofs huddled together. The dwellings were scattered all around the shore, reaching down to a small peninsula that jutted out into the sea. The city was surrounded by solid stone walls from which black cannons menacingly stuck out their barrels from large embrasures. Several pointed sentry boxes with flapping banners towered over the water.

Kamolea noticed many boats bobbing at anchor on the rippling sea's surface beneath the walls. As he compared their different seizes, several men emerged from the fortification gate, embarked in a gig, and rowed in the ship's direction. Soon, two of them, clad in red uniforms, climbed the wooden ladder and got on board. They saluted the captain and handed him a roll of paper, then they all disappeared into the great cabin. A while later, they came back, and the captain cried,

"Lower the pinnaces and take the pirates to the garrison! We'll stay for a week ashore. Have fun and make sure not to miss the hanging ceremony—it's gonna take place two or three days from now, so listen to the public crier's announcement. And go easy on the booze and whores, as next Monday at sunrise, I'll be mustering everybody onboard, rested and in top shape. Understood?"

"Aye, aye, Capitan!" bellowed the sailors as one, and then they hustled to lower the boats.

"No more than two captives by boat," ordered the officer who had come from the fortress.

"They were all chained together, colonel," said a guard.

"Then unchain them and put them in individual handcuffs and leg manacles. We brought enough shackles over there," said the colonel, waving towards a heap of iron.

The soldier took out a big black key, bent, and fiddled with the massive padlock for a moment. As the chain dropped loose, he removed the large round shackles that had been tightened around the pirates' ankles, while another marine cut the ropes behind their wrists. The moment he felt free, François delivered a heavy blow to the temple of the soldier who was still squatting over the chain, and the latter slumped on deck without letting out a sound. Under everyone's stunned gaze, in two mighty leaps, El Gabacho reached the bulwarks and jumped overboard, headfirst. A volley of muskets followed his splash into the water below, but the Frenchman disappeared under the water, and, although they searched a full glass of time for him, he had vanished without a trace, so they eventually gave up.

* * *

The gig glided swiftly towards the shore. Kamolea and Andreas were in the middle, their hands and legs in chains, between two sturdy young Spanish men, who had their pistols pointed against the captives' heads. Two other soldiers leaned hard on the oars, keeping up with the other boats. They all reached the shore simultaneously and disembarked on the rocky coast. After the pirates were put in rows two by two and surrounded by guards, they passed through a small wicket gate, walked several yards through a narrow passage with the stone walls on either side, and emerged onto a paved street, flanked by gorgeous two- and three-story houses. As he saw them, Kamolea let out a gasp. Despite his pain and the miserable situation in which he was caught, he gaped with sheer admiration, and his eyes grew wider to take in the large buildings, painted in bright colors and covered with porticos, arches, and colorful glass. The balconies were adorned with flowers and marble balustrades, and the red gabled roofs, the massive doors, even the metal bars on the windows, were all little wonders for him. While he shuffled on, puzzled about why his shipmates did not seem to be particularly impressed by Panama's beauty, the rumor about the captured pirates had spread like wildfire around the city, and within minutes it was crammed with people, curious to see the procession. The crowd spilled out onto the streets, overflowing within every space, terrace, and window. Men, women, and children shouted, cursed, and shook their fists; some even threw stones, eggs, and rotten fruit at them. Several times, young men jumped out at the pirates with cudgels, and only the surrounding soldiers saved them from being completely mangled.

Such a motley throng, Kamolea thought, delighted by the women, clad in their long, sophisticated dresses. He fixed his eyes on a beautiful young girl in a white bodice and pale blue skirt, but his reverie was interrupted by a rotten tomato hitting his cheek. He jumped, startled, trod on O'Reilly's foot, and felt his mighty push at his back. As he sprang off, he looked up and exclaimed,

"Almighty Kepolo, what is this?"

An enormous building of cut stones and bricks towered high in the sky. Two pairs of columns decorated the walls and flanked a large arch-shaped door. Kamolea gaped at the triangle gable, outlined against the sky, with a large circle in the middle from which a statue of a man looked down on the passengers. Atop the building shone a massive cross, similar to the one he had seen in the hand of the old man. As he looked up at the building, he felt small and insignificant like a fly, just as he had done on the day of his warrior's proof.

"Hey, Benito, what's this thing?" he asked, lifting his chained hands and brushing morsels of tomato from his cheek.

"What?" Benito turned around to face him. He represented a pitiful picture with his glasses askew, his face and clothes all stained, and the yolk of an egg slowly running down his chin.

Kamolea motioned with his head toward the building that they were passing by.

"Can't you read the inscription?" Benito glanced towards the building and rolled his eyes. "Of course you can't, savage. It's a temple, silly. The Lord's home. We don't worship trees, like you cannibals…"

"Silence!" shouted the guard and hit Benito on the shoulder with the butt of his musket. The latter cried out with pain and quickly turned around.

At that moment, Juan Carlos, who was last in the row, slumped down to his knees. The guard next to him kicked him in the ribs, yelling,

"Get up!" but he did not budge. The officer in charge squatted and put his hand on the pirate's face.

"He's burning with fever," he said. "Take him to the infirmary, but I won't bet my boots on his life."

The procession resumed, passed by the long brick fence surrounding the Santo Domingo convent, and turned right. After a few blocks, the beautiful houses disappeared, and they reached a vast paved square with a long, rectangular two-story building on the left, on top of which His Majesty's red and white colors whipped proudly in the sea breeze. Kamolea realized that they were headed toward the city's southern extremity, which was actually the fortified peninsula that stuck out into the sea. At the end of the extensive building was an adjoining stone one-story extension with metal bars on every orifice. The captives entered there, passed through a long corridor, halted before a solid oak door reinforced with a metal grill that rattled ominously as the guard opened it, and finally entered a dark room with only one small window near the ceiling. It stank of mold, piss, and excrement. The bare floor was covered with a bit of straw, and a bucket in the left corner marked the spot where they should see to their needs. At their appearance, rats and mice scurried around in all directions with loud squeals.

Shaggy and bloodstained, their wounded bodies hardly covered with tattered rags, the buccaneers collapsed on the filthy floor and fell into desperate silence.

After a while, O'Reilly spoke.

"I'm hungry as hell, mateys. If these bloody wretches don't fetch me something to eat, I'll rip the savage's throat and eat his heart while it's still pulsating. You did the same things on your island, didn't you, dunce?"

Kamolea shuddered with disgust at the memory of Akamui, smeared in blood and eating the heart of a Torago warrior. The others, however, thought that he was shivering with fear. Tom Brady let out a snort, and Andreas sniggered.

"Hands off him, you red-haired devil!" shouted Benito. "Nobody touches this boy 'til I'm around, clear? Oh, you'd better laugh in your sleeve, O'Reilly, or you're gonna get it."

"Easy, you, damn chaplain," chuckled O'Reilly. "Am I a savage like him to do such disgusting things? Just joking around, ain't I? But hear me out now, for I'm deadly serious: I won't let them hang me like the last bilge-sucking swab. So, let's scuttle that and be over, and that's all I'm saying."

"And how exactly are we gonna do that?" mockingly asked Andreas, a short young man with a round face and a thin, mossy mustache.

"Right, come over here, mateys, and I show you how," O'Reilly sniggered.

They sat in a tight circle, their heads close together, almost touching. O'Reilly cast a furtive glance around the room and said in a harsh whisper,

"You listen to the old Ron, and he'll let you all off the hook, right? Now, look at this."

He brought his chained hands to his dingy bandana, which had been bleached by the sun, and took it off. Then, like a magician, he conjured from behind his ear a small piece of wire that was painted the exact color of his ginger hair. The wire had a half-circle loop at one end and a slight hook-like curve on the other. The materialization of the metal line provoked muffled exclamations and great agitation. Kamolea could not understand why this weird object brought so much joy to his shipmates, but judging by their gleaming eyes, the thirst for life had returned to them.

"What's the fuss?" he asked Benito, who smiled.

"Well, with a little luck, that thing could unlock these shackles."

"But how…" began Kamolea, but Benito shut him up with an imperial gesture. The others let out joyful cries again as Lars van Halle produced a small clasp knife.

"Do you remember the lad who Gabacho knocked out? Well, in the commotion that followed, I rummaged him a bit," he said.

"So, what are we waiting for, then?" O'Reilly's eyes shone with an insane flame. "Let's make it happen, shall we? Beat it tonight. Here's my plan, short and sweet. The savage is gonna lie down and feign death, right? Soon, they're gonna bring us some grub, so they'll come in to check what's wrong with him. As they get in, we swoop on them and kill 'em all. Then we put their uniforms on and run away. It's child play, see? I did that before, in Portobello, and it worked—why wouldn't I do it again? What do you say?"

"Count me in! We've got nothing to lose, anyway," said Andreas.

"Let's get out of this dungeon!" said Tom Brady excitedly.

"I won't lay this course, mateys," Benito shook his head. "Neither will Junu. I'm not saying it's not worth trying, but I insist that first we stand the trial tomorrow and let the Lord decide our fate."

A low murmur met Benito's words, punctuated with a few murderous glances.

"Now you, bloody chaplain, listen to me!" O'Reilly jumped at his feet and spat on the stone floor before Benito. "We all know what our fate will be, so you shut up, right? I don't wanna hear 'bout God and punishment, and salvation, and all that bilge talk of yours. I've had enough of this nonsense. Where was your God when they caught you, eh? Where will He be tomorrow, when you dance with Jack Ketch?[30] Do your best, and the Devil will do the rest–that's my creed. Him, Creyente, not God or whatever! It's for us to take care of ourselves, but cowards like you would never understand that. So, you do whatever you want, but we're breaking out tonight."

"The only thing you're breaking is wind, you fools," hissed Benito angrily. "Tonight is not the moment to act. Tomorrow, when they get us to the tribunal, we need to inspect the sentries' position, the powder magazine, and a possible way out. After the trial, they'll bring us back to the cell for sure, so we'll have plenty of time to prepare for the escape."

"How do you know they'll take us back?" grunted Andreas.

"Did not you hear the town crier today, announcing that the execution would be in two days, at ten o'clock in the central square? They want to drag us through the whole city like monkeys on a chain to entertain people, that's why. So, they need time to organize all that.

---

30 To be hanged.

But they'll be surprised, though. I ain't saying Ron's plan is bad; all I'm saying is, let's do it tomorrow, on our way back to the cell."

The pirates fell silent, impressed by Benito's words. They were still brooding when the small opening in the low part of the door slid open, and a hand pushed in a jug filled with water, and a few chunks of bread on a plate.

"See? Nobody's coming into the cell, anyway," said Benito.

They all glared at him, and O'Reilly said,

"I'm just wondering what the real reason for postponing the break-out is. But let's go your way, chaplain."

"We need some elaboration of the plan, though," Benito said. "Come, I have something in mind."

The circle tightened, and their heads drew close once more, leaving Kamolea out. As nobody was paying attention to him, he went to the corner, took a leak in the bucket, then returned, grabbed a chunk of bread, and hungrily wolfed it down. It calmed his stomachache a bit and made him sleepy. The pirates' whispers rose to muffled outbreaks, but they had obviously found some common ground. Kamolea yawned, leaned against the far wall, and drifted off.

* * *

The next day, the prisoners were taken to the Real Audiencia, which was on the second story of the same building next to the dungeon. The guards led them to a vast hall with several rows of benches, and the first thing that greeted them was the immense portrait of his Catholic Majesty King Carlos II, hung on the far end wall just in front of the entrance. Below the picture stretched a long table, placed on a dais, with eight high empty chairs waiting for their masters. A man sat at a smaller table under the podium and scribbled something on a sheet of paper. The guards pushed the convicts towards the far end of the room. They walked past a dock that had been erected in front of the platform and sat on an extended bench, leaning their backs against the wall.

In the middle of the room, several rows of benches were occupied by a few people, including Señorita Isabella, her servants, and her cousin.

The young women looked haggard and crestfallen, especially Señorita Sara, who often pressed her white-snow handkerchief to her puffy eyes. Señor Felipe de Belmonte, pale and broken, was speaking with an angry-looking plump man who gesticulated vividly, his well-rounded belly jiggling up and down as he did. As Kamolea noticed him, he was immediately seized by a feeling of repulsion. The man looked pretty ordinary—medium height, almost bald, except for a little tuft of greasy black hair towards the back of his head, a short mustache, and lively black porcine eyes. Kamolea shifted his gaze and caught Señorita Isabella's stare boring into him.

What does this one want from me? he thought, trying to read her inscrutable expression. At that moment, the door on the right opened, and eight men walked in.

"All rise!" called out the clerk. At the front was a man wearing a long, crimson, richly embroidered coat, white breeches, and a matching cravat wrapped around his neck. He exuded power and confidence as he took the central place at the table. Most of the others were clad in black, sharply outlining their snow-white wigs. Last in line were three officers in military uniforms, but although they seemed familiar, Kamolea only recognized the captain of the ship that had kept them prisoner.

As everyone took their places, the recorder unrolled a piece of paper and started reading out loud,

"On the twenty-eighth of March, Anno Domini 1697, in the year thirty-six of the reign of his Catholic Majesty *Carlos II,* the Royal Audiencia of Panama in the judicial panel:

President: The Governor of Panama and Marquis of Mina, His Excellency, Pedro José de Guzmán Dávalos;

Oidores:[31] The Honorable Justices Juan Jose Fernandez; Luis Perez Garcia, and Cesar Clemente Forero;

Members: Colonel Manuel Caballero Perez, commander-in-chief of the city garrison, Captain Ricardo Romero, commander of the ship *Providencia*, and Captain Juan Sanchez Demara, commander of the ship *Santa Lucia*.

Prosecutor: The Most Excellent Señor Hugo Suarez.

Attorney-at-law of the defendants: Señor Gabriel Rolando Carillo.

"Here opens the trial for piracy, robbery, murder, and rape against five men and one boy, captured on the pirate ship *White Shark* on the 20th of March 1697 at or near the latitude of 2, North Latitude and 85, West Longitude, north-east of the Galapagos Islands."

The clerk finished and resumed his place at the table, his quill ready to move.

"Bring the first defendant to the bar," said the prosecutor, a tall man clad in black. The guards pushed Lars van Halle forward, and he shuffled into the dock. Señor Carillo, a short, thin bald man, stood aside, near to the accused.

"Name?" asked Justice Fernandez.

"Lars van Halle."

"Date and place of birth?"

"Seventh of July, sixteen fifty-one, Den Haag, Nederland."

"Freebooter then? What was your position in the pirate's crew?"

"A quartermaster."

"So, you were second-in-command of the crew after the captain, right?"

"Yes, Your Honor," muttered Van Halle.

"The defendant is yours, Señor Suarez," declared Justice Fernandez.

"Gracias, Your Honor," said the prosecutor and turned to Van Halle. "You, the said Lars van Halle, along with the other rogues here,

---

31 Judges of the Royal Audiencias.

are accused of seizing and taking by force and arms the merchantman *Santa Maria de Gracia,* sailing from El Callao and bound to Panama; and freighted with tobacco, sugar, cacao, wine, woolen blankets, and ponchos, 300 golden doubloons, 25,000 pieces-of eight and 284 pearls of medium and large size. This abhorrent deed happened on the 18th of March 1697, at or about the Equator latitude, eastward of the Galapagos Islands. Furthermore, you, Lars van Halle, and all other members of the crew currently alive, are accused of robbing and killing most of the passengers of the captured ship mentioned above, and of raping the females, one of which subsequently died. Do you admit your guilt and confirm that the crew has taken part in these abominable crimes?"

"I admit nothing," said Lars van Halle and spat on the floor. "I've never laid my eyes even on a single piece of eight, let alone the golden doubloon, for Captain Gonzalez hid everything and kept it for himself. As for the captives, I killed none of them, nor did I rape anyone." His eyes darted uneasily to Señorita Sara's bench.

"Silence!" cried the judge, banging his gavel several times until the buzz subsided. "The court calls the first witness—Señorita Sara Pérez Fernandez."

Señorita Sara rose and stepped forward.

"Do you solemnly swear in the name of God and His Catholic Majesty, Charles II of Spain, to tell the truth, the whole truth, and nothing but the truth?" asked Señor Suarez.

"I do," nodded Señorita Sara, her round face flushing.

"Do you know the defendant, the aforementioned Lars van Halle?"

"I do."

"How did you meet him?"

"He was on the pirate ship that attacked us."

"Do you see him killing or robbing anybody?"

"I did not see him do that, but..." her chin started quivering. She stared straight before her, not looking at anyone, tears running down her face. The hall was so quiet that one could hear a pin drop.

"This man beat me severely and raped me repeatedly," she said quietly at last, with a firm determination in her voice. "My whole back is furrowed by his belt. I don't know what he did to the other captives, but he is a savage, an animal, and he deserves to die for what he did to me."

"I understand your pain, Señorita Sara," said the prosecutor mildly. "Just one more question before you go, por favor. Did you see any of these other men here killing, robbing, or raping anyone?"

Señorita Sara looked at the other pirates.

"He killed Señor Davos," she said, pointing at O'Reilly. "And I saw this one killing a man too—cut him in pieces like a butcher," she shuddered, moving her finger across to Andreas.

"All right, you can go," Justice Fernandez said, taking some notes and looking at the paper in front of him. "The Audience calls the second witness, Señorita Isabella Diaz de la Cruz."

After Señorita Isabella was solemnly sworn and had answered approximately the same questions, she confirmed that the pirates had robbed everything from her father's ship.

"I saw this one shooting a sailor with his pistol," she said, nodding at Van Halle. "He was giving orders for the killings, as well. These four men are also murderers and robbers and deserve to be hanged."

Captain Romero delicately cleared his throat.

"I beg your pardon for the impudent inquiry, Señorita, but what about the rapes? There were rumors on board that all the women were raped that night. Could you shed some light on what exactly happened?"

"Well, I wasn't raped," said Señorita Isabella boldly. Sara glared at her, unable to believe her ears. Kamolea, who barely understood the young woman's quick talking, grasped perfectly the meaning of what she had said, and a faint smile ran across his lips.

Such a good liar, he thought with admiration, watching her beautiful, innocent face. *If I hadn't seen her in the captain's bed, I surely would have believed her.*

The loud bang of the gavel brought him out of his thoughts. "Silencio por favor," said Judge Garcia gravely from his seat to the left of Justice Fernandez, and he banged his gavel three times. Everybody waited until the last noise had died away.

"I can tell you that Captain Gonzalez behaved like a gentleman towards me, and he gave me his word that he would protect the other women," said Señorita Isabella. "Unfortunately, it was too late, as they were all gang-raped on the gun deck. Andrea, my attendant, lost her life that night, strangled to death..." She recited all this in the same breath, then stopped abruptly as her eyes met Kamolea's stare. Silence lingered for a while, then she blurted out,

"As I mentioned already, the other rogues deserve to die, but not the little one. He was the captain's servant and the one who saved us from certain death, freeing us from the cabin we had been locked in. He is a good boy, and I never saw him do ill to anyone."

"Thank you, Señorita Isabella," said Justice Fernandez. "The Audience calls the third witness, Señor Felipe de Belmonte."

After the majordomo's testimony, which only repeated the previous statements, the other defendants were called one by one and allowed to speak in their defense in conjunction with their lawyer. There wasn't much to be said. Benito was summoned the last.

"Name?" asked Justice Fernandes.

"Benito Ramires de Castilla."

"Date and place of birth?"

"August 21, 1658, Segovia, Spain."

"For how many years have you been engaging in piracy?"

"For 12 years, Your Honor," answered Benito.

"How many people have you killed during these years?"

"About twenty, Your Honor, most of them in self-defense," Benito stated.

"Quiet!" yelled the judge, knocking the gavel as the people in attendance started laughing at Benito's statement. "What have you to say as to why the sentence of death should not be passed on you?"

"I would be glad to say a few words, yes, but to this boy's defense, not mine." Benito pointed at Kamolea. "Señorita Isabella spoke truthfully about him. We found the lad about three months ago, lying unconscious in a boat that drifted in the sea. He does not belong to our crew; if you don't believe me, check his breast, and you'll see that he has no tattoo of the crew's totem. He was the captain's personal attendant and did all other sailor work, but he never killed, raped, or done any harm to anyone. Keeping all that in mind, I plead that the honorable jury acquit the boy and let him go. He barely speaks our language, so if he does not answer your questions properly, Your Honor should not consider his behavior as disrespectful toward the court."

"We have heard your plea. But what about you? Do you plead guilty to all these accusations?" asked Justice Fernandes.

"I do, Your Honor, except for the rape. I truly repent of my sins, and I understand I have wasted my precious life like a criminal and rascal. May God forgive me! I'm ready to meet my fate."

"All right, retake your seat," said the judge. "Bring the boy to testify!"

Benito stepped aside, and Kamolea took his place in the dock.

"What's your name?" the judge asked him.

"Kamolea."

"What kind of name is this? How do you spell it?"

Kamolea shrugged.

"We call him Junu the Savage," called out O'Reilly.

"Silence, please!" the judge said sternly. "Repeat your real name, please!"

"Kamolea."

"Date and place of birth?"

No answer.

"For how long have you been engaging in piracy?"

No answer again.

"Answer the questions, lad! Since when have you been with the pirates? What are you doing with such kind of men?"

"I'm the scourge of the Seven seas," explained Kamolea after a brief silence.

The spectators started giggling.

"Be quiet, please!" the clerk called.

"We found this bag with you. Is it yours?" asked Captain Demara, showing him the satchel.

"No, it's his." Kamolea pointed at Benito. "I just keep for him."

Captain Demara nodded, obviously satisfied.

"Have you killed or robbed anybody in your life?" asked the prosecutor.

"I killed nobody, Cap'n. I'm not man yet," Kamolea replied.

Everybody laughed again, and the hall hummed like a beehive. The judges put their heads together, discussing something.

"One last thing," said Justice Fernandez, as silence reigned again in the courtroom. "Everyone, open your shirts and show us your bare chests."

They all did as they had been ordered. The shark's skull grinned from every breast, save Kamolea's. Satisfied, the judge motioned to the clerk, who announced,

"The Honorable Audiencia will withdraw for deliberation."

The jury went out and returned half an hour later. His Excellency rose, unrolled a paper, and read,

"After careful consideration, the Audiencia found the five men, the aforementioned Benito Ramires, Tom Brady, Lars van Halle, Ron O'Reilly, and Andreas Perez, guilty of piracy, robbery, murder, and rape. Their sentence will be death by hanging and will be carried out tomorrow, 29th of March, Anno Domini 1697, at ten o'clock, at the Plaza Mayor.

"The Audiencia did not find the same guilt in the aforementioned Kamolea, and taking into account his youth, his assistance of Señorita Isabella and her companions, and the lack of direct evidence of piracy, we have adjudged him Not Guilty. However, living with criminals, being their friend, and sharing in their ill-gotten gains proves that he has corruptness in his heart, and it would only have been a matter of time before he became a pirate like them. Therefore, in the name of His Majesty Carlos II of Spain, the court sentences Kamolea to be given to Don Diego de la Cruz as a slave by way of small compensation for losing his ship *Santa Maria de Gracia*. The sentence will be carried out immediately; take off his irons and give him over to his master."

Kamolea looked at Benito and met his happy stare. He smiled at Kamolea and winked as O'Reilly grunted from behind,

"Better hanged than a slave."

One of the guards stepped up, took off Kamolea's shackles, and tossed him toward the benches on his left as the clerk handed the satchel with the Bible to the same bald chubby man that had disgusted Kamolea so much. Don Diego jerked his head back, and a burly, swarthy man with a sloppy black mustache grabbed Kamolea by the collar and pushed him towards the exit. The latter glanced at Benito for the last time, but he had bowed his head as he heard the governor of Panama saying solemnly,

"The convicts have a right to their last words..."

IN
SLAVERY

CHAPTER XIV

RAUL

—1704 AD, PANAMA, DON DIEGO'S PLANTATION.

Kamolea woke up wistful and ashamed of the tears that had wet his cheeks. At the beginning of his dream, a crowd of slaves had been carrying him on a stretcher, shouting, "Long live our hero!"

Afterward, the scene had shifted, and he was walking on lush tall grass reaching up to his waist. A handsome young man with lovely raven hair that spilled over his shoulders strode next to him. He was wearing brown leather pants but was naked from the waist upward. They emerged from the sea of supple green stems into a meadow studded with myriad unknown white flowers with delicate leaves attached to yellow rings. Kamolea wanted to ask his companion who he was and where they were, but as he turned to the stranger, no words came out of his mouth. Instead, the latter hugged him and said in a deep, pleasant timbre,

"Happy twentieth birthday, son. I brought you a special gift today."

The moment the long-haired man pressed him to his bare chest, Kamolea's heart melted, and he was moved to tears. Strong love towards this unknown fellow ran through him, so powerful that he longed to stay with him forever. He was still struggling to find words to express his feelings when the images distorted and faded away. As Kamolea gradually woke up, his eyes were still streaming, and the unbearable pain of leaving this man was tearing him apart.

He sat up in the hammock, listening closely to the familiar sounds outside. Scattered owl hoots, puny crickets' chirps, and a distinct lack of barking indicated the depth of night, around two hours from the dawn. The stale air in the cramped hut almost suffocated him after the vision of the lush, flowery meadow. He fought the temptation to go out and fill his lungs with fresh air for a moment, but eventually, he leaned back and brooded over his dream.

It's weird that this man said I'm turning twenty today. I've never had the slightest idea how old I am, let alone the day of my birthday. And he looked so familiar… I'm sure we've met before, but when or where, I cannot for the life of me remember… Pity the dream ended before he could give me the gift he mentioned.

His skin started itching underneath the two bracelets wrapped around his left wrist. He glimpsed at them and scratched his head in surprise.

It's like the shark teeth are gleaming and getting warmer, he thought. So many times, he had racked his brain in vain, trying to remember where, on earth, he had got that bracelet. At least, he could recall the origin of the pinkish one, which was made of seashells. It was a present from a girl who he had madly loved once, so long ago that it now seemed to be in another life. Maniha Komo was only a vague recollection, blurred fragments of broken memories and feelings, scattered scenes that felt like they had occurred in daydreams and nightmares. It was perfectly normal, as he had spent most of his conscious life on that fucking sugar plantation, known in slave jargon as *Don Diego's Shithole*, surrounded by wretches and sugar canes, and wishing to die almost every day.

As he swung gently in his hammock, scenes and memories from the past started rolling before his eyes. He recalled the arrival in the plantation as if it were yesterday. After they had ridden many miles north-east (actually, Raul had led his horse as Kamolea had been slumped like a sack of potatoes on its back), they had finally climbed to the top of a small plateau, where the most enchanting view had burst out in front of them.

Bathed in sunshine and surrounded by hills, a large valley stretched out below. In the bosom of the hill, amid majestic palms, tall magnolias, and mahogany trees, stood a splendid mansion, fenced by a stone wall. On the left side lay vast sugar crop farmland, pressing all the way up to the jungle. On the right, not far away from the field, a bunch of huts huddled together, and further on, some scattered long, low structures lurked. Small, dot-like cattle grazed around the buildings and a strange-looking tower rose in the distance, its four large rectangular wings moving slowly in the wind.

A building with sails? Can it fly? Or move like a ship? Kamolea had been amused back then, with no idea of the dreadful, backbreaking labor that lurked behind the walls of the sugar mill.

In the late afternoon, they reached a high fence made of sharp-pointing spikes, on top of which twisted a net of densely woven thorns. A wooden portcullis slid upward and fell immediately after the convoy had moved through the back entrance of the hacienda, cut into the logs, just large enough for two men to ride abreast. They continued and crossed a drawbridge that spanned a wide moat. It was crowded with armed men, some of them mounted, others afoot, keeping their angry hounds on tight leashes as they hurled forward, growling and snarling at the newcomers. The place echoed with shouts, curses, barks, and neighs. From lookout posts high in the trees stood guards with long guns, scrutinizing the situation below. Kamolea observed the surrounding setting with growing desperation, particularly unnerved by the raging hounds.

How did they manage to attach such wild beasts to a rope? It looks even more complicated than sitting atop these enormous animals they call caballos.[32] *These men have achieved incredible things, and as far as I can see, there will be no chance of escape with such high surveillance.* He brooded, and a foreboding feeling cut through him like a knife.

Raul took him directly to the slaves' village, which turned out to be the huts he had noticed from the plateau. The place looked deserted, as the workers were still in the field. A fat swarthy Spaniard with a whip in his hand, dressed in an open white shirt and breeches, awaited them.

"Holla, Facundo," greeted him Raul.

Facundo wiped his sweaty face, grunted back a greeting through his wet mustache, and his gold incisor flashed ominously. His mean piggy eyes scrutinized Kamolea spitefully.

"Forget about Raul!" he said. "From now on, *I'm* your boss, as *I'm* in charge of the village. What's your name?"

"Kamolea."

"Camofea?"

"Kamolea," repeated the boy patiently.

"Kama what? Bugger that name, you weird savage. Tu seras 'El Crespo,' y eso es todo!"[33] Do you like it, Raul?"

"Don't give a fuck 'bout savage's name," he snorted. "But mark my words, Facundo—he won't last long with us."

And from then on, everybody knew him as El Crespo, until he had even forgotten his own real name.

When Raul left them, Facundo led the newcomer to a thatched hut similar to those they had on his native island and growled at him to wait for the monkey man. It was dark and stifling inside, with two hammocks stretched between the supporting poles. A spare shirt and pair of trousers hung on a nail next to his quarters.

Kamolea waited for a long time, sitting on the floor and contemplating what his life would be like from then on. Eventually, he must

---

32 Horses.

33 You will be 'The Curly,' and that's that.

have dozed off, as he was startled when the door banged open, and a black giant of a man walked in. The Great Gobongo was so huge that there was hardly any space left after he had entered the hut. He looked down on Kamolea with the whites of his eyes bared, then ran his hand through his shaved head, which seemed to be planted directly on his shoulders. He wrinkled his smashed nose, and his fat lips barked something in an unknown language. Kamolea curled in the corner, numb with horror, expecting to be dragged outside and sacrificed to the frightful man's god at any moment.

The Great Gobongo lingered a bit, took something from the pocket of the hanging trousers, then strode out. In the gloom of the falling night, Kamolea strained his ears, listening to the joyful cries accompanied by the clatter of utensils outside, and his nostrils caught an appealing smell of cooked food wafting in the air. Dog-tired, all he wanted to do was curl up and sleep for ages, forgetting about the dreadful reality. Only he could not, as his belly rumbled and raged, denying him any peace. It had been almost two days since he had put a morsel of bread in his mouth. *Should I go out and look for something to eat?* He was still hesitating, when the Great Gobongo popped his head round the door again and beckoned him outside. Filled with dread, Kamolea followed obediently. The evening was warm and humid, and the heavy air promised rain. Gobongo strolled toward a big shed where at least forty people were already sitting around a long rectangular table. Next to the heated oven in the corner stood a fat black woman, ladling soup from an enormous cauldron and putting it in the wooden cups that men, waiting in line, handed to her. Once they had been served, they took their place at the table.

The Great Gobongo said something to the woman. She smiled, conjured a bowl from nowhere, and filled it generously. The giant took it, grunted his appreciation, passed it to the boy, and led him to the table, where the others shuffled to make a place for them both. Kamolea fell upon the hot chicken broth, feeling it descending like an ointment into his stomach. It was so delicious that he would forever remember the taste of his first meal at the plantation. He observed his new companions with curiosity as he partially appeased his hunger.

Most of them were black, clad in dingy rags that only half resembled shirts and baggy trousers. A different group sat at the far end of the table, with paler skin, long hair, and faces like carved masks. They were about ten men, five women, and several kids, chewing in silence, in contrast with the blacks, who were noisy and cheery, their laughter ringing in the night. They reminded him of his friend Bobo el Tuerto, and he immediately liked them.

What on earth are they laughing about? he wondered. *I can't understand a single word of their conversation; how will I communicate with these people?*

He must have fallen asleep on the table, for the next thing he remembered was the piercing whistle and shouts of, "Get up, you sluggards! Get ready for work!"

This first morning, which marked the beginning of seven years of a never-ending nightmare, was firmly embedded in his memory. He lay in the upper hammock, where he had apparently been placed by Great Gobongo, who was already on his feet, setting off toward the exit. He yelled out something in an urgent tone and left. Kamolea felt sleepy and exhausted. Instead of getting flustered, he closed his eyes and turned to the other side. A moment later, Facundo dashed in.

"Oh, His Majesty is still stretching. Beg your pardon for barging in, sire."

He lashed his whip at Kamolea, who shot off the hammock in response. Facundo gave him a kick to his behind, and the boy flew out at top speed, then tripped up outside and rolled over in the dust. The army of slaves was already ahead, and he ran to catch them up.

* * *

Facundo's pipe sounded, bringing Kamolea to reality. Seven years later, nothing had changed—the same damned toot every morning. Only now he knew better than to linger on. He jumped and quickly started dressing.

The years of heavy physical labor had turned the previous skinny boy into one of a sturdy, handsome man. Although he was of medium height, his supple and robust body, woven of bulging muscles, and his thick neck, large chest, and broad shoulders made him look far bigger.

The fucking brute, Kamolea scowled as he put his linen shirt on, his powerful pectoralis twitching nervously. The week before, Raul had flogged him again, and the marks of his scourge furrowed his entire body.

Every single slave was terrified to death of Raul and equally sick of him. The man was a mad sadist—an embodiment of the devil himself, as the others put it. In all those years, he had killed at least a dozen slaves, smashing each one into a bloody pulp. *Fool around with Raul, and you'll collide with a crazy bull,* was the motto that every newcomer had to learn first.

Crazy bull, indeed. There are plenty of them in the Shithole, but our Raul is a real piece of work. Kamolea grinned. For some unknown reason, and despite his recent tears, he felt elated and in an excellent mood that day.

The dawn was rising, chasing the gloom away with its crimson light. The next terrible day of hardship, sweat, and sorrow lay ahead. Still, for the first time since he had been enslaved, Kamolea's heart fluttered in anticipation that something incredible was going to happen.

* * *

Bent over the sugar stalks, Kamolea rose and wiped his front, glancing at the relentless midday sun. The work was feeling particularly burdensome, and the memories buzzed inside his mind like a bunch of angry wasps.

What the fuck is going on with me? he thought, irritated, overwhelmed by another recollection of his first day of slavery. He was marching with the other slaves under the supervision of several mounted overseers as the dawn emerged on the horizon, coloring the grey scenery with bright hues. After a long plod, they stopped before an infinite sea of green stems, twice the height of man, that swayed lightly in the morning breeze. The guards positioned the slaves approximately two yards away from each other, handed them curved knives, and warned them not to make a sound while they worked. A sharp blare urged them to start. Kamolea bravely stepped up and swung his knife at the first stem. Once. Twice. Three times. On the fourth slash, the cane finally fell. After taking down several others, his unhealed shoulder started hurting again. He felt clumsy and sluggish, dragging his wounded leg and gasping for air. The men either side of him had already made significantly more progress, cutting the plants down with one blow. Soon, they had disappeared out of sight among the thick greenery. A woman came to him with an armful of crops, picked up his modest harvest, and trotted down the road to carry them to an ox cart.

As Kamolea found out considerably later, the oxen would take the stalks to the weird building with wings, which was called *ingenio azucarero.*[34]

There, enormous grinding drums, turned slowly through human force, would squeeze the juice from the stems into large kettles, where it was boiled until it became a thick brown liquid called *melaza.*[35] The sticky substance was subsequently used for rum and sugar production. Finally, the end product was placed in kegs, transported to Portobello, loaded on ships, and sent to Spain. The work in the mill was a harrowing experience, and Kamolea dreaded the occasional moments that he had to go inside, in the sweltering heat, where a score of stink-

---

34 Sugar mill.

35 Molasses.

ing sweaty men pushed the gigantic horizontal levers that moved the drums.

On his first day, however, he was blissfully ignorant about the hell that awaited him. After an hour of work, he wanted only one thing—to stretch his exhausted, aching body on the ground and die. Breathing heavily, he stopped working and raised his eyes towards the heavens. It was getting hotter with every passing minute, and he craved a drop of water. As he toiled, a sharp neighing made him jump, and Raul popped up in front of him.

"Pero que demonios?"[36] he shouted as he deftly dismounted his steed and grabbed Kamolea by the throat.

"Why ain't you working, you lazy piece of shit?" he hissed, his black eyes only a few inches from Kamolea's face. "Are you here to work or to dawdle? Do you see where the others are, uh?" He shook him like a kitten.

"Aye-aye, Captain," Kamolea muttered.

"Captain? Are you making fun of me, sucker? If you don't catch up with the others by the break, I'll personally see to wringing your neck! Is that clear?" shouted Raul.

Kamolea delayed his response, which drove the overseer crazy.

"You need to learn some manners!" He hurled the skinny boy to the ground and started whipping him with his scourge and kicking him violently. "Now you'll fully understand me, you ugly, filthy little fuck!"

"Don't kill him yet, Raul!" cried one foreman who had been drawn by the shouting. "Leave him be, for God's sake; he's still a boy!"

"Si, caramba, chico!"[37] yelled Raul, panting. He snatched his hat from the ground, put it on, and mounted his cob. "Heed my words, Rodrigo, if he doesn't start moving his ass, he won't survive more than a week, your boy..."

---

36 What the hell?

37 Yes, dammit, boy!

A rustling from his right brought Kamolea to the present moment, and he shook off the unpleasant memory. As he looked in the direction of the noise, his heart jumped into his throat and started banging wildly.

Several yards from him, Uma, the most beautiful girl in the village, was gathering the canes and binding them in bunches. Every time she bent, her long braid bounced around her shoulders, and her large bust swung irresistibly. He gawked at her cleavage and swallowed, his member already stiff and aching.

"Gosh, what a piece of ass!" he muttered as Uma nimbly grabbed the bunch of canes, threw it over her shoulder, flashed him a playful smile, and turned around to lay it on the pile. Kamolea stared at her curvy bottom, which swayed rhythmically as she walked away, and a trickle of saliva formed at the corner of his mouth, causing him to brush it away.

Uma was in her twenties, a gorgeous slender mulatto slightly taller than him, and every time he thought about her supple body and heavy bosom, he got hard, and a sleepless, wet night would follow. He detested waking up like that, all smeared and sticky, but he could not help it. The women, still an unexplored area of his experience, took up almost his entire mind. As with everything unknown, women made him shy and anxious, even a little afraid, and his romantic, idealistic notions about them consumed a great deal of his energy. He liked several women in the village, but Uma was something special—she drove him crazy, as she blazed such a fire in his soul that he was ready to do whatever was necessary to impress her. He was aware, however, that playing with her would spell out imminent death.

Even though she had vanished among the dense sugar canes several minutes earlier, it had not eased his groin pain, and he felt like his testicles would explode. He resumed working, vigorously swishing his knife and felling stalks in quick succession, feeling an angry ball forming in his chest. Suddenly, he stopped and hurled his knife away, his eyes burning with a dangerous flame.

"How much I detest my bloody doom!" he spat through clenched teeth. "Everybody of my age has already a woman, but of course, not me, the fucking, curly wretch!"

Go to the brook and jerk off. You'll feel far, far better... whispered a tender voice in his mind and Kamolea stopped short, surprised.

"Where did that come from?" he muttered. "I've never done it, but many people say it's fun..."

"Get down the dell to the creek and do it so you can wash right afterward; otherwise, you'll wake up tonight smeared to your ears again," hinted the soft voice gently.

Leaving the workplace without permission was unthinkable, but neither foreman nor overseer were in sight, and Kamolea, out of his mind and blinded by passion, took a chance. He rushed toward the dell that descended on the other side of the large track that was used by the ox carts loaded with canes on their way to the sugar mill, but the moment he stepped on the road, a set of hooves clattered behind him. A stony ball hit his stomach. The punishment for being caught dawdling was thirty lashes and two nights in a cage without food. He had been through that twice already, so he expected more whips for his latest disobedience. His only hope was that the rider wasn't the hateful Raul...

"Where do you think you're going, you lazy son of a bitch?" shouted Raul behind him.

"I'm really sorry, señor," Kamolea turned around to face him. Hardly able to keep his rogue stallion calm, Raul was clutching the reins with one hand and aiming his shotgun at him with the other. "I just needed to take a..."

"I don't care what you needed!" Raul bellowed. "You're fooling around instead of working, and that's enough for me. Last week I flayed you again with no effect. Maybe it's time to end up your fucking little games once and for all, eh?"

A dangerous gleam flickered in Raul's eyes. In a flash, Kamolea realized that the brute had decided to kill him, but instead of being afraid, something snapped inside him. At that moment, he felt cold and detached, and he didn't give a damn whether he lived or died. He looked coldly at Raul and sensed that the last act of this seven-year-old drama had finally come to an end. One of them had to depart from this world. This was to be to the death.

He stepped forward, and Raul jerked at the reins, still aiming at him. The horse rose on his hind legs, whinnying.

"I think that you're just trying to escape, ain't you?" drawled Raul. "So, what are you waiting for? Run for your life, go!"

Kamolea knew Raul wanted to shoot him in the back—the only reason for wasting a slave's life was an attempted escape. In a heartbeat, he bent, grabbed a lump of dirt, and smashed it against the stallion's muzzle. The horse whinnied in pain and flung backward. Raul lost his balance and fell, discharging the gun in the air. He rolled over in the dust, and Kamolea leaped on him, ready to wring his neck, but before he could reach him, a gust of wind lashed against his face, and he bounced back as if he had hit an invisible wall.

Dart to the jungle, run! somebody screamed inside his mind. He turned and dashed up the road toward the dense tropical forest that started at the foot of the hill about half a mile away.

With a hammering heart and sinews taut to tearing point, he was almost flying, his feet hardly touching the ground.

Raul roared in the distance, and another shot resounded, the bullet buzzing past his ear by a whisker. The thud of hooves approached, and he strained with all his might. The road narrowed where the first trees began. Kamolea plunged into the mess of tangled creepers and low bushes, following the path, but it was hard for him to run. He tripped several times on snags and roots, made a sharp turn, caught a liana, and climbed swiftly inside the crown of an old oak, just as he had used to in his childhood.

He huddled there among the branches, panting, doubled over from the pain in his diaphragm caused by the stitches in his side. Visions of punishments he had witnessed over the years whirled in his mind—branded men and women with their noses cut off; bodies split in two, each half being dragged further away from the other by horses; screams of dread and pain from men and women beaten to death…

"They'll never take me alive," he whispered. The clatter of hooves got closer, and he saw Raul, hatless, clutching his shotgun and angrily spurring the poor stallion on as it barely managed to squeeze through the creepers. He passed Kamolea's vantage point when the horse suddenly reared up, let out a terrifying neigh, and collapsed backward, then rolled over, snorting and whinnying in pain, until it finally remained still.

The branches impeded Kamolea's vision, but he could see Raul's legs and a part of the animal. After nothing stirred for some time, he got down and approached cautiously. A long, spotted snake was still wrapped tightly around the stallion's neck. Raul lay on his back, clutching his gun firmly, his head smashed on a big round stone, and his eyes wide open, staring at the sky. A puddle of blood was forming steadily beneath his neck and shoulders. Kamolea was still gazing in disbelief at the dead man when he caught the sound of more hooves in the distance, accompanied by scattered shouts.

He plunged deep into the woods on his left, missing three mounted overseers by a fraction of a second as they rode along the path. They spotted Raul's body and stopped, yelling and gesturing. Kamolea could wait no longer. He crawled noiselessly until he was out of an earshot, then passed through the dell, crossed the track, and found his way to the place where he had been working before all the insanity had begun. Soon, Facundo arrived to check if any slaves were missing, and Kamolea gave him his warmest and most innocent smile.

CHAPTER XV

THE SORCERER

Kamolea had fooled the overseers, but it was not the case with his fellow sufferers. When he returned to the village the same evening, he noticed their furtive looks, shining eyes, and concealed smiles. The news had spread like wildfire around the camp, and in no time, every single person knew what Kamolea had done. At supper, he was seated in Great Gobongo's place at the head of the long rectangular table. It was a tremendous honor, considering that since his death, nobody had ever dared to sit there out of respect for the kind giant. Then Rita, who had been assigned the position of a master chef in the mansion, brought a part of a lamb's leg straight from the master's kitchen, especially for him. In doing so, she was risking her life, as stealing food was punishable by death.

Finally, for the first time since he had arrived at the plantation, the shiny eyes of the young women bored into him with real interest. Jubilant and glowing with pride, he repeatedly blushed, gazing bashfully at his plate every time he met a gaze.

They all seem to adore me tonight, so maybe, at last, I'll get my chance to fuck somebody, he thought. *This Kuna[38] pussy over there is ogling me*

---

38 Panamanian indigenous tribe.

pretty boldly and she's not bad at all… Aley's her name, I think? I wonder what her dad would say if he saw her leering at me like that.

The main reason for Kamolea's virginity was that the marriages were arranged between racial communities. Thus, blacks and Indians never mixed, and as he belonged to neither of them, they simply ignored him. Two years before, he had fallen for a nice black girl about his age, but it had ended in disaster. The day her father saw them speaking with their heads inches apart, he battered her pretty badly, and her brothers beat the shit out of him. *So much for the girls,* he had decided then.

But hopefully not anymore…

"Have you finished, Crespo?"[39] a familiar voice cut into his thoughts. He looked up, and Uma's piercing eyes drove straight into his heart. He flushed and looked to one side. Uma smiled knowingly and licked her juicy lips.

"Can I take your plate?" she asked.

"Of course, yes, I'm done. Thank you," he stammered.

She grabbed his dish and walked away, swinging her hips. Kamolea's eyes were glued to her bottom, but then, aware that he was the center of attention, he quickly averted his gaze.

"Shut your trap and stop drooling!" Niddi tapped him on the back and sat next to him, grinning.

"She's driving me crazy, man," muttered Kamolea.

"I hear you, but you'd better be careful with her," said Niddi, adopting his usual stone face. "Do you remember the hell around the camp before she got married? It was a nightmare, all that bickering and fighting for that cunt. My father said that somebody would get killed because of her, and that's what happened precisely."

"Really? And who was that?"

"How come you don't know? The village was on the verge of a riot when Khari stabbed Akuchi to death because of that bitch. Bron and

---

39 Curly.

Chuma were also injured in the brawl and couldn't work for weeks, so Don Diego finally woke up and forced her to marry. Afterward, everything settled down."

"Oh, now I understand." Kamolea slapped his forehead. "I heard Akuchi had got killed, but I didn't know she was involved."

"Yep, that's the whole story," nodded Niddi. "She had to wed the killer of her beloved because the brute threatened to slit the throat of everybody who dared approach her. No one had the guts to confront him, and as Don Diego had given her one week to choose her future husband, she had no choice. One thing I don't get, though, is how Khari got away with the murder. Raul and Don Diego did the investigation and beat him to a pulp, yet he has never admitted his crime. He's tough, that son of a bitch, and since he became one of Aka's bodyguards, he's been even worse. So, heed my advice, Crespo, and don't fool around with Uma if you value your life."

Kamolea regarded his friend's sharp-featured, chiseled face and nodded in agreement. Niddi, a long-haired, slender, wiry Kuna Indian about his age, smiled at him.

"You did it, man," he said, his black eyes, usually cold and derisive, glowing with happiness.

"Did what?" asked Kamolea innocently. "I don't know what you are talking about."

"I bet you don't," Niddi grinned. "Only Bolanie saw your little interaction with the wanker. To frighten his horse was a shrewd move, but enticing him to the jungle instead of killing him right on the spot was brilliant. I've always suspected that you're far smarter than you look, Crespo. And see, today everybody worships you more than Aka."

"Oh, come on," snorted Kamolea. "Frankly, I don't like so much attention."

"I'm so glad you killed the fucker. Do you remember how he dragged me down the hill? I will be forever in debt to you for jumping before his horse. Back then, you risked your life to save mine, and if it were not for you, I would have been a dead man long ago. That's why I pray every night to Babdummad[40] to give me an occasion to repay you the same way."

Kamolea patted him on the shoulder.

"Why, that's what friends do, no?"

"But where has everyone gone?" Niddi exclaimed suddenly, looking around. It was dark already, and only the two of them remained at the table.

"And what are they doing over there?" added Kamolea, eyeing four men suspiciously as they approached, carrying a large stretcher covered with fronds on their shoulders. A crowd of slaves followed several yards further behind, swinging their bodies and humming a sad, slow tune. Before Kamolea could react, two burly Negros grabbed him, mounted him on the litter, and the procession set off solemnly towards the edge of the village. A few women surrounded him and threw leaves and flowers as they advanced toward the outskirts, where a huge pyre similar to a small hut was already flaring up. The carriers put the stretcher in the center on a heap of cut branches, and accompanied by wild cheers and applause, two young girls hung a lei around Kamolea's neck and laid a wreath of leaves on his head. Then, both men and women whirled in a frenzied dance, singing and laughing.

"Our hero!" they cheered.

"Let's call today Crespo's day and always remember it as one of hope and freedom!" screamed Rita, who was singing along, clapping her paw-like hands and swaying her large fat bottom.

"Rita, what date is today?" asked her somebody, as they knew she kept track of the master's food in the pantry.

"It's the nineteenth of December seventeen four, el dia del Crespo!"[41] she cried and a volley of cheers and whistles exploded. Several dancers

---

40 The main male deity of the Kuna tribe, the creator of the universe.
41 The Curly's day.

dragged Kamolea off his perch, forcing him to join them, but he wasn't in the mood, and in a while, he had resumed his seat. Suddenly, he felt tired, lonely, and fed up with all this attention. He swept his eyes across the crowd in search of Niddi and met Aley's gaze again. She was a few years younger than him, willowy, with a cute round baby face flanked by two long plaits. He smiled at her, and she blushed and turned her gaze to the ground. He remembered now that it was not the first time he had caught her ogling him, but he had never paid heed to her. She vaguely reminded him of a girl from his native island, with whom he had fallen in love a long time before. But Aley simply wasn't fuckable—too young, too childlike, not really able to inflame him. He was into much riper, more experienced women... like Uma, for instance. Especially her.

God, I'd give two fingers on my left hand to spend a night with her, he thought, his member stiffening again.

But a moment later, his thoughts drifted to Aley and her resemblance to Illima.

Illima... Was she real, or was it some sweet daydream? he pondered to himself. It had been so long that he couldn't really remember. His fading memory worsened his loneliness, resulting in displeasure and a nagging irritation at himself. He got up and looked at all the cheerful people who were celebrating the end of the cursed overseer.

I'd never imagined that they loathed him so much, he thought. *Damned Raul. What a piece of shit he was.*

He headed to the bushes, took a leak, then quickly sneaked out and returned to the village. Then, he slipped into his hut, slumped into the remote corner, leaned cross-legged against the wall, and let out a sigh of relief.

"Alone is far better," he mumbled.

The tiny room he had shared for so many years with the Great Gobongo was stuffy and oppressive as usual, but since his demise, Kamolea had had the feeling that his spirit was still haunting the hut.

In the silence of the night, the memories of the black giant surged to the surface of his mind, and his eyes moistened as sheer love and gratitude overwhelmed him.

* * *

The first few months on the plantation had been a living hell. The days were an infinite string of backbreaking work, beatings, and floggings. In the evenings, he dragged himself to the hut, crawled to his hammock, and lay there, tired like a dog, not having any energy left to go and eat with the others. Gobongo had healed his wounds and regularly brought him food in the hut or carried him on his back to the common area for his meals. He was his guardian angel over all these years, and if it hadn't been for him, Kamolea would never have made it.

And now he had gone. Kamolea had witnessed his friend's terrible suffering, and the pain of the loss was tearing him apart.

"All because of this fucking wretch, Aka!" he spat.

Aka was a mysterious person. Don Diego had bought him about a year ago, and when the others saw him, everybody asked himself the same question: would the dotard survive for more than a month? Old, skinny, bald, and wrinkled like parchment, with ugly features resembling an ocelot's muzzle, Aka was all but redoubtable, and nobody took him seriously.

Yet, the surprises followed one after another. Aka performed so well on his first workday that he overshadowed the more forceful men, cutting almost twice as much sugar cane. Agile and sharp, he burst with energy and did not stop to rest for even a second. Nobody had seen such a thing before. A week had passed, then a month. Instead of being crushed and exhausted by the backbreaking work, Aka took a wife—a strong African woman, at least thirty years younger than him. A month after the marriage, she looked so weary that her girlfriends, seriously worried, asked her what was going on. She blushed, smiled shyly, and refused to talk, which was enough to spark the fire. The women went berserk, sneaking round Aka's hut all the time, and soon the camp exploded with juicy rumors that the old rogue did his youthful wife at least two or three times at night and some nights, around the time of the full Moon, even five or six. The other servants were in awe of his incredible stamina at his age, but after that daily work in the sweltering heat, it had to be impossible without the meddling of the dark forces. So, the gossip soon spread that Aka was a powerful sorcerer possessed by an evil spirit. Some would claim he practiced voodoo magic. Others swore that he could turn himself into an ocelot. But the most compelling reason to believe the rumors came in the third month, when his wife fell pregnant.

Gradually, Aka became the emperor of the village, surrounded by several personal servants and bodyguards who worshipped him to such a degree that they were ready to die for him. Overnight, everybody became afraid of him, ready to obey his whims, except for the Great Gobongo. He did not fear the old sorcerer, neither did he believe in his magic, but as the others did, little by little, Aka ousted Gobongo as the leader of the slaves and started making decisions in his place. He even overruled some of his orders, which drove Gobongo mad with fury. Kamolea pitied his friend, knowing how angry he was about losing his leadership, but there was nothing to be done—Aka was invincible, surrounded by his guards and magical secrets. Nevertheless, Kamolea knew Gobongo well, so he waited for the inevitable clash.

And it came, sure enough, with all the disastrous consequences that followed. It all started the day when Aka forced Kyra, a homely widow who had just lost her husband, to fetch him water.

Kyra was married to the young Jafari, a stand-up gentleman, and Gobongo's friend. There was talk that Jafari was indebted to Aka, and the latter claimed his wife for a servant to make things even. Nobody knew for sure if that was true, but it never happened. Both men quarreled and bickered for some time, then Jafari fell ill. Several days before he died, he went to see Gobongo, and Kamolea tactfully left, respecting their privacy. He sat near the entrance, not much interested in the faint whisper coming from inside, but then he heard Gobongo suddenly cry,

"How so? You look fine. What's wrong with you?"

Kamolea pricked up his ears.

"I think the filthy crook has cast a spell on me," Jafari was saying aloud, his voice strained and full of grief. "This nightmare is driving me crazy. How come it's always the same: While I'm working…" he switched to a whisper, mumbling, and Kamolea stopped paying attention, sinking back into his own thoughts. Then Gobongo cried again, making him jump.

"What do you mean your throat ached as if an ocelot had ripped it open?"

"It's true, Gobongo!" Jafari said crossly. "When I wake up, it hurts as if it's really torn; I can even feel the teeth of the cat on it." The voice lowered again, and the last words Kamolea overheard were, "My days are numbered… Promise me you'll take care of Kyra, please."

And Gobongo had promised. That's why he was so furious at the sight of the shuffling Kyra, crushed by grief over Jafari's death, and doubled over the heavy bucket on her way to Aka's hut. The sorcerer was sitting on a bench before the entrance, especially made for him, watching her mockingly. As she drew near, Gobongo stepped up, took the bucket from her, and splashed it into Aka's mug.

"Go fetch the water yourself, you scraggy back of bones!" Gobongo yelled. "If you dare to harass this poor woman once again, I'll smash your ugly head in!"

Aka rose slowly, his black, hypnotic eyes piercing Gobongo's. With his bald head, ashy visage with sunken cheeks, and skinny, sinewy body, he was the very personification of approaching death. He thrust his face a few inches from Gobongo's, almost touching him, then pulled his thin lips apart in a terrible grimace, revealing several rotten yellow teeth in his otherwise toothless mouth, and hissed,

"Within a week, you're a dead man, honey."

That evening, when he went back to the hut, Gobongo told Kamolea everything that had happened and admitted that he was a little scared. That very night, he woke up with a piercing scream, panting, clutching his throat and wailing,

"The ocelot… The ocelot! Get away from me, you beast…"

Kamolea shuddered at the memory of his shaking friend's sweaty face, his bulging eyes filled with horror, staring madly at him.

"Take my hand, Crespo," he had whispered hoarsely. "Don't let me go. I'm numb with terror, my friend. The wild cat is coming for my heart…"

This scene repeated the night after, and the following one, and every single one for the next ten days. Gobongo languished and became scatter-brained, constantly muttering to himself, unable to understand even a simple question or instruction. Within days, his skin was covered with blisters, scarring his body and face. The sores broke open in ulcers, making him howl in pain. Kamolea was already familiar with the awful disease that the Spaniard called "*bouba*,"[42] but he had never seen such a severe case. Doctor Ignacio, a tall, slim white-haired man with piercing blue eyes, who was the family physician of Don Diego but also took care of the sick slaves, came to examine him. He gave him some medicine, but it had no effect.

At the beginning of the third week, nothing was left of the Great Gobongo; he had turned into a skeleton covered with festering scabs. The stench in the hut was unbearable, and for the final few nights, Kamolea slept outside. Finally, after Doctor Ignacio shrugged his shoulders and said nothing else could be done, the overseers dragged him outside, and Raul blew out his brains.

Kamolea sighed. He could feel Gobongo's spirit in the room—he could even smell him. After his death, nothing was the same—dread

---

42 Yaws.

had taken a hold of the village, and everybody feared Aka like they would a natural disaster. He had deprived them of the only little piece of privacy and personal freedom they still had, thus making them slaves twice over, dependent on his whims.

I wish I could free them as I did with Raul, but the old rogue is too strong. Who could defeat his dark magic? Pensively, Kamolea yawned and soon drifted off. Suddenly, he jerked and woke with a start, aware of someone else's presence. The room was bright, filled with a mild glow.

Is it dawn already? he thought, still half-asleep. He tried to get up, but found himself unable to budge. He must still have been dreaming, as he could discern everything that was going on around him, but had no control over his limbs. The light intensified and became a silhouette, and the old man, wrapped in his red mantle, materialized in the center. Kamolea gasped. During all his years in slavery, he had completely forgotten about his existence. He tried to jump, but, to all his dismay, he still could not move.

The old man smiled, kindness streaming from his calm brown eyes. Judging by his snow-white hair and beard, he was ancient, but his pale skin was delicate and nearly translucent, and Kamolea was surprised to see that it was taut like that of a young person and not blotchy with age. As he observed the folds of his cloak, the man's voice echoed inside his head.

"It's been a long time since our last encounter, Kamolea."

"My name is Crespo," he thought mechanically, unable to move his agglutinated lips.

The old man lifted his eyebrows.

"Don't tell me you've forgotten your real name, son. A name is among the most important things in one's existence."

"What do you want?" Kamolea almost screamed inwardly. Was it his own voice or the shrill one that he had not heard for ages?

The man sighed.

"Hard time lies ahead, Kamolea," he said. "You have done extremely well up to now. It's an incredible feat to have survived seven years of living hell, enduring beatings, floggings, hunger, torture, humiliation, and backbreaking labor. You have suffered, it's true, but it was a necessary part of your training. This hardship has taught you humbleness and self-discipline to the point that you have achieved two challenging tasks: repressing the runt and defeating Raul.

"Now, the time has come to start my teaching, but first, I owe you an explanation of why you needed to go through this ordeal. You see, everyone who God chooses to be His warrior must pass through four stages of learning. The first one, called an *apprentice,* is when you start your training. The *apprentice* must be forced to do it because nobody wants to take the path of wisdom voluntarily. At this stage, he must be treated like a slave, and his own will must not be taken into consideration. That was your case so far, but it is over now. Thus, as a reward for your bravery, you will now proceed to the next level, and I will promote you as a *disciple.* At this stage, as a result of the accumulated energy, the *disciple* realizes that everything that happens to him makes sense. He begins to put together the lessons he has learned and draw logical conclusions about the events, so he ought to be left to his own devices and be helped only with advice when needed. Therefore, his stage of blind obedience is over, and his free will has to be given back to him with the encouragement to start seeking the truth by himself. Unfortunately, this is the most dangerous period for the learner, as he is still too weak to resist evil, so he will badly need his teacher's help and support. This is the time of a fierce fight when he amasses knowledge but still has no strength to resist temptation and could easily slip to the evil side."

"*What the fuck!*" shrieked the high-pitched voice inside Kamolea's head, this time clearly pronounced. "*So, you endured all that meaningless suffering to be promoted to a fucking disciple? Congratulations, jerk! What an honor, loser! Thank the crazy old man for your splendid life!*"

"Don't listen to *the runt*, Kamolea!" said the old man sternly. "Everything in life happens for a reason. Your struggle was not in vain, as it was preparation for the ultimate battle that awaits you in the future, when you'd face forces beyond your imagination, far mightier than yourself. This leads us to the third stage of the training when the disciple becomes a warrior. On this level, he must surmount one crucial challenge—to expel this nasty squealing thing called *the runt* from his body. Once that is done, *the warrior* will reach the fourth and final stage of his training, becoming a man of knowledge, also called *a sage*. On this ultimate achievement of perfection, the *sage* must accomplish the hardest assignment one could possibly face during their lifetime. He must confront *the runt's* master and resist his temptations."

"*I want no part of this shit!*" shrieked the voice. Kamolea stared at the old man in disbelief, unable to move.

"I'm sure you don't, but I'm not speaking to you," said the ancient one. "Kamolea, listen carefully. *The runt* possesses every human on Earth. It is a creature of a higher mind that comes from another universe. *It* has found an excellent host in humans. *It* blends so perfectly with one's personality that *its* existence is almost undetectable.

"You can consider *it* to be like a parasite that uses your body to nourish itself, and as all vermin, it ceaselessly corrupts your physical and mental health. The main problem with humans, though, is that they not only don't sense any harm, but they feel even comfortable with the runt. So, the first thing you should do to get rid of this, let's call it, *energy-sucker*, is to take control over your body and learn to fight the desires of the flesh. For the past seven years, you have done exactly that—without even realizing it, you have built inside you an iron wall of discipline that has repulsed the evil creature. It was a hard blow against *it*, which made *it* vulnerable and seriously shaken. So, now it's time for the next move: to go on the offensive and expel it from your body. It's easier said than done, though, because the runt and its master are far stronger than humans, and to defeat them, you will need to invoke an equally powerful force. Or, to put it simply, you must start praying to God for help. You still know nothing about His teachings, but you are about to see his might."

"I already have a god to pray to," Kamolea croaked, his voice strained as if it had come from the mouth of another person.

"I know your god," the old man replied. "Kepolo, the Supreme Evil One, also called Devil and Satan. But today, we have a more pressing matter to discuss. I came to warn you that your life is in grave danger. The Evil One manipulates the old magician, thus preparing a mortal blow for you, and if you don't turn to the *Only* and *True God*, you have no chance of surviving. You witnessed Gobongo's fate, so you've got the idea what has been lurking in the darkness, stalking you. Here, I have brought you a crucifix of the *Son of God* to protect you."

The old man produced a tiny object. Kamolea strained his eyes, but could not make out the details.

"*What is it?*" he wanted to ask through his cracked lips.

"It's called a crucifix. It depicts the final hours of the *Son of God*, who died on the cross for mankind, and his blood cleansed our sins."

"*What wrong did he do in order to be killed like this?*" Kamolea thought.

"He did nothing wrong," replied the old man. "He descended from heaven to teach us how to live and to show us the truth. But remember, those who preach the truth very often meet a cruel end, full of torture. Take you, for instance. What wrong have you done by refusing to kill and eat humans? It's the most disgusting thing in the world, yet they tried to sacrifice you to their evil god… The same thing happened with Jesus Christ, the *Son of the True God*."

"*Nonsense!*" screamed the sharp voice. "*The gods are immortal and invincible. No human could defeat a deity! This man was an imposter, a liar, and a coward, who preached only weakness and submission. No real man would listen to this fool…*"

"Do you hear how *the runt* blasphemes, Kamolea?" asked the old man sadly. "The awful part in all this is that, as it has taken a part of your brain, you can never guess which thoughts forming inside your mind are your own. It's extremely complicated, this duality—you, on the one hand, with your soul and character, and *it,* on the other, always trying to destroy the good in you. The only way to separate the true You from *it,* and to understand yourself, is through the exercises I will show you and the prayers I will teach you. But first, you must be aware of what's going on inside you."

Kamolea's mind was razor-sharp. He couldn't concentrate on the words but perfectly understood their meaning on some strange, supernatural level, as if waves of information were floating directly from the old man toward him. As his head was empty of thoughts, he struggled to formulate the question that intrigued him greatly for some time.

"I know what bothers you," said the old man. "You want to know what kind of creature *the runt* is, don't you?"

Kamolea nodded.

"Well, I call it this only for your convenience, as it is hard to understand *its* true nature. *The runt* is not actually a single creature—*it* is a combination of multiple evil spirits named demons, but calling all them *the runt* as a collective is far easier for the purpose of my lessons. There are many kinds of demons, and each is responsible for making you commit a particular sin. You could think of them as many different kinds of flies, and just like insects, they are more or less irritating."

In a flash, Kamolea saw the runt's bald head adorned with tiny horns and *its* bulging eyes staring at him from the bottom of the canoe.

That's why the ugly thing changed ceaselessly its colors and its features fluctuated all the time; because it consisted of many dark shadows, he thought, although he was not entirely sure how he had ended up with such a realization.

"Listen carefully, now," the old man continued. "*The runt* dwells a little above your heart; from there, *it* sends black waves out towards your brain at certain intervals. That's why our Lord Jesus Christ, Son of God, says, '*Out of the heart come evil thoughts.*' These dark waves travel through your body, reach your brain, and transform themselves into thoughts which, in turn, generate desires, obsessions, and feelings like spite, despair, hatred, jealousy, laziness, boredom, regret, anger, lust, and greed. Now, the process of converting *its* dark waves, which are nothing other than *its* thoughts, into your own mental images and grim feelings, is actually like nourishment to *the runt,* and the very core of *its* existence. Do you understand that, Kamolea? The specific energy released by transforming *the runt's* waves into negative feelings nourishes *it* and sustains *its* life. Those images of sex, for instance, which you see so often, are a classic example of *the runt* having a meal. And here is the key point—the more you succumb to these gloomy sentiments, the more you feed the parasite in you."

Something strange was starting to occur inside Kamolea's mind. The bleak room slowly started to revolve and grew bigger while his ears buzzed as if hundreds of moths fluttered inside them. Next, he felt himself become smaller than a bug, floating in total darkness. And then, in a flash, he realized that his mind had become an inner eye, and he was roving in the dark cavern of his own interior. He passed several dimly lit structures, clustered together like bunches of grapes, and found himself before a gigantic radiant egg woven by myriad luminous treads that spread in all directions. The egg pulsated slowly, two beats at the time, then a brief interval, and another two. Thud-thud.... thud-thud... thud-thud... thud-thud... Kamolea stared in awe at the source of his life, hypnotized.

"Focus every bit of your awareness on the upper part of the heart," he heard the old man's voice whisper from far away. Kamolea's concentration was superb. He fixed his gaze for a few seconds, and then he "*saw*" a dark spot the size of a hand span just above his heart. As he discerned it, he noticed several black waves detach from it and float upward, causing the brilliant egg to dim for a moment.

The next instant, Kamolea was in the room again, sitting on the floor. The effect of his brief journey had been incredible. Wrapped in blissful silence, he felt that something huge, similar to an age-old rock, had budged an inch inside his chest and had let out a trickle of living water that seeped through it and bedewed the desert of his soul.

"So, if you are successful in blocking your thoughts, you'll stop *the runt's* waves, and as a result, you'll deprive *it* of *its* food," continued the old man, as if nothing had happened. "And if you are successful in doing this for long enough, at a certain point, *the runt* will leave your body in search of other sources of subsistence. Once that happens, the actual change will begin, because your body, which has been kept in slavery your entire life, will finally taste freedom. Take time, now, to commit to memory your defense against *the runt*. In the evening, when you are most vulnerable, you must perform this exercise to stop *its* thoughts from occurring."

Stupefied, Kamolea sensed how part of him had left his body and moved towards the room's center. It was discernibly him, clad in the same clothes, only instead of eyes, he had two glowing amber orbs. His projection sat on the floor cross-legged, his hands interlaced before his navel. Then, he slowly bent down the upper part of his body, his head almost touching his legs. He stayed like that for a moment, then changed into a kneeling position, arched his back, and touched the floor with his forehead, his elbows closely tucked beneath his body. He began moving his hands slowly, still interlaced, and put them underneath his front, between his thumbs and forefingers, the former pressing against his temples. It was a strange posture; his bottom sticking out, his legs tightly clasped together, his upper arms firmly clinging to his ribs, and his forearms propped up against the dirt floor.

"Your spirit knows what to do, so leave it to guide you," said the aged one. "And here are the words you need to say to protect yourself from Aka's spell. The more you repeat them, the stronger you'll become."

Inside Kamolea's head, verses started to form and echo like bells, over and over.

"My heavenly Father,
Forgive my trespasses,
And help me fight the Evil One.
In You I believe, Almighty,
Only You I deify,
And for You, I'm ready to die.
Amen."

The recurrence of the stanzas continued for so long that when it finally stopped, his entire being was imbued with them.

"Our time is running out, my young disciple," said the old man abruptly. "Remember, the three weapons against the demons are firm belief, fervent prayer, and unbending intent to block out those negative thoughts. Always wear the cross on your chest, and you'll be invincible."

Then, the old man vanished. Darkness reigned in the room once again, and Kamolea fell into a deep sleep.

* * *

A sudden flash ignited within Kamolea's brain, and an ear-splitting scream woke him up. Panting and shaking, he was still unable to fully emerge from the terrible nightmare he had just had. He had been cutting canes in the field when Uma appeared. She was stark naked, her large, brown nipples bristling as her breasts swayed invitingly. She smiled and beckoned him with a luring grin, touched herself playfully between her thighs, and motioned with her head towards the dense thicket behind her.

"Don't go after her, you fool!" a faint voice urged him.

"Fuck you," muttered Kamolea, dropped his sugarcane knife, and followed Uma, burning with passion. The screech of a hawk resounded in the distance, and he glanced at the unblemished sky to see a flock of crows flapping their wings ominously as they alighted nearby.

Something's wrong, he thought, suddenly alert. He wanted to go back, but Uma grasped his hand, and they wadded into the green sea of rustling leaves and stalks. Her hand was warm and steady, and she intertwined her fingers with his. At her merest touch, Kamolea felt like he was going to come. At this moment Aka, the old sorcerer, materialized from nowhere. He glared at Kamolea spitefully and pulled his lips back into a leer, his countenance twisted into a hateful grimace resembling the muzzle of a wild cat. A beheaded white hen was swinging in his hand, her feathers slowly turning red from the blood dripping from her neck. Uma screamed and darted away.

Aka jerked the bleeding hen briskly toward Kamolea, and warm drops of blood spattered over his face. All of a sudden, the hen sprang to life, but instead of attacking him, she swooped at the sorcerer, madly flapping her wings, blood gushing from her severed neck. Smeared with red, Aka started shrieking, his bony hands shielding his ugly face. Kamolea rushed after Uma and lost himself in the forest of green stalks. He wandered for a long time until he found himself in a tiny clearing, an islet amid the dense vegetation. A small heap of dirt rose from the ground. He peered at it for a while, then kneeled and buried his bare hands in it, clawing lumps and clogs of dirt aside. Faster and faster, he scooped the earth, until he touched something soft. He impatiently swept the remaining soil aside and found himself peering at an arm covered with a white rag of a sleeve. On the wrist gleamed two bracelets, one white and one pinkish, made of seashells. He fervently started digging again, his heart thumping wildly. The head appeared, and he brushed the dirt off the face... His own, deathly pale face, covered with scabs and sores, stared back at him from the grave. His horrified screech shook the hut, and he awoke, screaming his lungs out and waving his arms as if to chase the terrible vision away.

He was still shaking when the familiar blare of Facundo's wake-up pipe pierced the night, and for once, Kamolea almost welcomed the hateful sound.

He got up, still dazed and confused, and noticed that something was lying at his feet. He picked it up and stepped outside to take a better look. At the light of the rising dawn, he peered downward and saw a small, exquisite wooden crucifix attached to a dark-brown leather cord. The cross was richly carved at the edges with creeping floral ornaments. The human figure was incredible—the man's hair reached his shoulders, his head tilted and decorated with a crown of thorns, and his face distorted in a grimace of anguish. The body was meticulously depicted to the slightest detail, from the outlined muscles to the minute toes and fingers. The man looked so natural that Kamolea could not tear his eyes away from him.

So incredibly done! he thought. *The beard, the locks, and this pained expression on his face! A real masterpiece! But how did it come to be there in the first place?*

He tried to remember the details of the night before. Somebody obviously had given him the cross, but who and why? Was it a gift from Niddi? He had spent much more time with him than anyone else. First, they had talked about Uma… then the others had taken him and made him their hero… Wild dances around the pyre… After that, Aley was ogling him… and finally, this horrible nightmare. He racked his brain for a while, unable to recall anything else, but the burning feeling that he must absolutely carry this strange thing with him was so strong that he shrugged and, without giving it a second thought, hung the cross around his neck.

"Hey, Crespo, what are you waiting for? A kick in the butt? It comes with an extra whip today!" shouted Miguel, the most hateful overseer after Raul. Kamolea hurried to catch up with the crowd of workers, who were about fifty yards ahead, their ringing laughs and joyful cries echoing in the air.

I've never seen them so happy, Kamolea thought as he joined them.

* * *

It was about a week since Raul's death, and the slaves' shitty lives were back to normal. For Kamolea, however, a significant change had been set underway. Now, he was considered a leader and a highly respected man. Even though he was still young, he possessed great self-control, concealed strength, and rational thinking—qualities that attracted people the same way the light drew the insects. The men loved chatting with him and asking him for personal advice, or his opinion on community matters. As for the women, some of them continued casting him unambiguous glances, which made him feel extremely uncomfortable.

Thus, Kamolea slowly rose in influence, and although this had never been his intent, he was gradually approaching the former position of the Great Gobongo, establishing himself as a community leader. On the one hand, he felt proud of his achievement, as the attention flattered his ego. On the other, however, he wasn't too thrilled about all the fuss about him, as he was convinced that it would bring him only trouble—the spiteful glares that Aka and his gang of thugs darted at him were an unmistakable sign that a clash was coming.

It all started about two weeks after Raul's death. It was nearly noon already, and Kamolea longed for a break. After the heavy rain from the day before, it was muddy, and the stalks were hard to cut. He stopped and wiped his face, wondering when the darned break signal would resound. Suddenly, the crucifix underneath his shirt heated up and burned his chest. Surprised, he brusquely took it out, asking himself how on earth the wood could get hot. He looked left and noticed the rustling of stalks, indicating that somebody was approaching. A moment later, Uma, hot and sweaty, emerged from the lush greenery. She cast a furtive look around and strode towards Kamolea, smiling at him. She was slightly taller than him, her body perfectly molded under her long white linen bodice, which she had unlaced just a trifle more than decency permitted, generously revealing the deep cleavage of her stunning bosoms. As usual, her presence made Kamolea nervous. He smiled back, his heart thumping like the frightened bird he had held in his cupped hand once.

"Hola, Crespo," she said, taking a step forward, her black eyes boring into him with a burning flame. "Como esta mi heroe hoy?"[43]

Kamolea blushed and tried to say "bueno,"[44] but nothing came out of his dry mouth. She licked her full lips and grabbed his right hand.

"Do you love me, Crespo?" she whispered. "I'm crazy about you… You're so smart, so brave and strong. Here, feel my heartbeat," she pressed his hand against her firm breast. "See how it's throbbing? That's because of you. How do you like it?"

She removed his hand and grabbed him unceremoniously between the legs.

"I seeee," she drawled, leering at him mockingly, and licked her lips again. "Harder than steel, as they say… Wait for me at midnight behind the stables, and I'll show you paradise…"

The canes on their right rustled again. Uma jerked nervously.

"Behind the stables, after everyone goes to sleep," she repeated and disappeared into the high stalks. Kamolea stood dumbfounded for a long while, unable to shake his stupor.

* * *

Despairing, exhausted, and resigned, the slaves were shuffling back to the village, dreaming of the most basic of needs—washing their tired bodies, having a meal, and getting some rest. Kamolea plodded along, bringing up the rear of the long row. Uma's supple body danced cease-

---

43 How is my hero today?
44 Good.

lessly before his eyes, and no matter how hard he tried, he could not get her out of his head. His imagination unleashed powerful, detailed images that made his erection almost permanent.

"I need to get a grip on myself," he muttered, irritated. "This passion is reducing me to ashes. Just like the moths that burn themselves in the candle's flame, I can't resist; except that I realize that I'm heading for disaster, and they don't…"

A tiny, muffled voice at the back of his mind screamed desperately about the consequences.

Let her go! Remember Niddi's warning, it pleaded. It was a weak voice, coming from far away, dull and cowardly, and easy to ignore. Instead, his brain conjured up more images of Uma's curved, supple body and ample breasts …

Deep in thought, he reached his hut without noticing. As he opened the door, he stopped dead—in the corner of the room stood Aka and three of his guards. Kamolea instinctively took a step back, but somebody pushed him from behind, and he staggered forward, waving his hand to keep his balance. One of Aka's guards, an enormous black man, gripped him by the throat.

"I heard you had groped my wife today. Is it true, Crespo?" he said.

Kamolea met Khari's bloodshot eyes and read in them his death sentence.

The colossus hit him in the belly. Kamolea doubled over, and a mighty blow to his neck sent him down. They all started kicking him fiercely, save Aka, who watched with a smile at how his victim's body was turning into a bloody mess.

"Enough," he raised his hand after a while. "We don't want him dead, do we? At least, not yet."

"Don't even dare look at my wife again, you fucking jerk!" yelled Khari and gave him a last kick in the head.

"Now, when all this is settled, it's my turn to speak with our little hero, the killer of the overseers," Aka said mockingly. He took a bucket full of water from the corner and poured it over Kamolea's head. Kamolea shook and struggled to get up as chuckles and snorts met his startled eyes.

"I have decided that from now on, you will be my errand boy," Aka drawled. "I want you to fill this bucket with water and bring it to my place. Then, our glorious hero is going to wash my feet, and drink the water afterward. It will be incredible entertainment for the entire village! I'll be waiting for you at my place, looser! Don't linger too long; I don't want to be late for supper. Go!"

He dropped the pail and left, followed by the others, except Khari. Kamolea lay still on the floor, considering what to do. He had no intention of being humiliated by the old fool and making himself a laughing stock, but the image of his scabby face from his dream refused to let go; not to mention Great Gobongo's horrifying fate…

A kick in the ribs announced that his thinking time was over.

"Get up and dance," said Khari. Kamolea realized from the anger in his voice that the sole reason he was still alive was the damned bucket and Aka's dirty feet.

He got up slowly, his body aching everywhere. Khari grinned,

"Still wanna fuck my wife, you kinky trash?" He punched Kamolea in the stomach again. Kamolea doubled up and slumped on his knees. Khari grabbed him by the rear of his shirt and hurled him through the entrance. Kamolea rolled over in the dust and moved aside just in time to see the bucket fly out from inside the hut and land inches from his head.

"Straight to the well, and then to Aka with a full pail!" ordered Khari. Kamolea rose, took the vessel, and staggered toward the well that lay on the outskirts of the village. Khari followed him several yards behind, watching him derisively. It was almost dark already, but Kamolea could see the sniggers of the men who eyed him along the road.

Only two weeks ago, they adored me so much and called me their hero! he contemplated. *Why do they hate me now? Why are they glad that I'm*

in trouble instead of defending me? But everybody fears Aka. One thing I know for sure, though—I would rather die than be the servant of my friend's killer. I will never betray you, Great Gobongo.

He filled up the bucket and dragged himself to Aka's hut. A small crowd had gathered around the old sorcerer, waiting to see what was going to happen. Aka was sitting in his usual place before the entrance, surrounded by his trusted men. Kamolea slammed down the pail before him.

"Wash my legs up to the knee, hero!" Aka sneered, dipped his skinny feet into the bucket, then added, "And then drink the slop straight from the pot."

Aka's bodyguards chuckled and leered. The crowd watched in deadly silence.

Kamolea stood motionless, like a statue, feeling the tension rising with every passing second. He knew he wouldn't touch Aka's limbs under any circumstances, so he desperately sought a way out of the situation.

They won't dare kill me here, in front of so many witnesses, he thought.

Everybody waited for Kamolea's reaction with bated breath, for what seemed to be an interminable amount of time. Then, something incredible happened. Just beside Aka, the Great Gobongo's spirit materialized. He seemed to be in perfect health, strong as a bull, without a trace of his illness. He pointed at Aka, then looked at Kamolea and shook his head. That instant, Kamolea was overwhelmed with an urge to urinate. Without even knowing what he was doing, he slowly unlaced his trousers. As though in a trance, he took out his member and started pissing, directing the jet into the bucket. The crowd let out a simultaneous gasp. Aka jerked his feet, but it was too late, and the steaming spurt poured over his shins. With a steady gurgle, the water sprinkled and slowly changed color from transparent to pale yellow. The spectators observed this sacrilege, frozen with terror. Kamolea's calm was stunning. Just as when he had confronted Raul, something snapped in him, and he felt cold and indifferent, his eyes shining like steel. In that instant, he did not give a damn whether he lived or died at the hands of Aka's thugs, who stared at him in disbelief, their jaws hanging half-open. Kamolea finished, shook himself off, and laced his pants back up.

"There," he said. "See to yourself, you old fool. Wash your feet in my piss now or take a sip if you're thirsty!"

Kamolea's voice finally summoned Aka's guards from their stupor, and two of them stepped forward, but Aka raised a bony hand and cried, "Halt!"

His eyes had become narrow slits, and his dark face had turned ashy.

"You are a dead man, you son of a bitch," he hissed as Kamolea turned around and strolled away without a care in the world.

THE POWER OF GOD

Kamolea woke up with a scream, trembling. Four days after the clash with the sorcerer things had gone from bad to worse. After he had urinated in Aka's bucket, he returned to his hut and hid behind the door with a heavy club that he had fashioned to defend himself. There, he waited for Aka's gang for almost the entire night. Luckily, nobody came, and when he finally drifted off to sleep, he found himself transported once again to the small mound that had turned out to be his grave.

A yellow and black ocelot was lying on the heap of earth, fixing him with its beady green eyes. Shivers started creeping down Kamolea's spine, and goosebumps rose all over his body. The spotted feline rose, advanced with a deep growl, and lowered its body to deliver an attack. Kamolea sensed the smell of death. With lightning speed, the ocelot jumped with a screech and sank its sharp teeth into his throat. Kamolea woke up, waving his hands, screaming, and shaking, his larynx throbbing with pain. After he had calmed down a bit, his memories took him back to Gobongo's suffering.

"The ocelot…," he whispered. "Every single night he wailed about it. Is the same fate awaiting me? If so, I may as well blow my head off now; it'd be a better end…"

The dream repeated the next two nights, getting more and more intense. Then, on the third morning, Kamolea made a grim discovery—his skin had started itching just below the elbow, and he noticed a small scab, similar to those that had beset Gobongo. When he saw it, his heart sank.

"The game is over," he whispered to himself. "Nobody can escape Aka's magic."

And sure enough, within several days, he felt so weak that he could hardly rise from his hammock. His skin had gradually become covered with purulent scabs that had split open, leaking and causing awful pain. In addition, his hair had started falling out, his vision had become blurry and, despite the heat, he constantly trembled with cold from the effects of a permanent fever.

The overseers informed Don Diego that Kamolea was sick and refusing to work, and the planter sent Doctor Ignacio to see him. After a thorough examination, the physician shook his head sadly and gave him quinine to combat the fever.

"The prognosis is not very optimistic," he reported to Don Diego. "The curly boy is dying."

* * *

This night, Kamolea had the worst nightmare ever. He was in a gloomy forest and running like mad, pursued by a dreadful shapeless *thing*, a blurry black shadow, the personification of horror itself. His skin was covered in goosebumps, the hairs on his neck stood straight up, and an acute primordial fear, the likes of which he had never before experienced, almost suffocated him. The dark terror gained swiftly on him despite his efforts, and he strained every muscle to escape. Dashing through lianas, shrubs, and creepers, he glimpsed a spot where the trees thinned out and soon emerged into the familiar clearing containing his grave. This time, however, the bulky heap of dirt had been replaced by a gaping oval pit. He stopped dead, staring at the brown earth, which formed a sharp outline against the green background of the grass, when the dark creature swooped at him from behind. He rolled over in the ditch, and lumps, clods, and stones flew all around him, striking his body and head. He writhed in pain, gasping for breath as the dirt, sour and salty, thrust into his mouth and nose, clogging his lungs. Seized by a claustrophobic fit, he desperately scrambled to escape being buried alive, his arms flapping and waving and his legs jolting and kicking. A primitive fear of darkness and death drove him crazy, and he fell out of his hammock, screaming at the top of his lungs. When he finally came to his senses, he curled up on the floor, trying to calm his shaking and suppress the childlike fear of the dark, which had very much come alive within him. He longed for the light of a single candle to dissipate the blackness of the cursed room, but there was nothing to abate the darkness.

I'm certainly losing my mind, he thought as he scratched himself all over and whined like a scabby dog. *I can't go on living like this anymore. What the fuck is the point of suffering further? I'll hang myself on the transversal pole over there, and it will finally be over.*

He tried to rise but fell to his knees and crawled, groping for the rope, when something warmed his chest. He reached and touched the cross. It was hot.

"But that's impossible!" he wailed out loud, forcing his memory to conjure up how the crucifix had ended up with him. And then suddenly, as if a veil had fallen from his eyes, he recalled everything—the presence of the old man with the red mantle, his lecture on Kamolea's warrior's path, the exercise of suppressing his inner dialogue, the prayer...

In a daze, he curled up on the floor, placed his forehead in his interlaced fingers, and drew his legs to his stomach. A weird melody flowed through his mind, and he started whispering the prayer that the ancient one had taught him. He couldn't remember it exactly, so he mumbled,

"Son of Benito's God,
Help me fight Aka, the old rogue.
In you I believe, and you I deify,
Almighty God, don't leave me to die."
He mumbled this stanza again and again until he finally fell asleep.

* * *

"Kamolea, wake up!" he heard a faint voice yelling. His eyes flew open. It was still pitch dark in the hut.

"Your prayer brought me to you," the voice said. The room filled with soft light, and a silhouette clad in white materialized in the center. Kamolea's blurry vision discerned a translucent, fluorescent creature with a fluid, human-like body and winglike structures attached to its shoulders. Above its head, a halo fluctuated in the darkness, constantly increasing and decreasing in size.

"Hurry up, Kamolea! The Devil's servant is coming for you," said the creature. *"Focus and do what I'm saying!"*

The creature disappeared, and Kamolea sensed a surge of strength, as though something had taken control over him. He jumped up and was surprised to discover that he felt no pain, weakness, or fear.

"Yesterday, they brought freshwater on the physician's request." This time, the voice was inside his mind. *"Bring the bucket from the corner."*

Kamolea grabbed the pail and brought it to the center of the room.

"Take the cross in your right hand, dip it into the bucket, and stir the water in a circular motion!" said the voice.

Kamolea removed the crucifix from his neck and did what he had been told.

"Yes, just like that. Now, repeat after me…" Kamolea found that his lips were moving, reciting the words as they formed in his head:

"My heavenly father,
Holy be your name,
May your will be done
Make evil be gone.

Burn Aka's vile magic at once,
And open my eyes to see the difference,
Between a good and an evil deed,
Between witchcraft and a true creed.

In you I believe, Almighty Lord,
And in Jesus Christ, Your Son and equal God,
He is the light of the world,
And the hope of the unheard.

Only you both, I deify,
And for you I'm ready to die.
Make this water holy for me,
Expel the demons and make me free.
Amen."

Kamolea fell into a trance. He repeated the verses over and over, staring straight ahead, clutching the cross, and turning the water over with his hand. Gradually the voice faded, and in his head reigned complete, blissful silence. Then, the voice appeared again.

"Put the crucifix back on your neck, make the sign of the cross three times, then pour three handfuls of the holy water over your head, wash your face, and sprinkle it all over your scabs."

Kamolea obeyed mechanically, feeling the water burning his skin like fire. The translucent creature exited his body and rematerialized near the entrance.

"It's time for you to see the power of God and to believe that those who invoke *His* name are invincible. When the old sorcerer comes to you in his skin-changing form to tear at your throat, splash him with the holy water and he will never bother you again."

The silhouette evaporated, and a dark shroud wrapped the room. Kamolea picked up the bucket, retreated to the corner, and waited there with a banging heart for something to happen. As time passed, he began wondering whether it had merely been another strange dream, when he heard a scratching noise.

He listened intently. A cat's feet were clawing up the wall outside; there was no doubt about it. The thatched roof shook amid more grating and scraping, then silence reigned for a moment. Kamolea stood up and leaned against the wall, holding the bucket ready. A minute later, something heavy landed on the floor inside the hut with a loud thump, and two shiny amber eyes stared at him from less than a yard away. A low growl filled the room. Kamolea felt the familiar shivers going down his spine and started shaking with inhuman fear. The next moment, a piercing screech rang out, and the eyes leaped toward him. Kamolea's hands shot forward in an instant, flinging the water from the bucket as he plunged left and rolled over, dodging the ocelot's claws by mere inches. The wild cat let out another shriek, but this time it was one of pain. Then, spitting and hissing, it swiftly climbed the central pole and disappeared through the roof. Kamolea jumped to his feet, his heart racing and adrenalin rushing through his veins. As soon as the hissing had faded into the distance, his energy left him, and he fainted.

* * *

When Kamolea came to, it was late afternoon. He was lying on the damp earthen floor, the empty bucket beside him. For the first time in nearly a week, his pain had considerably diminished, and the fever had passed. He rose, feeling a flow of energy rushing through his body. His stomach let out an angry rumble.

"I'm so hungry I could eat a cow," he muttered, then wrinkled his nose, "Blimey, what a stench. I stink worse than the bilge."

He took the pail and set off for the well, dragging his feet and walking at a snail's pace. He took his time to wash and scrub his fetid clothes, and when he had finished, the sun was already descending, so he hurried to eat with the others. Some women were bustling about, preparing supper, and most of the men had taken their places at the table and were chatting quietly. When they saw Kamolea, their jaws dropped, and they fell into silence. Uma, who was sitting with her back to him, setting the table, caught their stares, spun around, and let out a gasp, dropping a wooden spoon as she did. Her left eye was still half-closed, but the deep purple beneath it had disappeared, turning a shade of rose.

Kamolea grinned widely at her.

"He ain't joking, your man," he blurted out, but she hurriedly passed him by without a second glance.

"Come on, I'm not a ghost, and I'm starving," he chirped and grabbed an empty bowl.

"Crespo! What a surprise, my friend!" cried out Niddi, who had just arrived. "Every time I've been to see you, you have been unconscious or delirious. Doctor Ignacio told Rita that you wouldn't make it to the end of the week."

"Well, for once, he was wrong," Kamolea said and fell upon his meal, ravenous. "Stay away from me, though, as I could be still contagious." Niddi sat beside him, all the same.

"I don't give a shit," he said, eyeing him closely. "I'm so glad you're back, Crespo. You still don't look very well, though. Rather ugly, I would say."

Kamolea chortled and, catching the glares of two of Aka's guards, asked through a full mouth,

"What about the old fucker?"

"That's the weird thing," Niddi whispered, leaning against him. "He didn't come to work today. Said he ain't feeling well. So, you're here, getting much better, and he's not. What do you make of that?"

Kamolea shrugged and continued eating with relish.

"Listen, I gotta leave you," Niddi blurted out. "This girl, Aley, remember her? I think she's so head over heels in love with you that she fell ill as well. I'll go and bring her some calm with news that our hero is up and perky as a rat in cheese. Wanna come with me? She will be so happy to see you."

"No, I'll pass for now. As I said, I might be contagious, so why take a chance? But send her my regards and tell her that there's nothing to worry about."

"I certainly do. Are you going to work tomorrow?"

"One more bowl of this delicious beef stew and you can count me in," said Kamolea, before standing to fill his dish again.

When Niddi left, he tried to strike up a conversation with the others that were sitting around him, but nobody wanted to talk to him, so he retired early in the evening, frustrated and hurt.

* * *

One evening, about a week later, Kamolea was on his way to the well. There was nothing left of his previous clumsy plod—he walked briskly, bursting with energy. His scabs had healed and fallen off, his vision was back to normal, and he was strong and healthy again, working as hard as before. In contrast, the old sorcerer was nowhere to be seen. Despite mentally preparing himself for the next confrontation, Kamolea was surprised that Aka's faithful dogs never bothered him.

So much the better. One less trouble to worry about, he thought. The only cloud on the horizon was the other slaves' behavior towards him.

What the hell is wrong with them? he asked himself. They apparently still thought he was highly contagious, as everybody, including even his best friend Niddi, was avoiding him.

Engrossed in his thoughts, he didn't even notice Aley until he drew right alongside her. She was carrying two buckets that hung from a thick pole across her shoulders. That evening, she had plaited her long raven-black hair into two thin braids, and she looked fresh and pretty.

"Hi, Aley," said Kamolea.

"Hi, Crespo," she smiled, revealing her perfect white teeth.

"How are you doing?" Kamolea asked her.

"I'm fine, thanks," she responded.

"Do you need help with those pails?"

"No, I'm all right," she said.

An awkward silence set in. Aley slowed her pace, looking at her feet, obviously waiting for him to outpace her. A fireball of anger formed in Kamolea's chest and rushed through his body.

"What's going on, Aley? I thought we were friends?" he asked angrily.

Surprised, she lifted her big black eyes and looked at him shyly, as if she were asking him: *Are we?*

"Why does no one speak to me anymore?" he went on, his voice trembling. "They all said they liked me, and I was their hero a few weeks ago, but now everybody is avoiding me..."

"I *do* like you," uttered Aley. "Very much," she added, blushing.

"Tell me what's wrong, then!" said Kamolea.

While they were talking, they had reached the well. She put the bucket down, gave him a sidelong glance, then concentrated on examining her sandals.

"Dammit, Aley, speak your mind! What's the matter with all of you?" Kamolea shouted.

"If I tell you, what's in it for me?" Aley asked, her face red as a beet.

"Whatever you want!" he cried. "I'll carry out every wish of yours; just name it!"

"All right, then," said Aley quietly. "Aka is dying, Crespo. Same disease as you and the Great Gobongo. It's like *bouba*, but very severe, and he's going mad as well. Rumor has it he's almost blind, his body is covered with sores, his skin is flaking, and all his teeth are gone. They say he has no energy to get up. His wife is wailing like a wounded beast at night, mourning him and cursing you."

"Cursing me? But what for?" Kamolea looked really surprised.

"You still don't understand, do you?" said Aley. "There is talk around the village that you're a far more powerful magician than him and that his spell bounced off you and turned against him. I even overheard two of Aka's bodyguards considering whether to offer you their service. Everybody admires you for your bravery to confront Aka and to piss in his bucket, but at the same time, they fear you now. Nobody wants to talk to you in case they cross you."

"Oh, come on! What rubbish, Aley! You know me better than that! Are you afraid of me?" Aley raised her black eyes and smiled at him. That evening, there was some magic in the air, and he found her round, radiant face, with her small snub nose and cherry lips, particularly attractive. He knew she liked him, so... *She wants you, jerk! Go ahead!* screamed the shrill voice. Kamolea reached up and stroked her face, feeling her soft olive skin. The moment he touched her, his heart sped up, and his knees softened.

"No, I'm not scared of you, and I never could be," she said, looking him straight in the eye. "You promised to carry out a wish for me, remember? What about a kiss? Would you like to kiss me, Crespo?"

As if a thunderbolt had hit Kamolea. Her shining black eyes reminded him of somebody else's; a girl he had sworn to love forever. But Aley's longing look drew him like a magnet. He buckled, and their lips fused. She was not the first woman he had kissed, but her lips were definitely the sweetest he had ever tasted. He sucked her tongue, then pushed it back with his own, and she melted into his embrace, pressing her body firmly against his. Within a few seconds, the world had stopped revolving, and nothing existed beyond their new love. Then, some approaching voices brought them back to reality and they broke apart, flushed with passion and slightly trembling.

"I have to go," said Aley quickly, her eyes gleaming triumphantly.

"Wait; I'll help you fill them up," said Kamolea. "When can I see you again?"

"I don't know. We have to be extremely careful. My father will kill us if he finds out."

"We'll figure something out, don't worry," reassured Kamolea. "Take your buckets now."

"Thank you," said Aley and squeezed his hand, before glancing around. Then, she kissed him hastily on the mouth, turned, and walked hurriedly away. As she receded in the twilight, Kamolea observed her supple body, her back straight as a beam, the pails swinging on her yoke. He stood, flustered, until several people emerged from around the bend. Breathing heavily, he filled his bucket and left.

* * *

As he got back to the hut, Kamolea was still grinning at the memory of Aley's honey lips. He entered, slammed the pail down in the remote corner, then pivoted and shouted with surprise. The old man stood in front of him, his eyes flashing angrily and his gentle face sullen and menacing.

He looks pretty angry, the ancient one, thought Kamolea, who had begun to get used to the old man's unexpected visits.

"What is it now?" he asked out loud.

"It's time to stop fooling around with the women, son," said the aged man in a deep, serious voice.

"What do you mean?" asked Kamolea, surprised.

"You heard me, Kamolea," the old man's tone was rather menacing. "These women are an unnecessary distraction on your warrior's path. They are weapons that *the runt* will use very craftily against you. I'm going to tell you one of the most important secrets in your struggle with these demons: your sexual energy is the most powerful weapon in this fight. You cannot afford the luxury of wasting it, as it is a matter of life and death. Understand? It's not meant to be between you and this girl. Every man has a destiny, and believe me, yours is not to get married here and spend the rest of your life in slavery."

Kamolea's countenance clearly displayed his lack of understanding.

"I don't get what you want from me," he stammered.

"Today, you did something wrong without realizing it," rasped the old man. "There was a time you promised a girl named Illima that you would always be faithful to her, remember? She was not only your first, but also your true love. The lust you experience for Uma, for instance, is *the runt's* allure. It has nothing to do with the pure feeling of genuine love and only aims to destroy your happiness. And what about Aley? You should be ashamed of yourself, for you are playing with the heart of this innocent maiden, who has so deeply fallen for you."

"Why should I be ashamed?" asked Kamolea angrily.

"Don't play the fool," snapped the ancient one sternly. "You feel nothing for her, and you are perfectly aware of it. The only thing that interests you is getting underneath her underwear, losing your virginity, then leaving her all alone. Heed my words, though—it's not going to happen."

"And why not? Everybody needs a woman to play with," Kamolea yelled, but the old man raised his hand, and he froze with his mouth half-open.

"I know what you are thinking," he said. "Why do others do whatever they like, while you cannot? Because, my young disciple, to whom so much has been given, much is expected. God chose you to fight the elements, face eternity, and learn truth and wisdom, so you have to be stronger, braver, and wiser than your fellow men. God's warriors must be holy, impeccable, models of a perfect human being. I will not allow you to become like the rest of the manhood—unfaithful and treacherous, always looking aside. True love is a gift from the Lord to the pure in heart. It is eternal and unique, and in your case, it has only one name—Illima. So, from now on, I forbid you to be with another woman before I reunite you with her."

Kamolea could not believe his ears. A wild fury welled up in his chest and jolted through his body.

"But that's ridiculous!" he roared. "You know perfectly well that it's impossible to return to Mahiha Komo! I'm a slave, for God's sake, treated worse than Don Diego's dogs. But even if I were a free man, how would I find the way across that blue immensity over there! And why should I go back in the first place? The minute I set foot on Maniha Komo, I'm a dead man. And you, you bloody fool, you don't have any right to forbid me anything, not after everything you have done to me. I was cast out because of you; I've spent the best years of my youth as a fucking slave—your fault again; and now, when I finally catch a glimpse of hope and happiness, you come and want to deprive me of the most natural thing for every man—to have a woman?! What kind of twisted freak are you? Get out of my sight with your stupid admonitions! Beat it! I never wanna see you again."

The old man smiled. Kamolea went berserk.

"I said *go!*" he yelled, then, in a flash of rage, he grabbed the club he had prepared for Aka's guards and swung it at the old man. The weapon hit an invisible wall and shattered in hundreds of splinters, which flew across the hut. Kamolea shrieked with pain, covered his face, and fell to his knees. His cheeks were covered with tiny slivers, which were sticking out of him like a hedgehog's spines.

"Enough of your tantrums, my boy," said the aged one. He lifted his hand, and Kamolea's pain magically vanished. He froze, concentrated, and unable to move. All of a sudden, all he could do was listen to the old man's deep, enchanting timbre.

"What makes a man a man, Kamolea?" he asked. "It's neither the number of murdered foes nor the total of the women he has slept with. Your word and your honor measure your value and make you the model of a good man. You gave your word to Illima, and there is no way of backing out. You think you can't find your way back to your native home, but remember: you should never say the word 'impossible' when you are speaking about Lord. There is nothing impossible when God supports you, my son. Pray and believe, and *He* will show you how to return to your island. Let *Him* heal your wounded soul and lead you through the dark sea of your awareness because *He* is the only light on your arduous path. And if you are humble enough to listen to Him and follow His signs, He will bring you back to Maniha Komo, and to your beloved Illima. Promise me now that you will let go of Aley and never seek another woman until you see Illima again."

Kamolea did not respond. Something inside him furiously resisted the notion of giving up on women, but rather than responding, he just stood stock still, his thoughts like a whirlpool in his head, and his lips tightly pressed together. The old man gave him a deep look and said,

"You need to cope with *the runt*, my boy. Learn how to block out that voice that ceaselessly whispers to you, leads you by the nose, and prevents you from remembering Illima. Don't play the demons' game and don't go against me, 'cause it's hard for you to kick against the prick. Mark my words; you will do what I say, or you will suffer—it's as simple as that. Heed my warning, or you will regret it. You must know by now that I always get my way."

Then, the old man vanished in a puff of white smoke. The sharp pain from the splinters returned, and Kamolea collapsed onto the earthen floor, howling.

"Fuck you, you crazy old bastard!" he bellowed. The runt cackled inside his head and yelled triumphantly,

"Promise nothing and screw all the women in the world! You're the man!"

CHAPTER XVII

DONA LUCIA

"Pst... Aley! Over here," Kamolea beckoned her from inside the barn. It was pitch-dark. She groped toward the voice's direction and squeezed her way through the tiny hole towards the back wall. Kamolea gave her a hand and pulled her up in the hayloft. It was hot and smelled of fresh hay and cow shit. There, he hurled her on a haystack and started fervently kissing her, sliding his hand under her skirt.

"Stop," she mumbled, not convinced at all, catching his hand and tightly pressing her moist thighs together. "I told you already, not before you speak to my father. He'll kill us both if we do it before."

"I can't stand just kissing you anymore, Aley. It drives me crazy; my balls are gonna explode."

"And whose fault is that? You promised me last time you'd ask Father, but you've done nothing. You know how it works—you must vow to marry me, and if he agrees, we'll be officially betrothed..."

"Niddi told me today that he has arranged a meeting with your old man for tomorrow evening," Kamolea said.

"Finally! So, you can wait another day then, can't you? Let's see what he says."

"I really want to impress him, to show him I really care about you,"

Kamolea said. "How do you say in your language, 'I love your daughter'?"

"*An sabed be sisgwa*," Aley chirruped.

"Sabed what?"

"You'd better give up on that, Crespo," her intonation betrayed her grin. "I don't think that stuttering in our language would impress him much. He's been a little grumpy lately, and I'm pretty anxious about his reaction. The odds aren't in your favor as you aren't one of us, but because of your glory—and everybody being so afraid of you—it might work." She smiled lovingly and kissed him, pressing her body against his.

"Everybody's scared but you," smiled Kamolea, caressing her face.

"Well, maybe a little," she admitted. "To crush Raul and Aka within a month, is what I call the work of a vigorous man. In the end, Aka looked terrible, a mere skeleton. Tell me, how did you turn his spell against him?"

"I just prayed to the right god," Kamolea said, smiling. "But I advise you not to get me too angry, otherwise..." He growled and nipped her at the neck. She giggled with pleasure.

"I love you so much, Crespo," she said, her eyes shining in the dark-ness. "I'll pray to Nandummad[45] that tomorrow we finally get officially engaged. And you ought to pray to your mighty god too—if *He* saved you from Aka, *He* certainly wouldn't refuse you such a small favor as to be together, would *He*?"

"I'll pray for sure," said Kamolea. They kissed for a little longer, then she left. Kamolea got to his place and climbed into the hammock, careful not to wake his new roommate—a skinny black fellow in his thirties, snoring in the corner. He stared at the ceiling, unable to fall asleep. The adrenaline was coursing through his veins, making him anxious and alert. Tomorrow he would finally ask Wiga, Aley's father, for his permission to wed his daughter. How would he react? Would he

---

45 The main female deity of the Kuna tribe.

be angry or friendly? What if he said no? Kamolea clutched the cross, ran his index finger across the carved figure, pressed it to his lips, and began whispering,

"Please, Almighty Benito's God, and you, *His Son*, hung on wood, make Wiga accept me. Please, please, don't listen to the old man! Don't allow him to impede my happiness, as he has always done. I beg you, Jesus, let me be happy for once. If you do this for me, I'll ask Dona Lucia to convert me to your religion when the padre comes to the plantation next time."

Calmed by the gentle swing of his hammock, he drifted off to sleep and dreamt of Aley. When Facundo's whistle woke him, he was in a euphoric mood, carrying a broad smile on his lips. Later on, as he mechanically cut sugar cane in the field, he focused himself entirely on the upcoming meeting.

I have to crack his stony face, but as Aley said, the odds are against me, he thought. *Hopefully, Niddi will change his mind about me being an outsider... I must see my friend during the break for a final chat...*

Immersed in thought, he paid no heed to the scorching heat, nor to the insects that would otherwise have irked him. The hours dragged by, and it took an eternity for the lunch break to come. He ate under the shadow of the thatch with the others, but neither Aley nor Niddi were at the gathering. *Perhaps Niddi is in the woods, cutting down trees for Don Diego's new hacienda, but where is Aley?* Kamolea brooded, irritated. The pipe's blare announced that the break was over and he got up slowly, patting his full belly. As he rose, he saw the overseer Pedro Carreno cantering towards the slaves.

"Crespo, Amare, Escalador,[46] you, Perro Kuna,[47] and you, Cara Fea,[48] come with me!"

---

46 The Climber.

47 Dog of the Kuna tribe.

48 Ugly Face.

He wheeled his stallion around and Kamolea ran after him, followed by three black men and one Indian about his age. They went out onto the large road that separated the sugar cane field from the dell and continued towards the jungle. Pedro's horse raised a cloud of dust, which flew into their eyes and mouths, and they all coughed and sneezed, gasping for breath. As they entered the forest, the dust disappeared and Kamolea brushed his oozing eyes, realizing quite quickly that they had just passed the place of Raul's death. He glimpsed the stone where the hateful overseer had smashed his head. It was still stained with the brute's blood. Kamolea shuddered.

It's a bad omen, he thought. *Some more blood is coming.* The party penetrated deep into the forest, and in a little while, they could hear distant voices and the thud of axes. Soon, the narrow path took them to a small clearing, where four men were cutting an immense tree called Roble,[49] one of the toughest in the jungle. They were clearly exhausted, hardly lifting their axes to deliver hesitant, anemic blows to the trunk. Even their strongest efforts hadn't got through a third of the trunk's mighty diameter.

"They've been hewing it the whole morning and have broken three axes already," growled Pedro. "Must be done by sunset, and this one too," he pointed to a tall Kapok[50] about twenty yards to the right. "Cre-spo, Amare, start on it right away, and you three get down to the Roble. The others can have a break and a bite, but be quick; there's no time to waste." The men handed the axes to the newcomers and sat down to eat nearby. Kamolea and Amare, a young tall black man, faced each other on the same side of the tree and started hitting it with sharp, rhythmic blows.

Kamolea was bursting with energy. Thinking ahead about his upcoming engagement made him feel elated. The place rang with the

---

49 Oak.

50 Ceiba Pentranda, a gigantic tropical tree, reaching up to 250 feet.

axes' chimes as the splinters flew aside, and the blades sank deeper and deeper into the trunk. *It's weird to be so soft*, Kamolea thought. A suspicious crack made him halt abruptly and look up. The tremendous crown swayed ominously in the wind.

"Wait, Amare!" Kamolea shouted. "Something's wrong with the tree. It's like it's all rotten inside."

"So what?" grunted Amare back and hammered it again spitefully. The moment the blow found its mark, the Kapok cracked loudly and started falling in slow motion.

"Timber!" bellowed Kamolea. The men who were sitting in a semicircle on the ground gaped at the enormous tree closing in on them. They jumped or rolled over, shouting and jostling each other, as the Kapok crashed down with a mighty thud, crushing most of them under its crown. Screams and shouts filled the air, and total confusion reigned. Pedro's horse bolted, neighing sharply, and ran into the woods, carrying away the long gun of his master. The overseer went berserk.

"What the hell did you do, you bloody dunces?" he bellowed, tugging at the tree. "What are you staring at? Come and help me out! Bring some poles to lift the trunk!"

All the survivors rushed and fervently began pulling and tugging, straining every muscle, their eyes almost popping out from the superhuman efforts, but the damned thing did not budge an inch. From beneath came the loud groan of a dying man.

"Too heavy, master," panted Cara Fea, a giant Negro a head taller than Pedro. "We'd better cut some boughs first…"

"There's no time for that. Get down the tree and try to lift it against your backs," Pedro commanded.

Cara Fea grunted something that did not sound like agreement.

"Are you giving me backtalk, you ugly wretch? Under the trunk, I said!" Pedro shouted.

Cara Fea glared at him, clasped his fallen ax, pivoted quickly, and whacked the overseer in the temple with its blunt end. Pedro collapsed without so much as a sound, and when Cara Fea delivered the second blow, his skull audibly cracked.

"You go underneath, filthy son of a bitch!" hissed Cara Fea. He grabbed the limp body and hurled it under the fallen tree, then turned to the others, who stared at him, terrified. "The Kapok fell and crushed him, right? Wrong place at the wrong time, too bad for him. You are all witnesses, aren't you? Crespo, go and get help while we cut the branches."

Kamolea sprinted away, following the narrow path, his feet barely touching the ground. Leaves and low twigs furiously lashed his face and shoulders. A pointed knar snagged his sleeve and yanked at him, gashing his arm above the elbow. Oblivious to the blood and pain, he doubled his speed and had almost reached the end of the forest when, just before the last sharp turn, he heard a scream. A second later, a horse sprang out in front of him and he had to hurl himself aside to avoid being trampled by the spotted mare as it galloped past him, deep into the woods.

Wasn't that the mistress's horse? As the thought occurred to him, a screech came from around the corner and froze his blood, propelling him to an even high gear. He rounded the bend but stopped in his tracks at the terrifying scene that revealed itself to him. About ten yards ahead lay Dona Lucia, staring in horror at a large puma advancing towards her. Kamolea saw it stalking, its muscles twitching, its eyes focused on its prey. Then, it lowered its body, preparing to launch its mortal attack. Kamolea had no time to think. He dashed and hurled himself forward to shield Dona Lucia just at the moment the cat jumped. They clashed in the air and rolled over on the ground. The puma lost its balance for a split second, then sprang quickly to its feet again and, spitting and hissing, swooped on Kamolea, who raised his hands and ducked his head to hide his neck. The beast hit him with its paw and stunned him. Another blow stripped the flesh off his right shoulder, almost to the bone. The blood gushed from him like a geyser, and its smell drove the panther wild. With a low growl, it sank its fangs into Kamolea's arm and gnawed at his face, seeking his throat. The excruciating pain was so intense that he passed out as the sharp teeth neared its windpipe, when two gunshots in quick succession blew its head clean off. Dona Lucia's two guards rushed towards her, shaking with horror.

"Are you all right, Mistress? Your horse ran amok, and we could not keep up. Are you hurt?" asked Belisario, still aiming his gun at the beast.

"Estoy bien gracias.[51] This man gave his life to save mine. Is he dead?" she panted, pointing at Kamolea.

Carlos de Rima bent down over the lifeless body lying in a pool of blood and pressed his fingers against Kamolea's throat.

"He's still alive, but he's losing a lot of blood. We must hurry!" He tore off a piece of Kamolea's shirt and tied it around his arm and shoulder, fashioning a mock tourniquet.

"Carlos, take him directly to the mansion and call immediately for Doctor Ignacio!" said Dona Lucia. "Do everything possible to save him! Watch over him as if it were me! Go!"

"On your order, Mistress!" said Carlos de Rima. He lifted Kamolea, put him across his horse, and galloped towards the manor at breakneck speed.

"Come with me, Dona Lucia. I'll take you home," said Belisario. "Let me help you mount the horse."

At that moment, Amare rounded the bend and ran toward them.

"Help!" he cried. "People are dying in the clearing!"

"What happened?" asked Belisario and Dona Lucia simultaneously.

"A tree fell and crushed several men," panted Amare.

"Belisario, go seek help!" Dona Lucia ordered.

"And you, Mistress?"

"I'll be fine! Go!"

Belisario whirled his mount and spurred it, muttering, "God, what a shitty day!"

---

51 I'm fine, thanks.

* * *

Kamolea's head throbbed. Somebody grasped his hand, and an excited female voice cried,

"Look, Doctor, his lids are twitching!"

"Yes, and his pulse is more palpable," responded a male voice.

"I think he's coming around…. Thank God he's alive!" It was Dona Lucia's voice.

Kamolea opened his eyes with a groan, and thousands of knives stabbed his head, which was now swathed in bandages. The pain was excruciating. He tried to move, but his body was stiff, and his arms and left shoulder, both similarly bound, hurt severely. The pale face of Dona Lucia distorted as she bent over him, and he closed his eyes once again.

"It's a miracle, considering how much blood he has lost," the doctor was saying.

"My angel," warbled Dona Lucia. "God sent him to protect our family! First Isabella, and now me! I should have found him a suitable job in the mansion from the beginning but, God forgive me, I did nothing for him. That's going to change now. He will be my son, and I will treat him as a member of my family."

The male's voice replied, but all Kamolea could hear was the sound of a hundred bells ringing and, momentarily, he passed out again.

* * *

Two weeks later, Kamolea woke up without the usual excruciating pain in his head. He was getting better with every passing day, and Doctor Ignacio had removed his bandages.

He hauled himself into a sitting position, leaned against the down pillow, and glanced at the open window, through which came the intense chirping of birds and a sweet fragrance of Plumeria mixed with Alzatea. He inhaled eagerly, enjoying the glorious sunny morning and thinking that life was not so bad after all. Now he lived in the mansion and got the royal treatment compared with the other slaves. For the first time, he slept in a proper bed covered with sheets and laid his head on a pillow stuffed with goose feathers. The food was terrific, straight from the master's kitchen. Doctor Ignacio visited him every two days to clean his wounds and change his bandages. Dona Lucia saw him often, once or twice a day. She would sit with him for a while, smiling, and ask him how he felt. To Kamolea, she was the kindest person he had ever met, which was understandable—he had never been treated with such tenderness in his life.

A puff of wind filled the room with a sweet aroma that reminded him of that magic night when he had first kissed Aley. What was she doing now? He missed her so much! He knew he had to see her when he was feeling better and meet her father, as they had important things to discuss…

A quiet knock at the door took him out of his reverie, and Dona Lucia entered, carrying something faded green in color and vaguely familiar in shape.

"Oh, you've woken up," she smiled pleasantly. "How do you feel today?" This time, instead of taking the chair, she sat on the edge of his bed.

"Look what I brought for you. I think it's yours," she said after Kamolea assured her he was doing well.

She handed him Benito's satchel. Kamolea grinned with pleasure.

"Thank you, Mistress!" he mumbled as he took the black Bible out.

"I asked my husband to find all your belongings from the time you arrived, and he unearthed this bag. But that's not all—I have excellent news for you. Don Diego gave you to me, so you are my property now and I am the only one responsible for your destiny. You will live permanently in the house, in this room. You will not work in the field anymore. Instead, when you completely recover, you will look after the garden and, when necessary, you can help in the kitchen. From now on, nobody will lay a finger on you, and you won't be treated as a slave anymore. I will pay you a small wage for your labor every month, besides the food and clothes that you've been provided with."

"Thank you, Mistress," uttered Kamolea, moved. "Splendid news indeed. I'm very grateful…"

"No, Crespo, it's me who will be indebted to you forever," said Dona Lucia, squeezing his hand. She frowned as she mentioned his name.

"By the way, I have always wondered what your real name is? In the official court record, it's Junu, but I strongly doubt that's your native name. Is it?"

Kamolea shook his head.

"This was the name of a monkey that my captain gave me," he said.

"What is it, then?" insisted Dona Lucia.

"Kamolea," he uttered.

"What was that? Spell it for me, please!"

"Ka-mo-lé-a," he repeated slowly. "It means 'a new beginning' in my native language."

"Kamolea? It rings so euphoniously in my ears. And what a beautiful meaning! Kamoléa," she repeated. "Am I pronouncing it right?" He nodded.

"Good," she said, satisfied, "now I know your proper name. Tell me, Kamolea, what else can I do for you to show you my gratitude for saving me from the teeth of that beast? Ask whatever you want, and I'll grant it."

"It was nothing. Don't worry about it," Kamolea muttered. The news that he was going to work in the house had made him so happy that he needed nothing more.

"I appreciate your modesty," said Dona Lucia, "but you saved my life and suffered badly because of me, which merits the highest price. I understand I can never repay you completely for all you have done, but I promise you that from now on, you'll live better than many free men."

Kamolea looked intently at Dona Lucia. She was a slim, medium-height woman of middle age with a sharp, pinched face and thin, clenched lips, revealing a strict and ascetic character. Her hair, turning gray already, was lifted in a bun just above her neck. She would have been rather plain-looking if not for her black, blazing, mesmerizing eyes, which illuminated her features and gave her a noble and intelligent expression. He had once heard Rita saying that Dona Lucia was a highborn, very educated señora.

She took his hand between her two palms and smiled at him encouragingly.

"Tell me! Whatever you want," she urged him.

Kamolea could not believe his luck. For every slave, freedom was the most valuable price and a logical wish to ask. He knew of slaves who had been liberated on certain special merits. As he belonged to Dona Lucia now, she would undoubtedly have the power to set him free. And yet, he hesitated. His eyes flicked across at the Bible that he had tossed on the bed, and in a flash, he saw himself on the White Shark, talking with Benito that sunny morning about the book he was reading. *"If you could read, you would understand what a pleasure it is to discover new worlds through books."* Benito was saying.

"I would be happy if you could teach me to read, Mistress," he blurted out. "I'd like very much to read this book," he pointed to the Bible. As soon as he said it, his jaw dropped—he could not believe that such words had just come out of his mouth.

"What have you done, you fucking wanker! What about your freedom! You've blown a one-in-a-million chance!" screamed the familiar shrill voice.

"You want to read the Bible?" asked Dona Lucia, genuinely surprised.

He felt ashamed now.

"I know it's stupid, Mistress. Sorry, I just… I don't know what compelled me to ask this," he blushed and looked aside.

He sensed Dona Lucia's piercing eyes on him.

"Oh, my dear boy!" she whispered.

He looked up, expecting to meet her stern stare but was surprised to find she was crying! He had offended her for sure! This time, he had really overstepped the mark. He was a slave, after all, and was supposed to work, not read.

"I'm sorry, Mistress, I meant no offense," he muttered.

She stood up and hugged him. Her eyes were two blazing coals.

"You think you've offended me, Kamolea? You… Oh, Kamolea, you are the most amazing human being I have ever met in my life! After everything you've been through, this is the last thing I expected to hear from you! I was sure that you would claim your freedom. Now I know Lord has sent you to save me. But today, I realized something else. You are chosen by God, for it is written: '*Only those called by my Father would come to me*!' Be blessed, my boy! Of course I'll teach you to read and write as well, and much more. My own children have no interest in learning, which has hurt me a lot. But with you, it will be different! I'll give you a royal education, the same that I had when I was young, and this knowledge will open infinite horizons before you. As soon as you get better, we'll start. Oh, I am so happy you have asked me this!"

She squeezed his hand, wiped away her tears, and said,

"This will be an amazing journey, you'll see!"

* * *

After Dona Lucia left, Kamolea stared for a long time through the window, overwhelmed by the news.

I am on a roll for once! He wanted to scream with joy, his heart fluttering with happiness. *No more fucking sugar canes and bloody overseers to beat the shit out of me! No more struggling up in the evening with an aching body and cracked lips bleeding for water. That life is over! Oh, I can just imagine how much the others must envy me and seethe with jealousy, but frankly, I don't care. I'm going to find Aley and Niddi right away and tell them the splendid news! But I have to wash first.*

The adrenalin was pumping through his veins, and an upsurge in energy overpowered his body. He hauled himself out of bed and took several staggering steps to the table, where there was a large copper basin full of water. He dipped his hands in, bending over to splash his face… but then, he froze to the spot and stared at his reflection. Gradually, all his enthusiasm evaporated, and he became pale as a ghost.

From the water, the ugliest face he had ever seen gazed back at him. The worn skin was reddish-brown, cut, and covered with scars. A sizeable slash began at his left temple and crossed his cheek, reaching his chin. On the right cheekbone, a similar gash descended to the corner of his mouth. Several tiny stitches crisscrossed each other around his eyebrows and forehead, touching the lid of his half-closed left eye. Two different grooves marked his front, one of them running to his right temple, the other cutting vertically into his front and extending itself to the crown. The skin around this last scar was scabby, and the hair was missing. The lobe of his left ear was gone as well.

"Almighty God," he whispered.

The high-pitched voice burst out laughing, splitting his brain.

"That's the old geezer's gift to you, handsome boy!" it screamed. *"He warned you that you'd suffer if you didn't leave Aley alone, and he kept his promise. How do you like your ugly mug now?"*

Kamolea staggered back and crashed down on the bed, lying prone. Severe depression washed over him, clutching him in a pitiless grip.

"I'd rather have died," he uttered. The grief was pressing against his chest like a rock, and he had neither the energy nor the desire to move. About an hour later, Rita came with a tray of dishes and found him in the same position.

"Crespo!" she exclaimed. "The mistress told me you're doing well and gave me permission to visit you."

He turned to her, and she let out a faint cry, almost dropping the tray.

"It's hideous, my face, isn't it?" croaked Kamolea, a lump blocking his throat.

"It will heal, don't fret too much," Rita soothed him, but he perceived a touch of doubt in her low, deep-toned voice. "Look, I've brought you your favorite chicken broth. You must eat a lot now to regain your energy."

"Thanks, Rita. Leave it on the table, please. I'm not hungry right now."

"And to think I prepared it with so much love, especially for you," she muttered, hurt, and slammed the tray on the table.

"Don't be cross; I'll eat it later," Kamolea said. "Come, I want to ask you something."

Panting from the heat, Rita brushed a streak of sweat from her plump face and sat on the side of the bed.

"You all right?" she asked him

"I'll survive," Kamolea grinned wryly. "So, give me the news from the village. How are things going?"

"Not very well, hon," she shook her head sadly. "They tightened the discipline after the Kunas killed the foremen and escaped. Don Diego was so mad that he imposed a curfew, and now the overseers are sterner than ever. Imagine, after supper, they unleash their bloody hounds and set them on anyone who goes outside after sunset. Folks often miss meals or have no time to fetch water."

"But wait, what are you talking about? Some people escaped?" Kamolea asked.

"Yes, twelve Kunas fled the same day you saved the mistress. The tree that crushed Pedro Carreno and the others provoked such a commotion that they took their chances and killed the two gatekeepers, after which they scampered off into the jungle. By the time the over-seers understood what was going on, it was too late. So, they pursued them the whole night but eventually, they lost them."

"Which guards were killed?" Kamolea asked.

"Belisario and Rodrigo..."

"Rodrigo! Niddi will be glad to hear that!" cried Kamolea.

"I bet he will!" chuckled Rita. "They said that he and his friend Oller did it..."

"Almighty God! He was one of the fugitives then?"

"He was, and Oller also, with Duali, Udur, and Wiga..."

"Wiga? Aley's father?" Kamolea interrupted.

"Yes, of course, with his entire family..."

"Aley ran away with him?" cried Kamolea, stunned.

"Are you deaf, lad? She, and her mother and brothers..."

Kamolea stopped listening to Rita. The room swam before him, and his eyes grew moist.

"Aley's gone," he whispered.

"I have to go," Rita slapped herself on the forehead, got up clum-sily, then waddled toward the door. "I'll send somebody to collect the dishes later. So long, Crespo. I'm glad you've made it through!" She left and the draught slammed the door behind her.

Kamolea sank back and peered at the ceiling. His previous grief had multiplied by ten after the news about Aley. Tears started rolling down his injured face.

"Once again, I have lost somebody close to my heart," he sobbed.

A hoarse whisper came straight from the middle of his chest, as though his heartstrings were vibrating. But instead of music, words emerged.

"*It's time for you to end your miserable life, handsome boy,*" the buzzing sound vibrated inside him. "*What's the point of living? Such a pathetic coward, a slave, despised by everyone. No friends, no love, and ugly as hell. No woman will look at your disgusting face ever again. Such a failure you are. And it could have been a lot different if you hadn't obeyed the old fucker."*

Kamolea could not agree more. He was heartbroken, and his anguish crushed him like a slumping boulder.

"Stretch your hand under the bed, gorgeous," the voice whispered again, this time gentle and husky. *"I brought you Hugo's dagger. Remember Hugo? He sends you his regards. Take the dagger and open your veins, pretty boy. I want to hear your dripping blood making a lovely thumping sound against the floor. Drip… drip… drip… One drop at a time, bit by bit, draining your useless life away until we are reunited at last. Eternal brothers by blood. Your damn blood, you fool!"*

The intensity of the voice grew until the final words were almost screamed like the final cadenza of a soprano. Hypnotized, Kamolea rolled over on his stomach, reached under the bed, and wrapped his fingers around the cool steel of a knife. It wasn't Hugo's dagger, for sure. In fact, it rather resembled the knife that Doctor Ignacio used for taking blood.

He must have dropped it on his last visit, Kamolea thought.

"It will do the job!" screamed the voice.

He slowly brought the knife to his left wrist, and the blade touched the rose seashell bracelet. A bright light exploded in his mind, and the next instant, he found himself in a dark, hot, damp place that stank of rotten eggs. Somewhere near, a brook warbled its merry tune, and water dripped from the ceiling above him.

"The Steamy Cave," he whispered, surprised that he could speak. It was just like he remembered it, as the horror he had experienced then was forever engraved in his memory. Through the dense steam, Kamolea discerned the huge egg-shaped stone, rising from the floor in the center of the cavernous hall. He advanced warily, and sure enough, Kedia was there. The small, monkey-like figure, wrapped up in her own long white hair that trailed across the floor, leaned against the boulder and clutched her knees, her back arched like a cat. She was humming something hardly audible under her breath, but as Kamolea took another step, she cocked her head, alert, and croaked in the Tipihao language,

"Who's there?"

And then, through the thick wreaths of smoke, a young woman emerged, and Kamolea let out a gasp. Despite all these years, he recognized her at once.

"Illima! You have become so gorgeous!" he exclaimed as she advanced towards him. She was naked and willowy, blossomed to incredible beauty. Her black hair reached her calves, and her full, heavy breast had nothing in common with the skinny girl he remembered. Kamolea stared enchanted at her mesmerizing black eyes, admiring her perfect face and full lips, small nose, and high brow. Her countenance was pale and sad, though, and a tinge of sorrow shaded her eyes.

"Illima," he whispered, as a sharp pain stabbed his heart, and the love he had once experienced towards the black-eyed girl before him welled up inside like a mighty wave. At this moment, she was the only woman in the world who meant something to him. An overwhelming desire to take her in his arms and kiss her, again and again, shattered all his suicidal thoughts into pieces. He took a step towards her, but a loud cackle rang out, and suddenly he was in bed again, still clutching Doctor Ignacio's knife. The shrill voice continued tittering in his head and screaming,

"*Slash your wrists and die, you fool!*"

But this time, Kamolea paid no attention.

"Illima," he said quietly. "How could I have forgotten you all these years, my heart? What are you doing in that ghastly place with the dreadful witch? I am such a fool to want to end my life when you need me so badly! I'll find a way to return to Maniha Komo and save you, my love. And I swear that nothing will stop me!"

CHAPTER XVIII

THE CONVERSION

A year later, on a gorgeous sunny morning, Kamolea was sweating in the scorching heat as he bent over the tropical flowers in Dona Lucia's garden. That day, he had been tasked with weeding a large perimeter in front of the house, but the work was going annoyingly slowly. He rose, ran his backhand across his bedewed forehead, and looked around.

The view was magnificent. Behind him, the mansion, a huge two-story building painted pale rose, was glistening in the bright sun. Stone pillars and high arches supported a vast wooden terrace, forming a portico, at the far end of which Kamolea could see the glass door of the main entrance where the dining room and the saloon were located. A carved white parapet encircled the wide veranda on the upper floor, with several balcony doors leading to different bedrooms belonging to Don Diego's large family. Señorita Isabella was the youngest of the four siblings and the only one still unmarried, in contrast with her three brothers, who already had young children. The slaves who took care of the household slept in hammocks in the back of the house, the so-called "black wing," a miserable ramshackle annex adjacent to the kitchen and the laundry room.

As Kamolea admired the mansion, a two-wheeled carriage rattled down the large cobbled road.

It must be the padre who was supposed to come yesterday. The mistress will be happy; she was worried about him, Kamolea thought. The carriage passed along the lush tropical greenery that flanked the road, went past the central marble fountain, and stopped a bit further along. A man clad in black got out and walked down the alley leading to the round arbor—Dona Lucia's favorite place, where she, surrounded by flowers, spent a significant part of her time embroidering, knitting, reading, or meeting guests.

Kamolea squatted and continued pulling the rank grass and weeds, brooding about his dull life of slavery that dragged monotonously in the same mundane routine. Every morning, he would get up at sunrise and spend the day either working in the garden or helping out in the kitchen and stables.

The evenings were depressing, as he felt terribly lonely. He longed for a human company so badly that now he was even ready to return to the village and work on an equal footing with the other slaves. He missed their gatherings around the campfire, where the worn-out men and women would always find the strength to laugh, crack jokes, tease each other, and sing their long, sad songs, despite their awful lives.

But they had never accepted him back. He had joined them a few times, but it always finished with the same disastrous result—as soon as he approached them, they lapsed into silence and broke up the party almost immediately. Even Rita, his old friend, had not been too amiable of late.

"What's going on, Rita?" he had asked her once. "Why does everybody hate me? Why do they avoid me? What's wrong with me? Is it my face or what?"

"Your face has nothing to do with it," replied Rita grimly. "They are rather jealous of you—the mistress's pet that lives in the mansion, eats from the master's table, and sleeps wrapped in sheets. But there is something more, Crespo. They fear you. They do not understand how on earth you defeated Aka and survived the cougar's attack. People talk... You know how they are, them superstitious folks; they are so scared of you that they prefer to stay away from you."

"What kinds of yarns are they spinning about me?" Kamolea asked, but Rita waved him away with the words,

"You don't want to know."

Thus, he gave up on socializing and focused all his attention on his plan to return to his native island. During the long, lonely nights, he dreamed of Illima. The longing to see her had increased to an unbearable level, but no matter how hard he racked his brain, he could not find a way to get back to her.

How would I find Maniha Komo in this immensity? It's only water over there, nothing else. I have witnessed miracles not once in my life, but this still seems impossible...

"Hey, Crespo, the mistress has called you to the arbor." Startled, he glanced at Belade, one of Dona Lucia's servants, who was walking towards the mansion with an empty tray. She was young and pretty, but Kamolea did not like her, for she was always turning her head away, unable to bear the sight of his injured face.

"What?" he shouted back.

"Go to the arbor, the mistress has summoned you," repeated Belade and quickly vanished inside the house.

Kamolea lifted the rake across his shoulder and strode down the cobbled alley. At the very end of the garden, he spotted the white marble cross of the chapel, perched on the red gabble roof. The cross glistened in the sun, beautifully reflecting the sunshine rays.

"Fuck you!" spat Kamolea through clenched teeth, looking at it spitefully, and a sudden rage seethed inside his chest.

Why on earth did I say that? he wondered the next second, surprised by this unexpected surge of fury. Meanwhile, he turned right and took a narrow path, which led him to the small wooden rotunda covered with ivy and climbing roses.

Inside, Dona Lucia and a man wearing a black cassock sat at a round table, drinking a tricolor fruit cocktail.

"This is the boy I've been telling you so much about, Father," said Dona Lucia, as Kamolea walked into the arbor and greeted them with a bow. "Kamolea, let me introduce you to Padre Alberto del Monte, our family friend from Seville. He has come from Spain with a mission to convert our slaves to Christianity, at least the ones who are interested in doing so. He will stay at the plantation for three weeks to preach the Gospel, and the last Sunday before his departure, he will baptize everybody who is willing to embrace Jesus Christ. However, as you are so special to me, I insist on being your godmother and carrying out a special private ceremony for the upcoming Sunday."

"Thank you, Dona Lucia. I'm really moved, but I…"

"Oh, don't need to thank me, my boy. I assume you are ready to accept God, considering how much we have discussed the scriptures. The sacrament of baptism is the first and most important step to your conversion and your new spiritual life. Isn't that right, Father?"

"Indeed," Padre Alberto agreed.

Kamolea opened his mouth to say something, but no sound came out. Taking his silence as consent, Dona Lucia continued, her eyes shining with pride.

"I've been through many great topics of human history and culture with Kamolea. Every afternoon for the last year, I have taught him reading, writing, theology, Greek philosophy, myths and legends, the ancient history of Greece and Rome, Spanish customs, and so much more. He is a smart boy and a quick learner, and I am thrilled by his progress."

Padre Alberto allowed a slight smile, his bright blue eyes boring deeply into Kamolea.

"So, what have you liked most about your education, son?" the padre asked him. His voice was deep and calm, encouraging honesty.

"Almost everything sounds incredible to me, señor. Compared to the little island I was born on, with its ramshackle huts and simplicity, the pictures and drawings of the ancient temples and great cities that Dona

Lucia has shown me have left me speechless. The myths and legends about mighty warriors and great feats also... I adore the one about the two brothers who are raised by a she-wolf. The founders of the great empire, you know... I was so excited by this story that I could not sleep for days..."

"And what about God and the Christian religion?" asked Father Alberto.

"Well, this is certainly not so exciting," muttered Kamolea.

"Isn't it?" asked the padre. "I consider this the most important of all subjects."

"Kamolea has some doubts concerning the faith, and I don't want to force him into accepting Christianity only to please me," Dona Lucia said. "Now is the time to ask Padre Alberto everything that bothers you. Take a seat with us; don't be shy. Do you want some punch? No? It's all right. Fire away, now! Let the priest enlighten your soul!"

Kamolea sat clumsily at the edge of the bench and said, "Well, here is the thing—I'm not sure whether I want to adopt this religion at all."

"And why not, son?" asked Padre Alberto with a gentle smile. His white hair and open round face inspired trust, and Kamolea's fear disappeared, replaced by a certainty that this ascetic-looking man would understand his torment.

"Dona Lucia told me you had read some chapters of the Holy Book by yourself," continued the padre, "and that you have shown remarkable progress in your understanding and increasing belief. Is that so?"

"Frankly speaking, Master..."

"Father, son. You can call me Father Alberto."

"Honestly, Father, I find this teaching really stupid," Kamolea blathered, blushing, staring at the ground. "You see, our god, Kepolo, he is cool and never forbids us anything. He encourages us to be strong, fearless warriors and to keep the other tribes in subjection. And your religion is full of restrictions... Don't do this, don't do that... And this Jesus says strange things like *if somebody slaps you, offer him the other cheek.* I've never heard of something more stupid in my life. Am I so submissive and cowardly that I would do that? And then, there was another one, even better: *love your enemies and pray for them.* Sorry, but I could never accept loving my enemies or leaving somebody to beat me without hitting back. I wasn't raised like this, and it's not who I am."

"I understand your point," nodded Padre Alberto. "Tell me, what does your god look like, and how do you worship it?"

"Our God is a mighty man called *Kepolo,* who resides in *Rakapi,* the Sacred Tree. We bring our enemies there and sacrifice them to *him,* and then we eat their hearts and drink their blood. Thus, we receive their power and become invincible…" Kamolea's agitated voice trailed off as he saw the faces of his interlocutors had become elongated and deathly pale. The padre crossed himself.

"My god, you've never told me this," exclaimed Dona Lucia. "Have you ever committed such atrocities?"

"No, I wasn't allowed, and they cast me out just before I became a warrior."

"Have you killed anybody, my son?" asked the priest, frowning. The tension in his voice was palpable.

"No, as I said…"

"Good, good," said Father Alberto quickly, apparently relieved. "Because these are unpardonable sins, abominations of humanity. And did you say your tribe worships a tree?"

"That's God Kepolo's order," Kamolea confirmed. "We have worshipped the Sacred Tree since time immemorial."

"Another awful sin, my boy. Don't you know God's commandment: 'You shan't worship any idol, graven image or object on Earth or in the water beneath?' This commandment is so important that it comes second, immediately after the first one that forbids worshipping any other God than the true One. Why do you think this is so?"

"I don't know," Kamolea shrugged. "I like my god for leaving me to do whatever I want. Could I worship Him and your Christian God at the same time? It's not a big deal, is it? Why all the fuss?"

Padre Alberto stared at him in disbelief. In the awkward silence, Kamolea realized he had just said something quite absurd.

"You don't understand, do you?" the padre finally said. "Your god does not exist, son. It's a simple tree, and nobody dwells inside it! How could a tree be a deity? It's all made up. In reality, the man that your tribe worships is the Devil, the Evil One. In the Gospel, it is said: *'Whoever is not with me is against me, and whoever does not gather with me, scatters.'* You can't have it both ways. God is spirit and awareness; He is justice and light. But obviously, nobody on your island understands that, as they all have sold their souls to the Devil."

Kamolea considered his words for a moment, then he scratched his head and said, "You know, Father, I hear voices in my head, and they drive me nuts. The high-pitched one is the worse. I try to silence it, but sometimes it wakes me at night, yelling that I must not accept Jesus Christ, for I would vex Kepolo and terrible things would happen to me."

"Don't pay attention to it, son," said the padre. "This is a demon's voice. It is very much afraid that you'll do what is right, and it will lose control over you. You must fight it with prayer, and firm determination."

"I've heard about these demons, Father," Kamolea said, "but what are they? Do they really exist, or are they some imaginary things inside my head? At least, that's what the voice keeps telling me."

"You know, we are the hostages of forces we don't understand," sighed Padre Alfonso. "I can tell you this for sure: during my time as a priest, I have witnessed on countless occasions how these demons torture us, humans. And to answer your question, yes, they are real, conscious creatures that live inside us and ceaselessly use us for their goals. Whether they win or not depends on the strength of our spirit. In other words, the stronger your spirit, the weaker the demon inside you."

"I still can't believe that," Kamolea said.

"And that is precisely the goal of their master," said Padre Alberto. "All these demons have one ultimate ruler, the Devil, also called Satan and Lucifer. The last name derives from Latin and means *light-bringer* because he can transform into an angel of light. He wants to convince us that everything related to him is a fantasy and a lie, a figment of our imaginations. And I admit he is quite successful at doing this. Why? Because Satan is the ruler of our society, which is founded on lies, greed, and intrigue. The Devil makes people hard-hearted egoists who crave money, power, women, land, and so on—fake ambitions that ruin a man's life. Since time immemorial, all wars, slavery, abuse, destruction, and crimes have resulted from this vanity and selfishness.

"You asked me why there are so many rules in Christianity, and the answer is simple: they are a necessary part of the fight against the Devil. Religion teaches us how to live and behave, to be good people and, most importantly, how to resist the evil creature that blends so perfectly in with our personalities that it is almost impossible to detect. He sends us bad thoughts that provoke murder, adultery, fornication, theft, and lies. Blasphemy, malice, hypocrisy, anger, hatred, jealousy, envy, egoism, deceit, indifference, and greed—all these deeds and feelings are his invention.

"So, the more you give in to such sentiments, the more powerful the demons become inside you. These awful dark spirits devastate your soul, turning it into a desert. And this is the role of religion: it teaches you how to fight back. But this struggle, believe me, is the hardest thing in the world. 'Why so?' you might ask. It's because everybody has to confront themselves and face their vices and weaknesses. At first glance, this doesn't sound like a big deal, but I'll tell you now that the hardest victory in the world is the one over yourself. Make the glutton fast, the drunkard quit drinking, or the lecherous man refrain from adultery. They all go to church on Sunday, confess their sins, pray hypocritically, then go back and commit the same crimes, as they have no power to resist them. This makes their guilt thousands of times worse."

"But why do we need to repel these feelings?" asked Kamolea. "Can't we just accept them and live with them? In the end, we are who we are, aren't we?"

"No, we are not," the padre replied. "The truth is that we weren't created like that; we became evil after Satan has tempted us. That's why our earthly life is a trial in an arena, a hard, cruel battlefield. This is the way our Creator tests us in order to accept us back in His realm, and grant us eternity in Paradise. And when the fight is over, you arrive at the ultimate judgment of your performance, and then, believe me, you'd better be on the side of the winners. As the Romans says: '*Vae victis*,' which means: '*Woe to the vanquished*.'"

"And what do we have to do to win this battle?" Kamolea asked.

"The only way for us to succeed is to discipline ourselves to such a degree that we overcome the demon inside us," Padre Alberto responded. "We also need to accumulate all our mental energy and turn it into personal strength. Sexual energy, for instance, is the most powerful weapon in this struggle. Remember the seventh commandment: '*You shall not commit adultery*.' A man who is stingy with his seed is the greatest combatant against the evil."

"I'm not so sure about that," Kamolea muttered. "I've never been with a woman, and yet I cannot say I'm a great warrior..."

"Don't be sorry about the women, son," said Padre Alberto, smiling. "You will never be able to understand how strong you are until the moment of the ultimate battle. Dona Lucia pointed out that you are the only one who has survived so long on the plantation. Do you think this is by chance?"

"You have a point, Father," Kamolea said, agitated. "Look, although this Christian religion is for the weak and cowardly, and a part of me completely rejects it, I am sure your God is far mightier than Kepolo."

"What makes you think this?" asked the padre.

"Because He saved me several times. It all started on my native island, where He protected me from being torn to pieces. Then, He sent Benito to save me when this jerk Diego de Sylva was about to rape me; at least Benito said it was his God. I doubted his words for a long time, but then, after the last manifestation of His power, I am convinced that He and Jesus Christ are my protectors because what happened was incredible."

"And what was that?" Padre Alberto asked.

"There was a mighty magician, one of those Negros, Aka…"

"Aka? I've heard about him, yes. He caused a few problems," said Dona Lucia.

"Him exactly, Mistress. So, he cast black magic on me and tried to kill me just exactly as he did with the Great Gobongo. Then I have this cross," he took out the crucifix from inside his shirt, "so I prayed to the Almighty Lord and Jesus Christ. And it worked, Father!" Kamolea's eyes shone with wonder. "Instead of killing me, Aka dropped dead several days later, as though his magic had turned against him. At this moment, I understood Jesus is the one who protects me, even though He teaches us to be weak, obedient, and chicken-hearted."

"No, son, it's the contrary," said the padre. "Christianity has never been the religion of feeble and cowardly. To be a good Christian is the most difficult thing and only a few people achieve such perfection. You are obviously confused by the teaching that you must turn the other cheek, but imagine how strong you have to be not to answer to the evil with evil, and what perfect control over yourself you must have to withhold your instincts to strike back!"

"I still don't understand, Father," Kamolea said stubbornly. "Why do people who say they are good Christians not have any respect for God's commandments? For instance, it is written: *'You shall not kill.'* Nobody respects this. The White Shark's crew was a gang of butchers. My friend Benito was called *'Creyente'* because of his faith. He was the man who gave me the Holy Book, but he murdered many men. And the overseers? Since I have been here, they have killed scores of us! I overheard Raul bragging once that he was a good Christian and an impeccable husband and father, and that the slaves are closer to animals than humans, so it's not a sin to kill them. My point is, if our God Kepolo orders us to do something, we obey, right? Then, he grants us the freedom to do whatever we want. But with your God, it is the contrary—nobody obeys His rules, and in addition, He adds plenty of restrictions."

"That is true to a certain degree," agreed Padre Alberto. "I can see you are a clever boy, but don't let yourself be deceived by the Evil One. Everybody comes to the world with free will, and it's up to him to choose which side to take. However, as our Lord Jesus Christ revealed at the time, there will be consequences for those who do not respect God's commandments. I presume you are familiar with the narrative about Hell, the fiery pit into which evil people will be thrown to suffer? Everyone is responsible for their deeds, and I advise you to choose the right side. I see that you still have a long way to go, but the first step to repentance and purity begins with baptism—the most important ritual that will absolve you of your past sins and offer you a new life reunited with God. I feel that you are ready for it."

Kamolea got up, his lips tightly pressed together. The vein in his temple was twitching slightly. With his eyes fixed on the ground, he said,

"I will think about it, Father. Thank you for explaining to me all these religious riddles. It's a lot clearer now."

"So, we can you expect you on Sunday in the chapel? Your mistress and I will be glad to initiate you into your new life."

"I guess so," Kamolea said hesitatingly.

"Oh, I'm sure you will make the right decision, and this Sunday, your name will justify its meaning," said Dona Lucia. "You are free to go now, Kamolea."

Kamolea bowed, picked up his rake, and trotted toward the garden.

* * *

As though possessed by an evil spirit, Kamolea tossed and moaned in his sleep. It was two days before Sunday, and he had already firmly decided that Christianity was not the religion for him. This decision, however, instead of relieving him, had made him more miserable and restless.

In his dream, he found himself in a vast, gloomy hall, divided into three parts by wooden columns. In the center stretched two rows of pews, separated by an aisle, facing a small dais with a rectangular table. Behind the table, a richly carved wooden screen was flanked by a male and a female figure.

On the hall's left extremity, another full-size statue of a man hanging on an immense cross, drew Kamolea's attention. The crucifix resembled the one dangling from his neck. The man's head, tilted in a painful grimace, was crowned with a wreath of thorns.

Before the cross flickered many candles and Kamolea decided to ignite one for Benito. As soon as his fingers touched the candle, the crucified man glowed, and myriad rays started streaming from him. Kamolea fell to the floor, then looked up, frightened, and tightly shut his eyes.

"Kamolea, why don't you love me?" came a kind voice from above. "Why do you insult me and say that I am weak and cowardly? I taught people the truth and showed them the way to eternal life. I died on the cross for them. Do you think a coward could do that? In a world built on lies, preaching the truth is the most arduous thing. Accept me as your God and love me with all your heart, for I am the way, the truth, and the life, and you cannot ignore me anymore."

I prayed to you to give me Aley, and you didn't. I don't need such a God, Kamolea wanted to cry, a boiling rage seething in his breast.

"Be humble, Kamolea, and pure in your thoughts. God Almighty could move mountains and make the Earth shake. Who are you, little mite, to dare to challenge Him and lay down conditions? Accept your fate and forget about Aley—her destiny is not related to yours. You are linked to Illima, and if you accept me, I promise to bring you back to her and bestow upon you both five beautiful children."

"You can do that?" muttered Kamolea unbelievingly.

"If you truly believe in me, nothing is impossible," said the man.

A sudden flash blinded Kamolea, and he woke up moaning. The moment he opened his eyes, he was overcome with joy, and not even a shade of hesitation tortured his heart anymore. A light shone inside him as though a celestial ray had touched his soul. The rest of that night, he brooded over the promise of the man on the cross and wondered with excitement what the ritual of accepting his new faith would be like.

* * *

When the Sunday finally came, Kamolea jumped out of bed early in the morning and started dressing, still giddy from his sleepless night. He had eventually drifted off just before dawn, tormented by the nagging voice of the runt screaming and raging all the time, no matter how hard he tried to suppress it.

While he was putting on the new white embroidered shirt that Dona Lucia had prepared specially for the ceremony, he attempted to instill some order to his thoughts and ignore the new tantrum echoing in his ears.

"You can't do this to me, you dumb, ugly wretch! Where the hell do you think you're going? If you betray your god, prepare to meet Kepolo's wrath!"

"It was a blissful time when I couldn't hear this bloody voice," Kamolea muttered. "Of course, it's all the old man's fault, as usual—it all started when he reappeared."

He sighed and went outside. It was a glorious sunny morning, and as he walked past the multicolored flowers in the garden, their bright colors and sweet fragrance lifted his heart. He ascended the cobbled alley that led to the chapel, his eyes riveted on the marble cross gleaming in the distance, growing more prominent with every step. The chapel's small building gradually emerged; first, the red gabled roof, then the white walls, and finally, the wide-open door, flanked by two pillars plastered to the facade and connected with an arch in relief.

Padre Alberto del Monte and Dona Lucia stood at the entrance. His mistress waved at him, beaming.

"Come inside, my son," Padre Alberto invited him, and Kamolea, smiling bashfully back, stepped into a gloomy room with a row of benches in the center. From the wall just in front of him hung a massive crucifix with a church lamp lit beneath. Before the benches, on a solid oak table, were copies of the Holy Bible, a large copper kettle full of water, a silver cross inlaid with gems, a thick white candle, and a carafe, half-filled with yellowish chrism oil.

Padre Alberto motioned to him to stand beside the table.

"Did you eat or drink anything this morning?" he asked suspiciously.

"No, Father, just like you ordered me," Kamolea responded.

"Good," said Padre Alberto. "Have you invited somebody to be a witness to this glorious moment?"

Kamolea shook his head.

"All my friends are dead or gone," he said.

"So sad," murmured the padre, glancing at Kamolea's face. Then, he cleared his throat and said,

"Let us begin the rite now. Please, Dona Lucia, step forward to Kamolea's left."

Padre Alberto dipped the cross into the bucket and started sprinkling water everywhere, mumbling something in an unfamiliar language. A few drops fell on Kamolea's face, and he felt them burning him like a fire. The padre started reading the Bible and asked Kamolea something that he didn't understand at first, as his ears buzzed as though myriad insects were flapping their wings around him.

Padre Alberto repeated his question.

"Do you believe in God the Father, Creator of Heaven and Earth and his only son, Jesus Christ, who was born miraculously of the Virgin Mary?"

"I do," Kamolea muttered.

"Do you accept the Almighty Lord, within his three hypostases: the Father, the Son, and the Holy Spirit, for your one and only God?"

Kamolea's head was reeling. He was about to faint but still found the necessary energy to utter, "I do."

A sharp scream, "*Noooo!*" tore through his ears, and he slid to his knees, leaning his head against the table. Dona Lucia took him under his armpits and moved him under the kettle. Padre Alberto scooped water three times and poured it over his head as he repeated, "I baptize Kamolea, the servant of God, in the name of the Father, the Son, and the Holy Spirit. Amen."

At the third pour, Kamolea felt the heavens above open, and in a split second, past, present, and future merged, playing out scenes of his life in his mind.

He was a little boy, hunting a wild boar with Akamui; then shouting at Laggi to leave the divine parrots alone; he was lying in a boat, floating in the boundless sea; the ship was rocking while Benito handed him the Bible; on the deck, a roar of the guns almost deafened him, and a second later the splinters rained down, stabbing into his thigh; Raul was chasing him towards the jungle, and a slug whizzed past his ears; the cougar was chewing at his face; he was in the ocean, tossed by immense waves, gasping for breath and trying to cling to a log, until he was swept onshore. Then, finally, he was standing before Rakapi, clutching an enormous axe, surrounded by the men of his tribe.

After the final vision, his senses returned and he realized he wasn't clasping an axe, but Dona Lucia's hand in an attempt to rise to his feet. He rose, leaning on her unsteadily.

Padre Alberto poured out a little of the chrism oil onto his hand, and with his thumb, he painted a cross on Kamolea's forehead.

"Henceforth, you have become a new person who has united in Christ," cited Padre Alberto. "Lead a pure and unblemished life, and bring your soul unsullied to the judgment of our Lord Jesus Christ, so that you may have everlasting life. Amen."

He turned to Dona Lucia and said,

"Godmother, please introduce the newly baptized Kamolea to the light of Christ."

Dona Lucia took the massive white candle from the table, lit it from the lamp hanging before the crucifix, and handed it to Kamolea.

"Be a child of light, son, and carry the enlightenment of Christ in your heart," recited the padre in a singsong voice. "Be like the flame of this candle, a dazzling ray that disperses the darkness and warms the heart. Always keep the blaze of faith alive, and your life will be full of success and prosperity. Amen."

"Congratulations, Kamolea," Dona Lucia hugged him. "Today, I've got a new son and you a spiritual mother. And believe me, I love you like my child."

"Thank you, mistress," said Kamolea shyly. "I love you too. You are like a mother to me, as I have never had one."

"Oh, Kamolea," uttered Dona Lucia, moved, brushing her tears away. "Those were the most beautiful words I've ever heard."

"Congratulations, son," Padre Alberto shook his hand. "From this day onwards, you will be a new man, reborn in Christ. Therefore, be invincible and pure in thought, and may the Lord guide you to a new life."

Kamolea nodded and smiled as he felt the cross beneath his clothes pleasantly warming his chest. His heart was brimming over with joy. He knew that something incredible had happened that day, and that nothing would be the same from then on.

CHAPTER XIX

THE FAREWELL

Sitting cross-legged on his bed with a book in his lap, Kamolea was straining his eyes on the candle's flickering flame, trying to grasp the meaning of the text he was reading. It was a funny story about a strange man who imagined he was a knight, but Kamolea was unfamiliar with most of the words and struggled to understand what it was about.

More than a year had passed since the baptism, and he was getting more and more desperate as he still could not find a solution for getting back to Illima.

Besides, Jesus promised to take me back to her if I became Christian, and I held up my end of the bargain, so why is He so slow in fulfilling His? he brooded and often said a fervent prayer in the hope of seeing Illima again.

"Please, my Lord Jesus Christ, help me find my way back to my beloved Illima. From the bottom of my heart, I pray that you bring us together and let us be reunited again. I will do everything to find her; just show me the way!" He would repeat it until he fell asleep.

After his conversion, the shrill voice that had tortured him had lost some of its force, but Kamolea was under the impression that it had transformed into hissing inside his chest, producing an almost permanent boiling rage.

That night, the hissing was particularly strong, and Kamolea had become more and more frustrated for no obvious reason. He sought to distract himself with the book that Dona Lucia had lent him about a month before. He had made tremendous efforts to please and impress his mistress, but it was impossible to concentrate that day, so he put the book down, and his thoughts drifted to Dona Lucia herself. She had abruptly suspended her visits several weeks before, and he had not seen her since, which worried him a great deal.

Is she all right? She doesn't leave her room anymore. Rita told me once that she was sick... He brooded on and on until he finally dozed off again.

The answer came the next day. He was working in the garden when Belade told him Dona Lucia wanted to see him in her bedroom.

"Are you sure, Belade?" Kamolea asked. "I was specifically ordered not to go to the second floor."

"It's at her behest, Crespo," said the maid impatiently, looking to one side, as usual. "You'd better hurry, for she said right away; when you get upstairs, it's the second door from the left."

"All right, thanks," muttered Kamolea. He walked to the mansion, entered the vestibule, went past the dining room, and reached the spiral staircase that led to the second floor. There was only one corridor with several doors painted in white. Kamolea knocked on the second one on the left. No answer. He bent the handle and cautiously pushed it open. Dona Lucia lay in a big, framed bed in the middle of a vast room, sleeping. He hesitated for a second, wondering if he should wake her, then plucked up the courage to step inside.

She looked so fragile, shrunken in her vast bed like a little doll. Her face was pale and calm, and tiny drops bedewed her forehead.

As he watched her, her eyelids twitched slightly, and she opened her eyes.

"Kamolea," she whispered and smiled. "I'm so glad to see you."

"How are you doing, mistress?" Kamolea asked.

"I am dying, my dear boy," she spoke with effort, her voice hardly audible. "I've been sick for some time, but it's getting worse. Doctor Ignacio cannot help me; he has not seen such a disease before. It is as though all the evil we have done has come back upon me…"

"What evil? You are so pious, mistress, such a good Christian. Why don't you pray to Jesus Christ, and He will cure you, as He did to me?" Kamolea said.

A faint smile ran across Dona Lucia's lips before her face wrinkled with pain.

"You are so innocent," she sighed and tried to rise into a semi-reclined position. Kamolea adjusted her pillow against the metal bedframe and helped her lean on it. Then, seized by a sudden surge of energy, she grasped his hand and began speaking passionately, her black eyes ablaze.

"You know, when you ask God to spare you, you need to respect His will. Good people don't treat their neighbors worse than animals. They don't consider them objects, don't beat, rape, and kill them. No human being should suffer like this…"

"Are you speaking about us, Mistress?" asked Kamolea, astounded. "I think you're too hard on yourself. Don't fret much about us, slaves. As everybody says, we are closer to animals than humans; I mean, we are so far below you…"

"This is a terrible deception, Kamolea! God created us all equal, so don't you dare accept that you are a lesser being than anybody else, regardless of who they are. There are so many wonderful people among my servants, far better than us, their so-called masters! The only true master watches us from above, and believe me, He sees everything. I am convinced that my illness is His punishment for turning a blind eye to all the cruelty and injustice we have inflicted upon our slaves since we came to Panama and bought this cursed plantation. And then there's my money on top of that, from my dowry and heritage. Ignoring all these crimes makes me an accomplice, even more than the overseers. Oh, if only we could have stayed in Spain… But we had no choice after all my husband's affairs and then his bastard child…"

She sank back onto her pillow, exhausted. Kamolea waited, speechless, his mouth agape. The thought of losing this wonderful woman who had taken such immeasurable care of him formed a lump in his throat, and his heart ached with grief.

Dona Lucia closed her eyes for a moment. Her mental strength looked completely depleted.

"I can't bring back all the men and women we've killed," she whispered, "but at least I can do something for those who are still alive. I summoned you today to bid you farewell and to give you my goodbye present. Fetch me some water, please."

Kamolea poured some water from the carafe that was standing on her bedside table and lifted the glass to Dona Lucia's lips. She drank, watching him gratefully.

"Thank you," she said. "I have decided to grant liberty to all my slaves before it's too late, and regardless of my husband's opinion. You, however, are the most special—an angel sent from the heavens to save first my daughter, then me, from imminent death. I am so grateful to you, Kamolea! I love you even more than my sons. It was such an honor and a privilege to become your godmother! I am glad to have bequeathed all my knowledge to you and turned you into an educated person and a good Christian; It's the best deed I've ever done, and I'm happy that part of me will live on in you forever…"

She coughed and brushed the tears that were streaming from her eyes.

"Bring me the parchment and the leather purse from the second drawer down, please. Yes, the big cupboard over there. I've put them at the far end."

Kamolea went to the massive brown oak cupboard adjoined to the wall on his right and rummaged around in the drawer.

"There are many parchments, Mistress."

"That's the third drawer down, Kamolea. I told you the second. Did you find it? And the purse? Yes, that one. Give them to me."

She took the parchment, untied the red ribbon, and unrolled it.

"This is the official letter that grants your freedom," she said as she scanned it and rolled it back. "Keep it safe because you have no proof that you are a free man without it, and they will hang you as an escapee on the first tree. And this is your reward for your faithful service and for saving Isabella's life and mine."

She detached the heavily loaded purse and spilled several gleaming coins on the bed.

"Here, it's a lot of money, but I want you to live as a wealthy man for the rest of your days. Nobody is aware that I have it; it's my grandparents' heritage. God forbid I would deprive my children of such a treasure, but you deserve it more. You can buy a mansion like this one, and slaves of your own, and whatever else you like.

"I have already explained to you the difference between a doubloon, a ducat, and a piece of eight, remember? The golden pieces are more valuable than the silver ones and are for big things like horses or cows…"

Dona Lucia started coughing again. She put the coins back into the purse and handed it to Kamolea, along with the roll of paper. He did not budge. The sorrow at losing another beloved person again paralyzed him, and he was just staring at her, speechless.

Dona Lucia eyed him knowingly.

"Take it, Kamolea," she wheezed. "This is my last wish. I don't need any money now, anyway. My main concern is that you are still not ready for your liberty, as you know nothing about society. Don't trust anyone, son! People are predators, wild beasts who will tear you to pieces if you stand in their path. You've still got so much to learn… But time is always our most powerful enemy…"

Another fit of coughing interrupted her. Kamolea waited, rooted to the spot.

"Tomorrow morning, be ready to quit the plantation," she gasped finally. "I have an arrangement with Doctor Ignacio to take you to Panama City. I have told my husband already, and he has agreed to let you go, but I am not sure he will keep his promise after my death, so I've decided that now is the best time for you to leave. So many people hate you; it's dangerous for you to linger here any longer…"

Her voice trailed off. Kamolea slumped to his knees, torn apart. He took her limp hand, pressed it to his lips, and burst into tears.

"Gracias, señora. Eras más que una madre para mí,"[52] he wept. She lay pale and fragile, her eyes closed, her face drained of all emotions. Kamolea buried his face in the bed, still clutching her hand, shaking and weeping.

"Go now, my dear," she whispered and pushed him away slightly. Kamolea sniffed and composed himself, then stood up, brushed his tears away, took the purse with the money and the paper, and strode towards the exit. At the door, he turned back and looked at his mistress for the last time. As though she felt his gaze, she opened her eyes, smiled at him, and uttered,

"Adiós,[53] Kamolea."

---

52 You were more than a mother to me.

53 Farewell.

A NEW BEGINNING

CHAPTER XX

THE PRICE OF FREEDOM

—1706 AD, PANAMA CITY, PANAMA.

The two-wheeled carriage rattled along the cobbled road through the imposing stone walls of the city gate, and the magnificent buildings of Ciudad of Panama[54] loomed before Kamolea's eyes.

"You can leave me here, señor," he said to Dr. Ignacio, who was sitting next to him. "I'd like to investigate every corner of this great city by myself."

"Hold the horses!" called out the doctor, and the young mulatto perched on the coach's box pulled the reins back. Dr. Ignacio looked askance at Kamolea.

"Are you sure you don't wanna stay at home for a few days, Crespo?" he asked him pleasantly. "My wife would be pleased to make your acquaintance. Dona Lucia also demanded that I shelter you for some time and help you get familiar with the city.

---

54 Panama City.

"Much obliged, señor, but I won't trouble you with my presence," said Kamolea. "I'm a rich man now, and Dona Lucia explained to me about these houses where I can sleep and find a meal."

Doctor Ignacio smiled sadly.

"Yes, I know an inn nearby," he said. "Want me to take you there?"

"No, I'll come across it for sure. Thanks for everything, Doctor Ignacio." Kamolea took the old bag in which he had packed all his belongings and jumped lightly from the carriage.

"Be careful, Crespo," warned the physician. "Remember, freedom always comes at a price. I understand how excited you feel about this lucky turn in your life, but beware: the big city can be a dangerous place, even more hazardous than the plantation."

"Impossible!" exclaimed Kamolea.

"It is, believe me! To be a slave is a terrible hardship, but at least you get a meal and a roof over your head, whereas the city is like a jungle—it's every man for himself, and God help the losers. So don't trust anybody, my boy, and keep your eyes peeled, as troubles lurk around every corner. If you need my help, you are always welcome to pass by. Here, take my address, and don't lose it; but even if you do, just ask the locals where my house is—everybody knows me in Panama." Doctor Ignacio handed him a small, neatly written piece of paper.

"Gracias, señor," said Kamolea. He folded the note and put it in his purse. "I'll certainly come to visit you someday." He bowed, hardly able to hide his impatience to finally end the conversation. Dr. Ignacio gave him one last inquisitive look, then he nodded knowingly and waved him goodbye with the words:

"Good luck, Crespo."

The mulatto lashed the reins on the horse's back, and the gig rattled away. Kamolea took a deep breath, finally alone and free as a bird. In the late sunny morning, his heart leaped with joy.

"Freeman!" he cried, then he jumped and punched the air high above his head, his eyes shining with delight. It had all happened precisely as

Dona Lucia had foreseen it. The night before, he hadn't got a wink of sleep. Burning with excitement and making plans for the future, he had finally dozed off at dawn, and the physician found him still in bed.

"You're supposed to be ready by now," Doctor Ignacio scolded him.

"I am," said Kamolea, stifling a yawn, "Give me a few minutes to pack my clothes."

"All right, hurry up; I'll wait for you at the gig," the doctor said. "And don't forget the paper that Dona Lucia gave you, as we need to show it at the gate."

A while later, clad in his newest shirt and drab baggy trousers, Kamolea joined Doctor Ignacio, and they set off toward the central entrance.

"It's a great day for you, Crespo, isn't it?" the doctor asked him, smiling.

"It really is, señor," said Kamolea. Then, he glanced at him and said shyly, "By the way, my real name is Kamolea."

"Well, I find Crespo adorable," said the doctor. Meanwhile, they had reached the small sentry box that flanked the massive double-winged gate, and Herrado, who was standing guard, came out of the booth to meet them.

"What's this?" he barked as Doctor Ignacio handed him the roll of paper. He unfolded it and scanned the calligraphic handwriting that ended with the mistress's seal. "Where are you taking the curly one?"

"This is his release order," explained Doctor Ignacio. "He is a free man now. Don Diego was informed."

A trickle of sweat streamed down the keeper's temple, and Kamolea could not suppress his grin at his confused expression.

"All right then," he muttered, staring at the paper with the firm determination not to admit his illiteracy. "If Don Diego knows…"

He looked up and met Kamolea's smirk. His face grew darker.

"Jolly, eh? Pray you don't meet me outside, sucker," he drove his forefinger across his throat.

"That's enough, now," rasped Doctor Ignacio. "Give me the roll and let us out, please."

Muttering and casting spiteful glances, Herrado pushed the heavy wooden gate open.

* * *

As Kamolea was still grinning about the memory of Herrado's fury, a real-life cry caused him to jump aside, narrowly avoiding being smashed under a four-horse coach.

"Get out of the way, you fool!" the man yelled as the horses galloped away.

"Gosh, that was close," Kamolea muttered, looking around. How beautiful everything around him was! Elegant people strode importantly along the street, looking rich and happy. The colorful two-story houses painted in white, yellow, or rose glistened in the sunshine, majestically charming with their red-tiled roofs and sophisticated, wood-carved balconies adorned with flowers, but the splendid building just in front of him left him completely speechless. It was far taller than the surrounding houses, made of ashlars and flanked by two lofty towers with domed roofs. On the facade, two pairs of columns sat to the sides of the large, arch-shaped entrance. Another couple of pillars supported a frieze with a gable and a carved female figure inside. A metal cross shone atop the roof.

La Iglesia de La Merced, Kamolea read the inscription just above the open door. As he admired the imposing architecture of the church, the cross hanging on his neck underneath his shirt got warmer, and he felt that something mysterious was enticing him to take a peep inside. Seized by acute curiosity, he strolled toward the entrance.

Benito said the houses with a cross on top were temples, he thought, as the memory sprang to mind of their march to the dungeon, surrounded by soldiers. *How I would love to see this magnificent God's house again! Although the beauty of this one here is not so inferior.*

Once he stepped inside, he had a feeling of déjà vu—the dim, vast hall, the pillars that supported the wooden roof, the benches in the middle, and the candles scattered along the walls—the whole setting seemed pretty familiar to him.

But… I have already been here. Kamolea frowned, trying to remember. Then suddenly, the dream from the eve of his conversion hit him, right down to the slightest details. His eyes scanned the room, searching for the tall man's figure with his arms spread wide. He finally spotted it on his left, surrounded by many flickering candles.

Paying no attention to the several people who stood before the gorgeous wood-carved altar in the middle, he walked toward the wooden statue of the crucified Jesus, feeling more and more insignificant with every single step. About a yard from the crucifix, he dropped to his knees, bowed, wove his hands together, and closed his eyes, not daring to look up.

"Do you love me, Kamolea?" he heard a voice from above, and his heart started banging against his chest. He did not answer. His head was empty of thoughts, his mouth dry and sealed.

"You have made tremendous progress in your training," continued the voice, "but your invisible enemy is a monster with a hundred heads, and when you cut one off, two more sprout in its place. You must cope with the women now, for they are your weakest point. Beware of them and run away when they approach you, for they will ruin your life. I beg you, like a friend, be devoted to Illima! Be patient and don't look aside, and I'll bring you to your beloved, just as I promised. Give me your word as a man now that you will never betray Illima!"

"I give you my word," whispered Kamolea, trembling. "She is the love of my life, and I swear to be faithful to her."

"Keep that word and never break your oaths!" thundered the voice from above. "Go straight to Santo Domingo Convent now. There you'll find the answer to all of your questions! Don't stop or speak to anyone until you get there!"

The light faded away, and Kamolea opened his eyes to find himself lying prone on the stone floor. The church was deserted now, dim and quiet. As if roused from a deep slumber, he got up and staggered out.

The sun had passed its zenith, pouring down its fiery heat, and the bright light blinded him. He shadowed his eyes and, blinking, he tarried a little, observing the narrow street and hesitating over which path to take. Then, he heard a boy's voice shouting:

"Pretzels calientes,[55] señores, señoritas, scorching hot, you'll like 'em a lot!" Kamolea wended his way in the direction of the voice and soon, he spotted a teenage boy at the corner down the street, standing by a handcart. A delicious aroma of baked bread wafted through the air and Kamolea found his mouth was watering. He stopped before the lad and took out the purse from his pocket. The incredible feeling that he would buy something for the first time in his life made him proud and even a little haughty.

"Gimme one of these hot, sweet-smelling things," he said importantly to the boy.

"Aquí tiene, señor. Medio real."[56] the youngster handed him a round pretzel, seared on the lower side.

Kamolea rummaged in the purse, muttering to himself,

"Not the yellow ones; the mistress said you can buy a horse with them… The pale ones for the small stuff… Which one?" he produced three silver coins of different sizes.

"The smaller one, señor," said the boy, his eyes gleaming with amusement.

"Gracias, amigo!"[57] Kamolea gave him the coin, put the purse back

---

55 Hot pretzels.

56 Here you go, sir. Half a real (a small silver coin).

57 Thank you, my friend.

in his pocket, took a large bite, and nodded complacently.

"Excelente,"[58] he mumbled through a stuffed mouth and strolled importantly along the street, but the next second, he slapped himself on the forehead as he realized he had forgotten to ask the boy about the convent. He turned abruptly and crashed right into a pretty young woman who was walking just behind him.

"Lo siento,[59] señorita," he muttered.

"Hola, guapo,"[60] she said seductively. "What's the rush?"

"I forgot to ask the lad over there something."

"And what was that? Ask me, instead; perhaps I can help you?"

"Oh, that's very kind of you," said Kamolea, blushing. "I just came to the city, and I'm a little lost…"

"No problem, honey! Just tell me where you're going, handsome, and it will be my pleasure to be your guide."

Kamolea's jaw dropped. In Don Diego's plantation, the Spanish women only spoke to the slaves when giving them orders.

It's incredible to be a free man! his inner voice proudly observed. Yet, he sensed something was wrong—la señorita had called him '*handsome*' and '*honey*,' which was definitely weird. Kamolea scratched his head, bit into the pretzel, and said:

"I'm pretty confused, señorita. Of course, it will be a great honor to have such a highborn guide, but I find it a little weird that such a beauty even bothers to speak to an ugly man like me…"

"And who says you're ugly, chico? Oh, you mean your scars? Don't be silly! Your face appears so virile with them cuts! It speaks of a bold combatant who never flinches from danger; the lassies very much like brave niños[61] like you. Look at these broad shoulders and bulging muscles!"she chirruped, playfully squeezing his right biceps.

---

58 Excellent.

59 I am sorry.

60 Hi, handsome.

61 Boys.

cles!" she chirruped, playfully squeezing his right biceps. "You're so attractive, indeed! Are you hungry, dear? Do you want to share a meal with me? You need to take good care of your future guide, to be sure. Come, I know a decent tavern just over there. The most excellent wine you've ever tasted, I promise you."

The turbulent torrent of words was so vigorous that Kamolea felt slightly dizzy. He eyed the damsel with rising suspicion and growing anxiety, convinced that she was pulling his leg. She reminded him of Uma—tall and slim, with heavy bosoms, generously revealing themselves out of the plunging neckline of her long, blue-white dress. Her gorgeous black locks fell in waves over her shoulders, making a lovely contrast with her pale face, which emanated the cold beauty of an inveterate whore. Her black eyes were mesmerizing, but the more they bored into Kamolea, the more his heart sank with a foreboding feeling of impending calamity.

"Look, señorita, I'm not really hungry, and I don't have time now," he said resolutely. "I want to go to the Santo Domingo convent. Do you know where it is?"

"Of course I do. I'll take you there right after we have our meal together. A real one, not like this garbage. Here, let me taste this!"

Before Kamolea could react, she snatched the bun from his hand, took a huge bite, then threw it away.

"This stupid pretzel is not worthy of a sturdy guy like you!" she declared, shooing a flock of pigeons that had immediately landed to attack the rolling chunk of bread. Kamolea flushed with anger, but the beauty flashed him back a disarming smile and grabbed his hand. At her slightest touch, Kamolea's heart sped up and his member suddenly started stirring and twitching.

"Go straight to Santo Domingo Convent… Don't stop or speak to anyone until you get there!" Jesus's voice boomed in his head.

"What the fuck?!" screamed the familiar shrill voice. *"Look at her, sucker! Isn't she perfect? Check out those tits! Don't you want to grab them?*

How about her curvy ass? Go ahead, jerk! She's naked and wet underneath her dress!"

He hesitated for a second, torn between reason and passion, then ultimately gave up as the raven-haired enchantress pressed her hip against his crotch.

"What's your name, handsome?" she mumbled in his ear, her locks tingling against his face. But before he could answer, she continued, "I'm Angelina. Don't be afraid of me, sweetheart; I won't bite you." Her hand was warm and strong.

Beware of the women and run away when they approach you, as they will ruin your life. You swore you'd never betray Illima! The voice from the church was fading, and the sensation of Angelina's thighs clinging to his groin chased away the urge to run as quickly as a drop of water sucked in hot sand. Nevertheless, he attempted one last time.

"I'd better keep going," he muttered, not convinced at all.

"We're going together, honey," Angelina whispered in a husky voice as she pushed him towards the nearest house, and he leaned on the wall under the shadow of its balcony. "*El Gallo Cojo*[62] is a fine tavern, you'll see. The tenant is my friend and keeps me a room upstairs, so after our meal, I've got a surprise for you. Wanna brief hint what it is?"

She glanced around, assuring herself that nobody was watching them, then quickly lifted the hem of her dress and confidently moved Kamolea's hand underneath her skirt. The touch of her silky skin drove him crazy. His member pulsated, ready to explode, and he groped her aggressively, brushing the hair of her naked, wet pussy. *Just like I told you!* screamed the crazy voice inside his mind.

Angelina pushed his hand back again, then took his arm and, with a contemptuous leer, she dragged him through a labyrinth of tangled streets like a cougar hauling its prey.

---

62 The Lame Rooster.

"We'll have an unforgettable feast, my handsome curly boy," she muttered and licked her lips as her eyes darted in all directions, yet too often at the lump swelling in his pocket. Kamolea followed her obediently, his disquiet replaced by a daydream about his forthcoming loss of virginity, completely ignoring the muffled voice that screamed *"oath-breaker!"*

El Gallo Cojo was a dilapidated two-story building at the end of a long, somber street. Above the heavy door hung a bullet-riddled signboard of a one-leg motley rooster with a dangling saber, clutching a crutch under its wing. Angelina pushed the door and a wave of tobacco and roasted meat hit them as they stepped into a poorly lit, smoky hall. Kamolea squinted, waiting for his eyes to adjust to the gloom. Several men with dubious appearances sat in small groups around square wooden tables and drank ale or wine from wooden mugs. Angelina set off for the central, larger one, situated under a low-hanging, massive black chandelier. As they took a seat, a man with a tray and a towel dangling from his elbow materialized from nowhere.

"Hola,[63] Carlos!" cried out Angelina happily. "Bring us a pint of your best wine and a roasted fowl, por favor.[64] Same as last time, remember?"

"En seguida, señorita,"[65] nodded Carlos and disappeared as magically as he had arrived.

Muffled female cries, male grunts, and an accelerated rattling came from upstairs. Kamolea, all ears, looked up at the heavy round chandelier as it started swinging rhythmically.

"They seem to be having fun, the rascals!" Angelina smirked. "Wait, our turn is coming soon. Are you keen to have me in your arms, sturdy lad?"

"Here we go, the best wine in Panama," called out Carlos and

---

63 Hi.

64 Please.

65 Right away, missy.

slammed down a clay jug and two mugs. An old servant followed after him and laid down a large tray with roasted fowl covered with white rice, then distributed two empty plates before them.

"Gracias, Carlos," Angelina chirruped, "eres el major!"[66]

"Disfruten su comida, queridos invitados!"[67] replied Carlos, before bowing and retreating.

Angelina poured the wine earnestly into the cups and grinned at Kamolea. "Cheers! To our acquaintance."

They knocked mugs and drank. The wine was tart and strong and hit Kamolea straight in the head. Meanwhile, his companion fell on her food as if she had been starving for days.

"Eat!" she sputtered, her mouth stuffed full of food. "It's delicious!"

And it was, indeed. The tender meat melted in the mouth, and every bite of the savory rice was a magical explosion. While Kamolea enjoyed the meal, trying to remember if ever he had eaten something so tasty, Angelina had never stopped babbling despite her permanently full mouth. She generously ordered another pint of wine, heightening Kamolea's spirits. By the end of the second pitcher, the colors had gotten brighter, his self-esteem had hit a record high, and Angelina had become the gorgeous woman in the world. He laughed heartily at her blathering, but even in this drunken state, his wild-animal instincts kept telling him that something wasn't quite right. He noticed that for the past few minutes, Angelina's eyes had been ceaselessly flicking this way and that, and she had acquired an absentminded expression. But Kamolea did not care—the feast in the Lame Rooster was the happiest moment in his life. When they were finally done eating, Angelina moved onto his lap and wrapped her arms around his neck.

"I don't remember if you told me your name, but it doesn't matter,"

---

66 You're the best!

67 Enjoy your meal, dear guests!

she whispered in his ear, her wine-addled breath almost suffocating him. "Are you ready for adventures, my boy? I know you are." She shifted her bottom, rubbing her hips against his stiff cock as her eyes swept swiftly around the room over his shoulder. A man wrapped in a cloak, wearing a wide brim hat, sat alone at an empty table in the corner with his back leaning against the wall. As she caught his gaze, Angelina jerked her head toward the stairs. The man got up and lazily made his way to the second floor.

Giddy and flushed with passion, Kamolea glided his hand under Angelina's skirt, trying to cleave her tightly pressed thighs and reach into that so-coveted source of pleasure.

"Hey, not so fast," she giggled and removed his hand once more. "We need to pay Carlos for his hospitality first. Do you have any money, dear?" she glanced at his bulging pocket.

"Of course I do," declared Kamolea bullishly. He adjusted her to free his pocket and took out the leather purse. "How much?" he asked as he opened it up.

"Oh, these five will be enough." She took two silver pieces of eight and three golden doubloons out.

"Are you sure?" hesitated Kamolea. "The mistress said the yellow ones are for bigger stuff like cows or slaves."

"Do you think I'd lie to you?" Angelina pouted and fluttered her black eyelashes. "Be generous to me, and I'll take you to heaven. Come now, let's go upstairs!"

She flipped the silver coins to Carlos, leaped quickly from his lap, and pulled him towards the spiral staircase. Feeling vertiginous, Kamolea staggered behind her, pocketing the purse in motion. They climbed to the second floor, where they reached a lobby with many closed doors. Angelina opened the third on the left and they entered a large, dim room with tightly shut violet curtains, a vast bed in the middle, and a dresser in the corner. As soon as they got in, she turned quickly and pressed her lips to his. An acute pain pierced the back of his skull, and everything sank into darkness.

* * *

Kamolea was gradually coming to his senses. The first thing he thought was that he was lying in a boat, being tossed by the waves. The world bobbed up and down, again and again. A sharp neigh startled him, and he forced his eyes open, only to quickly shut them again, blinded by the bright light. His head throbbed and his ears buzzed. Somebody was speaking nearby. Carefully, he peeped out through slit eyes. There was no sea and no bobbing boat. Instead, he saw green grass moving beneath him, and it took him a while to realize that he was lying prone across a horse's back, his legs and arms firmly fastened. He curved his neck and looked upward. Three men rode ahead, the one in the middle, wearing a sombrero and a brown cloak, leading Kamolea's horse by the reins.

"… So we struck a deal with Don Alvaro, to find him only the best stock on the market," the one on the right was saying. "And this one here is a real treat—young, strong, and only just freed."

"Not for long, though," the man with the cloak chuckled. "How much do you think Don Alvaro will pay for the horny bastard, Pablo?"

"Oh, he always pays top prices, no worries about that," replied the one on the left. "But I hope he's recovered already, so we can do business with him, not the ginger devil who replaced him after he got hurt."

"Don Alvaro got hurt? What happened?"

"Come, Vicente, have you been living under a rock, man? A month ago, he and his two guards went to Panama's fair to buy a pony for his daughter and on his way back, he was ambushed."

"You don't say!"

"Si, amigo. Some riders found them by chance, shot, and stripped to their underwear. Money, horses, pony, everything's gone. Alvaro's two guards were stone dead, but the Don himself was miraculously alive despite three slugs in his hide."

"Some folks say they were five bullets," added the one on the right.

"Anyway, they drove him back to Panama's infirmary and saved his life," continued Pablo. "Later on, his men took him to the plantation in lamentable condition. Meanwhile, one of his overseers runs the show there—a nasty Irishman, cruel as hell and stingy as an old crone. Worse than the Devil himself, to be sure. But I heard that Don Alvaro is getting better, so maybe we'll be lucky enough to see him."

"I don't yield for less than three hundred pesos," said Vincente, and the other two grunted their agreement.

Kamolea listened to the strangers, shivers running down his spine. He had already heard dreadful rumors about Don Alvaro's plantation. He remembered an overseer who had previously worked there before coming to Don Diego's place, saying to Raul:

"I find your slaves pretty spoiled, amigo! There is no such pampering at Don Alvaro's hacienda. The bloody wretches work their asses off three times harder and they die like flies. And if somebody dares to break out, the hound hunt is a one-of-a-kind, man; it's definitely worth seeing."

Kamolea shuddered. *Out of the frying pan and into the fire,* he thought. *I must break away before we get there; I'd rather die than be a slave again. Why didn't I listen to Jesus? He warned me to go straight to the convent... What a fool I am! This time, I have nobody to blame but myself.*

Overcome with remorse, he closed his eyes and began whispering, hardly moving his lips:

Please, Jesus, I'm so sorry that I did not pay heed to your warning. Please, help me escape this time, and I swear on my dear life that I'll never let you down again. Don't let them make me a slave anew; I cannot bear it; not anymore, please God, please...

The road narrowed, and the horses started climbing up amid high bushes and trees. Kamolea twisted his head. They were riding through a hilly region toward hazy mountain ranges, outlined in the distance.

Judging by the descending sun and the direction of the elongated tree shadows, he concluded they were moving northeast.

"There's talk that the bloody Kunas are on the rampage around these hills," said one of the riders. "Two merchants disappeared several weeks ago, a little farther beyond this height over there."

"Why, the damn Kuna Mountain has always been a dangerous place!" grunted Vicente.

Kuna Mountain? It sounds familiar. Kamolea frowned. *Wait, isn't Niddi's tribe dwelling somewhere there? He told me once that they live north, beyond the ridge...*

A muffled swish interrupted his train of thought and Vicente cried out, grabbing at his throat and trying to pull out the arrow that had stuck there. Sniffing death, Vicente's horse bucked and reared up with a sharp neigh, and he fell off, gurgling and wheezing. Somebody shouted, then wild cries rent the air and the mounts bolted. A shot rang out, then another one, louder. The ground swung up and down as Kamolea rocked on the back of the horse, his chest smashing against its firm spine. A while later, there was another heavy thud amid whooping and neighing. Kamolea caught a glimpse of legs with striped sandals, running towards him. Then, somebody grabbed his horse's reins, forcing it to halt. Cold steel slid between his wrists, cutting the ropes loose, and firm hands lifted him and helped him to the ground. Still dizzy, his numb legs yielded and he slumped to his knees, glancing around. Then, he heard a familiar voice yelling in Spanish:

"Crespo? Is that you, amigo? What happened to your face?" Kamolea's jaw dropped as his swarthy best friend, clad in a white shirt and brown leather pants with dangling tassels, popped up in front of him.

"Niddi!" he exclaimed.

"What are you doing here, sprawled over a horse's back like a sack of potatoes?!?" grinned Niddi, his eyes gleaming happily. "So glad to see you, my old chum!" Kamolea rose unsteadily and gave him a hug. "Is this Oller over there? And Udur and Duali… You guys are the best!"

They all hugged him in turn, slapping his back and shoulders.

"I heard you killed that damned Rodrigo and the hateful Belisario! Great job, amigos!"

"Absolutely! You should have seen Rodrigo's stunned face—even when I ripped through his belly, he couldn't believe it was happening for real. But I'll tell you all that later. Oller, Udur, strip the corpses and let's go. Tell me, Crespo, why are you with those scum? Ain't you supposed to be in the shithole, working your ass off?"

"Long story, amigo. Do you know them?" Kamolea asked, nodding toward the three killed men.

"Bloody curs," Niddi kicked Pablo spitefully. "This one here was an overseer on Don Alvaro's plantation. And we've been tracking *this* dung for two moons already," he spat on Vicente's body. "He caught and sold one of our brothers to Don Alvaro."

"Really? How come?" Kamolea exclaimed.

"He owned a brothel and a pub, and a lot of *putas*[68] were working for him as decoys to lure foreigners, then rob them and sell them into slavery…"

"My case, exactly!" cried Kamolea, agitated. "She was so kind and beautiful, and then everything went dark and I found myself here, packed on this horse's back."

"Now you'll know better than to whore around," Niddi smirked. "But how did you get into the city's brothel in the first place?"

"Dona Lucia set me free because I saved her life. It all happened the same very day you broke free! What a day it was!"

"One of a kind," Niddi agreed. "So, how did you save her life?"

"A puma attacked her, but I confronted the beast, hence my scars."

"Wow, you fought and killed a cougar?" Niddi was impressed.

"Well, not really. As you can see, it mauled me pretty badly, but

---

68 Whores.

luckily for me, Dona Lucia's guards shot it."

"What a story, amigo!" exclaimed Niddi. "And then she set you free?"

"That's right, and gave me a lot of money as well. A purse stuffed with gold and silver... But wait, where is it?"

Kamolea started tapping his body fervently and rummaging through his pockets.

"They robbed me for sure," he muttered.

Niddi stared at him.

"They took your money? Maybe they still have it. Hey, Oller, did you find a purse with gold when you searched them?"

"Nah, no gold, brother. We found some pieces of eight on each one of them, but nothing that big."

Kamolea sighed.

"Now I have nothing again. Even my bag is gone. I have more chance of surviving by hunting in the jungle than returning to Panama City. They ask you for money for everything over there." "Don't worry, Crespo. Come with us and be my guest. You'll see how the free Kuna people live, and I'm sure you'll love it. The jungle provides us with everything, and we don't need any bloody Spanish money, that source of all evil and misery for our people." He turned to the others.

"All right, brothers, let's beat it. Duali, take the horses and go to Imali's camp; they will be glad to have them. Spend the night there, but tomorrow I want you in the village before noon. We will organize a big feast in honor of our great friend Crespo, with whom we have shared so many incredible moments in Don Diego's shithole, ain't we? Let's go!"

They set off north-east through the jungle, climbing up gradually toward the mountains.

"Do you know the name of these heights?" Kamolea asked Niddi.

"Yeah, we call them the Raptor's Mountain," Niddi replied. "Our village is just below the Monkey Rock, the left-hand one over there.

Do you see the highest peak yonder? It's the Eagle's Nest. But it's hard to get there; the forest is too messy and full of jaguars…"

"Full of what?" Kamolea asked.

"You've never heard of a jaguar?" Niddi chuckled. "It's a terrible beast, larger than a puma, and a lot fiercer. Especially the black ones. If you meet one like that, your encounter with the puma would seem like child's play to you."

"Wow! You don't say! Have you ever faced one?"

"I have not, but now and then, some of our brothers get killed by those beasts. Several days ago, we found Weggon, the shaman's son, torn and gnawed to the bones. Bad omen for the whole tribe, as they said. We chased the beast and even wounded it, but it escaped in the end."

A few hours later, they stopped to spend the night in the bosom of a jutting cliff, which sheltered them from the heavy rain as it continued through the night. The old friends didn't care a jot; huddled around a blazing fire, they had so many stories to tell each other that when they fell asleep, the sky had already lightened. Niddi's escape, of course, was the principal topic of the conversation.

"We took advantage of the total panic that broke when the tree fell and jammed the cutters," he said. "All the guards had left, save Belisario, who came to look for us, and Rodrigo, who kept the gate. We were ten, and they were only two, so by the time they realized it, it was too late for them. Then we took the river to deceive the hounds, and several days later, we were back home on the islands by the sea, where most of our people live. But as we've got great fighting plans for the future, some of us decided it was safer to settle down in the mountain's heart, where our enemies can't find us. Speaking of which, an idea just dawned on me. Why don't you stay with us forever? You'll become a member of our tribe, get married, and have your own family, with many children and all. It's very nice in the village, you'll see; I'm sure you're gonna like it. What a perfect happy end to your story, don't you think?"

"It's too good to be true," Kamolea sighed. "First, no woman on

Earth would want to be my wife; they're all too scared of my face."

"Don't be ridiculous, Crespo! I bet this will be the least of your problems," Niddi smirked. "Considering what a hero you are, your seed is priceless, and it would be a big honor for any woman to marry you. And there is one in particular that will be thrilled for sure."

Kamolea blushed.

"I just wanted to ask you what happened to Ally," he said.

"It's her I have in mind," Niddi replied. "I think she is still too much in love with you, so…"

"Tell me more about her!" Kamolea cried excitedly, but his friend, who was unusually conversational for the taciturn Indian Kamolea had known, changed the subject abruptly.

"So, here's the plan," he said. "We intend to visit the shithole and have a good long conversation with Don Diego and his stinkers. From there, we're going to Don Alvaro's place," a metallic note rang out in his voice, and his black eyes shone, reflecting the flames of the fire. "We'll free all the slaves and form an army that will join our alliance with the other tribes. We are about to negotiate with the Guaymi's chief and his son now, but that's only the beginning. Our goal is to create a common front, and then, all together, we'll put up a fight against the Spanish wankers. They should go back to their fucking country! Nobody invited them here to steal our land, rape our women, enslave us, and kill us like dogs. And what do we do in response? Nothing! The blood of our ancestors is calling for revenge! Are you with us in this fight, Crespo?"

"I hear you, my friend! Kill them all, bloody Spaniards! Count me in!" Kamolea cried excitedly.

"That's my boy!" Niddi slapped him on the back. Shortly after that, they retired to rest, but Kamolea was too excited and could not fall asleep. Niddi's invitation to start a new life as a member of Kuna's tribe and the happy memories of Ally, with their kisses and promises, whirled inside his head.

I can't believe my luck! Everything got fixed so suddenly and unexpect-

edly, and what a fortunate turn events have taken. Finally, I can find a home and a girl to marry. Aley will bear me many children, and my sons will be fine examples of men. All's well that ends well. Thank you, Jesus, for your mercy and the beautiful gift you have given me.

But as soon as he mentioned the son of God by name, it was as if a knife had penetrated his heart. The feeling of happiness evaporated, chased away by a sharp cry: "YOU PROMISED!" The pain was so acute that he gasped for air as a lump stuck in his throat.

"What is happening with me?" he mumbled, irritated. He felt dizzy and soon drifted into sleep.

In his slumber, he found himself once again in the Steamy Cave, at the same place where his previous vision had ended about two years before. Through the fleeces of vapor, he saw Illima leaning against the boulder, sitting with her legs tucked up to her chest. Surprised, his heart skipped a beat.

"Illima," he uttered. She was naked, concealed only by her long black hair. Her pinched face was sad and exhausted, martyr-like, her cheeks wet, and her eyes filled with moisture.

Is she's crying or are these just dew drops? he asked himself. The moment this thought occurred to him, she cocked her head and gazed in his direction. Their eyes locked, and a piercing pang of guilt stabbed his heart.

"Kamolea?" she whispered.

"Illima? Can you see me, my love?" he said, and he stretched out his hand, longing to touch her.

"Why do you call me 'love' when you came to bid me farewell?" she said, her voice tinged with indescribable sadness. "These words matter, Kamolea. A man who calls his beloved 'love' must mean it. What did you find in this girl more than you found in me? Why did you decide to leave me and break your oath that you'd love me forever? Don't leave me this way, sweetheart. I need you more than the sun and the air. Come back and save me from this stinking cave, where the best of my years have passed me by. I wept bitterly for you, year after year, waiting for the day that I would press you to my bosom again. Will you really leave me for her?"

"How do you know about her?" Kamolea mumbled.

She only smiled sadly.

"I wish I knew far less than I do," she said. "My spirit is often with you, especially when you are in great danger. I saw you when this man chased you on the back of his huge animal and when you fought the beast that almost killed you. I was also there when you were on the immense canoe with those thunderous things, spitting fire…"

"But how is this possible?" Kamolea exclaimed.

"I don't know," Illima wiped her moist cheek. "But you did not answer my last question. Will you leave me for her?"

Kamolea's inner fight was so intense that he had the impression he would burst into thousands of pieces at any moment. A part of him felt bitter remorse that he had cheated on Illima, and he longed to be with her, but the other part of him stubbornly refused to give up on Aley.

"This is only a dream, and dreams are not real, so you aren't real either," he said tenaciously, desperately trying to postpone the answer to her question. "And even if you were, it's impossible to be together; it's simply unthinkable that I could find my way back to Maniha Komo."

"You never know what's real and what's not," Illima got up and stretched out her arm toward him. "Don't fool yourself, my heart. I know about your doubts and fears, but hear me out: the day I decided to open my veins and watch my blood flow out and mix with the stream, the man with bleeding hands, stretched over thick wood, came to me and promised to reunite us. He gave me his word that I'd see you again, and it is only this hope that's kept me alive in this stinking hole during these interminable years. But now, you want to leave me, as though you don't care about my sacrifice. Please, be my savior; don't leave me behind…"

Kamolea woke up with a gasp and sat up. The dawn was breaking and the others were up, preparing to leave.

"Are you all right, brother?" Niddi bent over him, watching him with concern.

Kamolea shook his head.

"I have to go, Niddi. I cannot continue with you. My God wants me to return to my native place."

"Why?" asked Niddi, stunned. "I thought we were going to fight the Spaniards together…"

"I must leave right now," Kamolea cut him off and stood up. "Give me some weapons to survive in the jungle; I need nothing else."

"I don't understand," said Niddi, stunned. "I was counting on you so much, Crespo. Your reputation precedes you, man! You are the one who defeated Aka, and I'm convinced that we could be invincible with you by our side."

"I know I am disappointing you badly, my friend, but my fight is not against the Spaniards. I have another mission, and I must fulfill my destiny. That's the price of my freedom, and there is no way around it. Please, don't be mad at me, and don't think that I'm a coward, unable to keep his word."

"I've never thought of you as a coward," Niddi said sadly. "But what about Aley?"

"There will be no Aley," he said, trembling, still gasping for air. "Please, don't tell her we met. I am so sorry, brother…"

"I see," Niddi nodded, his voice filled with sadness, then turned to his friends, "Oller, give him your bow and arrows! And you, Udur, the machete, a flask with water, and a pouch with tinder. And this, my friend, is my special gift for you."

He unslung the knife he was wearing on a leather strap across his shoulder and handed it to Kamolea. It was a splendid weapon, about 8 inches long, with a polished deer-horn handle. Kamolea dragged it from its wooden sheath and cried with delight at the glare of the steel blade, which was curved at the point and notched with a deep blood groove.

"Do you like it, brother?" Niddi asked, smiling.

"Thank you, Niddi!" said Kamolea, moved. "I don't think I deserve such a wonderful present, after everything I've done."

"Oh, you certainly do," Niddi nodded. "You were born to be a leader, Crespo. Men so strong, smart, and brave like you are almost non-existent nowadays. I know that if you remember me through this knife and mentally wish me luck when you use it, so the spirits of my ancestors will bring me your love and positive feelings, and it will be a tremendous benefit for me. And it works the opposite way too—with this gift, which I offer you from the bottom of my heart, a part of me will always be with you, so we'll be together forever, inseparable by space and time."

Kamolea hugged him, hardly able to suppress his tears. Then they bid him farewell and sank into the lavish verdure of the jungle, leaving him alone with his fate.

CHAPTER XXI

ALONE AMID BEASTS

Just like years before, when Kamolea had been cast away, he was alone and on his own. But this time, instead of the immensity of the blue ocean, the greenery of the jungle surrounded him. The rainforest, a breathing mess of tangled creepers around soaring trees, reminded him of his carefree childhood. He felt at home there, far more confident than in the city, where society had imposed strange rules, and everything depended on money, not on one's strength and skills.

Kamolea stood in the obscure path among the gigantic boles, wondering which direction to take. The only compass he had was his inner feeling, and it was not being very helpful at that instant. He did not feel like returning to Panama; at least not right away, although he knew that there, inside the walls of the Santo Domingo Convent, some hope awaited him. But at that moment, he had had enough of people. He wished to be alone for a while and to take his time to think over his future, so instead of making his way south, he started northwest, towards the heart of the mountain. As he slowly hewed a path through the dense undergrowth, brooding where he could find a shelter, a deep, guttural howl echoed in the woods, wrenching him from his reverie. It was a frightening, wild, and unhinged roar, somewhere between barking and grunting. It started as a single holler, but soon the whoops came from all directions, resounding through the entire forest. Kamolea hurled himself behind the triangular buttress roots of a tree, known by the natives as *Urgo Dii,*[69] and huddled there. He drew his knife, shivering, remembering Niddi's words that *"the forest is enchanted and evil spirits bluster at night."*

"What the fuck is this mighty beast?" he whispered. "Is it the creepy jaguar, the killer of man? Luckily it's not dark yet." He desperately scanned the shroud of impenetrable bushes and creepers, searching in vain for a protective shelter. High above, the sunshine flickered here and there, blocked by the colossal canopy of the surrounding trees.

It could be lurking anywhere, he thought, and shuddered again. *I must find a safe place before nightfall.* As soon as the cries subsided, he put the knife back in the sheath, left his belongings by the roots, and climbed the massive trunk.

The awful roar started anew, coming this time from above. Kamolea froze and looked up, where he was surprised to see a large black ape staring at him, dangling from a branch just above his head. There could be no mistake now—it was this creature making the awful, guttural sound. In a flash, Bobo El Tuerto emerged before Kamolea's eyes, positioned at the helm as he steered the ship in the salty night, spinning yarns about Henry Morgan and the attack of Panama.

…They called them Howlers, the laziest monkeys in the world…

"Blimey, Bobo. I never could have imagined how terrible they sound," Kamolea let out a sigh of relief and, plucking up his courage, went on climbing.

Now, the whole jungle rang out with their screeches. The black primate that had started all the commotion bared its teeth in an attempt to stop Kamolea, but as it saw that the latter was advancing upward,

---

69 Aqua tree.

it jumped with a cry to the next tree, where it was met by a chorus of indignant roars. The cacophony was insane. Deftly squeezing through the branches, Kamolea had almost reached the middle of the tree when a considerably smaller monkey landed on his shoulder with a loud screech. Its white face and upper body contrasted with its black arms and torso, and its big, pleading eyes imparted an almost human-like expression on its cute face, distorted now with fear.

"Carita Blanca!"[70] exclaimed Kamolea, surprised. He knew this kind—Fernando, one of Señorita Isabella's brothers, had kept one for several years, and everybody in the village was amused by its intelligence. He tried to brush it off, but the monkey had grabbed his forearm so firmly that he could feel its fluttering heartbeat.

It clings to me like a child to its mother. It's scared to death, but of what? Kamolea's eyes moved upward and there, he quickly detected the reason. A dark brown snake with a flat head was dangling on one of the upper branches, its split tongue lazily moving in and out of its broad mouth. He had once seen a similar one, yellow and smaller, on the plantation. They called it *"Equis,"*—one of the deadliest snakes, so lethal that Chinaza, a female slave in her twenties, had died from its bite within several hours.

Kamolea froze for a moment, but quickly pulled himself together and wrapped a dangling liana around his left wrist. He took a firm grip on the branch and drew his knife, waiting. Anxiety throbbed through his veins, for he knew the snake was as quick as lightning, and his chances of outstripping it were close to zero. The monkey was still clutching desperately at his elbow, frozen with fear. Meanwhile, the serpent shifted to a lower bough and coiled downward, ready to strike. In a split second, the monkey squeezed his arm and screamed out. Without thinking, Kamolea's right hand shot forward. The knife flashed in the sunlight, meeting the snake in the air, and the rep-

---

70 White-faced capuchin.

tile fell, beheaded, still writhing on the ground in deathly agony. The white-faced capuchin gave a happy yelp and climbed onto its savior's shoulder.

"Thank you for your warning, little buddy. You saved my life as much as I saved yours." Kamolea kissed it on the head, and it leaped on the branch in front of him, grimacing.

"Wanna be friends?" Kamolea asked it as he wiped his knife against his trousers and put it back in the scabbard, sending his mental gratitude to Niddi as he did.

The monkey grinned and let out a joyful cry. Kamolea inspected the lower part of its belly.

"You're a boy, aren't you? I'll call you Captain Junu, in memory of Captain Gonzalez, who once named me Junu after his favorite monkey," he cackled and went on climbing. "Such a piece of work, my captain was, you know? Pity you didn't know him. Well, maybe he wasn't the nicest man in the world, but, peace to his ashes, he was always good to me and protected me from all them wankers, like Diego de Sylva and O'Reilly."

He continued climbing, twigs and foliage lashing at his face and his hands getting sticky from the bark's viscous clay. As he neared the top, the branches became perilously thin and swung dangerously on the wind. Kamolea clung to one wooden appendage like a leech, advanced a little, and observed the scenery below through the dense screen of leaves.

"Do you think we could find a small, cozy spot to spend the night?" he asked.

Captain Junu shrieked in agreement and jumped onto the upper branches. From atop the tree, the view was magnificent—a green sea of swaying canopy covering the nearby peaks as far as the eye could see. The peak of the Eagle's Nest towered above in the distance, majestic and unscalable, and the more Kamolea stared at it, the more he felt an overwhelming desire to conquer it. The mighty impulse to reach its top was so powerful that his eyes shone with determination when he finally turned to Captain Junu.

"Tomorrow, I'm attacking that peak, my furry friend," he declared to the monkey that gazed at him, beady-eyed. "I'm convinced that something exciting is hiding there. Are you coming with me?"

Captain Junu lifted a bug from some nearby bark and started chewing it, not bothering to answer. From his vantage point, Kamolea searched for a path through the mountain. On his left, about halfway toward the Eagle's Nest, he spotted a high cliff with a jutting rock that formed a small plateau and seemed like an excellent spot to spend the night.

"We must reach that rock before sunset," Kamolea decided and began his descent. Captain Junu followed him, and once he was on the ground, he jumped up onto Kamolea's shoulder.

Reaching the plateau was challenging and exhausting. There was no path and Kamolea advanced slowly, hacking and hewing the low bushes, lianas, and hanging branches left and right until his arms ached so much, he could barely lift them.

A gentle shroud of dusk was already descending over the jungle, impeding his vision. In the twilight, everything reminded him of Maniha Komo—the birds' screeches, the frogs' croaking, the rustling of the leaves, even the shadows cast by the trees. Every trunk, pebble, and root was a reminder of his past, making him feel like he had turned into a child again. And yet, he still felt a throbbing danger lurking in the forest.

I have to get there before dark, or I'll pass the night on a tree like a stupid sloth, he thought. Captain Junu had left him a while ago and was nowhere to be seen.

"So much for friends, as usual," Kamolea muttered.

He kept progressing, following a constant humming of falling water in the distance, which got louder with every step. As he sped up to find the source, he arrived at a small clearing and a beautiful view opened up before him.

From the cliffs that formed the plateau, a narrow waterfall tumbled down into a small, heart-shaped lake, from which the water flowed further downhill, becoming a meandering brook amid the woods. Kamolea kneeled and splashed his face, barely resisting the temptation to take his clothes off and throw himself into the crystal water. But he was running out of time—the twilight was getting denser with every single minute, so he explored the surroundings, trying to suppress his rising panic. The waterfall was blocking the way ahead; on his right, the forest seemed dark and hostile; glancing to his left, he noticed a narrow path that seemed to wind up through the trees. He cut a thick branch from a nearby tree, whittled it from the twigs, tore the lower part of his shirt, and wrapped it around the stick. Then, after some rummaging in his bag, he took out another priceless gift from Niddi—a small leather pouch filled with fine tinder dust, which he powdered all over the rag, and a flat flint attached to a horseshoe, which he struck several times quickly. A shower of sparks spilled out and the tinder burst into flames almost immediately. Kamolea raised his torch and started climbing, following the narrow track.

It was a steep slope, and he soon gasped for breath. The bright stars were already blinking in the blue-inked sky, and the full moon had risen to the east, casting its soft glowing magic over the cliff. Kamolea squeezed through trees, creepers, and thick bushes with his torch raised, occasionally tripping over snags and high stones as he progressed.

Finally, the trees thinned out, giving way to dense shrubs, and the path turned into a steep, narrow trail, which led him to the top of the protruding rock that formed the plateau. In the faint light, he could discern that the land was overgrown with high grass and scattered bushes. It wasn't particularly expansive either; about thirty yards wide and fifteen long.

It seemed bigger from below. He frowned and advanced left towards the sound of the falling water, but then he stopped abruptly. The stony ground was split, separated by an approximately seven-yard crack. Beyond it, glistening in the moonlight, a turbulent river cascaded down the slope and turned into a waterfall at the rock's edge.

That explains the track. The animals can't reach the water from here, so they have to go down to the pond, Kamolea thought.

He walked back to the cliff, where he kindled a fire and spent the night there.

* * *

In the morning, the calm grassy meadow looked fabulous, bathed in sunshine and studded with bright-colored tropical flowers with clouds of multi-colored butterflies fluttering around them. Kamolea looked around, delighted, listening to the rumbling waterfall in the distance, when he heard some strange sounds resembling faint yelps. They were coming from his left, where he noticed the outline of a pile of tumbled stones. He stood up and cautiously approached it, then he peeped behind the debris and let out a delighted gasp.

"That's exactly what I'm looking for," he muttered, observing the small, dark entrance into the main rock. He got across the heap and crawled inside. It was a crepuscular, cave-like rock shelter, consisting of one spacious room with a high ceiling, giving the false impression of vastness. It was dry and cool, but Kamolea wrinkled his nose, detecting a foul smell of carrion. As he waited for his eyes to adjust, something squealed and stirred to his left, and he spotted a whimpering cub, which trustfully pressed its fluffy body against his leg. Another one waddled over, waving its tail and looking at him with amber, pleading eyes. They were about three months old and incredibly cute, tan-colored, and dappled with black spots. In the far corner lay the huge, stiff corpse of a black panther, its muzzle frozen in a toothy grimace of pain.

It's weird to have a black parent but mottled children, Kamolea thought, and sadness pierced his heart. *Could this be the wounded jag-*

uar Niddi has told me about? What about the cubs? I cannot leave them just like that—they will die from starvation for sure. I'll stick around for a while and look after them until they get stronger and able to hunt.

His eyes swept the room.

It's a swell place to live; perfect protection from wind and rain. I'll put the hearth near the entrance so that the smoke will keep away all the snakes and vermin. And I'll sleep over there, at the far end, so during the rainy season, it'll be dry and cozy.

The cubs licked Kamolea's hands, whimpering quietly and interrupting his thoughts. He regarded them thoughtfully.

"I'm sorry for your loss," he whispered. "You must be hungry. I'll bring you some dry meat I have in my satchel. From now on, I'm going to take care of you."

He took the panther's carcass, carried it to the edge of the ground and threw it into the crack in the waterfall, then took his belongings and settled into his new home.

CHAPTER XXII

THE TEMPTATION

One hot morning, about three moons after he had settled down in his new rock home, Kamolea awoke at sunrise sullen and depressed. The last night, the frustration of his incapability to find a solution to return to Maniha Komo, which had been swelling inside him like an abscess for days, had finally reached its boiling point.

I've had enough of the lies of that crucified coward, who promised to take me back to her and did nothing, he had hissed, then he had removed his crucifix and hurled it into the remote corner of the room. After that, he had felt so content that he decided the stupid cross was the reason for all his troubles. But this morning, he was not so sure. As he was staring at the pink-shell bracelet, an overwhelming wave of rage directed toward Illima hit him.

"*Forget about that bitch!*" hissed an angry voice in his chest. "*Throw away that fucking bracelet and go back to Aley! She's on the brink of suicide because of you, jerk! Save her instead of dreaming about impossible things like returning to your island.*"

Maybe I've got to do exactly that, Kamolea sighed.

He glanced at the jaguars, which lay near the entrance. The fluffy cubs had grown up quickly and turned into graceful youngsters.

Kamolea had named them Gobo and Rita in honor of his friends from the plantation. In the beginning, he feared their father would pass by to visit them, but it never happened. After some time, Gobo and Rita started accompanying him on his rambles in the jungle, learning to hunt on their own, and when Gobo caught his first prey—a fat female coati[71]—it was celebration time. The siblings still lived with him, but they weren't around much, often leaving Kamolea alone for days. Cap-tain Junu was thrilled about their absence, as their resentful growl had become lately hard to endure.

"I'm going for a dip. Are you coming with me?" Kamolea asked the jaguars. It had become his daily routine to bathe in the lake, but this time, when he got up and strode outside, they did not follow him. As he was walking down the path, something landed on his back with a screech. Kamolea jumped, startled, and tried to shake it off, but the small dark-brown fur ball clung firmly to his forearm, letting out sharp squeals. The minute he recognized him, Kamolea grinned.

"Captain Junu, you traitor!" he exclaimed. "Where have you been the last three days? I turned the entire forest upside-down to find you, little scoundrel!"

He reached out to pet him, but the monkey jumped nimbly onto a nearby branch and bared his teeth in a grimace.

"I love you too, ugly phiz!" laughed Kamolea.

As Captain Junu did not respond, he rushed down to the pond. The waterfall fell with a roar in the small round basin. Kamolea stopped before it and lingered for a moment, admiring the beautiful rainbow that curved just above the spray. Then his stare moved and became riveted to the foaming whirlpool made by the falling jet. Enchanted, he gazed at the white swirl for a long time, the thunderous noise block-ing his thoughts, when a peripheral movement brought him out of his reverie. He spun brusquely and met the kind brown eyes of the old

---

71 A small mammal with a slender body and long tale, from the same family as the raccoon.

man, who was sitting on a boulder several yards away. He was clad in his usual red cloak and matching leather boots, the breeze ruffling his white beard and hair.

Kamolea cautiously approached him.

"Hello, old-timer," he said. "The last time we met, I specifically emphasized that I never wanna see you again. What part of that request you did not get, ah?"

The man smiled radiantly, not bothering to respond. Kamolea's temper rose.

"Do you like my face?" he shouted. "It's all your fault! You'd threatened me then, telling me I would regret it if I didn't leave Aley alone, and here I am, disfigured for the rest of my life!"

"At least I warned you," shrugged the old man, "and you left Aley anyway, so it would probably have been far easier if you had simply listened to me." His voice was deep and pleasant, much different from when he spoke inside Kamolea's head. "But don't think ill of me because of this incident," he went on. "Today is our farewell meeting, and there must be no hard feelings between us."

Kamolea pricked up his ears and lifted his eyebrows.

"Our last meeting? What excellent news," he mumbled.

His interlocutor rolled his eyes and spread his arms out in a desperate gesture.

"Your training is coming to a close, Kamolea, but you still behave like the most foolish man in the world. For somebody who has almost arrived at the end of his quest for wisdom, your attitude is outrageous. After all my efforts to teach you the core of all things and the secrets of life, the result is pretty discouraging. Heed my words, though: God has not invested so much in you to betray Him and act like a weakling and a spoiled brat, dancing to the runt's tune."

"I've never done so," objected Kamolea.

"Oh, really? And who gave up praying? Who blasphemes all the time? And what about the crucifix? That cross saved your life, remember? Is hurling it with such spite against the wall a way of expressing your gratitude? Look me in the eye and answer me!"

"He lied to me; that's why I threw it," said Kamolea stubbornly, his eyes fixed on the ground.

"Nonsense! Jesus has never lied! On the contrary, he was crucified because he never renounced the truth."

"But why does He not take me to Illima?" Kamolea cried.

"Because the time has not yet come. One more test remains, the hardest one of all, and unfortunately, you are far from ready to pass it—hence the reason I'm here, talking to you. A moment ago, you rejoiced like the biggest fool at the news that it would be our last encounter, without realizing that after I leave you, you will be on your own and I won't be able to help you anymore."

"Why not?" Kamolea asked.

"For when the disciple becomes a warrior and a man of knowledge, he is the only one responsible for his decisions," said the old man. "However, keep in mind that your success or failure will determine the fate of your tribe, for if you fail, God will raise the sea and submerge your island. He will annihilate every living thing. Do you understand that? Thousands of lives are at stake, lad!"

"And what the fuck do I care for them, the losers, who sent me to die?" Kamolea spat on the ground, then added quickly, "Besides Illima, of course, and Anuro, my best friend, and my father and grandmother, if they are still alive, that is."

"Don't call Akamui your father," said the old man sternly, "and don't talk like that about your tribe. Do you know why Maniha Komo still exists, despite all the atrocities and abominations that happen there? Because of the good people there, especially the women. They don't deserve such a cruel fate, but obviously, you're not inclined to save them. Your heart is like stone, for the demons are still strong with you. But don't worry, this will change swiftly," he chortled. "After our conversation, you'll be more Christian than the patriarch himself."

"Than what?" asked Kamolea.

"Never mind," the old man smiled, but it was a sad smile. "Now it's time to ask you for forgiveness for everything I have done to you over these years. Are you willing to forgive me, son?"

"Never!" Kamolea cried, trembling with rage. "How can I forgive you for forcing me to leave my native land? I'll never pardon you for separating me from Illima, for making me a slave, and for inflicting all this suffering upon me. Get out of my sight! I'm not even sure if you're real or not."

The man spread his hands in a gesture of despair.

"You are impossibly slow, my young warrior," he sighed. "This rock I'm sitting on is sharper than you. After everything that has happened, you still doubt that I exist? Come here, feel my arm."

Kamolea took two hesitant steps forward. As he neared the man, he smelled the delightful fragrance of sandalwood. The old man stretched out his arm, and Kamolea squeezed his firm biceps, feeling the soft, sleek fabric of his mantle rustling under his palm. The moment he touched the old man, it was as though the heavens had opened above him and an invisible light was streaming towards his stomach. Filled with awe, his anger disappeared, and his awareness increased hundreds of times over, leaving him so sharp that he immediately understood the meaning of everything the ancient one was trying to convey to him.

"You are real, no doubt about that," Kamolea confirmed, "and pretty strong and muscular for your age, I must say. So, if you can master the elements and show up whenever you like, I assume you are some powerful sorcerer like Aka... Are you?"

"Not at all! I'm far mightier than a simple magician. Believe it or not, I was born in Lycia, far, far away from here, by the name of Nicholas. That was over 1400 years ago."

"What?!" cried Kamolea, stupefied. "So, you're a ghost?!"

"Of course not! Ghosts are apparitions; they don't have a body. Am I like that?"

"How come you've lived for so long, then?"

"When I was young, I firmly believed in God and his Son, Jesus Christ. In return, Lord gave me supernatural force, and I have performed many miracles during my lifetime. My awareness broke the chains of my human limits, and when I left the empty shell of my body to continue my eternal life, it stayed intact and did not decay for centuries. Men like me are called saints, so I became Saint Nicholas."

"And what do they do, these saints?" Kamolea asked, intrigued.

"They help people fight against evil forces and keep their watch over the kind and humble," Saint Nicholas explained. "They also try to teach stupid boys wisdom and submission. An arduous task, indeed," he chuckled. "But although it has taken a little more time than I expected, and despite your stunning slowness and unresponsiveness, I'm confident I have done a good job with you. But let's return to my unpardonable sins towards you and consider them, shall we?"

"There's nothing to consider," muttered Kamolea, his rage foaming anew.

"First, about forcing you to stand up against your tribe, which provoked your exile," Saint Nicholas continued. "Have you ever asked yourself what the meaning of our existence is, Kamolea? I know you haven't, so I'll tell you now for free. No matter whether it's a bug, bird, or plant, every creature comes to the world to enhance its awareness through learning. And as you were chosen to be the savior of your tribe and teach them wisdom, your training required that you were taken from your natural setting. Look at you now! From a stupid, ignorant descendent of a cannibal tribe, you have turned into a knowledgeable man, familiar with human history, civilization, and Christian values. You don't consider your island to be the center of the universe anymore. Or, to put it simply, from a savage, you have become an exemplary human being, which must be the goal for everyone."

Kamolea listened, eagerly absorbing every word, his mouth half-open. He had never thought about his life from that perspective.

"As for Illima, the best lies ahead. For your scars, they have nothing to do with Aley—you got them in battle, saving your mistress's life, so they became your ticket to freedom from slavery. Now, concerning your suffering: I've already explained to you the main reasons for it, remember? About fighting the desires of the flesh, thus taking control over your body and acquiring an iron discipline? This was an essential step in your training, as it created a coat of energy that repelled the *runt*, this nasty parasite that has taken possession of your brain and part of your heart.

"There is something more, however, that I didn't tell you then, but that you must do now without flinching or wailing. The fight against the runt requires three essential techniques. You are already familiar with two of them: blocking out your negative thoughts and praying to our Heavenly Father. The third strategy requires that you restrain yourself from eating for a certain time. I've never made you do it before, as it was preposterous in your hard life of slavery. But now, your time is running out, so you need to do it for a couple of days and even limit your water intake for a short period…"

"What?!" shouted Kamolea.

"There's no way around it, son," said Saint Nicholas firmly. "Abstention is something that bewilders the demons in you. The process of weakening your body makes you less tasty to them, in a manner of speaking. This combination of praying, starving, and repelling their dark waves will drive *them* insane, and *they* will emerge on the surface in search of food."

"Woah, woah, hold your horses, you crazy old man!" Kamolea's heart raced, and his face flushed. "After everything you've done to me; after all the beating, suffering, and humiliation I've been through, you now want to deprive me of the most essential, natural things in life?"

"Oh, come on, Kamolea, stop whining like an old lady. Are you a warrior or what? Everything depends on a man's point of view, on his perception of the world. So, accept this task as a challenge—to starve a little is a small price for the reward that awaits you afterward, which will be to get back to Illima and have many beautiful children with her. But that's not all. If you succeed, you'll save your tribe, and eternal life will await you after your demise."

"Nonsense!" roared Kamolea, beside himself with rage. "I'm fed up with your gibberish! Fuck off, old timer!"

Saint Nicholas rose from the boulder and took a single step forward.

"Watch your language, young man," his voice rang out menacingly, and Kamolea shrank before his majestic presence. "Expelling the runt from your body is an impressive feat, but unfortunately, it's not enough to win the war," he went on in his usual tone. "The next step after you force the demons out of you is to confront their master, the Evil One."

"And why on earth should I do that?" cried Kamolea bellicosely.

"Because you cannot continue your journey without facing the Devil. Resisting *his* temptations is the utmost challenge that remains on your warrior's path. The confrontation with Satan will be your ultimate warrior's proof, your crucial, life-and-death battle that will require every bit of your mental strength and an unbending intent for victory. The strategy is simple—there must be nothing left in you that would allow him to cling on. Your spirit has to shine brighter than the sun with your virtue and your thoughts must be purer than crystal mountain water. That's why you have to pardon me—you cannot win if hatred and self-pity corrode your soul. To succeed, you have to be merciless toward yourself and compassionate toward your people, which is currently not the case at all.

"I hope, however, that the things you'll see presently will help you understand what is at stake. My last lesson will be to show you what will happen to you if you fail to resist the Devil's temptations. We're going to visit the most terrible place in the galaxy now, where no living creature is allowed. But first, put this back in its place, as it is essential to survive there."

Then, Saint Nicholas stretched out his arm and opened his fist. There, on his palm, lay Kamolea's crucifix.

"Thank you, Saint," Kamolea muttered. He took it and pulled the leather strap over his head. "As soon as I touched you, I realized what folly I had committed by throwing it away."

"Never do it again, son. This cross is your connection with God and the only compass that will get you to the safe shore of your salvation. It's the mightiest weapon against the demons; that's why they try to force you all the time to take it off. Give me your hand now!"

The saint squeezed Kamolea's extended hand and the lake with the waterfall vanished, being replaced by a desert. Interminable crimson dunes stretched far into the distance, reflecting the reddish sky that hung low, making the place ominous and creepy. It was scorching hot, and dense vapor rose from the earth, but despite the moisture, Kamolea could not perceive even a single cloud above them. Strangely enough, there was no trace of the sun either. A foul smell of rotten eggs wafted up, reminding him above the stench of Kedia's dwelling. He gasped for air, a sweaty palm pressed against his chest, as the most profound grief he had ever experienced entirely paralyzed him. Tired and desperate, his only desire was to lie down and die. He slumped on his knees and started weeping for no particular reason, as all the memories about his friends, acquaintances, and former life passed through his head.

"Pretty depressing place, isn't it?" he heard Saint Nicholas's voice, but he could not see him. "This is the afterworld of those who have committed the most terrible crimes against their neighbors. We'll take a stroll now, and you can greet some of your former friends. Do you miss them? Those real men that you have always admired are all here—pirates, overseers, cannibals, rapists, killers, and destroyers of all that is good."

A flash of lightning tore through the sky, a red light exploded forth, and the earth split in two with a blaring crash. A vast abyss gaped under Kamolea's feet, and he could barely keep his balance. Through the dense smoke coming from below, torrents of lava streamed down the glowing rocky walls and slowly flowed into a vast fiery river. At the bottom of the pit, millions of people were writhing in inhuman suffering, their awful screams and moans funneling upward and making Kamolea's hair stand up on the back of his neck. They desperately struggled to cling to any niche or jutting rock protruding here and there as they howled in pain and begged for mercy. It was boiling hot and stank of brimstone and scorching flesh. Kamolea stared, hypnotized at the wriggling crowd of naked men and women as they crept up the walls, trying desperately to escape from the blazing river. He pressed his hands against his ears, and his body rocked with sobs as a wave of sorrow overwhelmed him.

"Get me out of here!" he screamed. His anguish was so powerful that he sensed that staying for even a second longer would make his heart burst to pieces. He looked around to find a way out, and spotted three men standing on a small terrace on his right, waving at him. Peering toward them, he recognized Akamui, Momo, and Arataki, the former chieftains of his tribe. Akamui stretched his hand and shouted, "Kamolea! Come and help your father! Save us, son!"

His cry had not still subsided when a strange creature resembling a black goat but with a man's features, black goatee, and curved corns, appeared behind them. It held a fiery spear stuck between its hoofs, and with one mighty strike, it sent the three chieftains straight into the bubbling abyss, their gruesome shrieks echoing from the void.

"Out! Out!" Kamolea hollered, shaking with terror. He began to retreat, but the scene changed abruptly, and he found himself in a pool with three gorgeous young women. It was a warm evening, and the ink-blue sky covered them with a canopy of blinking stars. The beauties were all nude, pressing their splendid bodies against him, and he melted into their arms in an indescribable pleasure. An auburn-haired woman started kissing him, her tongue moving around in his mouth, her soft hand directing his pulsating member between her thighs… And then, just before he could explode with pleasure, the women disappeared and the scene shifted once again. Next, he was dangling upside down, attached by his penis on a dry bough of a weeping willow, hanging about a yard above a fiery lake filled with bubbling gore, which had replaced the pool. The pain in his groin was excruciating, the scorching heat was burning his face, and the stench of the evaporating blood suffocated him. The ghosts of the Tipihao warriors were there too, watching him scornfully. Some of them turned into snakes and crept onto the venerable tree, slowly wrapping their slithering bodies around him and pressing him harder and harder until his bones crunched. Kamolea's inhuman screams rent the air as he writhed up and down, the reptiles biting him all around his face, neck, and shoulders and hissing, "Why didn't you save us?" Every inch of his body hurt terribly, and he begged God to stop the torture and let him die. Then suddenly, the bough of the tree cracked and he plunged headfirst into the boiling blood, his insides turning into red hot embers in an instant.

Another change of scene and the next moment he was before the heart-shaped lake in the Panama jungle again, rolling over in the dirt, waving his limbs, and screaming his head off.

Saint Nicholas watched him from the rock, but no pity softened his eyes this time.

"So, how did you like it there, Kamolea?" he asked coldly, but it took a while before the boy calmed down and came to his senses.

"My body aches everywhere," he muttered, trembling. "What was that terrible place?"

"After one dies, one will be judged according to one's deeds," said Saint Nicholas gravely. "The people who have won their fight against evil will live forever in the heavenly garden. The others, like you and your friend Anuro, will pay the price for wasting their lives and not resisting the lure of the runt. Yes, all the Tipihao warriors will burn in eternal fire in the abyss you've just seen if you fail in your mission. Not the women, though—for most of them, including your grandmother Lalago, there is a different place, where they will stay until they realize and repent of all their mistakes. And for you, my feeble young warrior, as you have seen already, there is a special place in Hell that awaits you."

"No!" cried Kamolea, terrified. His stomach churned, and he bent over and vomited. When he lifted his head, his eyes were pleading and full of tears.

"Please, Saint Nicholas," he said, "please, don't let this happen. I'll do anything you ask me; just spare me this suffering."

"Do you forgive me for all I have done to you?" asked the old man once again.

"I do!" answered Kamolea willingly.

"Are you ready to starve and to drive the runt out of you?"

"I'll try," mumbled Kamolea.

"Do you promise me you'll do everything you can to return to your island and save your tribe from complete annihilation?"

"I promise," Kamolea said.

"Good. Now you know what your punishment will be if you yield to the Devil's seduction. It will be particularly severe because to whom much is given, much is expected. God saw that your spirit was pure and you could change the fate of your people, but if you blunder because of your whims and weak will, you will condemn thousands to terrible suffering, and their death will weigh on your conscience. But I believe in you, and I am convinced that you will win your battle. Beware of women, son! They are your weak link, and as you still haven't had sex, the Sly One will tempt you with them for sure. When the time comes, Illima will be your life belt and your only hope for salvation."

"Will she?" asked Kamolea dubiously.

"Absolutely! Because it's always about the people who you love and care for. Now, remember these parting words, Kamolea: the mightiest weapon against evil is *love*—the purest and the greatest feeling that flows directly from God to every living creature. *Love* is the feeling that makes a mother die for her children. Without love, there will be no existence. *Love* is an inseparable part of the awareness and spark of life. It incites incredible feats and is the driving force behind every good deed..."

The old man's words stirred indescribable sadness inside Kamolea. In his mind's eye, he saw a flashback from his childhood. First, he recalled how the dead parrot, killed by Loto while attempting to protect its chicken, thudded on the ground at his feet, and then another memory, which he had forgotten entirely, surfaced in its place. They were up the hill with Akamui, chasing a wild boar, when a sudden pouring rain forced them to shelter under a jutting rock. Several yards further on, a deep chasm opened and Kamolea could not resist crawling to the stony edge and taking a look. It was a breathtaking view—a ravine densely covered with greenery and a glistening river meandering far below. A sharp screech made him glance down to his right. On a small protruding slab, a female hawk had spread its wings over a nest, protecting her little chicks from the downpour. Kamolea could not see them, but judging by the sharp cries, there must have been two or three. The mother stood over them with a bowed head, waiting for the rain to stop. Instead, it took the full force, turning into a dense, white shroud of heavy hail, and Akamui yelled at Kamolea to get back under the rock. The latter, who had never seen such a phenomenon, watched on in fear at the egg-shaped chunks of ice bouncing from the ground. It lasted for a short while before transforming into rain again. As it slowly abated, Kamolea rushed again to the edge of the deep and glanced at the hawk. His heart missed a beat at the heartbreaking scene he witnessed—the mother lay dead in the nest, killed by the hailstorm, with her wings still spread over her little children. *She did it for love,* he had thought then, and now he perfectly understood what the old man meant.

"...Jesus taught us that '*There is no greater love than this, that someone lay down his life for his friends,*' and this is the core of your mission," Saint Nicholas was saying. "Teach the men of your tribe to live in peace and love. Turn them from savages into good human beings, just like I did to you. Show them the true God, destroy their cursed tree and evil legacy, and save Illima from the Steamy Cave. Be the new beginning for your people! Never forget that their lives depend on you! Remember: love is the key."

No sooner had he finished his speech than Saint Nicholas dissolved into the air, leaving Kamolea to stare blankly at the boulder on which he had been seated. Finally, emotionally drained by the morning's events, he decided to return to the shelter instead of bathing in the lake. Shaken to the core, he brooded over the things he had seen on his way back and mulled over the instructions of the saint while his brain swiftly gained its usual control over the situation.

"Frankly, I can't imagine how I could possibly stop eating," he mumbled to himself.

Oh, come on, don't be so pathetic! You know perfectly well that the things you saw were pure fantasy, don't you? Nobody dooms himself by starving voluntarily. It's sheer insanity! hissed the familiar voice ceaselessly.

Of course, it is, agreed Kamolea with himself. *Although, fantasy or not, the pain was pretty real when I was hung by the cock above that disgusting pond. Well anyway, I'll finish the half of a deer left from my last hunt first; then, I'll decide what to do...*

But after he returned to the shelter, another unpleasant surprise awaited him—the deer's carcass had disappeared. He bent down to observe the trail before the entrance, which indicated that some sort of large animal had dragged it toward the woods.

Gobo and Rita would never touch my food, he thought, irritated, and sniffed the air like a wild beast. *Maybe their father has finally dropped by.*

"... you must stop eating for several days...," Saint Nicholas's words echoed in his mind. He stopped short, thinking.

"The fuck I will," he hissed, grabbed his bow and quiver, and stepped outside. "That's the only thing missing in my shitty life—starving to death for no reason."

He took the path leading down to the lake, but he had barely made it a few yards before he slipped on a pebble. He stuck out his arms, then lost his balance, twisted his ankle, and slumped to the ground with a sharp cry. A sudden pain pierced his leg and he continued wailing as he crawled to a nearby tree, where he grabbed a low-hanging branch and hauled himself up, shifting all his weight on his good leg. His ankle was swelling up rapidly and in no time, it had doubled in size. He couldn't even put any weight on it, let alone walk. He hopped painfully back to the cave, using branches and creepers to support his weight. He had almost reached the end of the trees, where the bare cliff began, and was wondering how he'd make it any further one-legged through the thicket, when a severe stinging pain in the calf of his good leg made him shout with pain. He collapsed, howling, and his eyes leveled with the brown back of a snake. It was about two yards long and covered with yellowish rhomboid stripes. As it slowly slithered away with its ringed tail sticking up, it emitted a strange rattling sound.

Within a minute, Kamolea's leg was entirely paralyzed, and he stopped being able to feel it. Clawing at the dirt and pulling at snags and roots, he managed to crawl back to his shelter in the rock just before he was carried into unconsciousness by the rattlesnake's poison.

* * *

A terrible roar tore through his mind and he woke up shaking. It was night, but a small amount of faint light was filtering in from the entrance to the cave.

Is it already a full moon? Could I have been asleep for so long? he was sure the moon had been a waxing crescent the last time he remembered. But then, his thoughts quickly focused on more urgent matters. He was feverish, his face hot but his body shivering with cold, and his brain was projecting strange images of flying, fluctuating shadows in front of him.

Must be hallucinations from the snake's poison, he presumed. A loud rumble in his stomach suggested prolonged starvation, and he moaned, feeling like a stream of lava was burning his insides. He licked his cracked, bleeding lips and uttered "water," but no sound came from his dry mouth. His attempts to get up were unsuccessful, too, as he found his body was numb from his waist down. At least his arms were functioning, so he pressed his hands against his ears, trying to silence the cacophony that was echoing inside his head.

"What did you do, you fucking loser!" screamed a shrill voice. *"What are you going to eat now? How will you hunt? I'm so fed up with you, you jerk! I DETEST YOU, YOU USELESS WRETCH!"*

"Why are you doing this to me, my dear boy?" a pleading, child-like female voice wept. *"What's wrong with you? I've always been your friend, always wanted the best for you. It's the damned old man's fault; it's him that makes you suffer all the time. Please, dear, let me live inside you. I have nowhere to go. Please, let's be friends, like before. Please!"*

A profound depression overcame Kamolea. A lump formed in his chest and slowly moved towards his throat, causing him acute physical pain and suffocating him.

Where are my babies? his subconscious wailed, looking around for the jaguars. *I can't bear to be alone anymore…*

Despair is one of the runt's mightier weapons, flashed through his mind, and he cocked his head, astounded by this realization.

Where are all these thoughts and voices coming from? he asked himself. In response, a deep bass voice bellowed,

You ugly bastard, you can't do this to me! and Kamolea noticed a huge dark shadow passing onto the far wall. A second later, something swooped furiously over him. It was like a faint wind, but Kamolea's hair stood up on his neck, and goosebumps crawled all over him like living insects, as the same dread he had experienced when he met Aka in his ocelot form overwhelmed him again.

"Leave me alone," he whimpered.

"Bloody wretch!" came a different scream, and Kamolea, now numb with dread, saw a flock of shadows of various sizes circling over him like black bats. They hurled themselves at him, one after another, turning into spiteful memories that danced before his eyes. Diego de Sylva was there, grinning and fiddling with his aroused member inside his pants. Oh, how Kamolea detested him! If he had been able to move, he would have jumped at him and ripped his throat out. Uma was there, too, standing in the far corner, naked and sweaty, licking her lips. *"Go for her, sucker!"* screamed a voice. Two more shadows swooped on him with piercing screams, and he started shrieking like crazy when he heard Saint Nicholas yell from afar, "Sing, Kamolea, sing and pray, and they won't harm you."

But he had no energy left and, shaking with dread, he fainted once more.

* * *

When he came to his senses, it was dark again, but Kamolea suspected that it was a different night, for no moonlight entered the cave. Gobo and Rita licked his head and face vigorously, nudging him with their heads and paws the same way as they had done when they were cubs. He felt so weak that he had no strength even to stroke them, but at least he could move his legs, albeit with great effort. A whisper was constantly nagging in the back of his mind, telling him to crawl outside, reach the lake, dip his head in, and drink, drink, drink… But the mere thought of moving made him extremely tired. He tried to prop himself up on an elbow. Suddenly, the jaguars cocked their heads, sniffing nervously, then shot out of the cave, letting out a low growl. Kamolea gasped and strained with all his strength, hauling himself into a sitting position and leaning against the stone wall. He listened intently, alert and tense. His senses were telling him that something was wrong—an alien presence lurked in the darkness, invoking fear and exacerbating his feeling that there was an invisible danger nearby. He sat still, waiting, when all of a sudden, his eyes bulged, his face distorted in an ugly grimace, and he stuck his tongue out with a hissing sound.

"Fucker, the time has come. I refuse to put up with you anymore."

He roared at the top of his lungs and writhed on the floor, his tongue protruded, then he wheezed,

"Now you'll face the Ultimate One, your Master and God," the ominous whisper crescendoed into another horrendous bellow.

What's going on with me? he thought, trying to regain his normal face and roll his tongue back into his mouth. But then, he was seized by an urge to jump up and smash his head into the rocky wall. He rolled over, straining all his efforts to suppress it, as an unfamiliar language flowed from his mouth.

In tempore venit ad occursum,[72] he hissed. The presence of the horror itself was palpable in the darkness. His fingers wrapped firmly around his knife's hilt, as he waited in suspense. Gradually, the whole place filled with a faint reddish glow and a silhouette appeared, growing brighter and taking the form of a gigantic man, whose impossibly broad shoulders were outlined by the lively flickering of flames. His limbs did not stand out clearly, but his head, almost reaching the ceiling, was distinct, defined by two ember-blazing eyes.

The black giant emanated dread. Memories of *Rakapi*, the Sacred Tree, flooded Kamolea's mind, and he could hardly restrain himself from kneeling and kissing the ground before him. As he lowered his gaze, Kamolea noticed a small, ugly creature, about two hands high, standing at the man's feet. Lit up by the purple glow in the room, it was so grotesque and miserable looking that Kamolea could not help but pity it. Besides, it looked pretty familiar; these crooked legs and a strikingly bald head with bulging eyes and a frog mouth… In a flash,

---

72 The time has come to meet.

he saw himself lying in the boat again, observing the withered dwarf's face as it constantly fluctuated through multiple shapes and colors.

"Yes, when you uncovered my servant for the first time, I knew we would one day meet," the deep guttural voice of the shadow-like man confirmed his thoughts in perfectly enunciated Tipihao language. "Congratulations, young fellow. You have succeeded in chasing your companion out of you, and that, by any means, is a notable achievement, considering how stupid you humans are."

"Bow down and pay tribute to your master, fool!" squealed the ugly thing. "Worship your God and kiss the ground under *his* feet because the honor of seeing *him* in person is the greatest thing that could ever happen in your miserable life."

Kamolea felt the urge to do exactly that, but he could not budge.

"Who are you?" he wanted to ask, but his lips refused to part.

"I am the ruler of this world and your true God!" rang out the bass timbre, which seemed to come from the very depths of darkness. "I have many names, but Almighty Kepolo is enough for you."

"Are you the Evil One that the saint warned me I'd meet?" croaked Kamolea, his hoarse voice echoing hollowly in the small cave.

"There is no evil and no good, youngster!" responded the colossus. "It is all an invention of the human mind; empty words with no meaning. All that counts is to live your life and enjoy the present, but unfortunately, you have never got that.

"I've been watching you all these years, and I've never stopped marveling at your stupidity and delusion. Why did you waste the bright future I had intended for you? If you had only stayed at Maniha Komo, you would have been a chieftain now, glorified in many battles, handsome and powerful, respected and admired by your people! You would have had many women and fame, and everything else imaginable. But what did you do instead? You obeyed the crazy old man and threw away your brilliant destiny! Tell me now, after all the suffering and ill luck you have had, what have you gained? Look at you! A hermit in the mountains, ugly and lonely, disfigured, surrounded by beasts, starving and slowly dying. Your youth passed by in slavery, beating, and humiliation. And what about that pretty Indian who adored you? The old man forbade you from even having a girlfriend, which is the most natural thing for every man. What did you do to deserve such a dreadful ordeal? I'll tell you what—you listened to him and rejected *me*. You chose the crucified coward over *me*, the God of your ancestors, and you have paid the price. Have you enjoyed your life up to now? Even the animals live better than you!"

Kamolea caught himself rhythmically nodding in agreement.

So true, he thought. *I couldn't put it better myself.*

"But I can see that, although you're a bit confused, you're a smart lad," continued the dark man with a suddenly sympathetic tone. "Luckily for you, I'm not a vindictive person, and despite you snubbing me, I have decided to help you out. Enough suffering now! All these restrictions and stupid admonitions are over. I am the fun and the freedom! Believe me—the world will be a dull place without me. Tell me, have I ever forbidden my people anything? Have I ever betrayed them? I won't forsake you. Come back to me, and I'll make you a great man. Let me show you the glorious future I have in mind for you."

The next moment, Kamolea was flying at great speed, the wind lashing against his face. He soared above seas, forests, and mountains until a view of a magnificent palace made of gold and ivory met his eyes. As he descended, he observed himself sitting on a golden throne on a high platform before the palace. He was a king, dressed in stunning turquoise-blue clothes. A lion's hide covered his shoulders, and his head was adorned with a splendid gold crown studded with diamonds. He was surrounded by an army of black men stripped to the waist, who stood slightly astride, clutching spears with their shafts against the ground, their sharp blades pointing up. Two of the warriors flanked him, waving huge palm fronds before his face. Kamolea slowly floated towards the vision and merged into his king's body. Suddenly, he could sense the heat and the scent of unknowing flowers. He got up from the throne and stepped forward.

From the elevated ground, countless steps descended to a vast plain, where a swarm of men and women kneeled and touched their fronts rhythmically in prayer to their king. They were so many of them that Kamolea could not see the end of this swaying human sea.

"You are destined to be a great king and wise ruler," whispered a gentle voice in his ears. "Look at all these people! They will adore you and worship you as their God. Do you realize what I am offering you? You, the poor miserable hermit boy, will become a great emperor and a worshipped God! But wait, that's not all. The best is yet to come!"

All of a sudden, Kamolea was sitting at the center of an enormous table covered with fine dishes, surrounded by many people, who were laughing and talking animatedly. A bunch of servants scurried around, pouring wine from golden jugs and carrying overflowing golden plates. He could smell the delicious aroma of the meal, which was an irresistible temptation in itself, considering his long fast. His mouth watered. He raised a golden goblet, said something, and his companions burst into laughter. At this moment, six young women rushed into the large dining room, waving gossamer veils and twirling their graceful, half-naked bodies, covered only with flashing golden sequins that jingled with every twist. They all had different skin colors, from milky white to deep black, contrasting with their long, silky hair, which was dyed blonde, auburn, and jet-black. Their tresses, tossing around in frantic dance, bounced in all directions and spilled over their sculpted shoulders.

As Kamolea admired their supple figures and enchantingly lovely faces, he found himself relaxing in a large open pool covered with golden tiles. It was a tropical, starry night charged with passion. A sweet fragrance of blooming flowers drifted in the air, and he inhaled eagerly as the water wrapped him in a gentle hug, cooling his hot body pleasantly.

This place looks strangely familiar… He frowned, trying to shake the feeling of déjà vu. He glanced around for clues and noticed the same gorgeous dancers stretched out stark naked on ivory chaises longues alongside the pool. The moment he spotted them, three of the beauties got up and lazily approached, chatting and giggling.

Kamolea's heart started pounding in his throat—just watching their perfect shapes aroused him immediately. The women waded into the water and slowly swam in his direction, smiling, their eyes boring into him. Instead of being elated, though, he felt like he was panicking, so embarrassed was he by their perfection. But he had no time to react, as they quickly encircled him and pressed their lovely bodies against him, caressing him gently. Kamolea felt their full, firm breasts, their erect nipples, and their velvety skin, and a supreme pleasure burst within him. Wrapped between these gorgeous creatures, he melted in the water. The green eyes of the auburn-haired woman were mesmerizing. She squeezed his pulsating member and nodded approvingly, saying something in an unidentifiable language. The others sniggered and started kissing him. Kamolea sensed that he was about to come when suddenly, the world whirled around him, and something furiously stirred inside his chest.

Gradually, he became distracted and distant, and his lust vanished. His ears started buzzing as though thousands of butterflies were flapping their wings inside them. A sudden flash tore through the cloudless sky, and in a split second, he saw Illima lying in the Steamy Cave, her arm stretched out, her face distorted by anguish.

"Illima," he whispered. The next moment, he was in the pool again, surrounded and being caressed by the dazzling women, but the magic of the previous moment had disappeared, and their velvety, delightful bodies had become cold, slimy, and fishlike. He met the piercing gaze of the auburn-haired beauty and the memory of him dangling upside down above the boiling, bloody lake burst into view. A chilling fear stabbed his heart as a loud cackle resounded in the air and the gorgeous milky face of the green-eyed enchantress distorted into a goat's head with large, curved horns. A scream ran through his head, a strong wind blew through his nostrils, and everything went black. When he opened his eyes, he was lying on the cave's bare stone floor.

"Illima. There was so much sorrow in her eyes," he stuttered, his heart overwhelmed with love.

"So, how did you like your future, my young fellow?" asked the dark man pleasantly. "As I promised you, your life will be amazing from now on. What did you adore most? The girls weren't bad, were they? What about the delicious dishes? Lavish luxury and gold in a splendid palace? A crowd of subjects to worship you? Just say the word, and everything will be yours."

"It was incredible," Kamolea confirmed, still hypnotized by the bright images.

"That's my boy!" the black shadow hissed, and the dancing flames around him flared. "I assume we're all set now. The only thing you need to do is to accept me back as your God. Let's start by throwing away that stupid cross you've put back around your neck, and those two bracelets on your wrist. Then, I want you to spit on them. Afterward, you'll kneel before me, kiss the ground beneath my feet, and declare aloud that from now on, I will be your one and only God until your last breath. See how easy it is? No sweat, no pain. Think about it; it's no big deal, especially considering everything you'll receive in exchange. So don't hesitate, do it right away! Let's start by taking off the cross!"

Kamolea reached for the crucifix in a daze, but the moment he touched it, he felt his body swell as though some vital fluid was flowing into his veins. He grew bigger and stronger, his shoulders broadened, his legs elongated, and his head almost reached the ceiling, leveling with the giant's face. From up close, he realized that it wasn't a real face—it had no hair, and the features were fluid and fluctuating, just like those of the runt. Its beady red eyes were snake-like and mean, like two bright glowing coals in the darkness. Kamolea shuddered and averted his gaze. As he looked down, to his great surprise, he saw his physical body leaning against the wall. The second he noticed it, he immediately found himself back in it, watching the dark man from below, but at the same time, he retained his vision from within the giant form, equal in height to the dark being.

"I'm in two places simultaneously, no doubt about that!" his lower projection muttered. "So incredible! But how is it possible?"

A flow of feelings passed through him. His mind was quick and clear, but also split in two, corresponding with his two personalities. The lower being was superficial, light-headed, jolly, and adventurous, bursting with energy and searching for the pleasure of life. The giant, meanwhile, was stable, heavy, calm, and venerable, and Kamolea realized that this was the part of him that handled all his crucial decisions in life. The problem was that it was so deeply buried under the noisy, cheerful youngster that it was impossible to detect. The joyful one shouted ceaselessly,

"Glorious king! Splendid kingdom! Myriad women! Unfathomable wealth and everything that comes with it! You're on a roll, man! Lightning doesn't strike twice, so seize your luck and live happily ever after! What are you waiting for? Go ahead, accept!"

But the older, heavy part of him was not so eager.

"*Think what is at stake here,*" his ancient mind boomed, and Kamolea had the impression that he was standing before an immense ocean—mighty, inscrutable, and everlasting. "*Know thyself, lad. Look straight into your soul and feel what exactly it is that you long for.*"

And Kamolea did precisely that—he asked himself what would make him happy.

I'm certainly not thrilled by the prospect of being a king, he thought. *It must be dreadful to always be the center of attention; it's worse than slavery for me—I've always enjoyed the freedom of the jungle and the company of wild beasts rather than people. Except for the gorgeous women, of course... well, they were something for sure, especially the red-haired one... But what about Illima?*

Illima's face materialized before him once more, distorted with pain, her shiny eyes looking at him pleadingly.

I love her so much! he thought. *Everything I do is meaningless if I cannot share it with her. She is the only thing in this cruel world that matters to me.*

In that instant, Kamolea made his decision. He looked straight at the gleaming coals of the shadow.

"If I accept your proposition, will you bring Illima to me?" his gigantic self reverberated. "I want her always by my side, no matter whether I'm a king, chieftain, or a simple man. If you can bring us together, I'll worship you as my God again."

"Let her go!" thundered the dark man impatiently. "You don't need her! Did not you like all those dazzling beauties I'm offering you? They are hundreds of times more gorgeous than your Illima—no two ways about it. Come on, now, time is pressing. Throw the cross away and kneel before me, and tomorrow you'll wake up as a king."

Kamolea did not respond. An incredible force pulsated inside his body, and he felt like a mighty giant, stronger than this terrible man. The vision of the writhing bodies crawling from the fiery pit flashed through his mind, and for a split second, he spotted his childhood friend, Anuro, agonizing in the fire.

"What about the fiery river?" he asked. "I saw many men of my tribe down there."

"Don't pity them, lad," boomed the man. "They were the ones who cast you out, remember? They got what they deserved. But I can promise you that you aren't going there. I'll make you a vampire, and you'll live forever in this world."

"What is a vampire?" Kamolea asked.

"My servant. You'll keep your body and everything else; only you'll sleep mostly during the day. And you will be able to fly, turn yourself into animals, and much more. I'm sure you'll love it! But of course, this will be many years from now, after you have fully enjoyed a long life as a king—and all the pleasure that comes with it."

Kamolea considered this for a moment.

"It doesn't sound bad at all," he said. "But what about Illima? If I were to be this vampa or whatever, she should be one too. So, reunite us, and we have a deal."

"I can't do that," the dark man replied. "Illima belongs to another realm, and I have no power there. Ask anything else, but not that."

"What kind of kingdom is this?" Kamolea asked.

"It is the realm of love," the Evil One responded. "I have nothing in common with this corny, sleazy shit. I'm not interested at all in such nonsense. Love only makes people weak, sentimental fools; nothing else."

"If you can't take me to Illima or bring her here, then fuck off!" cried Kamolea angrily. "I certainly don't want a ruler who can't do such a simple thing."

"How dare to speak like that to the Great Kepolo!" the runt screamed from below, taking a step forward in protection of its master. "You're a dead man, you fool!"

"You are, indeed!" the shadow-man moved toward Kamolea. "If you refuse my offer, I'll crush you like a fly, and your bones will lie in this lair for time immemorial."

The dark giant emanated such dread and horror that Kamolea felt himself shrink. Within a heartbeat, he had curled up on the ground, trembling, his flesh covered with goosebumps, his head itching, and his hair sticking up. The monster bent down and a powerful gust caught Kamolea in a wild whirlwind, flinging him against the wall. His spine hit the solid rock and cracked, and he collapsed to the ground on his front, where he lay prone. The whirlwind raised the stones from the hearth and hurled them at his lifeless body, but the bracelet on his wrist flashed, and in a split second, Laia and Keoni appeared in the cave, holding hands. As they entered, a brilliant light suffused the dark room. They sheltered their son and shattered the flying rocks, which bounced back against the walls. The shimmering flames that danced around the giant flared in a blazing red that collided with the brightness emanating from Kamolea's parents. The runt's piercing scream rent the air, a blinding flash exploded, and everything went black.

CHAPTER XXIII

THE BURIED TREASURE

Kamolea floated across the black sky, surrounded by millions of stars.

"Remember Alina and her three children!" the booming voice from his childhood vision vibrated inside him. He noticed three blazing stars positioned in line, and as he focused on them, they turned into beautiful young girls with radiant smiles. Spellbound, he sped up towards them, but the more he longed to reach them, the more they receded until the innumerable blinking dots around him whirled with incredible speed before spitting him out on a bobbing raft in the swelling sea. He was now a little boy, sitting between Itaki and Lelando, his two younger half-brothers. Akamui leaned on the mast in front of them, pointing to the sky. The boys followed his raised hand and listened to him, enthralled.

"One day, if you succeed with your warrior's proof, and I'm sure you will, you'll need Alina, the brightest star over there, to lead you home," Akamui was saying. "It's pretty easy to locate her, as just below her are those three shining ones in a row, see? Her daughters, as the old woman says. So now, connect those four stars close to Alina in your mind."

"Which ones?" Lelando asked.

"Do you see the one on the right, two in the middle and the fourth below? They make an octopus. The five stars, including Alina, make its head, and her daughters are the tentacles."

The boys giggled with delight, rolling their eyes as they did.

"I see a crab instead," chuckled Itaki.

"No, it's a jellyfish!" cried out Lelando and punched him on the shoulder.

"Don't make fun of it, you little fools!" Akamui bawled angrily. "Carve that octopus into your memory as it's a matter of life and death when it comes to finding Maniha Komo."

Kamolea strained all his senses, striving to memorize the location of the stars, when a wave splashed his face, and he gradually came to his senses. He opened his eyes and met Rita's tongue, vigorously licking his cheek. Her low growl was the only clearly audible sound inside the dusky cave.

"Could you stop that, please," groaned Kamolea, barely recognizing his own croaking voice. His tongue was thick like the sole of a boot, and his mouth was dry like a sun-dried marlin. Still, he rejoiced at discovering he could move again. He propped himself up on one elbow, pushed Rita, and moaned, "Gosh, every inch of my body hurts."

His meeting with the Evil One was a blur, a deeply buried nightmare that had almost completely been wiped out by his childhood dream about Alina. He glanced at his ankle. The swelling had subsided, and it was getting better. He crawled to the wall and dug his nails into the cool rock, then, with clenched teeth, he braced himself against the surface, scrambling upward with his hands, yellow spots dancing before his eyes. To his surprise, his feet were firm, with no trace of the previous numbness. The good news gave him a boost of energy and he took a step towards the illuminated entrance, when Gobo emerged, dragging a brocket[73] fawn with him.

---

73 Small South and Central American deer.

"Oh, very kind of you, matey, but I need water first, for my insides are burning," Kamolea muttered as he slowly limped toward the exit. His twisted ankle still hurt a bit, but the pain was dull and tolerable. As for the bitten limb, it was healthy and steady, as if it had never been injured. Once outside, the breeze caressed his face and he eagerly inhaled the damp air, squinting in the bright sunshine. Using the overhanging branches for support, he reached the descending path and started on the steep, lumpy path, which was an overgrown mess of creepers, rolling stones, and protruded roots. Staggering, sliding, and falling, he finally reached the lake and plunged his head into the water, drinking fervently until a sharp abdominal cramp split his insides. He rolled on his back, clutching his fit-to-burst stomach and lay there for hours, watching the clouds dragging across the blue sky, listening to the roar of the waterfall, and waiting for the pain to subside.

After he felt better, he got into the lake, where he soaked himself and his stinking clothes under the falling jet for a long time. When he finally returned to the plateau, clean and fresh, it was already dusk. He built a huge fire and roasted the fawn, wolfing it down half-raw from hunger. By the time he had finished his feast, the cloudless, inky sky had turned into a shroud of millions of blinking stars. It was a magical night, replete with the chirping of cricket, the hooting of owl, and the rustling of leaves. The lively fire illuminated the spotted jaguars lying next to him, and soon, Captain Junu landed with a screech in his lap.

Moved to tears, Kamolea gave a spontaneous speech.

"Thank you for taking care of me, my children," he addressed them grandly. "As the whole family is united tonight, I'll seize the opportunity to express my gratitude for everything you've done for me." He scratched Rita behind the ears, stroked her fondly, and smiled sadly at Gobo that watched him, breathing heavily with his tongue out. "Soon, I will be obliged to leave you. I'm gonna miss you terribly, my hearties, but unfortunately, I cannot take you where I'm going. Don't be jealous of Captain Junu who, I assume, will be pleased to keep me company. As we will only have a few more days together, I'd truly appreciate it if you stay a bit longer with me."

Rita let out a low growl in agreement and Gobo yawned, seemingly consenting too. Captain Junu didn't make a sound; he simply wriggled in Kamolea's lap. Kamolea felt satiated and happy. He stretched out beside the fire and stared at the stars, going over his dream again and again. A new hope had arisen in him, as for the first time, he conceived a vague idea of how to return to Maniha Komo.

* * *

One afternoon, about two weeks later, Kamolea walked through the gate of Panama City for the second time. Since the memorable string of events, beginning with the encounter with the Evil One and followed by his healing, the change that had occurred in him was incredible, manifesting itself in several aspects.

First, the voices that had tortured him for years, had vanished and inside his head, blissful silence reigned. There were no nagging worries, no remorse or regret, no indecision, anger, or suicidal thoughts—only a delightful peace that anointed the deep cuts of his wounded soul with a marvelous balm.

The second alteration was the opening in his stomach, which he had first felt when he touched Saint Nicholas. It was a wonderful feeling, similar to a spring warbling inside him, connecting him to some immense source, like a torrential stream flowing directly from the heavens towards his abdomen. Brooding over this connection, Kamolea could not help but compare his experience with a phrase that he had read in the Scriptures back at the plantation: *"Whoever believes in me, out of his belly shall flow rivers of living water…"*

He had sneered at the assertion at the time, convincing himself that everything written in the Bible was bullshit.

I never believed that all those tales of demons, angels, miracles, hell, and the flow of living water had any meaning, he thought, astounded. *Now, based on my experience, I can swear that everything narrated in the Gospels is pure truth. The question is, why is it so hard to believe it?*

The living spring bubbling in him offered a tremendous boost of energy. It was a source of awareness that led him in a specific, strictly defined direction. The effect of this bursting vitality, combined with his inner silence, led to a third major shift, which strongly affected Kamolea's behavior. He became detached, bold, and determined, and he did not hesitate like before when it came to making a decision, as he immediately knew what he had to do. Thus, when he walked through the gate to Panama City, his inner compass took him southeast, and his mind focused on the invisible thread that led him through a tangled labyrinth of meandering streets. He passed by a tavern, where a bunch of loafers were cheering a fist fight between two sturdy drunkards, making bets, and shouting at the top of their lungs. After spending so much time as a hermit, the clamor of the city made him nervous and dizzy.

"It's far better living in the woods," he muttered to himself as several soldiers ran past him and swooped on the crowd, ending the fun. He was hurrying along a small narrow alley, when a woman yelled from a balcony and poured a washbasin full of stinking water out, several yards from him. Kamolea jumped and turned quickly down another street, then took another one and rambled for some time, until finally, he found himself before the Santo Domingo convent. It was the same majestic building of red bricks that had left him dumbstruck years ago, on his way to Panama dungeon.

Iglesia Santo Domingo, he read just above the door, remembering Benito's remarque: *Can't you read the inscription? Of course you can't, savage.*

This time I can, matey. Pity you can't see me now; I bet you would have been very proud of me, he smiled.

Kamolea glanced at the enormous figure of Saint Dominic, watching him sternly from atop the building, and once again, he felt small and insignificant. He tried the door to the church, but it was shut. Disappointed, he looked around, searching for another entrance. On his right, a high stone fence next to the church marked the start of the convent. He started walking along the wall and, several yards further, he noticed a massive dark oak door. He stopped in front of it, scratched his head, and hesitated for a second, then reached for the heavy metal ring dangling in the middle and banged it three times. After a while, he heard steps approaching, then the door screeched open and a bald, bearded man, clad in a brown cassock, popped his head through the narrow breach.

"God bless you, son. How may I help you?" he asked, suspiciously eyeing the scarred face of the broad-shouldered young man in the linen shirt and drab baggy trousers, with a bow and a quiver slung across his back, a shabby bag dangling at his hip, and a small monkey perched atop his left shoulder.

"I don't know how, but I hope you do, señor," said Kamolea cheerfully.

"Well, let's start with the reason you knocked on this door," said the monk. "This is God's abode, a monastery. Maybe you got the wrong building?"

"Is this Santo Domingo Convent?" Kamolea asked.

"It is," the monk confirmed.

"So, I'm in the right place, then. Jesus Christ sent me to you with the promise that in this very convent, I'd find the answer to all my questions."

"*Jesus* told you that?" the monk raised his brow doubtfully. "Are you sure that it was *Him* who spoke to you? Few people can claim such an honor, son."

"Well, I'm pretty sure, señor," Kamolea said, "but if you don't believe me, just tell me where I can stay overnight... Although I ain't got even a single real."

It was the monk's turn now to scratch his bald head. A firm believer, he contemplated,

God must be testing my faith, as this youngster is either delusional and mentally unstable, or he really has heard the Lord's voice. If I dismiss the lad now, and it later turns out that he's telling the truth, I will be certainly punished for my lack of faith, as God did with Moses when he doubted Him that the rock would yield water.

"Come inside, my young fellow," he said pleasantly. "Only the abbot can decide whether you will stay, but he is in the church now as the evening service will start soon. I'll take you to the refectory and you'll wait for him there. Just give me your bow and quiver, as weapons are not allowed in God's place."

Kamolea handed him his arms, and the monk led him through a neat, cobbled yard, edged with flowers. They passed a long one-story building with many small windows and multiple doors placed at equal intervals and set off towards a smaller square house made of stones at the far end of the yard. As they neared it, the bells started tolling. Captain Junu screamed with terror and clung to Kamolea's arm like a frightened child.

"I have to go," said the monk quickly. He pushed the door open and Kamolea stepped into a vast hall with a long table stretched out in the middle, flanked by two massive benches. Inside was somber and cool, the delicious aroma of a cooking meal filling the room.

"Wait for the end of the service here," said the man and he left hurriedly.

Kamolea sat on the edge of the bench and stared wistfully at the ashlars of the uncoated wall. The delightful scent came from the left, where a small door betrayed the position of the monastery kitchen. His stomach rumbled as if hundreds of cats were scratching his insides, and his mouth watered intensely. While he was wondering if he should peep into the kitchen, Captain Junu got overexcited for no apparent reason and jumped into the corner, climbing over the shelf crammed with cooking pots, bowls, and dishes.

"Stop that immediately, you scoundrel!" Kamolea cried, terrified. "If you break something, I'll wring your neck!"

With a triumphant screech, Captain Junu jumped back on the table and from there, he leaped onto Kamolea's shoulder, where he settled down and started rummaging in his master's tangled hair. Soon, he found something there, put it in his mouth, and grunted with pleasure.

Time dragged on. Kamolea, whose only occupation was to stare at the uncoated wall, had dozed off when the door finally flew open with a bang, startling him. About fifteen bearded men in brown cassocks, mostly above middle age, barged into the refectory and took their places around the table without uttering a word.

Two of the younger monks brought in a steaming cauldron, put it on a special three-legged metal stand, then took the bowls from the shelves, filled them one by one, and handed them to their seated brothers. The aroma of the steaming vegetable broth tickled Kamolea's nose, and he could hardly restrain himself from falling upon it. But a furtive glance to one side informed him that nobody was in a hurry to eat.

What the fuck are they waiting for? he thought angrily.

The bald monk who had received him turned to a majestic-looking old man with long white hair and a beard below the chest, who was sitting at the head of the table.

"This is the lad I told you about, Father," he said.

"Welcome to our abode, son," said the old man in a deep voice. Kamolea deduced that he was the abbot, judging by his confident I-am-in-charge-here intonation. "We invite you to share our supper with us in silence, and afterward, you will tell us what brings you here. But first, let us pray."

They all entwined their hands and lowered their eyes. Kamolea did the same. Captain Junu, however, did not feel like praying. Instead, he flung himself towards the shelves again, caught a large, painted earthen pot, half swung from it, then brought it crashing down amid a high-pitched screech and a thunderous noise. The jar shattered into pieces and shards flew everywhere, some landing on the table.

Kamolea wished he could sink through the floor, but to his surprise and utter relief, nobody reacted. The monks remained in the same posture, their eyes half-closed and their lips moving in silent prayer as if nothing had happened. Red in the face and seething with rage, Kamolea jumped up and hissed,

"That's enough, Captain Junu! Come here right now!"

The white-faced capuchin obediently jumped on his shoulder. Kamolea grabbed it by the scruff of the neck, opened the door, and threw it outside.

Still embarrassed, he returned to take his seat again, wondering if he should gather the scattered shards up, when he met the piercing gaze of a friar in his fifties, who was the only one at the table who had lifted his head from his prayer.

"I'm really sorry, señor. He has no manners, this rascal," Kamolea muttered, averting his gaze. But then, he stopped short, looked up, and stared back at the monk. There was something familiar in man's features, which were mostly covered under a thick, bushy beard. Although they weren't hidden under glasses, the calm brown eyes could only have belonged to one person. The blood slowly withdrew from Kamolea's face, and his jaw dropped as his saucer eyes stared in disbelief at the monk's equally stupefied countenance. Slowly, they both relaxed into broad grins.

"Junu," the monk mouthed and touched his lips with his forefinger, clearly indicating that he should be silent.

"Benito," Kamolea whispered, and his heart leaped with joy.

His shipmate had gotten a little older, his brow was more furrowed than before, and his chestnut hair had slightly receded into multiple, palpable white threads, but otherwise, he was the same—his savior and protector, his beloved Benito.

The majestic monk who presided at the table raised his head and said, "May God bless this food. Amen!" He crossed himself, and everybody repeated in chorus, "Amen."

"Don't worry about the monkey, son. Eat now; you must be hungry," said the abbot.

Kamolea did not wait to be asked twice. He gulped the broth down in less than a minute and accepted another bowl with great gratitude. While he devoured it, he cast furtive glances at Benito and a thousand thoughts whirled around his head.

What a surprise! How come he's still alive when he was sentenced to death? How did he escape the gallows? Where are his glasses? He's lost some weight, too… Is he the reason I'm here? Could he help me with my endeavor?

The abbot cleared his throat, breaking him from his reflection.

"Now, as we are done with the supper, let us hear your story, son," he said solemnly.

Kamolea had just opened his mouth to speak when Benito cut him off.

"Before our guest starts his narrative, I've got an important announcement to make. Two days ago, I dreamt this same boy would come here, and that I must take care of him."

"How strange! You did not mention it at your last confession," said the abbot, raising his hand to stop the agitated whisper that had broken out around the table.

"I had completely forgotten, but the moment I saw him, I suddenly remembered it to the slightest detail," Benito said. "For instance, the voice that ordered me to look after the lad mentioned that he was once a slave on Don Diego's plantation."

"Is that true, son?" the abbot turned toward Kamolea.

"It is, Father," Kamolea confirmed. "I was enslaved, but my mistress, Dona Lucia, set me free after I saved her life. But, unfortunately, as soon as I entered Panama City, bad people robbed me of all the money she had given me."

"Why did you decide to come to us?" asked the abbot. "Do you want to accept our God? To become a friar and lead an immaculate life?"

"I am already a baptized Christian, Father." Kamolea took out the crucifix from underneath his shirt. Muffled exclamations filled the room. "The first thing I did as a free man was to thank God with a prayer in the temple of Our Lady of Mercy. While I kneeled before the crucified Jesus, *He* spoke to me and commanded me to go to the Santo Domingo convent, where I'd find the answers to my questions."

"Well, this story is becoming more and more intriguing," said the abbot, stroking his long white beard pensively. "It's rare to see a former slave who wears a cross and speaks with God. We will consider the broken pot to be a sign of good luck and a new start. So, tell us your name, lad, and fire away; we will try to answer all the questions that torment you, to the best of our knowledge."

"My name is Kamolea. I was born far away from here, in a place called Half-Moon Island. I seek a way to return there, and if you would be so kind as to allow me to stay in the convent for a few days, I will pray to God to teach me how to do it."

"That could be arranged," said the abbot, still caressing his beard. "We have plenty of free rooms in which to accommodate you, on condition that you respect our statute. We get up before sunrise, do not eat breakfast, and require hard work in our small vegetable garden and livestock holding in exchange for our hospitality. As you are not a friar, you would not be mandatorily required to attend our services, and it would be up to you to decide, although I strongly encourage you to do so. Do you agree to our terms?"

"I do. After everything I've been through, this does not seem too hard," Kamolea said.

"Very good. Go with Brother Bernardino now, if it is God's will," the abbot waved his hand at Benito. "He'll help you with the lodging."

Benito stood up and bowed, then took a lantern and beckoned Kamolea, who thanked the monks for the meal, and followed his friend. Outside, it was a warm tropical night, lit by the mild moonlight and filled with the noisy chirping of crickets. They set off towards the extensive building with many doors, and Benito opened one of them, introducing his friend to a tiny cell with a small window, a single bed along the back wall, and a table with a stool in the corner. Above the bed hung a crucifix with a lit sanctuary lamp beneath it.

As they shut the door, Benito hugged him tightly and held him for a long time.

"So glad to meet you again, my little savage!" he said, his eyes gleaming. "I would have never been able to recognize you, but when you called your monkey Junu as if a veil fell from my eyes, and now I'm happy as a clam at high tide. Look at you! How strong and manly you've become! What about these scars? Tell me everything that has happened to you over the years!"

"There is not much to tell, Creyente. Constant thrashing and hard work were all that happened on Don Diego's shithole of a plantation. But how come you are alive? And where are your glasses? You were supposed to be hanged, remember?"

"Aye, but do you recall Ron O'Reilly and his little wire? He unshackled his wrists on our way to the cell and swooped on the two guards that were walking ahead. He killed them both with Lars van Halle's knife as the others attacked the other two. It was such a commotion! Eventually, we dragged them into the dungeon, took their clothes, and left them to feed the rats. Then, we scooted off under the nose of the entire garrison, in broad daylight at that. It took those stupid soldiers a long while to grasp what was going on, and when they finally realized that we were gone, night had fallen, and we had made a considerable advance. Good luck finding us in the jungle, matey."

"Wow! What a story, man!" cried Kamolea, delighted.

"We stuck together for some time, and then we broke apart," Benito went on. "The scoundrels planned to go to Portobello and then to Tortuga, the stomping ground of all the scum in the world. But me, I refused. I'd had enough of the pirate life, so I decided to withdraw into the mountains and die as a hermit. I found a small cave and settled there, praying day and night to God to forgive me for all the terrible things I had done in my life. And then, in response to my prayers, miracles started happening. First, my eyes became stronger, and I didn't need glasses anymore, although I have trouble reading up close if the letters are too small…"

"But how did you become a friar?" Kamolea cut him off impatiently.

"That was the second miracle. I was about to kill myself from starvation when I dreamt about you. You were a boy, as I remember you from the White Shark, and we were on a raft, surrounded by the blue immensity of the sea. Suddenly, a shining ray touched my soul, and a booming voice echoed, *'Benito, go to the Santo Domingo convent and wait for your shipmate to find you there. Your destiny from now on will be to help him in his quest for freedom. Don't ever dare to give up on him as he is the only reason you're still alive.'* When I woke up, I felt so excited! The Lord had spoken to me and given me an assignment! My life had a new purpose! So, I did what He bade me. I've been waiting for you for a long time, matey."

"Wow!" said Kamolea, impressed. "Does that mean that you're ready to help me again, Creyente?"

"Whatever you want! Just name it!"

"Gracias, amigo! Now I'm sure that the Lord sent me here because of you!"

"But what do you intend to do?" asked Benito.

"I'm planning to build a raft. It's crucial for my, or should I say, our mission. So first, I'll need you to lend me a helping hand with making her, and then you'll come with me on the most incredible journey in search of my pretty island," said Kamolea, nonchalantly.

"Say what?" cried Benito. "I've never heard a crazier story than this one."

"Yep, you heard me right! That's precisely what we're gonna do," Kamolea confirmed. "Only there are too many details that I still haven't figured out, and I doubt I ever will, without your precious aid."

"Details like what?" asked Benito.

"Well, first we need rigging, canvas, and weapons, right? Then we'll go down to the shore and cut a special kind of tree called *laupama*[74] in our language, which means light wood. We use them on Maniha Komo to build rafts. You can't imagine my joy when I discovered that the same tree also grows here. But the problem was that it should be near the shore—otherwise, how would we put the raft on the water? So, I searched for a long time on my way back to Panama city until I finally found the perfect spot where we could do the job."

"Oh, really?" said Benito mockingly.

"But here's the thing," continued Kamolea, not paying any attention to his friend's mocking smile. "I don't have a single real, for they robbed all the money that Dona Lucia gave me. Do you have any money, Creyente?"

"Friars and money!" Benito snorted. "We are worse than beggars, lad. But you have to knock this insanity out of your head, anyway. You simply don't understand what you are babbling on about! Nobody has crossed the ocean on a raft in a million years!"

"Why, according to the legend my grandmother told me, our ancestors came to Maniha Komo on immense rafts from Big Earth, from the same direction as the sunrise. And Akamui often talked about it, too. '*No boat could sustain the storms, but a raft made of laupama can,*' he used to say. He maintained that the currents and offshore winds are favorable for traveling towards the sunset, but the other way around is impossible. That's why our ascendants never had the chance to make it back to their land."

"Nonsense!" cried Benito angrily. "You cannot rely on rumors and legends about something so serious. But let's say we found what we needed and set sail for your bloody island. Then what? Where is your map? Your latitude? What course are we keeping? It's nothing but blue

---

74 Balsa tree.

immensity over there, my stupid savage, and we'll die and dry out under the scorching sun, floating on our foolish bark in search of the impossible!"

"Don't get so worked up, Creyente. I told you, I've got a plan. It's pretty easy, you'll see. We follow Alina, that's all."

"Follow what?"

"Alina. It's a star."

"Why should we follow it?"

"Well, Alina shines just above Maniha Komo. There is another legend about her…"

Benito roared with laughter.

"No, no, Junu, bugger that, matey!" the monk-pirate panted, shaking all over. "No way I am going to drown myself chasing some star with a weird name!" He brushed away a tear that oozed down from his eye. "Lord, my belly hurts; I haven't laughed like this for years… Listen," he went on in a more sober tone, "I *do* want to help you, but we need to think of another plan, because I'm simply not going to do something so stupid. No offense, matey, but you will always remain a hopeless savage with a small brain. Let me think of something else, will you?"

Kamolea grinned.

"You can babble about whatever you want, Creyente, and call me all the names under the sun, but in this case, it is you who are stupid, not me. Our main difference is that you may be a friar, but you don't believe in God. I do. Heed my words, amigo—everything will happen exactly as I told you. We'll build a raft together, and we'll get back to Maniha Komo to find my Illima. I dreamt about it, and the Lord confirmed it. If you don't trust me, at least have fate in Him. You told me *He* had sent you to the convent and ordered you to wait for me and help me, so you should follow my orders, shouldn't you?"

"Well, we'll see about that," snorted Benito. "But even if I do agree to share a berth with you, we don't have any money to put your crazy project in motion."

"Well, I have an idea how we could find money, but it's a really long shot," Kamolea said, eyeing his friend closely. "A few days ago, I remembered our last sea battle, when Bobo El Tuerto died in my arms. So, there he was, lying jammed beneath the ship's wheel, and I was kneeling beside him, trying to free him under a hail of round shots and crashing timbers. And then, believe it or not, I was inside his head, reading his thoughts."

"Impossible!" cried Benito.

"Hang me if I lie! At that time, I had the gift of seeing the thoughts of others. I saw most of your youthful adventures, Creyente, and how this man with the cross on his cloak sold you after you rolled the dice. Anyway, I was trying to free poor Bobo while he spoke to me about the church of Mercede, and then, I observed him burying some treasure here in Panama. He was with another man, and they were both digging a hole, when Bobo swung his spade and killed his shipmate."

"Ah, One-eyed, the old bucko," Benito shook his head disapprovingly.

"Aye, but do you catch my drift, Creyente? I saw the place where they hid the treasure, man!"

"Don't tell me you could find it, Junu!"

"We could try, at least! It was near to the church of Mercede, under an impressively wide tree." Kamolea's eyes shone in the gloom.

Benito gaped at him.

"But this is an incredible story!" he muttered. "Mind you, it's a long shot, as you said. Gosh, you've got me so overwhelmed with your yarns tonight that I feel seasick. Once I sleep on it, I'll feel better, I guess. Bugger that! We've got no time for slumber! Tell me about you now. What happened to your face? And how come they set you free?"

"Oh, it's a long story, man. But fortunately, we have the entire night ahead of us," Kamolea smiled, and began his story.

The dawn found them still talking, and soon, the bells had started clanging. Benito jerked and looked around.

"That was the shortest night of my life," he muttered. "I've gotta go to the service, but come, I'll bring you to your berth. Sling your lumbers there and get ready for the fieldwork."

They left in a hurry and Benito led him to another cell, six doors down on the left. The setup was the same as Benito's room, but it was obvious that nobody had lived there for a long while, as the air was stale and smelled of dust.

"What did they say about breakfast? My stomach is rumbling already," Kamolea said.

"We don't have breakfast, so tell your belly to calm down. I'll be back soon to take you to the garden. And don't forget to call me brother Bernardino before the others: never Benito."

"You bet," Kamolea grinned. "And you try to learn my real name as well, for Junu is my hairy mate now."

Benito simply waved at him hastily and slammed the door behind him.

* * *

A week later, in the late afternoon, the two friends were in Benito's cell. Kamolea had just returned from the garden, where he had dug up boniatos,[75] cucumbers, and eggplants the entire day.

"We need to hurry; the service will begin in a few minutes," Benito said. "Are you attending it this evening?"

"I'll skip this time," Kamolea said, stifling a yawn. "It's awfully boring, man; it drives me crazy."

"Yes, I know," grinned Benito, "but that's the way to discipline yourself. Look at what I found in the convent's archives."

He took one of two yellow parchments from the table and unfolded it on the bed.

---

75 A type of sweet potato.

"Pitch the tailed scoundrel out! He'll wreck the precious script," Benito said.

Captain Junu, resting on Kamolea's shoulder, puckered his nose in a resentful grimace.

"Nah, he'll be a good boy," Kamolea said, but Benito's glare was enough to dissuade him.

"I'm so glad I found it," Benito babbled on, as Kamolea returned from throwing Junu into the yard. "Luckily, I came upon it years ago, so now I knew what exactly I was looking for, but nevertheless, it took me four days rummaging in the archive to unearth it again."

Kamolea smoothed the parchment and scrutinized it. It was a detailed outline of an eight-log raft with a square sail in the middle. On the upper part, a faded sketch represented an Indian of full height, wrapped in a mantle, his head decorated with a crown of feathers.

"What a fleshy nose, man. Check out his flaring nostrils. It makes for a pretty distinct face compared with the Kuna people," Kamolea observed. "And the clothes as well. I've never seen cloaks like this one here."

"I bet you haven't. They call it *poncho* in their native language."

"They?"

"The Incas. Skilled warriors that lived south, high in the mountains, by the great lake Chucuito.[76] There, they had found the huge Imperio Inca that thrived for many years until Pizarro discovered them and put an end to their power."

"How far south?"

"Oh, pretty far. You have to get to El Callao and then make your way upward on a mule for several days."

"So, they built an empire over there?" asked Kamolea, surprised.

"Absolutely! They were advanced in many matters, like medicine, astronomy, and agriculture, not to mention how rich they were... I

---

76 Titicaca.

heard incredible stories about convoys loaded with gold and silver, passing from El Callao to Panama City and from there to Portobello. The ships were so heavy with gold that they plunged a yard below the waterline. Ah, glorious days for the pirates, my hearty… But it's been long since, almost two hundred years. Do you see the year here on the scroll? 1528. And guess where I found it? It comes from the personal archive of Francisco Pizarro!"

Kamolea looked with disinterest at Benito's blazing gaze.

"So what?" he asked.

"Arr, savage to the end! You've never heard about Pizarro, the conqueror of the Inca Empire, have you?" cried out Benito.

"I've never heard of him," Kamolea admitted.

"Never mind. But here's the thing—Pizarro lived in Panama for a couple of years, and it's a real stroke of luck that his archive was saved after Captain Morgan's carnage. Well, perhaps it wasn't exactly him who did the drawings, but all the same, it's his name here, so it belongs to him."

"Speaking of the carnage, I've always wondered how come the Almighty God allowed such destruction of this beautiful city," Kamolea said.

"I've asked myself the same question pretty often," Benito replied, "until the day I realized the hidden moral of God's lesson. I was on my way to the marketplace to buy some tools for the convent, and I walked across the newly built city, admiring its splendid buildings and churches when a celestial ray touched my heart and the answer dawned on me. It's true that the rogues tore the city down with Satan's help, but Panama City revived itself and rose from its ruins even more magnificent than before, like the phoenix arising from the ashes. And then, I understood that goodness and beauty would forever prevail over destruction and horror, and God's shining light will always disperse the darkness of Evil."

"Wow! So beautifully said!" Kamolea exclaimed. "You're full of surprises, Creyente! What eloquence flows from your mouth sometimes, man, until you switch to your usual tone and speak like the worst pirate again."

"Well, I was once an educated noble," Benito smirked. "So, let's concentrate on the picture now. It gives us a pretty good idea of how to build the raft, although I think it will be a tricky job."

They put their heads together over the drawing.

"Look, the logs are attached with ropes, and the mast is erected in the middle. How on earth are we gonna do that?"

Kamolea shrugged.

"These are all details that we should worry about later. For now, all I know is that I've found the perfect place, close to the shore, where these *laupama* trees that you call *balsa* grow. First things first, we're gonna build a hut and live there until we finish the raft."

"Good idea," said Benito enthusiastically, "but we'll need axes, ropes, canvas, and so many other things."

"We will for sure, so I think it's high time we left the convent to go and hunt for Bobo's treasure."

"I don't know, man," sighed Benito. "Let's say, by some miracle, we do get back to your cursed island. Then what? Do you reckon your cannibal friends will meet you with hugs, wine, and honey? Seriously, lad, if you think so, you are the biggest lubberhead. I can assure you that your tribemates will tear you to pieces, roast you over a slow fire, and gnaw you to the bones in the name of their bloody God. So, what's your choice, then? I'm curious to see how you will convince them to accept you back, renounce their God, and stop with their abominations."

"Unfortunately, I don't have a straightforward answer to your questions," Kamolea sighed. "And I know our journey is probably pure suicide. But if we somehow get there, the only thing I wish is to see Illima again and tell her how much I love her. Then we'll get you a lassie and flee to some desert island."

"Well, she'd better be a young and pretty one," Benito grinned.

"Absolutely! We'll live there as one big, happy family, and have many babies. As for preaching and teaching the cannibals about God, bugger that! They are a hopeless case, a lost cause. Even my friend Anuro would not believe me that Jesus Christ is a mighty God, especially when he hears about the other cheek crap, and submission, and so on. Frankly, I still have trouble processing that myself…"

"I hear you, matey," Benito said. "Well, your plan is not so bad, I must say, so let's give it a try. But about the treasure, look… I don't believe in such easy luck, but if nothing comes of it, at least we can get a job and earn some money."

"We don't have time for that," Kamolea shook his head. "I'm confident we'll find it. I dreamt we did."

"You and your weird dreams," Benito snorted. "I have one more surprise for you, though," he said, reaching over and spreading another scroll out on the bed. "Look what else I found in the archive."

"What's this?" asked Kamolea curiously.

"It's some charts of the sky, made by the sailors in the past century," Benito said. "I compared it with the picture of your constellation that you drew for me some days ago, and I think it's a pretty close match."

Kamolea peered at the tiny dots depicting the night sky. He discerned instantly the three stars in a row with a bigger one on the left, as well as the four smaller ones around it.

"Yes, pretty close," he confirmed, tracing them with his finger. "The angle here is much bigger than I remember, but this must be Alina, indeed."

"That's precisely what I expected to hear," Benito's face was beaming, and his voice was trembling with excitement. "Today is our lucky day, matey. When I explored the chart, I realized that Alina and her children are actually part of the Orion constellation. The only difference is that the stars, because of our position, are turned upside down and at a strange angle. That's why I didn't recognize Orion until now."

"How so?" Kamolea asked.

"It's normal, as the stars change all the time, depending on where you are. Even in summer and winter, they're slightly different. Lars Van Halle explained everything about them, and navigation, and showed me how to use the astrolabe and set the compass. Now, do you see these numbers below? *8°S125W.* That's the exact latitude and longitude where the chart was drawn. Do you understand what it means for us?"

"Not really," muttered Kamolea.

"We've made an amazing breakthrough, Kami. If the picture of the stars is close to your childhood memories, then the latitude, written here, indicates a point near to your island!" The triumph in Benito's tone was palpable. Kamolea met his blazing eyes and whispered,

"I can't believe that everything is arranging itself so easily for us."

"Indeed," Benito smiled, "and if we succeed at unearthing the treasure, I will firmly believe that God's grace is bestowed upon us. I think that now's a good time to announce our leave to the abbot."

Kamolea grinned.

"I agree. Now, with this clue about Maniha Komo's location and your navigating skills, we are surely unstoppable."

* * *

At dawn three days later, Benito and Kamolea walked out through the large door of the Santo Domingo convent. The farewell with the friars was heartbreaking, and Benito, who had spent many years with them, was moved to tears. Displeased by his decision to quit the monastery, the abbot spoke in a grave voice when they asked him to bless their enterprise.

"We, the mortal, often misinterpret God's will, but in the end, *He* is the major player in the game of life. Therefore, if you are sure of your choice, go ahead and stake your life on it! Then you'll see—if your deed pleases God, it will succeed. If not, you will smash your head against the wall that *He* will erect to stop your foolishness."

"Thank you for the wise words, Father, and for everything you have taught me during my stay here," Benito bowed. "I have one last favor to ask of you. Since we have no money, could you lend us a pick, a shovel, and an ax? We will search for a woodcutter's job, and I promise you that as soon as we are able to afford to buy our own tools, I will give yours back."

"Take whatever you need, Brother Bernardino, and may God bless your undertaking," said the abbot, making the sign of a cross before him.

When the monks went into the church for the morning service, the two friends set off toward La Iglesia de la Mercede. Deep in conversation, they ignored the passers-by, who stopped and watched them in astonishment. They were a strange couple indeed: Kamolea with a monkey on his shoulder, a long-shanked shovel resting on the other, and a bow and quiver swinging across his back, and Benito, clad in his drab cassock, shouldering a pick and an ax.

"The church is just beside the city gate, and there are watchmen day and night. I can't fathom how we're going to dig without attracting the guards' attention," Benito brooded.

"I have a strange feeling that we're heading in the wrong direction," Kamolea frowned.

But no sooner had he said it than the church loomed before them.

"Your feeling is wrong," smirked Benito.

"No, I mean the *place* is wrong," said Kamolea. "You see, when I entered Bobo's memories, I saw a church which he named 'Our Lady of Mercy.' Then, he repeated it twice while he was giving up the ghost. But I'm pretty sure that it wasn't the same building as this."

"What exactly was different?" Benito asked.

"It wasn't so tall and with fewer columns. There was an enormous tree as well, and houses were burning all around."

Benito stopped short, dropped the ax, and slapped himself on the forehead.

"Blimey, Kami, what lubbers we are!" he cried, and a passing elderly couple turned their heads, scrutinizing them suspiciously. "That was certainly the ancient Iglesia de la Mercede, in the old city that Captain Morgan burnt to the ground. You probably saw the church just before it caught fire! We have to go there, matey!"

"Is it far away?" Kamolea asked.

"It is, but who cares? We'll have to wait for nightfall to dig, anyway."

"Let's go, then," sighed Kamolea. "Meanwhile, I hope we kill some game as my stomach is already rumbling."

* * *

After several hours' tedious wandering about and asking for the exact location of the old Church of Our Lady of Mercy, they finally found the place—a heap of ruins, overgrown with grass and shrub. A flock of crows alighted upon the rubble and greeted them with harsh croaking.

"This is exactly the tree I saw in Bobo's memories," Kamolea said excitedly, pointing to an old, spreading fig tree several yards beyond. "I remember they dug somewhere here, around this spot. It's hard to tell, though."

"We'll wait until dusk to begin," Benito said. He looked around and shuddered. "Pretty ominous site; deserted, bleak and cursed, exactly as the old-timer we asked for directions described it. At least nobody will bother us."

"Aye, he said it was full of spooks and apparitions here," Kamolea grinned. "Do you believe in ghosts, Creyente?"

"I've lived long enough to know better than to deny their existence, although I've never seen one," Benito said gloomily. He sat underneath the tree and sighed, "But the spirits of those I've killed often chase me in my sleep."

"At night, it will be even spookier. Why don't we start digging right now?" Kamolea proposed.

"No, seeking a treasure must be done in the darkness of the night. Come now, we need to eat and sleep a bit. And remember, once we start, don't let a bloody sound escape from your big mouth until we find it. If you say even a word, the treasure will sink deeper, and we'll lose precious time. Savvy?"

"As you wish, captain," smirked Kamolea. "I don't believe such nonsense, though."

"Just do as I say," snapped Benito.

They built a small fire, plucked a fat Barbary duck that Kamolea had pierced with his arrow, roasted it, and after they had gnawed it to the bone, they stretched and snored merrily until dusk.

* * *

The waxing gibbous moon was hidden under thick layers of clouds, and when they started digging under the tree's large crown, it was hard to discern the details, but Benito refused to light a fire, nonetheless. The work progressed at a snail's pace, for the parched, stony earth was full of debris and hard to dig. Sweat-soaked, Kamolea brandished his mattock enthusiastically, enlarging the ditch by about two square yards. Benito shoveled and panted but remained in stubborn silence. A few times, they hit upon something solid, but it turned out to be only rocks or hewn stones from the ruins. As the night advanced, the wind increased, blowing dust and dirt into their faces. Kamolea was getting more and more frustrated with every swing of the pick. He snorted and grunted as Benito made desperate gestures to be silent. They had descended up to their chests already, but there was still no trace of the treasure, and their irritation was gradually turning into despair.

Kamolea had just begun wondering if they should change location when, shortly after midnight, he noticed something gleaming in the darkness in his peripheral vision. He stabbed the pick with a mighty swing, spun in the light's direction, and let out a gasp. Carlos, Bobo's shipmate, was sitting on the edge of the ditch. Clad in a long blue coat, breeches, and black leather boots, he was the same as Kamolea remembered him from the coxswain's memories. His tricorne hat was missing, though, and the bloody gash from Bobo's spade was clearly visible. His legs dangled from the ledge, and he stared at Kamolea with an expression of disgust, as though he was observing a miserable worm.

"Wrong spot, lubber!" said Carlos's apparition in a hoarse voice that had clearly not been used for a long time.

"What?" exclaimed Kamolea.

"Damn it, Kami!" shouted Benito angrily from the other side of the pit. "I knew that you'd be never able to shut your trap! Now it's sunk at least twenty…"

"Pipe down, Creyente!" Kamolea yelled back. Something in his tone silenced Benito immediately.

"Much better," said the ghost. "I was waiting for ages for somebody to come and dig out the bloody treasure. I'm curious, though; can you see me, or you only hear my voice?"

"I ain't only able to see you, but I know your name, Carlito," Kamolea said.

"Blood and thunder! Don't call me like that! You remind me of my mother. How come you know me?" Carlos croaked.

"I don't know, man. It's a gift. What about you?"

"Me? Well, I ain't got much to say, have I? My bloody spirit has been stuck at this shitty bilge since we buried the useless stuff…"

"What stuff?" asked Kamolea, raising his voice.

"Bloody hell, who you are talking to?" roared Benito as he approached, gazing into the darkness.

"Will you shut up?!" retorted Kamolea and the ghost in chorus. Benito sensed a chill creeping through his body. He said nothing and just watched, his mouth half open, as his friend gestured in the air to an invisible interlocutor.

"Where were we?" grunted Carlos. "Aye, the damned goblets and the cross. They've been consecrated to God, and somebody needs to get them back to Him and free me from this curse. Will you do this for me, lad? I'll show you where to find the plunder, and in return, you can keep the money and the gems. The only thing I ask of you is to take the two chalices, the casket, and the golden cross to the church."

"You mean you have dwelled here since you were killed?" Kamolea asked, stupefied.

"How do you know I was killed?" the ghost grunted. "By the way, how is my fucking shipmate Bobo doing? I assume you know him since you're swelling sails at this latitude?"

"He's dead," Kamolea replied.

"That's good!" the ghost chortled. "And when was that?"

"About eight years ago."

"Arr, that's a pity," said Carlos. "I hoped to meet the jackass in the afterlife and have a good long conversation with him, but it seems that he was taken to the blazing chasm before me. Listen, lad, you see me like this, buccaneer and all, but I gotta tell you I'm not such a wicked man. My hands weren't stained with blood when I died, and if I find a way to get the stolen things returned to the church, I will escape the inferno. But it's more complicated than it sounds, savvy? Up to now, nobody has been able to see or hear me, so if somebody found the treasure, how the hell would he know to give back the stupid goblets? But then, out of the blue, here you are, a fine lad, chatting with me like an old shipmate. So, I said to myself: *Hold onto him tight, Carlos, he's your only hope.* And it's true, matey—you are, for me, the beacon's light in the stormy sea and the ray that pierces the darkness that shrouds me."

"But where is the booty then?" Kamolea cried impatiently.

"Do you give me your word as a man, to give back to God which belongs to Him?" asked Carlos.

"I do," Kamolea nodded.

"Follow me, then!" the ghost beckoned him, detaching itself from the ground. Kamolea hauled himself up over the pit's edge and pursued him under Benito's staggered gaze. Carlos moved forward and stopped about ten yards to the left, nearer to the tree's trunk.

"It's just here, about the same depth you've reached over there," said Carlos. "Don't forget your promise, as I'll be watching you closely, both of you. You don't wanna experience the ghost's wrath, do you?" And with that, he dissolved into thin air.

Kamolea peered at the dark spot where the phantom had disappeared, then slowly scratched his head.

"Did you see him, Creyente?" he turned to Benito.

"After hushing me up twice, what the fuck I was supposed to see, besides you talking to yourself?" Benito sounded pretty annoyed.

"It was the ghost of the pal who One-eyed killed. He told me that the treasure is buried just here, below."

"Are you sure?" asked Benito dubiously. "I neither saw nor heard anything."

"Well, there's only one way to find out. Bring the pick and the shovel, and let's start over. I won't budge from this place until I dig a hole bigger than my height."

With redoubled strength and a new hope shining in their eyes, they did not stop the entire night. At the first gleams of the dawn, they were shoulder deep when Kamolea's pick clanged against a metal surface. Benito fervently shoveled the dirt and they both kneeled, frantically clearing the rest of the soil away with their bare hands until something glittered before them. Kamolea took out his knife and meticulously outlined the edges of the rectangular box. It was surprisingly big, and when they finally unearthed it, the sun had already risen above the horizon.

After they had cleaned up the last residue of soil, they both gasped in admiration.

"A repoussé," said Benito, gazing at it delightedly. The casket, made of wrought silver, was about two handspans wide and one in height. Two vine twigs twined their leaves over the middle of the cover, enclosed by a laurel wreath and creeping at the edges. The walls of the box were decorated with embossed cherubim and angels, surrounded by lush floral motifs.

"This box alone must be worth a fortune," Benito muttered. "Let's see what lies inside." He scrutinized the tiny lock just below the cover and murmured under his breath,

"Now I understand why the One-eyed always carried that silver key around his neck."

"Aye. He doesn't need it now, though, and neither do we," Kamolea grinned and put his knife in the hole. Part of the mechanism broke with a crunching noise. Kamolea inserted the blade into the slit between the box's wall and the cover, causing it to fly open.

"Oh my God!" whispered Benito and crossed himself.

Kamolea looked too, dumbstruck.

A heap of gold, mixed with colorful precious stones, which gleamed with all the colors of the rainbow, reflecting the bright rays of the rising sun. Kamolea took off his wet shirt, laid it on the ground, and buried his hands inside the casket. He scooped up a handful of gold coins and poured them on his shirt, then carefully separated them from the gems—mostly diamonds and rubies, as well as some amethyst, sapphires, and emeralds. At the same time, Benito set down a couple of golden rings, necklaces, and bracelets.

"Dear God, look at this beauty!" he cried as he lifted a gold chalice, whose sides were richly inlaid with red, blue, and green gems. "And here's another one!"

The shovel on the pit wall fell and made a rattling sound. Kamolea frowned.

"Don't get too excited, Creyente," he said darkly. "There is also a cross like this."

"Here it is!" cried Benito, lifting a big golden cross, inlaid at the four extremities with four different gems in the same fashion. "How did you know?"

"We must return them to the church," Kamolea sighed. "I thought about bringing them to the convent, but when the shovel fell, I saw us laying them before the altar of La Iglesia de la Mercede, so, they obviously belong there. But we can keep the gold and the money; at least, that's what the ghost said."

"Look what I found at the bottom," grinned Benito and he threw him three heavy purses. One of them was crammed with golden doubloons, and the others were loaded with pieces of eight.

"Wow, this is ten times more than Dona Lucia's money!" Kamolea exclaimed.

"With so much gold and all these gems, we can be the kings of the West Indies!" cried Benito. "Goodbye, friar hood, scanty portions, and misery! Please, you're your acquaintance with these new super-rich caballeros!"

"Pity that on my island, money is worth nothing," Kamolea said. "But I'll take these beautiful colorful stones and make a neckless for Illima. She'd certainly like such a gift. What do you think?"

"Bugger Illima, matey!" cried Benito, shaking, his eyes burning with an insane flame. "Each one of these little stones is worth a fortune. You can have ten Illimas with only one of them."

"You're talking exactly like the Evil One," Kamolea reproached him.

"Devil or not, I won't go to your bloody cannibal island to be eaten alive when I could live like a king to my last breath!"

"Are you telling me you'll turn again against God, as you have done so many times already?" Kamolea yelled. "Don't forget that I'm the only reason you are still alive!" Benito stopped short, processing the information, and his features gradually changed from excitement to sobriety as the color of his face grew paler.

"But… don't you want to be a rich man with many slaves and plantation, and everything else?" he stammered.

"I already refused an offer to be a king and live in a golden palace, and you're trying to impress me with a few coins," said Kamolea matter-of-factly. "Listen, Creyente, I think we both need a good, long sleep. Let's find an inn in the city where we can eat, wash, and rest. Tomorrow, we'll take the church belongings to their rightful place and return the tools to the convent. Afterward, we'll go straight to the city market. What do you say?"

"Sounds good," sighed Benito, watching the gleaming heap sadly. "Let's put the money back in the casket. I really feel like crying."

ALFREDO AND ALFONSO

In honor of Saint Sebastian's day, a fair had been arranged in the central marketplace of Panama City. Situated at the South protective wall close to the Saint Joseph porthole, the market buzzed like a beehive as traders and buyers praised and criticized merchandise, bargained, laughed, and quarreled.

Alfonso and Alfredo strolled lazily around the crammed middle section, observing the people as they hustled and bustled in all directions. They had just passed the green sector, where many sellers had spread their tropical fruits and vegetables on food carts, stands, or straight on the ground.

"Watch out, señor, you're trampling on my goods!" cried an elderly woman as Alfredo staggered and stepped over a bunch of plantains.

Alfredo gave her an apologetic wave and tugged at his brother's sleeve.

"Do you see the two fools over there?" he jerked his head to the left. "The one with the monkey on his shoulder, and the friar. I bet they are flush with cash."

Alfonso followed Alfredo's gaze. A stout, curly-haired man of medium height, clad in baggy trousers and a dirty linen shirt, was bargaining lively with the horse vendor. His companion, a middle-aged, delicate fellow wrapped in a drab monk's cassock, was shaking his head vigorously in disagreement.

"Why do you think so?" Alfonso grunted.

"First, the scar-faced one just brandished a full purse under the Jew's hooked nose, and second, behind the old vulture are fine, tethered horses, not bananas, right? Are you dumb or what? It's staring you in the face, but you're slower than a snail," Alfredo smirked.

Alfonso offered no comment.

"Let's go nearer and take a look," continued Alfredo. "The clown with the cassock rings a bell somehow. I think I saw him around once or twice before, buying fresh vegetables for the convent."

They advanced cautiously toward the livestock section, at the very end of the market, where the clamor of pigs, ducks, hens, goats, cows, donkeys, and ducks mixed in a terrible racket.

"Gosh, I wish I were deaf," muttered Alfonso, casting a sidelong glance at his brother.

The two men looked so different that it was hard to believe they were twins. Alfonso was a phlegmatic man, tall and skinny, with a distracted look and dumb smile that usually aroused pity and condescendence alike. Alfredo was just the opposite: sharp-witted, short, and chubby, with eyes that darted in all directions and a cunning smile permanently plastered on his fat, round face, he was the instigator of every evil deed.

They stopped behind the curly youth and the monk, who continued bargaining passionately with the dealer.

"If we buy these two horses, are you going to give us the mule at half price?" Benito was asking.

"I can't, señor. Four doubloons[77] for the three animals, and that's my last word," said the lanky, wizened old man with his vulture's face, spitting saliva through his trimmed beard.

---

77 A golden coin equal to 128 reals or 16 pieces of eight.

"What? Are you out of your mind, old man? This is daylight robbery!" Benito fumed.

"The packhorses are young and sturdy, and the mule is even stronger," moaned the seller, patting the mule's chestnut back. "Check out this thick-set body and them large hoofs! It's worth over two horses together."

The hinny cast Kamolea a melting glance, blinked its big black eyes, and snorted in agreement.

"A hopeless Jew," said Benito desperately. "Let's go to the other seller over there."

"What's the problem, Creyente?" Kamolea asked. "We have plenty of money. Give him whatever he wants and let's move on; there's so much left to buy."

"It's not about money!" hissed Benito angrily, casting a murderous glance at the old trader.

"So, what is it?" Kamolea was losing patience.

"He's taking us for fools, that's what. Nobody will make a fool of me. Let's go over there."

"No, we don't have time, and I want this hinny; it's a far better than a horse for hauling logs," Kamolea turned to the seller, "I'll give you four doubloons. Deal?"

"Absolutely!" cried the seller.

Kamolea took out his purse.

"Cup your hands," he said to Benito, and he poured a couple of golden and silver coins in them.

The orbs of the old Jew widened to twice their size. Meanwhile, Alfonso and Alfredo gaped at the gold, glowing with delight.

"Which ones?" Kamolea asked. Mumbling oaths under his nose, Benito wiggled four shining pieces between his fingers and handed them to the vendor.

"Much obliged!" the latter cried. "You can take the stock, caballeros; they're all yours."

While Kamolea and Benito untied the horses, Alfonso whispered to his brother,

"I've never seen so many *escudos*[78] in one place."

"So, let's do something about it," Alfredo grinned. "These guys definitely don't need so many of them. It'll be a piece of cake to deprive the two fools of their heavy load. Long live social justice!"

They lazily followed the two friends who had set out for the hardware section in the opposite direction, leading their steeds and mule through the crowded place. On their way, they bought two enormous baskets, which they attached to the mule as saddlebags, then stopped at a rope merchant and, after a long conversation, purchased all he had for sale.

"Oh, my, what will they do with all this rigging?" muttered Alfonso and added, agitated, "And look, they're buying canvas now!"

"If they continue to spend their dough like that, there will soon be no point in following them," Alfredo growled. "See how many axes and hatches they took?"

"And saws and hammers," added Alfonso.

Meanwhile, Kamolea and Benito had acquired an additional four machetes, two wedges, and six knives. Then, they had stopped before a large stand next to the hardware section, where two bearded subjects with weather-beaten faces and bandanas wrapped around their heads had scores of exposed weapons.

"Look at this, matey," said Benito, beaming like a kid in a candy store. "It's a wonderful week, isn't it? Fate has served us everything we need on a silver platter. I've just been wondering where we're gonna find arms, and here they are, waiting for us!"

"And so many at that!" said Kamolea enthusiastically. "I feel like I'm back in the White Shark's magazine."

On the counter, all kinds of steel weapons were arranged—daggers,

---

78 A golden coin equal to 16 reals.

boarding axes, cutlasses, rapiers, swords, halberds, a few arbalests, and several firearms.

"Let's say we get back to your island. How many people do you reckon you can convince to support us?" Benito asked.

"I doubt there will be any, aside from Anuro, eventually… if he's still alive," Kamolea said hesitantly. "But it's better to have some guns, anyway."

"Let's see, then. What have we here?" said Benito cheerfully, smiling at the sellers who, judging by their fierce gazes and flashing eyes, weren't men to be trifled with.

"Hola, señores, come estan?"[79] Benito greeted them. "We want to buy all your firearms and the total amount of ammunition that you can offer us. I see here six pistols, four muskets, and three blunderbusses. Do you have any more?"

"*All* of them? Did I understand you correctly, señor?" the merchant, a burly, husky man wearing a red bandana, said, pricking his ears up.

"Absolutely," confirmed Benito.

"Hey, Chico, these weirdos wish to buy all the firearms!"

"Shut up, Paco," the other man approached, his lips stretched out in a hungry smile, reminding the men of an alligator baring its teeth. "Ignore him, señor, as he is a little slow. Would you caballeros like to have a closer look?"

"If you don't mind, señor," Benito smiled back. "Let's start with these six flintlock pistols. I want to check the strikers first."

"Sure, of course." Chico's voice was greasier than butter. He took one of the pistols and, after a brief hesitation, said, "No offense, señores, but let me see your money first."

"No problem," said Benito, turning to his friend. "Show them the purse, Kamolea. Hey Kami, do you hear me, lad?"

Lost for words, Kamolea was staring at an enormous ax that

---

79 Hello, gentlemen, how are you doing?

leaned upright against some boxes behind the man they now knew to be Paco. The shaft was made of wood and about a yard and a half long, with carved helix motifs and some strange signs, somewhere between letters and images, running along its entire length. The shiny, curved blade, about two handspans across, was crescent-shaped and razor-sharp, made of forged steel that glinted like silver in the scorching sun. It captivated Kamolea's mind so powerfully that he could not tear his eyes away. His concentration was so sublime that his eyes became a hundred times sharper, and he had the impression that part of him had detached from his body and was nearing the ax. Now, he could discern that the entire blade was covered by the same bizarre symbols as the shaft, engraved on the metal and arranged in patterns of two, three, or four. As he observed them, they started moving as if they were alive, and a soft whisper glided into his ears. He didn't understand the meaning of the words, but he sensed how they crept inside him, turning into warm feelings of deep love, peace, and harmony, mixed with the absolute conviction that, dead or alive, he had to possess this ax. The next instant, he was back in his body, and the magic had gone, leaving only a lingering longing for a beautiful secret that he had to discover. With great effort, he shifted his gaze back to the spiral lines of the long chestnut haft, barely suppressing his desire to rush forward and grab the splendid weapon.

"Wake up, matey!" Benito pushed him hard on the shoulder.

"What?" Kamolea squinted as if he had just awakened from a daydream.

"They don't think we have enough money. Just show them the pouch," Benito said, watching him curiously.

"Here," Kamolea shook the heavy purse before the vendors' faces and allowed them a glance inside. "What we are buying, Creyente?"

"All firearms and possible ammunition they have, including this powder keg," said Benito.

"Right, and you can add these three daggers, the two harpoons, the two crossbows here, and all the boarding axes, as well as the biggest one, just behind you."

"The great ax is not for sale," Paco shook his head in refusal.

"For sure it is," Kamolea cried, "just name your price!"

"You don't understand," said Paco mildly, as his eyes flicked greedily at Kamolea's purse. "This is a family weapon that has been passed down from generation to generation for five hundred years. It belonged to my great-great-grandfather, one of the greatest blacksmiths of all time, who made it from special forged steel using secret Elvish magic. Now, see here," Paco took the ax and pointed at the strange signs, "these are Elvish runes. The saying goes that he engraved an incantation in their language, which makes the one who possesses this weapon invincible. Since then, it has saved the lives of many of my ancestors, and I'm afraid that no money on earth could buy its magical power."

"Your ax will save thousands of lives, my man!" Kamolea called out excitedly and stopped short, wondering why on earth such words had come out of his mouth. Then he squinted, unable to believe his eyes, as a man had materialized next to the ax. He was in his forties, dressed in a thigh-length blue tunic and baggy green trousers that reached down to his calves. Kamolea had never seen such an outdated outfit. The man gestured towards the ax, smiled at him, then stretched his hand forward. A current of pure energy flowed toward Kamolea, and he immediately understood the message.

"I think your great-great-grandfather is here," Kamolea stammered, pointing at the air behind Paco.

"What did you say? Where? What does he look like?" shouted Paco, alert and anxious.

"He is… Wait, he's telling me something about the ax…" Kamolea jumped over the stand. "Clutch the ax with one hand and give me your other one, quick!"

Under the stunned stares of Benito and Chico, Kamolea grasped Paco's free hand and clutched the air with his other.

"What's happening? Are you alright?!" exclaimed Paco as Kamolea slumped down on his knees. His eyes rolled upward, so only the sclera remained visible, and he foamed at the mouth as he thundered in a deep voice,

"Back at the time of my youth, I was a good friend with the elves, and they revealed to me their secrets. I forged the blade of this ax in the fiery flames of my burning love for the splendid elf woman, Glarindale. Every rune etched on this ax is one unforgettable moment of pure happiness with my beloved. The love spell cast over it is the mightiest of all magic and makes it an invincible weapon that must serve only magnanimous goals."

The booming voice that came from Kamolea's mouth grabbed the attention of the people around and soon, a small crowd surrounded the weapon's stall. Chico drew his saber and stepped before the stand, his eyes casting angry thunderbolts.

"You spoke truly about the ax, Paco, but you missed some important details," continued Kamolea, still kneeling, his face distorted in a painful grimace. "This weapon was destined to serve the brave and pure in heart; real men and ardent lovers who are ready to die for their beloveds. Are you such a man, Paco? You, who seduced that poor girl with your empty promises and then left her with your baby in her womb? You are a cowardly dunce and a great shame for our kin, unworthy of possessing the Ax of Love. However, as a trifle of my blood flows through your veins, I will make you rich and famous on condition that you marry your girlfriend, who has cried her eyes out over you. Be a perfect husband and father to your son, who misses you equally. Do you promise to do this?"

Paco was shaking with fear from head to toe.

"I do," he squealed.

"Good! Go back to our ancestors' land, to the old farm with the windmill that you, fool, intended to sell for a song. Hundreds of years ago, I buried a casket with Elvish treasure there—a lot of gold, emeralds, and diamonds from the Hallowed Mountains, The money will assure you an opulent life for generations to come. At the bottom of the chest, you'll find a parchment with the translation of the elvish spells. I'm convinced that even a mooncalf like you will understand its most precious wealth if you have enough wit to figure out how to use it."

As Kamolea conveyed the ghost's message, scenes from Paco's great-great-grandfather's life ran past his eyes. First, the man was strolling in a glade, hand in hand with a gorgeous woman with small, pointed ears and waist-long, pale-yellow hair in braids. The clearing was surrounded by ancient trees and studded with colorful flowers, emanating an incredible aroma. With every step they took, a cloud of butterflies rose from the soft grass and fluttered their mottled wings, sprinkling fine, brilliant particles around them. It was enchantingly beautiful. Then, the scene changed, and Kamolea saw the same man forging a hot piece of metal in a room full of iron tools. Finally, he was pacing towards a barn with a red rooster weathercock atop the roof, beside a massive windmill with impressive rotors. Under his arm, he was carrying a golden casket and clutching a shovel in his free hand. He entered the somber room, and the smell of cow shit and fresh hay hit Kamolea's nostrils. The man laid the casket in the corner opposite the door and started digging.

"I offer you as a gift my priceless treasure in exchange for the Ax of Love, which you will give to the lad whose hand you are holding right now," croaked Kamolea, his face still distorted. "He is the kind of man that the elves' magic was intended to assist. He will convey to you the exact place of the buried treasure. Farewell, Paco. I hope you will change from now on and become my worthy heir. Be brave and fair, as behooves my great-grandson!"

Kamolea collapsed on the ground, unconscious, his eyes rolled into the back of his head. Paco, dumbstruck, stared at the air before him. As Chico shooed the idlers away, Benito bent over Kamolea and Paco knelt to sprinkle some water over his face as he slowly came to his senses.

"What happened?" His voice was hoarse, but at least it was his own. "The heat, I suppose…"

"You don't remember, do you?" Benito asked him.

"Remember what?"

"You saw a ghost, amigo!" Paco cried out. "My great-great-grandfather. He spoke through your mouth…"

"Really?" Kamolea rubbed his front a little, then rose and said to Benito, "Let's get out of here."

"No, no, no, wait a minute!" Paco yelled. "Tell me where the treasure is hidden. My grandfather said I am supposed to swap this ax for the exact location of the gold."

"What ax? What gold?" Kamolea stared at him, his mouth half-open and his forehead furrowed under the effort of remembering. And then, in a twinkle, everything fell into place, and in his mind's eye, he saw the barn with the windmill on the left.

"Of course," he uttered. "I know what you are talking about."

He glanced at Chico, who had joined them, then bent over Paco's shoulder and whispered something in his ear. Paco nodded several times and muttered,

"Yes, the mill was still there when I left years ago, but the barn was gone. I wouldn't have any trouble locating it, though."

He took the heavy ax, glided his hand over the shaft as if to say goodbye, then handed it to Kamolea.

"Take it, buddy," he said in a sad voice. "If this is the wish of my ancestor, may his will be done. I'm curious, though; what do you intend to do with it?"

"I plan to fell a gigantic tree," said Kamolea. "It's a magical tree, a temple of evil that has enchanted and enslaved my people since time immemorial. The day I cut it down, I'll free them from its spell." He smiled at Paco's bewildered face. "It's hard to understand, isn't it?"

"So, it's for a magnanimous goal, then?" Paco asked.

"It's for what?" Kamolea was not familiar with this word.

"Yes, it's for a great, noble cause," chipped in Benito impatiently. "It's all about the glory of God and the triumph against evil. But we have to go now; the sun is getting low…"

"Be blessed, and may God help you in this endeavor," Paco said.

"So, señores, what else did you mention you wanted to buy?" Chico asked.

A while later, after they had loaded the mule with almost all the exposed arms, a keg of powder, and about 800 bullets, they were finally ready to set off.

"Gracias, señor. God bless you for your kindness!" Kamolea felt the ax's curved blade with his finger, gazing at it with admiration, and slung it over his shoulder. Then, he grabbed the mule's reins and followed Benito, who led the horses toward the exit of the marketplace.

* * *

The road leading to the shore ran through the small upland, covered with grass and low bushes, until it hit a small forest. The setting sun brought gloomy dusk over the Alvarez brothers, who shared a single horse whose uneven canter made them jiggle comically up and down on its back.

"I really don't get it, bro," Alfonso grunted discontentedly.

"Get what?" Alfredo growled.

"Why is everybody laughing their heads off when they look up at us?"

"I don't understand what's so funny either," Alfredo shrugged. "But better that than beating and shooting us, to be sure."

"Those clowns are heading toward the forest. Do you think we'll be able to track them there?" Alfonso waved toward Benito and Kamolea, who were riding far ahead.

"Of course we will," said Alfredo confidently. "They're gonna leave a trail as wide as the road to hell."

"It's hard riding in the jungle," Alfonso complained.

"It is," Alfredo agreed. "We'd better tether our mare before we get into the woods. Once we slit the fools' throats, we'll get their horses anyway."

"Yeah, and then we'll go back to the market and sell everything back. You're a genius, bro!" said Alfonso admiringly.

"You bet I am," Alfredo grunted complacently. "Listen to me and your life will be beautiful. Although, you see, I'm a little worried now…"

"What about?"

"I overheard one fellow in the market, who was buying two geldings, speaking with the nearby seller about Don Alvaro's health. He said that Don Alvaro is getting better with every single day!"

"Impossible!" exclaimed Alfonso. "We shot him at least three times, and when we left, he and the other two jerks were lying in a pool of blood."

"Did you shoot him in the head?" asked Alfredo.

"I didn't need to. He was as dead as a doornail."

"Well, obviously, that doornail has resuscitated miraculously, and if we don't disappear swiftly, we're gonna meet a sticky end."

"Disappear? Why should we?" Alfonso asked, surprised.

"Dumb as a rock!" snorted Alfredo. "Well, little brother, I'm pretty sure that your ugly face is firmly engraved in Don Alvaro's memory after you tortured him for so long to tell you where the money was. Wake up, muttonhead. He's getting better and soon, he'll be after us, with his ginger devil at the head."

Alfonso's face elongated in a grimace of dread.

"I didn't think about that," he muttered.

"Not your strong suit, thinking!" Alfredo grunted. "But here's the plan: once we take the golden purse from the monkey man, we beat it to Portobello. We'll find a ship bound for Tortuga, and good luck finding us there."

"Tortuga! You're the man, bro!" exclaimed Alfonso, his eyes gleaming with joy. "I had the best time in my life ever over there! Those cool taverns, full of fun! Do you remember the tall brunette harlot? She was something, man…"

"Shut up, Alfi! There's nothing but whores in your stupid head. Try to figure out what these guys are gonna do in the forest with all this stuff?"

"I don't know, bro. The jungle is not a place to dwell, and beyond the woods is the shore, yonder."

"I know, and that's the problem. Maybe they've moored a boat over there? Imagine if they load her and disappear tonight? We have to shorten the distance a bit." Alfredo rubbed his stubbed chin and spurred the horse.

* * *

As soon as Benito and Kamolea reached the first trees of the jungle, they dismounted their horses and led them through the narrow path that Kamolea had discovered on his way to Panama City. The mule, loaded with the heavy baskets, brought up the rear. They advanced slowly, squeezing their way through the dense creepers while deeply absorbed in conversation.

"I'm really pissed at you, matey," Benito was saying.

"What for?"

"With your gift of discovering treasures, we could be swimming in money."

"But you told me once that you were born with a silver spoon in your mouth, and you didn't care for money," Kamolea objected.

"It's true to a certain degree because wealth enslaves you, and when I was young, I longed for freedom. But when I discovered my independence, I craved to be rich again and to enjoy it fully. And now, when I'm finally able to have both freedom and wealth, I have to give up again and set off toward my imminent death. So, tell me, what's the point of having such a wonderful talent?

"I'll tell you what, Creyente. You are free to do whatever you like, just don't forget that this is your last chance to redeem your sins. If you leave me now, the ghosts of your victims will hunt you, not only in this, but in the other world as well."

"I know," Benito sighed. "After we returned the stolen wares to the church and you said that Carlos's ghost soared to the sky toward the shiny light, I couldn't stop thinking about it. If he was accepted into heaven, I believe there might still be hope for me too."

"My point exactly!" Kamolea said while vigorously cutting back a thick bush that was blocking their path. "Although he told me he had killed no one, and you have so many unpardonable sins… But listen, now we need to focus on the present moment. I was wondering why we didn't buy two or three slaves to help us?"

"It's a good idea," Benito agreed absentmindedly, still thinking about Kamolea's remark concerning his wrongdoing, "but slaves are a pain in the ass. It's too much care to take of—they are always hungry and grumpy and won't force themselves to work hard unless they're afraid of your whip. Not to mention that once we take them to the camp, we have no way to prevent them from escaping."

"Oh, they won't run away for sure. We'll promise to free them right after we've finished and give them a lot of money to boot…" Kamolea stopped talking abruptly as his sharp ear caught the snapping of a dry twig in the distance. The mule cocked its head and snorted nervously.

"Did you hear that?" Kamolea looked tensely around.

"Nothing," Benito said.

"We'd better keep going," Kamolea muttered, and pulled at his horse's bridle.

They walked in silence. Something ominous lingered in the air that reminded Kamolea of the creepy jungle from his childhood. He had the nasty feeling that they were observed, and his instincts turned him into a wild animal, sniffing the air like a dog and listening to every sound of the forest. Captain Junu sensed his nervosity and decided to jump into the trees and follow them from a distance. Luckily, the path, illuminated by the waxing moon, was easy to follow.

After about an hour, they emerged from the woods and the Pacific spread out before them, bathed in shimmering moonlight and rhythmically splashing its waves against the shore. At the site of the magical seascape, Benito let out a cry of delight.

"You nailed it, Kami! This place is perfect, just like you told me!"

The coast curved inward, forming a small, cozy cove. The sand band was large, with a lot of balsa trees growing at the far right of the sickle-shaped beach.

"We're gonna make camp over there, just out of the reach of high tide. Then, we'll drag the felled trees and work them up. Tomorrow, we'll build a hut to sleep in and a shed to shelter us from the sun," Benito babbled excitedly.

"Right!" Kamolea said. "And between the Balsas flows a freshwater brook; do you see its mouth over there, where it runs into the sea?"

"I do," Benito nodded.

"It seems like a lot of work, though," Kamolea sighed. "I wish we had at least three sturdy Negros to lend us a helping hand."

"Aye, we have to be ready before the rainy season," Benito agreed. "You could go tomorrow to the slave market while I'm setting up camp here."

"Nah, it's better to be with you," Kamolea said. "I could easily land myself on the wrong side of a bloody cage."

Kamolea paused and jerked his head, listening, but the everlasting crash of the waves and the swish of the breeze muffled every other sound.

"What's wrong?" Benito asked.

"I think somebody is watching us," Kamolea said.

"Nonsense," Benito exclaimed.

"Check out the horses, man! It's as clear as day."

"I noticed they were nervous, but it's normal so near the jungle. They can probably smell a jaguar…"

"Nah, it's more than that," Kamolea's voice was strained. "My instinct tells me something's wrong. I've heard several unusual sounds, and Captain Junu was excessively agitated tonight."

"So, what are we gonna do?" Benito asked.

"You stay here, with your pistol loaded and your eyes peeled," Kamolea said. "I'll go back and take a peek."

"Are you sure? I can help you…"

"No, Creyente. No offense, but you're clumsier than a mantled howler when it comes to creeping through the jungle. They'll hear you from a mile away, man."

"Well, I still think it's nonsense," said Benito stubbornly. "If somebody had traced us, they would have attacked us in the forest, not in the bright moonlight on the beach. Nobody can surprise us here."

"Perhaps they'll wait until we fall asleep or try to shoot us from a distance," Kamolea said. "Anyway, never mind. Stand by and use the horses as a shield if somebody fires on you. I'll see how the land lies."

Kamolea grabbed a rope and his machete and rushed towards the woods. He went right towards the Balsa trees and made a long left turn, squeezing like a snake through the tangled mess of overhanging branches, bushes, and creepers until he reached the path they had used to get to the shore. He progressed noiselessly, applying everything he had learned about the art of slinking through the jungle.

"My father was great at that. It's not by chance that one of his nicknames was 'The Creeping Dead,'" he shuddered at the memory of Akamui. He continued slipping between the trees, and then he stopped dead as he heard muffled voices ahead. His nerves tightened like a bowstring and he advanced stealthily, following every twist of the supple twigs.

As he got closer, he was able to make out two different voices, so he had a good idea about the location of the men. He halted and listened tensely, then crept forward again until he got so close that he could distinguish the words.

"Something's wrong over there," grunted one voice. "It's been an eternity since the Monkey man went into the woods. What the hell he was doing?"

"Taking a shit, maybe?" suggested a soft, sleepy voice.

"It must be pretty bad diarrhea if it's taking so long," said the first.

"I don't know, bro, but if nothing happens soon, I'll definitely pass out," responded the drowsy one.

Kamolea pulled aside a creeper and saw the two men: one lean and one chubby, lying prone at the very edge of the forest, watching the shore. He clutched the rope in his left hand and drew the pistol he had bought that day, then stepped out of the thicket and said,

"Not a single move, jerks. Put your hands behind your back, or you're dead."

He moved forward and pressed his knee against Alfonso's back, then swiftly bound his hands, doing the same with Alfredo straight after.

"Get up now and walk ahead without turning around," he ordered.

As they stepped through the opening, Benito immediately rushed toward them with a pistol and a cutlass in his hands.

"Look who I've brought for supper," grinned Kamolea.

"Down on your knees," Benito ordered after they had walked them to the horses. "So, let's see what we have here. Two ugly muttonheads, trying to harm us. Tsk-tsk-tsk," he shook his head in disapproving mockery, "Bad guys, eh? Real hoodlums, I must say."

"I think I saw them at the marketplace," Kamolea said. "It's hard to forget such beauties. So, what do you want, scoundrels? Why did you follow us?" He grabbed the blunderbuss lying next to him, shoved it under Alfonso's nose, and bellowed,

"Speak up or die!"

"We, we, the money, señor," Alfonso stammered. "We don't hate you; we are just after your purse."

"How do you know about it?"

"At the market, señor… We saw you there…"

"Let's drag them to the sea and finish them off," proposed Benito. "The morning tide will take them away."

"Benito! I thought you had become a good Christian, yet you speak like the ugliest rover!" Kamolea cried.

"Well, what should we do with them, then? We can't just let them go. What if they return and try again?" grunted Benito.

"Well, they won't because they aren't going anywhere," Kamolea said. Benito glanced at him, surprised. An inscrutable smile was tiptoeing across his friend's lips. "As you said today, fate has served us well. Now, we don't even need to buy slaves." He turned to the brothers and took out his purse. "So, you want this, right?"

"So be it," he said after they offered no reply. "Inside this small pouch is the sweat and blood of many beaten and murdered people because of these useless chunks of metal. And now you, like so many others, are ready to kill for them. So, enough blood, I say—this bloodshed has to stop once and for all. Let's make a deal. We will give you two similar purses, full of gold and silver, and make you rich men. However, you have to earn it. You will work your asses off, for you need to understand what it means to earn your daily bread. I'll hire you today, and once your work is done, you can have the money. Deal?"

"Wow! Such eloquence, matey! I remember you couldn't speak a word when I met you!" Benito exclaimed.

"We haven't worked even a day of our life," Alfonso complained. "Why should we now?"

"Shut up, fool!" Alfredo scolded him and turned to Kamolea, his eyes gleaming greedily. "We'll do whatever you ask us, señor. Just say the word, then lean back and watch us. Your wishes are our commands, señor; just tell us what we are required to do."

"You'll help us build a raft," Kamolea said, his eyes shining in the moonlight. "It will be a big one, so we need you to cut down many trees, then lop them off, peel the bark off, saw the logs up, and put them together. I want to see you drenched with sweat and your hands calloused, but always eager for more work. Got it?"

"Absolutely, señor. But how can we be sure that you'll reward us at the end instead of killing us? Why, in the first place, would you be inclined to give us so much money rather than keep it for yourself?" Alfredo asked, slyly watching him through his piggy, slit eyes.

"Because I don't need it. On my island, money is worth nothing," was Kamolea's response. "Besides, you have no choice," he shrugged. "You'll need to have a bit of faith."

CHAPTER XXV

THE WAY BACK

"Ha ha! Look at him, Benito, for God's sake!" Kamolea rolled over on the hot sand, clutching his stomach and screaming his head off with laughter. Alfredo, who was stripping the bark of the balsa tree they had felled a day ago, cast him a murderous glare and muttered something that no parent would want to hear from their child's mouth. He had just taken his shirt off, and his pale, naked torso, which was covered in a solid layer of grease, sharply contrasted with his brown neck and forearms.

"What tits, man, what an incredible body… A real ball of lard, our paunchy Alfi!" Kamolea gasped for breath, tears running down his face.

"Hey, don't make fun of my brother!" Alfonso shouted in mock anger, before tossing his shoulder-length greasy hair over his shoulder and joining Kamolea's laughter. His skinny but sinewy body outlined his muscles as he pulled the mule's reins. Eha strained with all her might to haul down the heavy balsa trunk, sinking her hoofs deeply into the sand.

It had been about two weeks since they had started working together. Alfonso, kind-hearted and slightly retarded, took his chores seriously and was engrossed in the raft project from the first day. Helpful and funny, with a fine sense of humor, he had the good-natured character of a seven-year-old, and the more Kamolea got to know him, the more he liked him.

Alfredo, though, was another story. Lazy, grumpy, and mean, he openly despised their work and barely concealed his hatred towards his employers. He would even turn on his brother now and then, particularly as Alfonso often took sides against him. On those occasions, Kamolea had the most fun, laughing until his stomach hurt. Watching them bickering and arguing was an incredible show, but Benito was not thrilled by any of it at all.

Now, noticing Kamolea still lying on the sand and shaking with laughter, a wave of anger overwhelmed the old buccaneer. He put his finger in his mouth, whistled sharply, and blurted out,

"Stop fooling about, lad! We don't have time for joshing and slobbering. Come here and hold this log for me!"

Kamolea got up and approached with a casual stroll, admiring the mighty swell of the Pacific. The breeze had increased, and heavy clouds covered the sky. Benito was on his knees, making deep grooves on the end of the log.

"Relax, Creyente," Kamolea drawled, still grinning. "You're so dry, man. What are these cuts for?"

"For the ropes," Benito explained. "Look here—the strings are tightly notched in the furrows; otherwise, they'll slide along the wood and get chafed by the friction."

Kamolea was impressed. "Wow! How did you realize that? You're so brilliant; you think of everything!"

"You just said I'm boring and dry," said Benito wryly, "but if you don't stop dawdling and joking around with the fools over there, we're doomed. I regret we didn't buy any slaves now and instead, we've got these two lazy muttonheads. And you're no better than them in terms of discipline! Get it into your head that we're running out of time! The bloody raft must get afloat before the rainy season!"

"Gosh, what a rant," grinned Kamolea. "Whatever you say, I'm glad we have Alfonso around. He's so much fun, that lanky man!"

Benito spread his hands out in a desperate gesture.

"I'm dealing with idiots," he mumbled, then slapped himself on the forehead. "I almost forgot. Last night, an idea dawned on me."

"What is it?" asked Kamolea.

"Once built, the raft will become too heavy. How do you think we'll haul it to the water? Even with the horses, it will almost be impossible."

"Lazy man thinks too much," called out Alfonso, approaching them. "I see you are too deep in conversation to notice that it's already lunchtime. What's the matter?"

"We'll build a U-shaped palisade near the sea and use the water as a natural lift to help us manipulate the heavy logs," said Benito. "We'll have our timbers in the water for several hours in the morning and evening, and the rest of the time, they'll be on firm ground."

"Genius!" cried Kamolea

"As if we don't have enough work already!" protested Alfonso. "It's gonna be hard to build a fence so close to the ocean, man. Why do we need such a stupid thing at all?"

"It will prevent the logs from being dragged away by the ebb," explained Benito.

"Perfect!" spat Alfonso. "So, after we've built a shack for Your Majesties to sleep inside and you've left us on the beach, we have to do *that*. It will take so many more trees and we need to hew them, chop them up, whittle spikes, dig holes… Gosh, I'm tired just thinking about it!"

"Stop whining, lanky one! You're getting on my nerves, man! Shut up and work, and your reward will be great at the end," Kamolea cried. "Benito's idea is good. When we finish, we're just gonna bring the palisades down, and the low tide will carry the raft away. Or do you want to haul her to the water yourself? Admit it: Benito is a smart man!"

"That he is! A smart guy is a smart guy, buddy; even in a privy, he will find something to eat," said Alfonso matter-of-factly, and he and Kamolea burst into frenzied laughter.

***

It took about two months of cutting, chopping, fastening, hauling, measuring, chiseling, carving, resining, rigging, hammering, whittling, accompanied by a lot of cursing, squabbling, and sweating, to get the job done. Benito's idea to use the tide for working in the water was crucial for implementing their task, as it was easier to bind the massive logs together while they were floating in their natural position. Once the timbers were fastened together, the raft was immense; about 10 yards long and 5 yards wide. Next, they nailed down a deck of thin bamboo poles and raised a mast with a large square sail and a considerably smaller topsail. As the work progressed, Benito proposed erecting a small shed covered with palm leaves at the rear to keep them sheltered from the scorching sun. Then came the details. They prepared oars and poles for rowing and fathoming; a large chest for the weapons and the powder keg, both sealed with resin and fastened to the logs and the mast's base; and three barrels for fresh water and one with salt meat, secured between the shed and the mast.

The last few days were dedicated to storing as much food and water as possible. Kamolea went hunting and Benito rode to the marketplace, returning with a swine and half a calf, which they salted and put inside the cask.

"This'll be enough for a year, or even more if I respect fasting," grunted Benito, contented.

Meanwhile, Alfredo and Alfonso were sent to gather fruit. After they had loaded a dozen baskets with fresh bananas, mango, papaya, and plenty of coconuts, everything was finally set, and they were ready to sail off for Maniha Komo.

On the eve of their departure, the entire team gathered onshore, including the horses, the mule, and Captain Junu, the latter an immutable member of the expedition despite his principal task of disturbing and impeding others' work. The sun touched the horizon, dying the sky in crimson glares and slowly sinking into the boundless ocean. Kamolea's heart welled up with longing and sorrow at the magnificent view. He hugged Eha, stroked her gently, and kissed her forehead. She snorted and nudged him with her head, her eyes big and moist, almost human.

"I'm gonna miss you, my faithful friend," Kamolea whispered in her ear, then patted the horses and turned to his companions, who remained silent, their eyes wandering into the distance as the evening breeze ruffled their hair.

"The day has come, my hearties." He turned dramatically to Benito and the siblings. "Tomorrow, our paths will separate, but I must say that building this raft has been an incredible amount of fun. I'll keep these memories of our teamwork in my heart, your enthusiasm and dedication, and especially the arguing skills of the skinny one. These moments will keep me fresh and amused during the long way back to my island. Thank you for helping us out and not trying to kill us even once during all the hard labor."

"That was definitely the hardest part," chortled Alfredo. "So, what about our money?"

"Tomorrow, you're gonna be rewarded for your hard labor," Kamolea replied.

"Why not right now?" Alfredo's voice rang out bellicosely.

"Because we still need your help tomorrow," Benito explained. "In the morning, after the tide flows and hoists the raft, you will break the fence and push us into the water. Thus, we'll take advantage of the ebb, which will take us out to the open sea. The moment you fell the spikes, you'll have your two fat purses full of gold and silver as promised. But there's more—on Kamolea's request, you will receive an extra bonus: a third purse full of golden bracelets, rings, necklaces, and earrings. They are stripped of their precious stones, but the gold still is worth a lot."

"Wow! Generous, indeed!" cried Alfonso.

"But this will be tomorrow," Kamolea said, smiling. "Tonight is party time. Let's celebrate the creation of this beauty!" he motioned to the huge raft stuck in the sand behind the sticks, her tall mast outlined against the setting sun. "I've been racking my brain about what to name her, and it finally dawned on me yesterday. We're going to call her '*Iluminacion*'[80] in honor of my mistress Dona Lucia, who taught me how to read and write, and in praise of an old saint who opened my eyes to the truth and led me down the path to wisdom. To me, 'enlightenment' is one of the most beautiful words. It brings the light of knowledge to a man's mind and is the opposite of ignorance, stupidity, destruction, and darkness."

The siblings did not react, but Benito was elated.

"Excellent speech, matey!" he cried, raising his fist in the air.

"Let's hope that this name will please God, and He'll help us in our endeavor," Kamolea responded, making the sign of a cross. "Let's celebrate now! And listen, no hard feelings, right?"

"I'll miss you too, Scarface, and the wacky Creyente as well," Alfonso pouted and made an exaggerated sad face, then brusquely brushed an imaginary tear from the corner of his eye and burst out laughing.

"I suppose we will," grinned Alfredo, cackling, his belly jiggling up and down despite the recent toil-induced weight loss.

"Muttonheads," muttered Benito and shouted, "Come on, let's build a fire!"

The twilight's shroud wrapped the beach in a gentle hug. The men collected all the lumber left from the construction and raised a pile as tall as a man.

---

80 Enlightenment.

"My God, they'll see us from Panama City!" cried Alfonso excitedly, then turned to Benito and said with a coy smile, "Hey, Benito, don't you want to share one of those bottles you were hiding in the shed with your beloved friends?" Benito, who had returned two days ago from a trip to Panama City's market, had brought back about a dozen bottles of rum among other provisions.

"How do you know about them, scoundrel?" asked Benito, genuinely surprised.

"No secrets in the family," grinned Alfonso.

"It'd be a shame if you didn't treat us to a bottle of strong rum after all the work on this bloody raft," whined Alfredo.

"Of course he will," chimed in Kamolea. Benito was not pleased.

"They're meant to be for the journey and, eventually, to bribe the men of your tribe," he said wryly, but then relented. "Only one then, and not a drop more." He grunted and walked over to the raft, where he had stored the crate with the liquor.

"I find him rather stingy, your matey," Alfonso nodded in Benito's direction, then he winked at Kamolea.

"Don't worry, it's just a facade," Kamolea smirked.

Several hours later, Kamolea and Alfonso were whirling around with linked elbows, jumping around in a jolly dance. Two empty bottles lay on the sand near the fire. Meanwhile, Benito and Alfredo sat on the beach, each with one arm over the other's shoulder, waving a bottle of rum in the other hand. In unison, they drunkenly sang an old pirate tune:

The fair winds blow,
the seas run high,
The sails are billowing out.

The sloop is rolling,
Tossed by the waves,

Closing in on bilander[81] now.

The old privateers,
And bold buccaneers,
Are sharping their sturdy cutlasses.

For a feast they prepare,
For fat booty's share,
And to have fun with beautiful lasses!

Captain Junu, frightened by the commotion, had long disappeared into the woods. After a lot of dancing and singing, followed by some slurred chat about how much they loved and respected each other, the night ended in a group hug and some rather loud snoring.

Benito woke up first in a sweat, the sun burning his face.

"Wake up, you rascals!" he yelled and jumped to his feet. "We're gonna miss the morning ebb." He kicked Alfredo vigorously on the posterior.

The low tide had already begun, and although the raft still floated in the water, it was a matter of minutes before they would be stranded.

"What's the rush? We'll wait until tomorrow," yawned Alfonso.

"No way! Bring the fence down. Quick! Fell the bloody fence down!" bellowed Kamolea.

"Give me the money!" shouted back Alfredo.

Kamolea took out a fat purse and tossed it to Alfredo. He snatched it, looked inside, and grinned.

"Perfect! You can square up the rest with my stupid brother! Good-bye, jerks!" And with that, he ran towards the forest. Alfonso gaped in disbelief at his twin as he watched him running away. "Where are you going, you crook? It's not fair!" he yelled after him.

---

81 A two-masted merchant ship.

Alfredo raised his middle finger and yelled back something, but they could only make out the words, "… against your brother…"

Alfonso shook his head. "That's him, my beloved sibling. A hopeless case."

He turned sharply to Kamolea and Benito, both of whom were already by the fence, hammering the poles.

"Wait, I'll help you. Shame on him, the swindler." He rushed towards the erected logs, grabbing an ax on his way. They fell the fence mere minutes before the water withdrew. *Iluminacion* glided lightly onto the shimmering surface, mounted the foamy crest of the first wave, and gracefully slid afloat.

"Go up and use the poles; I'm gonna push her further out!" Alfonso cried as he waded into the water, manhandling the raft. Kamolea and Benito leaned hard on the rod, and she moved away from the shore, catching the current and heading toward the open sea.

Submerged up to his chest already, Alfonso lost his footing and started swimming astern, still pushing the raft.

"I gotta go back!" he cried, panting, spouting water from his mouth. "Gimme the money, Monkey boy!"

"The monkey!" Kamolea roared. "Where is the monkey? Have you seen Captain Junu?"

He grabbed his seabag, fervently pulled out his spyglass, snapped it open, and brought it to his eyes, sweeping the shore.

"What the hell is going on over there?" he exclaimed.

Benito turned around and followed his gaze. There, Alfredo was running madly towards the sea, shouting and waving his hands, as though he wanted to stop them. From the forest behind him, five riders sprang out at full gallop, in hot pursuit and gaining on him quickly. One chaser swung a lasso over his head, flung it, and caught Alfredo just as he was about to wade into the water.

"Alfonso, climb up! Something's wrong!" Benito shouted and stretched the pole out. Alfonso, who had fallen behind by several yards, strained to swim faster. The waves lashed his face, and a jellyfish stung his neck as he tried twice to reach the pole. Finally, he grabbed the slippery rod, grasped Kamolea's hand, and clumsily crawled up.

"What's up?" he asked, gasping for air in fits and starts.

Kamolea handed him the spyglass without uttering a word.

Alfonso looked towards the shore and exclaimed, "What the fuck? Isn't that 'Fredo?"

Iluminacion had already moved quite a distance away from the shore, and the figures were getting smaller. The riders had dismounted their horses and were pushing Alfredo, who was tripping and staggering in the middle of a semi-circle they had made. At that moment, the wind blew the hat off a stout, broad-shouldered man, and his carrot red hair spilled over his shoulders.

"The Ginger Devil," groaned Alfonso. "My brother is doomed!"

"Let me see!" Benito impatiently snatched the spyglass from his hands and peered through the tube.

"Oh, my Lord Jesus Christ! Look, Kami, you won't believe your eyes!"

He gave him the spyglass.

"Wait, isn't that... Am I dreaming?" Kamolea's face betrayed his complete bewilderment as he peered through the telescope.

"Aye, that's him alright. The good old Ron O'Reilly in all his glory! I was convinced he'd caught the wind for Tortuga!" Benito said.

One man pointed at the raft, and three white clouds of smoke materialized from the shore. A second later, a bullet whizzed above Benito's head and hit the mast.

O'Reilly grabbed Alfredo, pointed at him, ran his index finger across his throat, and lifted his middle finger.

"What will he do with my 'Fredo?" whined Alfonso as he retook possession of the spyglass. "Look, they've bound him like a lamb and are carrying him toward the jungle. We have to go back and save him, Monkey boy! He's my brother, for God's sake! Let's do something about it!"

"Do you know these people, Alfonso?" asked Benito sharply.

"Don Alvaro's men. The ginger one, we call him the Red Devil. He's the most terrible of all of them cutthroats. We knew they were looking for us, because we shot Don Alvaro and robbed him, so working with you on the beach was a perfect hideout. If it weren't for that, you would have met dawn with slit throats the very first day you hired us."

"But now it will be *his* head on the spike," said Kamolea sadly.

Alfonso slumped to the deck and started sobbing, his body shaking uncontrollably.

"The Red Devil, indeed," said Benito. "Such a piece of work, our old shipmate."

"A real piece of shit," Kamolea agreed. "You know, now I remember that when they caught me in the whorehouse, they wanted to sell me to Don Alvaro, and they spoke about the red-haired overseer. So, he found his place there. I don't envy the slaves who have business with him."

"Neither do I," said Benito. "We also heard about the assault on Don Alvaro in the convent. So, it was these two blunderheads who attacked him, except they failed to kill him."

Kamolea kneeled and put his hand over Alfonso's slumping shoulders.

"I'm sorry about your brother, Alfi," he said quietly, "but we can't do anything for him. The currents, the breeze, and the ebb are all in the opposite direction. It's impossible to return ashore. Besides, it's too late for him; they've already taken him away. But there is still hope for you. Do you want to come with us? There are plenty of beautiful lassies on my island, and they would be glad to be your wives. You can have as many as you wish."

Alfonso looked up at Kamolea, his eyes still oozing.

"Don't treat me like a child," he sobbed. "I'm not the brightest, it's true, but we both know that we'll never make it to your place. Nobody has ever crossed the ocean on a raft, buddy. The crazy journey of the two crackpots, as 'Fredo and I called it behind your backs."

"Let it be the crazy journey of three crackpots, then," Kamolea smiled. "I like it very much, though; it's a perfect name for such a suicide expedition. Only you're missing one important point, matey—what is impossible for man is possible for God. I learned this the hard way, but I understood one thing: no matter how hopeless the situation seems to be or how desperate you feel, there is always a glimmer of hope. Man is not alone in this world, Alfi. Every single second, God is with us, helping us find our path. I realize how crazy our voyage looks, but you don't know all the details. Believe me, finding my island in the immensity of the ocean is no more difficult than standing up to my tribe and getting away alive or being cast away in a boat for weeks and rescued by a ship. All we need is to have faith in the force that rules our destiny. So, are you coming with us? Make up your mind quickly, because in a few minutes it'll be too late to swim back."

Alfonso did not move. He stayed still for a long while, staring into the void, then shrugged.

"What choice do I have, anyway? Returning to Panama is not an option anymore; they will kill me on the spot. My brother, the brains behind every heist, has always taken care of me. He's gone now, and I have nobody left in this shitty world. But if you treat me fairly and give me a mouthful of rum now and then to ease my sorrow, and if you keep your promise about the lassies, I could spend some more time in your company, I reckon."

"That's my man!" cried Kamolea and thumped him on the back.

A sharp screech of agreement made their heads turn in unison, just in time to see Captain Junu leap from inside the shed and alight on Kamolea's shoulder.

"The white-faced rascal is back!" exclaimed Alfonso.

"Captain Junu, you old scoundrel. How happy I am to see you back!" Kamolea cried and kissed him on the top of the head.

Benito rolled his eyes.

"More trouble on board," he muttered. "Now, as the lanky man has decided to stay, and the monkey has popped out from nowhere, we are no longer a skeleton crew."

"Aye, the crackpots have increased to four," said Kamolea, and they all roared with laughter.

"All right, enough spinning yarns for now!" Benito shouted. "All hands on deck! Hoist the sail! Feel the wind!"

"Aye, aye, Captain," cried out Kamolea, and the three men jumped to their feet.

Soon the sail filled out, catching the northeast trade wind, and *Iluminacion* cleaved the waves towards the never-ending horizon, marking the beginning of their insane journey.

* * *

Two moons later, Kamolea was on the first night-time lookout. Leaning against the mast and watching the full moon as it bathed the ocean in shimmering magic, his gaze wandered over the black sky strewn with stars. Millions of blinking dots descended low above the smooth sea surface, wrapping the small raft in a warm embrace as sky and water blended into one magnificent, eternal view.

The old saint told me once that we were only a speck of dust before this immensity, and now I understand what he meant. Today we are here, and tomorrow we disappear, but the stars will always shine in the heavens, sublime and everlasting, he contemplated, staring in awe at the twinkling lights. The constellations formed a gigantic map that sailors had used since time immemorial, and Kamolea focused his attention on *Orion's belt*.

"If I correctly remember the position of Alina and her surrounding stars, we're getting pretty close," he muttered.

The journey had been going well up to that point, and they had been lucky not to have encountered a significant storm. They had endured a few gales, though, and every time the sea ran high, they appreciated *Iluminacion* more and more. The raft was terrific—light and swift, she glided smoothly on the rippled sea surface and rode with ease over the waves' crests. No matter how big the swell was, she always stood on top like a cork, thus gradually dissipating their concerns that she would sink at the first surge.

Captain Junu landed in Kamolea's lap, interrupting his memories. Lately, his jolly screeches and sudden leaps over their backs and shoulders had fallen unusually quiet. Now, he huddled up, pressing his furry body against Kamolea's stomach, and wrapped his tiny fingers around his master's index, watching him pleadingly with his big brown eyes. As he met Captain Junu's sad gaze, Kamolea's heart sank with foreboding, and a whirlwind of emotion surged up inside him. He had never felt so fulfilled, happy, and free as on this journey, and yet he knew it would not last. Soon, he would have to face his death, either by the hands of the Tipihaos or by meeting the implacability of the elements.

"Are you going to be by my side then, little buddy?" he whispered and gently stroked the monkey's head. Captain Junu simply huddled more tightly, offering no reply. Kamolea's thoughts drifted back to the journey.

When they left Panama, the fair wind and the currents carried them southwest, and the Galápagos Islands were the last land they saw. The food had never been a problem. Besides the salted meat, fruits, and vegetables, the abundance of fish swimming around the raft secured the sailors a fresh supply of delicious meals every day. The water, though, was another story. When the reserve they had brought from Panama depleted, they drank coconut milk and used the shells to gather raindrops mixed with small amounts of seawater.

The gigantic swordfish and sharks, which occasionally swam along *Iluminacion*, made the seamen jumpy, especially when they glided calmly underneath the logs. Some of them were so huge that their heads emerged on the raft's edge while the tails were still on the opposite side. But the most thrilling encounter was with a blue whale. One morning at sunrise, it approached them, a floating rock with a dark blue back, glistening in the sun and jetting out water at intervals from the top of its head. In the silence of the calm morning, they listened to the deep, hoarse snorting sounds that the whale let out as it breathed.

"Gosh, what a fish!" exclaimed Alfonso, goggling his eyes.

"It's awe-inspiring, isn't it?" Benito said. "I've seen many of them from the ship, but never from such a close distance. Don't tease it in any manner, as one blow of its tail would be enough to shatter our little raft into splinters."

They couldn't tear their eyes away from the magnificent creature. It stayed for a moment and then dove graciously, waving its immense tail in a friendly goodbye and causing a minor storm of waves around *Iluminacion*.

Kamolea jerked his head, shaking off his drowsiness. He and his friends had important things to consider. During the long journey, he had told them his story from beginning to end, describing the setting, the customs, and the routine on the island, and strategizing with them how to land unnoticed.

"To avoid the lookouts the most secure approach would be from the north, as the cliffs impede the view from the island, and there are small caves that could hide us until nightfall," he had pointed out. "Otherwise, from south is a lot easier, but it's always under high surveillance, and they would spot us right off the bat. And from west, there's a strong current, and the steep slopes make almost impossible to reach the shore from there."

Kamolea sighed. These were details that they should not be worried about right now. The main question was whether they could find his native place at all. And if they somehow could, how would his tribe react to seeing them there? Would they be sacrificed before the Sacred Tree? What about Illima? Would she love him like before, despite his scars and hideous face?

Illima… His bright guiding star, the reason for everything he was doing. He touched the bulging pouch that was sewed on the reverse side of his trousers, just below the waist. It was Illima's gift, filled with the precious stones of Bobo's treasure. He had stripped every piece of jewelry of its gems after having the vague idea of making a necklace with them, but it turned out that it was far more complicated than he had imagined. He asked Benito for advice, but even he could not find a way to attach the different colored stones to a string.

"I'll offer her them as individual pieces then, and she can decide how to use them," Kamolea had concluded.

Suddenly, Captain Junu cocked his head, alert, and jumped up from Kamolea's lap onto the mast. Kamolea felt his bracelets tighten around his left wrist. He looked at it, surprised, and as so many times before, he had the impression that the shark teeth were gleaming with their own light. He frowned and tried to remember again how it had ended up on his wrist.

It's so frustrating that I can't recall who gave it to me. Obviously, I was very little when it came to me.

Deep in thought and still staring at the bracelet, he grew sleepy. His right hand, which had been steadying the steering oar to maintain their west-southwest course, became limp, and he fell into a deep slumber. In his dream, he found himself in the same lush meadow with tall grass and white-yellow flowers, walking next to the same man who had wished him a happy twentieth birthday. Kamolea looked at his handsome face and met his calm brown eyes. He felt a current of positive energy passing through him and thought,

This time I absolutely must find out who this incredible man is.

"We finally meet, my son," the latter said, smiling. "I'm so proud of you, my boy. You have become the exact model of the son I dreamed of—bold, humble, and wise."

"But who are you?" Kamolea asked.

"I am Keoni, your father."

"Akamui is my father," Kamolea objected.

"No, the cruel man just raised you. Akamui killed me the same day you were conceived, but I am your real father, and you have nothing in common with him. You resemble me in bravery and strength of mind, but you have much from your mother as well." They stood in silence for a moment, surrounded by swinging green stalks and listening to the swish of the wind, then Kamolea asked quietly, "If you are my father, can you help me find Maniha Komo?"

"Finding your native land is the easy part, son," Keoni replied. "The question is, what do you intend to do afterward? Don't tell me, because I know your plan: to run away with Illima to some remote island and have many children, far from the atrocities of this awful world. You resemble your mother so much in that regard. She offered me the same thing at the time, you know? It's a pretty selfish way of thinking, I must say. What about the others? Are you ready to leave all those thousands of people to die? You know the destiny that awaits them, and yet you don't have a single thought about saving them from death and disaster."

Kamolea was having trouble concentrating. Keoni's image became blurred, and the beautiful meadow distorted.

"Your ego is too strong, son," he heard Keoni saying. "It's all about you, your friends, and the girl you love. But you have to forgive your tribe that they forced you into exile and save them because this is the right thing to do. If you don't teach your people wisdom and peace and how to discern good from evil, the horror they sow all over the archipelago will go on forever. Don't worry about a thing, for as long as your mother and I keep watch over you, nothing is lost. Follow your destiny and don't give up on your people!"

His father's last words still echoed inside his mind as Kamolea slowly came to his senses. Alfonso was shaking him rudely by the shoulder.

"Wake up, ugly!" he said. "I see you've taken standing guard very seriously. You deserve no less than ten cats over your lazy back and I'd give 'em to you, too, sure as my name's Alfonso!"

* * *

The next day, Kamolea was so deep in thoughts that Benito, who was already used to his friend's strangeness, could not refrain from asking him what the matter was.

"There's been a change of plans, Creyente," Kamolea said. "I've tried to find a solution, but I can't seem to come up with one."

"Would you be so kind as to share the fresh development with your raftmates?" said Benito wryly. "As far as I'm concerned, we are also a part of any plan."

"Oh, I was about to tell you," said Kamolea blithely. "I've decided that we have to accomplish the mission the way God intended it."

"Which means…?"

"Which means that we can't run away with Illima, my friends, and their wives. On the contrary, we'll all be staying in Maniha Komo to preach the word of God, religion, and everything else."

"So, we're back to where we started then," Benito said. "Remember, when we considered your initial plan, we agreed it was pure suicide to try to convince your people that there is another God."

"I know," Kamolea sighed, "but we have no choice."

"Oh, of course we do," objected Benito. "We stick to our plan to run away with Illima and a few others, and that's that."

"Hey, check out the sail!" Alfonso cried from the shed.

The canvas had sagged like a rag, and, judging by the log Benito had thrown behind them, the raft was now bobbing in one place. Kamolea looked up. The sky was deep blue, with small fluffy clouds lazily dragging across the horizon. It was about noon, and there wasn't even a whiff of wind. The heat was terrible, and an ominous silence reigned in the air.

"The calm before the storm," Kamolea mumbled, and the world swirled around him.

Suddenly, the sky darkened, and the fluffy white lambs turned into heavy black beasts of clouds that hung menacingly low above the sea.

"Douse the sail, quick!" shouted Benito, and Alfonso rushed to climb the mast, when a sudden gust of wind swung the yard, which hit him hard. He staggered, lost his balance, and fell.

Kamolea and Benito, looked in his direction, and their eyes widened to twice their natural size.

"Almighty God," Benito whispered and crossed himself, watching the slowly approaching dark mountain with its snowy crest. It was at least 30 feet in height and growing bigger by the second.

"Mind the wave!" he bellowed and grabbed the nearby cable. Kamolea managed to cling to the mast pole just in time. *Iluminacion* soared up and plunged, bow first, splashing below the boiling trough. The next billow tossed it like a nutshell and shot it towards the sky, where the mighty gale took her up and turned her before she flew down again. Luckily, the raft rode the foaming crests, keeping herself above the surface. Pouring rain unleashed from all angles, pelting their faces as the wind sped up, shredding the sail. Now, it was blowing from all around, swiftly moving from gale to hurricane. *Iluminacion* plunged between the waves again when a gigantic mass of water collapsed straight on deck, sweeping away the bamboo shed with everything inside. A blinding light flashed through the sky, immediately followed by the blare of a terrific thunder. The mast crashed down, bursting into flames, and the upper part, about two-thirds of the pole, plummeted into the water, breaking the burning ropes. Through the roar of the wind, Kamolea detected a faint, frightened, childlike screech.

"Captain Junu! Captain Junu," he cried out. Clutching a rope, he rose and took two staggering steps before stumbling as *Iluminacion* dove anew into the abyss of foaming hell.

"Captain Junu!" bellowed Kamolea, his heart torn with grief. Another cry of sheer terror responded, and Alfonso, who had been clinging to the steering oar, was swept off his feet by the mass of water that smashed against the deck. At the last second, he grasped Kamolea's leg and clung tightly to it.

"Come here and grab the mast!" Benito yelled.

"Hold on tight, Alfi!" Kamolea pulled up the rope, dragging Alfonso with him. They reached the stump of the mast and grabbed it just before the next mountain of water crashed on deck.

"Let's pray for our dear lives!" shouted Benito, his voice hardly audible in the wind's roar.

They all gripped the base of the broken mast and pressed their foreheads to the pole in deep reverence, chorusing the words that every man, believer or not, has repeated at least once in his life when caught in mortal danger.

"Please, Lord, spare our lives and give us a second chance. Our Father, who art in heaven, hallowed be thy name..."

There was another thunderbolt, and in a split second, Kamolea received enlightenment. In a flash, he knew what God wanted from him.

"Let thy will be done, Almighty!" he cried. "If you spare our lives today, I'll lay down my life for my people. I'll show my folks the path of wisdom, as you did to me, and I'll convey your commandments to them."

The heavy rain drummed against their exhausted bodies, but the three friends did not move, their heads stuck to the mast and their eyes firmly shut. They remained silent for a long time, white knuckles clutching the remaining part of the pole until their hands ached, trembling in the chilly wind and stoically enduring the furious hailstorm as it bruised their bodies. *Iluminacion*, tossed by the immense billows like a nutshell, dove and heaved headlong at breakneck speed. But as Kamolea shouted his promise, the storm gradually started to abate. Bit by bit, the wind dwindled, and the raft slowed in its leaps. The black clouds reluctantly yielded southeast, and a single ray pierced the gloomy sky.

Finally, Kamolea dared to raise his eyes. The heavens were a magnificent grey white with a golden glare, lit up by the dissipated celestial beam. The ray went straight to his heart, and the euphoria he felt was indescribable. At that moment, he knew they were all safe.

"God has spared us once again!" he called out triumphantly, and Benito and Alfonso cocked their heads. But as they looked around, all their enthusiasm evaporated.

Iluminacion was a deplorable sight—a broken mast, missing sail, and bare deck that had been completely stripped, save the massive weapon's chest. It was a sight to inspire sadness and desperation.

"My, oh my!" Alfonso whispered. "The Almighty spared us from the storm only to kill us with starvation. Look, there isn't even a single barrel left! Without water, it won't be long before we meet *Him* up there."

"And the steering oar is broken," Benito chimed in. "With no sail, paddles, or steering oar, the raft is unmanageable. We haven't seen land for two months. We're doomed!"

"Aye, and they already know it," Alfonso said, motioning to the set of triangular fins cleaving the water towards the raft.

They lapsed into silence for a long time. The sun was already sinking, and the Evening Star blinked in the west. Crestfallen and desperate, the friends stared blankly at the swarm of sharks circling around *Iluminacion* like hungry vultures, multiplying with every single minute.

Then, just before the twilight ceded to darkness, something incredible happened. The water eastward started boiling and foaming, and all the sharks pulled out west as if under a silent command. From a distance came cheerful whistles, chirps, and clicking sounds, and the three survivors could soon see the arching silver backs of leaping dolphins. They were a large pod, at least thirty of them, with a powerful male at the lead. They approached the raft with incredible speed, and *Iluminacion* started bobbing up and down even more strongly, buoyed by the additional waves they had created. The dolphins swiftly surrounded the raft and, whistling to each other, started pushing it west-northwest.

"What's happening?! They chased the sharks away!" exclaimed Alfonso. "You see that, mateys? I would give two of my fingers to understand what they're talking about."

"I can't believe my eyes," Kamolea mumbled, stunned. "Tell me, Benito, how is this possible? Look, they're speaking to each other and deviating the course across the current. They communicate as we do. Do you think they know where we are going?"

"I believe they do," said Benito. "Has it really taken you this long to understand that God rules the whole Universe, and every living creature obeys *His* voice? *He* tells them, and they obey."

"Nonsense," snorted Alfonso.

"I'm not so sure either," Kamolea shook his head in disbelief. "I mean, we have nothing in common with these fish!"

"Well, first of all, they aren't fish, but mammals like us," Benito retorted. "Back in the convent, when I read the records, I found an incredible story about dolphins saving a shipwrecked sailor. He traveled for two days on a dolphin's back until he reached the shore. See what I mean? To be sure, they are far more intelligent than the other sea creatures. But don't ask me if they might know where we are going as even we don't have the slightest idea!"

"Well, I had hoped you might explain it somehow, as smart as you are…" Kamolea said.

"Nonsense! How can I explain the inexplicable, lad? Be humble and always keep in mind that we are too small to understand most things. That's why the word 'miracle' exists."

"I think we are very close, though," Kamolea said. "Yesterday, I watched the stars, and the configuration was almost the same as I remember it."

Benito shrugged.

"Well, the night is falling, and it looks like a cloudy one," he said.

"As the raft is uncontrollable, the only thing that I suggest is we take some rest and hope that our talkative saviors will bring us somewhere ashore, no matter if it's your island or not."

They lapsed into silence, each man sinking into his own dark thoughts. *Iluminacion* lulled rhythmically, pushed by the dolphins. There was no more whistling or giggling—they were also half-asleep. The wind was getting stronger again, and the smell of salt and hail was sharply pronounced. The three friends attached themselves with the remaining ropes from the mast, stretched out on the bare deck, and were soon snoring quietly as their sea saviors pushed them southwest where, somewhere ahead of them, the breakers violently lashed the rocky shore of Maniha Komo.

CHAPTER XXVI

THE PROPHECY

Under the top of the Carapace Hill, huddled in the bosom of the age-old rock and wrapped in dense mist, the Steamy Cave looked more ominous than ever. Deep below, in the heart of the crag, Illima lay prone on the hard, slippery floor. The faint light cast by a remote torch attached to the wall barely outlined Kedia, who was leaning on the imposing boulder nearby. The woman-like relic stood motionless, resembling a hewn monolithic statue, a constituent part of the stone. Suddenly, she cocked her head and listened closely. Her eyes flickered left and right, blinking, the very personification of a bird of prey, and then she blurted out:

"He's floating on the wrecks, a survivor in the ocean,
Creatures of the sea are leading him to land.
The prophecy of old times is now put in motion.
The scar-faced man is coming with a shining ax in hand."

Illima hauled herself into a sitting position.

"I saw the same thing," she uttered. "He's coming, Kedia! My hero will be here at dawn! And he's not alone—two other men are with him. Oh, how I long to meet him ashore!"

Kedia turned her bright brown eyes to her and croaked,

"Ahaki is the man who is supposed to meet him.
You need to help him out and guide him through his dream.
Go make his slumber vivid and lead him to the hero,
As they both have a mission: their people to redeem."

"I don't understand," Illima whispered. "How am I supposed to guide Ahaki through his dream?"

Nimble like a monkey, Kedia leaped up close and grabbed Illima's face between her claw-like wrinkled palms, peering at her. She fluttered her eyes, ensnaring Illima's attention, and started repeating faster and faster, passing from high-pitched falsetto to insane screaming,

"Your eyes you rivet on the rock and focus, focus, focus, FOCUS!"

Mesmerized but completely concentrated, Illima fixed her gaze on the boulder. The shape of the ancient stone started fluctuating and glowed with a soft amber light. The dark, steamy hall gradually distorted in slow motion, and the world span, picking up speed second by second. The next moment, the cave disappeared, replaced by a warm, tropical night, and Illima found herself in the center of the village, walking towards Ahaki's hut. She thirstily inhaled the fresh, fragrant air and squinted at the sky, turning her face against the wind to enjoy its gentle caress.

How beautiful everything is outside! She thought, enjoying the rustling of leaves, the shining moon, dimming and brightening with each bout of dragging raggy cloud, the croaking of toads and chirping of crickets, and even the shadows along the path. Everything was a miracle to her, no matter how trivial the surrounding details were.

The best years of my youth have passed by in this dark, damp hole while my peers were free and enjoyed their lives, she thought bitterly, feeling like crying, but no tears moistened her eyes. *Luckily, it's over now. After a few hours, I'll hold him in my arms.*

She cut across the small square, went past the copper Snake Gong that shone in the moonlight, and was soon at Ahaki's dwelling. She stretched her arm out to lift the mat that was blocking the entrance, but her hand sunk into the fabric, and she simply passed through the bamboo-woven switches, enjoying the smell of the raw material. The room was hot, stuffy, and gloomy, but she was used to seeing in the darkness, so she quickly spotted Ahaki. He was lying flat on his back on a straw mattress between his two wives, in a mess of tangled legs. Their limp arms were wrapped across his shoulders, and their heads rested on his chest, black hair spilling over his naked torso from all angles.

What am I supposed to do now? Illima thought, irritated.

"Get inside his dream! Lie down and fall asleep!" she heard a remote male voice.

But I am already dreaming, Illima objected in her mind.

"When the barriers of the everyday perception break, everything is possible." Now the voice was stronger, vibrating within her body. "Human beings can wake up in seven different dreams if they have enough energy, so you could fall asleep in six different places and still control your awareness. You can even move from one dream to another and act like you're still in your everyday life. I'll help you out. Just lie in the corner over there and think about merging into Ahaki's thoughts."

Illima understood nothing of the explanations, but she followed the instructions, nonetheless. She curled up in the corner, concentrating all her intent on entering Ahaki's mind, and a second later, she found herself walking through the jungle. It was day, and he was several yards to her left, stalking a wild boar in his dream. She caught a glimpse of the beast's rear as it quickly disappeared between the trees. Ahaki grunted discontentedly and bent over, looking for the trail, but then jumped and turned sharply, peering at Illima.

"What are you doing here, witch?" he asked roughly. His voice echoed as if he was in an empty cave.

"The prophecy is about to be fulfilled, Wise Ahaki," Illima said. "Go to the north shore and find the scar-faced man. You are predestined to help him in his endeavor, for many people are ready to follow you in fire and water. So, if you want to become the new chieftain, you must lead them against Kamani. Bring them before the curly-haired man, and he will teach you what to do."

"Why are you talking in a male voice, witch? Aren't you that girl from the cave?" Ahaki cried out.

"Wake up and follow me!" ordered Illima, still speaking in a deep, guttural timbre.

Ahaki jerked in his sleep and woke up. He pushed his wives away and they turned over, muttering and smacking their lips. He got up, staggering, still dizzy from the slumber, and force of habit compelled him to reach for his accouterments—a leather strap with a dangling knife attached to it, a pouch with touchwood, and a wooden canteen—which he slung across his shoulder before stepping out.

The damp night was cloudy and dark. Ahaki faltered a few yards and stopped, murmuring to himself, "What the fuck has caused me to go out in the heart of the night? I'd better go back to sleep…" He was about to turn around when he glanced ahead and jumped, frightened. Several yards from him, Illima's silhouette glowed in the darkness.

"Am I still dreaming?" He rubbed his eyes and slapped his cheek, but she was still there, skinny and shimmering. She beckoned him with an imperial gesture and pointed north.

"Follow me!" the male voice from his dream rang out, and a fit of anxiety hit his chest. He rushed after Illima, not seeing any path outlined but simply chasing the soft light as it gleamed here and there between the trees. As though guided by some invisible force, he squeezed between bushes, trees, and creepers, lashed and scratched by twigs and thorns, so that when he reached the shore, he was already puffy in the face, and deep bloody grooves covered his body.

Once on the beach, he stopped and listened. Although the storm had abated, the sea was still heavy, and the breakers crashed fiercely against the rocks. Illima had disappeared. Ahaki took off his sandals and walked eastward along the shore, burying his bare feet into the coarse sand.

I'm still not sure whether I have awoken, he contemplated, glancing at the lightening sky. *Today I'll send somebody to the cave to check that the two crazy hags haven't escaped somehow. But then, how it would be possible to see her otherwise… Wait a second, what are those wrecks over there?*

Several heavy-looking logs and an equally hefty chest were stranded onshore as the ebb tide had drawn the water back by several yards already. Ahaki rushed towards the debris, and he soon saw three men, sprawled unconscious among the wreck. Once there, he kneeled and scrutinized them. Both were lying flat on their backs, and the pale skin and bristly hair sprouting from their faces made Ahaki scratch his head in astonishment. They looked strange and exhausted with their peculiar, torn rags—especially the skinny one, whose forehead was colored by a large bloody blotch. The third survivor lay prone, his fists buried in the sand. Ahaki took him by the shoulder and turned over his heavy body. His face was covered with dirt and seaweed, but his skin was smooth, the right color, and his curly hair brought forth a vague memory. He wiped the man's face and stared at it for a long while.

"The man with scars will come, and he will cut the Tree," he whispered. "Exactly the way Kedia foresaw it. The same man from my childhood vision, the one I got out of the sea and carried on my back. But wait, isn't he… This curly hair… But how could he still be alive?"

As the thought flashed through his mind, Ahaki moaned and pressed his hands against his ears. The beach and the sea disappeared, and he was in the dark foggy cave, gazing at Kedia in dismay. Surrounded by hot steam, she writhed on the floor in ecstasies, advancing toward him.

There was another silhouette in the remote corner, but he could not make out the blurry figure. He strained his eyes, but his attention was drawn to Kedia's screeching voice as it tore through the air.

"A thousand full moons I waited for this day,
The day when he appears with a shining ax in hand,
The day of New Beginning, as stated by his name,
The prophecy set in motion is now a risky game.

That's why you have to help him, Ahaki, nobleman,
Without you, he won't be able to implement his plan.
Be always close to him and never let him down
And he will make you chieftain when comes the last countdown."

Ahaki opened his mouth, but somebody grabbed his ankle before he could ask for clarification. He looked down, expecting to see Kedia, and he realized he was back on the beach, staring at the curly-haired boy who had wrapped his fingers around his shin and was trying to rise.

"What happened? What happened?" he shouted in Spanish. "I heard the surf booming and woke up, and we were running straight towards the cliffs…"

"Wasn't your name Kamolea?" Ahaki squeezed his hand. "Do you recognize me, lad?"

In the gloom of the rising day, Kamolea peered at the slender man and immediately recognized him, although he could not recall his name. All the years had not brought any significant change to Ahaki's intelligent, open face. His hair was gray and longer now, reaching his shoulders, something unusual for the warriors of his tribe.

"Water," he stuttered in his native Maniha-Komo dialect. Ahaki detached his flask and moved it towards Kamolea's lips, who grabbed it and drank thirstily to the last dregs.

"Thank you!" he said as he gave it back to him. "I know you. What was your name?"

"Ahaki. I was your father's friend, remember?"

"So, this is Maniha Komo, then?"

"It is! Your native island, Kamolea! When we cast you off the island, I was sure you'd never return. It's so incredible that I am welcoming you back after so many years!"

"Absolutely," muttered Kamolea, apparently relieved. "I never really believed I'd land back here either."

"Pity that Akamui could not see this moment," Ahaki said. "I know that he missed you very much, although he never showed it."

"Is he alive?" Kamolea asked and rose slowly, feeling unsteady. He had the impression that the ground was moving as if he was still on the raft.

"No. It's been a long time since Kamani killed him."

"Kamani? It sounds familiar, this name," Kamolea frowned. "Wait, wasn't he one of the Laggi's gang?"

"He was, indeed. He is a chieftain now, in your father's place. You have a remarkable memory, you know?"

"I'm surprised that he killed the invincible Creeping Death," Kamolea said matter-of-factly. Since he had seen Akamui in Hell, something had snapped in him, and he felt nothing for the man who raised him and who he had admired so much as a child.

"Exactly! Nobody expected such an outcome. Kamani called him a traitor before the entire tribe because he did not kill you and spared Illima. He challenged him before the Council, and your father had no choice. They fought to the death, and he lost."

"You mentioned Illima. Where is she now? Don't tell me she's also dead!" Kamolea said anxiously.

Ahaki shook his head.

"She's alive. Do you remember the Steamy Cave? Kedia's dwelling, which we visited after your trial? They locked her there with the old crazy crone."

"Why?"

"She went berserk after your boat disappeared beyond the horizon and started shouting the same nonsense as Kedia and you, about the new God, and the punishment that awaits us all, and much more gibberish… So, first, they wanted to kill her, but Akamui said no. Nobody ever understood why he decided to protect her. But she continued disturbing the entire village, so they locked her in the cave. After a while, everybody forgot about her."

"I want to see her right away!" Kamolea cried and, as he remembered how Akamui had addressed the young warrior, he added, "Take me to her, Wise Ahaki!"

"No, you can't see her right now," objected Ahaki. "We must get out of here immediately, for if the lookouts see you here, it will be the end of your journey. I've got a hiding place in mind, so…"

A loud moan cut through his words, and Alfonso stirred. Kamolea glanced at him; then, his gaze swept the scenery. The jagged cliff nestling his small rocky shelter soared up in the distance, outlined against the brightening sky. The steady breeze blew from the sea, dragging tattered clouds and swinging the palm's fronds in hearty welcome, just as they had done ten years before, when they were waving him a heartbreaking goodbye. A swarm of memories swooped over him as he realized he was standing in the same place as the day of his exile. In a flash, he saw the loving gaze of Illima, the grief in Lalago's eyes, and the crowd throwing stones and rotten food at him. He shook his head, trying to rid himself of the painful recollections.

"What happened to Lalago?" he asked Ahaki.

"She died several moons after we cast you out. She loved you so much that she never got over the loss of you."

Kamolea nodded, and sorrow stabbed his heart. His eyes filled with tears and he found himself barely able to suppress the urge to throw himself in the water and swim straight to his little cave, as he had done in the old days when he felt sorrowful.

"I suspected she had passed away, as I met her once in my dream. She was pretty old, anyway," he said instead.

Another groan interrupted his thoughts, and Benito fidgeted, slowly coming to his senses. Kamolea kneeled beside him and took his hand.

"We did it, Creyente! We reached my island!" he said, trembling with excitement.

Benito's shirt was torn to pieces, revealing a deep blue discoloration on his left shoulder. He tried to prop himself up on one elbow but slumped back with a cry of pain.

"Where are we, by thunder?" His voice was hoarse and betrayed his discomfort. "Shit, my hand is numb as a transom beam. Who is this savage?" he yelled as he noticed Ahaki.

"Don't worry, he is a friend of mine," Kamolea reassured him.

"You said we've reached your island? I suppose this is good news." He rubbed his left shoulder. "The last thing I remember was the excruciating pain when we came upon the rocks and the raft shattered into pieces. Gosh, what a storm that was!"

"Blood and thunder! My darn coconut's gonna explode!" whined Alfonso, as he hauled himself into a sitting position and clutched his head between his two hands. He cast a suspicious look at Ahaki and muttered,

"When are they going to eat us? You said it was usually at sunset, so I reckon we have at least a few more hours to live."

"Listen, Kamolea, we have to get off the shore," said Ahaki in an urgent tone. "The timing of your arrival could not be better, as the chieftain, the elders, and most of the warriors are on a raid right now. But the lookouts will do their tour soon, and I don't want them to find us here. Up the Whelk Hill, there is a tree with a large hollow that will be a perfect place to shelter all of you."

"Are you talking about the Great Hollow Tree? Come, Wise Ahaki, every kid knows this place. We used to play there with Anuro; we even built a small watchtower on the top. It's not much of a hiding place if you ask me."

"Times have changed since you left," Ahaki replied. "Now nobody lets their kids wander on that part of the island, mainly because they know you played there. A bad omen, they say, everything you've touched…"

Kamolea slapped his forehead and cut him off.

"Anuro! I completely forgot about him! What's going on with him? Is he alive?"

"Well, as he was your best friend, he fell completely out of favor," Ahaki said darkly. "I'll give you all the details later, but we really need to get going."

"All right, let's go," Kamolea said. "We have to bring the chest as well."

"This long thing? It's gonna be hard through the tangled greenery over there."

"You just lead us, Wise Ahaki, and we'll take care of the rest," said Kamolea. He took out his knife—Niddi's gift—which he always carried on his waist, cut the ropes that fastened the chest to the logs, and thrust it between the cover and the wall. Then, he moved it along to cut the resin and finally flipped the heavy lid open. The cold steel gleamed in the early morning gloom.

"Here, take that." He handed a machete to Ahaki.

"Water," Alfonso moaned. "I'm thirsty as hell."

"What is he saying?" asked Ahaki.

"He wants water," explained Kamolea.

"I'll take you to a small brook not far from here. Just hurry up!" Ahaki was getting more anxious with every passing minute.

"All right, everybody, take a cutlass, two pistols, and a powder horn," Kamolea ordered in Spanish. "Ahaki is going to lead us through the jungle to a hiding place up to the hill."

"Just take us to water, dammit!" spat Alfonso.

They shouldered the long sea chest, crossed the sand band, and set off inland. It was hot, humid, and still dark in the forest. Soon, they reached the stream and plunged into the water, dipping their heads like animals and drinking thirstily for a long time. Ahaki watched them in dismay.

"How long has it been since you drank water?" he asked Kamolea.

"About two days, maybe more, for the bloody storm stripped the raft from everything."

After they rested a bit, they took up a narrow winding path that cut through the jungle, but soon the forest became so dense that it was impossible to carry the chest on their shoulders. They dragged and pushed it for some time, but after about a sandglass[82] of climbing, the three of them collapsed, half-dead and soaked with sweat.

"I can't take it anymore!" Benito panted. "My shoulder hurts like hell, and I can't feel my arm. Let's hide the weapons here and come back for them later."

Kamolea translated to Ahaki.

"You can leave them under the shrubs over there and conceal them with branches. I'll send my men to bring them afterward," he agreed.

"What he's saying?" Alfonso asked suspiciously.

Kamolea told them.

"How can we trust him?" Benito snorted. "I imagine he'll take the weapons and order his men to kill us."

"What for?" asked Kamolea, surprised.

"I don't know, man. Just to brag and boast in front of his folks."

"What's going on?" said Ahaki nervously.

"They're wondering if we can trust you," Kamolea said. "I really appreciate everything you are doing for us, Wise Ahaki, but you must be aware that your support could draw the ire of the chieftain and the other elders upon you. So, tell me, why are you so inclined to help us out and risk getting into trouble?"

Ahaki smiled.

---

82 Half an hour.

"I realize the danger, of course," he said, "but, you know, I have always believed that Kedia is telling the truth. Also, I had several similar dreams about her prophecy a long time ago, even before you were exiled. It went like this: the whole village was gathered before the Sacred Tree, and Kedia was there. Then, a curly-haired man with a disfigured face hammered Rakapi with an enormous ax, and just as he did, a thunderbolt hit the Tree top and some transparent, shimmering cloud descended from heaven, wrapping everyone in peaceful bliss. Do you believe me now?"

Kamolea nodded and drew the shining ax from the chest. As Ahaki saw it, his eyes grew twice the size.

"Is this the ax from your dream?" Kamolea asked him, smiling.

"The very same!" he exclaimed. "I can't believe it! May I?" He took the ax and scrutinized it, his eyes exuding awe and admiration as he muttered, "What an incredible weapon!"

"It's called 'The Ax of Love,'" said Kamolea and turned to his Spanish friends. "Shake a leg, mateys! We'll leave the chest with the powder cask here. I trust this man with my own life, so I don't want to hear even a single doubtful word about him."

They set off at a considerably faster pace. Along the way, Kamolea told Ahaki their sea adventures and the story of the ax. The time flew by, and it was about noon when they finally reached a small clearing near the top of the hill.

At the sight of the Great Hollow Tree, rising majestically in the middle of the clearing, its tangled trunks forming the immense cavity, Kamolea's childhood memories sprang back to him. He was a little boy again, hiding inside the vast hollow that was always dry and cozy, even during the rainy season, or climbing on the gigantic bole, made of twisted trunks.

He stepped on the soft turf covering the ground, and the pleasant smell of mushrooms and touchwood filled him with happiness.

"It's a perfect place for us to stay. Thank you for bringing us here, Wise Ahaki," Kamolea bowed.

"It's nothing. Stay still, and I'll be back soon with food and the rest of your weapons. I'll also bring some of my trusted people to see you."

"Before you go, let's do some planning," Kamolea motioned towards the ground, and they sat face to face. "You said that the army is on a raid, didn't you?"

"That's right, but we expect their return at any moment. They departed for the Lizard's Island about a fortnight ago. If you remember, it's the most remote island in the Archipelago. There was some trouble brewing, but I don't think Kamani will linger there too long."

"Tell me about him."

"Ah, he grew to such a terrible man, you simply can't imagine," Ahaki sighed. "A cold-hearted snake is now our chieftain."

"What do you mean?"

"He schemes and sows mystery and gossip all the time, sometimes even killing those who disagree with him. But perhaps his deceitfulness is your chance, as there is tough resistance against him, and half of the men secretly want me to replace him as the chieftain. In the last election, he only kept his place by a dozen votes, and that's because some of those who were in my favor suspiciously disappeared several sunsets before election day. Consequently, he hates me so much that he spreads all kinds of lies about me. He even banned me from participating in the raids! Such impudence! As you know, the biggest humiliation for a warrior is to be left behind with kids, the elderly, and women."

"It's a stroke of luck he's not here," said Kamolea thoughtfully. "How many men remain on the island that you can count on?"

"Not many. About twenty warriors and the others are worthless: too old or crippled. But those who stay here have fallen out of favor, so they are reliable. Kamani's argument to get rid of us was that we needed to keep the island safe. Fucking toad!" Ahaki spat with disgust.

"It's gonna heat up once he returns," Kamolea muttered. "Do you have any idea how to confront him? Could I evoke the old law, for instance, and challenge him to a fight to the death?"

"No, you don't belong to our tribe anymore, remember? You are an intruder and as such, your fate is the death penalty; you haven't even passed your warrior's proof, and to fight with him for the chieftain's position, you would have to be equal to him. I could have challenged him before, but now it's too late—I'm getting old, and he is too strong for me."

Kamolea considered the information for a moment.

"We need to implement a more cunning strategy, then," he said, "but first things first, I want to free Illima. Can you get us to the Steamy Cave? I can't find the way by myself."

"I can take you there tonight, but nobody should suspect I have helped you with this. It needs to look as if you have accomplished it alone, with your friends," said Ahaki after a brief reflection.

"Why not go right now?" asked Kamolea impatiently.

"No, it's too dangerous in daylight; the Carapace hill is too crowded during the day. Besides, you need some rest. By the way, what do you intend to do with Kedia?"

"I'll free her as well," said Kamolea.

"I advise you to think twice before doing that," Ahaki said, his eyes darting about uneasily.

"Why so?"

"Because, for our people, Kedia is a symbol of a supernatural disaster. After so many legends and rumors, she has turned into something incomprehensible and inhuman. The fact that she rejects our god and yet remains alive is gruesome enough. No one wants to deal with her."

"That's why I need her more than ever. She will confirm the prophecy and reiterate the truth about the true God," Kamolea said decisively.

"I'm starving, dammit! Let's go hunting!" Alfonso declared loudly, interrupting them.

"We need to eat something; it's been a few days since our last bite." Kamolea looked at Ahaki. "Should we hunt?"

"No, lie low for now. I don't want you to move from here. I'll bring you some food from the village." Then, he sprang up and disappeared into the jungle.

"What yarns were you guys spinning in your shitty language?" Alfonso asked, barging past Kamolea with a musket in hand.

"You wait here, lanky," Kamolea said. "Ahaki will be soon back with some food. Besides, there are only birds in the woods, and most of them taste awful."

"You told us there are wild boars…," Alfonso complained.

"So what? You'll never be able to catch one," Kamolea teased him.

"And why not?"

"'Cause you're a clumsy, skinny lubber who knows nothing about hunting. Let's cut some solid boughs and build a fence around the hollow's entrance while waiting for Ahaki. Then, if anybody attacks us, we can defend ourselves more successfully."

After some resentful grumbling, Alfonso agreed, and they fortified the entry with thick poles and trunks, cutting embrasures in the wood, and leaving a hole just big enough for one person to crawl inside. In the heat of their work, Ahaki returned with nine men, who brought the weapon chest, the powder keg, and several clay pots. As Kamolea stood up to greet them, Benito and Alfonso watched, filled with dread at the ominous-looking men with their shaved heads, naked and covered in tattoos and jewelry made of human bones. Each man clutched a spear in his hand, and stony knives on leather straps dangled around their waists.

"Shiver my timbers, matey," Benito whispered in Alfonso's ear. "I've seen a thing or two around the world—buccaneers, cut-throat thugs, Indians, and all, but never such terrible butchers like these here. Just look at their glaring eyes—there's nothing human in them."

"Never seen such perfect bodies, to be sure," observed Alfonso, nodding admiringly. "Slender but brawny and all bulging muscles. Look at their beautifully outlined abdomens! But they look like sheer savages, all the same…"

"Hey, Benito, Alfonso, come over here!" Kamolea beckoned them. The warriors had laid down the clay pots with fish stew, salt boar, roasted turtle, bananas, and mango. The three survivors fell upon the meal, grabbing the food with their hands and wolfing it down. Within a few minutes, everything was gone. Afterward, they all sat in a circle beneath the tree and began passing a pipe, as the welcome custom dictated. The stench of the smoldering herbs was terrible, but the mushrooms mixed with it had a relaxing effect. When the ceremony was over, Kamolea rose and bowed to Ahaki with gratitude.

"Thank you again, Wise Ahaki. So, these are your trusted men, right? Are you sure about them?"

"They'll stake their lives on me, and they loathe Kamani," replied Ahaki without hesitation.

"That's good. Now, I want to show you some interesting stuff that I brought across the ocean."

He took out a musket.

"This is a fiery stick," he explained. "When you pull this thing here, called 'gatillo'[83] in their language, the stick spews fire, and you can kill somebody from a distance."

"Show me!" cried Ahaki. An excited mutter passed around the circle.

"It's quite noisy when the fire comes out. Should we be cautious?" Kamolea asked.

"Oh, don't worry about the noise," said Ahaki. "The sky is cloudy, and if there is somebody nearby hunting, he'll think it's a thunderbolt. Anyway, the lookouts are near the shore and the surf will drown out any other sound. The only real danger is fire. Whatever happens, don't kindle a fire as the smoke will betray your presence."

"I'll warn my friends about that," Kamolea said. "But look now, how this works."

---

83 Trigger.

He put the long gun firmly against his shoulder, aimed at the sky, and shot. Everybody jumped back when the musket went off. The echo still hadn't died away when a royal pigeon thudded to the ground, landing at their feet. A wave of excitement passed through the Tipi-haos and one of them pulled the musket from Kamolea's hand with an approving murmur. He ran his fingers over the butt and barrel, his eyes shining with delight.

Next, Kamolea showed them the pistols, which piqued the warriors' interest even more. Alfonso and Benito watched the tough men with amusement as they turned the weapons in their hands like children. Kamolea instructed them how to load and aim the firearms and even allowed them to shoot. The shining cutlasses, the daggers and, of course, Kamolea's ax, were also objects of admiration. Each man took the ax in turn, tested its weight, swung it to check the trajectory, tried the blade, and feasted his eyes on the gleaming steel.

"This is a magical weapon that makes his owner invincible," Kamolea told them. "If you follow Ahaki and me, I promise to teach you incredible things and tell you amazing stories about the world of these pale men who I have brought with me. They live in vast, beautiful cities and dwell in coated houses made of stone or wood, many times taller than our huts. They have huge boats they call ships, which they use to sail across the ocean. And all this is because their God gives them strength and wisdom. So, remember, if you accept the same God, you will be undefeatable. With His support, you can achieve wonderful things and reach heights we thought were unattainable."

Kamolea's enthusiasm was so great that he enthralled his audience, but their primary interest remained the advantage of the weapons and the upcoming Ahaki's promotion, which would have assured them eventually a place in the Council. As for accepting a new god, the common opinion was that they would wait to see its signs, might, and power first.

Meantime, the sun had disappeared behind the hill, and gloom was slowly descending upon the forest. Kamolea felt some queasiness in his stomach. He glanced around, assessing the situation. His Spanish friends had retreated inside the hollow and were snoring, aided by full bellies and satisfied grins on their haggard faces. Ahaki was the center of attention, surrounded by his people and vividly gesticulating something to them. Kamolea broke through the circle and bent near his ear.

"It's time to disband the people and to get ready for tonight, Wise Ahaki," he whispered.

Ahaki nodded his agreement and turned to the men.

"My fellow warriors! Today, you have witnessed a prophetic moment in our history. The coming of the scar-faced man is a legendary event that will reverberate around our tradition for generations to come. But for now, I beseech you to keep your mouths shut and wait for my sign, as we must keep his arrival a secret. Remember that our enemies are everywhere, so not a single word to anyone about what happened today!"

"Can we have some of these fiery sticks?" asked one of them.

Ahaki cast an inquiring look at Kamolea.

"Not right away," he replied. "Come tomorrow to practice again, and on the eve of the fight you shall have them."

"Go to the village now!" ordered Ahaki. While he was giving the last instruction to his closest adherents, Kamolea woke up his friends.

"Brace yourself, mateys," he said. "We're setting off for the Steamy Cave."

* * *

The dense tropical forest was a cacophonous concert of nighttime sounds. The evening breeze had broken the clouds, and the moon shone brightly, casting a soft light over the almost invisible path. Ahaki was in the lead, cutting vigorously through the gigantic ferns and shrubs with his new cutlass, a gift from Kamolea, who followed directly behind him, brandishing his machete in a fierce fight with the creeping greenery. Alfonso was in the middle, and Benito brought up the rear. Ahaki had chosen the shortest way to Carapace Hill—an ancient overgrown trail nobody had used for years. Even at nightfall, the air was hot and damp, and they advanced in gloomy silence and at a snail's pace. After a few hours, the ascending track became less steep, and the creepers thinned out. Finally, Ahaki pushed aside a giant fern stem and stopped abruptly, raising his hand. In the moonlight, the ghostly scenery of the stony ground, wrapped in mist and surrounded by venerable trees, transported Kamolea back in time to memories of that awful night, on the eve of his expulsion. He cast a sidelong glance at his Spanish fellows and noticed that the view had had the same grim effect on them.

Through the dense misty veil, they made out the figure of a man sleeping on the ground and snoring so loudly that they could hear it even from such a distance. Kamolea knew that Kedia always had two guards, but the other was nowhere to be seen. Ahaki made a sign that they would wait until he appeared, and sure enough, he emerged a few minutes later from the bushes behind the cave, waddling complacently and caressing his belly. As he reached the cave entrance, he gave his snoring companion a light kick, causing him to stir discontentedly.

Ahaki waved toward the village and disappeared into the forest. As soon as he was out of sight, Kamolea pointed to the guards and they charged. The lookout froze, his mouth hanging half-open, looking in dismay at the three men in their strange clothes, materializing from the mist. He didn't even offer a reaction when Benito put his saber against his throat.

"Lie face down," Kamolea ordered, and Alfonso tied him up, while the other guard continued to sleep blissfully. Benito took his spear and kicked him in the ribs to wake him. The man started, trying immediately to jump to his feet, but Kamolea was too quick for him, landing a mighty punch on his face and pressing his knee to his chest.

"Toad's shit, who are you, bloody apparition?!" the man cried. "If I'm still dreaming, it's high time I woke up!"

There was no trace of fear in his boyish, mocking voice despite the tight spot he was caught in, though the intonation and his timbre sounded vaguely familiar to Kamolea's ears. He lifted an eyebrow and gazed at the warrior's face.

"Anuro," he whispered. There was no doubt. The face had become mature and manly, but the countenance, and especially his lively, cunning eyes, were the same.

"Anuro, my friend!" Kamolea cried and released his grip. "Do you remember me? It's me, Kamolea!" He gave him a hand up and grabbed him in a bear hug, then pushed him back and looked him all over, grinning with pleasure. Anuro's face slowly changed from a dumbfounded expression to a broad smile, and his eyes gleamed with wild joy.

"Kamolea!" he shouted. "Almighty Kepolo, but it's impossible! Come here, my friend!"

They hugged again, and time stood still as they became boys once again, transporting themselves to a feeling and a time from years before.

"Look at you, how strong you've become," said Anuro when they broke away. "You could have strangled me with this octopus hug of yours."

"Anuro, old buddy! I'm so happy to see you! You can't imagine how much I missed you!" Kamolea beamed.

"I missed you too in the beginning, but then I simply forgot about you!" Anuro said. "I am a simple boy, you know, and I never thought I'd see you ever again. After your departure, everybody said you would die within one or two sunsets on the sea, but here you are, sturdy and tough like a shark and covered with scars like a true warrior. So, tell me, how did you do this?"

"Not now, my friend," said Kamolea. "We have a mission to fulfill, and the night is advancing, so we need to hurry."

"You came for Illima, didn't you?" Anuro said with a mischievous flame in his eyes and stroked his shaved head. "If you knew how many times I wished to free her! But if I had done it, we would have had no chance of surviving."

"Let's do it now, then! Lead us!" cried Kamolea and glanced at his friends, who watched the emotional scene between Kamolea and the brawny savage with some confusion.

"He is my best friend," he explained. "We're going to break in. Don't be afraid of the screams of the old witch—she is insane but harmless. And try not to throw up at the smell. Follow me!"

They followed Anuro inside the dark mouth of the cavern. The awful stench of rotten eggs hit them in the nostrils, and Alfonso retched several times as Benito's face turned white as a sheet. It was steamy, hot, and damp, just as Kamolea remembered. Four torches, affixed to the walls, cast a faint light. Anuro took one and gave two others to Kamolea and Alfonso. They advanced through the narrow, slippery passage, hunched over and wary, splashing in the puddles and being careful not to bang their heads against the overhanging stalactites. Annoyed by the flames coming from the torches, a flock of bats rose with sharp screeches, flapping their wings around the explorers. Alfonso jumped back, frightened, and yelled as he smacked his nape on a protruded rock. After much grumbling, whining, and cajoling, he agreed to continue, and they soon heard a brook babbling in the distance.

"How on earth have they lived here for so many years? I couldn't bear to stay in this hole even for a sunset," Kamolea muttered.

"Well, they're crazy, aren't day?" Anuro's voice echoed ahead. "They live in another dimension, in a manner of speaking."

Kamolea did not respond, carried away by the memories of his first visit to this horrible place.

At least the dreadful witch isn't screaming her head off, he thought. *So many times, I woke up trembling in the night, still hearing her bloody screeches.*

They reached the spike fence and Anuro removed two poles from the middle, opening a gap big enough to squeeze through.

As they advanced, they heard a loud cackle coming from a distance. Goosebumps crawled down Kamolea's spine. On his left, Benito shivered and made a cross sign. The torches flickered, casting ghostly shadows around. They strained their eyes, trying to spot a human figure in the intense vapor that spread out all over the cavernous hall, but what they noticed first was the immense boulder rising up in the middle of the room.

"Illima!" Kamolea shouted. "Where are you, my love?"

He heard a scream and she materialized just in front of him, appearing from behind the rock. Kamolea threw his torch aside and hurled himself towards her. She jumped on him, wrapped her arms around his neck and her legs around his waist, and clung to him, almost suffocating him. He pressed her in a fervent embrace and kissed her vehemently all over her face until their lips fused in fiery passion, and his heart exploded with happiness. At this moment, the universe stopped, just like on the day of his warrior's proof, and for the second time in his life, he felt eternity. A wave of overwhelming love, gratitude, and awe, mixed with immense relief, suffused his entire being, and tears started rolling down his cheeks. Feeling his emotions, Illima wrapped her arms around him so tightly that he stopped breathing for a second. She dug her enormous, claw-like nails into his neck, back, and shoulders, tearing his shirt and scratching his skin as they continued to kiss, moaning and howling like wild animals. Kamolea never wanted it to end. He buried his fingers into her long, tangled hair, which reached down to her calves, and inhaled every bit of her, feeling her full, firm breasts as his hands ran all over her naked body. Now, she was a ripe woman, gorgeous and sensual, almost as tall as he was, but her shiny black eyes were those of the girl he remembered from over ten years before.

"My savior," she whispered in his ear, biting it slightly. "My superhero! I spent my entire conscious life in this miserable hole, waiting for you, for I knew you'd come and save me. It was written in the stars; and Kedia and I both foresaw it."

"I never believed I'll see you again, my love," Kamolea choked, his voice betraying his agitation. "I love you so much, Illima! You were the only reason I came back to this cursed place."

"I know," she smiled, caressing his cheek. "Are you crying, my handsome hero? You told me once that men never cry."

"Only this once, and they are tears of joy and happiness," he sniffed, wiping his cheeks and nose rapidly. "When I think of how difficult it was to decide to return! Man is the worst enemy of himself… But now, nothing else matters more than this wonderful moment, to hold you in my arms and tell you how much I love you. I am ready to trade my life for it, even if they kill me tomorrow."

"HE CAME! HE CAME! THE MAN WITH SCARS ARRIVED!" Kedia screamed from the remote corner of the cave, and everybody jumped, startled.

"Come on, love birds, leave your hugs for later and let's get out of here!" Anuro cried out.

"Wait!" Kamolea shouted. "We've got to take Kedia with us!"

"What for?" objected Anuro. "Leave the old bat here. Everyone fears her like a natural disaster."

"My point exactly. She's coming with us, no arguments."

"Do whatever you want, but I'm not touching this fossil!" Anuro declared. Then, he turned around and strode away.

"Halt, you coward! Where are you going like this?" Illima yelled after him, but he raised his hand, twisting his palm in an offensive gesture, and disappeared into the steam.

"Alfonso, you are the tallest; take her on your back," Kamolea said.

"But where is she?" Benito asked.

"Hey, Kamolea, hurry! The sky is brightening, and the watch will switch soon," came Anuro's voice from afar.

"Quick, we gotta go! Grab her, Alfonso! You're the man!" Kamolea cried.

Alfonso muttered inaudibly and stepped forward just as Kedia sprang out from the darkness with a wild scream. Alfonso leaped back, terrified. "What the fuck is this thing?" he whispered.

The small skinny creature that appeared through the dense vapor looked like a ghostly wraith. Swarthy, wizened skin contrasted with her long white hair, which trailed on the floor, entirely covering her naked body. Agile as a monkey and almost the same size, the shrill caws she was letting out were far from human speech, so it was no surprise that the instant she rushed towards Alfonso, the latter drew out his cutlass and lifted it, ready to strike.

"NOOOO!" bellowed Kamolea, launching himself forward and pushing Alfonso just as he swung his sword. They both tumbled to the ground as Kedia rolled over with a yelp and hid behind the stone again.

"What are you doing, you bloody wretch?!" Kamolea yelled at Alfonso. "She hasn't lived hundreds of years only for some fool like you to kill her! I told you to put her up on your back, not to…"

"On my *back?!* I wouldn't touch this apparition for all the gold on this godforsaken earth!" Alfonso resented.

"She's not a ghost. She's just an old woman," Kamolea said.

"Carry her yourself then or make your savage friend do it. I'm done with all this bullshit!" Alfonso spat on the floor.

"Kamolea!" the urgent tone in Anuro's distant voice was unmistakable.

"Damn it, man!" cried Kamolea and turned to Benito, but as he met his stare, the latter shook his head,

"No way am I carrying her, matey. You'd better leave her here."

"I won't. Kedia, come over here and jump on my back!"

No sooner had he finished talking than Kedia peeped out from behind the stone and cautiously approached, eyeing him closely.

"The one who'll change forever the thinking of the men," she breathed quietly. Kamolea looked at her wrinkled face and met her big, brown, intelligent eyes. He stretched his arm out and took her calloused, claw-like hand, trying to suppress a shudder. She thrust her long nails into his skin as she jumped nimbly and wrapped her bony hands around

his neck. Her stench was so terrible that Kamolea felt a fit of nausea overcome him for an instant. The others were already striding towards the exit, so he hurried to catch up with them, glad to get out of the awful place.

The fresh air outside was like an ointment to his lungs. Anuro did not hide his impatience, but his eyes gleamed with amusement when he saw Kamolea and Kedia.

"Such a pretty picture—the man with scars arrives, carrying the horror on his back," he chuckled.

Kamolea grinned.

"We have no equal, do we? Listen, we need to go back to the Great Hollow Tree on Whelk Hill. We played a lot there as boys, remember?"

"How could I forget the Hollow Tree?" Anuro cried. "You must've used the old track through the hills to get here, I suppose?"

"I don't know what you call the old path, but it took us almost the whole night to get through it," Kamolea replied.

"No surprise; nobody has used it for ages," Anuro said. "At least it'll be far easier now."

"What about him?" Kamolea pointed at the bound guard.

Anuro shrugged.

"Kill him and throw him in the abyss," he suggested. "He's not reliable, anyway."

"No, no more killing if it's up to me," Kamolea said. "We'll take him with us, so cut loose the ropes that bind his legs, but leave his hands tied. Benito, you take personal care of him, understand?" he said in Spanish, and Benito nodded in agreement.

Anuro bent down to free him, and the warrior cast him a murderous look.

"Follow me!" said Anuro, and they sank into the darkness of the jungle.

CHAPTER XXVII

THE NEW BEGINNING

Kamolea's moans mixed with Illima's as he sped up his movements, thrusting in and out faster and faster, firmly clutching her bottom. She twisted her pelvis upward, sinking her crooked nails into his back, and her body exploded with incredible pleasure at the exact moment that he came inside her. They clung together for a moment, completely still, before Kamolea rolled onto his back, still panting.

They lay on the soft grass beside the brook that passed about two hundred yards southwest of the Great Hollow Tree. The rippling sound of the water, the light breeze on their faces, the blue sky above, and the fragrance of the blooming flowers around them filled them with bliss. They stayed there for hours, making love and talking in between until the flame of their passion flared up again.

Kamolea's first attempt had not been particularly encouraging, as he had climaxed the moment he touched Illima between the legs. The second time, he had only lasted a couple of minutes and she had bled, which stressed him out.

"I imagined it would be something sublime," he had muttered, red in the face, thinking, *Gosh, how many times was I ready to risk my life for this?*

But the next attempt lasted longer, and a supreme delight shook their bodies. Now they had finished their fifth intercourse, and Kamolea was starting to get more excited about the deed.

"I love you so much, my savior," whispered Illima and laid her head on his chest. She watched him lovingly and stroked his face, before their lips fused in another passionate kiss.

"I waited an eternity for this day, and when now it has finally happened, I still can't believe it," she said after they had broken apart.

Kamolea smiled, unable to tear his eyes off her.

"Tell me, my love, how did you end up in this awful cave?" he asked, caressing her head.

"I went crazy when your boat disappeared. I started having visions and babbling in a male voice. I said things I don't remember," Illima said. "The elders didn't know what to do with me. They asked Kepolo, but the signs were ambiguous, so they didn't dare kill me. Then, Akamui had the idea of locking me away with Kedia, and the village settled down."

"Yes, Ahaki told me that," nodded Kamolea. "What a terrible destiny to live in such a miserable place with this crazy witch."

"You know, strangely enough, it wasn't so bad. I mean, she's insane all right, but so was I, and somehow, we understood each other. And with time, I adjusted to her presence and everything else—the foul stench, the gloom, the hunger as they barely fed us, but I never quenched the burning sorrow for you, or my longing to be with you again. Besides, I had all these enchanting dreams and visions! It was like traveling in different worlds and dimensions without limits of time and space. When we met in your dream, I told you I was with you many times, especially when you were in mortal danger. Lately, I saw on that raft, being tossed by the immense waves…"

"But how is this possible?" Kamolea exclaimed.

"I don't know, but I suspect that it's related to the steam. According to Kedia, one of the substances in the hot brook under ground provokes such visions. But I'm glad it's finally over! It was so tough in that horrid place."

"My beautiful flower," Kamolea whispered. "I can't bare knowing that at one point, I considered never coming back. I was so lucky that God didn't leave me alone and helped me to return. Even though I was unruly and unfaithful and always fought against *His* will, *He* was patient and forgave me so many times until *He* finally brought me to you. Without *His* guidance, I would've never made it."

"Yes, *He* was my defender as well," Illima said. "I was so mad at you when I foresaw you were ready to leave me for that girl. I had the dreadful feeling that I'd never see you again, so I prayed fervently to *Him*, and *He* brought you to the cave, giving me the possibility to speak to you."

"Yes, this dream changed everything," said Kamolea.

"It did! Because you've never realized how crucial the situation was," said Illima crossly. "If you had even spent one night with her, you would've been gone forever."

"I did wrong many times toward you, and I'm so ashamed about it now," Kamolea sighed, then he kissed her gently and whispered in her ear, "I beg you to forgive me, my love. Are you still mad at me?"

"A little. But I love you so ardently that I have already forgiven you everything." Smiling, she climbed on top of him and her hand reached between his legs, her eyes shining with passion.

* * *

It had been six days since Kamolea had landed at Maniha Komo. The rumors about his return had spread like wildfire throughout the village, and day after day, the crowd that gathered to see him grew bigger.

He preached ceaselessly, trying to convince the men to accept his new God, supporting his arguments with incredible stories from his life of adventures.

Lately, a score of women had also turned up, most of them Illima's friends from her childhood. She had summoned them, sending specific instructions through Ahaki, so they would bring as many boars' pelts as they could carry. As they hugged and kissed Illima, telling her about everything that had happened over the years, Alfonso gazed at them wistfully, delighted to see such an abundance of females assembled in one place.

"Hey, curly boy, don't forget you promised me three women if I came with you," he smirked at Kamolea. "Can I claim those two over there that smile so sweetly at me?"

"Shut up, you skinny fool." Kamolea cast a furtive look around. "Luckily, they don't speak a word of Spanish. How am I supposed to teach them Christian values if I allow you to have three women? Besides, I don't understand why on Earth you need more than one? They are all trouble, these wild lassies."

"They ought to be fiery as hell when they screw. Are they?" Alfonso swallowed and adjusted his trousers, his eyes gleaming lustfully.

"Well, they are hot-tempered almost all the time," shrugged Kamolea. "Believe me, Alfie, they will make your life a living hell with their grudges and brawls. When I was a little boy, there was a chieftain named Arataki, who had so many wives and mistresses that finally, one of them killed him out of jealousy. Such a shame, a great chief and brave warrior like him being murdered by a woman." He chuckled, watching Alfonso mockingly. "Do you want your life to be as tough as poor Arataki's?"

"What about this ladies' man?" Ahaki jumped in, recognizing the name of his former chieftain.

"Oh, I'm just telling stories about the good old days," smiled Kamolea. "So, how are things going, Wise Ahaki?"

"I just got the news that Kamani will be back tomorrow at about noon," Ahaki said and sighed, "I wished we had a bit more time."

"Is everything turning out according to our plan?" Kamolea asked nervously.

"I think so," Ahaki said. "The most important part is done: the stage is set, both fences are erected, and now, we are digging the trenches. After we finish, all that will remain is to disguise the trap, so we should be ready by tomorrow. What about you?"

Kamolea grinned.

"Come and see for yourself the surprises we've prepared," he said.

They entered the hollow. Inside was gloomy as usual, but besides the familiar smell of peat and rotten bark, Ahaki perceived an unknown odor—the sharp scent of powder.

They waited a bit for their eyes to adjust. Ahaki glanced curiously at the far corner of the nook, where Kedia rocked her body back and forth, humming something under her breath. During their return through the jungle, she had howled like a wounded animal, clawing at Kamolea's neck and shoulders, and almost suffocating him. Her eyes, accustomed to the cave's darkness for so many years, ached terribly, as though they were being stabbed by thousands of needles flying to earth from the rising sun. She had pressed her face down against Kamolea's back, whimpering and moaning, but nothing helped to ease the pain. Strangely enough, Illima, who had also spent a good portion of her life in the cave, did not have the same problem.

"I'm so much younger than she is," she shrugged when Kamolea asked her how she felt. "Maybe it's normal that her eyes have failed her."

When they had reached the Great Hollow Tree, Kedia had jumped from Kamolea's back, rushed inside to the darkest corner, and stayed there until nightfall.

Kamolea led Ahaki to the left, where Alfonso crouched before a bunch of coconuts. Nearby, over a straw mat, were scattered pellets, bullets, small pebbles, and several iron nails left from the weapon's chest.

"How many do we have, Alfi?" Kamolea asked.

"I've just finished the sixth," replied Alfonso proudly.

"Show Ahaki how you make it," said Kamolea.

"With pleasure. First, I pierce a hole in it, paying attention not to crack it," Alfonso took one coconut from the pile, laid the blade of his knife on the brown mossy shell, and hit the hilt with a stone. He repeated the process several times until he had made a gap large enough to thrust his two fingers through. He emptied the liquid into an already half-full bucket and said,

"Then, I leave the coco in the sun to dry completely, and when it's ready, I put a few pellets, bullets, and nails inside, then add the powder," he waved at the powder keg in the corner. "Finally, I attach this resin fuse to the hole and seal it with this sticky substance." He lifted another coconut and handed it to Ahaki. It looked like an ordinary one, only three times heavier, and from the middle of its shell, a short, thick thread protruded.

"I don't understand," Ahaki said. "What's the point of doing this?"

Kamolea translated for Alfonso.

Alfonso grinned.

"Tell him it's your welcome celebration fireworks," he said and burst out laughing.

Kamolea did not smile. The coconut bombs were Benito's invention, and they had argued a good part of the night about it.

"I don't want any more blood to be shed," he had insisted.

"You are completely disconnected from reality!" Benito snapped angrily. "You need to show them that your god is stronger than theirs and that He has given you a supernatural power. Only then will they believe and obey you. There will be a fight, no doubt about it, and if we fail to put Ahaki as a chieftain, we'll be slaughtered like Easter lambs."

"I don't see any other way either," Kamolea sighed.

"So, you agree then? That's my boy!" Benito had cried and slapped him on the back. "War is war, and when it comes down to it, you have no choice. Besides, the Bible says: *'Any tree that fails to produce good fruit is cut down and thrown into a fire,'* so it's better to cut down a few crooked trees instead of burning the entire forest."

"What do you mean?" Kamolea asked.

"Well, Kedia and Illima confirmed your assertion about the disaster that would befall your tribe," said Benito. "The time has come to separate the wheat from the chaff, my friend. If you spare the cruel chieftain and his supporters, you condemn your entire people to annihilation, and that will be the end of it, so think twice and stop complaining."

Kamolea tried hard to shake his nagging doubts and turned to Ahaki.

"Let's go and see Benito. Meanwhile, I'll explain to you how these bombs work," he said.

They found Benito near the forest, whittling a large funnel-shaped object.

"What's this for?" Ahaki asked.

Instead of replying, Kamolea took the funnel from Benito's hands, placed the thinner part to his lips, and called out,

"Men and women of Tipihao tribe."

His mighty voice echoed around the clearing, amplified tens of times. A flock of birds rose from the woods, and every single person turned to look at him.

"But this is amazing!" cried Ahaki enthusiastically. "I wondered how you captured the attention of so many people at *Kepolo's Belt*. How do you know such magic tricks?"

"It's him who knows everything." Kamolea pointed at Benito. "Look what else he has done."

He lifted several laths attached together with ropes, about two handspans long and three wide.

"This will be my armor," he explained, putting them against his breast and handing him the ends. Ahaki passed them over Kamolea's shoulders and tightened them up behind his back, looking critically at the wooden plates.

"You mean you'll wear this for protection?" he asked, mildly surprised.

"Absolutely! I'll hide it under the garment that Illima is about to prepare for me," Kamolea confirmed.

"I don't think it'll be very useful," Ahaki shook his head doubtfully. "It could work against arrows and knives, but it won't save you from a spear."

"Well, as you know, I have a place to hide from their lances," Kamolea said, smiling.

Ahaki nodded.

"Now we have an important job to attend to, Kamolea," he said as they walked away from Benito. "I want you to reassure my men the same way you convinced me. Tell them once again that your powerful God wants you to make me a chieftain, and you will be my shaman."

"Do you believe in this yourself, Wise Ahaki?" Kamolea asked, eyeing him closely. "Are you ready to follow me through fire and water so we can together change the mentality of our tribe?"

"I do! I've already pledged allegiance to you, and for me, there's no way back," said Ahaki, "but it's crucial now that we persuade the other warriors to believe you without hesitation, to such a point that they would be ready to die for you. Can you do that?"

"You bet!" Kamolea smiled, satisfied. "Gather them and watch me! My story, full of miracles, speaks for itself."

* * *

The next day, the entire village was buzzing like a beehive. The news that Kedia's prophecy was about to be fulfilled, and the man covered with scars had brought powerful foreigners, capable of incredible things, had made its way through the inhabitants. Old and young people alike had gathered in groups to passionately discuss the revelation, gesturing and speaking loudly. The women observed their husbands and sons from a distance with worried faces, their fine female intuition telling them that nothing good would come from such excitement.

Even the children were agitated and unruly. They ran back and forth, shouting about the curly-haired shaman and sneaking behind the gatherings, trying to overhear what the talk was about.

Inside Ahaki's hut, four men sat in a semicircle, their heads close together.

"So, is everything clear?" Ahaki whispered nervously. "Let's go over it one more time. Each one of you will draw a bead with Kamolea's fire sticks: Anuro aims at Kamani, Keoko at Scuro, and Hakahi at Keko. You lay still and wait for my signal to shoot them, right? Anuro, don't miss Kamani; as long as he lives, the others will never give up, and we will have no chance to win."

"I've been practicing a lot with the firestick, so I'm pretty confident I'll get him," said Anuro.

Ahaki raised his hand abruptly, and everybody listened intently. The big copper gong resounded four times in quick succession, and after a brief interval, it repeated twice more. When it started for a third time, they all jumped to their feet—three lots of four strokes meant the troops were returning from a raid.

"And so it begins," said Ahaki, a tinge of definitiveness in his voice. They looked at each other and nodded simultaneously.

"Stick to the plan!" barked Ahaki, and they rushed outside.

* * *

Under the Great Hollow Tree, Kamolea thoughtfully gnawed on a roasted loggerhead turtle flipper. Illima, Alfonso, and Benito sat in a circle next to him, already done with their lunch. Silent and gloomy, everyone had sunk into their own mirthless thoughts. Kedia nonchalantly snored several yards away from them.

"I feel like a man, convicted to death, who has just eaten his last meal," Alfonso muttered.

"So do I," echoed Benito.

"If we are destined to die, so be it," sighed Kamolea, "but the people deserve to hear what I have to say and choose with their hearts. Simply killing Kamani and his closest followers, and then replacing them with Ahaki and his men, is not a solution. It's nothing more than a simple takeover followed by a struggle for power. It will only lead to turbulence and more bloodshed, and we did not come for that."

"I can't believe you are so delusional, Kami," sighed Benito. "Have not you already understood that nobody gives a shit about God and His rules, neither on this cannibal island, nor in civilized Panama or the Great Spanish empire. No one will listen to you, lad. People are interested in power, wealth, and sex, and if you don't offer them those things, we'll all end up roasted on a spit."

Kamolea signed to him to keep silent.

"Somebody's coming," he whispered. Benito and Alfonso reached for their blunderbusses. Kamolea cupped his hands around his mouth and let out three parrot screeches. Almost immediately, two similar squeals came in response, and they all relaxed and exited into the clearing. After a moment, Anuro emerged, followed by seven other men.

"They're back," he said, still panting.

"Who?" Kamolea asked, although he knew the answer.

"Kamani, the elders, and the army," Anuro replied. "I brought Ahaki's trusted men to protect you. Give them the thunder sticks and let them keep you safe."

Kamolea looked at them inquisitively.

"Are they reliable? Wait, this one looks familiar. Isn't he…"?

"This is Fetu, the fatty. Remember him?" Anuro said, his facial muscles twitching as he tried to keep a straight face.

"Of course I do! How are you doing, Fetu? I'm glad you made it through your warrior's proof." Kamolea tapped him on the shoulder.

"I did," Fetu said and added modestly, "with a lot of luck."

"Should I trust you to protect me?" asked Kamolea mockingly.

"I swear I will. Besides, I have no choice—Kamani loathes my guts and is looking for an excuse to kill me. He would be surprised to know that I'm not as much of a coward as he thinks …"

"What's going on?" asked Alfonso anxiously.

"They're coming," said Kamolea. "Here are the men who will protect us. Keep two muskets for Benito and yourself and give all other available arms to Anuro."

While Benito and Alfonso distributed the weapons, Kamolea kissed Illima's worried face and whispered, "Let's go, my heart. The nightmare has begun."

* * *

Amid cheers and spears raised in hearty welcome, the warriors set foot on the shore, beached their canoes, and threw out the captives in the middle of the sandy strand, as they had done for thousands of years. As they arranged the prisoners in rows and slipped wooden loops over their necks, Ahaki stepped forward to meet Kamani.

The chieftain nicknamed "the Giant Death" inspired sheer dread. Incredibly strong, his shaved oily skull was visible amongst the crowd of men, a good handspan above the others. His nostrils and ears were decorated with small bones of his killed enemies, and his entire body was covered with scars and tattoos. A composition of the Sacred Tree, depicted with its dangling corpses and *circling burkans,* outlined his mighty chest, where a necklace made of human teeth lay, alternating with the phalanges of several fingers. The drawing of Rakapi was surrounded by the usual smaller tattoos representing the symbols of death—skulls, skeletons, and scenes of fights and killings. They crept all over the front part of his torso, arms, and legs. His back was covered with an explicit scene of a man entangled between two women.

He put his face as closely as possible to Ahaki's and growled,

"What's going on here, dunce? What's the fuss and what are these strange looks I'm getting? Speak up! You've been in charge here."

"Bad news, Chieftain." Ahaki bowed his head in submission. "While you were away, Kedia's prophesy started to be fulfilled. A mighty scar-faced man reached Maniha Komo and is now threatening to kill everybody who dares stand in his way. Moreover, he has brought some pale foreigners and fiery arms that can kill you from a considerable distance."

"Fucking moron!" Kamani bellowed. "How did you allow this to happen? You were supposed to protect our homeland and slaughter anyone who dares approach!"

"I know, but what could I have done?" mumbled Ahaki, making a rueful face. "It's impossible to kill this terrible intruder. We've tried everything, but the arrows and spears bounce off him, and nobody can get near him to slit his throat. A dark magic protects him, although he maintains that an alien god made him invincible. He is also claiming the position of shaman and declaring that everyone, even you, must bow before him."

"Of course he is. I can't wait to see that happen," said Kamani with a sneer, but there was some uneasiness in his voice. "Where is he now?"

"He is waiting for you in Kepolo's Belt," said Ahaki. "According to him, it's the perfect place to meet, as he wants to challenge your authority before Rakapi."

No sooner had he said these words, the copper gong started echoing again. Everybody fell silent and listened. Five bangs, then a pause, then another five. There was no doubt—it was the signal for a general meeting and a sacrifice before the Sacred Tree.

"Nobody may summon the tribe without my permission," Kamani mumbled, his Adam's apple jumping as he swallowed nervously.

"It's him," Ahaki said. "The snake's son is smooth-tongued and has lured some of our people onto his side. Perhaps it is one of them hitting the gong."

"These traitors will all be disemboweled and sacrificed to Kepolo! Let's go and finish him off!" roared Kamani and turned to the throng.

"You heard the signal!" he yelled. "Take the captives and follow me! We'll pay our tribute to Almighty Kepolo!"

* * *

In the meantime, Kamolea and his companions descended from the hill and set off for the Kepolo's Belt. Everyone but Kedia, who was sitting in a deep basket on Alfonso's back, was armed to the teeth; even Illima had a crossbow slung across her shoulders and a dagger at her thigh. Two pistols stuck out from Kamolea's waist, and the long shaft of the Ax of Love rested on his shoulder, its razor-sharp blade glinting in the scattered sunshine. Some of the warriors that brought up the rear were carrying bulky baskets full of coconut bombs, as well as Kamolea's outfit and stilts.

Anuro, who was the first to set foot in the clearing of Kepolo's Belt, turned quickly, and curiously squinted at the pale foreigners as they approached behind him. The reaction to the devastating effect that Rakapi exerted on every newcomer was always worth seeing, and this time was no different.

Benito fell to his knees, retching several times until the roasted turtle emerged as a yellowish-brown sludge. Alfonso stood frozen to the spot, his saucer eyes twice their normal size, unable to take even a single step towards the spreading horror in front of him. Kedia, upright in the basket, was muttering something to herself, waving her hands. Kamolea had put the heavy ax on the ground and was leaning on its shaft. A swarm of appalling childhood memories overwhelmed him, and his heart sank at the view of the dangling corpses and the awful stench of carrion that wafted in the air.

Nothing has changed, he thought, gazing at the giant tree, whose boughs, studded with corpses, spread out tens of yards across the vast clearing. The incessant flock of *burkans* circled the crown, letting out shrill, morbid screeches. The tree was so dreadful and imposing that the old desire to kneel before it seized Kamolea anew. This time, however, he only shook his head in disgust.

It's only a simple tree, he thought. Illima pressed her body to his and squeezed his hand.

"Welcome home, my heart. Did you find the answer to the question you asked me once: 'What makes people worship this gruesome thing?'" she whispered.

A faint smile ran across Kamolea's lips.

"I did, but you'd never believe it," he said. "It's a small ugly creature that dwells inside us. The old saint called it '*The Runt*.' Imagine, this tiny, grotesque thing is responsible for all the atrocity and perversion that happens inside the human mind."

"It sounds like a child's tale to me. Why is nobody aware of it? Kedia has never mentioned anything like it. And even if it's true, why would it make us do such deeds?" Illima asked.

"Oh, as far as I understand from all my training, this is its way of nourishing itself," shrugged Kamolea. "But there was something else that I never got. The old man who trained me called it '*The age-old game for the battle of the immortal part of us*.' They call it '*alma*'[84] on their language. The Evil One mentioned it too. It seems that we are a part of a fucking twisted game, my love, caught between a shark and a swordfish, and no matter what choice we make, we'll always lose and get hurt. Only after we die will we be judged and sent to different

---

84 Soul.

places, and believe me, it will matter then which deity you chose to worship during your earthly life. Are you all right, Benito? Don't faint, man. You look white as a sheet."

"I've never imagined such terror before," Benito uttered. "We have to put an end to all this, even if we are tortured and killed in the process. In the beginning, I was reluctant to come with you, but now I'm glad I did. It is the highest honor to die for such a noble cause, fighting against an evil like this."

"Oh, we'll die for sure, no doubt," Alfonso croaked. He licked his cracked lips and wiped his bedewed face. "I had a glimmer of hope before we arrived here, though. But one look at these swinging corpses and the gigantic crows that peck at them, and I already know what bright future awaits us."

"Well, I can't believe that the Gracious God brought us here only to feed the cannibals," Benito muttered. "But I have to admit that it will be a miracle if we survive tonight."

"Come, my hearties!" Kamolea called out. "We're all gonna die one day, so what's the fuss? Enough whining for now! We have a show to put on, so let's set the stage."

They all walked toward Rakapi. Before the giant tree and the nearby stone altar rose a large wooden platform, protected by two walls of sharp-pointed spikes in a semicircle, the first set of which were arranged at a 45-degree angle. In contrast, the second one, called *"the stockade,"* comprised sharpened vertical stakes that formed a smaller semi-arc, both extremities of which reached Rakapi's mighty trunk, thus making the tree a part of the fortification. Between the two walls, a trench had been dug about twice as deep as the height of a man, concealed by thin branches, turf, and leaves. The bottom of the pit was covered with sharp rocks, spears, and arrows, all stuck into the ground with their points up. Ahaki, who had composed the whole setup himself, was particularly proud of the improvised moat.

The party passed through a narrow opening to the left of the inclined snarling spikes, then crossed the wooden gangway that spanned the ditch. Finally, they climbed a rope ladder hanging from the second fence and stepped onto the log platform. Adjacent to the stage, tall, and imposing, the stockade hid them entirely and offered perfect protection against spears and arrows.

"Excellent!" Kamolea exclaimed. "Anuro, you take up position over there." He pointed at the left extremity of the stage, where several narrow loopholes were cut in the upper part of the stakes. "Benito, Alfonso, go to the other side! Alfonso, on my mark, you bring me Kedia, and I'll lift her so everybody can see her. Benito, you take care of the coconut bombs. Pile them over here, near to the fence."

"Where should we set the mortar with the fire?" asked Anuro.

"Let me think for a moment." Kamolea looked around. "The fire must be visible from afar and adjusted to my height, meaning it should stick about a yard above the poles."

"We need some support at this level," Anuro said. "Nobody has thought about that."

"I'll see to the stand," said Fetu. "I have something in mind." From his waist, he detached the small boarding ax he had taken for a weapon and rushed toward the jungle.

"All right! All set? My thunder funnel is here… Where are the stilts?" Kamolea was getting anxious with every word he shouted.

"Here there are." Hakahi stepped up and handed him a pair of long poles.

Kamolea took them and cried,

"Go and hit the gong, Anuro! Let the show begin!"

Anuro ran toward the village. Kamolea met Illima's tender stare.

"Are you ready, my glittery boy?" she said with a sad smile, touching one of the many diamonds glued to his cheek.

"Let's do it, my love! Bring me the armor and my festive garment!" he said with firm determination.

* * *

The late afternoon sun had cast elongated shades upon Kepolo's Belt when the first Tipihaos emerged. From the elevated platform, perched atop his stilts, Kamolea watched the crowd overflowing into the clearing like a turbulent sea.

He shuddered at his memory of a similar scene from years ago when the entire village had gathered to sacrifice him to Kepolo.

Now it's not so different, he thought bitterly, casting a glance around. Benito, Alfonso, Anuro, Keoko, and Hakahi had taken their positions at the two extremities of the fortification. The muzzles of their muskets poked through the narrow slots and were aimed at the crowd. Kedia was hidden below the erected platform. Illima was leaning against the stockade near him, holding her crossbow at the ready. Three of Kamolea's guards were on the stage, and the others crouched along the fence below, clutching pistols, blunderbusses, cutlasses, axes, and daggers.

He glanced at the stone mortar, filled with tinder, tarred twigs, and a few thicker sticks. It lay on a support made of two long vertical poles attached to the enclosure and two shorter ones put across them.

Everything was in place.

Kamolea directed his attention to the mass of men and women below. In a few minutes, the entire place had blackened with people and become so crammed that those who were packed in the middle could not move at all. The first row had stopped just before the pointed sticks and were so close that he could discern the expressions on their stunned faces. It seemed that nobody realized the constant pressure exerted by the pushing crowd behind, as every single stare was devouring Kamolea with dismay.

I bet they've never seen such a strange creature, he smiled inwardly.

The odd attire—a furry dress, made of many wild boars' pelts, stitched together in an immense cloth—was Illima's invention, made with the help of all her female friends, who had sewed it for three days in a row. It was so hot inside it that Kamolea was soaked with sweat and in constant danger of fainting. But it was worth the suffering, as the costume was so spectacular that he resembled an alien giant from a fantasy world, more than he did a human being. As the garment almost reached the ground, concealing his stilts, nobody was able to fathom how on earth he soared so high above the others. In addition, the wooden armor he had put on underneath his shirt made his shoulders impossibly broad. But the icing on the cake was his wide-brimmed furry hat, two handspans in height and three times larger in circumference than his head. It hid his curly hair and shadowed his glowing face, the most incredible invention in the entire masquerade.

It was Kedia who had proposed to paint Kamolea's visage with phosphorescent mushrooms.

"Your ghost-like countenance will glow green and provoke fear," she explained in her sing-song manner, and everybody had laughed their head off when they heard the plan. Then, Benito

had suggested gluing the precious stones from Bobo's treasure to his face, and the ensemble was complete.

The twilight was falling quickly. Kamolea noticed Ahaki cleaving his way through the multitude toward the front, accompanied by five other men. The first of them looked particularly terrifying, his face frozen in a grimace of a wild fury. There was no time to waste. Kamolea grabbed the large wooden funnel, attached to his waist, and cried,

"Men and women, Tipihaos!" His echoing voice fit his giant appearance, the sound reverberating so strongly that even the lookouts a mile away could hear it. "There are certain things written in the stars that we cannot change, nor can we disobey them. Many years ago, a man descended from the heavens and forbade me to kill people and worship Kepolo.

As a consequence, you cast me out from Maniha Komo in a small boat and left me at the mercy of elements. But here I am today, before your eyes, and the prophecy that I would come back and bring you a new God and a new beginning is happening right now! The elements were merciful to me, and instead of killing me, my destiny took me to a new, fascinating world. There, the heavenly man taught me wisdom and showed me the true God, the world's Creator, the one that everybody calls the God of Goodness and Justice.

"Today, I came back to convey to you the knowledge I gained during my journey. I have brought two aliens with me, men who belong to great people, the founders of amazing culture. They build ships as big as small hills; their temples, made of stone and wood, rise to the sky; and their large dwellings are of incomparable beauty. This was all possible because of their God, who bestowed upon them incredible abilities. The men who came with me can teach us their way of doing things, and armed with their knowledge, our uprising will know no end."

Kamolea stopped for a second. The multitude was so silent that you could have heard a pin drop. Even the familiar sounds of the jungle had fallen quiet, as though nature also wanted to hear what he had to say. It was almost dark now, and the nearly full moon was rising slowly from the east.

"Brothers and sisters, Tipihaos," Kamolea's voice resounded again, "I beg you today to accept me back as a member of your tribe and make me your new shaman and spiritual leader. Let me show you the true God, one far mightier than Kepolo, and let me convey His will to you. The new God commands that Kamani step down as a chieftain! If he refuses, I am ready to meet him in fair combat and to introduce him to my mighty weapon!" He bent down and took up the Ax of Love, which was attached to the stakes. The moment he raised it, the fire in the mortar flared up. Kamolea turned, surprised, but he saw nobody near the large stone vessel.

"Did you see the flames descending from the heavens?" he cried out, inspired. "This was a sign for you to believe my words. Bring your torches to me, and may the fire, falling from the sky, be a covenant between the new God and you!"

He motioned to Illima, who handed him a torch, fastened to a long pole. He lit it from the mortar and raised it towards the crowd, reaching beyond the first fence. The glare of the dancing flames from the mortar reflected off the precious stones, making his countenance glitter and his eyes sparkle and flash. He waited for a moment, clutching the pole in his outstretched hand, the torch burning in front of the throng. Nobody moved.

No one wants your heavenly fire, fool. The runt's cackle, which Kamolea had not heard since his encounter with the Evil One, echoed in his mind.

"The God I bring to you rules the life of every single creature," Kamolea continued, pulling the torch back, and placing it beside the mortar. "He will bring us peace and serenity, and will put an end to all these cruel wars, killings, abductions, and rapes. There will be no more slavery and oppression; instead, harmony and love will reign in Maniha Komo and all over the Turtle Archipelago. Everybody will be treated fairly, and the women, the best part of us, our precious flowers who bear our children and bring beauty and harmony to our ugly word, will have their place in the tribe's political life, as it was in Alina's time."

A wave of an indistinct murmur passed through the packed mass.

"Kamani, I await your response," declared Kamolea. "Accept me or die!"

The chieftain, surrounded by the elders, was watching from the first row. He hesitated, finding himself in a tight spot. Nobody could have labeled him a coward, but he wasn't thrilled to meet this towering creature with a glowing, sparkling face that spoke in such a booming voice, claiming he had the support of a mighty God. Moreover, the monstrous ax that he was waving had definitely won his respect, as it knew no equal in the whole arsenal of Tipihao's weapons. Even with his sophisticated mace and double-edged spear, Kamani strongly doubted his chance against this huge gleaming blade.

But the chief knew he had no choice but to confront the weird man if he wanted to keep the respect of his warriors. The crowd hushed, waiting for his response. He opened his mouth, but Hamaki, one of the few surviving members of the Council from Kamolea's trial, grabbed his hand and shouted,

"The traitor was cast out and banned from setting foot ever on our land. He has no place here and no right to challenge any warrior of our tribe in fair combat. Kill him and hang his stinking carcass on Rakapi as a sacrifice to our great God, Almighty Kepolo, and as an example to all betrayers!"

Kamani raised his spear and, with a mighty heave, threw it at Kamolea. Then, he hurled himself against the fence, roaring,

"Charge! Bring him down!"

The next moment, a rain of pikes and arrows whizzed all around. When the chieftain had flung his lance, Kamolea knew he would not miss. The weapon's trajectory pointed straight at him, and he hoped that the fur and his armor would at least soften the blow. But at the last second, it had deviated, and instead of hitting him, the spear had flown an inch past his right ear. Several arrows thudded against him, stabbing him in the wooden plates, and another spear hit him near the clavicle, but the impact was not particularly strong, and he was able to keep his balance.

Kamolea's men did not delay in their reply. All the muskets went off as one, and a red rose bloomed on Kamani's forehead. Keko, too, staggered and fell, and Hamaki grabbed his chest and rolled over in the dirt. Next to him, Scuro clutched his stomach and collapsed, his face twisted in pain. The other attackers stopped momentarily, dumbfounded by the scene, but in the heat of the assault, they recovered within a few seconds and proceeded.

A dozen warriors were already climbing the first barrier of inclined stakes while Kamolea's bodyguards put their heads above the fence and emptied their pistols and blunderbusses into the crowd. Several men dropped, shouting in pain, but a black wave of people submerged the first fortification in an overwhelming attack. Most of them plunged straight into the ditch, and within minutes, the trenches had filled with so many dead bodies that the trap became shallow, and the advancing men simply stomped over their dead fellows and continued to the stockade.

Inside the second wall, it was sheer bedlam. The defenders waiting by the loopholes fervently charged their muskets, pistols, and guns and emptied them on the attackers, but with minimal efficiency. Most of Kamolea's guards were engaged in fierce duels with their tribesmen, who had already topped the pointed stakes and were trying to jump over on the stage.

"The bombs!" Benito called out. "Kami, pass us the torch!"

Kamolea dropped the blazing firebrand and Anuro took it, lighting several slow matches before every available hand grabbed a coconut and threw it as far as he could.

The blinding glare of the first two bombs lit up the darkness in a mighty explosion, leaving a carpet of injured and dead. Screams of horror and pain filled the air, and all the assailants darted back, shrieking, "*Barkani! Barkani!*" [85]

Several other coconuts blasted in swift succession, setting the first protective wall ablaze. It was then that everything went wrong. Suddenly, Fetu let out a gurgling sound and fell down on the outer side of the stockade, a spear sticking out of his throat. But in his hand lay a bomb with a burning fuse.

"Watch out! Mind the explosion!" cried Kamolea and took two steps on his stilts towards the edge of the scene, as everyone near the fence hurled forward in the opposite direction. The next second, a powerful detonation shattered the defensive wall, which burst into flames along with the stage and lit up the whole clearing.

---

85 *Black magic* (in the Maniha Komo dialect).

Swept out by the shock wave, Kamolea rolled over on the grass, his stilts flying aside. He jumped on his feet, threw off his hat, and disentangled himself from the garment. Then he climbed quickly Rakapi and cast a glance from above.

The screaming sea of men and women are retreating towards the jungle, pushing and shoving in total panic and leaving scattered bodies trampled underfoot. Between the two protective walls, the entire area was crammed with corpses.

"How many people must die tonight?" Kamolea shouted angrily. He grabbed the funnel, still attached to his waist, brought it to his lips, and hollered,

"Tribesmen Tipihaos! Calm yourselves! Come here and listen to me! There will be no further killing and shooting. Kamani is dead, as well as most of those who dared to attack me.

"Brothers and sisters, listen to me! You cannot put out the inextinguishable. You couldn't kill me when I was a boy; how do suppose you will kill me now, as a grown man? The force that protects me is beyond your comprehension. The great new God that I have brought with me makes me invincible! *He* appointed Ahaki as a new chieftain and me as your shaman. Accept *His* choice and bow your heads in submission!"

The multitude had stopped running and now began returning timidly.

"Men and women, Tipihaos!" Kamolea roared. "God will speak to you through the mouth of His prophetess."

He beckoned Kedia, who had retreated with Illima near the Rakapi's gigantic trunk, and Alfonso lifted her to one of Rakapi's lower boughs. Despite her age, she was agile as a monkey and climbed with ease. As the crowd saw her, they let out a simultaneous gasp. Her tiny figure and long, wavy white hair gave her the ghost-like appearance of someone who had just risen from the grave. Kamolea handed her the blowhorn and she croaked,

"On your knees, non-believers!" The Tipihao warriors, famous for their refusal to bend to their foes, knelt as one. In a daze, they heard Kedia scream,

"For thousands of full moons, I waited for this day,
The scar-faced man to save us with a shining ax in hand,
The day when everybody must obey his command,
And if you don't comply, look what will be your end!"

The moment she finished speaking, the world stopped turning and the gate of eternity opened. Everyone's minds froze and their souls flew out of their bodies as though they had instantly died. They floated above Maniha Komo, transfixed by a terrible vision. It was late morning in bright daylight, close to noon. Suddenly, the earth rocked and a colossal billow of water rose from the bottom of the sea. It started slowly, taking its time, but growing bigger and bigger. When it approached Maniha Komo, the surge turned into a dark-green mountain of water, and the island looked like a tiny dot against its enormity. As it reached its peak, the monstrous mass lingered for a split second, as though it was enjoying the view for the last time, then collapsed over the island, sweeping away the entire forest. The trees flew like toothpicks, landing and smashing everything in their way, and the village disappeared, replaced by floating debris and hundreds of dead bodies. Under the inrush of the sea, the Sacred Tree crashed down, cracking and splitting, its gigantic roots leaving a deep crater in the earth, which immediately filled up with water, forming a small lake. Desperate cries filled the air as the island was sucked into a monstrous funnel and slowly sank under the water. Then, the abyss closed, and the only thing that remained was the shimmering blue-green ocean, colored with the tempestuous white foam of the waves' crests.

The Tipihaos' souls remained floating above the place their island had been, when they heard a voice from above them, thundering,

"I am the God of Good and Justice. Accept me, and this will never happen. Obey Kamolea and listen to him, as he is my beloved."

Then, in the blink of an eye, everybody was in the clearing again, dizzy and frightened, as if they had just awakened from a terrible nightmare. The stage came crashing down, consumed by the flames, and through the burning logs, everyone could see Kamolea, his pale friends, and the tribesmen-traitors who had joined them, gathered by Rakapi's trunk. The old witch had disappeared. While the Tipihaos were still asking themselves if it was a dream or reality, Kamolea's voice resounded from above.

"My dear friends! For thousands of years, our ancestors worshipped a simple tree, thinking that it was a god. They glorified a non-existent deity and praised Evil instead of Good. Since time immemorial, every generation has been introduced into the world with this deception, and the vicious circle never knew an end. But this is over now! I have brought you new hope and a new beginning. We'll start a brand-new life and never shed innocent blood again. We will never steal, rape, abduct, or kill our neighbors. Instead, we'll lead the lives of peaceful hunters, respected for their wisdom and prosperity all around the Turtle Archipelago. This new horizon will begin with the destruction of the cursed temple of Evil that we call Rakapi. Now, I will fulfill the prophecy and show you how delusional we all were. Watch me!"

He climbed down, took the ax from the ground and stepped toward the immense trunk. A dead silence reigned over the crowd. They watched him, submissive and still dizzy from the collective vision, but then, Kamolea heard a wild cry and spun to see a spear flying straight at him. In a heartbeat, Alfonso, who was standing near him, lunged forward as though pushed by an invisible force and sheltered his friend with his body. The spear plunged into his chest and emerged from the other side, the sound of crushing bones echoing in the air. Alfonso screamed and fell, his eyes, filled with pain, staring at the sky. Kamolea and Benito dashed forward and knelt beside him. Benito lifted his head and rested it on his thigh, and Kamolea grabbed his hand. He looked up and saw several men, who had detached themselves from the multitude, running towards them.

It's over, he thought.

But before he could fully accept his fate, a blinding flash ripped through the dark sky and hit Alfonso's killer in motion. The effect of the lightning piercing his head and scorching his body was so spectacular that the crowd let out a collective gasp. The men who had been running with him, stopped dead in their tracks and threw themselves on the ground.

Another glaring bolt hit one of Rakapi's spreading boughs, which burst into flames and came crashing down, landing a few yards from Kamolea and his friends. A flock of *burkans* flew out of the branches, screeching. The earth shook and split, forming a large furrow between the still burning fortification and the crowd, swallowing the first several rows of spectators in its womb amid screams and cries.

Kamolea had been watching the whole scene in awe, but Alfonso squeezed his hand, and he redirected his attention to his dying friend.

"I'm so sorry, Alfi," he sobbed.

Alfonso shifted his eyes from heaven to him and attempted a painful smile.

"Don't be," he whispered through the blood gushing out from his mouth. "I'm glad it ends this way. The debt to people I've killed… is paid."

His eyes rolled back, and he went limp. Kamolea felt chilling anger crawling inside his body. He stood up, lifted his heavy ax, and approached Rakapi's trunk. Amid the flames that consumed the bough, he raised the ax above his head. The steel gleamed in the moonlight, reflecting the fire, and the ancient runes glowed, outlining themselves against the blade. Kamolea heard a whisper, similar to a rippling brook, and a whiff of air caressed his face. At its touch, inhuman force filled his body. He took a deep breath, and with a mighty swing, he drove the ax into Rakapi's trunk. The tree shuddered, and the crowd let out a stifled sigh. An impaled head fell and rolled next to Kamolea's feet. He drew the ax, hit again, and the hollow thud echoed in the night. Anuro and Benito approached and raised their axes in synch with Kamolea's third swing. They buried them deep into Rakapi's flesh and continued to hew it with rhythmic movements. They knew it would take weeks, or even months until they felled the immense, age-old tree, but the foundations had been laid. A new era had dawned upon Maniha Komo, and a new life awaited the people of the Tipihao tribe.

EPILOGUE

—1712 AD, MANIHA KOMO

"**S**top crying, my love. You won't bring her back," Kamolea said. Illima wiped her eyes.

"It's easy for you to say that," she sniffed. "I spent almost my entire conscious life with her. She was so wise and kind, even if she was as crazy as *Manuka Lani* during nesting."

They were in the church, which had been erected several years before at the entrance to the village. It was an ordinary, log house with a small belfry on top where, instead of a bell, they had placed the old Snake's Gong. Benito had erected the building facing east and divided it inside into three separate naves, setting a few rows of pews in the central area. The altar was simple—a large table on a slightly elevated platform, with a massive wooden cross nailed on the wall behind it.

Kedia's remains rested in a coffin before the altar. The small church was crowded, as many people had gathered to take their final leave of the ancient Sybil. Benito had come with his young wife and their two children, and Anuro was present with his spouse and three-year-old son.

"I will be eternally in her debt for saving my boy's life," Anuro said.

"Me too, for healing my sweet girl," Benito added.

"Not to mention how many lives she saved with her herbs after I liberated her," Kamolea said. "How stupid the Tipihaos were to waste her talent, keeping her in that cave for so many years. She could have treated countless people during that time."

"I'm very grateful that she healed your scars, though," Illima said, looking lovingly at him. "After she taught me how to prepare this special balm, they have magically disappeared, and you are now the gorgeous man in the entire world."

"I bet I am!" Kamolea chuckled. "But I still pity Kedia for spending her life in that stinking hole. Her last request was that we bury her on the beach. She showed me the place several days ago when she informed me that her end was coming."

"And where was that?" asked Anuro.

"On the south shore, just on the boundary between the sandy strip and the beginning of the jungle."

"Why did she insist on being buried there?" exclaimed Anuro, surprised.

"For two reasons. First, she wanted to face the boundless ocean, and second, she wished to be the first one to welcome the men, who will arrive soon in ships."

"I hope she was right," said Benito. "We badly need some goods from civilization, especially powder and slugs, clothes, but also a bible, a crucifix, and candles for the temple."

"Well, her predictions were usually exact," Kamolea said. "She foretold that with Illima, I would have three boys and two girls, and so far, we have two boys and a girl, so I'm confident she got it right. The problem is that her time frame was pretty ambiguous, so the sailors could come tomorrow or in ten years, and meanwhile, we have to continue preaching the way we do."

"There's a lot of mockery about your preaching and the new God in the village," said Anuro, grinning widely. "Five years on, and you still haven't convinced them to turn the other cheek or love their enemies.

Not to mention monogamy! I don't see how the elders will ever accept it, as each of them has at least two wives. Besides, monogamy is a hard thing to respect, isn't it?" He winked at his wife and gave her a peck on the cheek.

"Well, step by step, my friend," Kamolea said. "We have made tremendous progress—at least they stopped the killings, the war, and the cannibalism. Frankly, I expected tougher resistance, but after the first three murder plots that I uncovered through my dreams and with Kedia's help, they now fear me even more than they dreaded her at the time."

They all smiled.

"It's a shame for Alfonso, though; he would have taken advantage of the polygamy. 'No fewer than three, remember?'" Benito mimicked his old friend.

"Damned Loto. I was shocked when I realized it was him who killed Alfi… But since Laggi's death, he has always brought me misfortune," said Kamolea sadly.

"Yes, but the thunderbolt that hit him was the pivotal point in our victory, so Alfonso's death was not in vain," said Benito, and Kamolea nodded in agreement.

"Should we proceed with the funeral? What are we waiting for?" Anuro asked.

"The chieftain," Kamolea responded and added, "Would you mind hitting the gong when we take her out? It will be more ceremonial."

"No problem," said Anuro. A second later, Ahaki entered, followed by the elders and a dozen men. The tiny space became so cramped that it was hard to breathe.

Ahaki raised his voice.

"Brave Tipihaos! The woman who lies here will leave a deep imprint on our history forever. Nobody was able to understand how she could predict the future, nor how she lived for so long. She was gifted with supernatural power beyond our comprehension, but instead of listening to her, we feared and rejected her. Many years passed until our priest, Kamolea, came and explained our ignorance to us, and revealed the hidden meaning in everything she foretold and foresaw. I now ask Illima, who spent so much time with her, and Kamolea, who understood her better than anyone, to say some words of farewell."

Everybody looked at Illima, who stepped forward, but when she opened her mouth, her chin started trembling and she burst into tears. Kamolea hugged and consoled her, and she merged with the other spectators, still weeping. Kamolea mounted on the elevation that represented the altar, and called out,

"Brothers and sisters, Tipihaos. Today, we have gathered to say a final goodbye to the most mysterious woman. She was the prophetess who predicted the end of the era of darkness in which our tribe lived. She was the first to announce the existence of the true God and the one who warned us that we were on the wrong path, worshiping Kepolo and his disgusting tree. But, most importantly, she taught us that our lives are predestined, and if God wants to change our fate, no matter how impossible it seems, it will happen the way He wishes. Keep bright memories about Kedia in your heart forever. She was the wisest seer who ever lived, and she accepted that she would spend her entire life in that stinking cave because she never renounced the truth! May God accept her into his Kingdom and repay her with a better life in Heaven! Amen!" Only He and Benito crossed themselves at the speech's conclusion; the others merely bowed their heads slightly.

Hopeless savages, Kamolea thought, irritated. *They'll never accept Jesus Christ in their hearts. The runt is so strong in them.*

He lifted the front of the coffin, and Ahaki took the far edge. It was neither large nor heavy, as Kedia had shrunk even more in her final days. Carrying the casket on their shoulder, they moved out under the ringing of the Snake Gong, which Anuro was hitting furiously, and set off solemnly towards the south coast. The crowd walked in silence, punctuated by Illima's occasional sobs.

When they reached the beach, they laid the coffin into the already digged grave. Kamolea was the first to scoop up and throw a handful of sand on the cover. He stepped aside to make room for the others, who passed one by one, mimicking the ritual. Ahaki was right after him, followed by Illima, the elders, Benito, and the rest of the crowd. As he watched them tossing the dirt, wondering why Anuro still hadn't caught up with them, Kamolea suddenly looked up and his jaw dropped. Beside the grave, a gorgeous young woman had appeared, clad in a white dress. She was of a medium height, with shoulder-length black hair that accentuated her prominent forehead and round, intelligent face. Kamolea stared at her small lips and slightly snub nose, trying to spot a resemblance to the old woman he had known, but it was hard to say for sure. What he could not find in her countenance, however, he detected unmistakably in her shining brown eyes, which were bright and kind, connected to the source of eternal wisdom, and turned inwardly toward her unique spiritual world. She met Kamolea's stare and, aware that only he could see her, smiled at him. He opened his mouth, wanting to ask her how it was on the other side, but her silhouette began to glow, and she slowly detached from the ground. Then, just before she soared up, she pointed towards the heavens. Following her sign, Kamolea looked up and gasped. Several gigantic fiery letters stood out against the azure sky, stretching from one end to the other and forming the sentence:

Conócete a ti mismo, y entonces conocerás la verdad,
y la verdad te hará libre.

Know thyself, and then you'll know the truth,
and the truth shall make you free.

THE END

ABOUT THE AUTHOR

Kris Nedy is a Canadian author and blogger. He has an M.A. in archaeology and a broad range of interests, such as philosophy, history, religion, biology, and literature. His versatility is evident in his diverse publications, including his scientific works based on his Ph.D. thesis in Archaeology, as well as the fairytale fantasy novel "The Fairy of the Enchanted Lake," published in London in 2023, and the present action/adventure historical novel, "The Savage." He lives in Montreal, Canada, with his wife. For more information about his blog and latest activities, visit https://krisnedy.com/.